D0941786

THE WORKS

OF

LEO TOLSTOI

One Volume Edition

BLACK'S READERS SERVICE COMPANY

ROSLYN, NEW YORK

Copyright, 1928,
By WALTER J. BLACK, Inc.

PRINTED IN THE UNITED STATES OF AMERICA

Contents

VOLUME I

TALES

VOLUME II

TALES

VOLUME III

NOVELS

VOLUME IV

VOLUME V

NOVELS

VOLUME VI

NOVELS

VOLUME VII

TALES

Too Dear!

NEAR the borders of France and Italy, on the shore of the Mediterranean Sea, lies a tiny little kingdom called Monaco. Many a small country town can boast more inhabitants than this kingdom, for there are only about seven thousand of them all told, and if all the land in the kingdom were divided there would not be an acre for each inhabitant. But in this toy kingdom there is a real kinglet; and he has a palace, and courtiers, and ministers, and a bishop, and generals, and an army.

It is not a large army, only sixty men in all but still it is an army. There were also taxes in this kingdom, as elsewhere: a tax on tobacco, and on wine and spirits, and a poll-tax. But though the people there drink and smoke as people do in other countries, there are so few of them that the King would have been hard put to it to feed his courtiers and officials and to keep himself, if he had not found a new and special source of revenue. This special revenue comes from a gaming house, where people play roulette. People play, and whether they win or lose the keeper always gets a percentage on the turnover; and out of his profits he pays a large sum to the King. The reason he pays so much is that it is the only such gambling establishment left in Europe. Some of the little German Sovereigns used to keep gaming houses of the same kind, but some years ago they were forbidden to do so. The reason they were stopped was because these gaming houses did so much harm. A man would

come and try his luck, then he would risk all he had and lose it, then he would even risk money that did not belong to him and lose that too, and then, in despair, he would drown or shoot himself. So the Germans forbade their rulers to make money in this way; but there was no one to stop the King of Monaco, and he remained with a monopoly of the business.

So now every one who wants to gamble goes to Monaco. Whether they win or lose, the King gains by it. "You can't earn stone palaces by honest labor," as the proverb says; and the Kinglet of Monaco knows it is a dirty business, but what is he to do? He has to live; and to draw a revenue from drink and from tobacco is also not a nice thing. So he lives and reigns, and rakes in the money, and holds his court with all the ceremony of a real king.

He has his coronation, his levees; he rewards, sentences, and pardons; and he also has his reviews, councils, laws, and courts of justice; just like other kings, only all on a smaller scale.

Now it happened a few years ago that a murder was committed in this toy King's domains. The people of that kingdom are peaceable, and such a thing had not happened before. The judges assembled with much ceremony and tried the case in the most judicial manner. There were judges, and prosecutors, and jurymen, and barristers. They argued and judged, and at last they condemned the criminal to have his head cut off as the law directs. So far so good. Next they submitted the sentence to the King. The King read the sentence and confirmed it. "If the fellow must be executed, execute him."

There was only one hitch in the matter; and that was that they had neither a guillotine for cutting heads off, nor an executioner. The Ministers considered the matter, and decided to address an inquiry to the French government, asking whether the French could not lend them a machine and an expert to cut off the criminal's head; and if so, would the French kindly inform them what the cost would be. The letter was sent. A week later the reply came: a machine and an expert could be supplied and the cost would be 16,000 francs. This was laid before the King. He thought it over. Sixteen thousand francs! "The wretch is not worth the money," said he. "Can't it be done somehow, cheaper. Why, 16,000 francs is more than two francs a head on the whole population. The people won't stand it, and it may cause a riot!"

So a Council was called to consider what could be done; and it was decided to send a similar inquiry to the King of Italy. The French government is republican, and has no proper respect for kings; but the King of Italy was a brother monarch, and might be induced to do the thing cheaper. So the letter was written, and a prompt reply was received.

The Italian government wrote that they would have pleasure in supplying both a machine and an expert; and the whole cost would be 12,000 francs, including traveling expenses. This was cheaper, but still it seemed too much. The rascal was really not worth the money. It would still mean nearly two

francs more per head on the taxes. Another Council was called. They discussed and considered how it could be done with less expense. Could not one of the soldiers, perhaps, be got to do it in a rough and homely fashion? The General was called and was asked: "Can't you find us a soldier who would cut the man's head off? In war they don't mind killing people. In fact, that is what they are trained for." So the General talked it over with the soldiers to see whether one of them would not undertake the job. But none of the soldiers would do it. "No," they said, "we don't know how to do it; it is not a thing we have been taught."

What was to be done? Again Ministers considered and reconsidered. They assembled a Commission, and a Committee, and a Sub-Committee, and at last they decided that the best thing would be to alter the death sentence to one of imprisonment for life. This would enable the King to show his mercy, and it would come cheaper.

The King agreed to this, and so the matter was arranged. The only hitch now was that there was no suitable prison for a man sentenced for life. There was a small lock-up where people were sometimes kept temporarily, but there was no strong prison fit for permanent use. However, they managed to find a place that would do, and they put the young fellow there and placed a guard over him. The guard had to watch the criminal, and had also to fetch his food from the palace kitchen.

The prisoner remained there month after month till a year had passed. But when a year had passed, the Kinglet, looking over the account of his income and expenditure one day, noticed a new item of expenditure. This was for the keep of the criminal; nor was it a small item either. There was a special guard, and there was also the man's food. It came to more than 600 francs a year. And the worst of it was that the fellow was still young and healthy, and might live for fifty years. When one came to reckon it up, the matter was serious. It would never do. So the King summoned his Ministers and said to them:

"You must find some cheaper way of dealing with this rascal. The present plan is too expensive." And the Ministers met and considered and reconsidered, till one of them said: "Gentlemen, in my opinion we must dismiss the guard." "But then," rejoined another Minister, "the fellow will run away." "Well," said the first speaker, "let him run away, and be hanged to him!" So they reported the result of their deliberations to the Kinglet, and he agreed with them. The guard was dismissed, and they waited to see what would happen. All that happened was that at dinner-time the criminal came out, and, not finding his guard, he went to the King's kitchen to fetch his own dinner. He took what was given him, returned to the prison, shut the door on himself, and stayed inside. Next day the same thing occurred. He went for his food at the proper time; but as for running away, he did not show the least sign of it! What was to be done? They considered the matter again.

"We shall have to tell him straight out," said they, "that we do not want to keep him." So the Minister of Justice had him brought before him.

"Why do you not run away?" said

the Minister. "There is no guard to keep you. You can go where you like, and the King will not mind."

"I daresay the King would not mind," replied the man, "but I have nowhere to go. What can I do? You have ruined my character by your sentence, and people will turn their backs on me. Besides, I have got out of the way of working. You have treated me badly. It is not fair. In the first place, when once you sentenced me to death you ought to have executed me; but you did not do it. That's one thing I did not complain about. Then you sentenced me to imprisonment for life and put a guard to bring me my food; but after a time you took him away again and I had to fetch my own food. Again I did not complain. But now you actually want me to go away! I can't agree to that. You may do as you like but I won't go away!"

What was to be done? Once more the Council was summoned. What course could they adopt? The man would not go. They reflected and considered. The only way to get rid of him was to offer him a pension. And so they reported to the King. "There is nothing else for it," said they; "we must get rid of him somehow." The sum fixed was 600 francs, and this was announced to the prisoner.

"Well," said he, "I don't mind, so long as you undertake to pay it regularly. On that condition I am willing to go."

So the matter was settled. He received one-third of his annuity in advance, and left the King's dominions. It was only a quarter of an hour by rail; and he emigrated, and settled just across the frontier, where he bought a bit of land, started market-gardening, and now lives comfortably. He always goes at the proper time to draw his pension. Having received it he goes to the gaming tables, stakes two or three francs, sometimes wins and sometimes loses, and then returns home. He lives peaceably and well.

It is a good thing that he did not commit his crime in a country where they do not grudge expenses to cut a man's head off, or to keeping him in prison for life.

Love

CHAPTER I

THE HUT

A SHOEMAKER named Simon, who had neither house nor land of his own, lived with his wife and children in a peasant's hut, and earned his living by his work. Work was cheap but bread was dear, and what he earned he spent for food. The man and his wife had but one sheepskin coat between them for winter wear, and even that was worn to tatters, and this was the second year he had been wanting to buy sheep-skins for a new coat. Before winter Simon saved up a little money: a three-rouble note lay hidden in his wife's box, and five roubles and twenty kopeks* were owed him by customers in the village.

So one morning he prepared to go to the village to buy the sheep-skins. He put on over his shirt his wife's wadded nankeen jacket, and over that he put his own cloth coat. He took the three-rouble note in his pocket, cut himself a stick to serve as a staff, and started off after breakfast. "I'll collect the five roubles that are due to me," thought

he, "add the three I have got, and that will be enough to buy sheep-skins for the winter coat."

He came to the village and called at a peasant's hut, but the man was not at home. The peasant's wife promised that the money should be paid next week, but she would not pay it herself. Then Simon called on another peasant, but this one swore he had no money, and would only pay twenty kopeks which he owed for a pair of boots Simon had mended. Simon then tried to buy the sheep-skins on credit, but the dealer would not trust him.

"Bring your money," said he, "then you may have your pick of the skins. We know what debt-collecting is like."

So all the business the shoemaker did was to get the twenty kopeks for boots that he had mended, and to take a pair of felt boots a peasant gave him to sole with leather.

Simon felt downhearted. He spent the twenty kopeks on vodka, and started homewards without having bought any skins. In the morning he had felt the frost; but now, after drinking the

---

* One hundred kopeks make a rouble. The kopek is worth about a farthing.

vodka, he felt warm even without a sheep-skin coat. He trudged along, striking his stick on the frozen earth with one hand, swinging the felt boots with the other, and talking to himself.

"I'm quite warm," said he, "though I have no skeep-skin coat. I've had a drop, and it runs through all my veins. I need no sheep-skins. I go along and don't worry about anything. That's the sort of man I am! What do I care? I can live without sheep-skins. I don't need them. My wife will fret, to be sure. And, true enough, it is a shame; one works all day long, and then does not get paid. Stop a bit! If you don't bring that money along, sure enough, I'll skin you, blessed if I don't. How's that? He pays twenty kopeks at a time! What can I do with twenty kopeks? Drink it—that's all one can do! Hard up, he says he is! So he may be—but what about me? You have house, and cattle, and everything; I've only what I stand up in! You have corn of your own growing; I have to buy every grain. Do what I will, I must spend three roubles every week for bread alone. I come home and find the bread all used up, and I have to fork out another rouble and a half. So just you pay up what you owe, and no nonsense about it!"

By this time he had nearly reached the shrine at the bend of the road. Looking up, he saw something whitish behind the shrine. The daylight was fading, and the shoemaker peered at the thing without being able to make out what it was. "There was no white stone here before. Can it be an ox? It's not too white; and what could a man be doing there?"

He came closer, so that it was clearly visible. To his surprise it really was a man, alive or dead, sitting naked, leaning motionless against the shrine. Terror seized the shoemaker, and he thought, "Some one has killed him, stripped him, and left him here. If I meddle I shall surely get into trouble."

So the shoemaker went on. He passed in front of the shrine so that he could not see the man. When he had gone some way, he looked back, and saw that the man was no longer leaning against the shrine, but was moving as if looking towards him. The shoemaker felt more frightened than before, and thought, "Shall I go back to him, or shall I go on? If I go near him something dreadful may happen. Who knows who the fellow is? He has not come here for any good. If I go near him he may jump up and throttle me, and there will be no getting away. Or if not, he'd still be a burden on one's hands. What could I do with a naked man? I couldn't give him my last clothes. Heaven only help me to get away!"

So the shoemaker hurried on, leaving the shrine behind him—when suddenly his conscience smote him, and he stopped in the road.

"What are you doing, Simon?" said he to himself. "The man may be dying of want, and you slip past afraid. Have you grown so rich as to be afraid of robbers? Ah, Simon, shame on you!"

So he turned back and went up to the man.

CHAPTER II

FAINTNESS

SIMON approached the stranger, looked at him, and saw that he was a young man, fit, with no bruises on his body, only evidently freezing and frightened, and he sat there leaning back without looking up at Simon, as if too faint to lift his eyes. Simon went close to him, and then the man seemed to wake up. Turning his head, he opened his eyes and looked into Simon's face. That one look was enough to make Simon fond of the man. He threw the felt boots on the ground, undid his sash, laid it on the boots, and took off his cloth coat.

"It's not a time for talking," said he. "Come, put this coat on at once!" And Simon took the man by the elbows and helped him to rise. As he stood there, Simon saw that his body was clean and in good condition, his hands and feet shapely, and his face good and kind. He threw his coat over the man's shoulders, but the latter could not find the sleeves. Simon guided his arms into them, and drawing the coat well on, wrapped it closely about him, tying the sash round the man's waist.

Simon even took off his torn cap to put it on the man's head, but then his own head felt cold, and he thought: "I'm quite bald, while he has long curly hair." So he put his cap on his own head again. "It will be better to give him something for his feet," thought he; and he made the man sit down, and helped him to put on the felt boots, saying, "There, friend, now move about and warm yourself. Other matters can be settled later on. Can you walk?"

The man stood up and looked kindly at Simon, but could not say a word.

"Why don't you speak," said Simon. "It's too cold to stay here, we must be getting home. There now, take my stick, and if you're feeling weak, lean on that. Now step out!"

The man started walking, and moved easily, not lagging behind.

As they went along, Simon asked him, "And where do you belong to?"

"I'm not from these parts."

"I thought as much. I know the folks hereabouts. But how did you come to be there by the shrine?"

"I cannot tell."

"Has some one been ill-treating you?"

"No one has ill-treated me. God has punished me."

"Of course God rules all. Still, you'll have to find food and shelter somewhere. Where do you want to go to?"

"It is all the same to me."

Simon was amazed. The man did not look like a rogue, and he spoke gently, but yet he gave no account of himself. Still Simon thought, "Who knows what may have happened?" And he said to the stranger: "Well, then, come home with me, and at least warm yourself awhile."

So Simon walked towards his home, and the stranger kept up with him, walking at his side. The wind had risen and Simon felt it cold under his shirt. He was getting over his tipsiness by now, and began to feel the frost. He went along sniffling and wrapping his wife's coat round him, and he thought to himself: "There now—talk about sheep-skins! I went out for sheep-skins and come home without even a coat to my back, and what is more, I'm bringing a naked man along with me. Matryona won't be pleased!" And when he thought of his wife he felt sad; but when he looked at the stranger and remembered how he had looked up at him at the shrine, his heart was glad.

CHAPTER III

THOUGHT

SIMON'S wife had everything ready early that day. She had cut wood, brought water, fed the children, eaten her own meal, and now she sat thinking. She wondered when she ought to make bread: now or tomorrow? There was still a large piece left.

"If Simon has had some dinner in town," thought she, "and does not eat much for supper, the bread will last out another day."

She weighed the piece of bread in her hand again and again, and thought: "I won't make any more today. We have only enough flour left to bake one batch. We can manage to make this last out till Friday."

So Matryona put away the bread, and sat down at the table to patch her husband's shirt. While she worked she thought how her husband was buying skins for a winter coat.

"If only the dealer does not cheat him. My good man is much too simple; he cheats nobody, but any child can take him in. Eight roubles is a lot of money—he should get a good coat at that price. Not tanned skins, but still a proper winter coat. How difficult it was last winter to get on without a warm coat. I could neither get down to the river, nor go out anywhere. When he went out he put on all we had, and there was nothing left for me. He did not start very early today, but still it's time he was back. I only hope he has not gone on the spree!"

Hardly had Matryona thought this, when steps were heard on the threshold, and some one entered. Matryona stuck her needle into her work and went out into the passage. There she saw two men: Simon, and with him a man without a hat, and wearing felt boots.

Matryona noticed at once that her husband smelt of spirits. "There now, he has been drinking," thought she. And when she saw that he was coatless, had only her jacket on, brought no parcel, stood there silent, and seemed ashamed, her heart was ready to break with disappointment. "He has drunk the money," thought she, "and has been on the spree with some good-for-nothing fellow whom he has brought home with him."

Matryona let them pass into the hut, followed them in, and saw that the stranger was a young, slight man, wearing her husband's coat. There was no shirt to be seen under it, and he had no hat. Having entered, he stood neither moving, nor raising his eyes, and Matryona thought: "He must be a bad man—he's afraid."

Matryona frowned, and stood beside the oven looking to see what they would do.

Simon took off his cap and sat down on the bench as if things were all right.

"Come, Matryona; if supper is ready, let us have some."

Matryona muttered something to herself and did not move, but stayed where she was, by the oven. She looked first at the one and then at the other of them, and only shook her head. Simon saw that his wife was annoyed, but tried to pass it off. Pretending not to notice anything, he took the stranger by the arm.

"Sit down, friend," said he, "and let us have some supper."

The stranger sat down on the bench.

"Haven't you cooked anything for us?" said Simon.

Matryona's anger boiled over. "I've cooked, but not for you. It seems to me you have drunk your wits away. You went to buy a sheep-skin coat, but come home without so much as the coat you had on, and bring a naked vagabond home with you. I have no supper for drunkards like you."

"That's enough, Matryona. Don't wag your tongue without reason! You had better ask what sort of man—"

"And you tell me what you've done with the money?"

Simon found the pocket of the jacket, drew out the three-rouble note, and unfolded it.

"Here is the money. Trifonof did not pay, but promises to pay soon."

Matryona got still more angry; he had bought no sheep-skins, but had put his only coat on some naked fellow and had even brought him to their house.

She snatched up the note from the table, took it to put away in safety, and said: "I have no supper for you. We can't feed all the naked drunkards in the world."

"There now, Matryona, hold your tongue a bit. First hear what a man has to say—!"

"Much wisdom I shall hear from a drunken fool. I was right in not wanting to marry you—a drunkard. The linen my mother gave me you drank; and now you've been to buy a coat—and have drunk it too!"

Simon tried to explain to his wife that he had only spent twenty kopeks; tried to tell how he had found the man —but Matryona would not let him get a word in. She talked nineteen to the

dozen, and dragged in things that had happened ten years before.

Matryona talked and talked, and at last she flew at Simon and seized him by the sleeve.

"Give me my jacket. It is the only one I have, and you must needs take it from me and wear it yourself. Give it here, you mangy dog, and may the devil take you."

Simon began to pull off the jacket, and turned a sleeve of it inside out; Matryona seized the jacket and it burst its seams. She snatched it up, threw it over her head and went to the door. She meant to go out, but stopped undecided—she wanted to work off her anger, but she also wanted to learn what sort of a man the stranger was.

CHAPTER IV

ALL MUST DIE

MATRYONA stopped and said: "If he were a good man he would not be naked. Why, he hasn't even a shirt on him. If he were all right, you would say where you came across the fellow."

"That's just what I am trying to tell you," said Simon. "As I came to the shrine I saw him sitting all naked and frozen. It isn't quite the weather to sit about naked! God sent me to him, or he would have perished. What was I to do? How do we know what may have happened to him? So I took him, clothed him, and brought him along. Don't be so angry, Matryona. It is a sin. Remember, we all must die one day."

Angry words rose to Matryona's lips, but she looked at the stranger and was silent. He sat on the edge of the bench, motionless, his hands folded on his knees, his head drooping on his breast, his eyes closed, and his brows knit as if in pain. Matryona was silent, and Simon said: "Matryona, have you no love of God?"

Matryona heard these words, and as she looked at the stranger, suddenly her heart softened towards him. She came back from the door, and going to the oven she got out the supper. Setting a cup on the table, she poured out some kvas. Then she brought out the last piece of bread, and set out a knife and spoons.

"Eat, if you want to," said she.

Simon drew the stranger to the table. "Take your place, young man," said he.

Simon cut the bread, crumbled it into the broth, and they began to eat. Matryona sat at the corner of the table, resting her head on her hand and looking at the stranger.

And Matryona was touched with pity for the stranger, and began to feel fond of him. And at once the stranger's face lit up; his brows were no longer bent, he raised his eyes and smiled at Matryona.

When they had finished supper, the woman cleared away the things and began questioning the stranger. "Where are you from?" said she.

"I am not from these parts."

"But how did you come to be on the road?"

"I may not tell."

"Did someone rob you?"

"God punished me."

"And you were lying there naked?"

"Yes, naked and freezing. Simon saw me and had pity on me. He took off his coat, put it on me and brought me here. And you have fed me, given

me drink and shown pity on me. God will reward you!"

Matryona rose, took from the window Simon's old shirt she had been patching, and gave it to the stranger. She also brought out a pair of trousers for him.

"There," said she, "I see you have no shirt. Put this on, and lie down where you please, in the loft or on the oven."

The stranger took off the coat, put on the shirt, and lay down in the loft. Matryona put out the candle, took the coat, and climbed to where her husband lay.

Matryona drew the skirts of the coat over her and lay down, but could not sleep; she could not get the stranger out of her mind.

When she remembered that he had eaten their last piece of bread and that there was none for tomorrow, and thought of the shirt and trousers she had given away, she felt grieved; but when she remembered how he had smiled, her heart was glad.

Long did Matryona lie awake, and she noticed that Simon also was awake—he drew the coat towards him.

"Simon!"

"Well?"

"You have had the last of the bread, and I have not put any to rise. I don't know what we shall do tomorrow. Perhaps I can borrow of neighbor Martha."

"If we're alive we shall find something to eat."

The woman lay still awhile, and then said, "He seems a good man, but why does he not tell us who he is?"

"I suppose he has his reasons."

"Simon!"

"Well?"

"We give; but why does nobody give us anything?"

Simon did not know what to say; so he only said, "Let us stop talking," and turned over and went to sleep.

CHAPTER V

MICHAEL

IN the morning Simon awoke. The children were still asleep; his wife had gone to the neighbor's to borrow some bread. The stranger alone was sitting on the bench, dressed in the old shirt and trousers, and looking upwards. His face was brighter than it had been the day before.

Simon said to him, "Well, friend; the belly wants bread, and the naked body clothes. One has to work for a living. What work do you know?"

"I do not know any."

This surprised Simon, but he said, "Men who want to learn can learn anything."

"Men work and I will work also."

"What is your name?"

"Michael."

"Well, Michael, if you don't wish to talk about yourself, that is your own affair; but you'll have to earn a living for yourself. If you will work as I tell you, I will give you food and shelter."

"May God reward you! I will learn. Show me what to do."

Simon took yarn, put it round his thumb and began to twist it.

"It is easy enough—see!"

Michael watched him, put some yarn round his own thumb in the same way, caught the knack, and twisted the yarn also.

Then Simon showed him how to wax the thread. This also Michael mastered. Next Simon showed him how to twist the bristle in, and how to sew, and this, too, Michael learned at once.

Whatever Simon showed him he understood at once, and after three days he worked as if he had sewn boots all his life. He worked without stopping, and ate little. When work was over he sat silently, looking upwards. He hardly went into the street, spoke only when necessary, and neither joked nor laughed. They never saw him smile, except that first evening when Matryona gave them supper.

CHAPTER VI

MY MEASURE

DAY by day and week by week the year went round. Michael lived and worked with Simon. His fame spread till people said that no one sewed boots so neatly and strongly as Simon's workman, Michael; and from all the district round people came to Simon for their boots, and he began to be well off.

One winter day, as Simon and Michael sat working, a carriage on sledge-runners, with three horses and with bells, drove up to the hut. They looked out of the window; the carriage stopped at their door, a fine servant jumped down from the box and opened the door. A gentleman in a fur coat got out and walked up to Simon's hut. Up jumped Matryona and opened the door wide. The gentleman stooped to enter the hut, and when he drew himself up again his head nearly reached the ceiling, and he seemed quite to fill his end of the room.

Simon rose, bowed, and looked at the gentleman with astonishment. He had never seen any one like him. Simon himself was lean, Michael was thin, and Matryona was dry as a bone, but this man was like some one from another world; red-faced, burly, with a neck like a bull's, and looking altogether as if he were cast in iron.

The gentleman puffed, threw off his fur coat, sat down on the bench, and said, "Which of you is the master boot-maker?"

"I am, your Excellency," said Simon, coming forward.

Then the gentleman shouted to his lad, "Hey, Fedka, bring the leather!"

The servant ran in, bringing a parcel. The gentleman took the parcel and put it on the table.

"Untie it," said he. The lad untied it.

The gentleman pointed to the leather. "Look here, shoemaker," said he, "do you see this leather?"

"Yes, your honor."

"But do you know what sort of leather it is?"

Simon felt the leather and said, "It is good leather."

"Good, indeed! Why, you fool, you never saw such leather before in your life. It's German, and cost twenty roubles."

Simon was frightened, and said, "Where should I ever see leather like that?"

"Just so! Now, can you make it into boots for me?"

"Yes, your Excellency, I can."

Then the gentleman shouted at him: "You can, can you?" Well, remember whom you are to make them for, and what the leather is. You must make me boots that will wear for a year, neither losing shape nor coming unsewn. If you can do it. take the leather and cut it up; but if you can't, say so. I warn you now, if your boots come un-sewn within a year, I will have you put in prison. If they don't burst or lose shape for a year, I will pay you ten roubles for your work."

Simon was frightened, and did not know what to say. He glanced at Michael and nudging him with his elbow, whispered: "Shall I take the work?"

Michael nodded his head as if to say "Yes, take it."

Simon did as Michael advised, and undertook to make boots that would not lose shape or split for a whole year.

Calling his servant, the gentleman told him to pull the boot off his left leg, which he stretched out.

"Take my measure!" said he.

Simon stitched a paper measure seventeen inches long, smoothed it out, knelt down, wiped his hands well on his apron so as not to soil the gentleman's sock, and began to measure. He measured the sole, and round the instep, and began to measure the calf of the leg, but the paper was too short. The calf of the leg was as thick as a beam.

"Mind you don't make it too tight in the leg."

Simon stitched on another strip of paper. The gentleman twitched his toes about in his sock, looked round at those in the hut, and as he did so he noticed Michael.

"Whom have you there?" asked he.

"That is my workman. He will sew the boots."

"Mind," said the gentleman to Michael, "remember to make them so that they will last me a year."

Simon also looked at Michael, and saw that Michael was not looking at the gentleman, but was gazing into the corner behind the gentleman, as if he saw someone there. Michael looked and looked, and suddenly he smiled, and his face became brighter.

"What are you grinning at, you fool?" thundered the gentleman. "You had better look to it that the boots are ready in time."

"They shall be ready in good time," said Michael.

"Mind it is so," said the gentleman, and he put on his boots and his fur coat, wrapped the latter round him, and went to the door. But he forgot to stoop, and struck his head against the lintel.

He swore and rubbed his head. Then he took his seat in the carriage and drove away.

When he had gone, Simon said: "There's a figure of a man for you! You could not kill him with a mallet. He almost knocked out the lintel, but little harm it did him."

And Matryona said: "Living as he does, how should he not grow strong? Death itself can't touch such a rock as that."

CHAPTER VII

THE BOOTS

THEN Simon said to Michael: "Well, we have taken the work, but we must see we don't get into trouble over it. The leather is dear, and the gentleman hot-tempered. We must make no mistakes. Come, your eye is truer and your hands have become nimbler than mine, so you take this measure and cut out the boots. I will finish off the sewing of the vamps."

Michael did as he was told. He took the leather, spread it out on the table, folded it in two, took a knife and began to cut out.

Matryona came and watched him cutting, and was surprised to see how he was doing it. Matryona was accustomed to seeing boots made, and she looked and saw that Michael was not cutting the leather for boots, but was cutting it round.

She wished to say something, but she thought to herself: "Perhaps I do not understand how gentlemen's boots should be made. I suppose Michael knows more about it—and I won't interfere."

When Michael had cut up the leather, he took a thread and began to sew not with two ends, as boots are sewn, but with a single end, as for soft slippers.

Again Matryona wondered, but again she did not interfere. Michael sewed on steadily till noon. Then Simon rose for dinner, looked around, and saw that Michael had made slippers out of the gentleman's leather.

"Ah!" groaned Simon, and thought, "How is it that Michael, who has been with me a whole year and never made a mistake before, should do such a dreadful thing? The gentleman ordered him boots, welted, with whole fronts, and Michael has made soft slippers with single soles, and has wasted the leather. What am I to say to the gentleman? I can never replace leather such as this."

And he said to Michael, "What are you doing, friend? You have ruined me! You know the gentleman ordered high boots, but see what you have made!"

Hardly had he begun to rebuke Michael, when "rat-tat" went the iron ring that hung at the door. Someone was knocking. They looked out of the window; a man had come on horseback, and was fastening his horse. They opened the door, and the servant who had been with the gentleman came in.

"Good day," said he.

"Good day," replied Simon. "What can we do for you?"

"My mistress has sent me about the boots."

"What about the boots?"

"Why, my master no longer needs them."

"Is it possible?"

"He did not live to get home after leaving you, but died in the carriage. When we reached home and the servants came to help him alight, he rolled over like a sack. He was dead already, and so stiff that he could hardly be got out of the carriage. My mistress sent me here, saying: 'Tell the bootmaker that the gentleman who ordered boots of him and left the leather for them no longer needs the boots, but that he must quickly make soft slippers for the corpse. Wait till they are ready, and bring them back with you.' That is why I have come."

Michael gathered up the remnants of the leather; rolled them up, took the soft slippers he had made, slapped them together, wiped them down with his apron, and handed them and the roll of leather to the servant, who took them and said: "Good-bye, masters, and good day to you!"

CHAPTER VIII

THE YEARS PASS

ANOTHER year passed, and another, and Michael was now living his sixth year with Simon. He lived as before.

He went nowhere, only spoke when necessary, and had only smiled twice in all those years—once when Matryona gave him food, and a second time when the gentleman was in the hut. Simon was more than pleased with his work. He never now asked him where he came from, and only feared lest Michael should go away.

They were all at home one day. Matryona was putting iron pots in the oven; the children were running along the benches and looking out of the window; Simon was sewing at one window, and Michael was fastening on a heel at the other.

One of the boys ran along the bench to work, turned to the window, and looked out of the window.

"Look, Uncle Michael! There is a lady with little girls! She seems to be coming here. And one of the girls is lame."

When the boy said that, Michael dropped his work, turned to the window, and looked out into the street.

Simon was surprised. Michael never used to look out into the street, but now he pressed against the window, staring at something. Simon also looked out, and saw that a well-dressed woman was really coming to his hut, leading by the hand two little girls in fur coats and woollen shawls. The girls could hardly be told one from the other, except that one of them was crippled in her leg and walked with a limp.

The woman stepped into the porch and entered the passage. Feeling about for the entrance she found the latch, which she lifted, and opened the door. She let the two girls go in first, and followed them into the hut.

"Good day, good folk!"

"Pray come in," said Simon. "What can we do for you?"

The woman sat down by the table. The two little girls pressed close to her knees, afraid of the people in the hut.

"I want leather shoes made for these two little girls, for spring."

"We can do that. We never have made such small shoes, but we can make them; either welted or turn-over shoes, linen lined. My man, Michael, is a master at the work."

Simon glanced at Michael and saw that he had left his work and was sitting with his eyes fixed on the little girls. Simon was surprised. It was true the girls were pretty, with black eyes, plump, and rosy-cheeked, and they wore nice kerchiefs and fur coats, but still Simon could not understand why Michael should look at them like that— just as if he had known them before. He was puzzled, but went on talking with the woman, and arranging the price. Having fixed it, he prepared the measure. The woman lifted the lame girl on to her lap and said: "Take two measures from this little girl. Make one shoe for the lame foot and three for the sound one. They both have the same sized feet. They are twins."

Simon took the measure and, speaking of the lame girl, said: "How did it happen to her? She is such a pretty girl. Was she born so?"

"No, her mother crushed her leg."

Then Matryona joined in. She wondered who this woman was, and whose the children were, so she said: "Are not you their mother, then?"

"No, my good woman; I am neither their mother nor any relation to them. They were quite strangers to me, but I adopted them."

"They are not your children and yet you are so fond of them?"

"How can I help being fond of them? I fed them both at my own breasts. I had a little son who died, and I was as fond of him as I now am of them."

"Then whose children are they?"

CHAPTER IX

HER TALE

THE woman, having begun talking, told them the whole story.

"It is about six years since their parents died, both in one week; their father was buried on the Tuesday, and their mother died on the Friday. These orphans were born three days after their father's death, and their mother did not live another day. My husband and I were neighbors of theirs, our yard being next to theirs. Their father was a lonely man; a wood-cutter in the forest. When felling trees one day, they let one fall on him. It fell across his body and crushed his bowels out. They hardly got him home before his soul went to God; and that same week his wife gave birth to twins—these little girls. She was poor and alone; she had no one, young or old, with her. Alone she gave them birth, and alone she met her death.

"The next morning I went to see her, but when I entered the hut, she, poor thing, was already stark and cold. In dying she had rolled on to this child and crushed her leg. The village folk came to the hut, washed the body, laid her out, made a coffin, and buried her. They were good folk. The babies were left alone. What was to be done with them? I was the only woman there who had a baby at the time. I was nursing my first-born—eight weeks old. So I took them for a time. The peasants came together, and thought and thought what to do with them; and at last they said to me: 'For the present, Mary, you had better keep the girls, and later on we will arrange what to do for them.' So I nursed the sound one at my breast, but at first did not feed this crippled one. I did not suppose she would live. But then I thought to myself, why should the poor innocent suffer? I pitied her, and began to feed her. And so I fed my own boy and these two—the three of them—at my own breast. I was young and strong, and had good food, and God gave me so much milk that at times it even overflowed. I used sometimes to feed two at a time, while the third was waiting. When one had had enough I nursed the third. And God so ordered it that these grew up, while my own was buried before he was two years old. And I had no more children, though we prospered. Now my husband is working for the corn merchant at the mill. The pay is good, and we are well off. But I have no children of my own, and how lonely I should be without these little girls! How can I help loving them! They are the joy of my life!"

She pressed the lame little girl to her with one hand, while with the other she wiped the tears from her cheeks.

And Matryona sighed, and said: "The proverb is true that says, 'One may live without father or mother, but one cannot live without God.'"

So they talked together, when suddenly the whole hut was lighted up as though by summer lightning from the corner where Michael sat. They all looked towards him and saw him sitting, his hands folded on his knees, gazing upwards and smiling.

CHAPTER X

A WOMAN'S SOUL

THE woman went away with the girls. Michael rose from the bench, put down his work, and took off his apron. Then, bowing low to Simon and his wife, he said: "Farewell, masters. God has forgiven me. I ask your forgiveness, too, for anything done amiss."

And they saw that a light shone from Michael. And Simon rose, bowed down to Michael, and said: "I see, Michael, that you are no common man, and I can neither keep you nor question you. Only tell me this: how is it that when I found you and brought you home, you were gloomy, and when my wife gave you food you smiled at her and became brighter? Then when the gentleman came to order the boots, you smiled again and became brighter still? And now, when this woman brought the little girls, you smiled a third time, and have become as bright as day? Tell me, Michael, why does your face shine so, and why did you smile those three times?"

And Michael answered: "Light shines from me because I have been punished, but now God has pardoned me. And I smiled three times, because God sent me to learn three truths, and I have learnt them. One I learnt when your wife pitied me, and that is why I smiled the first time. The second I learnt when the rich man ordered the boots, and then I smiled again. And now, when I saw those little girls, I learnt the third and last truth, and I smiled the third time."

And Simon said, "Tell me, Michael, what did God punish you for? and what were the three truths that I, too, may know them?"

And Michael answered: "God punished me for disobeying Him. I was an angel in heaven and disobeyed God. God sent me to fetch a woman's soul. I flew to earth, and saw a sick woman lying alone, who had just given birth to twin girls. They moved feebly at their mother's side, but she could not lift them to her breast. When she saw me, she understood that God had sent me for her soul, and she wept and said: 'Angel of God! My husband has just been buried, killed by a falling tree. I have neither sister, nor aunt, nor mother: no one to care for my orphans. Do not take my soul! Let me nurse my babes, feed them, and set them on their feet before I die. Children cannot live without father or mother.' And I hearkened to her. I placed one child at her breast and gave the other into her arms, and returned to the Lord in heaven. I flew to the Lord, and said: 'I could not take the soul of the mother. Her husband was killed by a tree; the woman has twins, and prays that her soul may not be taken. She says: "Let me nurse and feed my children, and set them on their feet. Children cannot live without father or mother." I have not taken her soul.' And God said: "Go—take the mother's soul, and learn three truths: Learn What dwells in man, What is not given to man, and What men live by. When thou hast learnt these things, thou shalt return to heaven." So I flew again to earth and took the mother's soul. The babes

dropped from her breasts. Her body rolled over on the bed and crushed one babe, twisting its leg. I rose above the village, wishing to take her soul to God; but a wind seized me, and my wings drooped and dropped off. Her soul rose alone to God, while I fell to earth by the roadside."

CHAPTER XI

THE LAST LESSON

AND Simon and Matryona understood who it was that had lived with them, and whom they had clothed and fed. And they wept with awe and with joy. And the angel said: "I was alone in the field, naked. I had never known human needs, cold and hunger, till I became a man. I was famished, frozen, and did not know what to do. I saw, near the field I was in, a shrine built for God, and I went to it hoping to find shelter. But the shrine was locked, and I could not enter. So I sat down behind the shrine to shelter myself at least from the wind. Evening drew on. I was hungry, frozen, and in pain. Suddenly I heard a man coming along the road. He carried a pair of boots, and was talking to himself. For the first time since I became a man I saw the mortal face of a man, and his face seemed terrible to me and I turned from it. And I heard the man talking to himself of how to cover his body from the cold in winter, and how to feed wife and children. And I thought: 'I am perishing of cold and hunger, and here is a man thinking only of how to clothe himself and his wife, and how to get bread for themselves. He cannot help me.' When the man saw me he frowned and became still more terrible, and passed me by on the other side. I despaired; but suddenly I heard him coming back. I looked up, and did not recognize the man: before, I had seen death in his face; but now he was alive, and I recognized in him the presence of God. He came up to me, clothed me, took me with him, and brought me to his home. I entered the house; a woman came to meet us and began to speak. The woman was still more terrible than the man had been; the spirit of death came from her mouth; I could not breathe for the stench of death that spread around her. She wished to drive me out into the cold, and I knew that if she did so she would die. Suddenly her husband spoke to her of God, and the woman changed at once. And when she brought me food and looked at me, I glanced at her and saw that death no longer dwelt in her; she had become alive, and in her too I saw God.

"Then I remembered the first lesson God had set me: 'Learn what dwells in man.' And I understood that in man dwells Love! I was glad that God had already begun to show me what He had promised, and I smiled for the first time. But I had not yet learnt all. I did not yet know What is not given to man and What men live by.

"I lived with you, and a year passed. A man came to order boots that should wear for a year without losing shape or cracking. I looked at him, and suddenly, behind his shoulder, I saw my comrade—the angel of death. None but me saw that angel; but I knew him, and knew that before the sun set he would take that rich man's soul. And I thought to myself, 'The man is making preparations for a year, and does not know that he will die before evening.'

And I remembered God's second saying: 'Learn what is not given to man.'

"What dwells in man I already knew. Now I learnt what is not given him. It is not given to man to know his own needs. And I smiled for the second time. I was glad to have seen my comrade angel—glad also that God had revealed to me the second saying.

"But I still did not know all. I did not know What men live by. And I lived on, waiting till God should reveal to me the last lesson. In the sixth year came the girl-twins with the woman; and I recognized the girls, and heard how they had been kept alive. Having heard the story, I thought, 'Their mother besought me for the children's sake, and I believed her when she said that children cannot live without father or mother; but a stranger has nursed them, and has brought them up.' And when the woman showed her love for the children that were not her own, and wept over them, I saw in her the living God, and understood What men live by. And I knew that God had revealed to me the last lesson, and had forgiven my sin. And then I smiled for the third time."

CHAPTER XII

AT HIS VOICE

AND the angel's body was bared, and he was clothed in light so that eye could not look on him; and his voice grew louder, as though it came not from him but from heaven above. And the angel said:

"I have learnt that all men live not by care for themselves, but by love.

"It was not given to the mother to know what her children needed for their life. Nor was it given to the rich man to know what he himself needed. Nor is it given to any man to know whether, when evening comes, he will need boots for his body or slippers for his corpse.

"I remained alive when I was a man, not by care of myself, but because love was present in a passerby, and because he and his wife pitied and loved me. The orphans remained alive, not because of their mother's care, but because there was love in the heart of a woman, a stranger to them, who pitied and loved them. And all men live not by the thought they spend on their own welfare, but because love exists in man.

"I knew before that God gave life to men and desires that they should live; now I understand more than that.

"I understand that God does not wish men to live apart, and therefore he does not reveal to them what each one needs for himself; but he wishes them to live united, and therefore reveals to each of them what is necessary for all.

"I have now understood that though it seems to men that they live by care for themselves, in truth it is love alone by which they live. He who has loved is in God, and God is in him, for God is love."

And the angel sang praise to God, so that the hut trembled at his voice. The roof opened, and a column of fire rose from earth to heaven. Simon and his wife and children fell to the ground. Wings appeared upon the angel's shoulders, and he rose into the heaven.

And when Simon came to himself the hut stood as before, and there was no one in it but his own family.

The Chinese Pilot

IN the town of Surat, in India, was a coffee-house where many travellers and foreigners from all parts of the world met and conversed.

One day a learned Persian theologian visited this coffee-house. He was a man who had spent his life studying the nature of the Deity, and reading and writing books upon the subject. He had thought, read, and written so much about God, that eventually he lost his wits, became quite confused, and ceased even to believe in the existence of a God. The Shah, hearing of this, had banished him from Persia.

After having argued all his life about the First Cause, this unfortunate theologian had ended by quite perplexing himself, and instead of understanding that he had lost his own reason, he began to think that there was no higher Reason controlling the universe.

This man had an African slave who followed him everywhere. When the theologian entered the coffee-house, the slave remained outside, near the door, sitting on a stone in the glare of the sun, and driving away the flies that buzzed around him. The Persian having settled down on a divan in the coffee-house, ordered himself a cup of opium. When he had drunk it and the opium had begun to quicken the workings of his brain, he addressed his slave through the open door:

"Tell me, wretched slave," said he, "do you think there is a God, or not?"

"Of course there is," said the slave,

and immediately drew from under his girdle a small idol of wood.

"There," said he, "that is the God who has guarded me from the day of my birth. Every one in our country worships the fetish tree, from the wood of which this God was made."

This conversation between the theologian and his slave was listened to with surprise by the other guests in the coffee-house. They were astonished at the master's question, and yet more so at the slave's reply.

One of them, a Brahmin, on hearing the words spoken by the slave, turned to him and said:

"Miserable fool! Is it possible you believe that God can be carried under a man's girdle? There is one God—Brahma, and he is greater than the whole world, for he created it. Brahma is the One, the mighty God, and in His honor are built the temples on the Ganges' banks, where his true priests, the Brahmins, worship him. They know the true God, and none but they. A thousand score of years have passed, and yet through revolution after revolution these priests have held their sway, because Brahma, the one true God, has protected them."

So spoke the Brahmin, thinking to convince every one; but a Jewish broker who was present replied to him, and said:

"No! the temple of the true God is not in India. Neither does God protect the Brahmin caste. The true God is not the God of the Brahmins, but of Abraham, Isaac, and Jacob. None does He protect but His chosen people, the Israelites. From the commencement of the world, our nation has been beloved of Him, and ours alone. If we are now

scattered over the whole earth, it is but to try us; for God has promised that He will one day gather His people together in Jerusalem. Then, with the Temple of Jerusalem—the wonder of the ancient world—restored to its splendor, shall Israel be established a ruler over all nations."

So spoke the Jew, and burst into tears. He wished to say more, but an Italian missionary who was there interrupted him.

"What you are saying is untrue," said he to the Jew. "You attribute injustice to God. He cannot love your nation above the rest. Nay rather, even if it be true that of old He favored the Israelites, it is now nineteen hundred years since they angered Him, and caused Him to destroy their nation and scatter them over the earth, so that their faith makes no converts and has died out except here and there. God shows preference to no nation, but calls all who wish to be saved to the bosom of the Catholic Church of Rome, the one outside whose borders no salvation can be found."

So spoke the Italian. But a Protestant minister, who happened to be present, growing pale, turned to the Catholic missionary and explained:

"How can you say that salvation belongs to your religion? Those only will be saved, who serve God according to the Gospel, in spirit and in truth, as bidden by the word of Christ."

Then a Turk, an office-holder in the custom house at Surat, who was sitting in the coffee-house smoking a pipe, turned with an air of superiority to both the Christians.

"Your belief in your Roman religion is vain," said he. "It was superseded twelve hundred years ago by the true faith; that of Mohammed! You cannot but observe how the true Mohammedan faith continues to spread both in Europe and Asia, and even in the enlightened country of China. You say yourselves that God has rejected the Jews; and, as a proof you quote the fact that the Jews are humiliated and their faith does not spread. Confess then the truth of Mohammedanism, for it is triumphant and spreads far and wide. None will be saved but the followers of Mohammed, God's latest prophet; and of them, only the followers of Omar, and not of Ali, for the latter are false to the faith."

To this the Persian theologian, who was of the sect of Ali, wished to reply; but by this time a great dispute had arisen among all the strangers of different faiths and creeds present. There were Abyssinian Christians, Llamas from Thibet, Ismailians and Fire-worshippers. They all argued about the nature of God, and how He should be worshipped. Each of them asserted that in his country alone was the true God known and rightly worshipped.

Every one argued and shouted, except a Chinaman, a student of Confucius, who sat quietly in one corner of the coffee-house, not joining in the dispute. He sat there drinking tea and listening to what the others said, but did not speak himself.

The Turk noticed him sitting there, and appealed to him, saying:

"You can confirm what I say, my good Chinaman. You hold your peace, but if you spoke I know you would uphold my opinion. Traders from your country, who come to me for assistance, tell me that though many religions have been introduced into China, you Chinese consider Mohammedanism the best of all, and adopt it willingly. Confirm, then, my words, and tell us your opinion of the true God and of His prophet."

"Yes, yes," said the rest, turning to the Chinaman, "let us hear what you think on the subject."

The Chinaman, the student of Confucius, closed his eyes, and thought a while. Then he opened them again, and drawing his hands out of the wide sleeves of his garment, and folding them on his breast, he spoke as follows, in a calm and quiet voice.

Sirs, it seems to me that it is chiefly pride that prevents men agreeing with one another on matters of faith. If you care to listen to me, I will tell you a story which will explain this by an example.

I came here from China on an English steamer which had been round the world. We stopped for fresh water, and landed on the east coast of the island of Sumatra. It was mid-day, and some of us, having landed, sat in the shade of some cocoanut palms by the seashore, not far from a native village. We were a party of men of different nationalities.

As we sat there, a blind man approached us. We learnt afterwards that he had gone blind from gazing too long and too persistently at the sun, trying to find out what it is, in order to seize its light.

He strove a long time to accomplish this, constantly looking at the sun; but the only result was that his eyes were injured by its brightness, and he became blind.

Then he said to himself:

"The light of the sun is not a liquid; for if it were a liquid it would be possible to pour it from one vessel into another, and it would be moved, like water, by the wind. Neither is it fire; for if it were fire, water would extinguish it. Neither is light a spirit, for it is seen by the eye; nor is it matter, for it cannot be moved. Therefore, as the light of the sun is neither liquid, nor fire, nor spirit, nor matter, it is—nothing!"

So he argued, and, as a result of always looking at the sun and always thinking about it, he lost both his sight and his reason. And when he went quite blind, he became fully convinced that the sun did not exist.

With this blind man came a slave, who after placing his master in the shade of a cocoanut tree, picked up a cocoanut from the ground, and began making it into a night light. He twisted a wick from the fiber of the cocoanut; squeezed oil from the nut into the shell, and soaked the wick in it.

As the slave sat doing this, the blind man sighed and said to him:

"Well, slave, was I not right when I told you there is no sun? Do you not see how dark it is? Yet people say there is a sun. . . . But if so, what is it?"

"I do not know what the sun is," said the slave. "That is no business of mine. But I know what light is. Here, I have made a night light, by the help of which I can serve you and find anything I want in the hut."

And the slave picked up the cocoanut shell, saying:

"This is my sun."

A lame man with crutches, who was sitting near by, heard these words and laughed:

"You have evidently been blind all your life," said he to the blind man, "not to know what the sun is. I will tell you what it is. The sun is a ball of fire, which rises every morning out of the sea and goes down again among the mountains of our island each evening. We have all seen this, and if you had had your eyesight you too would have seen it."

A fisherman, who had been listening to the conversation, said:

"It is plain enough that you have never seen beyond your own island. If you were not lame, and if you had been out as I have in a fishing boat, you would know that the sun does not set among the mountains of our island, but as it rises from the ocean every morning so it sets again in the sea every night. What I am telling you is true, for I see every day with my own eyes."

Then an Indian who was of our party, interrupted him by saying:

"I am astonished that a reasonable man should talk such nonsense. How can a ball of fire possibly descend into the water and not be extinguished? The sun is not a ball of fire at all, it is the Deity named Deva, who rides forever in a chariot round the golden mountain, Meru. Sometimes the evil serpents Ragu and Ketu attack Deva and swallow him, and then the earth is dark. But our priests pray that the Deity may be released, and then he is set free. Only such ignorant men as you, who have never been beyond their own island, can imagine that the sun shines for their country alone."

Then the master of an Egyptian vessel, who was present, spoke in his turn.

"No," said he, "you also are wrong. The sun is not a Deity, and does not move only round India and its golden mountain. I have sailed much on the Black Sea, and along the coasts of Arabia, and have been to Madagascar and to the Philippines. The sun lights the whole earth, and not India alone. It does not circle round one mountain, but rises far in the east, beyond the Isles of Japan, and sets far, far away in the west, beyond the islands of England. That is why the Japanese call their country 'Nippon,' that is 'the birth of the sun.' I know this well, for I have myself seen much, and heard more from my grandfather, who sailed to the very ends of the sea."

He would have gone on, but an English sailor from our ship interrupted him.

"There is no country," he said, "where people know so much about the sun's movements as in England. The sun, as every one in England knows, rises nowhere and sets nowhere. It is always moving round the earth. We can be sure of this for we have just been round the world ourselves, and nowhere knocked up against the sun. Wherever we went, the sun showed itself in the morning and hid itself at night, just as it does here."

And the Englishman took a stick and, drawing circles on the sand, tried to explain how the sun moves in the heavens and goes round the world. But he was unable to explain it clearly, and pointing to the ship's pilot said:

"This man knows more about it than I do. He can explain it properly."

The pilot, who was an intelligent man, had listened in silence to the talk till he was asked to speak. Now every one turned to him, and he said:

"You are all misleading one another, and are yourselves deceived. The sun does not go round the earth, but the earth goes round the sun, revolving as it goes, and turning towards the sun in the course of each twenty-four hours, not only Japan, and the Philippines, and Sumatra where we now are, but Africa, and Europe, and America, and many lands besides. The sun does not shine for some one mountain or for some one island, or for some one sea, nor even for one earth alone, but for other planets as well as our earth. If you would only look up at the heavens, instead of at the ground beneath your own feet, you might all understand this, and would then no longer suppose that the sun shines for you, or for your country alone."

Thus spoke the wise pilot, who had voyaged much about the world, and had gazed much upon the heavens above.

"So on matters of faith," continued the Chinaman, the student of Confucius, "it is pride that causes error and discord among men. As with the sun, so it is with God. Each man wants to have a special God of his own, or at least a special God for his native land. Each nation wishes to confine in its own temples Him, whom the world cannot contain.

"Can any temple compare with that which God Himself has built to unite all men in one faith and one religion?

"All human temples are built on the model of this temple, which is God's own world. Every temple has its fonts, its vaulted roof, its lamps, its pictures or sculptures, its inscriptions, its books of the law, its offerings, its altars and its priests. But in what temple is there such a font as the ocean; such a vault as that of the heavens; such lamps as the sun, moon, and stars; or any figures to be compared with living, loving, mutually-helpful men? Where are there any records of God's goodness so easy to understand as the blessings which God has strewn abroad for man's happiness? Where is there any book of the law so clear to each man as that written in his heart? What sacrifices equal the self-denials which loving men and women make for one another? And what altar can be compared with the heart of a good 'man, on which God Himself accepts the sacrifice?

"The higher a man's conception of God, the better will he know Him. And the better he knows God, the nearer will he draw to Him."

The Three Questions

It once occurred to a certain king, that if he always knew the right time to begin everything; if he knew who were the right people to listen to, and whom to avoid; and, above all, if he always knew what was the most important thing to do, he would never fail in anything he might undertake.

And this thought having occurred to him, he had it proclaimed throughout his kingdom that he would give a great reward to any one who would teach him what was the right time for every action, and who were the most necessary people, and how he might know what was the most important thing to do.

And learned men came to the King, but they all answered his questions differently.

In reply to the first question, some said that to know the right time for every action, one must draw up in advance, a table of days, months and years, and must live strictly according to it. Only thus, said they, could everything be done at its proper time. Others declared that it was impossible to decide beforehand the right time for every action; but that not letting oneself be absorbed in idle pastimes, one should always attend to all that was going on, and then do what was most needful. Others, again, said that however attentive the King might be to what was going on, it was impossible for one man to decide correctly the right time for every action, but that he should have a Council of wise men, who would help him to fix the proper time for everything.

But then again others said there were some things which could not wait to be laid before a Council, but about which one had at once to decide whether to undertake them or not. But in order to decide that, one must know beforehand what was going to happen. It is only magicians who know that; and, therefore, in order to know the right time for every action, one must consult magicians.

Equally various were the answers to the second question. Some said, the people the King most needed were his councillors; others, the priests; others, the doctors; while some said the warriors were the most necessary.

To the third question, as to what was the most important occupation: some replied that the most important thing in the world was science. Others said it was skill in warfare; and others, again, that it was religious worship.

All the answers being different, the King agreed with none of them, and gave the regard to none. But still wishing to find the right answers to his questions, he decided to consult a hermit, widely renowned for his wisdom.

The hermit lived in a wood which he never quitted, and he received none but common folk. So the King put on simple clothes, and before reaching the hermit's cell dismounted from his horse, and, leaving his bodyguard behind, went on alone.

When the King approached, the hermit was digging the ground in front of his hut. Seeing the King, he greeted him and went on digging. The hermit was frail and weak, and each time he stuck his spade into the ground and turned a little earth, he breathed heavily.

The King went up to him and said: "I have come to you, wise hermit, to ask you to answer three questions: How can I learn to do the right thing at the right time? Who are the people I most need, and to whom should I, therefore, pay more attention than to the rest? And, what affairs are the most important, and need my first attention?"

The hermit listened to the King, but answered nothing. He just spat on his hand and recommenced digging.

"You are tired," said the King, "let me take the spade and work a while for you."

"Thanks!" said the hermit, and, giving the spade to the King, he sat down on the ground.

When he had dug two beds, the King stopped and repeated his questions. The hermit again gave no answer, but rose, stretched out his hand for the spade, and said:

"Now rest awhile—and let me work a bit."

But the King did not give him the spade, and continued to dig. One hour passed, and another. The sun began to sink behind the trees, and the King at last stuck the spade into the ground, and said:

"I came to you, wise man, for an answer to my questions. If you can give me none, tell me so, and I will return home."

"Here comes some one running," said the hermit, "let us see who it is."

The King turned round, and saw a bearded man come running out of the wood. The man held his hands pressed against his stomach, and blood was flowing from under them. When he reached the King, he fell fainting on the ground moaning feebly. The King and the hermit unfastened the man's clothing. There was a large wound in his stomach. The King washed it as best he could, and bandaged it with his handkerchief and with a towel the hermit had. But the blood would not stop flowing, and the King again and again removed the bandage soaked with warm blood, and washed and rebandaged the wound. When at last the blood ceased flowing, the man revived and asked for something to drink. The King brought fresh water and gave it to him. Meanwhile the sun had set, and it had become cool. So the King, with the hermit's help, carried the wounded man into the hut and laid him on the bed. Lying on the bed the man closed his eyes and was quiet; but the King was so tired with his walk and with the work he had done, that he crouched down on the threshold, and also fell asleep—so soundly that he slept all through the short summer night. When he awoke in the morning, it was long before he could remember where he was, or who was the strange bearded man lying on the bed and gazing intently at him with shining eyes.

"Forgive me!" said the bearded man in a weak voice, when he saw that the King was awake and was looking at him.

"I do not know you, and have nothing to forgive you for," said the King.

"You do not know me, but I know you. I am that enemy of yours who swore to revenge himself on you, because you executed his brother and seized his property. I knew you had gone alone to see the hermit, and I resolved to kill you on your way back. But the day passed and you did not return. So I came out from my ambush to find you, and I came upon your bodyguard, and they recognized me, and wounded me. I escaped from them, but should have bled to death had you not dressed my wound. I wished to kill you, and you have saved my life. Now, if I live, and if you wish it, I will serve you as your most faithful slave, and will bid my sons do the same. Forgive me!"

The King was very glad to have made peace with his enemy so easily, and to have gained him for a friend, and he not only forgave him, but said he would send his servants and his own physician to attend him, and promised to restore his property.

Having taken leave of the wounded man, the King went out into the porch and looked around for the hermit. Before going away he wished once more to beg an answer to the questions he had put. The hermit was outside, on his knees, sowing seeds in the beds that had been dug the day before.

The King approached him, and said: "For the last time, I pray you to answer my questions, wise man."

"You have already been answered!" said the hermit, still crouching on his thin legs, and looking up at the King, who stood before him.

"How answered? What do you mean?" asked the King.

"Do you not see," replied the hermit. "If you had not pitied my weakness yesterday, and had not dug those beds for me, but had gone your way, that man would have attacked you, and you would have repented of not having stayed with me. So the most important time was when you were digging the beds; and I was the most important man; and to do me good was your most important business. Afterwards when that man ran to us, the most important time was when you were attending to him, for if you had not bound up his wounds he would have died without having made peace with you. So he was the most important man, and what you did for him was your most important business. Remember then: there is only one time that is important— now! It is the most important time because it is the only time when we have any power. The most necessary man is he with whom you are, for no man knows whether he will ever have dealings with anyone else; and the most important affair is, to do him good, because for that purpose alone was man sent into this life!"

Much Land

CHAPTER I

SISTERS TWO

An elder sister came from the town to visit a younger one. The elder one was married to a tradesman, and the younger to a peasant. As the two drank tea and talked the elder sister began to boast and make much of her life in town—how she lived and went about in ease and comfort, dressed her children well, had nice things to eat and drink, and went skating, walking, and to the theatre.

The younger sister was vexed at this, and retorted by running down the life of a tradesman's wife and exalting her own country one.

"For my part, I should not care to exchange my life for yours," she said. "I grant you ours is an uneventful existence and that we know no excitement; yet you, on the other hand, with all your fine living, must either do a very large trade indeed or be ruined. You know the proverb: 'Loss is Gain's elder brother.' Well, you may be rich to-day, but to-morrow you may find yourself in the street. We have a better way than that, here in the country. The peasant's stomach may be thin, but it is long. That is to say, he may never be rich, yet he will always have enough."

The elder sister took her up quickly. "'Enough' indeed?" she retorted. "'Enough'—with nothing but your wretched pigs and calves? 'Enough,' with no fine dresses or company? Why, however hard your man may work, you have to live in mud, and will die

there—yes, and your children after you."

"Oh, no," replied the younger. "'Tis like this with us. Though we may live hardly, the land is at least our own, and we have no need to bow and scrape to anyone. But you in town—you live in an atmosphere of scandal. To-day all may be well with you, but to-morrow the evil eye may look upon you, and your husband find himself tempted away by cards or wine or some light-of-love, and you and yours find yourselves ruined. Is it not so?"

Pakhom, the younger sister's husband, had been listening near the stove.

"That is true," he said. "I have been turning over our mother earth since my childhood, so have had no time to get any foolishness into my head. Yet I have one grievance—too little land. Only give me land, and I fear no man—no, not even the Devil himself."

The two women finished their tea, chattered a little longer about dress, washed up the crockery, and went to bed.

All this time the Devil had been sitting behind the stove, and had heard everything. He was delighted when the peasant's wife led her husband on to brag—led him on to boast that, once given land, not even the Devil himself should take it from him.

"Splendid!" thought the Devil. "I will try a fall with you. I will give

you much land—and then take it away
again."

CHAPTER II

TROUBLE

NEAR these peasants there lived a
lady landowner, with a small property
of 120 dessiatins. Formerly she had
got on well with the peasants and in
no way abused her rights; but now
she took as overseer a retired soldier,
who began to persecute the peasants
with fines. No matter how careful
Pakhom might be, one of his horses
would get into the lady's oats, or a
cow stray into her garden, or the calves
break into her meadows: and for all
these things there would be fines levied.
Pakhom paid up, and then beat and
abused his household. Much trouble
did he get into with the overseer for
the doings of the summer, so that he
felt devoutly thankful to have got his
cattle standing in the straw-yard again.
He regretted the cost of their keep
there, yet it cost him less anxiety in
other ways.

That winter a rumour went abroad
that the Barina was going to sell her
land, and that the overseer was arranging to buy both it and the highway
rights attached. This rumour reached
the peasants, and they were dismayed.
"If," they thought, "the overseer
gets the land he will worry us with
fines even worse than he did under
the Barina. We must get hold of the
property somehow, as we all live round
it in a circle."

So a deputation from the Mir went
to see the Barina, and besought her
not to sell the land to the overseer,
but to give them the refusal of it,

and they would outbid their rival. To
this the Barina agreed, and the peasants
set about arranging for the Mir to
purchase the whole of her estate. They
held a meeting about it, and yet another one, but the matter did not go
through. The fact was that the Unclean One always defeated their object
by making them unable to agree. Then
the peasants decided to try and buy
the land in separate lots, each man as
much as he could; and to this also
the Barina said she was agreeable.
Pakhom heard one day that a neighbour had bought twenty dessiatins, and
that the Barina had agreed to let half
the purchase money stand over for a
year. Pakhom grew envious. "If," he
thought, "the others buy up all the
land, I shall feel left out in the cold."
So he took counsel of his wife. "Everybody is buying some," he said, "so we
too had better get hold of ten dessiatins.
We can't make a living as things are
now, for the overseer takes it all out
of us in fines." So they took thought
how to effect the purchase.

They had 100 roubles laid by; so
that by selling a foal and half their
bees, in addition to putting out their
son to service, they managed to raise
half the money.

Pakhom collected it all together, selected fifteen dessiatins and a small
piece of timber land, and went to the
Barina to arrange things. The bargain
struck, they shook hands upon it, and
Pakhom paid a deposit. Then he went
to town, completed the conveyance
(half the purchase money to be paid
now, and half within two years' time)
—and lo! Pakhom was a landowner!
He also borrowed a small sum of his
brother-in-law, wherewith to purchase

seed. This he duly sowed in his newly acquired property, and a fine crop came up; so that within a year he had repaid both the Barina and his brother-in-law. He was now an absolute proprietor. It was his own land that he sowed, his own hay that he reaped, his own firewood that he cut, and his own cattle that he grazed. Whenever he rode out to his inalienable estate either to plough or to inspect the crops and meadows, he felt overjoyed. The very grass seemed to him different to other grass, the flowers to bloom differently. Once, when he had ridden over this land, it was just—land; but now, although still land, it was land with a difference.

CHAPTER III

THE RUMOUR

THUS did Pakhom live for a time, and was happy. Indeed, all would have been well if only the other peasants had left Pakhom's corn and pasture alone. In vain did he make repeated remonstrances. Shepherds would turn their flocks out into his meadows, and horses would somehow get into the corn at night. Again and again Pakhom drove them out and overlooked the matter, but at last he lost his temper and laid a complaint before the district court. He knew that the peasants only did it from lack of land, not maliciously; yet it could not be allowed, since they were eating the place up. He must teach them a lesson.

So he taught first one of them a lesson in court, and then another; had one fined, and then a second. This aroused feeling against him, and his neighbours now began, of set purpose,

to steal his crops. One man got into the plantation at night, and stripped the bark off no less than ten linden-trees. When Pakhom next rode that way and saw what had been done he turned pale. He drew nearer, and perceived that bark had been stripped off and thrown about, and trunks uprooted. One tree only had the miscreant left, after lopping all its branches, but the rest he had cleared entirely in his evil progress. Pakhom was furious. "Ah!" he thought, "if only I knew who had done this, I would soon get my own back on him!" He wondered and wondered who it could be. If anyone in particular, it must be Semka. So he went to see Semka, but got nothing out of him except bad language: yet he felt more certain than ever now that it *was* Semka who had done it. He laid a complaint against him, and they were both of them summoned to attend the court. The magistrates sat and sat, and then dismissed the case for want of evidence. This enraged Pakhom still more. He abused both the starshina and the magistrates. "You magistrates," he said, "are in league with thieves. If you were honest men you would never have acquitted Semka." Yes, there was no doubt that Pakhom was ill pleased both with the magistrates and with his neighbours. He began to live more and more apart on his land, and to have less and less to do with the Mir.

At this time there arose a rumour that some of the peasantry thereabouts were thinking of emigrating. This made Pakhom think to himself: "But there is no reason why I should leave *my* land. If some of the others go,

why, it will make all the more room
for me. I can buy up their land, and
so hedge myself in all round. I should
live much more comfortably then. At
present I am too cramped."

It happened soon afterwards that
Pakhom was sitting at home one day,
when a travelling peasant dropped in.
Pakhom gave him a night's lodging and
a meal, and then questioned him, in
the course of conversation, as to
whence in the name of God he had
come. To this the peasant replied that
he had come from lower down the
river—from a spot beyond the Volga,
where he had been in service. Then
he went on to relate how a settlement
was being formed there, every settler
being enrolled in the Mir and allotted
ten dessiatins of land. It was *such*
land, too, he said, and grew *such* rye!
Why, the straw of the rye was tall
enough to hide a horse, and thick
enough together to make a sheaf per
five handfuls! One peasant, he went
on, who had arrived there a poor man
and had had nothing but his two hands
to work with now grew his fifty dessiatins of wheat. Indeed, during the
past year that man had made 5000
roubles by his wheat alone!

Pakhom's soul was fired by this,
and he thought to himself: "Why
should I stay here, poor and cramped
up, when I might be making such a
fine living as that? I will sell out
here—both land and homestead—and
go build myself a new house and farm
there with the money. Here, in this
cramped-up spot, life is one long worry.
At any rate, I might take a trip there
and make inquiries."

So when the summer came he got
himself ready and set out. He took

a steamer down the Volga to Samara,
and thence tramped 400 versts till he
came to the place. It was all as had
been described. The peasants lived
splendidly, with ten dessiatins of free
land to each soul, and he was assured
of a welcome by the Mir. Moreover,
he was told that anyone who came
there with money could buy additional
land—as much as ever he wanted—
right out and in perpetuity. For three
roubles a dessiatin a man could have
the very finest land possible, and to
any extent.

All this Pakhom learnt, and then
returned home in the autumn. He
began straightway to sell out, and succeeded in disposing both of land, buildings, and stock at a profit. Then he
took his name off the Mir's books,
waited for the spring, and departed to
the new place with his family.

CHAPTER IV

THE SOWING

THEY duly arrived at their destination, and Pakhom was forthwith enrolled in the Mir of the great settlement (after moistening the elders'
throats, of course, and executing the
necessary documents). Then they took
him and assigned him fifty dessiatins
of land—ten for each soul of his family—in different parts of the estate,
in addition to common pasturage.
Pakhom built himself a homestead and
stocked it, his allotted land alone being
twice what he had formerly possessed
in the old place. It was corn-bearing
land, too. Altogether life was ten
times better here than where he had
come from, for he had at his disposal
both arable and pasture land—sufficient

of the latter always to keep as many cattle as he cared to have.

At first, while building and stocking, he thought everything splendid. Later, when he had settled down a bit, he began to feel cramped again. He wanted to grow white Turkish wheat as several others did, but there was hardly any wheat-bearing land among his five allotments. Wheat needed to be grown on grass, new, or fallow land, and such land had to be sown one year and left fallow for two, in order that the grass might grow again. True, he had as much soft land as he wanted, but it would only bear rye. Wheat required hard land, and hard land found many applicants, and there was not enough for all. Moreover, such land gave rise to disputes. The richer peasants sowed their own, but the poorer had to mortgage theirs to merchants. The first year, Pakhom sowed his allotments with wheat, and got splendid crops. Then he wanted to sow them with wheat again, but they were not large enough to admit both of sowing new land and of leaving last year's land to lie fallow. He must get hold of some more. So he went to a merchant, and took a year's lease of some wheat land. He sowed as much of it as he could, and reaped a magnificent crop. Unfortunately, however, the land was a long way from the settlement—in fact, the crop had to be carted fifteen versts; so, as Pakhom had seen merchant farmers living in fine homesteads and growing rich in the district where the land lay, he thought to himself: "How would it be if I took a longer lease of it and built a homestead there the same as they have done? Then I should be right

on the land." So he set about arranging to do so.

Thus did Pakhom live for five years, continually taking up land and sowing it with wheat. All the years were good ones, the wheat thrived, and the money came in. Yet just to live and live was rather tedious, and Pakhom began to tire of leasing land every year in a strange district and removing his stock there. Wherever there was a particularly good plot of land there would be a rush made for it by the other peasants, and it would be divided up before he was ready to lease and sow it as a whole. Once he went shares with a merchant in leasing a plot of pasturage of some peasants, and ploughed it up. Then the peasants lost it in a law suit, and his labour went for nothing. If only it had been his own land, absolutely, he need have given in to no one and been put to no trouble.

So he began to cast about where he could buy an estate outright. In this endeavour he fell in with a certain peasant who had ruined himself and was ready to let him have his property of 500 dessiatins cheap. Pakhom entered into negotiations with him, and after much discussion, closed at 1000 roubles—half down, and half to stand over. One day after they had thus clinched the matter, a merchant drove up to Pakhom's homestead to bate his horses. They drank a tea-pot empty and talked. The merchant said he had come a long, long way—from the country of the Bashkirs, in fact, where (so he said) he had just purchased 5000 dessiatins for only 1000 roubles! Pakhom went on to question him further and the merchant to answer. "All I did," said the latter, "was to make the

elders there a few presents (khalats, carpets, and a chest of tea), to distribute about a hundred roubles, and to stand vodka to anyone who felt inclined for it. In the result I got the land for twenty copecks a dessiatin," and he showed Pakhom the deed. "The property," he concluded, "fronts upon a river, and is all of it open, grass, steppe land." Pakhom questioned him still further.

"You would not," went on the merchant, "find such land as that in a year. The same with all the Bashkir land. Moreover, the people there are as simple as sheep. You can get things out of them absolutely for nothing."

"Well," thought Pakhom, "what is the good of my giving 1000 roubles for only 500 dessiatins, and still leaving a debt round my neck, when there I might become a proprietor indeed for the same money?"

CHAPTER V

THE CAMP

PAKHOM inquired of the merchant as to how to reach the country of the Bashkirs, and as soon as his informant had departed, got ready for the journey. Leaving his wife at home, and taking with him only his workman, he set out first for the town, where he bought a chest of tea, vodka, and other gifts, as the merchant had advised. Then the two drove on and on until they had covered 500 versts, and on the seventh day arrived at the camp of the Bashkirs. Everything turned out to be as the merchant had said. The people there lived in hide-tilted wagons, which were drawn up by the side of a river running through the open steppe. They neither ploughed the land nor ate corn, while over the steppe wandered droves of cattle and Cossack horses, the foals being tied to the backs of the wagons and their dams driven up to them twice a day to give them suck. The chief sustenance of the people was mare's milk, which the women made into a drink called kumiss, and then churned the kumiss into cheese. In fact, the only drink the Bashkirs knew was either kumiss or tea, their only solid food mutton, and their only amusement pipe-playing. Nevertheless they all of them looked sleek and cheerful, and kept holiday the whole year round. In education they were sadly deficient, and knew no Russian, but were kindly and attractive folk for all that.

As soon as they caught sight of Pakhom they came out of their wagons and surrounded the guest. An interpreter was found, and Pakhom told him that he had come to buy land. At once the people were delighted, and, embracing Pakhom fervently, escorted him to a well-appointed wagon, where they made him sit down on a pile of rugs topped with soft cushions, and set about getting some tea and kumiss ready. A sheep was killed, and a meal served of the mutton, after which Pakhom produced the gifts from his tarantass, distributed them round, and shared out also the tea. Then the Bashkirs fell to talking among themselves for a while, and finally bid the interpreter speak.

"I am to tell you," said the interpreter, "that they are greatly taken with you, and that it is our custom to meet the wishes of a guest in every possible way, in return for the presents given us. Since, therefore you have given us presents, say now what there is of ours which you may desire, so that we may grant it you."

"What I particularly desire," replied Pakhom, "is some of your land. Where I come from," he continued, "there is not enough land, and what there is is ploughed out, whereas you have much land, and good land, such as I have never before beheld."

The interpreter translated, and the Bashkirs talked again among themselves. Although Pakhom could not understand what they were saying, he could see that they kept crying out something in merry tones and then bursting into laughter. At last they stopped and looked at Pakhom, while the interpreter spoke.

"I am to tell you," he said, "that in return for your kindness we are ready to sell you as much land as you may wish. Merely make a gesture with your hand to signify how much, and it shall be yours."

At this point, however, the people began to talk among themselves again, and to dispute about something. On Pakhom asking what it was, the interpreter told him: "Some of them say that the Starshina ought to be asked first about the land, and that nothing should be done without him, while others say that that is not necessary."

CHAPTER VI

THE STARSHINA

SUDDENLY, while the Bashkirs were thus disputing, there entered the wagon a man in a foxskin cap, at whose entry everyone rose, while the interpreter said to Pakhom: "This is the Starshina

himself." At once Pakhom caught up the best khalat and offered it to the newcomer, as well as five pounds of tea. The Starshina duly accepted them, and then sat down in the place of honour, while the Bashkirs began to expound to him some matter or another. He listened and listened, then gave a smile, and spoke to Pakhom in Russian.

"Very well," he said, "pray choose your land wheresoever it pleases you. We have much land."

"So I am to take as much as I want!" thought Pakhom to himself. "Still, I must strengthen that bargain somehow. They might say, 'The land is yours,' and then take it away again."

"I thank you," he said aloud, "for your kind speech. As you say, you have much land, whereas I am in need of some. I only desire to know precisely which of it is to be mine; wherefore it might be well to measure it off by some method and duly convey it to me. God only is lord of life and death, and, although you are good people who now give it to me, it might befall that your children would take it away again."

The Starshina smiled.

"The conveyance," he said, "is already executed. This present meeting is our mode of confirming it—and it could not be a surer one."

"But," said Pakhom, "I have been told that a merchant visited you recently, and that you sold him land and gave him a proper deed of conveyance. Pray, therefore, do the same with me."

The Starshina understood now.

"Very well," he replied. "We have a writer here, and will go to a town and procure the necessary seals."

"But what is your price for the land?" asked Pakhom.

"Our price," answered the Starshina, "is only 1000 roubles per day."

Pakhom did not understand this day-rate at all.

"How many dessiatins would that include?" he inquired presently.

"We do not reckon in that way," said the Starshina. "We sell only by the day. That is to say, as much land as you can walk round in a day, that much land is yours. That is our measure, and the price is 1000 roubles."

Pakhom was astounded.

"Why, a man might walk round a great deal in a day," he said.

The Starshina smiled again.

"Well, at all events," he said, "it will be yours. *Only,* there is one condition—namely, that if on that same day you do not return to the spot whence you started, your money is forfeited."

"But how do you decide upon that spot?" asked Pakhom.

"We take our stand," replied the Starshina, "upon whatsoever spot you may select. I and my people remain there, while you start off and describe a circle. Behind you will ride some of our young men, to plant stakes wherever you may desire that to be done. Thereafter, a plough will be driven round those stakes. Describe what circle you wish; only, by the time of the setting of the sun you must have returned to the place from which you started. As much land as you may circle, that much land will be yours."

So Pakhom accepted these terms, and it was agreed to make an early start on the morrow. Then the company talked again, drank more kumiss, and ate more mutton, passing on thence to tea, and the ceremonies being prolonged until nightfall. At length Pakhom was led to a bed of down and the Bashkirs dispersed, after first promising to gather on the morrow beyond the river and ride out to the appointed spot before sunrise.

CHAPTER VII

THE DREAM

PAKHOM lay on his bed of down, but could not get a wink of sleep for thinking of the land which, as he said, "I am going to farm here."

"For I mean to mark out a very large 'Promised Land' to-morrow," he continued to himself. "I can cover at least fifty versts in the day, and fifty versts should enclose somewhere about 10,000 dessiatins. Then I shall be under nobody's thumb, and be able to afford a pair-ox plough and two labourers. I shall plough up the best land, and feed stock on the rest."

All that night Pakhom never closed his eyes, but dozed off for a short while just before dawn. The instant he did so he had a dream. He seemed to be lying in this identical wagon and listening to somebody laughing and talking outside. Wishing to see who it was that was laughing so much, he went outside, and saw the Starshina sitting on the ground and holding his sides as he rolled about in ecstasies of mirth. Then in his dream Pakhom walked up to him and asked him what the joke was—and immediately saw that it was not the Starshina at all, but the merchant who had so lately visited him to tell him about this land.

Then again, he had scarcely so much as said to the merchant, "Did I not see you at my home a little while ago?" when the merchant suddenly changed into the peasant from away down the Volga who had called at his farm in the old country. Finally Pakhom perceived that this peasant was not a peasant at all, but the Devil himself, with horns and hoofs, and that he was gazing fixedly at something as he sat there and laughed. Then Pakhom thought to himself: "What is he looking at, and why does he laugh so much?" And in his dream he stepped a little aside to look, and saw a man—barefooted, and clad only in a shirt and breeches—lying flat on his back, with his face as white as a sheet. And presently, looking yet more attentively at the man, Pakhom saw that the man was himself!

He gave a gasp and awoke—awoke feeling as if the dream were real. Then he looked to see if it were getting light yet, and saw that the dawn was near.

"It is time to start," he thought. "I must arouse these good people."

CHAPTER VIII

THE RAVINE

PAKHOM arose, awakened his workman in the tarantass, and told him to put the horse in and go round to call the Bashkirs, since it was time to go out onto the steppe and measure off the land. So the Bashkirs arose and got themselves ready, and the Starshina also arrived. They breakfasted off kumiss, and were for giving Pakhom some tea, but he could not wait. "If we are to go, let us go," he said. "It is fully time." So the Bashkirs harnessed up and set out, some on horseback, and some in carts, while Pakhom drove in his tarantass with his workman. They came out onto the steppe just as the dawn was breaking, and proceeded towards a little knoll—called in the Bashkir dialect a shichan. There the people in carts alighted, and everyone collected together. The Starshina approached Pakhom and pointed all round with his hand. "Whatsoever land you see from here," he said, "is ours. Choose whichsoever direction you like." Pakhom's eyes glowed, for all the land was grass, level as the palm of his hand, and black beneath the turf as a poppy-head. Only where there was a ravine was there a break in the grass—grass which was everywhere breast-high. The Starshina took off his foxskin cap, and laid it in the exact centre of the knoll. "This," he said, "will be the mark. Lay you your money in it, and your servant shall remain beside it while you are gone. From this mark you will start, and to this mark you will return. As much land as you circle, all of it will be yours."

Pakhom took out his money, and laid it in the cap. Then he divested himself of his cloak, stripped himself to his waistcoat, tightened his belt round his stomach, thrust a wallet with some bread into his bosom, tied a flask of water to his shoulder-strap, pulled up his long boots, and prepared to start. He kept debating within himself which direction it would be best to take, for the land was so good everywhere. "Oh, well, as it is all the same, I will walk towards the rising sun," he decided at length. So he turned his face that way, and kept trying his limbs while waiting for the sun to appear. "I must lose no time," he thought, "for I shall do my best walking while the air is yet cool."

Then the mounted Bashkirs also ascended the knoll, and stationed themselves behind Pakhom. No sooner had the sun shot his first rays above the horizon than Pakhom started forward and walked out into the steppe, the mounted men riding behind him.

He walked neither slowly nor hurriedly. After he had gone about a verst he stopped, and had a stake put in. Then he went on again. He was losing his first stiffness and beginning to lengthen his stride. Presently he stopped again, and had another stake put in. He looked up at the sun— which was now lighting the knoll clearly, with the people standing there —and calculated that he had gone about five versts. He was beginning to grow warm now, so he took off his waistcoat, and then fastened up his belt again. Then he went on another five versts, and stopped. It was growing really hot now. He looked at the sun again, and saw that it was breakfast time. "One stage done!" he thought. "But there are four of them in the day, and it is early yet to change my direction. Nevertheless, I must take my boots off." So he sat down, took them off, and went on again. Walking was easier now. "As soon as I have covered another five versts," he reflected, "I will begin to bend round to the left. That spot was exceedingly well chosen. The further I go, the better the land is." So he kept straight on, although, when he looked round, the knoll was almost out of sight, and

the people on it looked like little black ants.

"Now," he said to himself at length, "I have made the circle large enough, and must bend round." He had sweated a good deal and was thirsty, so he raised the flask and took a drink. Then he had a stake put in at that point, and bent round sharply to the left. On he went and on, through the high grass and the burning heat. He was beginning to tire now, and glancing at the sun, saw that it was dinnertime. "Now," he thought to himself, "I might venture to take a rest." So he stopped and ate some bread, though without sitting down, since he said to himself: "If I once sat down I should go on to *lying* down, and so end by going off to sleep." He waited a little, therefore, till he felt rested, and then went on again. At first he found walking easy, for the meal had revived his strength, but presently the sun seemed to grow all the hotter as it began to slant towards evening. Pakhom was nearly worn out now, yet he merely thought to himself: "An hour's pain may a century gain."

He had traversed about ten versts of this lap of the circle, and was about to bend inwards again to the left, when he caught sight of an excellent bit of land round a dry ravine. It would be a pity to leave that out. "Flax would grow so splendidly there!" he thought. So he kept straight on until he had taken in the ravine, and, having had a stake planted at the spot, again wheeled inwards. Looking towards the knoll he could see that the people there were almost indistinguishable. They could not be less than fifteen versts away. "Well," he thought, "I have covered the two long laps of the circuit, and must take this last one by the shortest cut possible." So he started upon the last lap, and quickened his pace. Once again he looked at the sun. It was now drawing near to the time of the evening meal, and he had only covered two versts of the distance. The starting point was still thirteen versts away. "I must hurry straight along now," he said to himself, "however rough the country be. I must not take in a single extra piece on the way. I have enclosed sufficient as it is." And Pakhom headed straight for the knoll.

CHAPTER IX

THE GRAVE

HE pressed on straight in its direction, yet found walking very difficult now. His feet were aching badly, for he had chafed and bruised them, and they were beginning to totter under him. He would have given anything to have rested for a while, yet knew that he must not if he was ever to regain the knoll before sunset. The sun at least would not wait. Nay, it was like a driver ever lashing him on. From time to time he staggered. "Surely I have not miscalculated?" he thought to himself. "Surely I have not taken in too much land ever to get back, however much I hurry? There is such a long way to go yet, and I am dead beat. It cannot be that all my money and toil have gone in vain? Ah, well, I must do my best."

Pakhom pulled himself together, and broke into a run. He had torn his feet till they were bleeding, yet he still ran on, ran on, ran further and further. Waistcoat, boots, flask, cap—

he flung them all away. "Ah!" was his thought, "I was too pleased with what I saw. Now everything is lost, and I shall never reach the mark before sunset." His fears served to render him only the more breathless, but he still ran on, his shirt and breeches clinging to his limbs with sweat, and his mouth parched. In his breast there were a pair of blacksmith's bellows working, and in his heart a steam hammer, while his legs seemed to be breaking under him and to be no longer his own. He had lost all thought of the land now. All that he thought of was to avoid dying from exertion. Yet, although he was so afraid of dying, he could not stop. "To have gone so far," he thought, "and then to stop! Why, they would think me a fool!" By this time he could hear the Bashkirs cheering and shouting to him, and their cries stirred his heart with fresh spirit. On, on he ran with his last remaining strength, while the sun was just touching the horizon. Ah, but he was close to the spot now! He could see the people on the knoll waving their hands to him and urging him on. He could see the foxskin cap lying on the ground, the money in it, the Starshina sitting beside it with his hands pressed to his sides. Suddenly Pakhom remembered his dream. "Yet I have much land now," he thought, "if only God should bring me safe to live upon it. But my heart misgives me that I have killed myself." Still he ran on. For the last time he looked at the sun. Large and red, it had touched the earth, and was beginning to sink below the horizon. Pakhom reached the knoll just as it set. "Ah!" he cried in his despair, for he thought that everything was lost. Suddenly, however, he remembered that he could not see from below so well as could the people on the knoll above him, and that to them the sun would still seem not to have set. He rushed at the slope, and could see as he scrambled up it that the cap was still there. Then he stumbled and fell—yet in the very act of falling stretched out his hands towards the cap—and touched it!

"Ah, young man," cried the Starshina, "you have earned much land indeed!"

Pakhom's servant ran to his master and tried to raise him, but blood was running from his mouth. Pakhom lay there dead. The servant cried out in consternation, but the Starshina remained sitting on his haunches—laughing, and holding his hands to his sides.

At length he got up, took a spade from the ground, and threw it to the servant.

"Bury him," was all he said.

The Bashkirs arose and departed. Only the servant remained. He dug a grave of the same length as Pakhom's form from head to heels—three Russian ells—and buried him.

Elias

In the Province of Oufa there lived a Bashkir named Elias. His father died a year after he had procured his son a wife, and left him a poor man. At that time Elias's property consisted only of seven mares, two cows, and twenty sheep, but now that he had become master he began to better himself. He and his wife worked hard from morning till night—rising earlier, and resting later, than any of their neighbours, and growing richer each year. For thirty-five years Elias lived this life of toil, and amassed a considerable fortune.

That fortune consisted of two hundred horses, a hundred and fifty head of cattle, and twelve hundred sheep. He had men to look after the droves of horses and the herds of cattle and sheep, and women to milk the mares and cows and to make kumiss, butter, and cheese. Indeed. he had much of everything, and everyone in the countryside envied him his lot. People said: "Elias must be a happy man. He has everything in abundance, and has no reason to desire death." The gentry sought his acquaintance, and cultivated it when made. Guests came from long distances to visit him, and each and all he received and entertained with food and drink. For everyone who arrived he would have kumiss, tea, sherbet, and mutton prepared. No sooner had a guest appeared than a sheep or two would be killed, or, if the guests were many, a mare.

The children of Elias numbered two sons and a daughter, all of whom he duly married off. In the days of his poverty his sons had worked with him, and themselves tended the droves and herds; but when they became rich, they began to indulge in dissipation, and one of them, in particular, to drink to excess. Eventually the eldest of the two was killed in a brawl, and the other one (who had fallen under the thumb of an upstart wife) became disobedient to his father, and was turned out in consequence.

Elias turned him out, but at the same time allotted him a house and cattle, so that his own wealth became diminished in proportion.

Soon afterwards his sheep became infected with disease, and numbers of them died. Next, there came a year of drought, when no hay grew, so that many cattle were starved during the following winter. Then the Khirgizes came and stole the best of his horses, and his property became diminished yet further. Lower and lower he sank, and his perseverance also; so that, by the time he had reached his seventieth year, he had been reduced to selling his sheepskin coats, his carpets, saddles, tilt-carts, and, eventually, his last remaining cattle, and had arrived at absolute penury. Then, when he saw that he had nothing left, he and his wife went to spend their declining years among strangers. All the property now left to him consisted of the clothes on his body (a sheepskin coat, a cap, a pair of breeches, and boots) and his wife, Sham Shemagi, who was as old as himself. The son whom he had turned out had gone to a distant land, and his daughter was dead; so that there was no one left to help the old people.

Yet a former neighbor of theirs, named Muhamedshah, felt sorry for them. He was neither rich nor poor, but lived plainly and was a respectable man. Remembering the days when he had partaken of bread and salt in the house of Elias, he felt his heart smite him, and said: "Come and live with me, Elias, and bring the old woman with you. In the summer you can do such work for me in the melon fields as you feel fit for, and in the winter you can tend my cattle, while Sham Shemagi can milk the mares and make kumiss. I will feed and clothe you both, and if you should need anything else you will merely have to tell me, and I will give it you.' Elias thanked his good neighbour, and went with his old wife to live in the service of Muhamedshah. At first it grieved them to do so, but in time they got used to it, and settled down to live there and to work as far as their strength permitted.

It suited their master to have them in his service, since the old people had been in authority themselves, and so knew how to do things. Moreover, they were never lazy, but worked the best they knew. Yet Muhamedshah used to feel sorry to see people formerly so high in the world now reduced to such a pass.

It happened once that some of Muhamedshah's relations came to visit him —people who lived in a distant spot—and with them a certain mullah. Muhamedshah bid Elias catch and kill a sheep; which duly slaughtered and skinned, Elias cooked, and sent in to dinner. The guests ate of the mutton, drank tea and passed on to kumiss. While they were sitting with their host on carpets and padded cushions as they drank cups of kumiss and conversed together, Elias happened to pass the door in the course of his duties. Muhamedshah saw him, and said to one of the guests: "Did you see that old man who passed the door just now?" "Yes," replied the guest; "but what of him?" "Well, this—that his name is Elias, and that once upon a time he was our richest man about here. Perhaps you have heard of him?" "Heard of him?" exclaimed the guest. "Yes, certainly I have, but this is the first time I have ever seen him, al-

though his fame used to be widespread."
"Well, now the old man has nothing at
all, but I keep him on as my servant,
and his old wife lives with him, and
milks the cows."

The guest clicked his tongue, shook
his head, and evinced much surprise.
Then he said: "Verily fortune is like a
wheel turning. It lifts up one man, and
sets down another. Does the old man
grieve about his plight?" "Who knows?
He lives quietly and peaceably, and does
his work well." "Might I, then, speak
to him?" inquired the guest. "I should
like to ask him about his former life."
"Certainly," replied the host, and called
behind the door-curtain: "Babai!"
(which means "Diediushka" in the Bashkir language), "come in and have some
kumiss, and call your wife also." So
Elias and his wife entered, and, having
greeted the guests and their master, the
old man said a grace and knelt down by
the door, while his wife went behind the
curtain where her mistress was sitting,
and seated herself beside her.

Elias was offered a cup of kumiss,
whereupon he wished the guests and his
master good health, bowed to them, drank
a little of the kumiss, and set the cup
down.

"Old man," said the guest, "tell me
whether it grieves you—now as you look
upon us—to remember your former fortunes and your present life of misery?"

Elias smiled and answered: "If I
were to speak to you of our happiness or
misery you might not believe me. You
should rather ask my wife. She has
both a woman's heart and a woman's
tongue, and will tell you the whole truth
about that matter."

Then the guest called to the old woman
behind the curtain: "Tell me, old

woman, what you think concerning your
former happiness and your present
misery."

And Sham Shemagi answered from
behind the curtain: "This is what I
think concerning them. I lived with
my husband for fifty years—seeking happiness, and never finding it; but now,
although we live as servants, and this is
only the second year since we were left
destitute, we have found true happiness,
and desire no other."

Both the guests and their host were
surprised at this—the latter, indeed, so
much so that he rose to his feet to draw
aside the curtain and look at the old
woman. There she stood—her hands
folded in front of her, and a smile upon
her face, as she gazed at her old husband
and he smiled back at her in return.
Then she went on: "I am but telling
you the truth, not jesting. For half a
century we sought happiness, and never
found it so long as we were rich; yet
now that we have nothing—now that
we have come to live among humble
folk—we have found such happiness as
could never be exceeded."

"Wherein, then, does your happiness
lie?" asked the guest.

"In this—that so long as we were rich
I and my husband never knew an hour's
peace in which we could either talk to
one another, or think about our souls,
or pray to God. We had too many cares
for that. If guests were with us we were
fully occupied in thinking how to entertain them and what to give them so that
they would not scorn us. Moreover,
when guests had arrived we had their
servants to look to—to see that they
should not compare their board and lodging with that given them elsewhere, and

compare it to our disadvantage, while at the same time we had to watch that they did not consume our entire substance—an act of sin on our part. Then again, there would be constant worries lest a wolf should kill one of our foals or calves, or thieves drive off the horses. If we lay down to sleep we could not do so for thinking that the ewes might overlay their lambs. Half the night we would be up and doing, and then, when we retired to rest once more, we would find ourselves beset with fresh anxieties as to how to procure fodder for the winter, and so on. Moreover, my husband and I could never agree together. He would say that a thing must be done in this way, and I that it must be done in that; and so we would begin to quarrel, and thus commit another act of sin. The life led us only from worry to worry, from sin to sin, but never to happiness."

"But how is it now?" asked the guest.

"Now," replied the old woman, "when I and my husband rise in the morning, we always greet each other in love and harmony. We quarrel over nothing, and are anxious about nothing. Our only care is how best to serve the master. We work according to our strength, and with a good will, so that the master shall suffer no loss, but on the contrary acquire gain. Then, when we come in, we find dinner, supper, and kumiss ready for us. Whenever it is cold we have fuel to warm us and sheepskin coats to wear. Moreover, we have time to talk to one another, to think about our souls, and to pray to God. For fifty years we sought happiness—but only now have we found it."

The guests burst out laughing, but Elias cried:

"Do not laugh, good sirs. This is no jest, but human life. Once I and my wife were gross of heart and wept because we had lost our riches, but now God has revealed unto us the truth, and we reveal it unto you again—not for our own diversion, but for your good."

To which the mullah added: "That is a wise saying, and Elias has spoken the truth—a truth which is found set down in Holy Writ."

Then the guests ceased to make merry, and became thoughtful.

Wisdom of Children

HOLY WEEK fell early. Sledding was only just over, and snow still lay in the shelter of the courtyards, or, melting, ran in rivulets down the village street. A large pool had oozed from beneath the slush, and collected in an alleyway between two yards. From those yards there hied them to this pool a couple of little girls—an elder and a younger. Their mothers had just dressed them in brand-new frocks (the younger one in a blue frock, and the elder in a yellow, embroidered one), and tied red handkerchiefs over their heads. The pair issued forth after dinner, and betook them to the side of the pool, where they first of all showed each other their fine clothes, and then fell to playing. They thought they would like to wade across the pool, and accordingly the younger one started to do so, shoes and all. The elder one, however, cried: "Don't go in like that, Malasha, or your mother will scold you. Take off your shoes first, and I will do the same." So they took off their shoes, tucked up their frocks, and waded across the pool from opposite sides. Malasha went in over her ankles, and called out: "It is so deep, Akulka dear, I am afraid." "No, no," replied the other, "it can't get any deeper. Come straight across to me." So they drew nearer. Then Akulka said: "Mind, Malasha, and don't splash me. Go gently." The words were hardly out of her mouth when Malasha gave a stamp with her foot, and splashed the water straight onto Akulka's frock. It was splashed all over, and so were her eyes and nose. When Akulka saw the stains on her frock she was very angry with Malasha, scolded her furiously, and ran towards her to give her a slap. Malasha, however, was frightened when she saw the damage she had done, and, jumping out of the pool, ran home. Now, Akulka's mother happened to pass that way, and saw her daughter with her frock all splashed and her petticoat mudded over. "How did you manage to get so dirty, you bad girl?' she asked. "Malasha splashed me. She did it on purpose," answered her little daughter. So Akulka's mother caught Malasha, and spanked her soundly, so that the street rang with her weeping. That brought her mother out. "What are you beating my child for?" she cried angrily to her neighbour, and the pair began bandying words. The peasants came out of their huts, and a small crowd collected in the street. Every one shouted, but no one listened, as the crowd wrangled and wrangled. At last one peasant pushed against another one,

and a fight was imminent, when an old woman—Akulka's grandmother—appeared on the scene. Running into the midst of the peasants, she cried protestingly: "Now then, good people! Is this the way in which this Holy Week should be spent? You ought all of you to be giving thanks to God, and not conspiring to sin like this." But the peasants would not listen to her, and almost pushed her off her legs. Indeed, she would never have dissuaded the two peasants from fighting but for Malasha and Akulka themselves. While the women had been quarreling, Akulka had gone in and wiped her frock, and then came out again to the pool in the alley-way. There she picked up a small stone, and began to dig out the earth by the side of the pool. While thus engaged, she was joined by Malasha, who began to help her to dig out a little channel with a chip of wood. The peasants were just starting to fight, when the water escaped out of the pool through the little channel dug by the children, and ran out into the street to the spot where the old woman was trying to separate the two peasants. The little girls came darting out of the alleyway, one on each side of the tiny stream. "Stop it, Malasha! Stop it!" cried Akulka. Malasha also was trying to say something, but could not speak for laughter.

Thus the two little girls came running along, laughing at the chip of wood as it bobbed about in the rivulet—and ran straight into the midst of the peasants. As soon as the old woman saw them she cried to the two disputants: "Have some respect for God! Here are you gathered together to fight about these same little girls, yet they themselves have long ago forgotten the whole matter, and are playing together again in peace and goodwill. They are wiser than you."

The two disputants looked at the little girls, and felt ashamed of themselves, while the other peasants burst out laughing at their own folly, and dispersed to their huts.

"If ye do not become as little children, ye shall not enter into the kingdom of Heaven."

The Right Way

AMONG the Patagonians there is current the following tradition.

At first (it runs) God created men so that they had no need to work, nor to provide themselves with shelter, clothing, or food. Every man lived to be a hundred exactly, and was immune from disease.

Time passed on, and when God looked down to see how mankind was faring, He found that, instead of rejoicing in their lot, men were thinking only of themselves, quarreling with each other, and ordering their existence in such a way that life was to them rather a curse than a blessing.

Then God said to Himself: "This comes of their living apart from one another, each man for himself." So, to put an end to that, He made it impossible for men to live without labour. If they would avoid suffering from cold and hunger they must build themselves dwellings, till the ground, and rear flocks and herds.

"Labour will unite them," thought God to Himself. "No man can hew and draw wood, build dwellings, forge implements, sow, reap, spin, weave, or make clothing, alone. Therefore men will be forced to recognize that the more they associate in labour, the more they will produce, and the more comfortable will their life be. This cannot but unite them."

Time passed on, and once more God looked down to see how mankind was faring, and whether it were now rejoicing in its lot. Yet He found men living even worse than before. True, they worked together (they could not do otherwise), but not all together, for they had divided themselves up into groups, each of which strove to depute its labour to another, as well as hindered its fellows, and wasted both time and energy in quarrelling. This was bad for all of them.

Seeing this, God decided to make men ignorant of the precise moment of their death, as well as liable to die at any age, instead of at a hundred exactly. This expedient He justified to Himself thus:

"When men know that they may die at any moment they will be too careful of their lives (hanging, as those lives will be, by a single thread) to rage against one another and so put in jeopardy those hours of life which may be allotted them."

Yet things turned out quite otherwise. When God looked down once more to see how mankind was faring He found that the life of men had in no way altered for the better.

Some men were stronger than others.

and so were able to avail themselves of the fact that death might come at any moment to intimidate those weaker than themselves, by killing a certain proportion of them and threatening the rest. Thus an order of life had arisen in which a certain number of strong men and their followers did no work at all, but consumed themselves in idleness, while the weaker were forced to work beyond their strength, and deteriorated for want of rest. Each of these two classes feared and detested the other, and the life of mankind had become more unhappy than ever.

Seeing how things stood, God determined to make use of the last remedy of all. That is to say, He sent every kind of disease among men; for He thought that when they had become subject to disease they would realize that the healthy man must pity and assist the sick, so that if he himself fell ill, he too might receive assistance from the healthy.

Then for a time God left mankind alone; but when He looked down once more to see how things were getting on, He found that from the very moment when men had been made subject to disease their life had been growing steadily worse. The diseases which God had thought would unite them had only served to sunder them more. Those who had been used to compelling others to work for them now compelled them also to wait upon them when sick, although they themselves took no thought whatever for other sufferers. At the same time, those who were thus compelled not only to work for others, but also to wait upon them when sick, were so overburdened with labour that they had no opportunity to attend to their own sick folk, and so had to leave them helpless. Moreover, some diseases were recognized to be infectious, so that, dreading the infection, many men would neither go near the sufferers nor consort with those who had come in contact with them.

Then God said to Himself:

"Since by these means I have failed to bring men to understand wherein lies their true happiness, I will leave them to arrive at that result through their tribulations."

Thenceforth, therefore, God left mankind alone.

Abandoned to their own devices, men lived for a long time without understanding the means by which it was both possible and right for them to live happily. But at last some of them began to realize that labour need not of necessity mean, for some a means of subjecting their fellows, and for others a kind of penal servitude, but rather a source of joy, uniting all men in one. Likewise, they realized that, in face of that death which threatened every man hourly, the only prudent course for them was to make up their minds to spend in concord and love such years, months, days, hours, or minutes as might be ordained them. Lastly, they realized, not only that disease should not be a source of division among men but that, on the contrary, it should be a source of loving good-fellowship.

The Grain

ONCE upon a time some children found, in a ravine, a little round something that was like an egg; but it also had a groove down the middle, and so was like a grain of corn. A passer-by saw this something in the children's hands, and bought it off them for a piatak. Then he took it away to town and sold it to the Tsar as a curiosity.

The Tsar sent for his wise men, and commanded them to examine the little round something and to say if it was an egg or a grain of corn. The wise men pondered and pondered, but could not solve the problem.

So the little round something was left lying on a window-sill, and a hen flew in, pecked at the little round something, and pecked a hole in it; so that everyone could now see that it was a grain of corn. Wherefore the wise men hastened to return and tell the Tsar that the little round something was nothing else than a grain of rye.

The Tsar was astonished, and commanded the wise men to ascertain where and when this grain was grown. So the wise men pondered and pondered, and searched their books, but could discover nothing. They returned to the Tsar, therefore, and said: "We cannot resolve those two questions, for we find nothing written in our books about them. But let your Imperial Majesty cause inquiry to be made among the peasantry, lest haply any one of them has ever heard from his elders where and when this grain was sown."

So the Tsar sent and commanded a very ancient elder of the peasantry to be brought to him. Such a one was searched for, and conducted to the Tsar's presence. The old man was livid and toothless, and walked with difficulty on crutches.

The Tsar showed him the grain, which was unlike anything that the old man had ever seen before. Indeed, he could hardly see it now, but half-examined it with his eyes, half-felt it with his hands. Then the Tsar asked him:

"Do you know, good grandfather, where this grain was grown? Did you yourself ever sow similar grain in your field, or did you ever in your time buy similar grain?"

The old man was deaf, and heard and understood only with great difficulty, so that he was slow in answering.

"No," he said at last, "it never befell me to sow such grain in my field, nor to reap such grain, nor to buy it. When we bought corn it was all of fine, small grain. But," he continued, "you would do well to ask my father. He may have heard where such a grain as this one was grown."

So the Tsar sent the old man to fetch his father, and commanded the latter to be brought to him. The father of the old man was duly found and conducted to the presence, and he entered it hobbling on one crutch only. The Tsar showed him the grain and, as the old man still had the use of his eyes, he was able to see it quite clearly. Then the Tsar asked him:

"Do you know, my good old man, where such a grain was grown? Did you ever yourself sow similar grain in your field? Or did you ever in your time buy similar grain from anywhere?"

The old man was a little hard of hearing, yet he could hear much better than his son.

"No," he said, "it never befell me to sow or to reap such grain; no, nor yet to buy it, since in my time money had not begun to be used in trade. Everyone grew his own bread, and, as regarded other needs, one shared with another. I do not know where such a grain as this one can have been grown, for, although our grain was larger than grain is now and gave more flour, I have never before seen such a grain. But I have heard my father say that in his time better corn was reaped than in mine, and that it was larger and yielded more flour. You would do well to send and ask him."

So the Tsar sent for the father of this old man, and the father was found and conducted to the presence. He entered it without crutches at all—walking easily, in fact—while his eyes were still bright and he spoke distinctly. The Tsar showed him the grain, and the old man looked at it and turned it over and over.

"Ah," he said, "but it is many a long day since I have seen a grain of olden times like this one!" Then he nibbled the grain and chewed a morsel of it. "It is the same!" he exclaimed.

"Tell me, then, grandfather," said the Tsar, "where and when such grain as this was grown? Did you yourself ever sow such grain in your field? Or did you ever in your time buy it anywhere of others?"

Then the old man replied:

"In my time such grain as this was reaped everywhere. It was on such grain that I myself lived and supported others. Such grain have I both sowed and reaped and ground."

And the Tsar asked him again:

"Tell me, good grandfather, was it ever your custom to buy such grain anywhere, or always to sow it yourself in your own field?"

The old man smiled.

"In my time," he said, "no one would ever have thought of committing so great a sin as to buy or to sell grain. We knew nothing of money. Each man had as much grain as he wanted."

Then the Tsar asked him again:

"Tell me, good grandfather, where it was that you sowed such grain—where, indeed, your field was?"

And the old man replied:

"My field was God's earth. Where I ploughed, that was my field. The earth was free, and no man called it his own. All that he called his own was the labour of his own hands."

"Tell me now," said the Tsar, "two other things: firstly, why it is that such grain once grew, but grows not now; and secondly, why it is that your grandson walked on two crutches, and your son on one, while you yourself walk easily without any at all, and have, moreover, your eyes still bright and your teeth still strong and your speech still clear and kindly. Tell me the reason for these two things."

Then answered the old man:

"The reason for those two things is that men have ceased to live by their labour alone, and have begun to hanker after their neighbours' goods. In the olden days they lived not so. In the olden days they lived according to God's word. They were masters of their own, and coveted not what belonged to another."

Martin Avdeitch

In a certain town there lived a shoe-maker named Martin Avdeitch. He lived in a basement room which possessed but one window. This window looked onto the street, and through it a glimpse could be caught of the passers-by. It is true that only their legs could be seen, but that did not matter, as Martin could recognize people by their boots alone. He had lived here for a long time, and so had many acquaintances. There were very few pairs of boots in the neighborhood which had not passed through his hands at least once, if not twice. Some he had resoled, others he had fitted with side-pieces, others, again, he had resewn where they were split, or provided with new toe-caps. Yes, he often saw his handiwork through that window. He was given plenty of custom, for his work lasted well, his materials were good, his prices moderate, and his word to be depended on. If he could do a job by a given time it should be done; but if not, he would warn you beforehand rather than disappoint you. Everyone knew Avdeitch, and no one ever transferred his custom from him. He had always been an upright man, but with the approach of old age he had begun more than ever to think of his soul, and to draw nearer to God.

His wife had died while he was still an apprentice, leaving behind her a little boy of three. This was their only child, indeed, for the two elder ones had died previously. At first Martin thought of placing the little fellow with a sister of his in the country, but changed his mind, thinking: "My Kapitoshka would not like to grow up in a strange family, so I will keep him by me." Then Avdeitch finished his apprenticeship, and went to live in lodgings with his little boy. But God had not seen fit to give Avdeitch happiness in his children. The little boy was just growing up and beginning to help his father and to be a pleasure to him, when he fell ill, was put to bed, and died after a week's fever.

Martin buried the little fellow and was inconsolable. Indeed, he was so inconsolable that he began to murmur against God. His life seemed so empty that more than once he prayed for death and reproached the Almighty for taking away his only beloved son instead of himself, the old man. At last he ceased altogether to go to church.

Then one day there came to see him an ancient peasant-pilgrim—one who was now in the eighth year of his pilgrimage. To him Avdeitch talked, and then went on to complain of his great sorrow.

"I no longer wish to be a God-fearing man," he said. "I only wish to die. That is all I ask of God. I am a lonely, hopeless man."

"You should not speak like that, Martin," replied the old pilgrim. "It is not for us to judge the acts of God. We must rely, not upon our own understanding, but upon the Divine wisdom. God saw fit that your son should die and that you should live. Therefore it must be better so. If you despair, it is because you have wished to live too much for your own pleasure."

"For what, then, should I live?" asked Martin.

"For God alone," replied the old man.

"It is He who gave you life, and therefore it is He for whom you should live. When you come to live for Him you will cease to grieve, and your trials will become easy to bear."

Martin was silent. Then he spoke again.

"But how am I to live for God?" he asked.

"Christ has shown us the way," answered the old man. "Can you read? If so, buy a Testament and study it. You will learn there how to live for God. Yes, it is all shown you there."

These words sank into Avdeitch's soul. He went out the same day, bought a large-print copy of the New Testament, and set himself to read it.

At the beginning Avdeitch had meant only to read on festival days, but when he once began his reading he found it so comforting to the soul that he came never to let a day pass without doing so. On the second occasion he became so engrossed that all the kerosene was burnt away in the lamp before he could tear himself away from the book.

Thus he came to read it every evening, and, the more he read, the more clearly did he understand what God required of him, and in what way he could live for God; so that his heart grew ever lighter and lighter. Once upon a time, whenever he had lain down to sleep, he had been used to moan and sigh as he thought of his little Kapitoshka; but now he only said—"Glory to Thee, O Lord! Glory to Thee! Thy will be done!"

From that time onwards Avdeitch's life became completely changed. Once he had been used to go out on festival days and drink tea in a tavern, and had not denied himself even an occasional

glass of vodka. This he had done in the company of a boon companion, and, although no drunkard, would frequently leave the tavern in an excited state and talk much nonsense as he shouted and disputed with this friend of his. But now he had turned his back on all this, and his life had become quiet and joyous. Early in the morning he would sit down to his work, and labour through his appointed hours. Then he would take the lamp down from a shelf, light it, and sit down to read. And the more he read, the more he understood, and the clearer and happier he grew at heart.

It happened once that Martin had been reading late. He had been reading those verses in the sixth chapter of the Gospel of St. Luke which run:

"And unto him that smiteth thee on the one cheek offer also the other; and him that taketh away thy cloke forbid not to take thy coat also. Give to every man that asketh of thee; and of him that taketh away thy goods ask them not again. And as we would that men should do to you, do ye also to them likewise."

Then, further on, he had read those verses where the Lord says:

"And why call ye Me, Lord, Lord, and do not the things which I say? Whosoever cometh to Me and heareth my sayings, and doeth them, I will show you to whom he is like: He is like a man which built an house, and digged deep, and laid the foundation on a rock: and when the flood arose, the storm beat vehemently upon that house, and could not shake it: for it was founded upon a rock. But he that heareth and doeth not, is like a man that without a foundation built an house upon the earth· against which the stream did beat vehemently, and immediately it fell; and the ruin of that house was great."

Avdeitch read these words, and felt greatly cheered in soul. He took off his spectacles, laid them on the book, leaned his elbows upon the table, and gave himself up to meditation. He set himself to measure his own life by those words, and thought to himself:

"Is my house founded upon a rock or upon sand? It is well if it be upon a rock. Yet it seems so easy to me as I sit here alone. I may so easily come to think that I have done all that the Lord has commanded me, and grow careless and—sin again. Yet I will keep on striving, for it is goodly so to do. Help Thou me, O Lord."

Thus he kept on meditating, though conscious that it was time for bed; yet he was loath to tear himself away from the book. He began to read the seventh chapter of St. Luke, and read on about the centurion, the widow's son, and the answer given to John's disciples; until in time he came to the passage where the rich Pharisee invited Jesus to his house, and the woman washed the Lord's feet with her tears and He justified her. So he came to the forty-fourth verse and read:

"And He turned to the woman, and said unto Simon, Seest thou this woman? I entered into thine house, and thou gavest Me no water for My feet: but she hath washed My feet with tears, and wiped them with the hairs of her head. Thou gavest Me no kiss: but this woman since the time I came in hath not ceased to kiss My feet. My head with oil thou didst not anoint: but this woman hath anointed My feet with ointment."

He read these verses and thought:

" 'Thou gavest Me no water for My feet' . . 'Thou gavest Me no kiss' . . . 'My head with oil thou didst not anoint' . . ."—and once again he took off his spectacles, laid them on the book, and became lost in meditation.

"I am even as that Pharisee," he thought to himself. "I drink tea and think only of my own needs. Yes, I think only of having plenty to eat and drink, of being warm and clean—but never of entertaining a guest. And Simon too was mindful only of himself, although the guest who had come to visit him was—who? Why, even the Lord Himself! If, then, He should come to visit *me*, should I receive Him any better?"—and, leaning forward upon his elbows, he was asleep almost before he was aware of it.

"Martin!" someone seemed to breathe in his ear. He started from his sleep.

"Who is there?" he said. He turned and looked towards the door, but could see no one. Again he bent forward over the table. Then suddenly he heard the words:

"Martin, Martin! Look thou into the street tomorrow, for I am coming to visit thee."

Martin roused himself, got up from the chair, and rubbed his eyes. He did not know whether it was dreaming or awake that he had heard these words, but he turned out the lamp and went to bed.

The next morning Avdeitch rose before daylight and said his prayers. Then he made up the stove, got ready some cabbage soup and porridge, lighted the samovar, slung his leather apron about him, and sat down to his work in the window. He sat and worked hard, yet all the time his thoughts were centred upon last night. He was in two ideas about the vision. At one moment he would think that it must have been his fancy, while the next moment he would find himself convinced that he had really heard the voice. "Yes, it must have been so," he concluded.

As Martin sat thus by the window he kept looking out of it as much as working. Whenever a pair of boots passed with which he was acquainted he would bend down to glance upwards through the window and see their owner's face as well. The doorkeeper passed in new felt boots, and then a water-carrier. Next, an old soldier, a veteran of Nicholas' army, in old, patched boots, and carrying a shovel in his hands, halted close by the window. Avdeitch knew him by his boots. His name was Stepanitch, and he was kept by a neighbouring tradesman out of charity, his duties being to help the doorkeeper. He began to clear away the snow from in front of Avdeitch's window, while the shoemaker looked at him and then resumed his work.

"I think I must be getting into my dotage," thought Avdeitch with a smile. "Just because Stepanitch begins clearing away the snow I at once jump to the conclusion that Christ is about to visit me. Yes, I am growing foolish now, old greybeard that I am."

Yet he had hardly made a dozen stitches before he was craning his neck again to look out of the window. He could see that Stepanitch had placed his shovel against the wall, and was resting and trying to warm himself a little.

"He is evidently an old man now and broken," thought Avdeitch to himself.

"He is not strong enough to clear away snow. Would he like some tea, I wonder? That reminds me that the samovar must be ready now."

He made fast his awl in his work and got up. Placing the samovar on the table, he brewed the tea, and then tapped with his finger on the window-pane. Stepanitch turned round and approached. Avdeitch beckoned to him, and then went to open the door.

"Come in and warm yourself," he said. "You must be frozen."

"Christ requite you!" answered Stepanitch. "Yes, my bones are almost cracking."

He came in, shook the snow off himself, and, though tottering on his feet, took pains to wipe them carefully, that he might not dirty the floor.

"Nay, do not trouble about that," said Avdeitch. "I will wipe your boots myself. It is part of my business in this trade. Come you here and sit down, and we will empty this tea-pot together."

He poured out two tumblerfuls, and offered one to his guest; after which he emptied his own into the saucer, and blew upon it to cool it. Stepanitch drank his tumblerful, turned the glass upside down, placed his crust upon it, and thanked his host kindly. But it was plain that he wanted another one.

"You must drink some more," said Avdeitch, and refilled his guest's tumbler and his own. Yet, in spite of himself, he had no sooner drunk his tea than he found himself looking out into the street again.

"Are you expecting anyone?" asked his guest.

"Am—am I expecting anyone? Well, to tell the truth, yes. That is to say, i am, and I am not. The fact is that some words have got fixed in my memory. Whether it was a vision or not I cannot tell, but at all events, my old friend, I was reading in the Gospels last night about Our Little Father Christ, and how He walked this earth and suffered. You have heard of Him, have you not?"

"Yes, yes, I have heard of Him," answered Stepanitch; "but we are ignorant folk and do not know our letters."

"Well, I was reading of how He walked this earth, and how He went to visit a Pharisee, and yet received no welcome from him at the door. All this I read last night, my friend, and then fell to thinking about it—to thinking how some day I too might fail to pay Our Little Father Christ due honour. 'Suppose,' I thought to myself, 'He came to me or to anyone like me? Should we, like the great lord Simon, not know how to receive Him and not go out to meet Him?' Thus I thought, and feel asleep where I sat. Then as I sat sleeping there I heard someone call my name; and as I raised myself the voice went on (as though it were the voice of someone whispering in my ear): 'Watch thou for me to-morrow, for I am coming to visit thee.' It said that twice. And so those words have got into my head, and foolish though I know it to be, I keep expecting *Him*—the Little Father —every moment."

Stepanitch nodded and said nothing, but emptied his glass and laid it aside. Nevertheless Avdeitch took and refilled it.

"Drink it up; it will do you good," he said. "Do you know," he went on,

"I often call to mind how, when Our Little Father walked this earth, there was never a man, however humble, whom He despised, and how it was chiefly among the common people that He dwelt. It was always with *them* that He walked; it was from among *them*—from among such men as you and I—from among sinners and working folk—that He chose His disciples. 'Whosoever,' He said, 'shall exalt himself, the same shall be abased; and whosoever shall abase himself, the same shall be exalted.' 'You,' He said again, 'call me Lord; yet will I wash your feet.' 'Whosoever,' He said, 'would be chief among you, let him be the servant of all. Because,' He said, 'blessed are the lowly, the peacemakers, the merciful, and the charitable.' "

Stepanitch had forgotten all about his tea. He was an old man, and his tears came easily. He sat and listened, with the tears rolling down his cheeks.

"Oh, but you must drink your tea," said Avdeitch; yet Stepanitch only crossed himself and said the thanksgiving, after which he pushed his glass away and rose.

"I thank you, Martin Avdeitch," he said. "You have taken me in, and fed both soul and body."

"Nay, but I beg of you to come again," replied Avdeitch. "I am only too glad of a guest."

So Stepanitch departed, while Martin poured out the last of the tea and drank it. Then he cleaned the crockery, and sat down again to his work by the window—to the stitching of a back-piece. He stitched away, yet kept on looking through the window—looking for Christ, as it were—and ever thinking of Christ and His works. Indeed, Christ's many sayings were never absent from Avdeitch's mind.

Two soldiers passed the window, the one in military boots, and the other in civilian. Next, there came a neighbouring householder, in polished goloshes; then a baker with a basket. All of them passed on. Presently a woman in woollen stockings and rough country shoes approached the window, and halted near the buttress outside it. Avdeitch peered up at her from under the lintel of his window, and could see that she was a plain-looking, poorly-dressed woman and had a child in her arms. It was in order to muffle the child up more closely—little though she had to do it with!—that she had stopped near the buttress and was now standing there with her back to the wind. Her clothing was ragged and fit only for summer, and even from behind his window-panes Avdeitch could hear the child crying miserably and its mother vainly trying to soothe it. Avdeitch rose, went to the door, climbed the steps, and cried out: "My good woman, my good woman!"

She heard him and turned round.

"Why need you stand there in the cold with your baby?" he went on. "Come into my room, where it is warm, and where you will be able to wrap the baby up more comfortably than you can do here. Yes, come in with you."

The woman was surprised to see an old man in a leather apron and with spectacles upon his nose calling out to her, yet she followed him down the steps, and they entered his room. The old man led her to the bedstead.

Sit you down here, my good woman," he said. "You will be near the stove, and can warm yourself and feed your baby."

"Ah, but I have no milk left in my breast," she replied. "I have had nothing to eat this morning." Nevertheless she put the child to suck.

Avdeitch nodded his head approvingly, went to the table for some bread and a basin, and opened the stove door. From the stove he took and poured some soup into the basin, and drew out also a bowl of porridge. The latter, however, was not yet boiling, so he set out only the soup, after first laying the table with a cloth.

"Sit down and eat, my good woman," he said, "while I hold your baby. I have had little ones of my own, and know how to nurse them."

The woman crossed herself and sat down, while Avdeitch seated himself upon the bedstead with the baby. He smacked his lips at it once or twice, but made a poor show of it, for he had no teeth left. Consequently the baby went on crying. Then he bethought him of his finger, which he wriggled to and fro towards the baby's mouth and back again—without, however, actually touching the little one's lips, since the finger was blackened with work and sticky with shoemaker's wax. The baby contemplated the finger and grew quiet—then actually smiled. Avdeitch was delighted. Meanwhile the woman had been eating her meal, and now she told him, unasked, who she was and whither she was going.

"I am a soldier's wife," she said, "but my husband was sent to a distant station eight months ago, and I have heard nothing of him since. At first I got a place as cook, but when the baby came they said they could not do with it and dismissed me. That was three months ago, and I have got nothing since, and have spent all my savings. I tried to get taken as a wet nurse, but no one would have me, for they said I was too thin. I have just been to see a tradesman's wife where our grandmother is in service. She had promised to take me on, and I quite thought that she would, but when I arrived to-day she told me to come again next week. She lives a long way from here, and I am quite worn out and have tired my baby for nothing. Thank, Heaven, however, my landlady is good to me, and gives me shelter for Christ's sake. Otherwise I should not have known how to bear it all."

Avdeitch sighed and said: "But have you nothing warm to wear?"

"Ah, sir," replied the woman, "although it is the time for warm clothes I had to pawn my last shawl yesterday for two grivenki."

Then the woman returned to the bedstead to take her baby, while Avdeitch rose and went to a cupboard. There he rummaged about, and presently returned with an old jacket.

"Here," he said. "It is a poor old thing, but it will serve to cover you."

The woman looked at the jacket, and then at the old man. Then she took the jacket and burst into tears. Avdeitch turned away, and went creeping under the bedstead, whence he extracted a box and pretended to rummage about in it for a few moments; after which he sat down again before the woman.

Then the woman said to him: "I thank you in Christ's name, good grandfather. Surely it was He Himself who sent me to your window. Otherwise I should have seen my baby perish with the cold. When I first came out the day was warm, but now it has begun to freeze. But He, Our Little Father, had placed you in your window, that you might see me in my bitter plight and have compassion upon me."

Avdeitch smiled and said: "He did indeed place me there: yet, my poor woman, it was for a special purpose that I was looking out."

Then he told his guest, the soldier's wife, of his vision, and how he had heard a voice foretelling that to-day the Lord Himself would come to visit him.

"That may very well be," said the woman as she rose, took the jacket, and wrapped her baby in it. Then she saluted him once more and thanked him.

"Also, take this in Christ's name," said Avdeitch, and gave her a two-grivenka piece with which to buy herself a shawl. The woman crossed herself, and he likewise. Then he led her to the door and dismissed her.

When she had gone Avdeitch ate a little soup, washed up the crockery again, and resumed his work. All the time, though, he kept his eye upon the window, and as soon as ever a shadow fell across it he would look up to see who was passing. Acquaintances of his came past, and people whom he did not know, yet never anyone very particular

Then suddenly he saw something. Opposite his window there had stopped an old pedlar-woman, with a basket of apples. Only a few of the apples, however, remained, so that it was clear that she was almost sold out. Over her shoulder was slung a sack of shavings, which she must have gathered near some new building as she was going home. Apparently, her shoulder had begun to ache under their weight, and she therefore wished to shift them to the other one. To do this, she balanced her basket of apples on the top of a post, lowered the sack to the pavement, and began shaking up its contents. As she was doing this, a boy in a ragged cap appeared from somewhere, seized an apple from the basket, and tried to make off. But the old woman, who had been on her guard, managed to turn and seize the boy by the sleeve, and although he struggled and tried to break away, she clung to him with both hands, snatched his cap off, and finally grasped him by the hair. Thereupon the youngster began to shout and abuse his captor. Avdeitch did not stop to make fast his awl, but threw his work down upon the floor, ran to the door, and went stumbling up the steps—losing his spectacles as he did so. Out into the street he ran, where the old woman was still clutching the boy by the hair and threatening to take him to the police, while the boy, for his part, was struggling in the endeavour to free himself.

"I never took it," he was saying. "What are you beating me for? Let me go."

Avdeitch tried to part them as he took the boy by the hand and said:

"Let him go, my good woman. Pardon him for Christ's sake."

"Yes, I will pardon him," she retorted, "but not until he has tasted a new birch-rod. I mean to take the young rascal to the police."

But Avdeitch still interceded for him.

"Let him go, my good woman," he said. "He will never do it again. Let him go for Christ's sake."

The old woman released the boy, who was for making off at once had not Avdeitch stopped him.

"You must beg the old woman's pardon," he said, "and never do such a thing again. I saw you take the apple."

The boy burst out crying, and begged the old woman's pardon as Avdeitch commanded.

"There, there," said Avdeitch. "Now I will give you one. Here you are,"— and he took an apple from the basket and handed it to the boy. "I will pay you for it, my good woman," he added.

"Yes, but you spoil the young rascal by doing that," she objected. "He ought to have received a reward that would have made him glad to stand for a week."

"Ah, my good dame, my good dame," exclaimed Avdeitch. "That may be *our* way of rewarding, but it is not God's. If this boy ought to have been whipped for taking the apple, ought not we also to receive something for our sins?"

The old woman was silent. Then Avdeitch related to her the parable of the master who absolved his servant from the great debt which he owed him, whereupon the servant departed and took his own debtor by the throat. The old woman listened, and also the boy.

"God has commanded us to pardon one another," went on Avdeitch, "or *He* will not pardon us. We ought to pardon all men, and especially the thoughtless."

The old woman shook her head and sighed.

"Yes, that may be so," she said, "but these young rascals are so spoilt already!"

"Then it is for us, their elders, to teach them better," he replied.

"That is what I say myself at times," rejoined the old woman. "I had seven of them once at home, but have only one daughter now." And she went on to tell Avdeitch where she and her daughter lived, and how they lived, and how many grandchildren she had.

"I have only such strength as you see," she said, "yet I work hard, for my heart goes out to my grandchildren —the bonny little things that they are! No children could run to meet me as they do. Aksintka, for instance, will go to no one else. 'Grandmother,' she cries, 'dear grandmother, you are tired'"—and the old woman became thoroughly softened. "Everyone knows what boys are," she added presently, referring to the culprit. "May God go with him!"

She was raising the sack to her shoulders again when the boy darted forward and said:

"Nay, let me carry it, grandmother. It will be all on my way home."

The old woman nodded assent, gave up the sack to the boy, and went away with him down the street. She had quite forgotten to ask Avdeitch for the money for the apple. He stood looking after them, and observing how they were talking together as they went.

Having seen them go, he returned to his room, finding his spectacles—unbroken—on the steps as he descended them. Once more he took up his awl and fell to work, but had done little before he found it difficult to distinguish the stitches, and the lamplighter had passed on his rounds. "I too must light up," he though to himself. So he trimmed the lamp, hung it up, and resumed his work. He finished one boot completely, and then turned it over to look at it. It was all good work. Then he laid aside his tools, swept up the cuttings, rounded off the stitches and loose ends, and cleaned his awl. Next he lifted the lamp down, placed it on the table, and took his Testament from the shelf. He had intended opening the book at the place which he had marked last night with a strip of leather, but it opened itself at another instead. The instant it did so, his vision of last night came back to his memory, and, as instantly, he thought he heard a movement behind him as of someone moving towards him. He looked round and saw in the shadow of a dark corner what appeared to be figures—figures of persons standing there, yet could not distinguish them clearly. Then the voice whispered in his ear:

"Martin, Martin, dost thou not know Me?"

"Who art Thou?" said Avdeitch.

"Even I!" whispered the voice again. "Lo, it is I"—and there stepped from the dark corner Stepanitch. He smiled, and then, like the fading of a little cloud, was gone.

"It is I!" whispered the voice again —and there stepped from the same corner the woman with her baby. She smiled, and the baby smiled, and they were gone.

"And it is I!" whispered the voice

again—and there stepped forth the old woman and the boy with the apple. They smiled, and were gone.

Joy filled the soul of Martin Avdeitch as he crossed himself, put on his spectacles, and set himself to read the Testament at the place where it had opened. At the top of the page he read:

"For I was an hungered, and ye gave Me meat: I was thirsty, and ye gave Me drink: I was a stranger, and ye took Me in."

And further down the page he read: "Inasmuch as ye have done it unto one of the least of these my brethren ye have done it unto Me."

Then Avdeitch understood that the vision had come true, and that his Saviour had in very truth visited him that day, and that he had received Him.

Efim and Elijah

CHAPTER I

JERUSALEM

Two old men took it into their heads to go and pray to God in ancient Jerusalem. One of them was a rich peasant named Efim Tarassitch Sheveloff, and the other was a poor man named Elijah Bodroff.

Efim was a sober man. He drank no vodka, smoked no tobacco, took no snuff, had never breathed an oath in his life, and was altogether a strict and conscientious citizen. Twice he had served a term as starosta, and left office without a figure wrong in his books. He had a large family (his two sons, as well as a grandson, were married), and they all lived together. In person he was an upright, vigorous muzhik, with a beard only begun to be streaked with grey now that he had attained his seventieth year. Old Elijah, on the other hand, was a man neither rich nor poor, who, formerly a travelling carpenter, had now settled down and taken to bee-keeping. One of his sons earned his living at home, and the other one

away. He was a good-hearted, cheerful old fellow, and drank vodka, smoked tobacco, took snuff, and loved a good song. None the less, he was of peaceable disposition, and lived on excellent terms both with his household and the neighbours. In himself he was a man of medium height, with a swarthy complexion and curly beard. Moreover, like his holy namesake, the Prophet Elijah, he was bald.

The two old men had long ago agreed to go upon this pilgrimage together, yet Efim had never been able to find time from his business. As soon as he had got one thing out of hand he would find himself hatching a new scheme. Now he would be marrying a grand-daughter, now expecting his younger son home from military service, now planning to erect a new hut.

One day the old men met at a festival, and seated themselves together on a bench.

"Well," said Elijah, "when are we

going to carry out that long-agreed-upon scheme of ours?"

Efim frowned. "We must wait a little yet," he said. "This last year has been a heavy one for me. When I planned to build that new hut I reckoned it would cost me about a hundred roubles only, but already the estimate is rising up to three times that amount, and it hasn't come in yet. I must certainly wait until the summer. *Then,* if God pleases, we will go."

"Well," replied Elijah, "it seems to me that we ought not to put it off any longer, but to go now. Spring is the very time for it.'

"Time or no time, the work is begun now. How can I go and leave it?"

"But have you no one to leave in charge? Surely your son could see to it?"

"*He* indeed! Why, that eldest son of mine is perfectly useless. He would spoil it all."

"No, no, my old friend. Even if you and I died to-morrow, the world would still go on without us. Your son only needs a little teaching."

"That may be; yet I want to see the work finished under my own eyes."

"Pooh, my dear sir! One never really gets to the end of things. Why, only the other day our women at home were washing the linen and getting ready for the festival—first one thing having to be done, and then another, as if there would never be an end to it all—when at last my eldest daughter-in-law (and she is a clever woman) exclaimed: 'Never mind if the festival *is* coming on and we shan't be ready. However much we do, we can't do everything.' "

Efim reflected a moment—then said: "I have laid out a lot of money already on this building scheme, and it would hardly do to set forth on a journey with empty hands. A hundred roubles is no light sum to raise, you know."

Elijah smiled.

"Yes, you must be careful," he said. "Why, your income is ten times as much as mine, yet you worry far more about money than I do. Look at me. Merely tell me when to start, and, little though I possess, I shall be there."

Efim smiled in his turn.

"Are you such a rich man, then, after all?" he said. "Where is it all going to come from?"

"Oh, I shall scrape it together somehow—raise it somehow. If there is no other way of doing so, I shall sell a dozen of my range of bee-hives to a neighbour. He has long been after them."

"And then the swarms will turn out well, and you will be sorry for it."

"Sorry for it? No, no. I have never been sorry for anything in my life except for my sins. There is nothing worth troubling about except one's soul."

"That may be; yet it is awkward to have things go wrong at home."

"But it is still more awkward to have things go wrong with one's soul. Come now! You have as good as promised me, so we must really go. It would be only right of us to do so."

CHAPTER II

CARES

THUS Elijah won over his comrade. Next morning Efim took counsel with himself, and then went to see Elijah.

"Yes, we will go very soon now," he

said. "You were quite right. In life or in death we are in God's hands. We ought to go while we are still alive and well."

A week later the two got themselves ready. Efim always kept his money at home, and of it he took 190 roubles for the journey, and left 200 for the old woman. Elijah likewise made his preparations. He sold the neighbour ten out of his range of bee-hives, together with whatever stock of honey they might produce. That brought him in seventy roubles. Another thirty he swept together from one corner and another. His wife gave up the whole of her funeral savings, and their daughter-in-law did the same.

Efim confided the entire direction of his affairs at home to his eldest son, telling him which crops to pull while he was away, and how much of them, where to spread the manure, and how to build and roof the new hut. He thought of everything, left directions for everything. Elijah, on the other hand, merely told his old wife to be careful to collect such young bees as might leave the hives which he had disposed of, and deliver full tale of them to the neighbour. On other domestic matters he said not a word. Circumstances themselves would show what was to be done, and how it was to be done, as circumstances arose. Housewives, he thought, know their own business best.

So the two old men made them ready for the journey. Home-made cakes were baked, wallets contrived, new leggings cut out, new boots procured, and spare shoes provided. Then they set off. Their respective households escorted them to the parish boundary, and there took leave of them. Thus the old men were fairly launched upon their way.

Elijah walked along in high spirits, and forgot all his domestic concerns immediately he had left the village. His only cares were how to beguile the way for his companion, to avoid uttering a single churlish word, and to arrive at his destination and return thence in perfect peace and goodwill. As he walked along he whispered silent prayers to himself or thought over his past life so far as he could remember it. Whether he fell in with a fellow-traveller, or whether he were begging for a night's lodging, with each and all he endeavoured to associate amicably and with a pious word upon his lips. As he went he rejoiced in heart. One thing, however, he could not do. He had resolved to leave off tobacco, and to that end had left his pipe at home—and he missed it sadly. On the way a man gave him one. Thereafter, lest he should cause his fellow-traveller to stumble, he would fall behind him and smoke quietly.

As for Efim, he walked circumspectly, determined to do nothing amiss and speak no light word, since frivolity was foreign to his soul. Likewise, his domestic cares never left his thoughts. He was forever thinking of how things might be going at home and of the directions he had given to his son, as well as wondering if those directions were being carried out. Whenever he saw peasants setting potatoes or carting manure he at once thought to himself: "Is my son doing as I instructed him?" Sometimes, indeed, he felt like turning back to give fresh directions and see them carried out in person.

CHAPTER III

THE CABIN

WHEN the old men had been on the tramp five weeks their home-made bast shoes gave out, and they had to buy new ones. In time they arrived at the country of the Khokhli, where, although by this time they were far from the district where they were known and had for some time past been accustomed to pay for their board and lodging each night, these good people vied with each other in entertaining them. They took them in and fed them, yet would accept no money, but sped them on their way with food in their wallets and sometimes new bast shoes as well. Thus the old men covered 700 versts with ease, until they had crossed another province and arrived in a bare and poverty-stricken land. Here the inhabitants were willing to take them in, and would accept no money for their night's lodging, yet ceased to provide them with food. Nowhere was even bread given to the travellers, and occasionally it could not be bought. Last year, the people said, nothing had grown. Those who had been rich had ploughed up their land and sold out; those who had been only moderately rich were now reduced to nothing; while those who had been poor had either perished outright or emigrated, with the exception of a few, who still eked out a wretched existence somehow. During the past winter, indeed, such people had lived on chaff and weeds.

One evening the old men stayed the night at a hamlet, and, having bought fifteen pounds of bread, went on before dawn, so as to get as far as possible while it was yet cool. They covered ten versts, and then sat down by a brook, ladled some water into a bowl, soaked and ate some bread, and washed their feet. As they sat and rested Elijah pulled out his horn tobacco-box, whereupon Efim shook his head in disapproval.

"Why not throw that rubbish away?" he said.

"Nay, but if a failing has got the better of one, what is one to do?" replied Elijah with a shrug of his shoulders.

Then they got up and went on for another ten versts. The day had now become intensely hot, and after reaching and passing through a large village, Elijah grew weary, and longed to rest again and have a drink. Efim, however, refused to stop, for he was the better walker of the two, and Elijah often found it difficult to keep up with him.

"Oh, for a drink!" said Elijah.

"Well go and have one. I myself can do without."

Elijah stopped. "Do not wait for me," he said. "I will run to that hut there and beg a drink, and be after you again in a twinkling."

"Very well," said Efim, and he went on along the road alone, while Elijah turned aside to the hut.

When he came to it he saw that it was a small, plastered cabin, with its lower part black and the upper part white. The plaster was peeling off in patches, and had evidently not been renewed for many a long day, while in one side of the roof there was a large hole. The way to the hut door lay through a yard, and when Elijah entered the latter he saw a man—thin, clean-shaven, and clad only in a shirt and breeches, after the fashion of the Kholkhi—lying stretched beside a trench. Somehow he looked as though he were lying there for coolness' sake, yet the sun was glaring down upon him. There he lay, but not as though asleep. Elijah hailed him and asked for a drink, but the man returned no answer. "He must be either ill or uncivil," thought Elijah, and went on to the door of the hut, within which he could hear the voices of two children crying. He knocked first with the iron ring of the door-knocker, and called out "Mistress!" No one answered. Again he knocked with his pilgrim's staff and called out, "Good Christians!" Nothing stirred within the hut. "Servants of God!" he cried once more, and once more received no response. He was just on the point of turning to depart when he heard from behind the door a sound as of someone gasping. Had some misfortune come upon these people? He felt that he must find out, and stepped inside.

CHAPTER IV

THE OLD WOMAN

THE door was unlocked, and the handle turned easily. Passing through a little entrance-porch, the inner door of which stood open, Elijah saw on the left a stove, and in front of it the living portion of the room. In one corner stood an ikon frame and a table, while behind the table stood a wooden bench. Upon this bench was seated an old woman—bare-headed, and clad in a simple shift. Her head was bowed upon her arms, while beside her stood a little boy—thin, waxen in the face, and pot-bellied—who kept clutching her

by the sleeve and crying loudly as he besought her for something. The air in the hut was stifling to the last degree. Elijah stepped forward and caught sight of a second woman stretched on a shelf-bunk behind the stove. She was lying face downwards, with her eyes closed, but moaned at intervals as she threw out one of her legs and drew it back again with a writhing movement. An oppressive odour came from the bunk, and it was clear that she had no one to attend to her. All at once the old woman raised her head and caught sight of the stranger.

"What do you want?" she asked in the Little-Russian dialect. "What do you want? Nay, my good man, we have nothing for you here."

None the less, Elijah understood her dialect, and took a step nearer.

"I am a servant of God," he said, "who crave of you a drink of water."

"Nay, but there is no one to get it for you," she replied. "You must take what you require and go."

"And is there no one well enough to wait upon this poor woman?" went on Elijah, presently.

"No, no one. Her man is dying in the yard yonder, and there are only ourselves besides."

The little boy had been stricken to silence by the entry of a stranger, but now the old woman had no sooner finished speaking than he clutched her again by the sleeve.

"Some bread, some bread, granny!" he cried, and burst out weeping.

Elijah was about to question the old woman further when a peasant staggered into the hut, supporting himself by the wall as he did so, and tried to sit down

upon the bench. Missing his footing
in the attempt, he rolled backwards
upon the floor. He made no attempt to
rise, but struggled to say something,
speaking a word only at a time, with
rests between each one.

"We have sickness here," he gasped,
"and famine too. That little one there"
—and he nodded towards the boy—"is
dying of hunger." He burst into tears.

Elijah unslung his wallet from his
shoulders, freed his arms from the strap,
and lowered the wallet to the floor.
Then he lifted it, placed it on the bench,
unfastened it, and, taking out some
bread and a knife, cut off a hunch and
held it out towards the peasant. Instead of taking it, the man made a
movement of his head in the direction
of the two children (there was a little
girl there also, behind the stove), as
much as to say, "Nay, give it to *them*."
Accordingly Elijah handed the piece to
the little boy, who no sooner caught
sight of it than he darted forward,
seized it in his tiny hands, and ran off,
with his nose fairly buried in the crumb.
At the same moment the little girl
came out from behind the stove, and
simply glued her eyes upon the bread.
To her too Elijah handed a piece, and
then cut off another for the old woman,
who took it and began to chew it at
once.

"I beseech you, get us some water,"
she said presently. "Our mouths are
parched. I tried to draw some water
this morning (or this afternoon—I
hardly know which), but fell down under its weight. The bucket will be there
now if you could only bring it."

Upon Elijah asking where the well
was, the old woman told him, and he
went off. He found the bucket there

as she had described, brought some
water, and gave each of them a drink.
Now that they had had the water, the
children managed to devour a second
hunch apiece, and the old woman too,
but the peasant would not touch anything. "I do not feel inclined," he said.
As for his wife, she lay tossing herself
to and fro on the bunk, unconscious of
what was passing. Elijah returned to
a shop in the village, bought some millet, salt, meal, and butter, and hunted
out a hatchet. Then, having cut some
firewood, he lighted the stove with the
little girl's help, cooked some soup and
porridge, and gave these poor people a
meal.

CHAPTER V

LIFE

THE peasant ate but little, but the
old woman did better, while the two
children cleared a bowlful apiece, and
then went to sleep in one another's
arms. Presently the man and the old
woman began telling Elijah how it had
all come upon them.

"We used to make a living," they
said, "poor though it was; but when
the crop failed last year we found we
had exhausted our stock by the autumn,
and had to eat anything and everything we could get. Then we tried to
beg of neighbours and kind-hearted folk.
At first they gave, but later they began
to refuse us. There were many who
would have given, but they had nothing
to give. In time, too, it began to hurt
us to beg, for we were in debt to everyone—in debt for money, meal, and
bread."

"I tried to get work," went on the
peasant, "but there was almost none to

be got. Everywhere there were starving men struggling for work. A man might get a little job one day, and then spend the next two in looking for another. The old woman and the little girl walked many a long distance for alms, though what they received was little enough, seeing that many, like ourselves, had not even bread. Still, we managed to feed ourselves somehow, and hoped to win through to the next season. But by the time spring came people had ceased to give at all, and sickness came upon us, and things grew desperate. One day we might have a bite of something to eat, and then nothing at all for two more. At last we took even to eating grass; and whether that was the cause or something else, the wife fell ill as you see. There she lay on the bed, while I myself had come to the end of my strength, and had no means of reviving it."

"Yes, I was the only one who held up," went on the old woman. "Yet hunger was pulling me down as well, and I was getting weaker every day. The little girl was in the same plight as I was, and taking to having nervous fits. One day I wanted to send her to a neighbour's, but she would not go. She just crept behind the stove and refused. The day before yesterday another neighbour came and looked in; but as soon as she saw that we were ill and starving she turned round and went away again. You see, her own husband had just died, and she had nothing to give her little children to eat. So, when you came, we were just lying here—waiting for death to come."

Elijah listened to their tale, and decided that, as it was doubtful whether he could overtake Efim that day, he had

better spend the night here. The next morning he rose and did the housework, as if he himself were the master. Then he helped the old woman to make dough, and lighted the stove. After that he accompanied the little girl to some neighbour's huts, to try and borrow what else was needed, but was unsuccessful everywhere. No one had anything at all—everything had been disposed of for food, down to household necessaries and even clothes. Consequently Elijah had to provide what was needed himself—to buy some things and make others. He spent the whole day like this, and then the next, and then a third. The little boy recovered himself, and began to walk along the bench and to frisk about Elijah, while the little girl grew quite merry and helped in everything. She was forever running after Elijah with her "Didu, Didusiu!" The old woman likewise picked up again, and went out to see a neighbour or two, while as for the husband, he progressed so far as to walk a little with the help of the wall. Only his wife still lay sick. Yet on the third day she too opened her eyes and asked for food.

"Now," thought Elijah to himself, "I must be off. I had not expected to be detained so long."

CHAPTER VI

OF WHAT AVAIL?

IT chanced, however, that the fourth (the next) day would be the first of the rozgovieni, or days of flesh-eating and Elijah thought to himself: "How would it be if I were to break my fast with these people, buy them some presents for the festival, and then go on my way in the evening?" So he went to the village again, and bought milk, white meal, and lard. Everyone, from the old woman downwards, boiled and baked that day, and next morning Elijah went to Mass, returned to the hut, and broke his fast with his new friends. That day, too, the wife got up from her bed, and walked about a little. As for the husband, he shaved himself, put on a clean shirt (hastily washed for him by the old woman, since he had only one), and went off to the village to beg the forbearance of a rich peasant to whom both corn and pasture-land had been mortgaged, and pray that he would surrender them before the harvest. Towards evening the husband returned with a dejected air, and burst into tears. The rich peasant, it seemed, had refused his request, saying. "Bring me the money first."

Elijah took counsel with himself again. "How are these people to live without land?" he thought. "Strangers will come and reap the crops, and leave nothing at all for them, since the crops are mortgaged. However good the rye may turn out to be (and Mother Earth is looking well now), strangers will come and harvest it all, and these people can look to receive nothing, seeing that their one dessiatin of corn-land is in fee to the rich peasant. If I were to go away now, they would come to rack and ruin again."

He was so distressed by these thoughts that he did not leave that evening, but deferred his departure until the next morning. He went to sleep in the yard as usual, and lay down after he had said his prayers. Nevertheless his eyes would not close.

"Yes, I ought to go," he thought "for I have spent too much time and money here already. I am sorry for these people, but one cannot benefit everyone. I meant only to give them a drop of water and a slice of bread; yet see what that slice has led to! Still," he went on, "why not redeem their corn- and meadow-land while I am about it? Yes, and buy a cow for the children and a horse for the father's harvesting? Ah, well, you have got your ideas into a fine tangle Elijah Kuzmitch! You are dragging your anchors, and can't make head or tail of things."

So he raised himself, took his cloak from under his head, turned it over until he had found his horn tobacco box, and smoked to see if that would clear his thoughts. He pondered and pondered, yet could come to no decision. He wanted to go, and at the same time felt sorry for these people Which way was it to be? He really did not know. At last he refolded his cloak under his head and stretched himself out again. He lay like that until the cocks were crowing, and then dozed off to sleep. Suddenly some one seemed to have aroused him, and he found himself fully dressed and girded with wallet and staff—found himself walking out of the entrance-gate of the yard. But those gates were so narrow, somehow, that even a single person could hardly get through them First his wallet caught on one of the gates, and when he tried to release it the gate on the other side caught his legging and tore it right open. Turning to release it also, he found that after all, it was not the gate that was holding it, but the little girl, and that he was crying out, "Didiu! Didiusiu! Give me some bread!" Then he looked at his leg again, and there was the little boy also holding on to the legging, while their father and the old woman were looking from a window. He awoke, and said to himself: "I will buy out their land for them to-morrow —yes, and buy them a horse and cow as well. Of what avail is it to go across the sea to seek Christ if all the time I lose the Christ that is within me here? Yes, I must put these people straight again'—and he fell asleep until morning. He rose betimes, went to the rich peasant, and redeemed both the rye-crop and the hay. Then he went and bought a scythe (for these people's own scythe had been sold, together with everything else) and took it home with him. He set a man to mow the hay, while he himself went hunting among the muzhiks until he found a horse and cart for sale at the inn-keeper's. He duly bargained for and bought it, and then continued his way in search of a cow. As he was walking along the street he overtook two Kholkhi women, who were chatting volubly to each other as they went. He could hear that it was of himself they were speaking, for one of the women said:

"When he first came they could not tell at all what he was, but supposed him to be a pilgrim. He only came to beg a drink of water, yet he has been there ever since. There is nothing he is not ready to buy them. I myself saw him buying a horse and cart today at the innkeeper's. There cannot be many such people in the world. I should like to see this marvellous pilgrim."

When Elijah heard this, and understood that it was himself they were praising, he forbore to go and buy the cow, but returned to the innkeeper and paid over the money for the horse and cart. Then he harnessed the horse, and drove home to the hut. Driving right up to the gates, he stopped and alighted. His hosts were surprised to see the horse, and although it crossed their minds that possibly he might have bought it for themselves, they hesitated to say so. However, the husband remarked as he ran to open the gates: "So you have bought a new horse, then, grandfather?" To this Elijah merely answered: "Yes, but I only bought it because it happened to be going cheap. Cut some fodder, will you, and lay it in the manger for its food to-night?" So the peasant unharnessed the horse, cut some swathes of grass, and filled the manger. Then everyone lay down to rest. But Elijah lay out upon the roadway, whither he had taken his wallet beforehand; and when all the people were asleep he arose, girded on his wallet, put on his boots and cloak, and went on his way to overtake Efim.

CHAPTER VII

RESUMPTION

WHEN Elijah had gone about five versts, the day began to break. He sat down under a tree, opened his wallet, and began to make calculations. According to his reckoning, he had seventeen roubles and twenty kopeks left. "Well," he thought, "I can't get across the sea on that, and to raise the rest in Christ's name would be a sin indeed. Friend Efim must finish the journey alone, and offer my candle for me. Yes, my vow must remain unfulfilled now until I die; but, thanks be to God, the Master is merciful and long-suffering."

So he rose, slung his wallet across his shoulders, and went back. Yet he made a circuit of the village—of *that* village —so that the people should not see him. Soon he was near home again. When he had been travelling *away* from home, walking had been an effort, and he had hardly been able to keep up with Efim; but now that he was travelling *towards* home it seemed as if God helped his steps and never let him know weariness. As he went along he jested, swung his staff about, and covered seventy versts a day.

So he came home. A crowd gathered from the fields, far and near, and his entire household ran to greet their old head. Then they began to ply him with questions—as to how, when and where everything had happened, why he had left his comrade behind, why he had returned home without completing the journey, and so on. Elijah did not make a long story of it.

"God did not see fit to bring me to my goal," he said. "I lost some money on the road, and got separated from my companion. So I went no further. Pardon me, for Christ's sake,"—and he handed what was left of the money to his old goodwife. Then he asked her about his domestic affairs. All was well with them, everything had been done, there had been no neglect of household management, and the family had lived in peace and amity.

Efim's people heard the same day that Elijah had returned, and went to him to ask about their own old man.

Elijah merely told them the same story. "Your old man," he said, "was quite well when he parted from me. That was three days before the Feast of Saint Peter. I meant to catch him up later, but various matters intervened where I was. I lost my money, and had not enough to continue upon, so I came back."

Everyone was surprised that a man of such sense could have been so foolish as to set out and yet never reach his journey's end, but only waste his money. They were surprised—and then forgot all about it. Elijah did the same. He resumed his household work —helping his son to get firewood ready against the winter, giving the women a hand with the corn-grinding, roofing the stable, and seeing to his bees. Likewise he sold another ten hives, with their produce, to the neighbour. His old wife wanted to conceal how many of the hives had been swarmed from, but Elijah knew without her telling him which of them had swarmed and which were barren, and handed over seventeen hives to the neighbour instead of ten. Then he put everything straight, sent off his son to look for work for himself, and sat down for the winter to plait bast shoes and carve wooden clogs.

CHAPTER VIII

THEFT

ALL that day when Elijah found the sick people in the hut and remained with them, Efim had waited for his companion. First he went on a little way and sat down. There he waited and waited, dozed, off, woke up again, and went on sitting—but no Elijah appeared.

He looked and looked about him, while the sun sank behind a tree—yet still no Elijah. "Can he have passed me," thought Efim, "or have been given a lift and so have *driven* past me, without noticing me where I sat asleep? Yet he could not have helped seeing me if that had been the case. In this steppe country one can see a long way. It would be no good my going back for him, since he might miss me on the road, and we should be worse off than ever. No, I will go on, and we shall probably meet at the next halting-place for the night." In time Efim came to a village, and asked the Desiatnik there to see to it that if such and such an old man (and he described Elijah) arrived later he should be directed to the same hut as himself. But Elijah never arrived to spend the night, so Efim went on again the next morning, asking everyone whom he saw if they had come across a baldheaded old man. No one had done so, however. Efim was surprised, but still pushed on alone. "We shall meet somewhere in Odessa," he thought, "or on board the ship," and forthwith dismissed the matter from his mind.

On the road he fell in with a travelling monk who, dressed in skull-cap and cassock, had been to Athos, and was now on his way to Jerusalem for the second time. They happened to lodge at the same place one night, and agreed henceforth to go together.

They arrived at Odessa without mishap, but were forced to wait three days for a ship. There were many other pilgrims waiting there, come from all parts of Russia, and among them Efim made further inquiries about Elijah, but no one had seen him.

The monk told Efim how he could get a free passage if he wished, but Efim would not hear of it. "I would much rather pay," he said. "I have made provision for that." So he paid down forty roubles for a passage out and home, as well as laid in a stock of bread and herrings to eat on the way. In time the vessel was loaded and the pilgrims taken on board, Efim and the monk keeping close to one another. Then the anchor was weighed, sail set, and they put out to sea. All that first day they had smooth sailing, but towards evening the wind arose, the rain came down, and the vessel began to roll heavily and ship water. The passengers were flung from side to side, the women began wailing, and those of the men whose stomachs were weaker than those of their fellows went below in search of berths. Efim too felt qualms, but repressed any outward manifestation of them, and remained sitting the whole of that night and the following day in the same position on deck which he had secured on embarking, and which he shared with some old people from Tamboff. They held on to their baggage, and squatted there in silence. On the third day it grew calmer, and on the fifth they put into Constantinople, where some of the pilgrims landed and went to look at the Cathedral of Saint Sophia, now a Mahomedan mosque. Efim did not land, but remained sitting where he was. After a stay of twenty-four hours they put to sea again, and, calling only at Smyrna and Alexandria, arrived without mishap at their port of destination, Jaffah. There all the pilgrims disembarked for the seventy versts' tramp to Jerusalem, the business of landing being a nerve-shaking one for the poor people, since they had to be lowered into small boats, and, the ship's side being high and the boats rocking violently, it always looked as though the passenger would overshoot the boat. As a matter of fact, two men did get a ducking, but eventually everyone came safely to land. Once there, they lost no time in pushing forward, and on the fourth day arrived at Jerusalem. They passed through the city to a Russian hostel, showed their passports, had some food, and were conducted by the monk around the Holy Places. To the actual Holy Sepulchre itself there was no admission that day, but they first of all attended Matins at the Greek Monastery of the Patriarch (where they said their prayers and offered votive candles) and then went to gaze at the outside of the Church of the Resurrection, in which lies the actual Sepulchre of the Lord, but which is so built as to conceal all view of the Sepulchre from outside. That first day also they were afforded a glimpse of the cell where Mary of Egypt took refuge, and duly offered candles there and recited a thanksgiving. They next wished to return to Mass at the Church of the Holy Sepulchre, but found that they were too late, and so went on to the Monastery of Abraham in the Garden of Saveki, where Abraham once wished to sacrifice his son to the Lord. Thence they proceeded to the place where Christ appeared to Mary Magdalene, and thence to the Church of Saint James, the brother of Our Lord. At all these places the monk acted as their guide, telling them everywhere how much to pay and where to offer candles. At length they returned to the hostel, and had just retired to rest when the monk suddenly sprang up, and began rummaging among his clothes. "Someone has stolen my purse and money!" he exclaimed. "The purse had twenty-three roubles in it—two ten-rouble notes and three roubles in coin!" He raged and stormed for some time, but there was no help for it, and eventually they all lay down to sleep.

CHAPTER IX

DOUBT

EFIM lay down with the rest, and a temptation fell upon him. "I do not believe," he thought to himself, "that the monk was robbed, for he had nothing which thieves could take. He never gave anything anywhere. He told *me* to give, but never gave anything himself, and even borrowed a rouble of me."

But almost instantly he began to reproach himself for thinking so. "Who am I," he said, "to judge another? It is sinful of me, and I will refrain from these thoughts." It was not long, however, before he found himself remembering again how watchful of money the monk had been, and how unlikely it was that his tale of being robbed could be true. "He had nothing to be robbed of," thought Efim once more. "It was a mere excuse."

In the morning they rose and went to early mass at the great Church of the Resurrection—at the Holy Sepulchre itself. The monk never left Efim, but walked by his side all the way. When they entered the church they found a great crowd there, both of monks and pilgrims—Russian, Greek, Armenian, Turkish and Syrian, as well as of obscurer nationalities. Efim approached the Holy Gates with the others, passed the Turkish guards, and reached the spot where the Saviour was taken down from the Cross, and where now stood nine candlesticks with lighted tapers. There he offered a candle, and was then conducted by the monk up the steps on the right to Golgotha, to the spot where the Cross had stood. There Efim knelt down and prayed. Then he was shown the cleft where the earth was rent, the spot where Christ's hands and feet were nailed to the Cross, and the Tomb of Adam, where Christ's blood had trickled down upon Adam's bones. Next they came to the stone on which Christ sat while the Crown of Thorns was being placed upon His head, and then to the pillar to which He was bound for the scourging. Finally Efim saw the stone with the two holes for the feet of Christ. They would have shown him something more had not the crowd hurried forward, for all were eager to reach the acual catacomb of the Lord's Sepulchre. There a foreign Mass had just ended, and the Orthodox was beginning. Efim entered the Sepulchre with the rest.

He wanted to get rid of the monk, for he found himself continually sinning in his thoughts against him; but the monk still kept by his side, and entered with him into the Holy Sepulchre to hear Mass. They tried to get nearer to the front, but found it impossible, since the people were so closely packed that any movement either backward or forward was out of the question. As Efim stood gazing to the front and trying to pray, he found himself continually feeling for his purse. Two thoughts kept passing through his mind. The first was—"Is the monk cheating me all the time?" and the second was—"If he has not been cheating me, and really had his purse stolen, why did they not do the same to me as well?"

CHAPTER X

THE HOLY SEPULCHRE

As Efim stood thus, praying and gazing towards the chapel in which the actual Sepulchre stood, with thirty-six lamps always burning above it—suddenly, as he stood peering through the heads in front of him, he saw a strange thing. Immediately beneath the lamps, and ahead of all the congregation, he perceived an old man, dressed in a rough serge kaftan, and with a shining bald head like Elijah Bodroff's. "How exactly like Elijah he is!" thought Efim to himself. "Yet it cannot possibly be he, for it would have been impossible for him to get here before myself. The last ship before our own sailed a whole week before we did, so he could never have caught it. And he certainly was not on our own, for I looked at every pilgrim on board."

Just as these thoughts had passed through Efim's mind, the old man in front began to pray, with three bows as he did so: one forwards, to God, and one on either side of him, to the whole Orthodox world. And lo! as the old man turned his head to bow towards his right, Efim recognized him beyond all possibility of doubt. It *was* Elijah Bodroff! Yes, that *was* Elijah's curly black beard—those *were* his eyebrows, his eyes, his nose—those *were* his features altogether! Yes, it *was* he, and nobody else—Elijah Bodroff!

Efim was overjoyed at having found his comrade, though also not a little surprised that Elijah could have arrived before him.

"He must have slipped past me somewhere, and then gone on ahead with someone who helped him on the way," thought Efim. "However, I will catch him as we pass out, and get rid of this monk in the skull-cap. After that Elijah and I will keep together again. He might have got me to the front now if he had been with me."

So he kept his eyes fixed upon Elijah, determined not to lose sight of him. At last the Mass came to an end, and the people began to move. Indeed, there was such a crush as everyone pressed forward to kiss the Cross that Efim got jammed into a corner. Once more the thought that his purse might be stolen from him made him nervous, so he squeezed it tightly in his hand and set himself to force his way clear of the throng. Succeeding at last, he ran hither and thither, seeking Elijah, but eventually had to leave the church without having come across him. Next he visited the various hostels, to make inquiries about him, but, although he traversed the whole city, he could not find him anywhere. That evening, too, the monk did not return. He had departed without repaying the rouble, and Efim was left alone.

Next day, Efim went to the Holy Sepulchre again, accompanied by one of the old men from Tamboff who had been with him on the ship. Once more he tried to get to the front, and once more he got thrust aside, so that he had to stand by a pillar to say his prayers. He peered, through the heads in front of him again, and, behold! ahead of all the congregation, and under the very lamps of the Lord's Sepulchre, stood Elijah as before! He had his arms spread out like those of a priest at the altar, and his bald head was shining all over.

"Now," thought Efim, "I do not mean to lose him this time." So he started to worm his way forward, and eventually succeeded—but Elijah had vanished. He must have left the church.

The third day also Efim went to Mass, and once more looked for Elijah. And once mroe there stood Elijah, in the same position as before, and having the same appearance. His arms were spread out and he was gazing upwards, as though beholding something above him, while his bald head again shone brightly.

"Well," thought Efim, "come what may, I am not going to lose him this time. "I will go straight away and post myself at the entrance, where we cannot possibly miss each other."

So he did so, and stood waiting and waiting as the people passed out; but Elijah did not come with them.

Efim remained six weeks in Jerusalem. He visited all the holy spots— Bethlehem, Bethany, the Jordan, and the rest—as well as had a new shirt stamped with a seal at the Holy Sepulchre (to be buried in one day), took away water from the Jordan in a phial, took away also earth and candles from the Holy Place, and spent all his money except just what was sufficient to bring him home again. Then he started to return, reached Jaffah, embarked, made the passage to Odessa, and set out upon his long overland tramp.

CHAPTER XI

MEMORY

EFIM travelled alone, and by the same route as on the outward journey. Gradually as he drew nearer home there came back to him his old anxiety to know how things had been faring in his absence. "So much water passes down a river in a year!" he thought. "A home may take a lifetime to build up, and an hour to destroy." So he kept constantly wondering how his son had managed affairs since his departure, what sort of a spring it had been, how the cattle had stood the winter, and whether the new hut was finished.

When in time he arrived where he had parted from Elijah he found it hard to recognize the people of the locality. Where last year they had been destitute, to-day they were living comfortably, for the crops had been good everywhere. The inhabitants had recovered themselves, and quite forgotten their former tribulations. So it came about that one evening Efim was drawing near to the identical village where Elijah had left him a year ago. He had almost reached it, when a little girl in a white frock came dancing out of a hut near by, calling out as she did so, "Grandfather! Dear grandfather! Come in and see us." Efim was for going on, but she would not let him, and, catching him by the skirt of his coat, pulled him laughingly towards the hut. Thereupon a woman and a little boy came out onto the steps, and the former beckoned to Efim, saying: "Yes, pray come in, grandfather, and sup and spend the night." So Efim approached the hut, thinking to himself, "I might get news of Elijah here, for surely this is the very hut to which he turned aside to get a drink." He went in, and the woman relieved him of his wallet, gave him water to wash in, and made him sit down at the table; after which she produced milk, and dumplings, and porridge, and set them before him.

Efim thanked her kindly, and commended her readiness to welcome a pilgrim. The woman shook her head in deprecation of this. "We could do no otherwise," she answered, "for it was from a pilgrim that we learnt the true way of life. We had been living in forgetfulness of God, and He so punished us that we came very near to death's door. It was last year, in the summer, and things had gone so hard with us that we were, one and all, lying ill and starving. Of a surety we should have died, had not God sent to us just such another old man as yourself. He came in at midday, to beg a drink of water, and was seized with compassion when he saw us, and remained here. He gave us food and drink and set us on our feet, redeemed our land for us, bought us a horse and cart—and then disappeared."

The old woman entered the hut at this moment, and the younger one broke off.

"Yes," went on the old woman, "to this day we do not know whether that man may not have been an angel of God. He loved us, pitied us, and yet went away without saying who he was, so that we know not for whom to pray. Even now it all passes before my eyes. I was lying there, waiting for death, when I chanced to look up and saw that an old man—an ordinary-looking old man, except for his baldness—had entered to beg some water. I (may God forgive me for my sinfulness!) thought to myself: 'Who is this vagabond?' Yet listen now to what he did. No sooner had he seen us than he took off his wallet, and, laying it down here—yes, here, on this very spot—unfastened it and—"

"No, no, granny," broke in the little girl, eagerly. "First of all he laid the wallet in the *middle* of the hut, and *then* set it on the bench"—and they fell to vieing with one another in recalling Elijah's every word and deed—where he had sat, where he had slept, and all that he had said and done to everybody.

At nightfall the master of the house came riding up to the hut on horseback, and soon took up the tale of Elijah's life with them. "Had he not come to us then," he said, "we should all of us have died in sin; for, as we lay there dying and despairing, we were murmuring both against God and man. But this holy pilgrim set us on our feet once more, and taught us to trust in God and to believe in the goodness of our fellow men. Christ be with him! Before, we had lived only as beasts: 'twas he that made us human."

So these good people entertained Efim with food and drink, showed him to a bed, and themselves lay down to sleep. But Efim could not sleep, for the memory of Elijah—of Elijah as he had three times seen him at the head of the congregation in Jerusalem—would not leave him.

"Somewhere on the road he must have passed me," he thought. "Yet, however that may be, and no matter whether my pilgrimage be accepted or not, God has accepted *him.*"

In the morning his hosts parted with Efim, loaded him with pasties for the journey, and went off to their work, while Efim pursued his way.

CHAPTER XII

RE-UNION

JUST a year had passed when Efim arrived home—arrived home in the spring. The time was evening, and his son was not in the hut, but at a tavern. At length he came home in drink, and Efim questioned him. There was abundant evidence that his son had been living a dissolute life in his absence. He had wasted all the money committed to his care, and neglected everything. His father broke out into reproaches, to which the son replied with insolence.

"You went gaily off on your travels," he said, "and took most of the money with you. Yet now you require it of *me!*" The old man lost his temper and struck him.

Next morning, as he was going to the starosta to give up his passport, he passed Elijah's yard. On the lodge-step stood Elijah's old wife, who greeted Efim warmly.

"How are you, my good sir?" she said. "So you have returned safe and well?"

Efim stopped. "Yes, I have returned, glory be to God," he replied. "But I lost sight of your good husband, although I hear that he is back now."

The old woman responded readily, for she loved chatting.

"Yes, he is back, good sir," she said. "He returned some while ago—it was just after the Feast of the Assumption—and glad we were that God had brought him safely! We had been sadly dull without him. He can work but little now, for his best years lie behind him, but he remains always our head, and we are happier when he is here. How delighted our boy was! 'Life without daddy,' said he 'is like having no light to see by.' Yes, we found it dull indeed without Elijah. We love him too well not to have missed him sorely."

"Then perhaps he is at home at this moment?"

"Yes, he is at home, and busy at his hive-bench, taking a swarm. He says that the swarms have been magnificent this year—that God has given the bees such health and vigour as he has never known before. Truly, he says, God does not reward us after our sins. But come in, my dear sir. He will be delighted to see you."

So Efim stepped through the lodge, crossed the courtyard, and went to find Elijah in the bee-garden. As he entered it he caught sight of him—unprotected by netting or gloves, and clad only in a grey khaftan—standing under a young birch tree. His arms were spread out and his face turned upwards, with the crown of his bald head shining all over, as when he had stood those three times by the Lord's Sepulchre in Jerusalem; while above him—as also in Jerusalem— the sun was playing through the birch branches like a great burning lamp, and around his head the golden bees were dancing in and out and weaving themselves into a diadem, without stinging him. Efim stood still where he was.

Then Elijah's wife called out: "Hus-band! A friend has come to see you." Elijah looked round, his face broke out into smiles, and he ran to meet his comrade, gently brushing some bees from his beard as he did so.

"Good day to you, good day to you, my dear old friend!" he cried. "Then did you get there safely?"

"Yes, of a surety. My feet carried me safely, and I have brought you home some Jordan water. Come and see me some time and get it. Yet I know not if my task has been accepted of God, or—"

"Surely, surely it has. Glory be to Him and to Our Lord Jesus Christ!"

Efim was silent a moment; then continued: "Yes, my feet carried me thither; but whether I was there also in spirit, or whether it were another who—"

"Nay, nay. That is God's affair, my old comrade—God's affair."

"Well, on my way back," added Efim, "I stopped at the hut where you parted from me."

Elijah seemed frightened, and hastened to interrupt him. "That also is God's affair, my friend—God's affair," he said. "But come into the hut, and I will get you some honey"—and he hurried to change the conversation by talking of household matters.

Efim sighed, and forebore to tell Elijah of the people in the hut or of his having seen him in Jerusalem. But this clearly did he understand: that in this world God has commanded everyone, until death, to work off his debt of duty by means of love and good works.

The Vision At Sea

AN Archbishop was making the voyage from Archangel to Solovki, and on the ship were several pilgrims. The wind was favourable, the weather bright, and the vessel steady. The pilgrims were chatting to one another—some lying down, some eating, some sitting in groups. The Archbishop came on deck, and began pacing to and fro on the fore-and-aft bridge. Presently, as he drew near to the forecastle, he perceived a knot of passengers gathered there, among whom a little muzhik was pointing towards something on the sea and relating some tale or other, while the crowd listened. The Archbishop halted and looked in the direction in which the muzhik was pointing, but could see nothing except the sea glittering in the sun. Then he drew nearer and began to listen, but as soon as the muzhik saw him he took off his cap and became silent. His listeners also saw the Archbishop, took off their caps, and did him reverence.

"Do not be disturbed, my brethren," said the Archbishop. "I did but come to join the others in listening to what you, my good friend, were saying."

"The little fisherman was telling us about the old men," ventured a merchant more daring than the rest.

"What of them?" asked the Archbishop as he crossed over to the side and seated himself on a chest. "Tell me, for I should like to hear. What were you pointing to just now?"

"To the little island showing faintly over there," replied the little peasant as he pointed forward and to starboard. "On that little island over there there live some old men who are servants of God."

"Point out that island to me exactly. will you?" said the Archbishop.

"Be so good, then, your Holiness, as to glance along my hand. You will see a little cloud, and below it and to the left of it something which looks like a dark streak on the horizon."

The Archbishop looked and looked, yet the water was so specked with sunlight that his unaccustomed eye could make out nothing.

"No, I cannot see it," he said. "But what are they like, those old men who live there?"

"They are holy men," replied the peasant. "I heard of them first a long, long while ago, but it was not until last summer that I ever obtained a sight of them."

And the fisherman repeated the story of how he had been sailing in his boat after fish, when it struck upon this island, although he did not know at the time where he was. In the morning, he said, he landed to look about him, and came upon a little mud hut, beside which an old man was sitting, and out of which two others emerged presently. They gave him food, dried his clothes, and helped him to repair his boat.

"What were they like to look at?" asked the Archbishop further.

"One of them was small and hunchbacked, as well as very, very old, and dressed in a cassock of ancient style. He must have been over a hundred years old at the least, for the grey hairs in his beard had begun to show green; yet he was as bright and cheer-

ful of countenance as an angel of
Heaven. There was a second old man,
likewise very ancient, but taller than
the first, and dressed in a ragged khaftan. His long beard was half yellow,
half grey, yet he was clearly a strong
man, for he turned my boat over as
though it had been a pail, and my assistance was quite unnecessary. He too
was of cheerful countenance. As for
the third old man, he was of great
height, with a beard reaching to his
knees and as white as the plumage of
a ger-falcon; yet his countenance was
gloomy, with beetling brows, and he was
naked save for a loin-cloth."

"And what did they say to you?" inquired the Archbishop.

"Most of what they did they did in
silence, and seldom spoke, even to one
another. One of them would look at
the other, and the other one would
understand him at once. I asked the
tallest of them whether they had lived
there long, and he frowned and said
something, as though vexed, but the
little old man—the eldest of the three—
took him by the hand and smiled: and
for a moment there was a great silence.
All that the eldest one said then was,
'Pardon us;' and then he smiled again."

While the peasant had been speaking
the ship had been drawing nearer to a
group of islands.

"It is quite visible now," put in the
merchant. "Pray look over yonder,
your Holiness," he added as he pointed
forward. The Archbishop did so, and
could clearly distinguish a little island
like a dark streak on the water. At this
island he gazed intently, and then went
aft from the forecastle to the poop, and
approached the helmsman.

"What is the name of that island
over there?" he asked.

"That island? It has no name. There
are many such about here."

"Then is it true what they say—that
some holy men live there?"

"It is said so, your Holiness, but I
do not know if it be true. There are
fishermen who say that they have seen
them, but it often happens that they are
only spinning yarns."

"I should like to touch at that island
and see the old men," said the Archbishop. "Could that be done?"

"Well, your Holiness, no ship can
put in there, only a small boat, and you
would need to ask the captain's leave."

So the captain was sent for.

"I should like to go and see those
old men," said the Archbishop. "Could
you land me there?"

The captain demurred. "Whether I
could or not," he said, "it would cost
us much time. Besides, I would represent to your Holiness that it would not
be worth your while to go and see the
old men, for I have heard that they
are imbeciles who understand nothing
and are as dumb as the fishes of the
sea."

"Nevertheless, I should like to see
them," replied the Archbishop, "and
would pay you well for your trouble if
you could land me there."

After that it only remained to give
orders to the crew and to have the sails
put about. The helmsman also altered
his course, and the ship headed for the
island. A chair was set for the Archbishop on the forecastle, so that he
might sit there and look towards the
island, and round him gathered the
ship's company, all gazing in the same
direction. Already those with keener

eyes could see the rocks fringing the shore and point out the little hut, out of which one of the three old men was already peering. The captain produced a telescope, and, having looked through it, handed it to the Archbishop. "I think," said the captain, "that I can make out three men standing on the beach, just to the right of a large rock." So the Archbishop also looked through the telescope towards the spot indicated. Yes, there seemed to be three men there—one of them very tall, one rather shorter than he, and one a man of small stature. They were standing hand-in-hand upon the beach.

The captain now approached the Archbishop. "Here, your Holiness," he said, "we must heave the ship to, but if you still wish to land, you can do so by small boat, while we remain at anchor here."

So a cable was run out and the sails furled. Then the anchor was let go, and the barque swung to and fro at the cable's end as her course was checked. A boat was lowered, the rowers jumped in, and the Archbishop began to let himself down the companion-ladder. Rung by rung he descended until he had seated himself in the stern sheets of the boat, whereupon the rowers gave weigh and headed for the island. Arrived under the large rock for which they had been steering, they saw standing there three old men—one of them tall and naked but for a loin-cloth, a second one shorter and clad in a ragged khaftan, and a very, very old hunchback in an antiquated cassock. There the three stood, hand in hand.

The rowers grappled the shore with a boat-hook, and made fast, after which the Archbishop stepped out. The old

men made obeisance to him, and he blessed them in return, whereupon they bowed still lower. Then the Archbishop spoke.

"I heard," he said, "that you three holy men were living the devout life here and praying to Christ for the sins of mankind; wherefore I—also an unworthy servant of Christ, called to feed His flock—am here by the mercy of God, that I might see you and, if possible, impart to you instruction."

The old men said nothing—only smiled and looked at one another.

"Tell me, will you," went on the Archbishop, "what your devotions are and how you serve God?"

The old man of medium height sighed and looked at the most ancient of the three, while the tallest of them knit his brows and also looked at the most ancient. The latter smiled once more and said:

"O servant of God, we know not how to serve Him. We know but how to serve ourselves, to support ourselves."

"In what form, then, do you pray to God?" asked the Archbishop, and the eldest replied:

"We pray thus: 'Ye are three, and we are three. Have Ye mercy upon us.'"

And instantly as the old man said this, the three raised their eyes to heaven and said in unison: "Ye are Three, and we are three. Have Ye mercy upon us."

The Archbishop smiled and said: "It seems that you have heard of the Blessed Trinity: yet that is not the way in which you should pray. I feel drawn towards you, O old men of God, and perceive that you wish to please Him, yet know not rightly how to serve

Him. It is not thus that you should pray, but rather in the manner that I will teach you, if you will listen to me. Yet not of myself comes this knowledge which I am about to impart to you, but of Holy Writ, wherein God has set forth how all men should pray unto Him."

So the Archbishop began to expound to the old men how God revealed Himself to mankind, as well as to speak at length concerning God the Father, God the Son, and God the Holy Ghost. Then he said:

"God the Son, who came to earth to save mankind, did thus command that all men should pray unto Him. Listen, and repeat it after me."

"Our Father," began the Archbishop, and "Our Father" repeated the first old man, "Our Father" repeated the second, and "Our Father" repeated the third.

"—Which art in Heaven," continued the Archbishop, and "—Which art in Heaven" re-echoed the three old men. None the less, the one of medium height kept mixing up his words and pronouncing them incorrectly, while the tall, naked old man could not speak distinctly for the beard which covered his mouth and hindered his utterance. As for the eldest and toothless old man, he only stammered out his words in a meaningless sort of way.

The Archbishop repeated the sentence a second time, and the old men after him. Then he sat down upon a rock, and the old men stood round him, looking attentively into his face, and learning by rote what he taught them. All that afternoon until evening did the Archbishop labour with them. Ten, twenty—even a hundred—times would he repeat a single word, until the old

men had learnt it by heart. They would keep stumbling over it and he correcting them, after which he would bid them repeat the whole again from the beginning.

Indeed, the Archbishop did not leave them until he had taught them the whole of the Lord's Prayer, so that they could recite it both after him and by themselves. The eldest of the three was the first to grasp it in its entirety, yet the Archbishop made him say it again, and then repeat it again and yet again. So with the others also.

When at length the Archbishop rose to return to the ship it was beginning to grow dark and the moon was rising out of the sea. He took leave of the old men, and they prostrated themselves at his feet. He raised them, kissed them each on the forehead, bid them pray as he had instructed them, and re-entered the boat to return to the ship.

All the while that he was being rowed thither he could hear them reciting aloud, and in three different voices, the Lord's Prayer; but by the time the boat had reached the ship their voices had faded out of hearing, and only their forms were discernible in the moonlight. They were still standing in the self-same spot, those old men; one—the shortest—in the middle, the tallest on the right, and the one of medium height on the left.

The Archbishop reached the ship and climbed aboard. The anchor was weighed and the sails hoisted, until presently, as the wind filled out the canvas, the ship began to move and continued on her voyage. The Archbishop went onto the poop, sat down, and fixed his eyes upon the island. For a time the three old men remained still visible, but gradually they disappeared from view, and only the outline of the island could be seen. Then it too disappeared, and the lonely sea played in the moonlight.

The pilgrims had now turned in for the night, and all was quiet on deck. Yet the Archbishop did not feel sleepy as he sat alone on the poop and gazed at the sea in the direction of the vanished island and thought of the good old men. He remembered how pleased they had been to learn the Lord's Prayer, and thanked God that it had been vouchsafed him to bring aid to those pious hermits and teach them God's Word.

Thus did the Archbishop sit thinking and gazing towards the sea-line where the island had disappeared. Then something far away in the distance began to flicker in his eyes, and a light seemed to come stealing thence over the face of the waters. Suddenly that something became definite—became something which shone and showed white in the track of the moon. Surely it was either a sea-bird or the tiny sail of a fishing-boat. The Archbishop gazed attentively at it. "It is a boat sailing to catch us up," he thought: "nor will it be long before it does so. A moment ago it was a long, long way off, yet now it is drawing near to us so quickly that it will soon be plainly visible. But no," he went on presently, "that boat, as I took it to be, is no boat, nor does that resemble a sail. Whatever it is, it is pursuing us, and will quickly overhaul us." Yet still the Archbishop could not make out for certain what the thing was—whether a boat, or not a boat; whether a bird, or not a bird; whether a fish, or not a fish. Hold! There was something there, looking like a man and very large! Yet it could not be a man—a man out there in the middle of the waters! The Archbishop rose and crossed to the helmsman. "Look," he said to him. "What is that thing there?"

"Ay, my man, what is it, what is it?" asked the Archbishop again—and then saw for himself that it was the three old men running on the sea, their grey beards showing dazzlingly bright, and their feet overhauling the ship as though it had been standing still!

The helmsman started, let fall the tiller in his fear, and shouted at the top of his voice: "Oh, God of Heaven! There are three old men running upon the sea as upon dry land!"

The ship's company heard him, rushed on deck, and crowded to the poop. Everyone could see the old men running and holding each other by the hand as they did so.

Then the two outer ones of the three held up each of them a hand, and commanded the ship to stop. They ran upon the sea as upon dry land, yet without moving their feet at all.

The ship had not been brought to when the old men reached it, approached the bulwark, raised their heads above it, and cried with one voice:

"O servant of God, we have forgotten, we have forgotten all that you taught us. So long as we repeated it we remembered it, but for an hour we ceased to repeat it, and every word escaped us. We have forgotten it all— it is all gone from us. None of it can we recall. Teach us thou it again."

Then the Archbishop crossed himself, bent over the bulwark to the old men, and said:

"Your prayer too, O ancient men of God, was profitable unto the Lord. It is not for me to teach you. Pray you rather for us sinners."

And the Archbishop bowed to his feet before the old men. For a moment they stood motionless—then turned, and went back across the sea. And until morning a light could be seen glowing in the direction in which they had departed.

The Confessed Crime

In the town of Vladimir there lived a young merchant named Aksenoff, who possessed two shops and a house.

In person Aksenoff was ruddy, curly-haired, and altogether handsome. Moreover, he was a singer and wit of the first order. From his youth upward he had been given to drinking habits, and, when drunk, to brawling; yet, as soon as ever he married, he foreswore liquor, and only occasionally broke out in that direction.

One summer he was taking leave of his family before setting out for the fair at Nizhny, when his wife said to him:

"Ivan Dmitrievitch, do not go to-day. I had such an evil dream about you last night."

But Aksenoff laughed and said:

"Are you afraid, then, that I am going to make too merry at the fair?"

"Nay," she replied, "I hardly know what it is I am afraid of. Only, I saw such a dreadful thing in my dream! You were coming home from the town, and as you lifted your cap I could see that your hair had turned grey!"

Aksenoff laughed again.

"So much the better," he said. "See now if I don't drive some prudent bargains there, and bring you home some valuable presents."

And he kissed his family and departed. Half-way on the road he fell in with another merchant of his acquaintance, and they stopped to spend the night together at an inn. They drank tea, and then went to bed in adjoining rooms. Aksenoff, who was anything but a stay-abed, awoke in the middle of the night, and, since travelling was pleasanter while it was cool, aroused the ostler, and told him to put his horse in. Then he went into the office, settled up with the landlord, and departed.

After going about forty versts he stopped to bait his horse, and, having refreshed himself with a sleep in the lodge of the inn-yard, went indoors to dine on the verandah. He ordered a samovar of tea, laid hands upon a guitar, and proceeded to play it. Suddenly a troika hung with bells drove into the courtyard, and from the body of it alighted a tchinovnik and two soldiers. The man walked up to Aksenoff and asked him who he was and where he had come from, to which queries Aksenoff duly replied, and then inquired, in his turn, if the tchinovnik would care to join him in a samovar of tea. The official's only answer was to ply him with further questions—where he had slept last night, was he alone or with a merchant, had he seen the merchant in the morning before he left, why he had started so early, and so on. Aksenoff was a good deal surprised at being examined in this way, but told the official all he knew, and then said:

"Why do you want these particulars? I am neither a thief nor a highwayman, but a merchant travelling on business of my own, and have given no cause for being questioned like this."

The tchinovnik merely called the soldiers to him and said:

"I am an ispravnik, and the reason I am questioning you is that the merchant in whose company you were last night has had his throat cut. Show me all your things; and do you" (here he turned to the soldiers) "search him."

So Aksenoff was conducted indoors, and his trunk and hand-bag taken from him, opened and searched. Suddenly the ispravnik lifted a knife from the bag and cried:

"What is this knife of yours?"

Aksenoff stared, and saw that a blood-stained knife had been produced from his baggage. He was simply thunder-struck.

"And how comes there to be blood on the knife?" pursued the ispravnik.

Aksenoff tried to answer, but the words stuck in his throat.

"I—I do not know. I—I—that knife—does—does not belong to me at all," he stammered at length; to which the ispravnik retorted:

"This morning the merchant was found murdered in his bed, and no one but you could have done it, for the door of the sleeping-hut was locked on the inside, and there was no one in it, besides him, but yourself. Now we find this blood-stained knife in your bag, and, in addition, your face betrays you. Tell me how you murdered this man and how much money you stole from him."

Aksenoff vowed to God that he had not committed the deed, that, as a matter of fact, he had seen nothing of the merchant after taking tea with him, that he had nothing upon his person beyond 8000 roubles of his own, and that the knife was not his. Yet his voice kept breaking, his face was deadly pale, and he shook with fear like a guilty man.

Despite his tears and protestations, the ispravnik ordered the soldiers to handcuff him and conduct him outside to the vehicle. All his baggage and money were taken from him, and he was dispatched to gaol in the neighbouring town. Inquiries were made in Vladimir as to his character, and the inhabitants and merchants of the place unanimously testified that, although he had been a free drinker and roisterer from his boyhood up, he was nevertheless a most respectable man. Then the trial came on, and in the end he was convicted both of the murder and of stealing 20,000 roubles.

His wife was distracted about her husband, and hardly knew what to think about the affair. Nevertheless, although her children were all of them young—one, indeed, being still at the breast—she set off with them to the town where her husband was confined. At first she could not obtain permission to see him, but after petitioning the superior authorities, she was at length admitted to the prison. As soon as she caught sight of him dressed in prison clothes, fettered, and surrounded by criminals, she fell to the floor in a faint, and it was a long time before she recovered. Then she gathered her children about her, sat down with them by her husband's side, and began to tell him of domestic matters and to ask him about all that had happened to him. When he had told her she said:

"And what ought we to do now?"

"We must petition the Tsar," he replied. "They cannot let an innocent man suffer."

Then she broke it to him that she had already done so, and that the petition had been rejected. He said nothing, but sat looking at the floor. She went on:

"So, you see, it was not for nothing that I saw in my dream that your hair had turned grey. It is growing a little so already with your troubles. Ah, if only you had not gone that day!"

Then she began to stroke his hair as she added:

"My own darling Ivan, tell me, your wife, the truth. You did this deed, did you not?"

"That *you* should ever have thought it of me!" was all that Aksenoff could say as he covered his face with his hands and burst into tears. At that moment a soldier entered and said that it was time for the wife and her children to leave. So, for the last time, Aksenoff parted with his family.

When she had gone Aksenoff began to think over their conversation; and when he remembered that even his wife had thought him guilty and had

actually asked him whether he had not murdered the merchant he said to himself:

"It is clear that God alone knows the truth. To Him only must I pray, and from Him only expect mercy."

And from that moment Aksenoff abandoned all hope or thought of further petitions, and prayed only to God.

He had been sentenced to the knout and penal servitude, and the sentence was duly carried out. First he was flogged, and then, when the wounds from the knout had healed, he was dispatched with other convicts to Siberia.

In Siberia he lived in penal servitude for twenty-six years. The hair of his head turned as white as snow, and his beard grew long, straight, and grizzled. All his old cheerfulness left him, and he became bent, taciturn, and grave—yet constant always in his prayers to God.

In prison he learnt to make boots, and with the money thus earned he bought a Testament, and read it whenever there was sufficient light in the prison; while on feast days he went to the prison church, read the Gospel there, and sang in the choir, for his voice was still good. The authorities liked him for his quiet demeanour, while his prison comrades respected him so much that they called him "Diediushka" and "the man of God." Whenever petitions were being drawn up in the prison his comrades always sent Aksenoff with them to the authorities, and whenever quarrels were afoot among the convicts they always appealed to him to settle them.

No one ever wrote to Aksenoff from home, so that he had no means of knowing whether his wife and children were alive or dead.

One day a batch of new convicts arrived at the prison, and in the evening the old prisoners gathered around the latest arrivals to ask them who they were, what town or village they had come from, and for what offences. Aksenoff likewise came and sat down upon a pallet near the newcomers, and listened, with his eyes upon the floor, to what one or another of the prisoners might be saying. One convict in particular—a tall, vigorous old man of sixty, with a grey, close-cropped beard —was relating the story of the offence for which he was arrested.

"So, my friends," he said, "you see that I have been sent here for nothing. All that I did was to take a post-boy's horse out of a sledge in an inn-yard. They arrested me, saying that I had stolen it. Of course I told them that my only object in taking the horse was to arrive the quicker at my journey's end, after which I should have returned it; yet they said, 'No, you have stolen it'—and that, too, without so much as knowing at the time where or how I had 'stolen' it! Well, I was tried, and, if only they could have got the necessary evidence, should have been here long ago. But they couldn't, so they packed me off contrary to the law. Ah, well," he added, "I have been in Siberia before—and didn't make a long stay there either."

"Where do you come from?" asked one of the other prisoners.

"From Vladimir, where I was a register burgher. My name is Makar, and my surname Semenovitch."

Aksenoff raised his head at this, and asked him:

"Did you ever hear, in Vladimir, of some merchants called Aksenoff? Are they still alive?"

"How could I *not* hear of them? They are well-to-do people, although, unfortunately, their father is in Siberia. He is in the same plight as ourselves, in fact. But you—what was *your* crime?"

Aksenoff was not fond of talking about his own troubles, so he only sighed and said:

"I, for my sins, have now lived in penal servitude for twenty-six years."

"But for *what* sins?" pursued Makar.

"For sins that earned me *this*," replied Aksenoff, and would say no more. His comrades, however, went on to tell Makar the story of a merchant being murdered while travelling, of the knife being planted upon Aksenoff, and of the latter's wrongful conviction for the deed.

When Makar heard this he stared at Aksenoff, clapped his hands to his knees, and exclaimed:

"Wonderful! Wonderful! But it has aged you, little father, a good deal."

Yet, when asked what had surprised him so, and whether he had ever seen Aksenoff before, he would not answer, but merely said:

"It is marvellous, my friends, what meetings take place in this world."

Immediately the idea occurred to Aksenoff that possibly this man might know who had been the actual murderer. So he said:

"Did you ever hear of this affair before, Semenovitch, or see me before?"

"Did I ever hear of it before indeed? Why, the world rang with it at the time. Still, it all happened a long while ago, and if I heard much of it then, I have forgotten much of it now."

"But did you ever chance to hear who really murdered the merchant?" pursued Aksenoff.

Makar smiled as he said:

"The man who murdered him must have been the man in whose bag the knife was found. If someone had planted the knife on you, you would not have been arrested (as you were) for the robbery as well. Besides, to plant the knife on you, the murderer would have had to stand by your very bedside, would he not?—in which case you would have heard him."

As soon as Makar said this, Aksenoff began to suspect that Makar himself had been the actual murderer. He got up and moved away. All that night he could not sleep. Restlessness had him in its grip, and he began making mental pictures of the past. First there presented herself to his vision his wife, looking just as she had done when she saw him off for the last time to the fair. He could see her before him as though actually alive—could see her eyes and face, could hear her laughing and talking to him. Then he saw his children as they had been in those days—little things, one of them in a tiny fur jacket, and the youngest one sucking at its mother's breast. Next he pictured himself as he was then—young and high-spirited. He remembered sitting on the verandah and playing the guitar in the inn where he had been arrested. How light-hearted he was then! Next he went on to recall the place of execution where he had been flogged, the executioner, the crowd gathered around, the fetters, the other convicts, all his

twenty-six years' life in prison, his old age. And such a spasm of despair shook him that he almost laid hands upon himself.

"And all because of that villain yonder," he thought to himself. Indeed, at that moment, his rage against Makar Semenovitch could almost have driven him to fall upon the man and avenge himself forever. The whole night long he recited his prayers, yet that could not calm him. Next day he never went near Makar nor looked at him.

Two more weeks passed. Aksenoff could not sleep at nights, and such restlessness would come upon him that he hardly knew what to do with himself. One night he was roaming about the prison when he saw some earth being thrown out from under one of the pallets. He stopped to look. Suddenly Makar Semenovitch leapt from beneath the bed and glared at him with a terrified air. Aksenoff was about to pass on, to avoid looking at him, when Makar seized him by the arm, and told him that he was digging a passage under the walls. The earth, he said, he conveyed outside each day in his boot-tops, and got rid of it on the roadway as they were being marched to work.

"Say nothing about this," he went on, "and I will take you with me; but if, on the other hand, you inform—well, I will never let you go until I have killed you."

As Aksenoff looked upon the man who had wronged him so terribly his whole form trembled with rage. He withdrew his arm from the other's grasp and said:

"I have nothing to gain by escaping, nor could you kill me again. You did that long ago. As to whether or no I inform against you, that will be as God may put it into my heart."

Next day, when the prisoners were being marched to work, some soldiers noticed that Makar Semenovitch was strewing earth upon the ground. This led to the prison being searched and the hole discovered. The Governor arrived, and began to question every man in turn, in the hope of finding out who had made the hole. All of them denied it. Those who knew the truth would not betray Makar, since they knew that for such an offence as that he would be nearly flogged to death. Then the Governor turned to Aksenoff. He knew that Aksenoff was a truthful man, and therefore said:

"Old man, you are one of those who speak the truth. Tell me now, before God, who did this thing."

Makar was standing by, looking as if he had had nothing to do with it; yet he kept his eyes fixed upon the Governor, and never glanced at Aksenoff Aksenoff's hands and lips were trembling, and it was some time before he could get a word out. All the while he was thinking to himself:

"If I shield him, I shall be pardoning the man who ruined me Why should I do that? Let him pay at last for all my suffering. Yet, if I denounce him, it means that he will be flogged. What, too, if my suspicions of him should be wrong? And, in any case, should I feel any the easier after it?"

The Governor spoke again. "Tell me the truth, old man," he said. "Who dug this hole?"

Aksenoff looked for a moment at Makar and answered:

"I cannot tell you, your Excellency.

God does not bid me do so, so I will not. Do with me as you please. I am in your power."

And, in spite of all the Governor's threats, Aksenoff would say nothing more; so that they never discovered who had dug the hole.

The same night, as Aksenoff was lying on his pallet, half-asleep and half-awake, he heard someone approach him and sit down at the foot of the bed. He peered through the darkness and recognized Makar.

"What more do you want with me?" he said. "Why are you there at all?"

Makar returned no answer, so Aksenoff raised himself a little and repeated:

"What do you want? Away with you, or I will call the soldiers!"

Then Makar leant over towards him and said in a whisper:

"Ivan Dmitrievitch, pardon me!"

"Pardon you for what?" asked Aksenoff.

"Because it was I who murdered the merchant and then planted the knife on you. I meant to murder you too, but a noise arose in the courtyard, and I thrust the knife into your bag and escaped out of the window again."

Aksenoff said nothing, for, indeed, he knew not what to say. Presently Makar slipped from the pallet, crouched on the floor, and went on:

"Ivan Dmitrievitch, pardon me, pardon me, for the love of God! I am going to confess to the murder of the merchant, and then they will pardon you and let you go home."

But Aksenoff answered:

"It were easy enough for you to speak, yet what could I suffer more?

Moreover, where could I go? My wife is dead, and my children will have forgotten me. I should have nowhere for the sole of my foot to rest."

Still crouching upon the floor, Makar beat his head against it as he repeated:

"Ivan Dmitrievitch, pardon me, pardon me! Even if I had been knouted, the blows would not have hurt me as does the sight of you now. To think that you could still have compassion upon me—and would not say—! Pardon me, for Christ's sake, abandoned villain though I am!"—and he burst into tears.

When Aksenoff heard Makar weeping he too wept and said:

"May God pardon you! It may be that I am a hundred times worse than you."

And on the instant his heart grew lighter. He ceased to yearn for home, and felt as if he never wished to leave the prison. All that he thought of henceforth was his latter end.

Nevertheless, in spite of what Aksenoff has said, Makar confessed to the murder. Yet, when the official order came for Aksenoff to return home, he had passed to the last home of all.

Promoting A Devil

A POOR peasant went out to plough. He had had no breakfast, and took with him only a crust of bread for dinner. He canted the plough over, unfastened the sheeting, laid it under a bush, placed the crust on the top of it, and covered the whole over with his coat.

By-and-by the horse grew tired and the man hungry, so he stuck the nose of the plough into the soil, unhitched the horse, turned it loose to graze, and went to his coat to get his dinner. He lifted up the coat—but, behold! no crust of bread! He searched and searched about, turned the coat over and shook it—and yet no crust. He was greatly astonished. It seemed such a strange thing.

"I never saw anyone go and take it," he said to himself. Yet, as a matter of fact, a little devil had snatched the crust away while the peasant was ploughing, and sat himself down behind the bush to enjoy hearing the peasant curse and swear at his loss.

The peasant was greatly disappointed, yet all he said was: "Well, I shan't die of hunger. Whoever took the crust must have needed it, so let him eat it and good luck to him!"

Then he went to the well, had a drink of water, and rested himself. After that he caught his horse, reyoked it to the plough, and started ploughing again. The little devil was greatly put out at not having led the peasant into sin, and hied him off to Hell to see the Chief Devil and tell him how he had carried off the peasant's crust with no better results than to hear the peasant bless the thief. The Chief Devil was greatly annoyed.

"If," said he, "the peasant worsted you in this affair it must have been your own fault entirely. You cannot have gone the right way about it. It will be a bad look-out for us indeed if first the peasants, and then their old women, adopt this non-swearing habit. We shall not be able to live at all. Well, the matter must not be left where it is. Go you up again," he said, "and restore to the peasant his crust of bread: and if within three years from this date you have not got the better of him somehow, I will souse you in holy water."

Terrified by the bare mention of holy water, the little devil scurried back to earth, where he fell to thinking how he could best expiate his fault. He thought and thought, and at last hit upon a plan. He assumed the outward appearance of a pilgrim, and entered the service of the peasant as a labourer. He taught him first to provide against a dry summer by sowing his seed in a swamp, so that when all the other peasants' crops were being burnt up by the sun our poor peasant's corn was still growing tall and thick and its ears bursting with grain. Indeed, the peasant lived upon that store of grain until the next season, and yet had plenty to spare. The next summer the "pilgrim" advised the poor peasant to sow his crop on high ground. It turned out to be a very rainy season, and while the other peasants' corn became flooded or mildewed and never ripened, our peasant's crop on the hill was a splendid one, and he was left with more grain than he either needed or knew what to do with.

Then the "pilgrim" induced the peasant to waste his grain by distilling vodka from it. First he distilled the liquor, and then he drank it, and then he treated others to it. The little devil lost no time in repairing to his principal and bragging to him that he had now atoned for the matter of that crust of bread. So the Chief Devil went up to look.

Arrived at the peasant's homestead, he found that the owner had invited some rich peasants into the hut, and was about to regale them with vodka, which the goodwife was preparing to take round. Just as she started to do so, however, she caught her foot against the table and upset a glassful. The peasant flew into a rage, and rated his wife soundly.

"Hi!" he said. "What a slop you have made! To think of spilling all that good stuff upon the floor, you clumsy-footed fool!"

The little devil nudged his superior. "Please note," he said, "that it is not exactly crusts of bread that he is regretting now."

Having chidden his wife, the peasant started to take round the vodka himself. At this moment there entered the hut a poor labourer, returned from work. He entered uninvited, but nevertheless sat down and greeted the company; until, suddenly perceiving that the guests were drinking vodka, he began to long for a drink too, for he was very tired. There he sat and sat, with his mouth watering and watering—yet the goodwife brought him nothing, and he could only sit muttering under his breath: "My word, but they take good care to keep it all to themselves!"

The Chief Devil was pleased enough with this, so far as it went, but his subordinate said proudly: "Wait a little, and you will see something better."

So the rich peasants drank their first glassful of vodka, and their host did the same. Then they began to catch hold of and flatter one another, and to speak smooth, oily words.

The Chief Devil listened attentively, and commended this too. "If," said he, "they can get so foxy on this one glassful apiece, they will soon go on to cheating one another—and then we have the lot of them!"

"Yes, but wait and see what is to come next," said the little devil. "You will see it, right enough, after they have drunk their next glassful. At present they are curling their brushes over their backs like foxes, and trying to get the better of one another; but see what truly wolfish brutes they will become presently."

So the peasants had another glassful each, and their talk grew more noisy and less civil. In place of oily speeches they began to utter curses and threats, as well as to strike one another and tweak one another's noses. Their host too joined in the quarrel, and got set upon by the rest.

The Chief Devil beheld this with delight. "It is altogether excellent!" he cried. But the little devil answered: "Wait until they have had their third glassful. At present they are like angry wolves: but only give them time—only let them drink a third glassful—and you will see them become sheer pigs."

So the peasants had a third glassful all round, and grew completely fuddled. They clamoured and shouted, without either knowing what they said themselves or listening to what their companions were saying. Finally, they all left the hut, and went their several ways—some singly, some in twos, some in threes, and all of them rolling about the roadway as they walked. Their host stepped outside to speed the parting guests, and immediately fell flat on his nose in a puddle. Splashed from head to foot, he lay there like a wild boar and grunted. The Chief Devil was now in absolute raptures.

"This was a most splendid scheme you invented," he exclaimed to the little devil. "You have more than atoned for that crust of bread. But tell me now—How did you make this liquor? I take it your first ingredient was fox's blood, to make the peasant grow cunning; your next, wolf's blood, to make him grow cruel; and your third, swine's blood, to make him grow into a pig?"

"Not at all," rejoined the little devil. "The recipe I used was quite a different one. I merely made the peasant grow too much corn. That was all. You see, the right stuff (that is to say, the blood of wild beasts) was in him already—is always in him, in fact—only it had no outlet so long as he grew corn merely for food. There was a time, you may remember, when he did not even repine over the loss of his only crust; yet he had no sooner come to possess a surplus of grain than he came also to cast about how to divert himself. Then *I* stepped in—stepped in and taught him a new diversion— namely, drinking; with the result that, as soon as ever he had distilled God's gift into idle liquor, there arose in him both the fox's blood and the wolf's and the pig's. And now that he has once tasted liquor, he will remain a beast for ever."

The Chief Devil congratulated the little one warmly, pardoned him for the crust of bread, and awarded him promotion in the hierarchy of devils.

Repentance

ONCE upon a time a man lived in the world for seventy years, and lived all his life in sin. Then this man fell sick, but did not repent—except that, when death came to him in the last hour of all, he burst into tears and cried: "O Lord, pardon me as Thou didst the thief upon the cross." That was all he had time to say before his soul departed. Yet the soul of that sinner loved God, and trusted in His mercy, and thus it came to the doors of Paradise.

And the sinner began to knock thereat and beseech admittance to the Kingdom of Heaven. Then he heard a voice from within the doors saying: "What manner of man is this who is knocking at the doors of Paradise, and what deeds hath he performed during his lifetime?"

Then the voice of the Accuser answered, and recounted all the sinful deeds of the man, and named no good ones at all.

Thereupon the voice from within the doors spoke again. "Sinners," it said, "may not enter into the Kingdom of Heaven. Depart thou hence."

And the man cried: "O Judge, thy voice I hear, but thy face I cannot see, and thy name I do not know."

And the voice answered: "I am Peter the Apostle."

Then said the sinner: "Have compassion upon me, O Peter the Apostle, and remember the weakness of men and the mercy of God. Wert thou not a disciple of Christ, and didst thou not hear from His own lips His teaching, and didst thou not behold the example of His life? Dost thou not remember also the time when He was in agony of soul and did thrice ask of thee why thou didst sleep and not pray, and yet thou didst sleep, for thine eyes were heavy, and thrice He found thee sleeping?"

"Dost thou not remember also how thou didst promise Him that thou wouldst not deny Him unto death, and yet how thou didst thrice deny Him when He was brought before Caiaphas? Thus hath it been with me."

"Dost thou not remember also how the cock did crow, and thou didst go out and weep bitterly? Thus hath it been with me. Thou canst not deny me admittance."

But the voice from within the doors of Paradise was silent.

Then, after waiting a little while, the sinner began once more to beseech admittance to the Kingdom of Heaven. Thereupon a second voice was heard from within the doors and said: "Who is this man, and in what manner hath he lived in the world?"

The voice of the Accuser answered, and once more recited all the evil deeds of the sinner, and named no good ones.

Thereupon the voice answered from within the doors: "Depart thou hence. Sinners such as thou may not live with us in Paradise."

But the sinner cried: "O Judge, thy voice I hear, but thy face I cannot see, and thy name I do not know."

Then the voice said to him: "I am King David the Prophet." Yet the sinner would not desist nor leave the doors, but cried again:

"Have compassion on me, O King David, and remember the weakness of men and the mercy of God. God loved thee and exalted thee above thy fellows. Thou hadst all things—a kingdom, glory, riches, wives, and children—yet didst thou look from thy roof upon the wife of a poor man, and sin did enter into thee, and thou didst take the wife of Uriah, and didst slay Uriah himself with the sword of the Ammonites. Thou, the rich man, didst take from the poor man his one ewe lamb, and didst put the man himself to death. Thus also hath it been with me."

"But dost thou not remember also how thou didst repent and say—'I acknowledge my transgressions, and my sins are ever before me'? Thus is it with me now. Thou canst not deny me admittance."

But the voice from within the doors of Paradise was silent.

Then, after waiting a little while, the sinner began once more to knock and beseech admittance to the Kingdom of Heaven.

Thereupon a third voice was heard from within the doors and said: "Who is this man, and in what manner hath he lived in the world?"

And the voice of the Accuser answered, and for the third time recited the evil deeds of the man, and named no good ones.

Then the voice spoke again from within the doors. "Depart thou hence," it said. "Sinners may not enter into the Kingdom of Heaven."

But the sinner cried: "O Judge, thy voice I hear, but thy face I cannot see, and thy name I do not know."

And the voice answered: "I am John the Divine, the disciple whom Jesus loved."

Then the sinner rejoiced and said: "Now canst thou not deny me admittance. Peter and David might have let me in because they know the weakness of men and the mercy of God: but thou wilt let me in because in thee there is abounding love. Didst not thou, O John the Divine, write in thy book that God is Love, and that whoso loveth not, the same knoweth not God? Didst not thou in thy old age give to men this saying—'Brethren, love one another'? How, therefore, canst thou hate me or drive me hence? Either must thou love me and yield me admittance to the Kingdom of Heaven, or thou must deny what thou thyself hast said."

Then the doors of Paradise were opened, and John received the penitent sinner, and admitted him to the Kingdom of Heaven.

Cruelty Avenged

THIS happened in the time of the masters. Of masters there were different kinds. There were those who, remembering God and the hour of death, showed mercy to their serfs, and there were others—sheer brutes—who remembered neither. Of these overlords, the worst were those who had themselves been serfs—men who had risen from the mire to consort with princes. Life under them was the hardest of all.

Such an overseer was appointed to a seigniorial estate, the peasantry on which worked on the barstchina system. The estate was a large and fine one, comprising as it did both meadow and forest land, as well as a good water supply. Both its owner and the peasantry were contented, until the former appointed one of his house-serfs from another estate to be overseer.

This overseer assumed office, and began to press the peasants hardly. He had a family—a wife and two married daughters—and meant to make money, by fair means or by foul, for he was both ambitious and thoroughly wicked. He began by compelling the peasants to exceed their tale of days under the barstchina, and, having started a brick factory, nearly worked the people (women as well as men) to death, that he might sell and make money by the bricks. Some of the peasants went to Moscow to complain to the owner of the estate, but their representations availed nothing. The owner sent his petitioners away empty-handed, and did nothing to check the overseer. Soon the overseer heard that the peasants had been to complain, and started to take vengeance upon them, so that their daily lot became worse than ever. Moreover, some of them were untruthful men, and began telling tales of one another to the overseer and intriguing among themselves, with the result that the whole district was set by the ears, and the overseer only grew the more cruel.

Things grew steadily worse, until at last the overseer was as much feared by the peasantry as though he had been a raging wild beast. Whenever he rode through the village, every man shrank away from him as from a wolf, and endeavoured at all costs to avoid his eye. The overseer saw this, and raged all the more because they feared him so. He flogged and overworked the peasants, and many a one suffered sore ill at his hands.

In time, however, it came to pass that the peasants became desperate at these villainies, and began to talk among themselves. They would gather together in some secluded spot, and one of the more daring of them would say, "How much longer are we going to put up with this brute who is over us? Let us end it, once and for all. It would be no sin to kill such a man."

Once the peasants had been told off to clear the undergrowth in the forest. It was just before the beginning of Holy Week, and when they gathered together for the mid-day meal they began to talk once more.

"How can we go on like this?" they said. "That man is driving us to desperation. He has so overworked us of late that neither we nor our women have had a moment's rest by day or night. Besides, if anything is not done exactly to his liking, he flies into a passion and beats us. Simon died from his flogging, and Anisim has just undergone torture in the stocks. What are we to look for next? That brute will be coming here this evening, and we shall feel the rough side of his tongue. Well, all we need do is to pull him from his horse, bash him over the head with an axe, and thus end the whole thing. Yes, let us take the body somewhere, cut it up, and throw the limbs into the water. The only thing is—we must all be agreed, we must all stand together. There must be no treachery."

Vassili Minaeff was especially insistent in the matter, for he had a particular spite against the overseer. Not only did the latter flog him every week, but he had also carried off his wife to be his cook.

So the peasants talked among themselves, and in the evening the overseer arrived. He had hardly ridden up when he flew into a rage because the chopping had not been done to his liking. Moreover, in one of the piles of faggots he detected a hidden bough.

"I told you not to cut the lindens," he said. "Which of you has done this? Tell me, or I will flog the whole lot of you."

So, on his asking them again in whose tale of trees the linden had been included, the peasants pointed to Sidor; whereupon the overseer lashed him over the face till it was covered with blood, gave Vassili also a cut because his pile of faggots was too small, and rode off home again.

That evening the peasants collected together as usual, and Vassili said:

"What fellows you are! You are sparrows rather than men. You keep saying to one another, 'Stand ready, now, stand ready,' and yet, when the moment comes, you are every one of you afraid. That is just how the sparrows got ready to resist the hawk. 'Stand ready, now, stand ready—no betrayal of one another,' they said; and yet, when the hawk stooped, they scurried off into the nettle-bed, and the hawk took the sparrow he wanted, and flew off with it dangling in his talons. Then the sparrows hopped out again. 'Tweet, tweet!' they cried—

and then saw that one of their number was missing. 'Which of us is gone?' they said. 'Oh, only little Vania. Well, it was fated thus, and he is paying for the rest of us.' The same with you fellows, with your cry of 'No betrayal, no betrayal.' When that man hit Sidor you should have plucked up heart of grace and finished him. But no; it was 'Stand ready, stand ready! No betrayal, no betrayal!'—and yet, when the hawk stooped, every man of you was off into the bushes."

The peasants talked more and more frequently on this subject, until they were quite prepared to make an end of the overseer.

Now, on the Eve of Passion Week he sent word to them that they were to hold themselves in readiness to plough the barstchina land for oats. This seemed to the peasants a desecration of Passion Week, and they gathered together in Vassili's backyard and debated the matter.

"If he has forgotten God," they said, "and orders us to do such things as that, it is our bounden duty to kill him. Let us do it once for all."

Just then they were joined by Peter Michieff. Peter was a peaceable man, and had hitherto taken no part in these discussions. Now, however, he listened, and then said:

"You are meditating a great sin, my brothers. To take a man's life is a terrible thing to do. It is easy enough to destroy another's life, but what about your own? If this man does evil things, then evil awaits him. You need but be patient, my brothers."

Vassili flew into a passion at these words.

"For you," he said, "there is but one

consideration—that it is a sin to kill a man. Yes, of course it is a sin, but not in such a case as the present one. It is a sin to kill a *good* man, but what about a dog like this? Why, God has commanded us to kill him. One kills a mad dog for the sake of one's fellows. To let this man live would be a greater sin than to kill him. Why should he go on ruining our lives? No matter if we suffer for killing him, we shall have done it for our fellows, and they will thank us for it. Yours is empty talk, Michieff. Would it be a less sin, then, for us to go and work during Christ's holy festival? Why, you yourself do not intend to go, surely?"

"Why should I *not* go?" answered Peter. "If I am sent to plough I shall obey. It will not be for myself that I shall be doing it. God will know to whom to impute the sin, and, for ourselves, we need but bear Him in mind as we plough. These are not my own words, brothers. If God had intended that we should remove evil by evil, He would have given us a law to that effect and have pointed us to it as the way. No. If you remove evil by evil, it will come back to you again. It is folly to kill a man, for blood sticks to the soul. Take a man's soul, and you plunge your own in blood. Even though you may think that the man whom you have killed was evil, and that thus you have removed evil from the world—look you, you yourselves will have done a more wicked deed than any one of his. Submit yourselves rather to misfortune, and misfortune will submit itself to you."

After this, the peasants were divided in opinion, since some of them agreed with Vassili, and some of them respected Peter's advice to be patient and refrain from sin.

On the first day of the festival (the Sunday) the peasants kept holiday, but in the evening the starosta arrived from the manor house with his messengers, and said:

"Michael Semenovitch, the overseer, has sent us to warn you that you are to plough to-morrow in readiness for the oat sowing."

So the starosta and his men went round the village and told all the peasants to go to plough next day— some of them beyond the river, and some of them starting from the highroad. The peasants were in great distress, yet dared not disobey, and duly went out in the morning with their teams, and started ploughing. The church bells were ringing to early mass, and all the world was observing the festival; but the peasants—they were ploughing.

The overseer awoke late that morning and went to make his round of the homestead as usual. His household tidied themselves up and put on their best clothes, and, the cart having been got ready by a workman, drove off to church. On their return a serving-woman set out the samovar, the overseer returned from the farm, and everyone sat down to tea-drinking. That finished, Michael lighted his pipe and called for the starosta.

"You set the peasants to plough?" he asked.

"Yes, Michael Semenovitch."

"They all of them went, did they?"

"Yes, all of them, and I divided up the work myself."

"Well, you may have done that, but

are they actually *ploughing?* That is the question. Go and see whether they are, and tell them that I myself am coming when I have had dinner. Tell them also that each two ploughs must cover a dessiatin, and that the ploughing is to be good. If I find anything done wrong I shall act accordingly, festival or no festival."

"Very good, Michael Semenovitch," and the starosta was just departing when Michael called him back. He called him back because he wanted to say something more to him, though he hardly knew how to do it. He hemmed and ha'ed, and finally said:

"I want you to listen, too, to what those rascals are saying of me. If you hear anyone abusing me, come and tell me all he said. I know those brigands well. They don't like work—they only like lying on their backs and kicking up their heels. Guzzling and keeping holiday, that is what they love, and they will think nothing of leaving a bit of land unploughed, or of not finishing their allotted piece, if I let them. So just you go and listen to what they are saying, and mark those who are saying it, and come and report all to me. Go and inspect things, report to me fully, and keep nothing back—those are your orders."

The starosta turned and went out, and, mounting his horse, galloped off to to the peasants in the fields.

Now, the overseer's wife had heard what her husband had said to the starosta, and came to him to intercede for the peasants. She was a woman of gentle nature, and her heart was good. Whenever she got an opportunity she would try to soften her husband and to defend the peasants before him.

So she came now to her husband, and interceded.

"My dearest Michael," she implored, "do not commit this great sin against the Lord's high festival, but let the peasants go, for Christ's sake."

But Michael disregarded what she said, and laughed at her.

"Has the whip become such a stranger to your back," he said, "that you are grown so bold as to meddle with what is not your business?"

"Oh, but, Michael dearest, I have had such an evil dream about you. Do listen to me, and let the peasants go."

"All I have to say to you," he replied, "is that you are evidently getting above yourself, and need a slash of the whip again. Take that!" And in his rage he thrust his glowing pipe-bowl against her lips, and, throwing her out of the room, bid her send him in his dinner.

Jelly, pies, shtchi with bacon, roast sucking-pig, and vermicelli pudding—he devoured them all, and washed them down with cherry-brandy. Then, after dessert, he called the cook to him, set her down to play the piano, and himself took a guitar and accompanied her.

Thus he was sitting in high spirits as he hiccuped, twanged the strings, and laughed with the cook, when the starosta returned, and, with a bow to his master, began to report what he had seen in the fields.

"Are they ploughing, each man his proper piece?" asked Michael.

"Yes," replied the starosta, "and they have done more than half already."

"No skimping of the work, eh?"

"No, I have seen none. They are ploughing well, for they are afraid to do otherwise."

"And is the up-turn good?"

"Yes, it is quite soft, and scatters like poppy-seed."

The overseer was silent a moment.

"Well, and what do they say of me?" he went on presently. "Are they abusing me?"

The starosta hesitated, but Michael bid him tell the truth.

"Tell me everything," he said. " 'Tis not your own words that you will be reporting, but theirs. Tell me the truth, and I will reward you; but screen those fellows, and I will show you no mercy—I will flog you soundly. Here, Katiushka! Give him a glass of vodka to encourage him."

The cook went and fetched a glassful and handed it to the starosta, whereupon the latter made a reverence to his master, drank the liquor down, wiped his mouth, and went on speaking.

"Anyway," he thought to himself, "it is not my fault that they have nothing to say in praise of him, so I will tell the truth since he bids me do so."

So the starosta plucked up courage and went on:

"They are grumbling, Michael Semenovitch. They are grumbling terribly."

"But what exactly do they say? Tell me."

"There is one thing they all of them say—namely, that you have no belief in God."

The overseer burst out laughing.

"Which of them say that?" he asked.

"They all do. They say, in fact, that you serve the Devil."

The overseer laughed the more.

"That is excellent," he said. "Now tell me what each of them separately has to say of me. What, for instance, does our friend Vassili say?"

The starosta had been reluctant hitherto to inform against his own friends, but between him and Vassili there was an old-standing feud.

"Vassili," he replied, "curses you worse than all the rest."

"Then tell me what he says."

"I am ashamed to repeat it, but he hopes you may come to a miserable end some day."

"Oh, he does, does he, that young man?" exclaimed the overseer. "Well, he won't ever kill me, for he will never get a chance of laying his hands upon me. Very well, friend Vassili, you and I will have a settling together. And what does that cur Tishka say?"

"Well, no one says any good of you. They all curse you and utter threats."

"What about Peter Michieff? What did he say? I'll be bound the old rascal was another one of those who cursed me."

"No, but he was not, Michael Semenovitch."

"What did he say, then?"

"He was the only one of them who said nothing at all. He knows a great deal for a peasant, and I marvelled when I saw him to-day."

"Why so?"

"Because of what he was doing. The others marvelled at him too."

"What was he doing?"

"A most strange thing. He was ploughing the grass dessiatin by the Tourkin ridge, and as I rode up to him I seemed to hear someone singing in a low, beautiful voice, while in the middle of his plough-shaft there was something burning."

"Well?"

"This thing was burning like a little tongue of fire. As I drew nearer I saw that it was a five-kopek wax candle, and that it was fastened to the shaft. A wind was blowing, and yet the candle never went out."

"And what did he say?"

"He said nothing, except that when he saw me he gave me the Easter greeting, and then began singing again. He had on a new shirt, and sang Easter hymns as he ploughed. He turned the plough at the end of the furrow, and shook it, yet the candle never went out. Yes, I was close to him when he shook the clods off the plough and lifted the handles round. Yet, all the time that he was guiding the plough round, the candle remained burning as before."

"What did you say to him?"

"I said nothing, but some of the other peasants came up and began laughing at him. 'Get along with you!' they said. 'Michieff will take a century to atone for ploughing in Holy Week.'"

"And what did he say to that?"

"Only 'On earth peace, and goodwill toward men'; after which he bent himself to his plough, touched up his horse, and went on singing to himself in a low voice. And all the time the candle kept burning steadily and never went out."

The overseer ceased to laugh, but laid aside the guitar, bowed his head upon his breast, and remained plunged in thought.

He dismissed the cook and the starosta, and still sat on and on. Then he went behind the curtain of the bed-chamber, lay down upon the bed, and fell to sighing and moaning as a cart may groan beneath its weight of sheaves. His wife went to him and pleaded with him again, but for a long time he returned her no answer.

At last, however, he said, "That man has got the better of me. It is all coming home to me now."

Still his wife pleaded with him.

"Go out," she implored him, "and release the peasants. Surely this is nothing. Think of the things you have done and were not afraid. Why, then, should you be afraid of this now?"

But he only replied again, "That man has conquered me. I am broken. Go you away while you are yet whole. This matter is beyond your understanding."

So he remained lying there.

But in the morning he rose and went about his affairs as usual. Yet he was not the same Michael Semenovitch as before. It was plain that his heart had received some shock. He began to have fits of melancholy, and to attend to nothing, but sat moodily at home. His reign did not last much longer. When the Feast of St. Peter arrived the owner came to visit his estate. He called on his overseer the first day, but the overseer lay sick. He called on him again the second day, but still the overseer lay sick. Then the owner learnt that Michael had been drinking heavily, and deposed him from his stewardship. The ex-overseer still hung about the homestead, doing no work and growing ever more melancholy. Everything which he possessed he drank away, and descended even to stealing his wife's shawls and taking them to the tavern to exchange for drink. Even the peasants pitied him, and gave him liquor. He survived less than a year and died at last of vodka.

Payment

CHAPTER I

BIRTH

A POOR peasant had a son born to him. Greatly delighted, he went off to a neighbour's to ask him to stand godfather; but the neighbour refused, since he was unwilling to stand godfather to a poor man's son. Then the father went to another neighbour with the same request, but this man too refused.

In fact, the peasant made the round of the village, but no one would stand godfather, and he was driven to pursue his quest elsewhere. On the way to another village he fell in with a chance wayfarer, who stopped when he met him.

"Good-day to you, friend peasant," he said. "Whither is God taking you?"

"He has just given me a child," replied the peasant, "that it may be a joy to me in my prime, a comfort to me in my old age, and a memorial to my soul when I am dead. Yet, because of my poverty, no one in our village will stand godfather, and I am just off to seek godparents elsewhere."

"Take myself as a godfather," said the stranger.

The peasant was delighted, and, thanking him for the offer, inquired: "Whom, then, shall I ask to be godmother?"

"A merchant's daughter whom I know," replied the other. "Go to the town, to the stone building with the shops in it which fronts the square. Enter and ask the proprietor to give his daughter leave to stand godmother."

The peasant demurred to this.

"But, my good friend," he said, "who am I that I should go and call upon a rich merchant? He will only turn away from me in disgust, and refuse his daughter leave."

"That will not be *your* fault. Go and ask him. Arrange the christening for to-morrow morning, and I will be there."

So the poor peasant returned home, first of all, and then set out to the merchant's in the town. He was fastening up his horse in the courtyard when the merchant himself came out.

"What do you want?" he said.

"This, sir," replied the peasant. "God has just given to me a child, that it may be a joy to me in my prime, a comfort to me in my old age, and a memorial to my soul when I am dead. Pray give your daughter leave to stand godmother."

"When is the christening to be?"

"To-morrow morning."

"So be it. God go with you. To-morrow my daughter will be at the christening Mass."

And, sure enough, on the following morning both the godfather and the godmother arrived, and the child was christened; but as soon as ever the christening was over, the godfather departed without revealing his identity, and they never saw him again.

CHAPTER II

YOUTH

THE child grew up to be a delight to his parents, for he was strong, industrious, intelligent and peaceable. When he was ten years old his parents sent him to learn his letters, and he learnt in a year what others took five years to master. His education was soon completed.

One Holy Week the boy went as usual to visit his godmother and give her the Easter embrace. But when he had returned home he said:

"Dear father and mother, where does my godfather live? I should like to go and give him the Easter greeting."

But his father said: "We do not know, little son, where your godfather lives. We ourselves have often been troubled about that. Never since the day of your christening have we set eyes upon him, nor heard of him; so that we neither know where he lives nor whether he be alive at all."

Then the boy knelt down before his father and mother.

"Let me go and look for him, dear parents," he said. "I might find him and give him the Easter greeting."

So the father and mother gave their boy leave to go, and he set off in quest of his godfather.

CHAPTER III

LIFE

LEAVING the hut, he started along the highroad, and had been walking about half the day when he met a stranger.

The stranger stopped.

"Good-day to you, my boy," he said. "And whither is God taking you?"

"This morning," answered the boy, "I went to visit my godmother and give her the Easter greeting, after which I returned home and asked my parents: 'Where does my godfather live? I should like to go and give him also the Easter greeting.' But my parents said to me: 'Little son, we do not know where your godfather lives. As soon as ever you had been christened he left our house, so that we know nothing about him nor whether he be alive at all.' Yet I felt a great longing to see my godfather, and now have come out to seek him."

Then the stranger said, "I am your godfather."

The boy was overjoyed, and straightway gave his godfather the Easter embrace.

"But where are you going now, dear godfather?" he asked. "If in our direction, come with me to our hut; and if to your own home, let me come with you."

"Nay, I have no time now to go to your home," replied his godfather; "for I have business to do in the villages; but I shall be back at my own home to-morrow, and you may come to me then."

"And how shall I find the way to you, dear godfather?"

"Walk straight towards the rising sun, and you will come to a forest, and in the middle of the forest to a clearing. Sit down there and rest yourself, and observe what happens in that spot. Then come out of the forest, and you will see in front of you a garden, and in that garden a pavilion with a golden roof to it. That is my home. Walk straight up to the garden gates, and I will meet you there."

Thus spake the godfather, and then vanished from his godson's eyes.

CHAPTER IV

IN THE FOREST

So the boy went by the way that his godfather had told him. On and on he went, until he reached the forest, and then a little clearing in the middle of it. In the centre of this clearing stood a pine tree, to one branch of which a rope was fastened, and to the other end of the rope an oaken log some three poods in weight. Exactly beneath the log there was placed a pail of honey. Just as the boy was wondering why the honey had been put there, there came a crackling sound from the forest, and he saw some bears approaching. In front walked the mother bear, behind her a young yearling bear, and behind him again three little bear cubs. The mother bear raised her muzzle and sniffed, and then made straight for the pail, with the young ones behind her. First she plunged her own nose into the pail, and then called the young ones. Up they ran, and fell to work on the honey; but their doing so caused the log to swing a little, and to thrust the cubs away as it swung back. Seeing this, the old she-bear thrust it away again with her paw. It swung further this time, and, returning, struck two of the cubs—one of them on the head, and the other one on the back—so that they squealed and jumped aside. This angered the mother bear, and, raising both paws to the log, she lifted it above her head and flung it far away from her. High up it swung, and immediately the yearling bear leapt to the pail, buried his nose in the honey, and munched

away greedily, while the cubs also began to return. Before, however, they had reached the pail the log came flying back, struck the yearling bear on the head, and killed him outright. The mother bear growled more fiercely than ever as she seized the log and flung it away from her with all her strength. Up, up it flew—higher than the branch itself, and well-nigh breaking the rope. Then the she-bear approached the pail, and the cubs after her. The log had gone flying upwards and upwards, but now it stopped, and began to descend. The lower it came, the faster it travelled. Faster and faster it flew, until it struck the mother bear and crashed against her head. She turned over, stretched out her paws, and died, while the cubs ran away.

CHAPTER V

THE SEALS

THE boy marvelled at what he saw, and then went on until he came to a large garden, in the middle of which stood a lofty pavilion with a golden roof to it. At the entrance gates of the garden stood his godfather smiling, who greeted his godson, drew him within, and led him through the grounds. Never, even in a dream, had the boy seen such beauty and delight as were contained in that garden.

Next, his godfather conducted him into the pavilion, the interior of which was even more beautiful than the garden had been. Through every room did his godfather lead him—each one more magnificent, more enchanting than the last—until he had brought him to a sealed door.

"Do you see this door?" he said

"There is no lock upon it—only seals. Yet, although it can be opened, I bid you not do so. You may live here and play here, where you like and how you like, and enjoy all these delights; but this one charge do I lay upon you— that you do not enter that door. If ever you should do so, you will remember what you have so lately seen in the forest."

Thus his godfather spake, and disappeared. Left alone, his godson lived so happily and contentedly that he seemed only to have been there three hours when in reality he had been there thirty years. At the end of those thirty years the godson drew near to the sealed door and thought within himself, "Why did my godfather forbid me to enter that room? Suppose I go in now and see what it contains?"

So he pushed at the door, the seals parted, and the door flew open. As he entered he could see rooms larger and more splendid even than the others, and that in the midst of them there was set a golden throne. On and on he walked through those rooms, until he had come to the throne. Ascending the steps, he sat down upon it. Hardly had he done so when he perceived a sceptre resting against the throne. He took this sceptre into his hand—and lo! in a moment all the four walls of all the surrounding rooms had rolled away, and he could look right round him, and see the whole world at a glance and all that men were doing in it. In front of him he could see the sea and the ships sailing over it. To his right he could view the life of all foreign, non-Christian nations. To his left he could watch the doings of all Christian nations other than the Russian. And

lastly, on the fourth side, he could behold how our own—the Russian—nation was living.

"Suppose," he said to himself, "I look to see what is happening in my own home, and whether the crop has come up well?"

So he looked towards his own native field, and saw sheaves standing there; whereupon he began to count them, to see how many there were. While he was doing this he caught sight of a cart going across the field, with a peasant sitting in it. At first he thought it must be his father going to carry sheaves home by night, but when he looked again he saw that it was Vassili Kudnishoff, the thief, who was driving the cart. Up to the sheaves he drove, and began to load them on to the cart. The godson was enraged at this, and cried out: "Father dear! they are stealing sheaves from your field!"

His father awoke in the middle of the night. "Somehow I dreamt that my sheaves were being stolen," he said. "Suppose I go and look?" So he mounted his horse and set off. As soon as he came to the field he perceived Vassili there, and raised the hue and cry. Other peasants came, and Vassili was beaten, bound, and carried off to prison.

Next, the godson looked towards the town where his godmother was living, and saw that she was now married to a merchant. There she lay asleep, while her husband had got out of bed and was sneaking off to his paramour's room. So the godson cried out to the merchant's wife: "Arise! your husband is about an evil business."

His godmother leapt out of bed, dressed herself and went to look for her husband. She shamed him utterly, beat his paramour, and turned him out of doors.

Then the godson looked to see how his mother was faring, and saw her lying asleep in the hut. Presently a robber entered, and began to break open her strong-box. At this moment she awoke and cried out, whereupon the robber seized a hatchet, flourished it over her, and seemed on the point of killing her.

The godson could not restrain himself, but flung the sceptre towards the robber. Striking him right on the temple, it killed him on the spot.

CHAPTER VI

CONSEQUENCES

INSTANTLY that the godson had killed the robber the walls of the pavilion closed in again, and the place became as before.

Then the door opened, and the godfather entered. He went up to his godson, and, taking him by the hand, led him down from the throne.

"You have not obeyed my commands," he said. "One thing you have done which you ought not: you have opened the forbidden door. A second thing you have done which you ought not: you have ascended the throne and taken my sceptre into your hands. And a third thing you have done which you ought not: you have caused much evil in the world. Had you sat there but another hour you would have ruined the half of mankind."

Then the godfather led his godson back to the throne, and took the sceptre into his hands. Once again the walls

rolled back, and all the world became visible.

"Look first at what you have done to your father," said the godfather. "Vassili lay for a year in prison, and there learnt every kind of villainy and became embittered against his fellow-man. Now, look you, he has just stolen two of your father's horses, and is at this very moment in the act of firing his farm also. That is what you have done to your father."

Yet, hardly had the godson perceived that his father's farm was blazing up before his godfather hid the spectacle from him and bade him look in another direction.

"Look there," he said. "It is just a year since your godmother was deserted by her husband for an unlawful love, and she has been driven by her grief to drink, and her husband's paramour to utter ruin. That is what you have done to your godmother."

Then this picture also was hid from the godson by his godfather as he pointed towards the godson's own home. In it sat his mother, weeping tears of remorse for her sins and saying: "Far better had it been had the robber killed me, for then I should have sinned the less."

"That is what you have done to your mother," added the godfather. Then he hid this spectacle also from his godson, and pointed below it. There the godson saw the robber standing before a dungeon, with a warder holding him on either side.

And the godfather said to his godson: "This man has taken nine lives during his career. For those sins he would have had to atone had you not killed him. But now you have transferred those sins to yourself, and for them all must answer. That is what you have done to *yourself.*"

Then the godfather went on:

"The first time that the old she-bear pushed away the log, she only frightened her cubs a little. The second time that she pushed it away, she killed the yearling bear by doing so. But the third time that she pushed the log away, she killed herself. So also have you done. Yet I will set you now a term of thirty years in which to go forth into the world and atone for the sins of that robber. Should you not atone for them within that time, then it will be your fate to go where he has gone."

And the godson said: "In what manner shall I atone for his sins?"

To this the godfather replied: "When you have relieved the world of as much evil as you have brought into it, then will you have atoned for the sins of that robber."

"But in what manner," asked his godson again, "am I to relieve the world of evil?"

"Go you towards the rising sun," replied his godfather, "until you come to a field with men in it. Note carefully what those men do, and teach them what you yourself have learnt. Then go forward again, still noting what you see, and on the fourth day you will come to a forest. Within that forest there stands a hermit's cell, and in that cell there lives an old man. Tell him all that has befallen you, and he will instruct you. When you have done all that he bids you do, then will you have atoned both for the sins of that robber and for your own."

Thus spoke his godfather, and dismissed him from the entrance gates.

CHAPTER VII

THE LESSON

THE godson went on and on, and as he walked he kept thinking to himself: "How am I to relieve the world of evil? The world relieves itself of evil by sending evil men into exile, by casting them into prison, by executing them upon the scaffold. How, then, will it be possible for me to rid the world of evil without taking upon myself the sins of others?"

Thus did he ponder and ponder, yet could not resolve the problem.

On and on he went, until he came to a field in which the corn had grown up rich and thick, and was now ready for the harvest. Suddenly he perceived that a calf had wandered into the corn, and that some peasants, having also seen it, had mounted their horses and were now chasing the calf from one side of the field to the other through the corn. Whenever the calf was on the point of breaking out of the corn a man would come riding up and the calf would double back in terror. Then once more the riders would go galloping about through the crop in pursuit of it. Yet all this time an old woman was standing weeping on the highway and crying out: "My calf is being driven to death!"

So the godson called out to the peasants:

"Why ride about like that? Come out of the corn, all of you, and then the old woman will call her calf back to her."

The peasants listened to his urging, and, advancing to the edge of the corn, the old woman cried aloud, "Here, here, little madcap! Come here, then!" The calf pricked up its ears and listened. For a little while it listened, and then ran to the old woman and thrust its head against her skirt, almost pushing her from her feet. And it all ended in the peasants being pleased, and the old woman likewise, and the calf was well.

As the godson went on he thought to himself:

"'I see now that evil cannot be removed by evil. The more that men requite evil, the more does evil spread. Thus it is manifest that evil is powerless against evil. Yet how to remove it I know not. It was pleasant to see the calf listen to the old woman's voice. Yet, had it not listened, how could she ever have recovered it from the corn?"

Thus the godson pondered and pondered as he went.

CHAPTER VIII

FLAMES

ON and on he walked, until he came to a village, where he asked at the first hut for a night's lodging, and was admitted by the goodwife. She was all alone in the hut, and engaged in washing it and the furniture.

Having entered, the godson went quietly to the stove, and stood watching what the woman was doing. She had finished the floor and was now starting to wash the table. First of all she swilled it over, and then began wiping it with a dirty clout. She rubbed it vigorously one way, but still it was not clean, since the dirty clout left streaks upon its surface. Then she rubbed it the other way about, and cleared off some of the streaks, while making fresh ones. Lastly, she rubbed

it lengthways, and back again, yet only with the result of streaking its surface afresh with the dirty clout. One piece of dirt might be wiped away here and there, yet others would be rubbed in all the firmer.

The godson watched her for a time, and at last said:

"My good woman, what are you doing?"

"Do you not see?" she said. "I am cleaning against the festival day, but, although I am tired out, I cannot get this table clean."

"But you should first of all rinse the clout, and *then* rub the table with it."

The woman did so, and very soon had the table clean.

"I thank you," she said, "for what you have taught me."

In the morning the godson took leave of his hostess, and went on. He walked and walked, until he came to a forest. There he saw some peasants bending felloes. The godson drew near them and saw that, however much they kept walking round the felloe-block, a felloe would not bend. So he watched them, and perceived that this was because the felloe-block kept turning with them, since it lacked a stay-pin. As soon as he saw this he said:

"My brothers, what are you doing?"

"We are bending felloes," they replied. "Twice have we soaked these felloes, and worn ourselves out, yet they will not bend."

"But you should first of all make fast the felloe-block," said the godson, "and then the felloe will bend as you circle round."

Hearing this, the peasants made fast the felloe-block, and thereafter their work prospered.

The godson spent the night with them, and then went on again. A whole day and a night did he walk, until just before dawn he came up with some cattle-drovers, and lay down beside them. He saw that they had picketed their cattle and were now trying to light a fire. They kept taking dry twigs and setting fire to them, yet the flames had no sooner sprung up than they put wet brushwood upon them. The brushwood only gave a hiss, and the flames went out. Again and again the drovers took dry twigs and lit them, yet always piled wet brushwood on the top, and so extinguished the flames. For a long time they laboured at this, yet could not make the fire burn up.

At length the godson said, "Do not be so hasty in piling on the brushwood. First draw up the fire into a good flame. When it is burning fiercely, *then* put on the brushwood."

The drovers did so. First of all they drew up the flames to a good heat, and then applied the brushwood, so that the latter caught successfully, and the whole pile burst into a blaze.

The godson stayed with them for a while, and then went on again. He kept wondering and wondering why he should have seen these three incidents, yet could not discern the reason.

CHAPTER IX

THE HERMIT'S COUNSEL

For the whole of that day he pressed on, until he came to the forest in which stood the hermit's cell. He approached the cell and knocked at the door, whereupon a voice from within called out to him: "Who is there?"

"A great sinner," replied the godson, "who has come hither to atone for the sins of another."

Then an old man came out and asked him further:

"What sins of another are those which have been laid upon you?"

So the godson told him all—about his godfather, and the bear and her young, and the throne in the sealed room, and the command which his godfather had given him, and the peasants whom he had seen in the field, and their trampling of the corn, and the calf running to the old woman of its own accord.

"It was then," said the godson, "that I understood that evil cannot be removed by evil. Yet still I know not how to remove it. I pray you, teach me."

And the old man said: "Yet tell me first what else you have seen by the wayside as you came."

So the godson told him about the woman and the washing of the table, as also about the peasants who were bending felloes and the drovers who were lighting a fire. The old man heard him out, and then, turning back into the cell, brought out thence a little notched axe.

"Come with me," he said.

He went across the clearing from the cell, and pointed to a tree.

"Cut that down," he said.

So the godson applied the axe until the tree fell.

"Now split it into three."

The godson did so. Then the old man went back to the cell, and returned thence with a lighted torch.

"Set fire," he said, "to those three logs."

So the godson took the torch, and set fire to the three logs, until there remained of them only three charred stumps.

"Now, bury them half their length in the ground. So."

The godson buried them as directed.

"Under that hill," went on the old man, "there runs a river. Go and bring thence some water in your mouth, and sprinkle these stumps with it. Sprinkle the first stump even as you taught the woman in the hut. Sprinkle the second one even as you taught the felloes-makers. And sprinkle the third one even as you taught the drovers. When all these three stumps shall sprout, and change from stumps to apple trees, then shall you know how evil may be removed from among men, and then also will you have atoned for your sins."

Thus spoke the old man, and retreated to his cell again, while the godson pondered and pondered, and yet could not understand what the old man had said to him. Nevertheless, he set about doing as he had been bidden.

CHAPTER X

THE ROBBER

GOING to the river, and taking a full mouthful of water, he returned and sprinkled the first stump. Again, and yet again, he went, and sprinkled the other two. Now he began to feel tired and hungry, so he went to the cell to beg bite and sup of the old man; yet, hardly had he opened the door, when he saw the old man lying dead across his praying-stool. The godson looked about until he found some dry biscuits, which he ate. Then he found also a spade, and began to dig a grave for the old man. By night he brought water and sprinkled the stumps, and by day he went on digging the grave. Just when he had finished it and was about to bury the old man, some peasants from a neighbouring village arrived with presents of food for the aged hermit.

Learning that the old man was dead, and believing that he had blessed the godson as his successor, they helped to inter the body, left the food for the godson's use, and departed after promising to bring him some more.

So the godson lived in the old man's cell, subsisting upon food brought him by the people, and doing as he had been bidden—that is to say, bringing water in his mouth from the river and sprinkling with it the stumps.

He lived thus for a year, and many people began to come to him, since it had got abroad that a holy man was living the devout life in the forest who brought water in his mouth from under the hill to sprinkle with it three charred stumps. Very many folk visited him, and even rich merchants brought presents, but the godson would accept nothing for himself beyond necessaries. All other things which were given him he handed to the poor.

Thus his order of life became as follows. Half the day he would spend in fetching water in his mouth for the sprinkling of the stumps, and the other half he would spend in resting or receiving visitors. In time he began to believe that this must really be the way in which it was appointed him to live, and that by his very mode of life he would succeed both in removing evil form the world and in atoning for his own sins.

A second year passed without his once omitting, on any single day, to sprinkle the stumps: yet none of the three had yet begun to sprout.

Once he was sitting in his cell, when he heard a man ride by on horseback, singing to himself as he went. Going out to see what manner of man this was, the godson beheld a fine, strong young man, well-dressed, and mounted on a valuable horse and saddle. So the godson hailed him, and asked him what his business was, and whither he was going. The man drew rein.

"I am a highwayman," he said, "and ride the roads and kill people. The more I kill, the merrier is my singing."

The godson was horrified, and thought to himself: "How am I to remove the evil that must lie in such a man? It is easy for me to counsel those who visit me, because they are themselves repentant, but this man glories in his wickedness."

However, he said nothing, but went on reflecting as he walked beside the man:

"What is to be done now? If this highwayman takes to riding this way, he will frighten the people, and they will cease to visit me. What use will it be for me then to go on living here?"

So he stopped, and said to the highwayman:

"People come here to visit me—not to glory in their wickedness, but to repent and to pray for their sins' forgiveness. Do you also repent if you have any fear of God. But, if you will not, then ride the roads elsewhere, and never come this way again, so that you may not trouble my peace and terrify the people. Should you not hearken to me, assuredly God will chastise you."

The highwayman laughed.

"I neither fear God nor will listen to *you*," he said. "You are not my master. *You* live by your prayers and piety, and *I* by murder. Everyone must live somehow. Do you go on with your teaching of the old women who come to you, but do not attempt to teach *me*. Yet because you have reminded me of God this day, I will kill two people the more to-morrow. I would have killed you yourself this instant, but that I do not wish to soil my hands. For the rest, keep out of my way."

Having uttered these threats, the highwayman rode away. Yet he came no more in that direction, and the godson went on living quietly as of old for another eight years.

CHAPTER XI

ESCAPE

ONE night the godson had been sprinkling the stumps, and then returned to his cell to sit and rest a while. As he sat there he kept looking along the little forest path to see if any of the peasants were coming to visit him. Yet none came that day, and the godson sat alone until evening. Growing weary, he began to think over his past life. He remembered how the highwayman had reproached him for living by his piety, and began to recall his whole career.

"I am not living as God meant me to," he thought. "The old man laid upon me a penance, but that penance I have turned into a source both of bread and of public repute. I have been so led into temptation by it that I find time hangs heavy on my hands if no visitors come. Yet, when they come, I am pleased only if they extol my piety! It is not thus that I must live.

I have been led astray by the praise of men. So far from atoning for my past sins, I have been incurring new ones. I will go away into the forest—away to some new spot where the people cannot find me, and there I will live entirely alone, so that I may both atone for my past sins and incur no fresh ones."

Thus the godson pondered in his heart. Then he took a little bag of biscuits and the spade, and set out from the cell towards a ravine, in some remote corner of which he hoped to dig for himself an earthen hut, and so hide himself from the people.

As he was walking along with the bag of biscuits and the spade, there came riding towards him the highwayman. The godson was afraid, and tried to flee, but the highwayman overtook him.

"Whither are you going?" asked the brigand.

The godson replied that he wished to hide himself in some spot where no one could visit him. The highwayman was surprised at this.

"But how will you subsist," he asked, "when no one can come to visit you?"

The godson had not thought of this before, but as soon as the highwayman put the question he remembered the matter of food.

"Surely God will give me the wherewithal," he replied.

The highwayman said nothing more, but started to ride on his way.

"What can I be thinking of?" said the godson suddenly to himself. "I have said not a word to him about his mode of life. Maybe he is repentant now. He seemed softened to-day, and never once threatened to kill me."

So he called after the highwayman:

"Yet I beseech you to repent, for never can you escape God."

Upon this the highwayman turned his horse, seized a dagger from his belt, and brandishing it at the godson, who straightway fled in terror into the forest. The highwayman did not pursue him, but said:

"Twice now have I let you go, old man; but the third time, look to yourself, for I will kill you."

This said, he rode away.

That evening the godson went to sprinkle the stumps as usual—and, behold! one of them had put forth shoots, and a little apple tree was growing from it!

CHAPTER XII

A SECOND GROWTH

So the godson hid himself from men, and entered upon a life wholly solitary. When his small stock of biscuits came to an end he bethought him: "I must go out and search for roots." Yet, hardly had he set forth upon this quest, when he saw hanging from a bough in front of him a little bag of biscuits. He took them down and ate them. No sooner had he done so than he saw another little bag hanging on the same bough.

Thus the godson lived on, with no anxieties to trouble him, save one—fear of the highwayman. Whenever he heard him coming he would hide himself, thinking: "If he were to kill me I should die with my sins unpurged."

He lived in this manner for ten years. The apple tree on the one stump grew apace, but the other two stumps remained as they had always been.

One day he rose early, and went out

to perform his task of sprinkling the stumps. He had done this, when he felt weariness overcome him, and sat down to rest. As he sat resting there, the thought occurred to him: "Surely I have sinned the more, since now I have begun to fear death. Yet it may be that it is by death itself that God means me to atone for my sins."

Hardly had he thought this, when of a sudden he heard the highwayman riding towards him, and cursing as he came. As soon as he heard him the godson thought: "None but God Himself can work me weal or woe," and so went straight to meet the robber.

Then he saw that the highwayman was not riding alone, but was carrying a man behind him, and that the man's hands were bound and his mouth gagged. The man could utter no word, but the highwayman was cursing him without ceasing. The godson advanced towards them, and stood in the horse's path.

"Whither are you carrying this man?" he said.

"Into the forest," replied the highwayman. "He is a merchant's son, and refuses to say where his father's money is concealed, so I am going to flog him until he tells me."

And the highwayman tried to ride on, but the godson seized his bridle, and would not let him pass. "Let the man go," he said.

The highwayman was enraged at this, and shook his fist at the godson.

"Do you want the same as he?" he asked him. "I promised you long ago that I would kill you. Let me pass."

But the godson felt no fear now.

"I will *not* let you pass," he said. "I fear not you, but only God, and God has bidden me detain you. Let this man go."

The highwayman knit his brows, then seized his dagger, cut the bonds, and released the merchant's son.

"Away with you both," he said, "and never cross my path again."

The merchant's son leapt to the ground and fled, but when the highwayman tried to ride on again the godson still detained him, and told him that he must abandon his wicked life. The highwayman sat quietly listening, but said nothing in reply, and then departed.

In the morning the godson went to sprinkle the stumps as usual—and behold! another one of them had sprouted, and from it a second little apple tree was growing.

CHAPTER XIII

REDEMPTION

ANOTHER ten years passed, and one day, as he was sitting free from anxiety or fear of any kind, and with his heart light within him, the godson thought to himself: "What blessings are given to men by God! Yet they vex themselves in vain when all the time they should be living in peace."

He thought of the vast sum of human wickedness, and how men distressed themselves to no purpose. And he felt a great pity for men.

"I ought not to be living thus," he thought. "Rather ought I to go forth and tell men what I know."

Just as this had passed through his mind he heard once more the highwayman approaching. At first he was for avoiding the brigand, thinking: "It is bootless to say anything to this man."

Thus he thought at first, but presently he changed his mind, and stepped forth into the road. The highwayman was riding along with downcast mien and with his eyes fixed upon the ground. As the godson looked upon him he felt a great pity for him, and, running to his side, clasped him by the knee.

"Dear brother," he cried, "have mercy upon your own soul, for in you too there dwells a God-given spirit. If you continue thus to torment yourself and to torment others, assuredly worse torments than all await you. Yet think how God yearns towards you, and what blessings He has laid up for you! Do not destroy yourself, my brother, but change your way of life."

But the highwayman only frowned and turned away. "Leave me," he said.

Yet the godson clasped him still closer by the knee, and burst into tears.

At that the highwayman raised his eyes and looked at the godson. He looked and looked, and then suddenly slid from his horse and threw himself upon his knees on the ground.

"Old man," he said, "you have overcome me at last. Twenty years have I striven with you, but you have gradually taken away my strength, until now I am not master of myself. Do what you will with me. The first time that you pleaded with me I was but the more enraged. It was not until you withdrew from the eyes of men, and recognised that you needed not their help, that I began to think over your words. But from that moment I began to hang the bags of biscuits for you on the bough."

Then the godson remembered how it was only when the clout was rinsed that the table was cleaned. Even so, he saw it was only when he had ceased to take thought for himself that his heart had been purified, and he had been able to purify the hearts of others.

And the highwayman went on:

"But the first real change of heart took place in me when you ceased to fear death at my hands."

Instantly the godson remembered that it was only when the felloes-makers had fastened firmly the felloes-block that they had been able to bend the felloes. Even so, he saw it was only when he had established firmly his life in God and humbled his presumptuous heart that he had ceased to have any fear of death.

"And," said the highwayman, in conclusion, "it was when your heart went out to me in pity, and you wept before me, that my own heart was changed entirely."

Rejoicing greatly, the godson led the highwayman to the spot where the three stumps were—and behold! from the third stump also an apple tree had sprouted!

Then the godson remembered that it was only when the drovers' fire had kindled to a blaze that the wet brushwood had kindled with it. So also, he saw, had his heart within him kindled to a blaze, and with its flame had set fire to the heart of another.

With joy he recognised that his sins were at last redeemed.

All this he related to the highwayman and died. The highwayman laid him in his grave, and lived thereafter as the godson had bidden him, and taught men to do likewise.

Croesus and Fate

In olden times—long, long before the coming of Christ—there reigned over a certain country a great king called Croesus. He had much gold and silver, and many precious stones, as well as numberless soldiers and slaves. Indeed, he thought that in all the world there could be no happier man than himself.

But one day there chanced to visit the country which Croesus ruled a Greek philosopher named Solon. Far and wide was Solon famed as a wise man and a just; and, inasmuch as his fame had reached Croesus, also, the king commanded that he should be conducted to his presence.

Seated upon his throne, and robed in his most gorgeous apparel, Croesus asked of Solon: "Have you ever seen aught more splendid than this?"

"Of a surety have I," replied Solon. "Peacocks, cocks, and pheasants glitter with colours so diverse and so brilliant that no art can compare with them."

Croesus was silent as he thought to himself: "Since this is not enough, I must show him something more, to surprise him."

So he exhibited the whole of his riches before Solon's eyes, as well as boasted of the number of foes he had slain, and the number of territories he had conquered. Then he said to the philosopher:

"You have lived long in the world, and have visited many countries. Tell me whom you consider to be the happiest man living?"

"The happiest man living I consider to be a certain poor man who lives in Athens," replied Solon.

The king was surprised at this answer, for he had made certain that Solon would name him himself; yet, for all that, the philosopher had named a perfectly obscure individual!

"Why do you say that?" asked Croesus.

"Because," replied Solon, "the man of whom I speak has worked hard all his life, has been content with little, has reared fine children, has served his city honourably, and has achieved a noble reputation."

When Croesus heard this he exclaimed:

"And do you reckon my happiness as nothing, and consider that I am not fit to be compared with the man of whom you speak?"

To which Solon replied:

"Often it befalls that a poor man is happier than a rich man. Call no man happy until he is dead."

The king dismissed Solon, for he was not pleased at his words, and had no belief in him.

"A fig for melancholy!" he thought. "While a man lives he should live for pleasure."

So he forgot about Solon entirely.

Not long afterwards the king's son went hunting, but wounded himself by a mischance, and died of the wound. Next, it was told to Croesus that the powerful Emperor Cyrus was coming to make war upon him.

So Croesus went out against Cyrus with a great army, but the enemy proved the stronger, and, having won the battle and shattered Croesus' forces, penetrated to the capital.

Then the foreign soldiers began to pillage all King Crœsus' riches, and to slay the inhabitants, and to sack and fire the city. One soldier seized Crœsus himself, and was just about to stab him, when the king's son darted forward to defend his father, and cried aloud:

"Do not touch him! That is Crœsus, the king!"

So the soldiers bound Crœsus, and carried him away to the Emperor; but Cyrus was celebrating his victory at a banquet, and could not speak with the captive, so orders were sent out for Crœsus to be executed.

In the middle of the city square the soldiers built a great burning-pile, and upon the top of it they placed King Crœsus, bound him to a stake, and set fire to the pile.

Crœsus gazed around him, upon his city and upon his palace. Then he remembered the words of the Greek philosopher, and, bursting into tears, could only say:

"Ah, Solon, Solon!"

The soldiers were closing in about the pile when the Emperor Cyrus arrived in person to view the execution. As he did so he caught these words uttered by Crœsus, but could not understand them.

So he commanded Crœsus to be taken from the pile, and inquired of him what he had just said. Crœsus answered:

"I was but naming the name of a wise man—of one who told me a great truth—a truth that is of greater worth than all earthly riches, than all our kingly glory."

And Crœsus related to Cyrus his conversation with Solon. The story touched the heart of the Emperor, for he bethought him that he too was but a man, that he too knew not what Fate might have in store for him. So in the end he had mercy upon Crœsus, and became his friend.

Quench the Spark

In a certain village there lived a peasant named Ivan Shtchevbakoff. He lived comfortably enough, for he himself was strong and the best worker in the village, and, moreover, he had three sons of full age. One of these sons was married, another one engaged to be married, and the third one a youngster old enough to look after the horses and to have begun to learn to plough. Likewise, Ivan's wife was a sensible, managing woman, and his daughter-in-law had proved herself a peaceable, hardworking girl. So he and his family did very well. The only mouth in the homestead that did not feed itself was that of the old father, who suffered from asthma, and had now been lying seven years by the stove. Ivan possessed plenty of stock—three mares and their foals, a cow with a weaning calf, and fifteen sheep—and, while the women of the family made boots for the household, sewed the men's clothing, and helped in the fields, the men of the family did the rough work of a peasant's life. If the stock of grain gave out before the next harvest was due, the sale of a few sheep soon put the family's requirements to rights; so that, what with one thing and what with another, the household did well.

Unfortunately, however, there lived next door to them a certain Gabriel Chromoi, the son of Gordei Ivanoff, and between him and Ivan there arose a feud.

So long as old Gordei—this Gordei's father—had been alive, and Ivan's father still ruled the roost at Ivan's place, the two households had lived on neighbourly terms. If the women had need of a sieve or a bucket, or the men of an axle-tree or a wheel, the one household would send and borrow them of the other, and help each other as neighbours should do. Again, if a calf strayed from its rightful premises into the other family's threshing-floor, it would merely be driven out again with the request, "Please do not let your calf stray here, for we have not yet stacked our rick." But as for filching anything from one another, or for shutting up anything belonging to the other in barn or stable, such things were unknown in either establishment.

That is how things were in the time of the old men; but when their sons came to be master things were otherwise.

It all arose from a trifle.

A young pullet belonging to Ivan's daughter-in-law began to lay early. In fact, the young woman was collecting eggs even before Holy Week, and went every day to the shed, where she would find an egg laid in the wagon. But one day, it appeared, the children frightened the pullet, so that she flew over the fence into the neighbours' yard, and laid there. The young woman heard the cackling, but thought to herself, "I have no time to get the egg now, for I have so much to get ready for the festival. I will go at supper-time and fetch it."

So in the evening she went to the wagon under the shed—but there was no egg there. She asked her mother- and brothers-in-law if they had taken it, but they said no. Tarass, the youngest one, added, "The pullet must have laid in the neighbours' yard, for I heard her cackling there, and saw her fly back again."

So the young woman went to look for the pullet, and found her roosting on the beam with the cock. Her eyes were closing already, and she was preparing for her night's rest. The young woman would have asked her where she had laid if it had been possible for the pullet to answer, but, as it was, she went round to the neighbours', and was met at the door by the old woman.

"What do you want, my girl?" she asked.

"Only this, grandmother, that my pullet flew over into your place to-day, and we think she must have laid an egg there."

"We haven't seen it, then. We have our own eggs, and God sent that they were laid hours ago. All those that we collected were our own, and we have no need of other people's. We do not go collecting eggs in yards which don't belong to us, my girl."

The young woman was greatly offended at this, and said the unnecessary word. Her neighbour capped this with two more, and in a moment they were at it hammer and tongs. Presently Ivan's wife came out with a bucket of water, and of course joined in the fray.

Next, Gabriel's wife ran out of the door, and gave her neighbours the rough side of her tongue, regardless of what was fact and what was fiction. In short, there was a general uproar. Everyone shouted at the top of her voice, gabbling two words to the other's one, and every word a term of abuse. "You are this!" could be heard, or "You are that!" "You are a thief and a slut!" "May you and your father-in-law die of the plague together!" and "You are a cadger of other people's things!" were some of the other expressions used.

"You everlasting borrower, you have worn my sieve simply to shreds!" would cry one of the women.

"Well, you have got our yoke in your place at this moment," would retort the other. "Give us back our yoke at once."

So, wrangling about the yoke, they managed to upset the water, tore each other's clothes, and came in good earnest to blows. At this moment Gabriel arrived from the field, and took his wife's part, whereupon Ivan and one of his sons issued from the other hut, and likewise swelled the tumult. Ivan was a muscular peasant, and thrust everyone aside. Eventually other peasants came running in to part the combatants, but not before Ivan had torn out a handful of Gabriel's beard.

That was how it all began. Gabriel wrapped his tuft of beard in newspaper, and went off to institute proceedings in the district court.

"I did not grow that piece of beard," he said, "for any tow-headed Ivans to pull out."

As for his wife, she did not let her neighbours forget that Ivan would assuredly be convicted and sent to Siberia.

So the feud went on.

Yet from the very first day the old man by the stove preached to them reconciliation. Yet the young people would not listen to him.

"You are acting foolishly, my children," he said. "You are making a great matter out of a trifle. Bethink yourselves—the whole affair has arisen out of an egg—an egg that was run off with only by the little bairns! One egg is no great loss. Yet, although you have spoken in enmity, there is yet time to smooth it away and to learn better things. So long as you remain at variance you remain in sin. It must always be so. Go, then, and ask pardon of one another, and let our houses have but one roof again. If you harbour malice it cannot but be the worse for you as time goes on."

But the young people would not listen to him, for they thought that he did not understand the matter, and that he spoke with the garrulity of an old man.

Ivan also would not cry quits with his neighbour.

"I did not tear his beard," he declared. "He tore it out himself. On the other hand, he *did* tear the skirts of my blouse, not to speak of my shirt. Just look at it!"

So Ivan instituted proceedings in *his* turn, and the matter came before both the local and the district courts. While the case was still pending, a linch-pin chanced to disappear from Gabriel's cart. For this his womenkind blamed one of Ivan's sons.

"We saw him pass the window last night," they declared, "and go in the direction of the cart. Besides, a neighbour has given us the word that he went to an inn last night and pawned a linchpin with the inn-keeper."

So another suit was instituted, and every day there would be quarrels and fighting between the two huts. Even the children got set by the ears, in imitation of their elders, while the women could never meet by the brook without falling to with their rolling-pins and showering abuse—most evil abuse—upon one another.

In time these peasants went on from making accusations against one another to filching each other's property whenever they were short of anything. The women and children learnt to do likewise, and things went from bad to worse. Ivan and Gabriel brought constant suits against one another, both at parish assemblies and before the local and district courts, until everyone was sick to death of their quarrels. One day Gabriel would have Ivan fined or imprisoned, and the next day Ivan would do the same by Gabriel. The more they hurt one another, the more embittered they grew. We all know that when dogs fight, they fight the more furiously if struck, for the one struck thinks that it is the other one biting him, and hangs on the more determinedly. In the same way these two peasants would sue each other, and one of them be punished with fine or imprisonment—with the result that the enmity of the pair would be more deadly even than before. "Wait a little, and I will be even with you!" was their mutual attitude.

Things went on thus for six years. Yet the old man by the stove never altered his advice.

"What are you doing, my children?" he would say. "Have done with old scores, and let the matter drop. Cease to be bitter against these neighbours of ours, and all will go well with you. On the other hand, the longer you cherish your bitterness the worse will things become."

Yet they would not listen to the old man.

In the seventh year of the feud matters were brought to a head by Ivan's daughter-in-law putting Gabriel to shame before the whole company at a wedding-feast by accusing him of horse-stealing. Gabriel was drunk at the time, and not master of himself, so that he struck the woman—struck her with such clumsy aim, moreover, that she was laid in bed for a week, for she was pregnant. Ivan was overjoyed at this, and at once set off to the public prosecutor with an indictment, thinking: "Now at last I shall get rid of this precious neighbour of mine. He is bound to get either prison or Siberia." Yet his plea did not wholly succeed, for the public prosecutor declined to receive the indictment on the ground that, as the woman had recovered and showed no marks of injury when examined, it was a matter for the local courts only. So Ivan went to the mirovoi, who passed the case on to the district court. Ivan fussed about the precincts of the court, regaled the clerk and the usher on half a gallon of sweet cider, and pressed for a sentence of flogging to be awarded. And eventually the sentence was read out.

"The court ordains," read the clerk, "that Gabriel Gordieff, peasant, do receive twenty strokes within the precincts of the district police-station."

When Ivan heard the sentence h

glanced at Gabriel. "How does he like it now?" he thought.

As for Gabriel, he turned as white as a sheet when the sentence was declared. Then he turned and went out into the corridor. Ivan followed him, and was just moving towards his horse when he heard Gabriel saying something.

"Very well," were Gabriel's words. "He is going to have my back flogged for me, and it will burn sorely; yet I pray that he and his may burn more sorely still."

When Ivan caught these words he at once returned into court.

"Your worship," he said, "this man has just threatened me with arson. Pray take the evidence of witnesses before whom he did it."

So Gabriel was sent for.

"Is it true that you said this?" he was asked.

"I said nothing," replied Gabriel. "Flog me if you wish. It seems that I only am to suffer, though in the right, whereas *he* may do what he pleases."

And he was about to say more, when his lips and cheeks started quivering, and he turned his face to the wall. Even the magistrates were moved as they looked at him. "Can he really have threatened evil against his neighbour," they thought, "or was he only cursing at himself?"

So the senior magistrate said:

"See here, my good fellows. Would it not be better for you to be reconciled? For, look you, my good Gabriel, was it right what you did, to strike a pregnant woman? If you had right on your side, God has pardoned the deed, however sinful. But had you such right? No, assuredly you had not. Yet, if you will plead guilty and express

your contrition to the prosecutor, I feel sure that he will pardon you, and we will then annul the sentence."

Hearing this the clerk intervened.

"That cannot be done," he said. "The 117th Article of the Penal Code forbids reconciliation of the parties when once sentence has been passed. Therefore the sentence must be carried out."

But the magistrate paid no attention to him.

"Enough!" he said. "Hold your tongue! The article which chiefly concerns us is this: In all things remember God. And God has commanded us to be reconciled, the one with the other."

So he tried again to persuade the two peasants to see reason, but without success, for Gabriel would not listen to him.

"I am a man wanting but a year of fifty," he said, "and have a married son. Never since my boyhood have I been beaten. Yet now, when this scoundrel Ivan has brought me under the lash, I am to cry pardon to him! Nay, let things be. But he shall have cause to remember me."

Again his voice broke, and he could say no more, but turned and left the court-room.

From the district town to Ivan's home was a distance of ten versts, so that it was quite late when Ivan reached there, and the women had gone to bring the sheep home. He unsaddled his horse and stabled it, and then entered the hut. There was no one within, since his sons were not yet back from the fields, and the women had gone to fetch the sheep. Seating himself upon a bench, he plunged into thought. He recalled the passing of the sentence upon Gabriel, and how Gabriel had blanched as he heard it and turned his face to the wall. Ivan's heart suddenly contracted. He pictured to himself what it might have been like if he himself had been sentenced to be flogged, and he felt sorry for Gabriel. At that moment he heard the old man on the stove begin coughing, and then turn himself over, put his feet to the floor, and stand up. Having risen, the old man dragged himself to the bench, and sat down beside Ivan. The effort of getting so far had exhausted him, and for a moment or two he could only cough. At length, when his coughing fit was passed, he leaned forward over the table and said:

"Well? Did the court try the case?"

"Yes," answered Ivan, "and sentenced Gabriel to twenty strokes."

The old man shook his head.

"That is bad, Ivan," he said, "as also is *all* this that you are doing. You are harming yourself even more than him. Even when he has been flogged, how will you be the better off?"

"This much—that he will refrain from doing such things again."

"But what things? What worse things has he done than you?"

"Nay, but what has he *not* done?" cried Ivan. "He nearly killed my daughter-in-law, and now threatens to fire my farm! Why should I knuckle under to him?"

The old man sighed, and said:

"You, Ivan, can walk and ride about the world, while I have to lie the year round on the stove; so that perhaps you think that you see everything and I nothing. But no, my son, it is not so. There is very little that you see, for hatred has blinded your eyes. Others'

sins you see, but not your own, for *them* you place behind your back. You said just now that Gabriel has done you much evil. Yet, if he had been the only one who had done evil, there would have been no quarrel between you. Can a dispute between two men arise from one side only? No, it takes two to make a quarrel. *His* wrong-doing you see, but not your own. If all the wrong had been on his side, and all the right on yours, bad blood could never have been made. Who was it tore his beard? Who was it overturned his rick when stacked? Who was it first haled the other before the courts, and is haling him still? Nay, but your own way of life is wrong, and that is whence the ill comes. I never lived so, my son, and never taught you to do so. How did I live with the old man, his father? Why, on neighbourly terms, as neighbours should do. If they ran short of meal, his wife would come to me and say: 'Good Uncle Frol, our meal has given out.' 'Go, then, young woman,' I would say, 'to the binn and take as much as you require.' Again, if they were lacking a hand to lead the horses at ploughing, I would say to you: 'Go, little Ivan, and help them with the horses.' Then, in my turn, if I were short of anything, I would go to his father and say: 'Uncle Gordei, I am put to it for such and such an article.' 'Take it, then, good Uncle Frol,' he would reply; and thus it always was with us, and life went smoothly. But how does it go now? Only to-day a soldier was speaking to me of Plevna; yet you and Gabriel are waging a more grievous battle than ever there was fought at Plevna. Is this the proper way to live, then? No, it is not—it is sinful. You are a peasant and the master of a home. I would ask you, then—what sort of a lesson are you teaching to your women-kind and children? Why, you are but teaching them to fight as dogs fight. To-day I saw that little rascal Tarass make a face at his Aunt Arina before his mother, and yet his mother only laughed at him. Is *that* right, I ask you? Are such things as *that* to be? Are you to say a word to me, and I two in return to you, and you then to strike me, and I to strike you twice for your one blow? No, no, my dear son. That was not how Christ taught us poor fools when He walked this earth of ours. He taught us that to abuse we should return no answer, and his own conscience would convict the offender. Yes, that is what Our Little Father taught us. And if a man should smite us on the one cheek, we should turn to him the other also, and even submit ourselves to death at his hands if need be. His own conscience would convict him some day, and he would become reconciled and beg for pardon. Yes, that is what Christ taught us, and not pride. But why are you thus silent? Is it not as I say?"

But Ivan returned no answer as he listened.

The old man coughed, cleared his throat with difficulty, and went on:

"Maybe you think that Christ taught us amiss? Yet his teaching was meant for us all, and for our good. Consider now your worldly substance; has it increased or decreased since this Plevna was begun between you two? Cast up how much you have spent on law-costs, on journeying to court and expenses. Here are you, with three sons strong as eagles, and with plenty to live upon; yet, for all that, you must go seeking misfortune and wasting your means! And why? Simply through pride. You ought to be out in the fields with your sons—ploughing and sowing; yet you spend your time forever haling your enemy to court over some trifle or another. The ploughing is delayed, and the seeding, and so our Mother Earth does not bear. Why are the oats not sprouting yet? When were they sown? You had to go to town, forsooth. Yet what have you gained by your law-suiting? Only a load round your own neck. Ah, my son, remember what is your proper work in life. Turn again to your ploughing and your sons and your home, and if any man offends you, pardon him as God has bidden us do. Then will everything go better with you, and there will always be peace in your soul."

Still Ivan said nothing.

"But see here, now, dear Ivan," went on his father. "Listen to me who am an old man. Saddle the roan horse, and go back to the police-station and cancel your suit. Then, in the morning, go to Gabriel and ask pardon of him in God's name, and invite him to your home for the festival. To-morrow, the birthday of Our Lady, set out the samovar, take a half-bottle, and renounce this sinfulness forever. Ay, and bid the women and children do the same."

Ivan sighed as he thought to himself: "Assuredly the old man is right, only I know not how to do this—how I am to become reconciled."

The old man seemed to have guessed his thoughts, for he said:

"Nay, but do not delay, dear Ivan. A fire should be quenched at the start.

else, if it burn up, it may never be mastered."

He was going on to say more, when the women entered, chattering like magpies. Already they had heard the whole story of Gabriel being sentenced to a flogging and of his making threats of arson. Yes, they knew all about it, and had hastened to put their oar in by getting up a quarrel with Gabriel's womenfolk at the pasture-ground. Now they burst out with the news that Gabriel's daughter-in-law had threatened them with the public prosecutor, whom she declared to be intervening on Gabriel's behalf. The public prosecutor (so said the women) was reviewing the whole case, and the schoolmaster had written out a petition to the Tsar in person, and in this petition every suit was set forth from the beginning—the one about the linch-pin, and the one about the garden-ground, and so on—and half Ivan's land would be given to Gabriel as compensation.

When Ivan heard all this his heart grew hard again, and he thought better of being reconciled to his adversary.

A farmer always has much to do on his farm, so, instead of discussing matters with the women, Ivan rose and left the hut. By the time he had cleared up things in the barn and stable the sun had set and his sons were returning from the fields, where they had been ploughing a double tilth during the winter in readiness for the spring corn. Ivan met them and asked them about their work, after which he helped them to take the harness off the horses, laid aside a broken horse-collar for repairs, and was for stowing away some poles in the stable, but it was getting too dark to see. So he left the poles till the

morning, and, after feeding the stock opened the gates for young Tarass to take the horses across the roadway to their night pasture. Finally, he closed the gates, put up the board which fastened them, picked up the broken horse-collar and walked towards the hut, thinking: "It is time now for supper and bed." At the moment he had forgotten all about Gabriel, as well as about his father's words; yet he had no sooner laid his hand upon the door-knob to enter the porch, than he heard his neighbour shout out in a hoarse voice to someone on the other side of the fence: "To the devil with him! I could kill him!"

These words aroused in Ivan all his old enmity against his neighbour, and he waited to hear what more he might say. But nothing further came from Gabriel, so Ivan went indoors. The lamp had just been lit, the young woman was sitting at her loom in the corner, the goodwife was preparing supper, the eldest son was putting a patch into his bast shoes, the second son was reading a book at the table, and little Tarass was getting himself ready to go and sleep in the horse-stable over the way. Everything would have looked cosy and cheerful had it not been for that one blighting influence—their wicked neighbour.

Ivan came in tired, turned the cat off the bench, and rated the women for having put the stove-couch out of its place. He sat down with knitted brows to mend the horse-collar, but felt restless somehow. Gabriel's words would keep running through his head—both the threats he had uttered in the court-house, and the words he had just shouted in a hoarse voice to someone behind the fence: "I could kill him!"

Meanwhile the goodwife was bustling about to give young Tarass his supper. As soon as he had eaten it, he put on his little sheepskin and kaftan, belted them round, took a hunch of bread, and went out to drive the mares down the street. His eldest brother was for going with him, but Ivan himself rose and accompanied him out on to the steps. It was quite dark now in the yard, for the sky was overcast and a wind was rising. Ivan descended from the steps to mount his little son, and, having shoo'ed the foals after him, stood watching them depart. He could hear Tarass go riding along the street, until joined by other boys, and then the sound of them die away. Yet he still hung about the gates, for Gabriel's words would not leave his mind: "I pray that he and his may burn more sorely still."

"He would not hesitate to do it," thought Ivan. "Everything is standing dry now, and there is a wind blowing, so that if he were to get in somewhere at the back, and fire things from there, it would make a terrible blaze. The wind would fan it too fiercely for it ever to stop. Yes, once it were alight there would be no putting it out."

The idea took such a hold upon Ivan that, instead of returning to the steps, he went out into the roadway, and then round behind the gates.

"Suppose I make a complete inspection of the place?" he thought. "Who knows what that man may not be up to?" So he left the gates, and went along with stealthy tread until he came to the corner. There, as he glanced along the wall, he thought he could discern something moving—something

which jutted out at one moment, and became hidden in a recess the next. He stopped and remained absolutely still as he listened and watched. Yet all was quiet. Only the wind kept shaking the leaves of a vine-stock and moaning through its stems. It was very dark, yet not so completely so but that, by straining his eyes, Ivan could distinguish the outlines of things—of the back wall, a plough, and the eaves overhead. He listened and watched, but there seemed to be no one there.

"I cannot help thinking that I saw a glimmer just now," he said to himself. "Suppose I were to go right round the place?" So he crept stealthily along under the stable, walking so softly in his bast shoes that he could not even hear his own footsteps. He had almost reached the recess when lo! something flashed for a moment beside the plough, and then disappeared. Ivan's heart gave a thump, and he stopped dead. Yet even as he did so there came a brighter glimmer at that spot—a glimmer which revealed a man in a cap—a man kneeling back upon his heels and engaged in lighting a tuft of straw which he held in his hands. Ivan's heart beat in his breast like a bird fluttering, as, stiffening himself all over, he darted forward with long strides, but too softly for him even to hear his own footsteps. "He shall not escape me!" he thought. "I will catch him in the very act!"

He had not advanced another couple of strides when suddenly a brilliant light flared up—but not from the spot low down in the recess, for the wattling of the wall flamed up in the eaves, and thence the fire was carried on to the roof. In the light of the flames Gabriel stood revealed as clear as day.

Ivan made for the lame man as a hawk stoops to a lark. "I will wring his neck now," he thought, "for he cannot escape me." Yet the lame man must suddenly have heard his footsteps, for he glanced round, and then, with a sudden turn of speed, limped away like a hare.

"You shall not escape me!" shouted Ivan as he flew in pursuit. Just as he was on the point of seizing him by the collar, the hunted man doubled, and Ivan's hands clutched the tail of his coat only. The tail tore away, and Ivan fell forwards. Instantly leaping up again, he shouted, "Watchman! Hold him!" and resumed the chase.

Yet, while he had been scrambling to his feet, Gabriel had regained his own yard. Ivan pursued him there, and was once more on the point of seizing him, when something crashed down upon his head, like a rock falling from above. Gabriel had picked up an oaken stake lying in the yard, swung it aloft to the full extent of his arm, and brought it down upon Ivan's head just as the latter ran in upon him.

Ivan blinked his eyes, and sparks flashed before them. Then all grew dark as he staggered and fell to the ground. When he came to himself again Gabriel had disappeared, and it was as light as day, while from the direction of his own yard there came a crackling, rattling sort of a sound, like a machine at work. Ivan turned his head and saw that the whole of the back shed was ablaze, and that the side shed too had caught, while flames and smoke and bits of burning straw in the smoke were being carried in a stream on to the hut.

"Help, neighbours!" cried Ivan, rais-

ing his hands in despair and smacking them down upon his thighs. "Pull the burning stuff from the eaves for me, and stamp it out! Help, good neighbours!"

He tried to keep on shouting, but his breath failed him and his voice choked. Then he tried to start running, but his legs refused to move, and kept catching against one another. Whenever he took a step forward he staggered, and his breath failed, so that he had to stand still and recover it before he could move again. At last, however, he managed to get round the shed and approach the fire. The side shed was a mass of flames, as also were one corner of the hut and the porch. Indeed, the flames were bursting so furiously from the hut that the yard was impassable. A large crowd had collected, but had done nothing. Only the neighbours had succeeded in removing their stock and furniture from their own premises.

Gabriel's place was the next one after Ivan's to be consumed, and then, the wind carrying the flames across the roadway, half the village became involved. The old man had been got out of Ivan's hut only just in time, while the others had had to rush forth exactly as they were, and abandon everything. The whole of the stock except the horses at night pasture had been consumed, as well as the poultry on the roosting beams, the carts, the ploughs, the harrows, the women's chests, and the grain in the bins. On the other hand, Gabriel's stock was saved, and a certain amount of his other belongings.

The fire lasted for a long time—all night, in fact—and for a while Ivan stood watching his place being consumed, and reiterating at intervals:

"Help, good neighbours! Pull out the burning stuff and stamp upon it!" But when at length the roof of the hut fell in, he rushed into the very heart of the fire, and, seizing hold of a blazing beam, tried to drag it out. The women had seen him and called to him to come back, but he nevertheless dragged out the beam, and was about to drag out another, when he suddenly staggered and fell into the flames. His son went in after him, and got him out, but although his hair and beard had been singed, his clothes half burnt away, and his hands injured, he had felt nothing. "He has gone mad with grief," said the peasants. In time the fire began to die down, yet Ivan still stood there, repeating: "Help, neighbours! Pull out the burning stuff!"

Next morning the starosta sent his son to him.

"Uncle Ivan," said the son, your father is dying, and bade me fetch you to take leave of him."

Ivan had forgotten all about his father, and could not understand who was referred to.

"Whose father?" he asked. "And who is it he wants?"

"Yourself. He bade me fetch you to take leave of him. He is dying in our hut. Come, Uncle Ivan"—and the starosta's son held out his hand to him. Ivan went with him.

Some blazing straw had fallen upon the old man as he was being carried out of the hut the previous night, and burnt him badly. They had then removed him to the starosta's hut, which stood in the far outskirts of the village, and had escaped the fire.

When Ivan reached his father there was no one in the hut but an old woman, and some children lying on the stove; for everyone else was busy at the ruins of the fire. The old man was lying in a bunk, with a candle in his hands, and his face turned towards the door. As soon as his son entered the outer door he stirred a little, and when the old woman went to tell him that his son had come, he bade him draw nearer. Ivan did so, and the old man said:

"What did I tell you, dear Ivan? Who was it fired the village?"

"*He,* dear father. *He,* for I found him at it. With my own eyes I saw him put the kindling into the eaves. Ah, if only I had stopped to pull out the burning straw and stamp upon it! But I had no time."

"Ivan," went on the old man, "my end is near, and I would have you reconciled. Whose was the fault?"

Ivan gazed fixedly at his father, but remained silent. Not a word could he utter.

"Before God, speak," said his father again. "Whose was the fault? What did I say to you but lately?"

Then at length Ivan came to himself and understood all. He gave a sob and replied:

"Mine was the fault, dear father."

Then, bursting into tears, he fell upon his knees and exclaimed:

"Pardon me, O my father! I have sinned both against you and against God!"

The old man moved his hands and changed the candle into his left. Then he raised his right hand towards his forehead as though to cross himself, but could not stretch it so far, and desisted.

"Glory be to Thee, oh, Lord! Glory

be to Thee!" he murmured as he turned his eyes again upon his son. "But, Ivan. dear Ivan—"

"What is it, my father?"

"What shall you do now?"

Ivan burst out weeping afresh.

"I know not, dear father," he said. "How, indeed, are we to live, now that this has happened?"

The old man closed his eyes, moistened his lips a little, as though he were collecting all his strength, and then said, as he re-opened his eyes:

"Live on and prosper. So long as your life be with God, you will prosper."

He was silent for a moment, then smiled gently and continued:

"Look you, dear Ivan—*never* say who started the fire. If you should shield the sins of another, God will pardon you two of your own"—and, taking the candle in his two hands, the old man folded them upon his breast, sighed, stretched himself out, and passed away.

Ivan never told of Gabriel, and so no one ever knew whence the fire originated.

Indeed, Ivan's heart went out to Gabriel, while Gabriel, for his part, was amazed that Ivan had never informed against him. At first he went in fear of him, but gradually grew accustomed to the new order of things; with the result that the two peasants abandoned their feud, and their families did the same. While their new homesteads were being built, the two families lived as one, under the same roof; and when the whole village had been rebuilt, with its huts put wider apart, Ivan and Gabriel still remained neighbours, with contiguous homesteads.

Indeed, they lived as good neighbours as their fathers had done. Never did Ivan Shtchevbakoff forget the advice of the old man and the law of God—that a fire should be quenched when it is but a spark.

If any man did him wrong, he would strive, not to avenge himself, but to right the matter; and if any man flung him an evil word, he would strive, not to return a word more evil, but to teach that man a better one. And in like manner also he taught his women-folk and sons to do.

Thus Ivan Shtchevbakoff put straight his way of life, and prospered as he had never done before.

The Death of Ivan Ilyitch

CHAPTER I

NEWS

INSIDE the great building of the Law Courts, during the interval in the hearing of the Melvinsky case, the members of the judicial council and the public prosecutor were gathered together in the private room of Ivan Yegorovitch Shebek, and the conversation turned upon the celebrated Krasovsky case. Fyodor Vassilievitch hotly maintained that the case was not in the jurisdiction of the court. Yegor Ivanovitch stood up for his own view; but from the first Pyotr Ivanovitch, who had not entered into the discussion, took no interest in it, but was looking through the newspapers which had just been brought in.

"Gentlemen!" he said, "Ivan Ilyitch is dead!"

"You don't say so!"

"Here, read it," he said to Fyodor Vassilievitch, handing him the fresh still damp-smelling paper.

Within a black margin was printed: "Praskovya Fyodorovna Golovin with heartfelt affliction informs friends and relatives of the decease of her beloved husband, member of the Court of Justice, Ivan Ilyitch Golovin, who passed away on the 4th of February. The funeral will take place on Thursday at one o'clock."

Ivan Ilyitch was a colleague of the gentlemen present, and all liked him. It was some weeks now since he had been taken ill; his illness had been said to be incurable. His post had been kept open for him, but it had been thought that in case of his death Alexyeev might receive his appointment, and either Vinnikov or Shtabel would succeed to Alexyeev's. So that on hearing of Ivan Ilyitch's death, the first thought of each of the gentlemen in the room was of the effect this death might have on the transfer or promotion of themselves or their friends.

"Now I am sure of getting Shtabel's place or Vinnikov's," thought Fyodor Vassilievitch. "It was promised me long ago, and the promotion means eight hundred roubles additional income, besides the grants for office expenses."

"Now I shall have to petition for my brother-in-law to be transferred from Kaluga," thought Pyotr Ivanovitch. "My wife will be very glad. She won't be able to say now that I've never done anything for her family."

"I thought somehow that he'd never get up from his bed again," Pyotr Ivanovitch said aloud. "I'm sorry!"

"But what was it exactly was wrong with him?"

"The doctors could not decide. That's to say, they did decide, but differently. When I saw him last, I thought he would get over it."

"Well, I positively haven't called there ever since the holidays. I've kept meaning to go."

"Had he any property?"

"I think there's something, very small, of his wife's. But something quite trifling."

"Yes, one will have to go and call. They live such a terribly long way off."

"A long way from you, you mean. Everything's a long way from your place."

"There, he can never forgive me for living the other side of the river," said Pyotr Ivanovitch, smiling at Shebek. And they began to talk of the great distances between different parts of the town, and went back into the court.

Besides the reflections upon the changes and promotions in the service likely to ensue from this death, the very fact of the death of an intimate acquaintance excited in every one who heard of it, as such a fact always does, a feeling of relief that "it is he that is dead, and not I."

"Only think! he is dead, but here am I all right," each one thought or felt. The more intimate acquaintances, the so-called friends of Ivan Ilyitch, could not help thinking too that now they had the exceedingly tiresome social duties to perform of going to the funeral service and paying the widow a visit of condolence.

The most intimately acquainted with their late colleague were Fyodor Vassilievitch and Pyotr Ivanovitch.

Pyotr Ivanovitch had been a comrade of his at the school of jurisprudence, and considered himself under obligations to Ivan Ilyitch.

Telling his wife at dinner of the news of Ivan Ilyitch's death and his reflections as to the possibility of getting her brother transferred into their circuit,

Pyotr Ivanovitch, without lying down for his usual nap, put on his frock-coat and drove to Ivan Ilyitch's.

At the entrance before Ivan Ilyitch's flat stood a carriage and two hired flies. Downstairs in the entry near the hat-stand there was leaning against the wall a coffin-lid with tassels and braiding freshly rubbed up with pipeclay. Two ladies were taking off their cloaks. One of them he knew, the sister of Ivan Ilyitch; the other was a lady he did not know. Pyotr Ivanovitch's colleague, Shvarts, was coming down; and from the top stair, seeing who it was coming in, he stopped and winked at him, as though to say: "Ivan Ilyitch has made a mess of it; it's a very different matter with you and me."

Shvarts's face, with his English whiskers and all his thin figure in his frockcoat, had, as it always had, an air of elegant solemnity; and this solemnity, always such a contrast to Shvarts's playful character, had a special piquancy here. So thought Pyotr Ivanovitch.

Pyotr Ivanovitch let the ladies pass on in front of him, and walked slowly up the stairs after them. Shvarts had not come down, but was waiting at the top. Pyotr Ivanovitch knew what for; he wanted obviously to settle with him where their game of "screw" was to be that evening. The ladies went up to the widow's room; while Shvarts, with his lips tightly and gravely shut, and amusement in his eyes, with a twitch of his eyebrows motioned Pyotr Ivanovitch to the right, to the room where the dead man was.

Pyotr Ivanovitch went in, as people always do on such occasions, in uncertainty as to what he would have to

do there. One thing he felt sure of—
that crossing oneself never comes amiss
on such occasions. As to whether it
was necessary to bow down while doing
so, he did not feel quite sure, and so
chose a middle course. On entering
the room he began crossing himself, and
made a slight sort of bow. So far as
the movements of his hands and head
permitted him, he glanced while doing
so about the room. Two young men,
one a high school boy, nephews probably, were going out of the room, crossing themselves. An old lady was standing motionless; and a lady, with her
eyebrows queerly lifted, was saying
something to her in a whisper. A deacon in a frockcoat, resolute and hearty,
was reading something aloud with an
expression that precluded all possibility
of contradiction. A young peasant who
used to wait at table, Gerasim, walking
with light footsteps in front of Pyotr
Ivanovitch, was sprinkling something
on the floor. Seeing this, Pyotr Ivanovitch was at once aware of the faint
odour of the decomposing corpse. On
his last visit to Ivan Ilyitch Pyotr Ivanovitch had seen this peasant in his room;
he was performing the duties of a sick-
nurse, and Ivan Ilyitch liked him particularly. Pyotr Ivanovitch continued
crossing himself and bowing in a direction intermediate between the coffin,
the deacon, and the holy pictures on
the table in the corner. Then when
this action of making the sign of the
cross with his hand seemed to him to
have been unduly prolonged, he stood
still and began to scrutinize the dead
man.

The dead man lay, as dead men always do lie, in a peculiarly heavy dead
way, his stiffened limbs sunk in the
cushions of the coffin, and his head bent
back forever on the pillow, and thrust
up, as dead men always do, his yellow
waxen forehead with bald spots on the
sunken temples, and his nose that stood
out sharply and, as it were, squeezed
on the upper lip. He was much
changed, even thinner since Pyotr Ivanovitch had seen him, but his face—as
always with the dead—was more handsome, and, above all, more impressive
than it had been when he was alive.
On the face was an expression of what
had to be done having been done, and
rightly done. Besides this, there was
too in that expression a reproach or a
reminder for the living. This reminder
seemed to Pyotr Ivanovitch uncalled
for, or, at least, to have nothing to do
with him. He felt something unpleasant; and so Pyotr Ivanovitch once
more crossed himself hurriedly, and,
as it struck him, too hurriedly, not quite
in accordance with the proprieties,
turned and went to the door. Shvarts
was waiting for him in the adjoining
room, standing with his legs apart and
both hands behind his back playing
with his top hat. A single glance at
the playful, sleek, and elegant figure
of Shvarts revived Pyotr Ivanovitch.
He felt that he, Shvarts, was above it,
and would not give way to depressing
impressions. The mere sight of him said
plainly: the incident of the service
over the body of Ivan Ilyitch cannot
possibly constitute a sufficient ground
for recognizing the business of the session suspended,—in other words, in no
way can it hinder us from shuffling and
cutting a pack of cards this evening,
while the footman sets four unsancti-
fied candles on the table for us; in fact,
there is no ground for supposing that

this incident could prevent us from spending the evening agreeably. He said as much indeed to Pyotr Ivanovitch as he came out, proposing that the party should meet at Fyodor Vassilievitch's. But apparently it was Pyotr Ivanovitch's destiny not to play "screw" that evening. Praskovya Fyodorovna, a short, fat woman who, in spite of all efforts in a contrary direction, was steadily broader from her shoulders downwards, all in black, with lace on her head and her eyebrows as queerly arched as those of the lady standing beside the coffin, came out of her own apartments with some other ladies, and conducting them to the dead man's room, said: "The service will take place immediately; come in."

Shvarts, making an indefinite bow, stood still, obviously neither accepting nor declining this invitation. Praskovya Fyodorovna, recognizing Pyotr Ivanovitch, sighed, went right up to him, took his hand, and said, "I know that you were a true friend of Ivan Ilyitch's . . ." and looked at him, expecting from him the suitable action in response to these words. Pyotr Ivanovitch knew that, just as before he had to cross himself, now what he had to do was to press her hand, to sigh and to say, "Ah, I was indeed!" And he did so. And as he did so, he felt that the desired result had been attained; that he was touched, and she was touched.

"Come, since it's not begun yet, I have something I want to say to you," said the widow. "Give me your arm."

Pyotr Ivanovitch gave her his arm, and they moved towards the inner rooms, passing Shvarts, who winked gloomily at Pyotr Ivanovitch.

"So much for our 'screw'! Don't complain if we find another partner. You can make a fifth when you do get away," said his humorous glance.

Pyotr Ivanovitch sighed still more deeply and despondently, and Praskovya Fyodorovna pressed his hand gratefully. Going into her drawing-room, which was upholstered with pink cretonne and lighted by a dismal-looking lamp, they sat down at the table, she on a sofa and Pyotr Ivanovitch on a low ottoman with deranged springs which yielded spasmodically under his weight. Praskovya Fyodorovna was about to warn him to sit on another seat, but felt such a recommendation out of keeping with her position, and changed her mind. Sitting down on the ottoman, Pyotr Ivanovitch remembered how Ivan Ilyitch had arranged this drawing-room, and had consulted him about this very pink cretonne with green leaves. Seating herself on the sofa, and pushing by the table (the whole drawing-room was crowded with furniture and things), the widow caught the lace of her black fichu in the carving of the table. Pyotr Ivanovitch got up to disentangle it for her; and the ottoman, freed from his weight, began bobbing up spasmodically under him. The widow began unhooking her lace herself, and Pyotr Ivanovitch again sat down, suppressing the mutinous ottoman springs under him. But the widow could not quite free herself, and Pyotr Ivanovitch rose again, and again the ottoman became mutinous and popped up with a positive snap. When this was all over, she took out a clean cambric handkerchief and began weeping. Pyotr Ivanovitch had been chilled off by the incident with the lace and the struggle with the ottoman springs, and he sat looking sullen. This awkward position was cut short by the entrance of Sokolov, Ivan Ilyitch's butler, who came in to announce that the place in the cemetery fixed on by Praskovya Fyodorovna would cost two hundred roubles. She left off weeping, and with an air of a victim glancing at Pyotr Ivanovitch, said in French that it was very terrible for her. Pyotr Ivanovitch made a silent gesture signifying his unhesitating conviction that it must indeed be so.

"Please, smoke," she said in a magnanimous, and at the same time, crushed voice, and she began discussing with Sokolov the question of the price of the site for the grave.

Pyotr Ivanovitch, lighting a cigarette, listened to her very circumstantial inquiries as to the various prices of sites and her decision as to the one to be selected. Having settled on the site for the grave, she made arrangements also about the choristers. Sokolov went away.

"I see to everything myself," she said to Pyotr Ivanovitch, moving on one side the albums that lay on the table; and noticing that the table was in danger from the cigarette-ash, she promptly passed an ash-tray to Pyotr Ivanovitch, and said: "I consider it affectation to pretend that my grief prevents me from looking after practical matters. On the contrary, if anything could—not console me . . . but distract me, it is seeing after everything for him." She took out her handkerchief again, as though preparing to weep again; and suddenly, as though struggling with herself, she shook herself, and began speaking calmly: "But I've business to talk about with you."

Pyotr Ivanovitch bowed, carefully keeping in check the springs of the ottoman, which had at once begun quivering under him.

"The last few days his sufferings were awful."

"Did he suffer very much?" asked Pyotr Ivanovitch.

"Oh, awfully! For the last moments, hours indeed, he never left off screaming. For three days and nights in succession he screamed incessantly. It was insufferable. I can't understand how I bore it; one could hear it through three closed doors. Ah, what I suffered!"

"And was he really conscious?" asked Pyotr Ivanovitch.

"Yes," she whispered, "up to the last minute. He said good-bye to us a quarter of an hour before his death, and asked Volodya to be taken away too."

The thought of the sufferings of a man he had known so intimately, at first as a light-hearted boy, a schoolboy, then grown up as a partner at whist, in spite of the unpleasant consciousness of his own and this woman's hypocrisy, suddenly horrified Pyotr Ivanovitch. He saw again that forehead, the nose that seemed squeezing the lip, and he felt frightened for himself. "Three days and nights of awful suffering and death. Why, that may at once, any minute, come upon me too," he thought, and he felt for an instant terrified. But immediately, he could not himself have said how, there came to his support the customary reflection that this had happened to Ivan Ilyitch and not to him, and that to him this must not and could not happen; that in thinking thus he was giving way to depression, which was not the right thing to do, as was evident from Shvarts's expression of face. And making these reflections, Pyotr Ivanovitch felt reassured, and began with interest inquiring details about Ivan Ilyitch's end, as though death were a mischance peculiar to Ivan Ilyitch, but not at all incidental to himself.

After various observations about the details of the truly awful physical sufferings endured by Ivan Ilyitch (these details Pyotr Ivanovitch learned only through the effect Ivan Ilyitch's agonies had had on the nerves of Praskovya Fyodorovna), the widow apparently thought it time to get to business.

"Ah, Pyotr Ivanovitch, how hard it is, how awfully, awfully hard!" and she began to cry again.

Pyotr Ivanovitch sighed, and waited for her to blow her nose. When she had done so, he said, "Indeed it is," and again she began to talk, and brought out what was evidently the business she wished to discuss with him; that business consisted in the inquiry as to how on the occasion of her husband's death she was to obtain a grant from the government. She made a show of asking Pyotr Ivanovitch's advice about a pension. But he perceived that she knew already to the minutest details, what he did not know himself indeed, everything that could be got out of the government on the ground of this death; but that what she wanted to find out was, whether there were not any means of obtaining a little more? Pyotr Ivanovitch tried to imagine such means; but after pondering a little, and out of politeness abusing the government for its stinginess, he said that he believed that it was impossible to obtain more.

Then she sighed and began unmistakably looking about for an excuse for getting rid of her visitor. He perceived this, put out his cigarette, got up, pressed her hand, and went out into the passage.

In the dining-room, where was the bric-à-brac clock that Ivan Ilyitch had been so delighted at buying, Pyotr Ivanovitch met the priest and several people he knew who had come to the service for the dead, and saw too Ivan Ilyitch's daughter, a handsome young lady. She was all in black. Her very slender figure looked even slenderer than usual. She had a gloomy, determined, almost wrathful expression. She bowed to Pyotr Ivanovitch as though he were to blame in some way. Behind the daughter, with the same offended air on his face, stood a rich young man, whom Pyotr Ivanovitch knew, too, an examining magistrate, the young lady's *fiancé*, as he had heard. He bowed dejectedly to him, and would have gone on into the dead man's room, when from the staircase there appeared the figure of the son, the high school boy, extraordinarily like Ivan Ilyitch. He was the little Ivan Ilyitch over again as Pyotr Ivanovitch remembered him at school. His eyes were red with crying, and had that look often seen in unclean boys of thirteen or fourteen. The boy, seeing Pyotr Ivanovitch, scowled morosely and bashfully. Pyotr Ivanovitch nodded to him and went into the dead man's room. The service for the dead began—candles, groans, incense, tears, sobs. Pyotr Ivanovitch stood frowning, staring at his feet in front of him. He did not once glance at the dead man, and right through to the end did not once give way to depressing influences, and was one of the first to walk out. In the hall there was no one. Gerasim, the young peasant, darted out of the dead man's room, tossed over with his strong hand all the fur cloaks to find Pyotr Ivanovitch's, and gave it him.

"Well, Gerasim, my boy?" said Pyotr Ivanovitch, so as to say something. "A sad business, isn't it?"

"It's God's will. We shall come to the same," said Gerasim, showing his white, even, peasant teeth in a smile, and, like a man in a rush of extra work, he briskly opened the door, called up the coachman, saw Pyotr Ivanovitch into the carriage, and darted back to the steps as though bethinking himself of what he had to do next.

Pyotr Ivanovitch had a special pleasure in the fresh air after the smell of incense, of the corpse, and of carbolic acid.

"Where to?" asked the coachman.

"It's not too late. I'll still go round to Fyodor Vassilievitch's."

And Pyotr Ivanovitch drove there. And he did, in fact, find them just finishing the first rubber, so that he came just at the right time to take a hand.

CHAPTER II

WHO HE WAS

THE previous history of Ivan Ilyitch was the simplest, the most ordinary, and the most awful.

Ivan Ilyitch died at the age of forty-five, a member of the Judicial Council. He was the son of an official, whose career in Petersburg through various ministries and departments had been such as leads people into that position in which, though it is distinctly obvious that they are unfit to perform any kind of real duty, they yet cannot, owing to their long past service and their official rank, be dismissed; and they therefore receive a specially created fictitious post, and by no means fictitious thousands—from six to ten—on which they go on living till extreme old age. Such was the privy councilor, the superfluous member of various superfluous institutions, Ilya Efimovitch Golovin.

He had three sons. Ivan Ilyitch was the second son. The eldest son's career was exactly like his father's, only in a different department, and he was by now close upon that stage in the service in which the same sinecure would be reached. The third son was the unsuccessful one. He had in various positions always made a mess of things, and was now employed in the railway department. And his father and his brothers, and still more their wives, did not merely dislike meeting him, but avoided, except in extreme necessity, recollecting his existence. His sister had married Baron Greff, a Petersburg official of the same stamp as his father-in-law. Ivan Ilyitch was *le phénix de la famille,* as people said. He was not so frigid and precise as the eldest son, nor so wild as the youngest. He was the happy mean between them—a shrewd, lively, pleasant, and well-bred man. He had been educated with his younger brother at the school of jurisprudence. The younger brother had not finished the school course, but was expelled when in the fifth class. Ivan Ilyitch completed the course successfully. At school he was just the same as he was later on all his life—an intelligent fellow, highly good-humoured and sociable, but strict in doing what he considered to be his duty.

His duty he considered whatever was so considered by those persons who were set in authority over him. He was not a toady as a boy, nor later on as a grown-up person; but from his earliest years he was attracted, as a fly to the light, to persons of good standing in the world, assimilated their manners and their views of life, and established friendly relations with them. All the enthusiasms of childhood and youth passed, leaving no great traces in him; he gave way to sensuality and to vanity, and latterly when in the higher classes at school to liberalism, but always keeping within certain limits which were unfailingly marked out for him by his instincts.

At school he had committed actions which had struck him beforehand as great vileness, and gave him a feeling of loathing for himself at the very time he was committing them. But later on, perceiving that such actions were committed also by men of good position, and were not regarded by them as base, he was able, not to regard them as good, but to forget about them completely, and was never mortified by recollections of them.

Leaving the school of jurisprudence in the tenth class, and receiving from his father a sum of money for his outfit, Ivan Ilyitch ordered his clothes at Sharmer's, hung on his watchchain a medallion inscribed *respice finem*, said goodbye to the prince who was the principal of his school, had a farewell dinner with his comrades at Donon's, and with all his new fashionable belongings—travelling trunk, linen, suits of clothes, shaving and toilet appurtenances, and travelling rug, all ordered and purchased at the very best shops—set off to take the post of secretary on special commissions for the governor of a province, a post which had been obtained for him by his father.

In the province Ivan Ilyitch without loss of time made himself a position as easy and agreeable as his position had been in the school of jurisprudence. He did his work, made his career, and at the same time led a life of well-bred social gaiety. Occasionally he visited various districts on official duty, behaved with dignity both with his superiors and his inferiors; and with exactitude and an incorruptible honesty of which he could not help feeling proud, performed the duties with which he was intrusted, principally having to do with the dissenters. When engaged in official work he was, in spite of his youth and taste for frivolous amusement, exceedingly reserved, official, and even severe. But in social life he was often amusing and witty, and always good-natured, well-bred, and *bon enfant,* as was said of him by his chief and his chief's wife, with whom he was like one of the family.

In the province there was, too, a connection with one of the ladies who obtruded their charms on the stylish young lawyer. There was a dressmaker, too, and there were drinking bouts with smart officers visiting the neighbourhood, and visits to a certain outlying street after supper; there was a rather cringing obsequiousness in his behaviour, too, with his chief, and even his chief's wife. But all this was accompanied with such a tone of the highest breeding, that it could not be called by harsh names; it all came under the rubric of the French saying, *Il faut que la jeunesse se passe.* Everything was done with clean hands, in clean shirts, with French phrases, and, what was of most importance, in the highest society, and consequently with the approval of people of rank.

Such was Ivan Ilyitch's career for five years, and then came a change in his official life. New methods of judicial procedure were established; new men were wanted to carry them out. And Ivan Ilyitch became such a new man. Ivan Ilyitch was offered the post of examining magistrate, and he accepted it in spite of the fact that this post was in another province, and he would have to break off all the ties he had formed and form new ones. Ivan Ilyitch's friends met together to see him off, had their photographs taken in a group, presented him with a silver cigarette-case, and he set off to his new post.

As an examining magistrate, Ivan Ilyitch was as *comme il faut*, as well-bred, as adroit in keeping official duties apart from private life, and as successful in gaining universal respect, as he had been as secretary of private commissions. The duties of his new office were in themselves of far greater interest and attractiveness for Ivan Ilyitch. In his former post it had been pleasant to pass in his smart uniform from Sharmer's through the crowd of petitioners and officials waiting timorously and envying him, and to march with his easy swagger straight into the governor's private room, there to sit down with him to tea and cigarettes. But the persons directly subject to his authority were few. The only such persons were the district police superintendents and the dissenters, when he was serving on special commissions. And he liked treating such persons affably, almost like comrades; liked to make them feel that he, able to annihilate them, was behaving in this simple, friendly way with them. But such people were then few in number. Now as an examining magistrate Ivan Ilyitch felt that every one—every one without exception—the most dignified, the most self-satisfied people, all were in his hands, and that he had but to write certain words on a sheet of paper with a printed heading, and this dignified self-satisfied person would be brought before him in the capacity of a defendant or a witness; and if he did not care to make him sit down, he would have to stand up before him and answer his questions. Ivan Ilyitch never abused this authority of his; on the contrary he tried to soften the expression of it. But the conscious-ness of this power and the possibility of softening its effect constituted for him the chief interest and attractiveness of his new position. In the work itself, in the preliminary inquiries, that is, Ivan Ilyitch very rapidly acquired the art of setting aside every consideration irrelevant to the official aspect of the case, and of reducing every case, however complex, to that form in which it could in a purely external fashion be put on paper, completely excluding his personal view of the matter, and what was of paramount importance, observing all the necessary formalities. All this work was new. And he was one of the first men who put into practical working the reforms in judicial procedure enacted in 1864.

On settling in a new town in his position as examining magistrate, Ivan Ilyitch made new acquaintances, formed new ties, took up a new line, and adopted a rather different attitude. He took up an attitude of somewhat dignified aloofness towards the provincial authorities, while he picked out the best circle among the legal gentlemen and wealthy gentry living in the town, and adopted a tone of slight dissatisfaction with the government, moderate liberalism, and lofty civic virtue. With this, while making no change in the elegance of his get-up, Ivan Ilyitch in his new office gave up shaving, and left his beard free to grow as it liked. Ivan Ilyitch's existence in the new town proved to be very agreeable; the society which took the line of opposition to the governor was friendly and good; his income was larger, and he found a source of increased enjoyment in whist, at which he began to play at this time; and having a faculty for playing cards good-humouredly, and being rapid and exact in his calculations, he was as a rule on the winning side.

After living two years in the new town, Ivan Ilyitch met his future wife. Praskovya Fyodorovna Mihel was the most attractive, clever, and brilliant girl in the set in which Ivan Ilyitch moved. Among other amusements and recreations after his labours as a magistrate, Ivan Ilyitch started a light, playful flirtation with Praskovya Fyodorovna.

Ivan Ilyitch when he was an assistant secretary had danced as a rule; as an examining magistrate he danced only as an exception. He danced now as it were under protest, as though to show "that though I am serving on the new reformed legal code, and am of the fifth class in official rank, still if it comes to a question of dancing, in that line, too, I can do better than others." In this spirit he danced now and then towards the end of the evening with Praskovya Fyodorovna, and it was principally during these dances that he won the heart of Praskovya Fyodorovna. She fell in love with him. Ivan Ilyitch had no clearly defined intention of marrying; but when the girl fell in love with him, he put the question to himself: "After all, why not get married?"

The young lady, Praskovya Fyodorovna, was of good family, nice-looking. There was a little bit of property. Ivan Ilyitch might have reckoned on a more brilliant match, but this was a good match. Ivan Ilyitch had his salary; she, he hoped, would have as much of her own. It was a good family; she was a sweet, pretty, and perfectly *comme il faut* young woman. To say that Ivan Ilyitch got married because he fell in love with his wife and found in her sympathy with his views of life, would be as untrue as to say that he got married because the people of his world approved of the match. Ivan Ilyitch was influenced by both considerations; he was doing what was agreeable to himself in securing such a wife, and at the same time doing what persons of higher standing looked upon as the correct thing.

And Ivan Ilyitch got married.

The process itself of getting married and the early period of married life, with the conjugal caresses, the new furniture, the new crockery, the new house linen, all up to the time of his wife's pregnancy, went off very well; so that Ivan Ilyitch had already begun to think that so far from marriage breaking up that kind of frivolous, agreeable, light-hearted life, always decorous and always approved by society, which he regarded as the normal life, it would even increase its agreeableness. But at that point, in the early months of his wife's pregnancy, there came in a new element, unexpected, unpleasant, tiresome and unseemly, which could never have been anticipated, and from which there was no escape.

His wife, without any kind of reason, it seemed to Ivan Ilyitch, *de gaité de cœur,* as he expressed it, began to disturb the agreeableness and decorum of their life. She began without any sort of justification to be jealous, exacting in her demands on his attention, squabbled over everything, and treated him to the coarsest and most unpleasant scenes.

At first Ivan Ilyitch hoped to escape from the unpleasantness of this position by taking up the same frivolous and well-bred line that had served him well on other occasions of difficulty. He endeavored to ignore his wife's ill-humour, went on living light-heartedly and agreeably as before, invited friends to play cards, tried to get away himself to the club or to his friends. But his wife began on one occasion with such energy, abusing him in such coarse language, and so obstinately persisted in her abuse of him every time he failed in carrying out her demands, obviously having made up her mind firmly to persist till he gave way, that is, stayed at home and was as dull as she was, that Ivan Ilyitch took alarm. He perceived that matrimony, at least with his wife, was not invariably conducive to the pleasures and proprieties of life; but, on the contrary, often destructive of them, and that it was therefore essential to erect some barrier to protect himself from these disturbances. And Ivan Ilyitch began to look about for such means of protecting himself. His official duties were the only thing that impressed Praskovya Fyodorovna, and Ivan Ilyitch began to use his official position and the duties arising from it in his struggle with his wife to fence off his own independent world apart.

With the birth of the baby, the attempts at nursing it, and the various unsuccessful experiments with foods, with the illnesses, real and imaginary, of the infant and its mother, in which Ivan Ilyitch was expected to sympathize, though he never had the slightest idea about them, the need for him to fence off a world apart for himself outside his family life became still more imperative. As his wife grew more irritable and exacting, so did Ivan Ilyitch more and more transfer the centre of gravity of his life to his official work. He became fonder and fonder of official life, and more ambitious than he had been.

Very quickly, not more than a year after his wedding, Ivan Ilyitch had become aware that conjugal life, though providing certain comforts, was in reality a very intricate and difficult business towards which one must, if one is to do one's duty, that is, lead the decorous life approved by society, work out for oneself a definite line, just as in the government service.

And such a line Ivan Ilyitch did work out for himself in his married life. He expected from his home life only those comforts—of dinner at home, of housekeeper and bed which it could give him, and, above all, that perfect propriety in external observances required by public opinion. For the rest, he looked for good-humoured pleasantness, and if he found it he was very thankful. If he met with antagonism and querulousness, he promptly retreated into the separate world he had shut off for himself in his official life, and there he found solace.

Ivan Ilyitch was prized as a good official, and three years later he was made assistant public prosecutor. The new duties of this position, their dignity, the possibility of bringing any one to trial and putting any one in prison, the publicity of the speeches and the success Ivan Ilyitch had in that part of his work,—all this made his official work still more attractive to him.

Children were born to him. His wife became steadily more querulous and ill-tempered, but the line Ivan Ilyitch had taken up for himself in home life put him almost out of reach of her grumbling.

After seven years of service in the same town, Ivan Ilyitch was transferred to another province with the post of public prosecutor. They moved, money was short, and his wife did not like the place they had moved to. The salary was indeed a little higher than before, but their expenses were larger. Besides, a couple of children died, and home life consequently became even less agreeable for Ivan Ilyitch.

For every mischance that occurred in their new place of residence, Praskovya Fyodorovna blamed her husband. The greater number of subjects of conversation between husband and wife, especially the education of the children, led to questions which were associated with previous quarrels, and quarrels were ready to break out at every instant. There remained only those rare periods of being in love which did indeed come upon them, but never lasted long. These were the islands at which they put in for a time, but they soon set off again upon the ocean of concealed hostility, that was made manifest in their aloofness from one another. This aloofness might have distressed Ivan Ilyitch if he had believed that this ought not to be so, but by now he regarded this position as perfectly normal, and it was indeed the goal towards which he worked in his home life. His aim was to make himself more and more free from the unpleasant aspects of domestic life and to render them harmless and decorous. And he attained this aim by spending less and less time with his family; and when he was forced to be at home, he endeavored to secure his tranquility by the presence of outsiders. The great thing for Ivan Ilyitch was having his office. In the official world all the interest of life was concentrated for him. And this interest absorbed him. The sense of his own power, the consciousness of being able to ruin any one he wanted to ruin, even the external dignity of his office, when he made his entry into the court or met subordinate officials, his success in the eyes of his superiors and his subordinates, and, above all, his masterly handling of cases, of which he was conscious,—all this delighted him and, together with chats with his colleagues, dining out, and whist, filled his life. So that, on the whole, Ivan Ilyitch's life still went on in the way he thought it should go—agreeably and decorously.

So he lived for another seven years. His eldest daughter was already sixteen, another child had died, and there was left only one other, a boy at the high school, a subject of dissension. Ivan Ilyitch wanted to send him to the school of jurisprudence, while Praskovya Fyodorovna to spite him sent him to the high school. The daughter had been educated at home, and had turned out well; the boy too did fairly well at his lessons.

CHAPTER III

THE QUARREL

SUCH was Ivan Ilyitch's life for seventeen years after his marriage. He had been by now a long while prosecutor, and had refused several appointments offered him, looking out for a more desirable post, when there occurred an unexpected incident which utterly destroyed his peace of mind. Ivan Ilyitch had been expecting to be appointed presiding judge in a university town, but a certain Goppe somehow stole a march on him and secured the appointment. Ivan Ilyitch took offence, began upbraiding him, and quarrelled with him and with his own superiors. A coolness was felt towards him, and on the next appointment that was made he was again passed over.

This was in the year 1880. That year was the most painful one in Ivan Ilyitch's life. During that year it became evident on the one hand that his pay was insufficient for his expenses; on the other hand, that he had been forgotten by every one, and that what seemed to him the most monstrous, the cruelest injustice, appeared to other people as a quite commonplace fact. Even his father felt no obligation to assist him. He felt that every one had deserted him, and that every one regarded his position with an income of three thousand five hundred roubles as a quite normal and even fortunate one. He alone, with a sense of the injustice done him, and the everlasting nagging of his wife and the debts he had begun to accumulate, living beyond his means, knew that his position was far from being normal.

The summer of that year, to cut down his expenses, he took a holiday and went with his wife to spend the summer in the country at her brother's.

In the country, with no official duties to occupy him, Ivan Ilyitch was for the first time a prey not to simple boredom, but to intolerable depression; and he made up his mind that things could not go on like that, and that it was absolutely necessary to take some decisive steps.

After a sleepless night spent by Ivan Ilyitch walking up and down the terrace, he determined to go to Petersburg to take active steps and to get transferred to some other department, so as to revenge himself on *them,* the people, that is, who had not known how to appreciate him.

Next day, in spite of all the efforts of his wife and his mother-in-law to dissuade him, he set off to Petersburg.

He went with a single object before him—to obtain a post with an income of five thousand. He was ready now to be satisfied with a post in any department, of any tendency, with any kind of work. He must only have a post—a post with five thousand, in the executive department, the banks, the railways, the Empress Marya's institutions, even in the customs duties—what was essential was five thousand, and essential it was, too, to get out of the department in which they had failed to appreciate his value.

And, behold, this quest of Ivan Ilyitch's was crowned with wonderful, unexpected success. At Kursk there got into the same first-class carriage F. S. Ilyin, an acquaintance, who told him of a telegram just received by the governor of Kursk, announcing a change about to take place in the ministry—Pyotr Ivanovitch was to be superseded by Ivan Semyonovitch.

The proposed change, apart from its significance for Russia, had special significance for Ivan Ilyitch from the fact that by bringing to the front a new person, Pyotr Peterovitch, and obviously, therefore, his friend Zahar Ivanovitch, it was in the highest degree propitious to Ivan Ilyitch's own plans. Zahar Ivanovitch was a friend and schoolfellow of Ivan Ilyitch's.

At Moscow the news was confirmed. On arriving at Petersburg, Ivan Ilyitch looked up Zahar Ivanovitch, and received a positive promise of an appointment in his former department—that of justice.

A week later he telegraphed to his wife: *"Zahar Miller's place. At first report I receive appointment."*

Thanks to these changes, Ivan Ilyitch unexpectedly obtained, in the same department as before, an appointment which placed him two stages higher than his former colleagues, and gave him an income of five thousand, together with the official allowance of three thousand five hundred for travelling expenses. All his ill-humour with his former enemies and the whole department was forgotten, and Ivan Ilyitch was completely happy.

Ivan Ilyitch went back to the country more light-hearted and good-tempered than he had been for a very long while. Praskovya Fyodorovna was in better spirits, too, and peace was patched up between them. Ivan Ilyitch described what respect every one had shown him in Petersburg; how all those who had been his enemies had been put to shame, and were cringing now before him; how envious they were of his appointment, and still more of the high favour in which he stood at Petersburg.

Praskovya Fyodorovna listened to this, and pretended to believe it, and did not contradict him in anything, but confined herself to making plans for her new arrangements in the town to which they would be moving. And Ivan Ilyitch saw with delight that these plans were his plans; that they were agreed; and that his life after this disturbing hitch in its progress was about to regain its true, normal character of light hearted agreeableness and propriety.

Ivan Ilyitch had come back to the country for a short stay only. He had to enter upon the duties of his new office on the 10th of September; and besides, he needed some time to settle in a new place, to move all his belongings from the other province, to purchase and order many things in addition; in short, to arrange things as settled in his own mind, and almost exactly as settled in the heart too of Praskovya Fyodorovna.

And now when everything was so successfully arranged, and when he and his wife were agreed in their aim, and were, besides, so little together, they got on with one another as they had not got on together since the early years of their married life. Ivan Ilyitch had thought of taking his family away with him at once; but his sister and his brother-in-law, who had suddenly become extremely cordial and intimate with him and his family, were so pressing in urging them to stay that he set off alone.

Ivan Ilyitch started off; and the light-hearted temper produced by his success, and his good understanding with his wife, one thing backing up another, did not desert him all the time. He found a charming set of apartments, the very thing both husband and wife had dreamed of. Spacious, lofty reception-rooms in the old style, a comfortable, dignified-looking study for him, rooms for his wife and daughter, a schoolroom for his son, everything as though planned on purpose for them. Ivan Ilyitch himself looked after the furnishing of them, chose the wall-papers, bought furniture, by preference antique furniture, which had a peculiar *comme-il-faut* style to his mind, and it all grew up and grew up, and really attained the ideal he had set before himself. When he had half finished arranging the house, his arrangement surpassed his own expectations. He saw the *comme-il-faut* character, elegant and free from vulgarity, that the whole would have when it was all ready. As he fell asleep he pictured to himself the reception-room as it would be. Looking at the drawing-room, not yet finished, he could see the hearth, the screen, the *étagère,* and the little chairs dotted here and there, the plates and dishes on the wall, and the bronzes as they would be when they were all put in their places. He was delighted with the thought of how he would impress Praskovya and Lizanka, who had taste too in this line. They would never expect anything like it. He was particularly successful in coming across and buying cheap old pieces of furniture, which gave a peculiarly aristocratic air to the whole. In his letters he purposely disparaged everything so as to surprise them. All this so absorbed him that the duties of his new office, though he was so fond of his official work, interested him less than he had expected. During sittings of the court he had moments of inattention; he pondered the question which sort of cornices to have on the window-blinds, straight or fluted. He was so interested in this business that he often set to work with his own hands, moved a piece of furniture, or hung up curtains himself. One day he went up a ladder to show a workman, who did not understand, how he wanted some hangings draped, made a false step and slipped; but, like a strong and nimble person, he clung on, and only knocked his side against the

corner of a frame. The bruised place ached, but it soon passed off. Ivan Ilyitch felt all this time particularly good-humoured and well. He wrote: "I feel fifteen years younger." He thought his house-furnishing would be finished in September, but it dragged on to the middle of October. But then the effect was charming; not he only said so, but every one who saw it told him so too.

In reality, it was all just what is commonly seen in the houses of people who are not exactly wealthy but want to look like wealthy people, and so succeed only in being like one another—hangings, dark wood, flowers, rugs and bronzes, everything dark and highly polished, everything that all people of a certain class have so as to be like all people of a certain class. And in his case it was all so like that it made no impression at all; but it all seemed to him somehow special. When he met his family at the railway station and brought them to his newly furnished rooms, all lighted up in readiness, and a footman in a white tie opened the door into an entry decorated with flowers, and then they walked into the drawing-room and the study, uttering cries of delight, he was very happy, conducted them everywhere, eagerly drinking in their praises, and beaming with satisfaction. The same evening, while they talked about various things at tea, Praskovya Fyodorovna inquired about his fall, and he laughed and showed them how he had gone flying, and how he had frightened the upholsterer.

"It's as well I'm something of an athlete. Another man might have been killed, and I got nothing worse than a blow here; when it's touched it hurts, but it's going off already; nothing but a bruise."

And they began to live in their new abode, which, as is always the case, when they had got thoroughly settled in they found to be short of just one room, and with their new income, which, as always, was only a little—some five hundred roubles—too little, and everything went very well. Things went particularly well at first, before everything was quite finally arranged, and there was still something to do to the place—something to buy, something to order, something to move, something to make to fit. Though there were indeed several disputes between husband and wife, both were so well satisfied, and there was so much to do, that it all went off without serious quarrels. When there was nothing left to arrange, it became a little dull, and something seemed to be lacking, but by then they were making acquaintances and forming habits, and life was filled up again.

Ivan Ilyitch, after spending the morning in the court, returned home to dinner, and at first he was generally in a good humour, although this was apt to be upset a little, and precisely on account of the new abode. Every spot on the table-cloth, on the hangings, the string of a window blind broken, irritated him. He had devoted so much trouble to the arrangement of the rooms that any disturbance of their order distressed him. But, on the whole, the life of Ivan Ilyitch ran its course as, according to his conviction, life ought to do—easily, agreeably, and decorously. He got up at nine, drank his coffee, read the newspaper, then put on his official uniform, and went to the court. There the routine of the daily work was ready mapped out for him, and he stepped into it at once. People with petitions, inquiries in the office, the office itself, the sittings—public and preliminary. In all this the great thing necessary was to exclude everything with the sap of life in it, which always disturbs the regular course of official business, not to admit any sort of relations with people except the official relations; the motive of all intercourse had to be simply the official motive, and the intercourse itself to be only official. A man would come, for instance, anxious for certain information. Ivan Ilyitch, not being the functionary on duty, would have nothing whatever to do with such a man. But if this man's relation to him as a member of the court is such as can be formulated on official stamped paper—within the limits of such a relation Ivan Ilyitch would do everything, positively everything he could, and in doing so would observe the semblance of human friendly relations, that is, the courtesies of social life. But where the official relation ended, there everything else stopped too. This art of keeping the official aspect of things apart from his real life, Ivan Ilyitch possessed in the highest degree; and through long practice and natural aptitude, he had brought it to such a pitch of perfection that he even permitted himself at times, like a skilled specialist, as it were in jest, to let the human and official relations mingle. He allowed himself this liberty just because he felt he had the power at any moment if he wished it to take up the purely official line again and to drop the human relation. This thing was not simply easy, agreeable, and decorous; in Ivan Ilyitch's hands it attained a positively artistic character. In the intervals of business he smoked, drank tea, chatted a little about politics, a little about public affairs, a little about cards, but most of all about appointments in the service. And tired but feeling like some artist who had skillfully played his part in the performance, one of the first violins in the orchestra, he returned home. At home his daughter and her mother had been paying calls somewhere, or else some one had been calling on them; the son had been at school, had been preparing his lessons with his teachers, and duly learning correctly what was taught at the high school. Everything was as it should be. After dinner, if there were no visitors, Ivan Ilyitch sometimes read some book of which people were talking, and in the evening sat down to work, that is, read official papers, compared them with the laws, sorted depositions, and put them under the laws. This he found neither tiresome nor entertaining. It was tiresome when he might have been playing "screw"; but if there were no "screw" going on, it was anyway better than sitting alone or with his wife. Ivan Ilyitch's pleasures were little dinners, to which he invited ladies and gentlemen of good social position, and such methods of passing the time with them as were usual with such persons, so that his drawing-room might be like all other drawing-rooms.

Once they even gave a party—a dance. And Ivan Ilyitch enjoyed it, and everything was very successful, except that it led to a violent quarrel with his wife over the tarts and sweetmeats. Praskovya Fyodorovna had her own plan; while Ivan Ilyitch insisted on getting everything from an expensive pastry-cook, and ordered a great many tarts, and the quarrel was because these tarts were left over and the pastry-cook's bill came to forty-five roubles. The quarrel was a violent and unpleasant one, so much so that Praskovya Fyodorovna called him, "Fool, imbecile." And he clutched at his head, and in his anger made some allusion to a divorce. But the party itself was enjoyable. There were all the best people, and Ivan Ilyitch danced with Princess Trufonov, the sister of the one so well known in connection with the charitable association called, "Bear my Burden." His official pleasures lay in the gratification of his pride; his social pleasures lay in the gratification of his vanity. But Ivan Ilyitch's most real pleasure was the pleasure of playing "screw," the Russian equivalent for "poker." He admitted to himself that, after all, after whatever unpleasant incidents there had been in his life, the pleasure which burned like a candle before all others was sitting with good players, and not noisy partners, at "screw"; and, of course, a four-hand game (playing with five was never a success, though one pretends to like it particularly), and with good cards, to play a shrewd, serious game, then supper and a glass of wine. And after "screw," especially after winning some small stakes (winning large sums was unpleasant), Ivan Ilyitch went to bed in a particularly happy frame of mind.

So they lived. They moved in the very best circle, and were visited by people of consequence and young people.

In their views of their circle of acquaintances, the husband, the wife, and the daughter were in complete accord; and without any expressed agreement on the subject, they all acted alike in dropping and shaking off various friends and relations, shabby persons who swooped down upon them in their drawing-room with Japanese plates on the walls, and pressed their civilities on them. Soon these shabby persons ceased fluttering about them, and none but the very best society was seen at the Golovins. Young men began to pay attention to Lizanka; and Petrishtchev, the son of Dmitry Ivanovitch Petrishtchev, and the sole heir of his fortune, an examining magistrate, began to be so attentive to Lizanka, that Ivan Ilyitch had raised the question with his wife whether it would not be as well to arrange a sledge drive for them, or to get up some theatricals. So they lived. And everything went on in this way without change, and everything was very nice.

CHAPTER IV

NOCTURNAL PAIN

ALL were in good health. One could not use the word ill-health in connection with the symptoms Ivan Ilyitch sometimes complained of, namely, a queer taste in his mouth and a sort of uncomfortable feeling on the left side of the stomach.

But it came to pass that this uncomfortable feeling kept increasing, and became not exactly a pain, but a continual sense of weight in his side and irritable temper. This irritable temper, continually growing and growing, began at last to mar the agreeable easiness and decorum that had reigned in the Golovin household. Quarrels between the husband and wife became more and more frequent, and soon all the easiness and amenity of life had

fallen away, and mere propriety was maintained with difficulty. Scenes became again more frequent. Again there were only islands in the sea of contention—and but few of these—at which the husband and wife could meet without an outbreak. And Praskovya Fyodorovna said now, not without grounds, that her husband had a trying temper. With her characteristic exaggeration—she said he had always had this awful temper, and she had needed all her sweetness to put up with it for twenty years. It was true that it was he now who began the quarrels. His gusts of temper always broke out just before dinner, and often just as he was beginning to eat, at the soup. He would notice that some piece of the crockery had been chipped, or that the food was not nice, or that his son put his elbow on the table, or his daughter's hair was not arranged as he liked it. And whatever it was, he laid the blame of it on Praskovya Fyodorovna. Praskovya Fyodorovna had at first retorted in the same strain, and said all sorts of horrid things to him; but on two occasions, just at the beginning of dinner, he had flown into such a frenzy that she perceived that it was due to physical derangement, and was brought on by taking food, and she controlled herself; she did not reply, but simply made haste to get dinner over. Praskovya Fyodorovna took great credit to herself for this exercise of self-control. Making up her mind that her husband had a fearful temper, and made her life miserable, she began to feel sorry for herself. And the more she felt for herself, the more she hated her husband. She began to wish he were dead; yet could not wish it, because then there would be no income. And this exasperated her against him even more. She considered herself dreadfully unfortunate, precisely because even his death could not save her, and she felt irritated and concealed it, and this hidden irritation on her side increased his irritability.

After one violent scene, in which Ivan Ilyitch had been particularly unjust, and after which he had said in explanation that he certainly was irritable, but that it was due to illness, she said that if he were ill he ought to take steps, and insisted on his going to see a celebrated doctor.

He went. Everything was as he had expected; everything was as it always is. The waiting and the assumption of dignity, that professional dignity he knew so well, exactly as he assumed it himself in court, and the sounding and listening and questions that called for answers that were foregone conclusions and obviously superfluous, and the significant air that seemed to insinuate —you only leave it all to us, and we will arrange everything, for us it is certain and incontestable how to arrange everything, everything in one way for every man of every sort. It was all exactly as in his court of justice. Exactly the same air as he put on in dealing with a man brought up for judgment, the doctor put on for him.

The doctor said: This and that proves that you have such-and-such a thing wrong inside you; but if that is not confirmed by analysis of this and that, then we must assume this and that. If we assume this and that, then—and so on. To Ivan Ilyitch there was only one question of consequence. Was his condition dangerous or not? But the doctor ignored that irrelevant inquiry. From the doctor's point of view this was a side issue, not the subject under consideration; the only real question was the balance of probabilities between a loose kidney, chronic catarrh, and appendicitis. It was not a question of the life of Ivan Ilyitch, but the question between the loose kidney and the intestinal appendix. And this question, as it seemed to Ivan Ilyitch, the doctor solved in a brilliant manner in favour of the appendix, with the reservation that analysis of the water might give a fresh clue, and that then the aspect of the case would be altered. All this was point for point identical with what Ivan Ilyitch had himself done in brilliant fashion a thousand times over in dealing with some man on his trial. Just as brilliantly the doctor made his summing-up, and triumphantly, gaily even, glanced over his spectacles at the prisoner in the dock. From the doctor's summing-up Ivan Ilyitch deduced the conclusion—that things looked bad, and that he, the doctor, and most likely every one else, did not care, but that things looked bad for him. And this conclusion impressed Ivan Ilyitch morbidly, arousing in him a great feeling of pity for himself, of great anger against this doctor who could be unconcerned about a matter of such importance.

But he said nothing of that. He got up, and, laying the fee on the table, he said, with a sigh, "We sick people probably often ask inconvenient questions. Tell me, is this generally a dangerous illness or not?"

The doctor glanced severely at him with one eye through his spectacles, as though to say: "Prisoner at the bar, if you will not keep within the limits of the questions allowed you, I shall be compelled to take measures for your removal from the precincts of the court." "I have told you what I thought necessary and suitable already," said the doctor; "the analysis will show anything further." And the doctor bowed him out.

Ivan Ilyitch went out slowly and dejectedly, got into his sledge, and drove home. All the way home he was incessantly going over all the doctor had said, trying to translate all these complicated, obscure, scientific phrases into simple language, and to read in them an answer to the question, Is it bad—is it very bad, or nothing much as yet? And it seemed to him that the upshot of all the doctor had said was that it was very bad. Everything seemed dismal to Ivan Ilyitch in the streets. The sledge-drivers were dismal, the houses were dismal, the people passing, and the shops were dismal. This ache, this dull gnawing ache, that never ceased for a second, seemed, when connected with the doctor's obscure utterances, to have gained a new, more serious significance. With a new sense of misery Ivan Ilyitch kept watch on it now.

He reached home and began to tell his wife about it. His wife listened; but in the middle of his account his daughter came in with her hat on, ready to go out with her mother. Reluctantly she half sat down to listen to these tedious details, but she could not stand it for long, and her mother did not hear his story to the end.

"Well, I'm very glad," said his wife; "now you must be sure and take the medicine regularly. Give me the pre-

scription; I'll send Gerasim to the chemist's!" And she went to get ready to go out.

He had not taken breath while she was in the room, and he heaved a deep sigh when she was gone.

"Well," he said, "may be it really is nothing as yet."

He began to take the medicine, to carry out the doctor's directions, which were changed after the analysis of the water. But it was just at this point that some confusion arose, either in the analysis or in what ought to have followed from it. The doctor himself, of course, could not be blamed for it, but it turned out that things had not gone as the doctor had told him. Either he had forgotten or told a lie, or was hiding something from him.

But Ivan Ilyitch still went on just as exactly carrying out the doctor's direction, and in doing so he found comfort at first.

From the time of his visit to the doctor Ivan Ilyitch's principal occupation became the exact observance of the doctor's prescriptions as regards hygiene and medicine and the careful observation of his ailment in all the functions of his organism. Ivan Ilyitch's principal interest came to be people's ailments and people's health. When anything was said in his presence about sick people, about deaths and recoveries, especially in the case of an illness resembling his own, he listened, trying to conceal his excitement, asked questions, and applied what he heard to his own trouble.

The ache did not grow less; but Ivan Ilyitch made great efforts to force himself to believe that he was better. And he succeeded in deceiving himself so long as nothing happened to disturb him. But as soon as he had a mischance, some unpleasant words with his wife, a failure in his official work, an unlucky hand at "screw," he was at once acutely sensible of his illness. In former days he had borne with such mishaps, hoping soon to retrieve the mistake, to make a struggle, to reach success later, to have a lucky hand. But now he was cast down by every mischance and reduced to despair. He would say to himself: "Here I'm only just beginning to get better, and the medicine has begun to take effect, and now this mischance or disappointment." And he was furious against the mischance or the people who were causing him the disappointment and killing him, and he felt that this fury was killing him, but could not check it. One would have thought that it should have been clear to him that this exasperation against circumstances and people was aggravating his disease, and that therefore he ought not to pay attention to the unpleasant incidents. But his reasoning took quite the opposite direction. He said that he needed peace, and was on the watch for everything that disturbed his peace, and at the slightest disturbance of it he flew into a rage. What made his position worse was that he read medical books and consulted doctors. He got worse so gradually that he might have deceived himself, comparing one day with another, the difference was so slight. But when he consulted the doctors, then it seemed to him that he was getting worse, and very rapidly so indeed. And in spite of this, he was continually consulting the doctors.

That month he called on another celebrated doctor. The second celebrity said almost the same as the first, but put his questions differently; and the interview with this celebrity only redoubled the doubts and terrors of Ivan Ilyitch. A friend of a friend of his, a very good doctor, diagnosed the disease quite differently; and in spite of the fact that he guaranteed recovery, by his questions and his suppositions he confused Ivan Ilyitch even more and strengthened his suspicions. A homoeopath gave yet another diagnosis of the complaint, and prescribed medicine, which Ivan Ilyitch took secretly for a week; but after a week of the homoeopathic medicine he felt no relief, and losing faith both in the other doctor's treatment and in this, he fell into even deeper depression. One day a lady of his acquaintance talked to him of the healing wrought by the holy pictures. Ivan Ilyitch caught himself listening attentively and believing in the reality of the facts alleged. This incident alarmed him. "Can I have degenerated to such a point of intellectual feebleness?" he said to himself. "Nonsense! it's all rubbish. I must not give way to nervous fears, but fixing on one doctor, adhere strictly to his treatment. That's what I will do. Now it's settled. I won't think about it, but till next summer I will stick to the treatment, and then I shall see. Now I'll put a stop to this wavering!" It was easy to say this, but impossible to carry it out. The pain in his side was always dragging at him, seeming to grow acute and ever more incessant; it seemed to him that the taste in his mouth was queerer, and there was a loathsome smell even from his breath, and his appetite and strength kept dwindling. There was no deceiving himself; something terrible, new, and so important that nothing more important had ever been in Ivan Ilyitch's life, was taking place in him, and he alone knew of it. All about him did not or would not understand, and believed that everything in the world was going on as before. This was what tortured Ivan Ilyitch more than anything. Those of his own household, most of all his wife and daughter, who were absorbed in a perfect whirl of visits, did not, he saw, comprehend it at all, and were annoyed that he was so depressed and exacting, as though he were to blame for it. Though they tried indeed to disguise it, he saw he was a nuisance to them; but that his wife had taken up a definite line of her own in regard to his illness, and stuck to it regardless of what he might say and do. This line was expressed thus: "You know," she would say to acquaintances, "Ivan Ilyitch cannot, like all other simple-hearted folks, keep to the treatment prescribed him. One day he'll take his drops and eat what he's ordered, and go to bed in good time; the next day, if I don't see to it, he'll suddenly forget to take his medicine, eat sturgeon (which is forbidden by the doctors), yes, and sit up at 'screw' till past midnight."

"Why, when did I do that?" Ivan Ilyitch asked in vexation one day at Pyotr Ivanovitch's.

"Why, yesterday, with Shebek."

"It makes no difference. I couldn't sleep for pain."

"Well, it doesn't matter what you do it for, only you'll never get well like that, and you make us wretched."

Praskovya Fyodorovna's external attitude to her husband's illness, openly expressed to others and to himself, was that Ivan Ilyitch was to blame in the matter of his illness, and that the whole illness was another injury he was doing to his wife. Ivan Ilyitch felt that the expression of this dropped from her unconsciously, but that made it no easier for him.

In his official life, too, Ivan Ilyitch noticed, or fancied he noticed, a strange attitude to him. At one time it seemed to him that people were looking inquisitively at him, as a man who would shortly have to vacate his position; at another time his friends would suddenly begin chaffing him in a friendly way over his nervous fears, as though that awful and horrible, unheard-of thing that was going on within him, incessantly gnawing at him, and irresistibly dragging him away somewhere, were the most agreeable subject for joking. Shvarts especially, with his jocoseness, his liveliness, and his *comme-il-faut* tone, exasperated Ivan Ilyitch by reminding him of himself ten years ago.

Friends came sometimes to play cards. They sat down to the card-table; they shuffled and dealt the new cards. Diamonds were led and followed by diamonds, the seven. His partner said, "Can't trump," and played the two of diamonds. What then? Why, delightful, capital, it should have been— he had a trump hand. And suddenly Ivan Ilyitch feels that gnawing ache, that taste in his mouth, and it strikes him as something grotesque that with that he could be glad of a trump hand.

He looks at Mihail Mihailovitch, his partner, how he taps on the table with his red hand, and affably and indulgently abstains from snatching up the trick, and pushes the cards towards

Ivan Ilyitch so as to give him the pleasure of taking them up, without any trouble, without even stretching out his hand. "What, does he suppose that I'm so weak that I can't stretch out my hand?" thinks Ivan Ilyitch, and he forgets the trumps, and trumps his partner's cards, and plays his trump hand without making three tricks; and what's the most awful thing of all is that he sees how upset Mihail Mihailovitch is about it, while he doesn't care a bit, and it's awful for him to think why he doesn't care.

They all see that he's in pain, and say to him, "We can stop if you're tired. You go and lie down." Lie down? No, he's not in the least tired; they will play the rubber. All are gloomy and silent. Ivan Ilyitch feels that it is he who has brought this gloom upon them, and he cannot disperse it. They have supper, and the party breaks up, and Ivan Ilyitch is left alone with the consciousness that his life is poisoned for him and poisons the life of others, and that this poison is not losing its force, but is continually penetrating more and more deeply into his whole existence.

And with the consciousness of this, and with the physical pain in addition, and the terror in addition to that, he must lie in his bed, often not able to sleep for pain the greater part of the night; and in the morning he must get up again, dress, go to the law-court, speak, write, or, if he does not go out, stay at home for all the four-and-twenty hours of the day and night, of which each one is a torture. And he had to live thus on the edge of the precipice alone, without one man who would understand and feel for him.

CHAPTER V

HATRED!

IN this way one month, then a second, passed by. Just before the New Year his brother-in-law arrived in the town on a visit to them. Ivan Ilyitch was at the court when he arrived. Praskovya Fyodorovna had gone out shopping. Coming home and going into his study, he found there his brother-in-law, a healthy, florid man, engaged in unpacking his trunk. He raised his head, hearing Ivan Ilyitch's step, and for a second stared at him without a word. That stare told Ivan Ilyitch everything. His brother-in-law opened his mouth to utter an "Oh!" of surprise, but checked himself. That confirmed it all.

"What! have I changed?"

"Yes, there is a change."

And all Ivan Ilyitch's efforts to draw him into talking of his appearance his brother-in-law met with obstinate silence. Praskovya Fyodorovna came in; the brother-in-law went to see her. Ivan Ilyitch locked his door and began gazing at himself in the looking-glass, first full face, then in profile. He took up his photograph, taken with his wife, and compared the portrait with what he saw in the looking-glass. The change was immense. Then he bared his arm to the elbow, looked at it, pulled the sleeve down again, sat down on an ottoman and felt blacker than night.

"I mustn't, I mustn't," he said to himself, jumped up, went to the table, opened some official paper, tried to read it, but could not. He opened the door, went into the drawing-room. The door into the drawing-room was closed. He went up to it on tiptoe and listened.

"No, you're exaggerating," Praskovya Fyodorovna was saying.

"Exaggerating? You can't see it. Why, he's a dead man. Look at his eyes—there's no light in them. But what's wrong with him?"

"No one can tell. Nikolaev" (that was another doctor) "said something, but I don't know. Leshtchetitsky" (this was the celebrated doctor) "said the opposite."

Ivan Ilyitch walked away, went to his own room, lay down, and fell to musing. "A kidney—a loose kidney." He remembered all the doctors had told him, how it had been detached, and how it was loose; and by an effort of imagination he tried to catch that kidney and to stop it, to strengthen it. So little was needed, he fancied. "No, I'll go again to Pyotr Ivanovitch" (this was the friend who had a friend a doctor). He rang, ordered the horse to be put in, and got ready to go out.

"Where are you off to, Jean?" asked his wife with a peculiarly melancholy and exceptionally kind expression.

This exceptionally kind expression exasperated him. He looked darkly at her.

"I want to see Pyotr Ivanovitch."

He went to the friend who had a friend a doctor. And with him to the doctor's. He found him in, and had a long conversation with him.

Reviewing the anatomical and physiological details of what, according to the doctor's view, was taking place within him, he understood it all. It was just one thing—a little thing wrong with the intestinal appendix. It might all come right. Only strengthen one sluggish organ, and decrease the undue activity of another, and absorption

would take place, and all would be set right. He was a little late for dinner. He ate his dinner, talked cheerfully, but it was a long while before he could go to his own room to work. At last he went to his study, and at once sat down to work. He read his legal documents and did his work, but the consciousness never left him of having a matter of importance very near to his heart which he had put off, but would look into later. When he had finished his work, he remembered that the matter near his heart was thinking about the intestinal appendix. But he did not give himself up to it; he went into the drawing-room to tea. There were visitors; and there was talking, playing on the piano, and singing; there was the young examining magistrate, the desirable match for the daughter. Ivan Ilyitch spent the evening, as Praskovya Fyodorovna observed in better spirits than any of them; but he never forgot for an instant that he had the important matter of the intestinal appendix put off for consideration later. At eleven o'clock he said good night and went to his own room. He had slept alone since his illness in a little room adjoining his study. He went in, undressed, and took up a novel of Zola, but did not read it; he fell to thinking. And in his imagination the desired recovery of the intestinal appendix had taken place. There had been absorption, rejection, re-establishment of the regular action.

"Why, it's all simply that," he said to himself. "One only wants to assist nature." He remembered the medicine, got up, took it, lay down on his back, watching for the medicine to act beneficially and overcome the pain. "It's only to take it regularly and avoid injurious influences; why, already I feel rather better, much better." He began to feel his side; it was not painful to the touch. "Yes, I don't feel it—really, much better already." He put out the candle and lay on his side. The appendix is getting better, absorption." Suddenly he felt the familiar, old, dull, gnawing ache, persistent, quiet, in earnest. In his mouth the same familiar loathsome taste. His heart sank, and his brain felt dim, misty. "My God, my God!" he said, "again, again, and it will never cease." And suddenly the whole thing rose before him in quite a different aspect. "Intestinal appendix! kidney!" he said to himself. "It's not a question of the appendix, not a question of the kidney, but of life and . . . death. Yes, life has been and now it's going, going away, and I cannot stop it. Yes. Why deceive myself? Isn't it obvious to every one, except me, that I'm dying, and it's only a question of weeks, of days—at once perhaps. There was light, and now there is darkness. I was here, and now I am going! Where?" A cold chill ran over him, his breath stopped. He heard nothing but the throbbing of his heart.

"I shall be no more, then what will there be? There'll be nothing. Where then shall I be when I'm no more? Can this be dying? No; I don't want to!" He jumped up, tried to light the candle; and fumbling with trembling hands, he dropped the candle and the candlestick on the floor and fell back again on the pillow. "Why trouble? it doesn't matter," he said to himself, staring with open eyes into the darkness. "Death. Yes, death. And they—all of them—don't understand, and don't want to understand, and feel no pity. They are playing. (He caught through the closed doors the far-away cadence of a voice and the accompaniment.) They don't care, but they will die too. Fools! Me sooner and them later; but it will be the same for them, And they are merry. The beasts!" Anger stifled him. And he was agonisingly, insufferably miserable. "It cannot be that all men always have been doomed to this awful horror!" He raised himself.

"There is something wrong in it; I must be calm, I must think it all over from the beginning." And then he began to consider. "Yes, the beginning of my illness. I knocked my side, and I was just the same, that day and the days after; it ached a little, then more, then doctors, then depression, misery, and again doctors; and I've gone on getting closer and closer to the abyss. Strength growing less. Nearer and nearer. And here I am, wasting away, no light in my eyes. I think of how to cure the appendix, but this is death. Can it be death?" Again a horror came over him! gasping for breath, he bent over, began feeling for the matches, and knocked his elbow against the bedside table. It was in his way and hurt him; he felt furious with it, in his anger knocked against it more violently, and upset it. And in despair, breathless, he fell back on his spine waiting for death to come that instant.

The visitors were leaving at that time. Praskovya Fyodorovna was seeing them out. She heard something fall, and came in.

"What is it?"

"Nothing. I dropped something by accident."

She went out, brought a candle. He was lying, breathing hard and fast, like a man who has run a mile, and staring with fixed eyes at her

"What is it, Jean?"

"No—othing, I say. I dropped something."—"Why speak? She won't understand," he thought.

She certainly did not understand. She picked up the candle, lighted it for him, and went out hastily. She had to say good-bye to a departing guest. When she came back, he was lying in the same position on his back, looking upwards.

"How are you—worse?"

"Yes."

She shook her head, sat down.

"Do you know what, Jean? I wonder if we hadn't better send for Leshtchetitsky to see you here?"

This meant calling in the celebrated doctor, regardless of expense. He smiled malignantly, and said no. She sat a moment longer, went up to him, and kissed him on the forehead.

He hated her with all the force of his soul when she was kissing him, and had to make an effort not to push her away.

"Good night. Please God, you'll sleep."

"Yes."

CHAPTER VI

DESPAIR

IVAN ILYITCH saw that he was dying, and was in continual despair.

At the bottom of his heart Ivan Ilyitch knew that he was dying; but so far from growing used to this idea, he simply did not grasp it—he was utterly unable to grasp it.

The example of the Syllogism that he had learned in Kiseveter's logic—Caius is a man, men are mortal, therefore Caius is mortal—had seemed to him all his life correct only as regards Caius, but not at all as regards himself. In that case it was a question of Caius, a man, an abstract man, and it was perfectly true, but he was not Caius, and was not an abstract man; he had always been a creature quite, quite different from all others; he had been little Vanya with a mamma and papa, and Mitya and Volodya, with playthings and a coachman and a nurse; afterwards with Katenka, with all the joys and griefs and ecstasies of childhood, boyhood, and youth. What did Caius know of the smell of the leathern ball Vanya had been so fond of? Had Caius kissed his mother's hand like that? Caius had not heard the silk rustle of his mother's skirts. He had not made a riot at school over the pudding. Had Caius been in love like that? Could Caius preside over the sittings of the court?

And Caius certainly was mortal, and it was right for him to die; but for me, little Vanya, Ivan Ilyitch, with all my feelings and ideas—for me it's a different matter. And it cannot be that I ought to die. That would be too awful.

That was his feeling.

"If I had to die like Caius, I should have known it was so, some inner voice would have told me so. But there was nothing of the sort in me. And I and all my friends, we felt that it was not at all the same as with Caius. And now here it is!" he said to himself.

"It can't be! It can't be, but it is! How is it? How's one to understand it?" And he could not conceive it, and tried to drive away this idea as false, incorrect, and morbid, and to supplant it by other, correct, healthy ideas. But this idea, not as an idea merely, but as it were an actual fact, came back again and stood confronting him.

And to replace this thought he called up other thoughts, one after another, in the hope of finding support in them. He tried to get back into former trains of thought, which in old days had screened off the thought of death. But, strange to say, all that had in old days covered up, obliterated the sense of death, could not now produce the same effect. Latterly, Ivan Ilyitch spent the greater part of his time in these efforts to restore his old trains of thought which had shut off death. At one time he would say to himself, "I'll put myself into my official work; why, I used to live in it." And he would go to the law-courts, banishing every doubt. He would enter into conversation with his colleagues, and would sit carelessly, as his old habit was, scanning the crowd below dreamily, and with both his wasted hands he would lean on the arms of the oak arm-chair just as he always did; and bending over to a colleague, pass the papers to him and whisper to him, then suddenly dropping his eyes and sitting up straight, he would pronounce the familiar words that opened the proceedings. But suddenly in the middle, the pain in his side, utterly regardless of the stage he had reached in his conduct of the case, began its work. It riveted Ivan Ilyitch's attention. He drove away the thought of it, but it still did its work, and then *It* came and stood confronting him and looked at him, and he felt turned to stone, and the light died away in his eyes, and he began to ask himself again, "Can it be that It is the only truth?" And his colleagues and his subordinates saw with surprise and distress that he, the brilliant, subtle judge, was losing the thread of his speech, was making blunders. He shook himself, tried to regain his self-control, and got somehow to the end of the sitting, and went home with the painful sense that his judicial labours could not as of old hide from him what he wanted to hide; that he could not by means of his official work escape from *It*. And the worst of it was that It drew him to itself not for him to do anything in particular, but simply for him to look at It straight in the face, to look at It and, doing nothing, suffer unspeakably.

And to save himself from this, Ivan Ilyitch sought amusements, other screens, and these screens he found, and for a little while they did seem to save him; but soon again they were not so much broken down as let the light through, as though It pierced through everything, and there was nothing that could shut It off.

Sometimes during those days he would go into the drawing-room he had furnished, that drawing-room where he had fallen, for which—how bitterly ludicrous it was for him to think of it! —for the decoration of which he had sacrificed his life, for he knew that it was that bruise that had started his illness. He went in and saw that the polished table had been scratched by something. He looked for the cause, and found it in the bronze clasps of the album, which had been twisted on one side. He took up the album, a costly one, which he had himself arranged with loving care, and was vexed at the carelessness of his daughter and her friends. Here a page was torn, here the photographs had been shifted out of their places. He carefully put it to rights again and bent the clasp back.

Then the idea occurred to him to move all this *établissement* of the albums to another corner where the flowers stood. He called the footman; or his daughter or his wife came to help him. They did not agree with him, contradicted him; he argued, got angry. But all that was very well, since he did not think of It; It was not in sight.

But then his wife would say, as he moved something himself, "Do let the servants do it, you'll hurt yourself again," and all at once It peeped through the screen; he caught a glimpse of It. He caught a glimpse of It, but still he hoped It would hide itself. Involuntarily though, he kept watch on his side; there it is just the same still, aching still, and now he cannot forget it, and *It* is staring openly at him from behind the flowers. What's the use of it all?

"And it's the fact that here, at that curtain, as if it had been storming a fort, I lost my life. Is it possible? How awful and how silly! It cannot be! It cannot be, and it is."

He went into his own room, lay down, and was again alone with It. Face to face with It, and nothing to be done with It. Nothing but to look at It and shiver.

CHAPTER VII

LONGING

How it came to pass during the third month of Ivan Ilyitch's illness, it would be impossible to say, for it happened little by little, imperceptibly, but it had come to pass that his wife and his daughter and his son and their servants and their acquaintances, and the doctors, and, most of all, he himself—all were aware that all interest in him for other people consisted now in the question how soon he would leave his place empty, free the living from the constraint of his presence, and be set free himself from his sufferings.

He slept less and less; they gave him opium, and began to inject morphine. But this did not relieve him. The dull pain he experienced in the half-asleep condition at first only relieved him as a change, but then it became as bad, or even more agonising, than the open pain. He had special things to eat prepared for him according to the doctors' prescriptions; but these dishes became more and more distasteful, more and more revolting to him.

Special arrangements, too, had to be made for his other physical needs, and this was a continual misery to him. Misery from the uncleanliness, the unseemliness, and the stench, from the feeling of another person having to assist in it.

But just from this most unpleasant side of his illness there came comfort to Ivan Ilyitch. There always came into his room on these occasions to clear up for him the peasant who waited on table, Gerasim.

Gerasim was a clean, fresh, young peasant, who had grown stout and hearty on the good fare in town. Always cheerful and bright. At first the sight of this lad, always cleanly dressed in the Russian style, engaged in this revolting task, embarrassed Ivan Ilyitch.

One day, getting up from the night-stool, too weak to replace his clothes, he dropped on to a soft low chair and looked with horror at his bare, powerless thighs, with the muscles so sharply standing out on them.

Then there came in with light, strong steps Gerasim, in his thick boots, diffusing a pleasant smell of tar from his boots, and bringing in the freshness of the winter air. Wearing a clean hempen apron, and a clean cotton shirt, with his sleeves tucked up on his strong, bare young arms, without looking at Ivan Ilyitch, obviously trying to check the radiant happiness in his face so as not to hurt the sick man, he went up to the night-stool.

"Gerasim," said Ivan Ilyitch faintly.

Gerasim started, clearly afraid that he had done something amiss, and with a rapid movement turned towards the sick man his fresh, good-natured, simple young face, just beginning to be downy with the first growth of beard.

"Yes, your honour."

"I'm afraid this is very disagreeable for you. You must excuse me. I can't help it."

"Why, upon my word, sir!" And Gerasim's eyes beamed, and he showed his white young teeth in a smile. "What's a little trouble? It's a case of illness with you, sir."

And with his deft, strong arms he performed his habitual task, and went out, stepping lightly. And five minutes later, treading just as lightly, he came back.

Ivan Ilyitch was still sitting in the same way in the armchair.

"Gerasim," he said, when the latter had replaced the night-stool all sweet and clean, "please help me; come here." Gerasim went up to him. "Lift me up. It's difficult for me alone, and I've sent Dmitry away."

Gerasim went up to him; as lightly as he stepped he put his strong arms round him, deftly and gently lifted and supported him, with the other hand pulled up his trousers, and would have set him down again. But Ivan Ilyitch asked him to carry him to the sofa. Gerasim, without effort, carefully not squeezing him, led him, almost carrying him, to the sofa, and settled him there.

"Thank you; how neatly and well . . . you do everything."

Gerasim smiled again, and would have gone away. But Ivan Ilyitch felt his presence such a comfort that he was reluctant to let him go.

"Oh, move that chair near me, please. No, that one, under my legs. I feel easier when my legs are higher."

Gerasim picked up the chair, and without letting it knock, set it gently down on the ground just at the right place, and lifted Ivan Ilyitch's legs on to it. It seemed to Ivan Ilyitch that he was easier just at the moment when Gerasim lifted his legs higher.

"I'm better when my legs are higher," said Ivan Ilyitch. "Put that cushion under me."

Gerasim did so. Again he lifted his legs to put the cushion under them. Again it seemed to Ivan Ilyitch that he was easier at that moment when Gerasim held his legs raised. When he laid them down again, he felt worse.

"Gerasim," he said to him, "are you busy just now?"

"Not at all, sir," said Gerasim, who had learned among the town-bred servants how to speak to gentlefolks.

"What have you left to do?"

"Why, what have I to do? I've done everything, there's only the wood to chop for to-morrow."

"Then hold my legs up like that—can you?"

"To be sure, I can." Gerasim lifted the legs up. And it seemed to Ivan Ilyitch that in that position he did not feel the pain at all.

"But how about the wood?"

"Don't you trouble about that, sir. We shall have time enough."

Ivan Ilyitch made Gerasim sit and hold his legs, and began to talk to him. And, strange to say, he fancied he felt better while Gerasim had hold of his legs.

From that time forward Ivan Ilyitch would sometimes call Gerasim, and get him to hold his legs on his shoulders, and he liked talking with him. Gerasim did this easily, readily, simply, and with a good-nature that touched Ivan Ilyitch. Health, strength, and heartiness in all other people were offensive to Ivan Ilyitch; but the strength and heartiness of Gerasim did not mortify him, but soothed him.

Ivan Ilyitch's great misery was due to the deception that for some reason or other every one kept up with him— that he was simply ill, and not dying, and that he need only keep quiet and follow the doctor's orders, and then some great change for the better would be the result. He knew that whatever they might do, there would be no result except more agonising sufferings and death. And he was made miserable by this lie, made miserable at their refusing to acknowledge what they all knew and he knew, by their persisting in lying over him about his awful position, and in forcing him too to take part in this lie. Lying, lying, this lying carried on over him on the eve of his death, and destined to bring that terrible, solemn act of his death down to the level of all their visits, curtains, sturgeons for dinner . . . was a horrible agony for Ivan Ilyitch. And, strange to say, many times when they had been going through the regular performance over him, he had been within a hair's-breadth of screaming at them: "Cease your lying! You know, and I know, that I'm dying; so do, at least, give over lying!" But he had never had the spirit to do this. The terrible, awful act of his dying was, he saw, by all those about him, brought down to the level of a casual, unpleasant, and to some extent indecorous, incident (somewhat as they would behave with a person who should enter a drawing-room smelling unpleasant). It was brought down to this level by that very decorum to which he had been enslaved all his life. He saw that no one felt for him, because no one would even grasp his position. Gerasim was the only person who recognised the position, and felt sorry for him. And that was why Ivan Ilyitch was only at ease with Gerasim. He felt comforted when Gerasim sometimes supported his legs for whole nights at a stretch, and would not go away to bed, saying, "Don't you worry yourself, Ivan Ilyitch, I'll get sleep enough yet," or when suddenly dropping into the familiar peasant forms of speech, he added: "If thou weren't sick, but as 'tis, 'twould be strange if I didn't wait on thee." Gerasim alone did not lie; everything showed clearly that he alone understood what it meant, and saw no necessity to disguise it, and simply felt sorry for his sick, wasting master. He even said this once straight out, when Ivan Ilyitch was sending him away.

"We shall all die. So what's a little trouble?" he said, meaning by this to express that he did not complain of the trouble just because he was taking this trouble for a dying man, and he hoped that for him too some one would be willing to take the same trouble when his time came.

Apart from this deception, or in consequence of it, what made the greatest misery for Ivan Ilyitch was that no one felt for him as he would have liked them to feel for him. At certain moments, after prolonged suffering, Ivan Ilyitch, ashamed as he would have been to own it, longed more than anything for some one to feel sorry for him, as for a sick child. He longed to be petted, kissed, and wept over, as children are petted and comforted. He knew that he was an important member of the law-courts, that he had a beard turning grey, and that therefore it was impossible. But still he longed for it. And in his relations with Gerasim there was something approaching to that. And that was why being with Gerasim was a comfort to him. Ivan Ilyitch longs to weep, longs to be petted and wept over, and then there comes in a colleague, Shebek; and instead of weeping and being petted, Ivan Ilyitch puts on his serious, severe, earnest face, and from mere inertia gives his views on the effect of the last decision in the Court of Appeal, and obstinately insists upon

them. This falsity around him and within him did more than anything to poison Ivan Ilyitch's last days.

CHAPTER VIII

THE DOCTOR'S VISIT

IT was morning. All that made it morning for Ivan Ilyitch was that Gerasim had gone away, and Pyotr the footman had come in; he had put out the candles, opened one of the curtains, and begun surreptitiously setting the room to rights. Whether it were morning or evening, Friday or Sunday, it all made no difference; it was always just the same thing. Gnawing, agonising pain never ceasing for an instant; the hopeless sense of life always ebbing away, but still not yet gone; always swooping down on him that fearful, hated death, which was the only reality, and always the same falsity. What were days, or weeks, or hours of the day to him?

"Will you have tea, sir?"

"He wants things done in their regular order. In the morning the family should have tea," he thought, and only said—

"No."

"Would you care to move on to the sofa?"

"He wants to make the room tidy, and I'm in his way. I'm uncleanness, disorder," he thought, and only said—

"No, leave me alone."

The servant still moved busily about his work. Ivan Ilyitch stretched out his hand. Pyotr went up to offer his services.

"What can I get you?"

"My watch."

Pyotr got out the watch, which lay

just under his hand and gave it to him.

"Haif-past eight. Are they up?"

"Not yet, sir. Vladimir Ivanovitch" (that was his son) "has gone to the high school, and Praskovya Fyodorovna gave orders that she was to be waked if you asked for her. Shall I send word?"

"No, no need. Should I try some tea?" he thought.

"Yes, tea . . . bring it."

Pyotr was on his way out. Ivan Ilyitch felt frightened of being left alone. "How keep him? Oh, the medicine. Pyotr, give me my medicine. Oh well, may be, medicine may still be some good." He took the spoon, drank it. "No, it does no good. It's all rubbish, deception," he decided, as soon as he tasted the familiar, mawkish, hopeless taste. "No, I can't believe it now. But the pain, why this pain; if it would only cease for a minute." And he groaned. Pyotr turned round. "No, go on. Bring the tea."

Pyotr went away. Ivan Ilyitch, left alone, moaned, not so much from the pain, awful as it was, as from misery. Always the same thing again and again, all these endless days and nights. If it would only be quicker. Quicker to what? Death, darkness. No, no. Anything better than death!

When Pyotr came in with the tea on a tray, Ivan Ilyitch stared for some time absent-mindedly at him, not grasping who he was and what he wanted. Pyotr was disconcerted by this stare. And when he showed he was disconcerted, Ivan Ilyitch came to himself.

"Oh yes," he said, "tea, good, set it down. Only help me to wash and put on a clean shirt."

And Ivan Ilyitch began his washing. He washed his hands slowly, and then his face, cleaned his teeth, combed his hair, and looked in the looking-glass. He felt frightened at what he saw, especially at the way his hair clung limply to his pale forehead. When his shirt was being changed, he knew he would be still more terrified if he glanced at his body, and he avoided looking at himself. But at last it was all over. He put on his dressing-gown, covered himself with a rug, and sat in the armchair to drink his tea. For one moment he felt refreshed; but as soon as he began to drink the tea, again there was the same taste, the same pain. He forced himself to finish it, and lay down, stretched out his legs. He lay down and dismissed Pyotr.

Always the same. A gleam of hope flashes for a moment, then again the sea of despair roars about him again, and always pain, always pain, always heartache, and always the same thing. Alone it is awfully dreary; he longs to call some one, but he knows beforehand that with others present it will be worse. "Morphine again—only to forget again. I'll tell him, the doctor, that he must think of something else. It can't go on; it can't go on like this."

One hour, two hours pass like this. Then there is a ring at the front door. The doctor, perhaps. Yes, it is the doctor, fresh, hearty, fat, and cheerful, wearing that expression that seems to say, "You there are in a panic about something, but we'll soon set things right for you." The doctor is aware that this expression is hardly fitting here, but he has put it on once and for all, and can't take it off, like a man who has put on a frockcoat to pay a round of calls.

In a hearty, reassuring manner the doctor rubs his hands.

"I'm cold. It's a sharp frost. Just let me warm myself," he says with an expression, as though it's only a matter of waiting a little till he's warm, and as soon as he's warm he'll set everything to rights.

"Well, now, how are you?"

Ivan Ilyitch feels that the doctor would like to say, "How's the little trouble?" but that he feels that he can't talk like that, and says, "How did you pass the night?"

Ivan Ilyitch looks at the doctor with an expression that asks—

"Is it possible you're never ashamed of lying?"

But the doctor does not care to understand this look.

And Ivan Ilyitch says—

"It's always just as awful. The pain never leaves me, never ceases. If only there were something!"

"Ah, you're all like that, all sick people say that. Come, now I do believe I'm thawed; even Praskovya Fyodorovna, who's so particular, could find no fault with my temperature. Well, now I can say good morning." And the doctor shakes hands.

And dropping his former levity, the doctor, with a serious face, proceeds to examine the patient, feeling his pulse, to take his temperature, and then the tappings and soundings begin.

Ivan Ilyitch knows positively and indubitably that it's all nonsense and empty deception; but when the doctor, kneeling down, stretches over him, putting his ear first higher, then lower, and goes through various gymnastic evolutions over him with a serious face, Ivan Ilyitch is affected by this, as he used

sometimes to be affected by the speeches of the lawyers in court, though he was perfectly well aware that they were telling lies all the while and why they were telling lies.

The doctor, kneeling on the sofa, was still sounding him, when there was the rustle of Praskovya Fyodorovna's silk dress in the doorway, and she was heard scolding Pyotr for not having let her know that the doctor had come.

She comes in, kisses her husband, and at once begins to explain that she has been up a long while, and that it was only through a misunderstanding that she was not there when the doctor came.

Ivan Ilyitch looks at her, scans her all over, and sets down against her her whiteness and plumpness, and the cleanness of her hands and neck, and the glossiness of her hair, and the gleam full of life in her eyes. With all the force of his soul he hates her. And when she touches him it makes him suffer from the thrill of hatred he feels for her.

Her attitude to him and his illness is still the same. Just as the doctor had taken up a certain line with the patient which he was not now able to drop, so she too had taken up a line with him— that he was not doing something he ought to do, and was himself to blame, and she was lovingly reproaching him for his neglect, and she could not now get out of this attitude.

"Why, you know, he won't listen to me; he doesn't take his medicine at the right times. And what's worse still, he insists on lying in a position that surely must be bad for him—with his legs in the air."

She described how he made Gerasim hold his legs up.

The doctor smiled with kindly condescension that said, "Oh well, it can't be helped, these sick people do take up such foolish fancies; but we must forgive them."

When the examination was over, the doctor looked at his watch, and then Praskovya Fyodorovna informed Ivan Ilyitch that it must, of course, be as he liked, but she had sent to-day for a celebrated doctor, and that he would examine him, and have a consultation with Mihail Danilovitch (that was the name of their regular doctor).

"Don't oppose it now, please. This I'm doing entirely for my own sake," she said ironically, meaning it to be understood that she was doing it all for his sake, and was only saying this to give him no right to refuse her request. He lay silent, knitting his brows. He felt that he was hemmed in by such a tangle of falsity that it was hard to disentangle anything from it.

Everything she did for him was entirely for her own sake, and she told him she was doing for her own sake what she actually was doing for her own sake as something so incredible that he would take it as meaning the opposite.

At half-past eleven the celebrated doctor came. Again came the sounding, and then grave conversation in his presence and in the other room about the kidney and the appendix, and questions and answers, with such an air of significance, that again, instead of the real question of life and death, which was now the only one that confronted him, the question that came uppermost was of the kidney and the appendix, which were doing something not as they ought to do, and were for that reason being attacked by Mihail Danilovitch and the celebrated doctor, and forced to mend their ways.

The celebrated doctor took leave of him with a serious, but not a hopeless face. And to the timid question that Ivan Ilyitch addressed to him while he lifted his eyes, shining with terror and hope, up towards him, Was there a chance of recovery? he answered that he could not answer for it, but that there was a chance. The look of hope with which Ivan Ilyitch watched the doctor out was so piteous that, seeing it, Praskovya Fyodorovna postively burst into tears, as she went out of the door to hand the celebrated doctor his fee in the next room.

The gleam of hope kindled by the doctor's assurance did not last long. Again the same room, the same pictures, the curtains, the wall-paper, the medicine-bottles, and ever the same, his aching suffering body. And Ivan Ilyitch began to moan; they gave him injections, and he sank into oblivion. When he waked up it was getting dark; they brought him his dinner. He forced himself to eat some broth; and again everything the same, and again the coming night.

After dinner at seven o'clock, Praskovya Fyodorovna came into his room, dressed as though to go to a *soirée,* with her full bosom laced in tight, and traces of powder on her face. She had in the morning mentioned to him that they were going to the theatre. Sarah Bernhardt was visiting the town, and they had a box, which he had insisted on their taking. By now he had forgotten about it, and her smart attire was an offence to him. But he concealed this feeling when he recollected that he had himself insisted on their taking a box and going, because it was an æsthetic pleasure, beneficial and instructive for the children.

Praskovya Fyodorovna came in satisfied with herself, but yet with something of a guilty air. She sat down, asked how he was, as he saw, simply for the sake of asking, and not for the sake of learning anything, knowing indeed that there was nothing to learn, and began telling him how absolutely necessary it was; how she would not have gone for anything, but the box had been taken, and Ellen, their daughter, and Petrishtchev (the examining lawyer, the daughter's suitor) were going, and that it was out of the question to let them go alone. But that she would have liked much better to stay with him. If only he would be sure to follow the doctor's prescription while she was away.

"Oh, and Fyodor Dmitryevitch" (the suitor) "would like to come in. May he? And Liza?"

"Yes, let them come in."

The daughter came in, in full dress, her fresh young body bare, while his body made him suffer so. But she made a show of it; she was strong, healthy, obviously in love, and impatient of the illness, suffering, and death that hindered her happiness.

Fyodor Dmitryevitch came in too in evening dress, his hair curled à la Capoul, with his long sinewy neck tightly fenced round by a white collar, with his vast expanse of white chest and strong thighs displayed in narrow black trousers, with one white glove in his hand and a crush opera hat.

Behind him crept in unnoticed the little high school boy in his new uniform, poor fellow, in gloves, and with that awful blue ring under his eyes that Ivan Ilyitch knew the meaning of.

He always felt sorry for his son. And pitiable indeed was his scared face of sympathetic suffering. Except Gerasim, Ivan Ilyitch fancied that Volodya was the only one that understood and was sorry.

They all sat down; again they asked how he was. A silence followed. Liza asked her mother about the opera-glass. An altercation ensued between the mother and daughter as to who had taken it, and where it had been put. It turned into an unpleasant squabble.

Fyodor Dmitryevitch asked Ivan Ilyitch whether he had seen Sarah Bernhardt? Ivan Ilyitch could not at first catch the question that was asked him, but then he said, "No, have you seen her before?"

"Yes, in *Adrienne Lecouvreur*."

Praskovya Fyodorovna observed that she was particularly good in that part. The daughter made some reply. A conversation sprang up about the art and naturalness of her acting, that conversation that is continually repeated and always the same.

In the middle of the conversation Fyodor Dmitryevitch glanced at Ivan Ilyitch and relapsed into silence. The others looked at him and became mute, too. Ivan Ilyitch was staring with glittering eyes straight before him, obviously furious with them. This had to be set right, but it could not anyhow be set right. This silence had somehow to be broken. No one would venture on breaking it, and all began to feel alarmed that the decorous deception was somehow breaking down, and the facts would be exposed to all. Liza was the first to pluck up courage. She broke the silence. She tried to cover up what they were all feeling, but inadvertently she gave it utterance.

"*If we are going,* though, it's time to start," she said, glancing at her watch, a gift from her father; and with a scarcely perceptible meaning smile to the young man, referring to something only known to themselves, she got up with a rustle of her skirts.

They all got up, said good-bye, and went away. When they were gone, Ivan Ilyitch fancied he was easier; there was no falsity—that had gone away with them, but the pain remained. That continual pain, that continual terror, made nothing harder, nothing easier. It was always worse.

Again came minute after minute, hour after hour, still the same and still no end, and ever more terrible the inevitable end.

"Yes, send Gerasim," he said in answer to Pyotr's question.

CHAPTER IX

A STRANGE IDEA

LATE at night his wife came back. She came in on tiptoe, but he heard her, opened his eyes, and made haste to close them again. She wanted to send away Gerasim and sit up with him herself instead. He opened his eyes and said, "No, go away."

"Are you in great pain?"

"Always the same."

"Take some opium."

He agreed, and drank it. She went away.

Till three o'clock he slept a miserable sleep. It seemed to him that he and his pain were being thrust some-

where into a narrow, deep, black sack, and they kept pushing him further and further in, and still could not thrust him to the bottom. And this operation was awful to him, and was accompanied with agony. And he was afraid, and yet wanted to fall into it, and struggled and yet tried to get into it. And all of a sudden he slipped and fell and woke up. Gerasim, still the same, is sitting at the foot of the bed halfdozing peacefully, patient. And he is lying with his wasted legs clad in stockings, raised on Gerasim's shoulders, the same candle burning in the alcove, and the same interminable pain.

"Go away, Gerasim," he whispered.

"It's all right, sir. I'll stay a bit longer."

"No, go away."

He took his legs down, lay sideways on his arm, and he felt very sorry for himself. He only waited until Gerasim had gone away into the next room; he could restrain himself no longer, and cried like a child. He cried at his own helplessness, at his awful loneliness, at the cruelty of people, at the cruelty of God, at the absence of God.

"Why hast Thou done all this? What brought me to this? Why, why torture me so horribly?"

He did not expect an answer, and wept indeed that there was and could be no answer. The pain grew more acute again, but he did not stir, did not call.

He said to himself, "Come, more then; come, strike me! But what for? What have I done to Thee? what for?"

Then he was still, ceased weeping, held his breath, and was all attention; he listened, as it were, not to a voice uttering sounds, but to the voice of his soul, to the current of thoughts that rose up within him.

"What is it you want?" was the first clear idea able to be put into words that he grasped.

"What? Not to suffer, to live," he answered.

And again he was utterly plunged into attention so intense that even the pain did not distract him.

"To live? Live how?" the voice of his soul was asking.

"Why, live as I used to live before— happily and pleasantly."

"As you used to live before—happily and pleasantly?" queried the voice. And he began going over in his imagination the best moments of his pleasant life. But strange to say, all these best moments of his pleasant life seemed now not at all what they had seemed then. All—except the first memories of childhood—there, in his childhood there had been something really pleasant in which one could have lived if it had come back. But the creature who had this pleasant experience was no more; it was like a memory of some one else.

As soon as he reached the beginning of what had resulted in him as he was now, Ivan Ilyitch, all that had seemed joys to him then now melted away before his eyes and were transformed into something trivial, and often disgusting.

And the further he went from childhood, the nearer to the actual present, the more worthless and uncertain were the joys. It began with life at the school of jurisprudence. Then there had still been something genuinely good; then there had been gaiety; then there had been friendship; then there

had been hopes. But in the higher classes these good moments were already becoming rarer. Later on, during the first period of his official life, at the governor's, good moments appeared; but it was all mixed, and less and less of it was good. And further on even less was good, and the further he went the less good there was.

His marriage . . . as gratuitous as the disillusion of it and the smell of his wife's breath and the sensuality, the hypocrisy! And that deadly official life, and anxiety about money, and so for one year, and two, and ten, and twenty, and always the same thing. And the further he went, the more deadly it became. "As though I had been going steadily downhill, imagining that I was going uphill. So it was in fact. In public opinion I was going uphill, and steadily as I got up it life was ebbing away from me. . . . And now the work's done, there's only to die.

"But what is this? What for? It cannot be! It cannot be that life has been so senseless, so loathsome? And if it really was so loathsome and senseless, then why die, and die in agony? There's something wrong.

"Can it be I have not lived as one ought?" suddenly came into his head. "But how not so, when I've done everything as it should be done?" he said, and at once dismissed this only solution of all the enigma of life and death as something utterly out of the question.

"What do you want now? To live? Live how? Live as you live at the courts when the usher booms out: 'The Judge is coming!' . . . The judge is coming, the judge is coming," he repeated to himself. "Here he is, the judge! But I'm not to blame!" he shrieked in fury. "What's it for?" And he left off crying, and turning with his face to the wall, fell to pondering always on the same question, "What for, why all this horror?"

But however much he pondered, he could not find an answer. And whenever the idea struck him, as it often did, that it all came of his never having lived as he ought, he thought of all the correctness of his life and dismissed the strange idea.

CHAPTER X

NO EXPLANATION

ANOTHER fortnight had passed. Ivan Ilyitch could not now get up from the sofa. He did not like lying in bed, and lay on the sofa. And lying almost all the time facing the wall, in loneliness he suffered all the inexplicable agonies, and in loneliness pondered always that inexplicable question, "What is it? Can it be true that it's death?" And an inner voice answered, "Yes, it is true." "Why these agonies?" and a voice answered, "For no reason." Beyond and besides this there was nothing.

From the very beginning of his illness, ever since Ivan Ilyitch first went to the doctor's, his life had been split up into two contradictory moods, which were continually alternating—one was despair and the anticipation of an uncomprehended and awful death; the other was hope and an absorbed watching over the actual condition of his body. First there was nothing confronting him but a kidney or intestine which had temporarily declined to perform their duties, then there was nothing but unknown awful death, which there was no escaping.

These two moods had alternated from the very beginning of the illness; but the further the illness progressed, the more doubtful and fantastic became the conception of the kidney, and the more real the sense of approaching death.

He had but to reflect on what he had been three months before and what he was now, to reflect how steadily he had been going downhill, for every possibility of hope to be shattered.

Of late, in the loneliness in which he found himself, lying with his face to the back of the sofa, a loneliness in the middle of a populous town and of his numerous acquaintances and his family, a loneliness than which none more complete could be found anywhere—not at the bottom of the sea, not deep down in the earth;—of late in this fearful loneliness Ivan Ilyitch had lived only in imagination in the past. One by one the pictures of his past rose up before him. It always began from what was nearest in time and went back to the most remote, to childhood, and rested there. If Ivan Ilyitch thought of the stewed prunes that had been offered him for dinner that day, his mind went back to the damp, wrinkled French plum of his childhood, of its peculiar taste and the flow of saliva when the stone was sucked; and along with this memory of a taste there rose up a whole series of memories of that period—his nurse, his brother, his playthings. "I mustn't . . . it's too painful," Ivan Ilyitch said to himself, and he brought himself back to the present. The button on the back of the sofa and the creases in the morocco. "Morocco's dear, and doesn't wear well; there was a quarrel over it. But the morocco was different, and different too the quarrel when we tore father's portfolio and were punished, and mamma bought us the tarts." And again his mind rested on his childhood, and again it was painful, and he tried to drive it away and think of something else.

And again at that point, together with that chain of associations, quite another chain of memories came into his heart, of how his illness had grown up and become more acute. It was the same there, the further back the more life there had been. There had been both more that was good in life and more of life itself. And the two began to melt into one. "Just as the pain goes on getting worse and worse, so has my whole life gone on getting worse and worse," he thought. One light spot was there at the back, at the beginning of life, and then it kept getting blacker and blacker, and going faster and faster. "In inverse ratio to the square of the distance from death," thought Ivan Ilyitch. And the image of a stone falling downwards with increasing velocity sank into his soul. Life, a series of increasing sufferings, falls more and more swiftly to the end, the most fearful sufferings. "I am falling." He shuddered, shifted himself, would have resisted, but he knew beforehand that he could not resist; and again, with eyes weary with gazing at it, but unable not to gaze at what was before him, he stared at the back of the sofa and waited, waited expecting that fearful fall and shock and dissolution. "Resistance is impossible," he said to himself. "But if one could at least comprehend what it's for? Even that's impossible. It could be explained if one were to say that I hadn't lived as I ought. But that can't be alleged," he said to himself, thinking of all the regularity, correctness, and propriety of his life. "That really can't be admitted," he said to himself, his lips smiling ironically as though some one could see his smile and be deceived by it. "No explanation! Agony, death. . . . What for?"

CHAPTER XI

CONFESSION

So passed a fortnight. During that fortnight an event occurred that had been desired by Ivan Ilyitch and his wife. Petrishtchev made a formal proposal. This took place in the evening. Next day Praskovya Fyodorovna went in to her husband, resolving in her mind how to inform him of Fyodor Dmitryevitch's proposal, but that night there had been a change for the worse in Ivan Ilyitch. Praskovya Fyodorovna found him on the same sofa, but in a different position. He was lying on his face, groaning, and staring straight before him with a fixed gaze.

She began talking of remedies. He turned his stare on her. She did not finish what she had begun saying; such hatred of her in particular was expressed in that stare.

"For Christ's sake, let me die in peace," he said.

She would have gone away, but at that moment the daughter came in and went up to say good morning to him. He looked at his daughter just as at his wife, and to her inquiries how he was, he told her drily that they would soon all be rid of him. Both were silent, sat a little while, and went out.

"How are we to blame?" said Liza to her mother. "As though we had done it! I'm sorry for papa, but why punish us?"

At the usual hour the doctor came. Ivan Ilyitch answered, "Yes, no," never taking his exasperated stare from him, and towards the end he said, "Why, you know that you can do nothing, so let me be."

"We can relieve your suffering," said the doctor.

"Even that you can't do; let me be."

The doctor went into the drawing-room and told Praskovya Fyodorovna that it was very serious, and that the only resource left them was opium to relieve his sufferings, which must be terrible. The doctor said his physical sufferings were terrible, and that was true; but even more terrible than his physical sufferings were his mental sufferings, and in that lay his chief misery.

His moral sufferings were due to the fact that during that night, as he looked at the sleepy, good-natured, broad-cheeked face of Gerasim, the thought had suddenly come into his head, "What if in reality all my life, my conscious life, has been not the right thing?" The thought struck him that what he had regarded before as an utter impossibility, that he had spent his life not as he ought, might be the truth. It struck him that those scarcely detected impulses of struggle within him against what was considered good by persons of higher position, scarcely detected impulses which he had dismissed, that they might be the real

thing, and everything else might be not the right thing. And his official work, and his ordering of his daily life and of his family, and these social and official interests,—all that might be not the right thing. He tried to defend it all to himself. And suddenly he felt all the weakness of what he was defending. And it was useless to defend it.

"But if it's so," he said to himself, "and I am leaving life with the consciousness that I have lost all that was given me, and there's no correcting it, then what?" He lay on his back and began going over his whole life entirely anew. When he saw the footman in the morning, then his wife, then his daughter, then the doctor, every movement they made, every word they uttered, confirmed for him the terrible truth that had been revealed to him in the night. In them he saw himself, saw all in which he had lived, and saw distinctly that it was all not the right thing; it was a horrible, vast deception that concealed both life and death This consciousness intensified his physical agonies, multiplied them tenfold. He groaned and tossed from side to side and pulled at the covering over him. It seemed to him that it was stifling him and weighing him down. And for that he hated them.

They gave him a big dose of opium; he sank into unconsciousness; but at dinner-time the same thing began again. He drove them all away, and tossed from side to side.

His wife came to him and said, "Jean, darling, do this for my sake" (for my sake?). "It can't do harm, and it often does good. Why, it's nothing. And often in health people——"

He opened his eyes wide.

"What? Take the sacrament? What for? No. Besides . . ."

She began to cry.

"Yes, my dear. I'll send for our priest, he's so nice."

"All right, very well," he said.

When the priest came and confessed him he was softened, felt as it were a relief from his doubts, and consequently from his sufferings, and there came a moment of hope. He began once more thinking of the intestinal appendix and the possibility of curing it. He took the sacrament with tears in his eyes.

When they laid him down again after the sacrament for a minute, he felt comfortable, and again the hope of life sprang up. He began to think about the operation which had been suggested to him. "To live, I want to live," he said to himself. His wife came in to congratulate him; she uttered the customary words and added—

"It's quite true, isn't it, that you're better?"

Without looking at her, he said, "Yes."

Her dress, her figure, the expression of her face, the tone of her voice,—all told him the same: "Not the right thing. All that in which you lived and are living is lying, deceit, hiding life and death away from you." And as soon as he had formed that thought, hatred sprang up in him, and with that hatred agonising physical sufferings, and with these sufferings the sense of inevitable, approaching ruin. Something new was happening; there were screwing and shooting pains, and a tightness in his breathing.

The expression of his face as he uttered that "Yes" was terrible. After uttering that "Yes," looking her straight in the face, he turned on to his face, with a rapidity extraordinary in his weakness, and shrieked—

"Go away, go away, let me be!"

CHAPTER XII

DEATH IS OVER

FROM that moment there began the scream that never ceased for three days, and was so awful that through two closed doors one could not hear it without horror. At the moment when he answered his wife he grasped that he had fallen, that there was no return, that the end had come, quite the end, while doubt was still as unsolved, still remained doubt.

"Oo! Oo—o! Oo!" he screamed in varying intonations. He had begun screaming, "I don't want to!" and so had gone on screaming on the same vowel sound—oo!

All those three days, during which time did not exist for him, he was struggling in that black sack into which he was being thrust by an unseen resistless force. He struggled as the man condemned to death struggles in the hands of the executioner, knowing that he cannot save himself. And every moment he felt that in spite of all his efforts to struggle against it, he was getting nearer and nearer to what terrified him. He felt that his agony was due both to his being thrust into this black hole and still more to his not being able to get right into it. What hindered him from getting into it was the claim that his life had been good. That justification of his life held him fast and would not let him get forward, and it caused him more agony than all.

All at once some force struck him in the chest, in the side, and stifled his breathing more than ever; he rolled forward into the hole, and there at the end there was some sort of light. It had happened with him, as it had sometimes happened to him in a railway carriage, when he had thought he was going forward while he was going back, and all of a sudden recognised his real direction.

"Yes, it has all been not the right thing," he said to himself, "but that's no matter." He could, he could do the right thing. "What is the right thing?" he asked himself, and suddenly he became quiet.

This was at the end of the third day, two hours before his death. At that very moment the schoolboy had stealthily crept into his father's room and gone up to his bedside. The dying man was screaming and waving his arms. His hand fell on the schoolboy's head. The boy snatched it, pressed it to his lips, and burst into tears.

At that very moment Ivan Ilyitch had rolled into the hole, and caught sight of the light, and it was revealed to him that his life had not been what it ought to have been, but that that could still be set right. He asked himself, "What is the right thing?"—and became quiet, listening. Then he felt some one was kissing his hand. He opened his eyes and glanced at his son. He felt sorry for him. His wife went up to him. He glanced at her. She was gazing at him with open mouth, the tears unwiped streaming over her nose and cheeks, a look of despair on her face. He felt sorry for her.

"Yes, I'm making them miserable," he thought. "They're sorry, but it will be better for them when I die." He would have said this, but had not the strength to utter it. "Besides, why speak, I must act," he thought. With a glance to his wife he pointed to his son and said—

"Take away . . . sorry for him. . . . And you too . . ." He tried to say "forgive," but said "forgo" . . . and too weak to correct himself, shook his hand, knowing that He would understand Whose understanding mattered.

And all at once it became clear to him that what had tortured him and would not leave him was suddenly dropping away all at once on both sides and on ten sides and on all sides. He was sorry for them, must act so that they might not suffer. Set them free and be free himself of those agonies. "How right and how simple!" he thought. "And the pain?" he asked himself. "Where's it gone? Eh, where are you, pain?"

He began to watch for it.

"Yes, here it is. Well, what of it, let the pain be.

"And death. Where is it?"

He looked for his old accustomed terror of death, and did not find it. "Where is it? What death?" There was no terror, because death was not either.

In the place of death there was light.

"So this is it!" he suddenly exclaimed aloud.

"What joy!"

To him all this passed in a single instant, and the meaning of that instant suffered no change after. For those present his agony lasted another two hours. There was a rattle in his throat, a twitching in his wasted body. Then the rattle and the gasping came at longer and longer intervals.

"It is over!" some one said over him.

He caught those words and repeated them in his soul.

"Death is over," he said to himself. "It's no more."

He drew in a breath, stopped midway in the breath, stretched and died.

Polikushka

CHAPTER I

ONE MUST GO!

"It's as you're pleased to command, madam, only I'm sorry for the Dutlovs! They're all—every one of them —good lads; but since there's not a house-serf to send, one of them's bound to go," said the bailiff. "As it is, every one's pointing to them. It's as your honour wills, of course."

And he shifted his right hand over his left, holding both before his stomach, bent his head on the other side, drew in his thin lips, almost with a whistle, turned up his eyes, and sank into silence, with the unmistakable intention of remaining silent a long while and hearing without comment all the nonsense his mistress would be sure to say upon the subject. He was a bailiff, a serf, a close-shaven man in a long coat, of the peculiar bailiff cut, who was standing one autumn evening before his mistress with his report. Receiving the report consisted from the lady's point of view in listening to the accounts of past agricultural operations and giving directions for future ones. From the point of view of Yegor Mihalovitch, the bailiff, the presentation of the report was a ceremonial that consisted of standing evenly on both bandy legs, in a corner, with his face to the sofa, listening to all sorts of irrelevant chatter, and leading the mistress by various devices up to the point of saying quickly and impatiently, "Very well, very well," to all Yegor Mihalovitch's suggestions.

At that moment the question was the furnishing of conscripts. Three had to be sent from Pokrovskoe. Two were unmistakably pointed out by the very finger of fate, by the conjunction of domestic, moral, and financial considerations. As regards them, there could be no hesitation nor dispute on the part of the mir, on the part of their mistress, or on the part of public opinion. The third was the subject under discussion. The bailiff wanted to save Dutlov, who had three lads in his household eligible, and to send the family house-serf Polikushka, who had a very bad reputation, and had more than once been guilty of stealing bags, harness, and hay. The mistress, who had often petted Polikushka's ragged children, and was attempting to reform his morals by exhortations from the gospel, did not want to give him up. At the same time, she had no ill-will towards the Dutlovs, whom she did not know, and had never noticed. But for some reason she was unable to grasp the fact that, if Polikushka did not go, Dutlov must go, and the bailiff hesitated to explain this point in so many words to her. "Oh, I don't wish the Dutlovs to be unhappy!" she said with feeling. "If you don't wish it, then pay the three hundred roubles in lieu of a recruit," was the answer that ought to have been made to that. But policy forbade it.

And so Yegor Mihalovitch remained standing quietly, leaned a little towards the doorpost, and fell to gazing at his mistress's lips moving, at the ruche in her cap dancing up and down, together with her shadow on the wall under the picture. But he did not feel it in the least necessary to penetrate to the meaning of her remarks. The lady talked a long while, and said a great deal. He felt a twitching impulse to yawn behind his ears, but he adroitly changed this nervous quiver into a cough, covering his mouth with his hand, and affecting to clear his throat. I had not long before seen Lord Palmerton sitting with his hat on, while a member of the Opposition thundered against the ministry; then, suddenly rising, he replied in a three hours' speech to every point his adversary had made. I saw this, and did not marvel at it, because I had seen something like it a thousand times over between Yegor Mihalovitch and his mistress. Either because he was afraid of dropping asleep, or because it struck him that she was getting very much wrought up, he shifted the weight of his person from the left leg to the right, and began with the time-honoured formula with which he used always to begin:—

"It's as you will, madam, only, only—the mir meeting's standing before the counting-house now, and one must make an end. In the order it says they must take recruits before Intercession to the town. And of the peasants it's the Dutlovs that all point to, and no one else. The mir cares nothing for your interests; it's all one to them if we do ruin the Dutlovs. I know, to be sure, what a struggle they've had. Why, ever since I've been bailiff, they've always been living in poverty. The old man's gone on, only reckoning on his younger nephews growing up to be a help, and now we must put them back to ruin again. But I, as your honour's well aware, care for your property as for my own. It's a pity, madam, it's as you're pleased to command! They're no kith nor kin to me, and I've taken nothing from them— -"

"Oh, I never thought of such a thing, Yegor," put in his mistress, and she suspected at once that he had been bribed by the Dutlovs.

"Only it's the best homestead in all Pokrovskoe—God-fearing, hard-working peasants. The old man was for thirty years church elder, never touches a drop, nor uses a bad word, goes to church" (the bailiff knew what sop would be acceptable); "and what's the great thing I put before you, he has only two sons, and then the nephews. The mir pitches on him, but in reality he ought to be reckoned among the households of two. Others with three sons have divided into separate households in their foolishness, and now they're right enough, while these have to suffer for their prudence."

Here his mistress failed to grasp anything; she had no notion what "separate households" and "households of two" meant in this connection. She simply heard the sound of the bailiff's voice, and looked at the nankin buttons on his coat; the top one he probably did not often button, so it was quite firmly on; but a middle one was dragged out and hanging, and ought to have been sewed on long ago. But as we are all aware, for purposes of conversation, especially on matters of business, it is not at all necessary to understand what is said to you—the only thing necessary is to remember what you want to say yourself. And that the lady did on this occasion.

"How is it you won't understand me, Yegor Mihalovitch?" she said; "I don't in the least desire a Dutlov to be sent for a soldier. I should have thought you might judge from what you know of me, that I do all I can to assist my peasants, and don't desire their unhappiness. You know that I'm ready to make every sacrifice to escape from this melancholy necessity, and not to let either Dutlov go or Horyushkin." (I don't know whether it occurred to the bailiff that to escape from this melancholy necessity there was no need to make *every* sacrifice, the sacrifice of three hundred roubles would be sufficient; but that reflection easily might have occurred to him.) "But one thing I tell you plainly, that I won't let Polikey go on any account. After that affair with the clock, when he confessed of himself to me, and wept and swore that he would reform, I talked a long while to him, and saw

that he was touched and sincerely penitent." ("Well, she's off now!" thought Yegor Mihalovitch, and he began scrutinizing the marmalade which had been put in her glass of water—orange or lemon was it? "Bitter it's sure to be," he thought.) "Here it's seven months since then, and he's never once been tipsy, and his conduct is excellent. His wife told me that he's become a different man. And how would you have me punish him now when he's reformed? And besides, wouldn't it be inhumanity to send a man who has five children and only he to keep them? No; you'd better not talk to me about that, Yegor."

And the lady took a sip from the glass. Yegor Mihalovitch watched the progress of the water down her throat, and then replied shortly and drily—

"Then your orders are to fix upon Dutlov?"

His mistress flung up her hands.

"How is it you can't understand me? Do I want to make the Dutlovs miserable? Do you suppose I have anything against them? God is my witness that I'm ready to do anything for them." (She glanced at the picture on the wall, but bethought herself that it was not God. "Well, that's no matter, though," she thought. It was strange again that she did not stumble upon the idea of the three hundred roubles.) "But what am I to do? Do I know how and why? I can't know that. Well, I rely upon you, you know what I want. You act so that all may be content according to law. What's one to do? They're not the only ones, all have their painful moments. Only Polikey can't be sent away. You understand that would be a horrid thing for me to do."

She would have gone on longer—she was so deeply stirred; but at that moment a maidservant came into the room.

"What is it, Dunyasha?"

"A peasant has come, bid me ask Yegor Mihalovitch is it his orders the meeting's to wait?" said Dunyasha, and she glanced wrathfully at Yegor Mihalovitch. ("Ugh, that bailiff!" she thought, "upsetting the mistress; now she won't let us get to sleep till one o'clock again.")

"You can go then, Yegor," said the lady. "Do the best you can."

"Yes, ma'am." He said no more now of Dutlov. "And whom do you bid me send to the gardener for the money?"

"Is Petrusha not yet back from the town?"

"No, ma'am."

"Can't Nikolay go?"

"Father's laid up with lumbago," said Dunyasha.

"Wouldn't your honour desire me to go myself to-morrow?" asked the bailiff.

"No; you're wanted here, Yegor." The lady pondered. "How much is it?"

"Four hundred and sixty-two roubles."

"Send Polikey!" said the lady, glancing resolutely into the face of Yegor Mihalovitch.

Yegor Mihalovitch, without parting his teeth, drew his lips back, as though he smiled, and did not change countenance.

"Yes, ma'am."

"Send him to me."

"Yes, ma'am," and Yegor Mihalovitch went off to the counting-house.

CHAPTER II

HORSE-DOCTOR

POLIKEY, being a man of no importance, and of tarnished reputation, and coming, too, from another village, had had no chance of obtaining privileges through the housekeeper or the butler, through the bailiff or the lady's-maid, and his corner was of the very poorest, although he and his wife and children made a family of seven. The corners had been built by the late master in this way. In a stone hut twenty-three feet square a Russian stove was placed in the centre; all round it was the collider (as the house-serfs called it), and at each angle a corner was partitioned off with boards. Space was consequently not plentiful, especially in Polikey's corner, which was nearest the door. The conjugal couch with quilted counterpane and cotton chintz pillows, the hanging cradle with the baby, the three-legged table at which the cooking and the washing were done, and on which all the household goods were put, and at which Polikey himself did his work (he was a horse-doctor), tubs, clothes, fowls, a calf, and the seven of themselves filled up the whole corner; and they could not have stirred had not the common stove offered them one quarter of its surface on which things and persons could impartially be laid, and had it not been possible, too, to find an outlet on the steps. That, though, was hardly possible; in October it was cold, and their winter clothes consisted of a solitary sheepskin for the seven; but then the children could keep warm by running, and the grown-up folks by work, and both could creep on to the stove where the warmth rose to forty degrees Réaumur. It must be terrible, one imagines, to live in such conditions, but it did not trouble them —one could get on all right. Akulina washed and mended for her husband and children, spun and wove and bleached her linen, cooked and baked in the common oven, quarrelled and gossiped with the neighbours. There were not only monthly rations enough for the children, but litter for the cow as well. Kindling wood was free, and food for the beasts, too. Hay, too, from the stable sometimes came their way. There was a strip of kitchen garden. Their cow had calved; they had their own chickens. Polikey worked in the stables, looked after two colts, and bled the horses and cattle; cleaned their hoofs, cured them of worms, and applied an ointment of his own invention, and a few coppers and provisions were bestowed on him for this. There were leavings of the oats, too, to be picked up. In the village there was a peasant who regularly, every month, gave him twenty pounds of mutton for two measures of oats. One could have got on well enough if there had been no trouble at heart. But trouble there was, and plenty of it for all the family. Polikey had been in his youth in another village at a stud stable. The stable-keeper into whose hands he came was the greatest thief in the whole district; at last he was sent away to a penal settlement. From this stable-keeper Polikey received his training; and owing to his youth, he had grown so used to "such silly ways," that he couldn't give them up even when he'd have been glad to. He was a young man, and weak; he had no father or mother, and no one

to teach him. Polikey liked drink, and did not like anything lying about in the wrong place. Whether it was a rope or a pad, or a lock or a bolt, or something of more value, Polikey Ilyitch found a place for everything. There were people everywhere who would take these articles and pay for them in spirits or money, according to agreement. Such wages are the easiest earned, as the people say; no apprenticeship nor labour—nothing is needed —and if once you try it, you never care for other work after. There's only one drawback to such gains, though everything's to be had cheap and without toil, and the life's pleasant as a rule; all of a sudden this line of business will come to grief through evil-disposed folk, and one has to pay for everything, and may find life a burden.

That was just what happened with Polikey. Polikey had married; God had given him good luck; his wife, the cowherd's daughter, had turned out a healthy, clever, hard-working woman, had borne him children, each finer than the last. Polikey still stuck to his line of business, and all went well. All at once a mischance befell him, and he was caught. And caught for the merest trifle; he had popped away some leather reins at a peasant's. They found them, beat him, reported it to the mistress, and began to keep an eye on him. A second and a third time he was caught. Folk began to cry shame on him, the bailiff threatened sending him for a soldier, the mistress reprimanded him, his wife began crying and fretting. . . . Everything went utterly wrong! He was a good-natured fellow, and no harm in him, only weak, liked a drop of drink, and had dropped into such a habit of this sort of thing that he could not give it up anyhow. Sometimes his wife would start rating at him, even beating him when he came home drunk, and he'd cry. "Unlucky fellow I am," he would say. "What can I do? Blind my eyes, but I'll give it up, I will." A month later you'd see him leaving home again, going off drinking, and staying away for two days. "He must have got the money from somewhere for his spree," folks reasoned. His last exploit was with the counting-house clock. There was in the counting-house an old clock hanging on the wall; it hadn't gone for a long while. He chanced to go into the counting-house alone; he took a fancy to the clock, carried it off, and disposed of it in the town. As ill-luck would have it, the shopkeeper to whom he sold the clock happened to be related by marriage to one of the house-serfs, and he came to the village for a feast-day, and told them about the clock. Folks began making inquiries, just as though it were any concern to anybody. The bailiff in particular did not like Polikey. And they found the culprit. They reported it to the mistress. The mistress sent for Polikey. He fell at her feet at once, and with feeling, touchingly, made a full confession, as his wife had told him to do. He carried out all her instructions very well. The mistress began reasoning with him, talked away, preached away; talked of God, and of virtue, and of the future life, and of his wife, and of his children, and reduced him to tears. The mistress said—

"I forgive you; only promise me you will never do it again.'

"I never will; damn my soul, con-found me, rip me open if I do!" said Polikey, and he wept pathetically.

Polikey went home, and lay on the stove, bellowing like a calf all day. Since then nothing had once been traced to Polikey. But his life had not been a gay one; folks looked on him as a thief, and as the time for levying recruits drew near, every one began to point to him.

Polikey was a horse-doctor, as already stated. How he had all at once become so no one knew, and he less than any one. In the stud stables, under the man who had been sent to a settlement, he had performed no duty except clearing the dung out of the horse-boxes, sometimes rubbing down the horses, and bringing water. There he could not have learnt his art. Then he had been a weaver; then he had worked in the garden, weeding paths; then, as a punishment, he had been sent to the brickyard; then, being allowed to go off on payment of a fixed sum a year to his master, he went into service as house-porter to a merchant. So there, too, he could not have had practice in his art. But the last time he came home a belief gradually somehow gained ground in his extraordinary, almost supernatural, in fact, knowledge of the veterinary art. He let blood—once, and a second time—then laid a horse on its back, and probed something in its leg, then insisted on the horse being fastened to a bench, and began cutting its pastern till the blood came, in spite of the struggles and even screams of the horse, and said that this meant "letting off the under-hoof blood." Then he explained to the peasant that it was essential to take blood from both veins "for greater ease," and began tapping with a mallet on his blunt lancet. Next he bound a bandage made of the selvedge of a woman's headkerchief round the belly of the porter's horse. Finally he took to sprinkling all sorts of sores with vitriol, wetting rags from a bottle, and sometimes giving internally what he thought fit. And the more horses he tortured and did to death, the more they believed in him, and the more horses were brought to him.

I feel that it's not quite for us gentlefolks to laugh at Polikey. The means to which he resorted to inspire confidence were exactly the same as those which have been effectual with our fathers and with us, and will be so with our children. The peasant lies with his belly on the head of his solitary nag, who is not merely his chief wealth, but almost one of his family, and gazes with faith and horror at Polikushka's significantly puckered-up face, and his thin arms with the sleeves tucked up, as he purposely pinches the very spot that is painful, and boldly cuts into the living flesh, with the private reflection, "Here goes, come what may!" while he puts on an air of knowing where there is blood, and where matter, and where a dry vein, and where a wet one, holding in his teeth a healing rag or a bottle of vitriol. The peasant, watching him, cannot conceive that Polikushka's hand is raised to cut in ignorance. Himself he could not do that. And as soon as the wound is made, he cannot face the self-reproach of having given the poor beast to be wounded for nothing. I don't know how it may be with you, reader, but in my dealings with a doctor, torturing at my request those dear-

est to my heart, I have had precisely the same experience. The lancet and the mysterious whitish bottle of corrosive sublimate, and the words, "the staggers," "farcy," "let blood," "matter," and so on, are not they much the same as *neurosis, rheumatism, organisms,* and so on? *Wage du zu irren und zu träumen*—that does not apply so much to poets as to doctors and to veterinary surgeons.

CHAPTER III

SOBS OF AKULINA

On the same evening, while the village meeting buzzed round the counting-house in the still October darkness, choosing the recruits, Polikey was sitting on the edge of the bed, pounding with a bottle on the table a horse mixture which was new to himself. It contained corrosive sublimate, sulphur, Glauber's salts, and a herb which Polikey had gathered, bethinking himself all at once that this herb would be very good for a broken-winded horse, and fancying it would not be amiss to give it also for other ailments. The children were already in bed—two on the stove, two in the bed, and one in the hanging cradle, at which Akulina was sitting busy with her yarn. A candle-end, a relic of some candles from the mistress's house that had been left lying about, stood in a wooden candlestick in the window; and that her husband might not break off from his important occupation, Akulina got up to snuff it with her fingers. There were independent spirits who considered Polikey a poor sort of doctor and a poor sort of man. Others, and they were the majority, regarded him as not much of a man, but a great master in his own line. Akulina, although she often scolded and even beat her husband, believed him to be incontestably the best horse-doctor and the best man in the world. Polikey scattered in a handful of some simple. (He never made use of weights, and would allude ironically to Germans, who use weights. "This," he would say, "is not an apothecary's!") Polikey weighed his simple in his hand, and shook it; but it seemed too little to him, and he scattered in ten times as much. "I'll put it all in; it'll pick it up," he said to himself. Akulina looked round quietly at the voice of her lord and master, expecting some command; but seeing that the matter did not concern her, she shrugged her shoulders. "He's a deep one! How does he come by it all?" she thought, and took up her spinning again. The paper from which the drug was shaken fell under the table. Akulina did not let that pass unnoticed.

"Anyutka!" she called; "see what father's lost; pick it up."

Anyutka drew her thin, bare legs from under the old gown that served her as a quilt, crept like a kitten under the table, and picked up the paper.

"Here, daddy," she said, and dived into the bed again with her frozen little feet.

"Why are you pushing me?" whined her younger sister, lisping in a sleepy voice.

"I'll give it you!" said Akulina, and both heads vanished under the old gown.

"Three silver roubles he'll give," said Polikey, corking the bottle. "I shall cure the horse. Cheap, too," he added. "You rack your brains, and see! . . .

Akulina, run round and ask Nikita to lend me a pinch of tobacco. I'll pay him back to-morrow."

And Polikey took out of his trousers a limewood pipe, once painted, with sealing-wax at the mouthpiece, and began filling it.

Akulina left her spindle and went out without coming into collision with anything, which was a feat of some difficulty. Polikey opened a cupboard, put the bottle in it, and raised to his lips an empty flask, but there was no spirit left in it. He groaned; but when his wife brought the tobacco, and he had filled up his pipe, lighted it, and sat down on the bed, his face beamed with the pride and satisfaction of a man who has completed his day's work. Whether he was thinking how next day he would catch hold of the horse's tongue and pour into its mouth that amazing mixture, or whether he was reflecting that when a man's an indispensable person no one will refuse him anything, and Nikita had just sent him the tobacco,—anyway he was in good spirits. Suddenly the door, which hung on one hinge, was flung back, and into their *corner* came a maid from *up yonder*—not the second maid, but the third, the little one who was kept for errands. *Up yonder,* as every one knows, always means the master's house, even though it be downhill. Aksyutka (that was the girl's name) always flew like a bullet; and as she ran, her arms hung straight and swung like a pendulum in time with her rapid movement, not at her sides, but in front of her person. Her cheeks were always rosier than her pink dress; her tongue always moved as rapidly as her legs. She flew into the room, and clutching for some reason at the stove, began swaying to and fro; and as though she were in such haste that she seemed to try to bring out two or three words at once, she suddenly articulated breathlessly, addressing Akulina:—

"Mistress gave orders for Polikey Ilyitch to come this minute; up yonder she gave orders . . ." She stopped, and drew a deep breath. "Yegor Mihalovitch has been with the mistress; they've been talking of the recruits, mentioned Polikey Ilyitch. . . . Avdotya Mikolavna sent word to come this minute. . . . Avdotya Mikolavna sent word . . ." (again a breath); "he's to come this minute."

For half a minute Aksyutka stared at Polikey, at Akulina, at the children, who peeped out from under the quilt, snatched up a nutshell which was lying on the stove, flung it at Anyutka, and articulating once more, "To come this minute," she flew like a whirlwind out of the room, and the pendulums swung with their usual rapidity before the line of her flight.

Akulina got up again and got her husband his boots—they were wretched, torn, soldiers' boots—took his coat from the stove and gave it him, without looking at him.

"Ilyitch, won't you change your shirt?"

"No," said Polikey.

Akulina did not once glance at his face while he was putting on his boots and his coat, and she did well not to glance at him. Polikey's face was pale, his lower jaw was twitching, and in his eyes there was that tearful, meek, profoundly unhappy expression which is only seen in good-natured, weak, sinful persons. He combed his hair and would have gone out, but his wife stopped him and tucked in a tape of his shirt, which was hanging out on his coat, and put on his cap.

"What, Polikey Ilyitch, is it the mistress is wanting you?" they heard the voice of the carpenter's wife asking behind the screen. The carpenter's wife had only that morning had an intensely unpleasant scene with Akulina over a pot of soapsuds, which the Polikey children had upset in her place, and she was delighted at the first minute to hear that Polikey was summoned to the mistress; it was sure to be for no good. Moreover, she was a subtle, diplomatic, and malignant lady. No one knew better than she did how to take the shine out of any one with a word; such, at least, was her own conviction about herself.

"I suppose they want to send to town for some purchases," she went on. "I imagine that they choose a trustworthy man, and so they're sending you. You might buy me a quarter of a pound of tea there, Polikey Ilyitch."

Akulina suppressed her tears, and her lips tightened into an expression of fury. She could have pulled the nasty hair of that wretch, the carpenter's wife. But as she glanced at her children and thought that they would be left orphans, and she a soldier's widow, she forgot the spiteful carpenter's wife, hid her face in her hands, sat down on the bed, and her head sank into the pillows.

"Muvver, you're squashing me," lisped the little girl, pulling the covering from under her mother's elbows.

"I wish you were all dead! For sorrow I brought you into the world!"

cried Akulina, and the whole corner was filled with her sobs, to the glee of the carpenter's wife, who had not yet forgotten the soapsuds of the morning.

CHAPTER IV

ROUBLES

HALF an hour passed by. The baby began to cry. Akulina got up and fed it. She was not crying now; but with her still handsome, thin face propped in her hand, she sat still with her eyes on the burnt-down candle, and pondered the question why she had married, why so many soldiers were wanted, and how, too, she was to pay out the carpenter's wife.

She heard her husband's steps; she wiped away the traces of her tears and got up to make way for him. Polikey came in as bold as brass, flung his cap on the bed, drew a long breath, and began undoing his belt.

"Well, why did she send for you?"

"H'm . . . we all know! Polikushka's the least of men; but when there's business to be done, then who's wanted? —Polikushka."

"What sort of business?"

Polikey was in no haste to reply; he lighted his pipe and spat.

"I'm to go to the merchant's to fetch some money."

"To fetch money?" asked Akulina.

Polikey chuckled and wagged his head.

"A clever one she is, too, with words. . . . 'You,' says she, 'were under observation that you were an untrustworthy man, but I trust you more than any other.'" (Polikey spoke loudly, so that the neighbours might hear.) "'You promised me to reform,' says she, 'so here's the first proof that I trust you; set off,' says she, 'to the merchant, take the money, and bring it here.' I says, 'madam,' says I, 'we are all your serfs, and bound, as we would serve God, so to serve you, whereas I feel myself that I can do anything for your welfare, and from no duty could I cry off; what you command, that I do, since I am your slave.'" (Again he smiled that peculiar smile of a weak, good-natured, and guilty man.) "'So,' says she, 'you'll do it faithfully? You understand,' says she, 'that your fate depends on it?' 'Could I fail to understand that I can do everything? If they have slandered me, why, there's none that can't be blamed; but I never could, I do believe, ever think of anything against your welfare.' . . . So, to be sure, I talked to her, till my lady became quite soft. 'You,' says she, 'shall be my chief man . . .'" (He paused, and again the same smile lingered on his face.) "I know just how to talk to them. When I was away working for hire, didn't I come across queer customers! But only let me come to talk to them. I'd soften them till they were like silk."

"And is it a lot of money?" asked Akulina.

"Fifteen hundred roubles," Polikey responded carelessly.

She shook her head.

"When are you to go?"

"To-morrow, she said. 'Take a horse,' says she, 'which you like, go to the counting-house, and set off in God's name.'"

"Praise be to Thee, O Lord!" said Akulina, getting up and crossing herself. "God help you, Ilyitch," she added in a whisper, that they might not hear the other side of the partition, and pulling him by the sleeve of his shirt. "Ilyitch, listen to me! For Christ's sake, I beseech you, kiss the cross when you set off, that you won't let a drop of anything pass your lips."

"As if I would drink with all that money with me!" he snorted. "But, I say, there was some one playing away smartly on the piano there, grand!" he added, pausing and chuckling. "The young lady, no doubt. I stood like this before the old lady, at the what-not; while the young lady there, through the door, didn't she rattle up and down the piano, and dash it off in fine style. I should like to play, upon my word I should. I know I could do it, that I could. I'm a smart chap at such things. Give me a clean shirt for to-morrow."

And they went to bed happy.

CHAPTER V

YOU STOLE IT!

THE meeting meanwhile was noisy about the counting-house. It was no jesting matter that was in question. The peasants were almost all present; and while Yegor Mihalovitch had gone to their mistress, they put their hats on, more voices were audible in the general buzz and talk, and the voices were louder. The roar of bass voices, broken now and then by a breathless, husky, shrill speech, filled the air; and that roar floated across, like the sound of a booming sea, to the windows of the mistress, who was sensible of a nervous uneasiness at that sound, like the feeling before the outbreak of a violent storm. It was a feeling between

dread and dislike. She kept fancying that now the voices were growing louder and noisier, and that something was happening. "As though they couldn't do it all quietly, peaceably, without strife and shouting," she thought, "according to the Christian law, in brotherly love and meekness."

Many voices were speaking at once, but loudest of all shouted Fyodor Ryezun, the carpenter. He was the head of a household with two sons, and was attacking the Dutlovs. Old Dutlov was defending himself; he stepped out in front of the crowd, behind which he had at first been standing; and waving his arms and pulling his beard, he talked with such frequent snufflings in his throat and nose, that it would have been hard for him to make out himself what he was saying. His children and nephews, strapping fellows, stood huddled behind him, and old Dutlov suggested the hen in the game of "Hawk and Chickens." The hawk was Ryezun, and not Ryezun only, but all the heads of families of twos and fathers of only sons, almost all the meeting, in fact, pouncing down on Dutlov. The point was that Dutlov's brother had, thirty years before, been sent for a soldier, and so he did not want to take his turn with the families with three eligible members, but wanted his brother's service to be reckoned, and said that he should be put on an equality with the families of two only for a general drawing of lots, and that from that drawing of lots the third recruit should be taken. There were four other families with three men eligible for recruits in them besides Dutlov's. But one was the village elder, and he had been exempted by the mistress;

from another family a recruit had been sent at the last levy; from the remaining two families two recruits had been chosen, and one of them had not even come to the meeting, though his wife was standing mournfully behind every one, blankly awaiting some turn in her fortunes. The father of the other chosen recruit, red-haired Roman, in a torn smock, though he was not poor, stood leaning against the steps with downcast head, mute all the time, though he sometimes gazed intently at any one who was talking loudly, and looked down again. His whole figure was eloquent of misery. Old Semyon Dutlov was a man to whom any one who had the slightest acquaintance with him would have readily intrusted hundreds and thousands of roubles. He was a steady, God-fearing, responsible man; he was, moreover, the church elder. All the more striking was his violent excitement at this moment.

Ryezun, the carpenter, was, on the contrary, a tall, black-haired, drunken, turbulent man, bold and particularly clever in disputes and discussions at village meetings, at bazaars, with workmen, merchants, peasants, and gentry alike. Now he was self-possessed and malignant; and with all the height of his tall figure, all the force of his loud voice and oratorical talent, he overpowered the husky church elder, who was so completely thrown out of the steady groove he always moved in. Among others taking part in the discussion was a round-faced, squat, youngish fellow, with a square head and curly beard. Garaska Kopilov, one of the regular talkers of the younger generation, who followed Ryezun's lead. He was always conspicuous for his abrupt speech, and had already gained a certain weight in the village meetings. Then there was Fyodor Melnitchny, a long, thin, yellow-faced, stooping peasant, young too, with a scanty beard and little eyes, always bitter and gloomy, always seeing the bad side of everything, and often bewildering the meeting by his unexpected and disconnected questions and remarks. Both these speakers were on the side of Ryezun. Besides these, there were two chatterboxes, who put in their word continually; one with a good-natured face and a bushy flaxen beard, Hrapkov, who was always beginning, "But, my dear fellow!" and the other, a little man, with a bird-like countenance, Zhidkov, who also began with an invariable preface, "It follows, my lads!" addressing every one, and talking away without rhyme or reason. Both of these were first on one side and then on the other, but no one heeded them. There were others of the same sort, but these two seemed to pervade the whole crowd. They shouted louder than all, alarming the mistress; they were listened to less than any; and intoxicated with the noise and shouting, gave themselves up entirely to the pleasure of letting their tongues wag. There were many more peasants of different characters; they were gloomy, decorous, indifferent, and depressed. There were peasant-women, too, behind the men, with sticks in their hands, but of all of them, please God, I will tell another time. The bulk of the crowd consisted of peasants, who stood in the meeting, as they did in church, talking in a whisper behind the others of domestic matters, of when they will cart home the faggots in the copse, or waiting in silence for the racket to be soon over. There were rich ones, too, for whom the meeting could do nothing to increase or detract from their prosperity. Such was Yermil, with his broad, shiny face, whom the peasants nicknamed Fat Belly, because he was rich. Such, too, was Starostin, whose face wore a complacent expression of power. "You may talk as you like," he seemed to say, "but no one can touch me. I've four sons, but not one of them will they take." Now and then some freelance, like Kopilov and Ryezun, would try to pick a quarrel with them, and they answered, but calmly and firmly, with a sense of their own security. If Dutlov were like the hen in the game of "Hawk and Chickens," his lads did not quite suggest chickens; they did not fidget uneasily, nor cackle, but stood calmly behind him. The elder, Ignat, was thirty years old; the second, Vassily, was married, too, but not suitable for a recruit; the third, Ilyushka, the nephew, who had only just been married, a pink-and-white young fellow in a smart sheepskin (he used to go out as a driver), stood watching the people, and sometimes scratching his head under his hat, as though it were all no concern of his, though he it was whom the hawks were trying to pounce upon.

"And so did my grandfather go for a soldier," said one, "and so I'll cry off the lots, too."

"There's no law like that, brother! Last levy they took Miheitchev, and his uncle's not come home yet."

"You've neither father nor uncle that served the Tsar," Dutlov was saying at the same time. "No, and you your-self have served neither your masters nor your mir. You do nothing but drink, and your children have parted from you because there's no living with you; so, do you point to others? But I was village constable ten years; I've been elder; twice I've been burned out—no one helped me; and just because in our house it's all peaceable and honest, am I to be ruined? Give me back my brother. He's dead out there, for sure. Judge in truth, in God's way, brethren in the faith, and be not led away by a drunkard's ravings."

At precisely the same moment Garaska was saying to Dutlov—

"You talk about your brother, but he wasn't sent by the mir, but the masters sent him for his debauchery; so he's nothing for you to get off by."

Garaska had not finished when the lank, bilious Fyodor Melnitchny, stepping forward, began—

"Yes, the gentry send whom they think they will, and then the mir may choose. The mir has decreed for your son to go; and if you don't like it, ask the mistress. She'll maybe send me, single-handed as I am, to shave my head and leave my children. That's your law!" he said bitterly, and waving his arm again, he went back to his former position.

Red-haired Roman, whose son had been chosen, lifted his head, and brought out, "Yes, that's so, that's so!" and sank back on to the step in vexation.

But these were not all the voices that were speaking at once. Besides those who, standing in the background, were talking of their own affairs, the chatterboxes, too, did not forget to do their part.

"To be sure, brethren in the faith," said little Zhidhov, repeating Dutlov's words, "we must judge like Christians. Like Christians, to be sure, my lads, we must judge."

"We must decide by our conscience, my good friend," put in the simple-hearted Hrapkov, repeating the words of Kopilov, and pulling Dutlov by his sheepskin; "that was a matter of the master's will, and not the decision of the mir."

"True! So it was, sure," said others.

"Who's a drunkard raving?" retorted Ryezun. "Did you give me drink, eh? or is your son, who's been picked up by the roadside, going to reproach me for drinking? Come, lads, we must come to a decision. If you want to spare Dutlov, you'd best pitch on a lad of a family of two, or an only son, while you're about it; and he'll make a laughing-stock of us."

"It's for a Dutlov to go. Why talk about it?"

"We all know it's for those that have three sons to take the lots first," said voices.

"It's still to see what the mistress's orders are. Yegor Mihalovitch was saying they meant to send a house-serf," said a voice.

This remark checked the dispute a little, but soon it flickered up again, and again passed into personalities.

Ignat, of whom Ryezun had said that he had been picked up by the roadside, began proving to Ryezun that he had stolen a saw from some travelling carpenters, and had almost beaten his wife to death when he was drunk.

Ryezun replied that he beat his wife both drunk and sober, and even so never beat her enough, and made every one laugh thereby. But about the saw, he became suddenly offended, stepped closer up to Ignat, and began asking—

"Who stole it?"

"You stole it!" the sturdy Ignat answered boldly, stepping still nearer up to him.

"Who stole it? Wasn't it you?" shouted Ryezun.

"No, you!" shouted Ignat.

After the saw they passed to the theft of a horse, to a sack of oats, to a certain strip of vegetable garden in the big village, to a certain dead body; and the two peasants said such awful things of each other, that if a hundredth part of their accusations had been true, they ought both by the law to be at least sent to Siberia.

Old Dutlov meanwhile had chosen another line of defence. He did not like his son's shouting. Stopping him, he said, "Shame! give over, I tell you!" and himself began to argue that families of three were not only those who had three sons living together, but those families which had broken up, too; and he referred too to Starostin.

Starostin smiled faintly, cleared his throat, and stroking his beard with the manner of a well-to-do peasant, answered that the mistress's will had decided that. His son must have deserved it if the order was to pass him over.

As to divided families, Garaska too shattered Dutlov's arguments, observing that families ought never to have been allowed to break up, as it was in the old master's time; but that after the summer was over, there was no picking raspberries; that, as it was, families of only one couldn't send a recruit.

"Is it to please themselves they're divided? Why utterly ruin them now?" cried the voices of members of divided families, and the regular chatterboxes joined those voices.

"You buy a recruit, if you don't like it; you can afford it," said Ryezun to Dutlov.

Dutlov wrapped his coat about him despairingly, and stood behind the other peasants.

"You've counted my money, it seems," he remarked malignantly. "Let's see what Yegor Mihalovitch will say from the mistress."

CHAPTER VI

THE LAW

YEGOR MIHALOVITCH did in fact come out of the house at that moment. One cap after another was lifted over the heads, and as the bailiff approached one head after another uncovered—bald, at the top and in front, grey, grizzled, red, black, and flaxen—and gradually the voices subsided, till at last all were perfectly still. Yegor Mihalovitch stood on the steps, and made a sign that he was going to speak. In his long coat, with his hands thrust awkwardly into his front pockets, in a town-made forage cap, pulled down in front, Yegor Mihalovitch stood firmly, his legs wide apart, and in his elevated position towering above those mostly old and mostly handsome bearded faces, raised and turned towards him. He looked very different from the way he had looked before his mistress. He was majestic.

"Here, lads, is the mistress's deci-sion. It's not her pleasure to punish any of the house-serfs; but when you fix on one of yourselves, he will go. This time we want three; by rights, two and a half, but a half will have to go in advance. It's all the same; if not now, it would be next time."

"To be sure, that's the fact!" said voices.

"In my judgment," continued Yegor Mihalovitch, "for Horyushkin and Mityuhin's Vaska to go, is God's own will."

"And so it is, indeed!" said voices.

"The third must be Dutlov, or else one out of the families with two sons. What do you say?"

"Dutlov," said voices—"the Dutlovs have three!"

And again little by little the shouting began, and again it came back to the strip of garden in the big village, and to certain pieces of sacking stolen from the mistress's yard. Yegor Mihalovitch had managed the estate now for twenty years, and was a shrewd and experienced man. He stood a while listening for a quarter of an hour, and all at once commanded all to be silent, and the Dutlovs to draw lots which of the three they would send. The lots were cut. Hrapkov began to draw them out of a hat in which they were shaken, and he drew Ilyushka's. All were silent.

"Mine, is it? Show it here," said Ilyushka in a breaking voice.

All were silent. Yegor Mihalovitch bade them bring on the morrow the recruit's money, seven kopecks from each family, and announcing that all was at an end, dismissed the meeting. The crowd moved off, putting on their caps round the corner, with a hum of talk and footsteps. The bailiff stood on the steps, looking after the retreating figures. When the younger Dutlovs had gone round the corner, he beckoned to the old man, who had of his own accord lingered, and went with him into the counting-house.

"I'm sorry for you, old man," said Yegor Mihalovitch, sitting down in an elbow chair before the table; "it was your turn. Will you buy your nephew off or not?"

The old man glanced significantly at Yegor Mihalovitch without replying.

"There's no getting out of it," Yegor Mihalovitch said in reply to his look.

"And glad we'd be to buy him off, but we haven't the money to do it, Yegor Mihalovitch! Two horses died in the summer, and my nephew's wedding. It seems our fate would have it so . . . because we live honestly. It's very well for him to talk." (He meant Ryezun.)

Yegor Mihalovitch rubbed his face with his hand and yawned. He was unmistakably weary of the business, and it was time for his tea.

"Ah, old man, don't fall into sin!" he said. "Look well under your floor, may be you'll find the old silver roubles to make up the four hundred. I'd buy you such a substitute, a perfect wonder! The other day a man offered himself. . . ."

"In the *province?*" asked Dutlov, meaning by *province* the provincial town.

"Why, will you buy him?"

"And I'd be glad to, before God, but . . ."

Yegor Mihalovitch cut him short sternly.

"Well, then, listen to me, old man; mind Ilyushka doesn't do himself a mischief, and produce him at once when I send for him—either to-day or to-morrow. You produce him, you will have to answer for him; but if, God forbid, anything were to happen to him, I shall take your elder son to be shaved for a soldier. You hear?"

"But can't any of the families of two, Yegor Mihalovitch? Why, it's unfair!" he said after a pause—"when my brother's dead a soldier, to take the son, too, why should such a calamity fall on me?" he said, almost weeping, and ready to fall at his feet.

"Come, go along, go along," said Yegor Mihalovitch; "there's nothing can be done, it's the law. Keep an eye on Ilyushka; you must answer for him."

Dutlov went homewards, mournfully flicking at the clods of the road with a limewood switch.

CHAPTER VII

THE ENVELOPE

NEXT day, early in the morning, there stood at the steps of the house-serfs' quarters the cart in which the bailiff used to drive about on his rounds, with a big-boned bay gelding, for some unknown reason called Drum, in the shafts. In spite of the rain and hail and the cold wind, Anyutka, Polikey's eldest daughter, was standing barefoot at the horse's head, in obvious alarm, holding him a long way off with one hand on the bridle, while with the other she kept on her head the yellow-green wadded jacket, which filled in the family the functions of quilt, cloak, headdress, carpet, overcoat for Polikey, and many other uses. A great bustle was going on within. It was still dark; the morning light of the rainy day faintly glimmered in at the window, pasted up here and there with paper. Akulina had left for a while her baking in the oven; and her children, of whom the smaller ones were shivering in bed, as their covering had been taken to be used as a garment, and in its place they had been given only their mother's head shawl. Akulina was busy in getting her husband ready for the journey. His shirt was clean. His boots, which, as they say, were begging for porridge, caused her particular anxiety. To begin with, she took off her own solitary pair of thick woollen stockings and gave them to her husband; and secondly, out of a saddle cloth, which had been lying about in the stable, and been brought to their hut by Polikey a couple of days before, she had contrived to make inner soles in such a way as to stop up the holes, and to preserve Polikey's feet from getting wet. Polikey, seated with his feet on the bedstead, was engrossed in twisting his sash round him so that it should not look like a dirty cord. And the cross, lisping little girl in a cloak, which even put on her head still tripped up her feet, had been despatched to Nikita to beg the loan of a cap. The bustle was increased by house-serfs coming in to ask Polikey to buy for them in the town—needles for one, tea for another, olive oil for a third, tobacco for a fourth, and sugar for the carpenter's wife, who had already managed to have the samovar ready; and to propitiate Polikey, had brought him in a jug a decoction which she called tea. Though Nikita refused to lend the cap, and it was necessary to get his own into

a fit state, that is, to poke in the stuffing that had burst and was hanging out, and with a veterinary needle to sew up the hole; though the boots with the saddle-cloth patches would not at first go on to his feet; though Anyutka got too frozen and was letting go Drum, and then Mashka had to go in the cloak to take her place, and then Mashka had to take off the cloak, and Akulina herself went to hold Drum—in the end Polikey had at last put on all the clothing of the family, leaving only one jacket and a pair of slippers, and fully equipped, seated himself in the cart, wrapped himself up, arranged the hay, once more wrapped himself up, picked up the reins, wrapped himself still more compactly, as very precise persons do, and started.

His little boy, Mishka, running out on to the steps, begged for a ride. The lisping Mashka too began begging, "Let me wide and I sall be warm wivout a cloak"; and Polikey pulled up Drum, smiled his weak smile, while Akulina sat the children in beside him; and bending over to him, besought him in a whisper to remember his oath and not to touch a drop on the way. Polikey took the children as far as the smithy, put them down, muffled himself up again, again set his cap straight, and drove off alone at a steady little trot, his cheeks quivering with the jolting, and his feet knocking on the bark lining of the cart. Mashka and Mishka ran bare-foot home down the slippery hillside with such swiftness and such shrieks, that a dog, running from the village to the serf's quarters, stared at them; and suddenly putting its tail between its legs, fled home barking, at which the heirs of Polikey redoubled their shrieks.

It was miserable weather, the wind cut his face, and something between snow and rain and hail beat persistently in Polikey's face and on his bare hands, which he stuffed, holding the chilly reins, up the sleeves of his coat. The wet sleet blew on the leather cover of the horse-collar too, and on the head of old Drum, who twitched his ears and blinked.

Then it suddenly ceased and cleared all in an instant; bluish snow clouds could be seen distinctly; and the sun began as it were to peep out, but uncertainly and cheerlessly, like the smile of Polikey himself. In spite of that, Polikey was plunged in agreeable reflections. He whom they'd wanted to send to a settlement, whom they threatened to send for a soldier, whom every one, not too lazy, abused and beat, whom they always shoved into the worst place,—he was driving now to receive a sum of money, and a large sum too, and the mistress trusted him, and he was driving in the bailiff's cart with Drum, with whom the mistress drove out sometimes, driving like some upper servant, with leather straps and reins. And Polikey sat up straighter, set the stuffing in his cap right, and wrapped himself up once more. If Polikey supposed, however, that he was exactly like some well-to-do upper servant, he was in error. It is true, indeed, as every one knows, that men who do business with tens of thousands drive about in carts with leather harness, but that's the same thing with a difference. A man with a beard, in a blue or a black long coat, comes along driving a sleek horse and sitting alone

on the box. One's only to look whether his horse is well fed, whether he's well fed himself, how he's sitting, how the horse is harnessed, what the tyres of the wheels are like, how the man is belted; and one can see at once whether it's a peasant who's doing business with hundreds or with thousands. Any man of experience would only have had to look close at Polikey, at his hands, at his face, at his beard that he had lately let grow, at his sash, at the hay flung anyhow in the cart, at thin Drum, at the worn tyres, to see at once that this was a poor serf driving, and not a merchant, not a drover, not a hall-porter; nor was he doing business with thousands, nor even with hundreds, nor with tens of roubles. But Polikey did not think so. He was in error, and the error was an agreeable one. He was to carry back fifteen hundred paper roubles in his bosom. If he liked, he could turn Drum's head towards Odesta instead of homewards, and drive off God knows where. Only that he would not do, but would faithfully bring the money to his mistress, and would tell people that larger sums than that he'd had to bring. On reaching an inn, Drum began pulling at the left rein, slackening his pace, and turning towards it. But Polikey, although he had the money given him to make purchases with, cracked the whip at Drum and drove by. He did the same thing too at another inn, and towards midday got out of the cart, and opening the gate of the tavern at which all his mistress's people used to stop, he led in the horse, unharnessed the cart, gave the horse some hay, dined with the innkeeper's workmen, not omitting to mention what imortant business he had come about, and went off with the letter in his cap to the gardener's. The gardener, who knew Polikey, read the letter, and with evident doubt cross-questioned him, whether he really had been told to take the money. Polikey would have liked to resent this, but did not know how to, and simply smiled his smile. The gardener read the letter again and handed him the money. Polikey took the money, put it in his bosom, and went back to the tavern. Neither beer-house nor gin-shop—nothing tempted him. He was conscious of an agreeable tension in all his being, and more than once he stopped at shops with tempting wares—boots, coats, caps, cotton goods, and things to eat. And after stopping a little while, he walked away with an agreeable feeling, "I can buy it all, but see I'm not doing it." He went to a bazaar to buy what he had been commissioned, got everything, and discussed the price of a lined cloak, for which he was asked twenty-five roubles. The salesman, staring for some reason at Polikey, did not believe that he could buy it; but Polikey pointed to his bosom, saying he could buy up all the shop if he liked, and asked to try on the cloak, fingered it, stroked it, blew into the fur, even smelt at it, and at last with a sigh took it off.

"The price doesn't suit me. If you'd say a little less than fifteen roubles," said he. The shopkeeper angrily flung the cloak across a table, while Polikey went out, and in excellent spirits made his way to the tavern. After having supper, giving water and oats to Drum, he got up on the stove; and pulling out the envelope, looked at it a long while, and asked a man who could read

to read him the address and the words, "With enclosure of a thousand, six hundred, and seventeen roubles in notes." The envelope was made of plain paper, the seal was of brown wax, with anchors on it; one big one in the middle, four at the corner; there was a drop of sealing wax on the side. Polikey gazed at all this and studied it, and even felt the sharp edges of the notes. He felt a sort of childish pleasure in knowing there was so much money in his hands. He thrust the envelope into the lining of his cap, put the cap under his head, and lay down. But even in the night he waked up several times and felt the envelope. And every time finding the envelope in its place, he had an agreeable sensation in realising that here was he, Polikey, disgraced, degraded, taking such a sum, and bringing it faithfully— more faithfully than if the bailiff him-self had brought it.

CHAPTER VIII

THE RECRUITS

ABOUT midnight the innkeeper's servants and Polikey were waked by a knocking at the gate and the shouting of peasants. It was the recruits who were being brought from Pokrovskoe. There were ten men: Horyushkin, Mityuhin, and Ilya (Dutlov's nephew), a couple of men to replace them in case of accident, the village elder, old Dut-lov, and three peasants who drove them. A night light was burning in the hut; the cook was asleep on the locker under the holy images. She jumped up and began lighting a candle. Polikey, too, waked, and stooping over from the stove, began looking at the peasants as they came in. They all came in, crossed themselves, and sat down on the benches. They were all quite self-possessed, so that no one could have said which were the recruits and which were their escorts. They greeted the persons in the hut, chatted merrily, and asked for something to eat. Some, it is true, were silent and depressed; but others were exceptionally lively, having unmistakably been drinking. Among the latter was Ilya, who had never drunk spirits before.

"Well, lads, will you sup or go to sleep?" asked the elder.

"Supper!" answered Ilya, throwing open his overcoat and settling himself on a bench. "Send for some vodka."

"Nonsense with your vodka!" the elder dropped casually, and he turned again to the others. "Take a bite of bread then, lads. Why wake the folk up?"

"Give me some vodka!" repeated Ilya, not looking at any one in particular, and speaking in a tone that suggested that he would not easily give way.

The peasants followed the elder's advice, got their bread out of the cart, ate a little, and asked for some rye-beer, and lay down, some on the stove, and some on the floor.

Ilya kept repeating at intervals, "Give us some vodka; I tell you, vodka!" Suddenly he caught sight of Polikey. "Polikey, hey Polikey! You here, my dear fellow? I'm going for a soldier, you see; I've said the last good-bye to my mother and my wife. . . . How she did wail! They've sent me for a soldier. . . . Stand us some vodka."

"No money," answered Polikey;

"but still, please God, they may reject you," added Polikey, to comfort him.

"No, brother, I'm like a clean birch-tree; never a sign of any disease have I in me. What chance of my being rejected? What better soldier could the Tsar want?"

Polikey began to tell an anecdote of how a peasant had given the doctor a bribe, and he had got him off for it.

Ilya moved nearer the stove and began to be talkative.

"No, Polikey, it's all over now, and I don't want to stay myself. Uncle's sent me off. Do you suppose he couldn't have bought me off? No, he grudged his son, and he grudged his money. They're giving me up. . . . Now, I don't care to stay myself." (He talked softly, confidentially, under the influence of subdued sadness.) "The only thing is, I'm sorry for mother; she's simply broken-hearted! And my wife too; they've simply ruined the poor wench for nothing; she's done for now—a soldier's wife, that's all you can say. Better not have married. What did they marry me for? They're coming to-morrow."

"But why did they bring you away so early?" asked Polikey; "there was nothing heard about it, and now all of a sudden you're off."

"They're frightened, d'ye see, I might do myself a mischief," answered Ilyushka, smiling. "No fear, I'll not do anything. I shall be all right if I'm a soldier, only it's mother I'm sorry for. Why did they marry me?" he said softly and dejectedly.

The door opened, shut with a slam,

and old Dutlov, shaking his cap, walked in in his immense basket-work shoes, which were like boats on his feet.

"Afanasy," said he, crossing himself and addressing the innkeeper's man, "haven't you a lantern for me to put the oats out by?"

Dutlov did not glance at Ilya, and began quietly lighting a candle end. His gloves and whip were stuffed into his belt, and his smock was carefully belted; he looked as collected as though he had come on some other business; his hard-working face was as simple, peaceable, and occupied with his work as usual.

Ilya, seeing that his uncle had ceased speaking, again let his eyes rest gloomily on the locker, and began again, addressing the elder—

"Give us some vodka, Yermila. I want drink."

His voice was gloomy and wrathful.

"Drink at this time?" answered the elder, sipping his cup. "Don't you see folks have eaten and laid down, and why are you making a row?"

The word "row" obviously suggested an idea to Ilya.

"Elder, I'll do a mischief if you don't give me vodka."

"If you'll just make him listen to reason," said the elder to Dutlov, who had lighted his candle, but was stopping still, evidently to hear what would come next; and was looking askance, with commiseration at his nephew, as though marvelling at his childishness.

Ilya, looking down, said again—

"Give me vodka; I'll do mischief."

"Give over, Ilya!" said the elder mildly, "give over Really now, it will be better."

But he had hardly uttered these words when Ilya jumped up, struck his fist into the window, and shouted with all his might—

"You wouldn't listen, so there you are!" and rushed to the other window to smash that one too.

Polikey, in the twinkling of an eye, rolled over twice and hid himself in the furthest corner of the stove, so that he frightened all the beetles. The elder flung down his spoon and ran up to Ilya. Dutlov slowly put down the candle, untied his belt, and shaking his head and clucking with his tongue, he went up to Ilya, who was by now struggling with the elder and the innkeeper's man, who would not let him get near the window. They had caught hold of him by his arms, and held him, it seemed, firmly; but as soon as Ilya saw his uncle with his belt, his strength seemed redoubled, he tore himself away and, with rolling eyes, stepped with clenched fists up to Dutlov.

"I'll kill you; don't come near me, brute! You've been the ruin of me; you with your ruffianly sons, you've ruined me. Why did you marry me? . . . Don't come near, I'll kill you."

Ilyushka was terrible. His face was purple, his eyes were wild, all his healthy young body was shaking as though in fever. He would, it seemed, and could have killed all the three peasants who were approaching him.

"You'll drink your own brother's blood, bloodsucker!"

There was a gleam of something in Dutlov's ever-serene face. He took a step forward.

"If you won't obey of yourself . . ." he said suddenly. With inexplicable energy he caught hold of his nephew by a sudden movement, rolled with him on the ground, and with the help of the elder began to bind his hands. They were struggling for five minutes. At last Dutlov, with the peasant's assistance, got up, pulling Ilya's hands away from his coat, at which he was clutching; he got up himself, then lifted up Ilya with his hands tied behind him, and seated him on the locker in a corner.

"I said it would be the worse for you!" he said, still breathing hard from the struggle, and setting straight his shirt band. "Why sin? We shall all come to die. Put a cloak under his head," he added, turning to the innkeeper's man, "or else his head will ache"; and he took up the candle, tied a bit of cord round his waist, and went out again to the horses.

Ilya, with ruffled hair, with a pale face and rumpled shirt, looked about the room, as though trying to remember where he was. The innkeeper's man collected the broken bits of windowpane and stuffed a coat into the window to prevent a draught. The elder sat down to his cup again.

"Ay, Ilyuha, Ilyuha! I'm sorry for you, truly. What can one do? Here's Horyushkin too a married man; there was no getting you off, it seems."

"It's to my scoundrelly uncle I owe my ruin!" Ilya repeated with intense fury. "He wouldn't give his own son. Mother told me, the bailiff bade him buy a recruit. He won't; he can't do it, he says. Have my brother and I brought so little into the house? He's a scoundrel!"

Dutlov came into the hut, said his prayer to the holy pictures, took off his overcoat, and sat down with the elder.

The servant gave him some rye-beer too, and a spoon. Ilya was silent, and shutting his eyes, lay down on the cloak. The elder pointed to him without speaking and shook his head. Dutlov made a gesture with his hand.

"Do you suppose I'm not sorry? My own brother's son. As if it's not sorrow enough, they've made me out a scoundrel to him. It's been put into his head by his wife, I suppose—a sly wench, for all she's so young—that we've money, so that we could buy a recruit, and so here he brings it up against me. But how sorry I am for the lad!"

"Ah, a fine lad!" said the elder.

"But I can do nothing with him. To-morrow I shall send Ignat to him, and his wife wanted to come."

"Send them; it'll do him good," said the elder, and he got up and went to the stove. "What is money? Money's dust and ashes."

"If one had the money, who would grudge it?" said one of the workmen, lifting up his head.

"Ah, money, money! Many a sin comes from it," Dutlov responded. "Nothing in the world brings so much sin as money is said indeed in the Scriptures."

"All is said there," assented the workman. "And so a man told me; there was a merchant, he piled up a great deal of money, and did not want to leave anything behind; he so loved his money that he took it with him to the grave. When he came to die, all he bade them do was to lay his pillow with him in the coffin. They suspected nothing, and so they did. Then the sons began looking for his money; there was none anywhere. One son guessed that the money must be in the pillow.

The matter was brought to the Tsar—he allowed them to dig him up. And would you believe it? They opened the coffin; there was nothing in the pillow, but the coffin was full of maggots; so they buried it again. So that's what money brings!"

"To be sure, many a sin it brings," said Dutlov, and he got up and began saying his prayers.

When he had prayed, he looked at his nephew. He was asleep. Dutlov went up, took the belt off his hands, and lay down. The other peasant went off to sleep with the horses.

CHAPTER IX

NIGHT

As soon as everything was still, Polikey crept stealthily out, as though he were somehow guilty, and began making ready to set off. For some reason he felt wretched at spending the night here with the recruits. The cocks were already crowing to one another more often. Drum had eaten all his oats, and was trying to get to the drinking-trough. Polikey harnessed him and led him past the peasants' carts. The cap with its contents was in safety, and the wheels of the cart rattled again along the half-frozen Pokrovskoe road. Polikey felt more at ease only when he had driven out of the town. Till then he kept fancying for some reason that he would hear pursuers behind him, that they would stop him, and tie his hands behind him, and take him next day to the recruiting station in Ilya's place. A chill ran down his back, half from cold, half from fright, and he kept urging on and urging on Drum. The first man to meet him was a priest, in a high winter cap, walking with a one-eyed workman. Polikey felt still more uneasy. But outside the town this terror gradually passed away. Drum went at walking pace; the road could be seen more distinctly in front. Polikey took off his cap and began feeling the money. "Should I put it in my bosom?" he thought; "I should have to undo my belt again. Let me get beyond the turning uphill, and I'll get out of the cart and set myself to rights. The cap's sewed up strongly at the top, and it couldn't come out below under the lining. And I won't take my cap off till I get home." As he approached the turning, Drum of his own accord galloped uphill; and Polikey, who was as eager as Drum to get home, did not hinder his doing so. Everything was right—so at least it seemed to him—and he abandoned himself to dreams of the gratitude of his mistress, of the five roubles she would give him, and of the joy of all at home. He took off his cap, felt the letter once more, stuck it more firmly on to his head, and smiled. The cloth of the cap was rotten, and just because Akulina had sewed it up so carefully where it was torn, it began to go at the other end; and the very movement by which Polikey, when he took the cap off, thought to thrust the letter further under the stuffing—that very action made a hole in the stuff and drove the letter at one corner out of the cloth.

It began to get light; and Polikey, who had not slept all night, dozed. Pulling his cap forwarder, and in so doing driving the letter further out, Polikey, half asleep, began nodding his head against the side of the cart. He waked up near home. His first action was to clutch at his cap; it was sitting firmly on his head; he did not even take it off, feeling certain that the envelope was in it. He touched up Drum, set the hay in order, assumed once more the air of an upper servant, and looking about him with dignity, rattled homewards.

Here he could see the kitchens, here the servants' wing, yonder the carpenter's wife carrying linen; yonder the counting-house; and over there the mistress's house, where Polikey would prove immediately that he was a trustworthy and honest man, "that any one may be slandered." And the mistress would say, "Well, thank you, Polikey, here's for yourself three"—or may be five, or may be even ten roubles, and would tell them to give him some tea too, and may be a drop of vodka. And it wouldn't be half bad in the cold. For ten roubles we can have a spree on the holiday, buy boots; and Nikita too, to be sure, we'll pay back his four and a half roubles, for he's begun to be very worrying. A hundred paces from home, Polikey wrapped himself up again, set his belt straight and his collar, took off his cap, smoothed his hair, and without hurry thrust his hand under the lining. His hand fumbled about in the cap, more and more quickly; the other was thrust in there too, his face grew paler and paler, one hand was poked through. Polikey fell on his knees, stopped the horse, and began looking about the cart, the hay, the parcels, fumbling in his bosom, in his trousers; the money was nowhere.

"Heavens! What does it mean? What will happen?" he howled, clutching at his hair.

But then recollecting that he might be seen, he turned Drum's head round, pulled his cap down, and drove the astonished and disgusted Drum back along the road.

"I can't stand being driven by Polikey!" Drum must have been thinking. "For once in my life he has fed me and watered me at the right time, and only to deceive me so horribly. How I tried to race home! I'm tired, and I'd hardly got a whiff of our hay, and he drives me back."

"Come up, you devil's jade!" Polikey shrieked through his tears, standing up in the cart, tugging at Drum's mouth with the reins, and lashing him with the whip.

CHAPTER X

STRANGULATION

THE whole of that day no one in Pokrovskoe saw Polikey. The mistress made inquiries several times after dinner, and Aksyutka flew to Akulina. But Akulina said that he had not come; that doubtless the merchant had detained him, or something had gone wrong with the horse. "Hasn't it gone lame!" she said. "Last time Mihail was gone full twenty-four hours just the same; he had to come the whole way on foot!" And Aksyutka swung her pendulums back to the house again; while Akulina sought for causes for her husband's being detained, and tried to soothe her fears, but did not succeed. She had an ache at her heart, and no sort of work for the holiday on the morrow went well in her hands. She was the more worried because the carpenter's wife affirmed that she had seen with her own eyes "a man exactly like Polikey come into view, and then turn back again." The children, too, awaited their father with impatience and uneasiness, though on other grounds. Anyutka and Mashka were left without either cloak or overcoat, which articles had enabled them, if only by turns, to get out into the street; and so, wearing nothing but their frocks, they were forced to confine themselves to making circles with exaggerated speed round the house, occasioning thereby no little inconvenience to all the inhabitants of the servants' lodge in their comings in and goings out. Once Mashka darted into the lap of the carpenter's wife as she was carrying water; and though she roared beforehand on knocking against her knees, she still received a good cuffing about her curly head, and cried still louder. When she did not run up against any one, she flew straight indoors, and, by means of a tub, clambered on to the stove. Only the mistress and Akulina were genuinely anxious about Polikey individually; the children's anxiety related to the question of his wearing apparel. But Yegor Mihalovitch, going with his report to his mistress, in reply to her question, "Has not Polikey come, and where can he be?" smiled as he answered, "I can't say," and was obviously pleased that his presuppositions were realised. "He ought to have come by dinner-time," he said significantly. All that day no one in Pokrovskoe knew anything about Polikey; only later it was learned that some neighbouring peasants had seen him without a cap running along the road and asking every one, "Hadn't they found a letter?" Another man had seen him asleep by the wayside, near a cart and horse tied up to a post. "And I did think, too," this man said, "that he was drunk, and the

horse had had no food or water for two days, so lean it looked." Akulina did not sleep all night; she was listening all the time; but even in the night Polikey did not come. If she had been alone, or if she had had a cook and a housemaid, she would have been even more miserable. But as soon as the cocks had crowed for the third time, and the carpenter's wife was stirring, Akulina was obliged to get up and to set to work at the stove. It was a holiday, before daylight she must have her bread out, must make rye-beer, bake cakes, milk the cow, iron out frocks and smocks, wash the children, bring in water, and not let her neighbour keep the oven all to herself. Akulina, though she never ceased listening, set to work on those duties. Daylight came, the bells had begun ringing, the children were getting up, and still Polikey had not come. The day before had been like winter, the snow in patches covered the fields, the road, and the roofs; but to-day, as though for the holiday, it was fine, sunny and frosty, so that one could see and hear at a distance. But Akulina, standing at the stove, poking her head into its opening, was so busy with the baking of the cakes that she did not hear Polikey come in, and only found out from the children's shouts that her husband had returned. Anyutka, being the eldest, had greased her head and dressed herself. She was in a pink chintz gown, new but crumpled, a present from the mistress, which stood out as stiffly as the bark of a tree, and was the envy of all beholders. Her hair glistened, she had rubbed half a candle end on it; her slippers, though not new, were elegant. Mashka was still in the old jacket and dirty, and Anyutka would not let her come near her for fear of her making her in a mess. Mashka was out of doors when her father drove up with the sack full of his commissions. "Daddy's come," she shrieked, and dashed headlong in at the door past Anyutka, making her dirty. Anyutka, laying aside her fears of getting dirty, at once proceeded to beat Mashka, while Akulina could not tear herself away from her work. She only shouted to the children, "Now, then, I'll thrash you all!" and looked round at the door. Polikey, with a sack in his hands, came into the entry, and at once made his way to his corner. Akulina fancied that he was pale, and his face looked as though he were half crying, half smiling. But she hadn't time to make it out.

"Well, Polikey, successful?" she asked him from the oven. Polikey muttered something that she did not catch.

"Eh?" she called. "Have you seen the mistress?" Polikey in his corner sat down on the bed, looked wildly round him, and smiled his guilty and intensely miserable smile. For a long time he made no answer.

"Polikey, why so long gone?" Akulina's voice called again.

"I gave the money to the mistress, Akulina. How she did thank me!" he said suddenly, and began still more uneasily looking about him and smiling. Two objects particularly caught his restless, feverishly wide-open eyes—the cord tied to the hanging cradle, and the baby. He went up to the cradle, and with his deft fingers began hurriedly untying the knot of the cord. Then his eyes rested on the baby; but at that moment Akulina came into the "corner" with a tray of cakes. Polikey quickly hid the cord in his bosom and sat down on the bed.

"How is it, Polikey, you don't seem yourself?" said Akulina.

"I haven't slept," he answered.

Suddenly something flashed by the window, and in an instant the girl from up yonder, Aksyutka, darted in like an arrow.

"The mistress gave orders for Polikey Ilyitch to come to her this minute," she said. "This minute, Avdotya Mikolavna said, this minute."

Polikey looked at Akulina, at the girl.

"Directly! What more does she want?" he said so simply, that Akulina was reassured. "Perhaps she wants to reward me. . . . Say I'll come directly."

He got up and went out. Akulina took a deep tub, set it on the locker, poured water in from the buckets standing at the door, and from a caldron of hot water on the stove, tucked up her sleeves, and tried the water.

"Come, Mashka, I'll wash you."

The cross, lisping little girl began to roar.

"Come, you dirty girl, I'll put you on a clean smock! Now then, none of your nonsense. . . . Come, I've your sister to wash too."

Polikey meanwhile had not followed the errand-girl to the mistress, but had gone to quite a different place. In the entry close to the wall was a steep ladder leading to the loft. Polikey, going out into the entry, looked round, and seeing no one, bending nearly double, climbed nimbly and quickly, almost running, up this ladder.

"What can be the meaning of Polikey's not coming?" said the mistress, impatiently turning to Dunyasha, who was combing her hair. "Where is Polikey? Why is it he doesn't come?"

Aksyutka again flew to the serfs' quarters, and again flew into the entry, and summoned Polikey to go to the mistress.

"But he went long ago," answered Akulina, who had finished washing Mashka, and at that moment had just sat her baby boy in the trough, and, in spite of his screams, was wetting his scanty locks of hair. The baby screamed, puckering up its face, and tried to clutch at something with its helpless little hands.

With one large hand Akulina supported his fat, soft little back, all in dimples, while with the other she washed him.

"Look and see if he's dropped asleep anywhere," she said, looking round with anxiety.

At that moment the carpenter's wife, with her hair uncombed and her bosom open, went, holding up her petticoats, to the loft, to get down her clothes that were drying there. Suddenly a shriek of horror was heard in the loft; and, like one possessed, the carpenter's wife, with her eyes shut, came flying backwards on all fours, falling rather than running down the ladder.

"Polikey!" she shrieked.

Akulina let the baby drop out of her hands.

"Strangled himself!" roared the carpenter's wife.

Akulina, not noticing that the baby had fallen backwards all of a heap, and was head downwards in the water, kicking its legs, ran out into the entry.

"On the beam . . . hanging," brought out the carpenter's wife, but she stopped short on seeing Akulina.

Akulina rushed to the ladder; and before they had time to prevent her she had run up, but with a fearful scream she fell down the ladder like a dead body, and would have been killed, if the people who ran in from everywhere had not been in time to catch her.

CHAPTER XI

SILVER CHILDREN

FOR some minutes it was impossible to distinguish anything in the general uproar. Masses of people ran together, all were shouting, all were talking, children and old people were crying. Akulina lay unconscious. At last some men, the carpenter, and the bailiff, who had run up, went up above; and the carpenter's wife for the twentieth time described how she, "thinking nothing, went after my cape, looked round like this: what do I see?—a man; I stared; a cap lies beside him, turned inside out. Mercy! why, the legs are swinging! A cold shudder ran down me. To think of a man's hanging himself, and I must be the one to see him! How I flew down, I couldn't say myself. And a marvel it is how God's mercy preserved me. Truly, the Lord had mercy on me. To think of it; so steep, and such a height! It might have been my death."

The men who had gone up told the same story. Polikey was hanging from a beam, wearing nothing but his shirt and his breeches, by the very cord he had taken from the cradle. His cap, turned inside out, lay there too. His coat and cloak had been taken off, and were tidily folded up beside him. His feet reached the ground, and there were no signs of life.

Akulina came to herself and made a dash again towards the ladder, but they did not let her go.

"Mammy, Syomka's choked himself," the lisping child whined suddenly from the "corner." Akulina broke away again, and ran to the "course." The baby lay quite still, face downwards, in the tub, and its legs were not kicking now. Akulina snatched him out, but the baby did not breathe or move. Akulina threw him on the bed, leaned on her hands, and broke into such a loud, piercing, and terrible peal of laughter, that Mashka, who at first laughed too, stopped up her ears and ran crying out into the entry. The neighbours thronged into the "corner" with weeping and wailing. They carried the baby out and began rubbing it, but it was all useless. Akulina rolled on the bed and laughed, laughed so that horror came upon all who heard that laugh. Only seeing this heterogeneous crowd of men and women, old people and children, thronging the hut, could one conceive of the mass of folk of all sorts living in the "serfs' quarters." Every one fussed, every one talked, many cried, and no one did anything. The carpenter's wife still found persons who had not heard her story, and described anew what a shock her sensitive feelings had received, and how providentially she had been preserved from falling down the ladder. A little old footman, wearing a woman's jacket, described how, in the old master's days, a woman had drowned herself in the pond. The bailiff sent messengers to the village constable and to the priest, and picked out men to keep a watch on the place. The errand-girl Aksyutka, her eyes starting out of her head, kept peering up the opening into the loft; and though she saw nothing there, she could not tear herself away and go to her mistress. Agafea Mihalovna, a maid in the last mistress's time, wept and demanded tea to restore her shattered nerves. Old Granny Anna, with her practised fat hands, reeking with olive oil, laid the little corpse out on the table. The women stood round Akulina and stared mutely at her. The children huddled in corners, peeped at their mother and fell to roaring, then subsided, peeped again, and huddled further away than ever. Boys and men crowded about the steps, and with scared faces gazed at the door and at the windows, seeing and understanding nothing, and asked each other what was the matter. One said that the carpenter had chopped off one of his wife's legs with an axe; another declared that the washerwoman had been brought to bed of triplets; a third asserted that the cook's cat had gone mad and bitten folks: but the truth gradually spread, and at last reached the mistress's ears, and it appears they had not even the wit to break it to her. Yegor in his coarse way had told her bluntly straight out, and so upset the lady's nerves that it was a long while before she could recover from the shock. The crowd was beginning to subside; the carpenter's wife had set her samovar, and was wetting the tea, which made outsiders, not invited to partake of it, feel it unseemly to linger longer. Boys had begun scuffling at the steps. Every one knew by now what had happened; and crossing themselves, they began to separate, when suddenly the cry was heard, "The mistress, the mistress!" and they all crowded together and squeezed close to make way for her, but every one wanted too to see what she was going to do. The mistress, pale and tearful, crossed the threshold into the entry and into Akulina's "corner." Dozens of heads squeezed in and gazed in the doorway. One woman, big with child, was so crushed that she shrieked, but promptly took advantage of the very circumstance to gain a place in front. And who would not want to stare at the mistress in Akulina's "corner"? For the house-serfs it was precisely what the fireworks are at the end of an entertainment. It's sure to be worth seeing if they're letting off fireworks; and sure to be worth seeing if the mistress, in silk and lace, has gone into Akulina's "corner." The mistress went up to Akulina and took her by the hand; but Akulina pulled it away. The old house-serfs shook their heads disapprovingly.

"Akulina!" said the mistress, "you have children, have pity on yourself."

Akulina laughed and got up.

"My children are all silver, all silver. . . . I don't keep paper money," she muttered, speaking rapidly. "I said to Polikey, don't take the paper, and now they've smeared you, smeared you with pitch, pitch and soap, madam. Any scabbiness you've got, it will get rid of directly." And again she chuckled more than ever.

The mistress turned away and asked for the apothecary to come with mustard. "Bring some cold water!" and she began looking for water herself; but catching sight of the dead baby, before whom was standing old Granny Anna, the mistress turned away, and all saw how she hid her face in her handkerchief and burst into tears. Granny Anna (it was a pity the mistress didn't see, she would have appreciated it—it was all done for her benefit too) covered the baby with a piece of linen, straightened his little arm with her fat deft hand; and so shook her head, so pursed up her lips, so sympathetically dropped her eyelids and sighed, that no one could help seeing the goodness of her heart. But the mistress did not see this, and indeed she was incapable of seeing anything. She burst into sobs, was overcome by nervous hysterics, and was supported out into the entry and supported home. "And that was all that came of her visit!" many people reflected, and they began to disperse. Akulina still laughed and talked nonsense. She was led away into another room; they bled her and put mustard plasters on her, applied ice to her head. Yet she remained still understanding nothing, not weeping, but laughing, talking, and doing such things that the good folks who were looking after her could not restrain themselves, and laughed too.

CHAPTER XII

FRIGHT

THE holiday was not a lively one in Pokrovskoe. In spite of the fine weather, people did not come out walking; the girls did not meet together to sing choruses; the factory lads, who came over from the town, did not play on the harmonica nor the balalaica, or flirt with the girls. They all sat in corners; and if they talked, they talked softly, as though some evil one was about and might hear them. In the daytime it was not so bad; but in the evening, when it got dark, the dogs began to howl, and then, as ill-luck would have it, a wind sprang up and howled in the chimneys, and such a panic came over all the inhabitants of the serfs' quarters that those who had candles lighted them before the holy pictures. And who lived alone in a "corner" went in to neighbours to ask them to let him stay the night where there were more people, while those who had to go out to the sheds to feed the cattle would not go, and did not scruple to leave the cattle unfed that night. And the holy water, of which every one kept a bottle, was all used up during that night. Many positively heard some one pacing heavily about the loft that night, and the blacksmith saw a snake fly straight to the loft. In Polikey's "corner" none of the family were left; the children and the mad woman had been removed. There was only the dead baby lying there, and two old women watching over it, and a pilgrim woman, who, in the fervour of her piety, read the Psalter aloud, not over the baby, but simply as a tribute to the whole occasion. This was by the wish of the mistress. These old women and the pilgrim woman heard with their own ears a beam begin shaking and some one groaning overhead just as the verse was being read. When the words, "And God is risen," were read, all became still again. The carpenter's wife invited a crony of hers, and sitting up together, they drank, in the course of that night, all the tea she had laid in to last her a week. They, too, heard the beams creaking overhead, and a noise as though sacks were falling down. The peasant watchmen kept up the courage of the house serfs, or they

would have died of fright that night. The peasants lay in the entry on hay; and afterwards asserted that they too had heard wonderful things in the loft, though on the night itself they conversed very calmly together about the recruiting, munched bread, scratched themselves, and, worst of all, made the entry so reek of the peculiar peasant smell, that the carpenter's wife when she passed spat in disgust and abused them for it. However that might be, the suicide was still hanging in the loft, and it seemed as though the evil one himself had spread huge wings over the serfs' quarters that night, making his power manifest, and coming closer than ever before to these people. So at least they all felt. I can't say whether this was true. I believe indeed that it was altogether untrue. I believe that if on that terrible night some brave soul had taken a candle or a lantern, and sanctifying himself, or even not sanctifying himself, with the sign of the cross, had gone up into the loft, and slowly putting to flight the terrors of the night with the candle, and lighting up the beams, the sand, the fluepipe covered with cobwebs, and the cape forgotten by the carpenter's wife, had made his way to Polikey; and if, mastering his terrors, he had raised the lantern to level of the face, he would have seen the familiar, lean body, with the legs touching the ground (the cord had grown slack), bending lifeless on one side, the shirt collar unbuttoned and no cross to be seen under it, the head sunk on the breast, and the good-natured face with its open sightless eyes, and the meek, guilty smile and stern repose, and stillness over everything. In reality, the carpenter's wife, huddled up in the corner of her bed, with dishevelled locks and scared eyes, describing how she heard the sacks falling, was a great deal more awful and terrible than Polikey, though his cross had been taken off and was lying on the beam.

Up yonder, that is, at the mistress's house, the same terror reigned as in the serfs' quarters. The old lady's room reeked of eau-de-cologne and medicine. Dunyasha was melting yellow wax and making ointment. What the ointment was for precisely, I don't know; but I know it was always made when the mistress was unwell. And now she was so upset that she was quite ill. Dunyasha's aunt had come to stay the night with her to keep up her courage. There were four of them with the errand-girl in the maid's room talking softly together.

"Who's to go for the oil?" said Dunyasha.

"Not, on any account, Avdotya Mihalovna—I'm not going!" the second maid answered resolutely.

"Nonsense! Aksyutka and you go together."

"I'll run alone, I'm not afraid of anything," said Aksyutka; but her heart failed her as she spoke.

"Well, run along, there's a good girl; ask Granny Anna for a glassful, and don't spill it as you bring it," Dunyasha said to her.

Aksyutka picked up her skirt with one hand; and though she was consequently unable to swing both arms, she swung one with twice the energy in front of her line of advance, and flew off. She was frightened; and she felt that if she were to see or hear anything whatever, even her own living mother,

she would drop with terror. Shutting her eyes, she flew along the familiar path.

CHAPTER XIII

THE PEASANT

"Is the mistress asleep, or not?" was suddenly asked close to Aksyutka in a peasant's deep voice. She opened her eyes, which had till then been closed, and saw a figure that seemed to her taller than the hut before her. She squealed, and whisked back so quickly, that her petticoat could not keep pace with her. In one bound she was on the steps, in another she was in the maid's room, and with a wild yell she flung herself on the bed. Dunyasha, her aunt, and the other maid were numb with terror; but before they had time to recover themselves, slow, heavy, and hesitating steps were heard in the passage and at the door. Dunyasha rushed in to her mistress, dropping the ointment; the second maid hid herself behind the skirts hanging on the wall; the aunt, a person of stronger will, would have held the door, but the door opened, and a peasant came into the room. It was Dutlov, in his boats of shoes. Taking no notice of the girls' terror, he looked about for the holy picture; and not making out the little image in the left corner, crossed himself, bowing to the shelf with the tea-cups, laid his cap down in the window, and thrusting his hand far under his coat, as though he wanted to scratch his armpit, he took out the letter with the five brown seals, stamped with the anchor. Dunyasha's aunt clutched at her chest; with effort she articulated—

"How you did terrify me, Semyon Naumitch! I can't utter a wo—ord. I fairly thought the end had come."

"How could you?" protested the second girl, popping her head out from under the skirts.

"And you've upset the mistress too!" said Dunyasha, coming in at the door. "Why do you come creeping up the maids' staircase without asking leave? A regular peasant!"

Dutlov, making no apology, repeated that he wanted to see the mistress.

"She's not well," said Dunyasha.

At that moment Aksyutka went off into such an unseemly loud crowing laugh that she had to stuff her head again into the pillows of the bed, from which, in spite of the threats of Dunyasha and her aunt, she could not remove it for a whole hour without a loud crow, as though something had exploded in her rosy throat and red cheeks. It struck her as so funny that they had all been so scared, and she hid her head again, and flapped her slipper, and writhed all over, as though she were in convulsions.

Dutlov stopped, looked at her attentively, as though he wanted to ascertain what was happening to her; but unable to discover what was wrong, he turned away, and continued speaking.

"To be sure, then, it's a matter of great importance," he said. "Only tell her that a peasant has found the letter with the money."

"What money?"

Before taking this message, Dunyasha read the address and cross-examined Dutlov as to where and how he had found the money, which Polikey was to have brought from the town. After having learnt every detail, and

thrust the errand-girl, still guffawing, out into the passage, Dunyasha went in to her mistress; but, to her surprise, her mistress still would not see him, and said nothing coherent to Dunyasha.

"I know nothing about it, and I don't want to know," said the old lady. "What peasant or what money? I can see no one, and I want to see no one. Let him leave me in peace."

"What am I to do?" said Dutlov, turning the envelope over; "it's not a trifling sum. Is anything written on it?" he asked Dunyasha, who once more read him the address.

Dutlov still seemed incredulous. He had hoped that may be the money did not belong to the mistress, and that the address had not been read him right, but Dunyasha confirmed the reading of it. He sighed, put the envelope in his bosom, and was about to leave.

"I suppose I must give it to the police constable," he said.

"Stay, I'll try again; I'll speak to her," Dunyasha stopped him, attentively watching the disappearance of the envelope into the peasant's coat. "Give the letter here."

Dutlov drew it out again, but did not at once put it into Dunyasha's outstretched hand.

"Say it was found on the road by Dutlov—Semyon."

"Oh, give it here?"

"I did think it was just—a letter, but a soldier read that there was money in it."

"Oh, give it me!"

"I didn't even venture to go home, so as. . . ." Dutlov began again, still not parting from the precious envelope. "So you put it before her."

Dunyasha took the envelope, and once more went in to her mistress.

"Oh, mercy Dunyasha!" said her mistress in a reproachful voice; "don't talk to me about that money. If I but think of that little babe . . ."

"The peasant, madam, doesn't know to whom it's your pleasure for him to hand it," Dunyasha said again.

Her mistress broke open the envelope, shuddered as soon as she saw the money, and pondered.

"Horrible money! what evil it does!" she said.

"It's Dutlov, madam. Do you bid him go, or is it your pleasure to come out and speak to him? Is the money all safe?" inquired Dunyasha.

"I don't want this money; it's unlucky money. Think what it's done! Tell him to take it himself if he likes," the lady said suddenly, feeling for Dunyasha's hand. "Yes, yes, yes!" she repeated to the amazed Dunyasha; "let him take it altogether, and do what he likes with it."

"Fifteen hundred roubles," observed Dunyasha, smiling as though at a child.

"Let him take them, all of them!" her mistress repeated impatiently. "How is it you don't understand me? That money's unlucky; never speak to me of it! Let that peasant take what he found. Go long! There, do go now!"

Dunyasha went into the maid's room.

"Was it all there?" asked Dutlov.

"You count them yourself," said Dunyasha, giving him the envelope. "My orders are to hand it to you."

Dutlov put his cap under his arm, and, bending forward, he began counting the money.

"Has she no reckoning beads?"

Dutlov supposed that his mistress was so stupid that she could not reckon the money, and so had told him to do so.

"You can count it at home! It's for you—your money!" said Dunyasha angrily. "'I don't want,' says she, 'to see it; give it to the man who brought it.'"

Dutlov, still in his stooping posture, fixed his eyes on Dunyasha. Dunyasha's aunt fairly flung up her hands.

"My goodness gracious! What luck God's given you! My gracious goodness!"

The second maid would not believe it.

"Why, you're joking, Avdotya Nikolaevna, surely?"

"Joking, indeed! She told me to give it to the peasant. There, take your money, and get along, do," said Dunyasha, not disguising her annoyance. "One man's sorrow is another's luck!"

"It's no joking matter, fifteen hundred roubles!" said the aunt.

"More," put in Dunyasha. "Well, now you can put up a ten kopeck candle to Saint Mikola," said Dunyasha sarcastically. "Why, are you struck silly? And a good thing if it had been a poor man, but he has a lot of his own."

Dutlov at last grasped that it was not a joke, and began to put together and fold up in the envelope the notes he had unfolded to count; but his hands shook, and he kept glancing at the maids to assure himself it was not a joke.

"Why, he hardly knows what he's doing, he's so pleased," said Dunyasha, affecting to feel none the less contemptuous both of the peasant and the money. "Let me put them up for you."

And she would have taken the notes; but Dutlov would not give them her. He crumpled up the notes, stuffed them still further into his bosom, and took up his cap.

"Are you glad?"

"I don't know what to say! Why really . . ."

He could not finish; he waved his hand, grinned, and, almost crying, went out.

The bell rang in the old lady's room.

"Well, have you given them to him?"

"Yes."

"Well, was he very much pleased?"

"He's quite beside himself."

"Oh, fetch him in. I'll ask him how he found them. Fetch him here; I can't come out."

Dunyasha ran and found the peasant in the entry. Without waiting to put on his cap, he had pulled out his purse, and was bending down, untying it, while he held the notes in his teeth. He fancied, perhaps, that the money was not quite his own till he had it in his purse. When Dunyasha called him, he was panicstricken.

"What is it, Avdotya—Advotya Mikolavna? Does she want to take them back? If only you'd stand up for me, for God's sake, and I'll bring you some honey."

"I dare say!"

Again the door was opened, and the peasant was led in to see his mistress. He felt anything but cheerful. "Oh, she's going to take it back!" something made him believe, as he walked through the room, lifting his whole leg high up as though getting through high grass, and trying not to let his plaited shoes creak. He did not take in, did not even see anything around him. He walked by a looking-glass, saw flowers of some sort, saw a peasant in bark shoes kicking up his feet, a gentleman with one eye painted on the wall, some sort of green tub, and something white . . . And behold that something white began talking; it was his mistress. He could make out nothing of what she said; he simply stared with round eyes. He did not know where he was, and saw everything in a sort of fog.

"Is that you, Dutlov?"

"Yes, madam. As it was, I never touched it," said he. "I'm not glad at having found it, so help me God. How I did drive the horse home!"

"Well, you're in luck!" she said, with a smile of supercilious good-nature. "Take it, take it for yourself!"

He could only roll his eyes blankly.

"I'm glad that you've got the money. God grant it has come when it was wanted! Well, are you glad?"

"Glad! Oh, so glad, ma'am! I'll always be praying to God for you! I'm so glad that, thank God, our lady's alive. That's all I had to do with it."

"How did you find it?"

"To be sure, we could always try our best for our lady, not but . . ."

"He's in a regular muddle, madam," said Dunyasha.

"I'd taken my nephew as a recruit, I was driving back, and on the road I found it. Polikey must have dropped it by accident."

"Well, you can go, you can go, my good man! I'm glad you found it."

"So glad, ma'am!" said the peasant. Afterwards he recollected that he had not thanked her, and did not know how to repair this omission properly. The old lady and Dunyasha smiled while he stepped back again as though over high grass, and with difficulty refrained from breaking into a trot. He still kept fancying they would stop him and take the notes back.

CHAPTER XIV

POLICE!

On getting into the fresh air, Dutlov moved off the road to the lime-trees, untied his sash so as to get at his purse more easily, and began putting away the notes. His lips twitched and worked, though he did not utter a sound. After putting away the money and fastening his sash, he crossed himself and walked away along the path, staggering like a drunken man, so absorbed he was in the thought that surged in his brain. Suddenly he saw the figure of a peasant coming to meet him. He called; it was Efim, who was walking round the serfs' quarters with an oak cudgel, as a watchman.

"Ah, Uncle Semyon!" Efimka cried joyfully, coming closer. (Efimka had been feeling scared all alone.) "Well, have you been seeing the recruits off, uncle?"

"Yes. And what are you doing?"

"Why, they've set me here to watch over Polikey, who's hanged himself."

"Where is he?"

"Yonder in the loft, they say he's hanging," answered Efimka, pointing with his stick in the darkness towards the roof of the hut.

Dutlov looked in that direction; and though he saw nothing, he puckered his brows, screwed up his eyes, and shook his head.

"The police constable has come," said Efimka; "the coachman was saying so. They're going to take him away at once. It's a fearful thing at night, uncle! I won't go at night—not for anything—if they tell me to go up to the loft. Yegor Mihalovitch may be the death of me, but I won't go."

"A sin it is, a sin indeed!" Dutlov repeated, evidently for the sake of doing the proper thing, without in the least thinking of what he was saying, and he would have gone on his way. But the voice of Yegor Mihalovitch stopped him.

"Hi, watchman, come here!" Yegor Mihalovitch shouted from the step.

Efimka called back in reply.

"But who is there with you?"

"Dutlov."

"You come too, Semyon."

As he came closer into the light of the lantern carried by the coachman, Dutlov made out Yegor Mihalovitch and an undersized functionary in a cap with a cockade and a cloak; it was the district police constable.

"Here's the old man will come with us," said Yegor Mihalovitch, on seeing him.

The old man felt qualms; but there was no getting out of it.

"And you, Efimka, you're a bold young fellow, run up into the loft where he hanged himself, and set the ladder straight for his honour to get up."

Efimka, who was most unwilling to go into the hut, ran towards it, his bark shoes stumping like logs of wood.

The police constable struck a light and lit a pipe. He lived two versts away, and had only lately been cruelly reprimanded by the police captain for drunkenness, and was therefore just now in a very fever of zeal. He arrived on the scene at ten o'clock in the evening, and insisted on viewing the body without delay. Yegor Mihalovitch asked Dutlov what brought them there. On the way Dutlov told the bailiff about finding the money and what the mistress had done. Dutlov said that he was coming to ask Yegor Mihalovitch's sanction. The bailiff, to Dutlov's horror, asked for the envelope and examined it. The police constable, too, took the envelope into his hands and shortly and drily inquired into details.

"Come, the money's lost!" thought Dutlov, and he even began to apologise for his part in the affair. But the police constable gave him back the money.

"Well, the peasant's in luck!" said he.

"It's come just right for him," said Yegor Mihalovitch; "he's just taken his nephew for a recruit; now he'll buy him out."

"Oh," said the police constable, and he went on in front.

"You'll buy him out, Ilyushka, won't you?" said Yegor Mihalovitch.

"Buy him out? Will the money be enough? and may be it's too late."

"That's for you to decide," said the bailiff, and both of them followed the police constable.

They reached the serf's hut, in the porch of which the stinking watchmen were waiting with a lantern.

Dutlov walked behind them. The watchmen had a guilty air, possibly due only to a consciousness of the odour they had introduced into the place, for they had done no harm. Every one was silent.

"Where is he?" asked the police constable.

"Here," whispered Yegor Mihalovitch. "Efimka," he added, "you're a bold young chap, go on ahead with a lantern."

Efimka had already put the board straight above, and seemed to have lost all fear. Taking two or three steps at a time, he clambered up in front with a cheerful face, looking round to light the way for the police constable, who was followed by Yegor Mihalovitch. When they were out of sight, Dutlov, who had put one foot on the first step, sighed and stopped short. Two minutes passed, their steps died away in the loft; they had, doubtless, reached the body.

"Uncle, he's calling you!" Efimka shouted through the hatch.

Dutlov went up. The police constable and Yegor Mihalovitch stood in the light of a lantern with their upper part only visible behind a beam; behind them stood some one else with his back turned. It was Polikey. Dutlov climbed over the beam and stood still, crossing himself.

"Turn him round, lad!" said the police constable. No one moved.

"Efimka, you're a bold young chap!" said Yegor Mihalovitch.

The bold young chap strode across the beam; and turning Polikey round, stood beside him, looking with the most cheerful expression for Polikey to the authorities, as a showman exhibiting an albino or Julia Fastrana looks from the public to the monster he is showing them, ready to execute all the wishes of the spectators.

"Turn him again!"

Polikey was turned again, with a slight swing of the arms and a scrape of the foot on the sand.

"Lift him; take him down!"

"You bid them cut him down, Vassily Borisovitch?" said Yegor Mihalovitch. "Give me an axe, mates!"

The watchmen and Dutlov had to be told twice before they came up. The bold young chap dealt with Polikey as though he were a sheep's carcass. At last they cut the rope, took down the body, and covered it up. The police constable said that the doctor would come next day, and dismissed them all.

CHAPTER XV

THE DISCHARGE

DUTLOV walked homewards, moving his lips. At first he felt uneasy; but, as he got nearer the village, this feeling passed away, and the feeling of gladness sank more and more deeply into his heart. In the village he heard sounds of singing and drunken voices. Dutlov never drank, and now he went straight home. It was late when he walked into the hut. His old wife was asleep. The elder son and the grandsons were asleep on the stove, the second son in the loft. Ilyusha's wife was the only one not asleep. In her dirty working-day blouse, with nothing on her head, she was sitting on the bench wailing. She did not come out to open the door to her uncle, but only went on more vigorously with her dirge and her wailing as he entered the hut. In the opinion of the old mother, her dirge was an exceedingly fine and

creditable performance, in spite of the fact that at her years she could not have had much practice.

The old woman got up and began getting supper for her husband. Dutlov drove Ilyushka's wife away from the table. "Sh! sh!" he said. Aksinia got up, and lying down on the bench, did not cease wailing. Without uttering a word, the old woman laid the table and cleared it again. The old man too did not say a word. After praying to God, he washed his hands; and taking his reckoning frame from a nail, he went off to the loft. There he first whispered to the old woman, then the old woman went out, and he began rattling the reckoning beads. At last he closed the lid of a chest with a bang, and crept down into the storeroom under the floor. He was a long while busily engaged in the loft and the underground storeroom. When he came back to the living-room it was all dark—the splinter was not burning. The old woman, by day usually so quiet and unobtrusive, lay outstretched near the stove, and filled the whole hut with her snoring. The noisy young wife too was asleep, and her breathing could not be heard. She had fallen asleep on the bench, just as she was, without undressing or putting anything under her head. Dutlov said his prayers, then looked at Ilyushka's wife, shook his head, put out the splinter he had lighted, clambered on to the stove, and lay down beside his little grandson. In the darkness he dropped his bark shoes down from the stove and lay down on his back, looking at the crossbeam, over the stove, which was faintly visible above his head, and listening to the beetles rustling over the walls, to the sighs, to the snoring, to the scratching of one foot against another, and to the sounds of the cattle in the yard. For a long while he could not get to sleep; the moon rose, it grew lighter in the room, he could see Aksinia in the corner, and something which he could not clearly distinguish; he could not see whether it was a cloak his son had forgotten, or a tub the women had set there, or some one standing there. Whether he were dozing or not, he looked more intently again. . . . It seemed as though the spirit of darkness, who had driven Polikey to his fearful deed, and whose proximity the serfs had been aware of that night,—it seemed that that spirit had winged his way to the village, to Dutlov's hut, where lay the money *he* had used for Polikey's ruin. Anyway Dutlov felt *him* there, and Dutlov was ill at ease. He couldn't sleep nor move. Seeing something which he could not make out clearly, he thought of Ilyushka with his hands tied, thought of the face of Aksinia and her creditable dirge, thought of Polikey with his swaying wrists. Suddenly, it seemed to the old man that some one passed by the window. "What's that?" he thought. "Or is it the village elder come to give notice of something?" "How did he open the door?" wondered the, old man hearing steps in the passage, "or didn't the old woman put up the bar when she went out into the passage?" The dog howled in the backyard, and *he* walked about the passage, as the old man used to tell afterwards, as though he were looking for the door, passed it by, began fumbling about the wall again, stumbled against a barrel, and it rumbled. And again *he* fumbled about as

though feeling for the handle. Then *he* got hold of the handle. A shiver ran down the old man. Then *he* pulled at the handle and entered in the shape of a man. Dutlov knew that it was *he*. He tried to make the sign of the cross, but could not. *He* went up to the table on which there lay a cloth, pulled it off, flung it on the floor, and climbed on to the stove. The old man became aware that *he* had taken the shape of Polikey. He grinned, his arms dangled. He climbed on to the stove, lay down straight on the old man, and began strangling him.

"My money!" cried Polikey.

"Let me go, I won't do any harm," Semyon tried to say, and could not.

Polikey was crushing him with all the weight of a mountain of stone pressing on his chest. Dutlov knew that if he were to repeat a prayer, *he* would let him go, and he knew what prayer he ought to recite, but the prayer would not be uttered. His grandson was sleeping beside him. The boy screamed shrilly and began to cry—his grandfather was squeezing him against the wall. The child's cry freed the old man's lips. "May the Lord arise," articulated Dutlov. *He* fell back a little. "And scatter His enemies," mumbled Dutlov. *He* got off the stove. Dutlov heard his two feet thud on the floor. Dutlov went on repeating prayers he knew; he repeated them all in succession. *He* went towards the door, passed by the table, and slammed the door so that the hut shook. Yet every one slept on except the old man and his grandchild. The grandfather repeated his prayers, trembling all over, while the child cried as he dropped asleep and clung to the old man. Everything was quiet again. The grandfather lay without stirring. The cock crowed on the other side of the wall just at Dutlov's ear. He heard the hens beginning to stir, heard the young cock trying to crow like the old one and failing. Something moved at the old man's feet. It was the cat; she leapt on her soft pads from the stove to the floor, and began mewing at the door. The grandfather got up, raised the window; it was dark and dirty in the street; he saw the shafts of the cart close to the window. Crossing himself, he went out barefoot to the horses; and here it was evident that it was the Evil One that had come to them. The mare, standing under cover in the lean-to shed, had caught her leg in the reins, and spilt over her chaff. Lifting her leg, she turned her head looking for her master. The colt was rolling in the dung-heap. The old man put him on his legs, freed the mare from the reins, put the food for her, and went back into the hut. The old woman had got up and lighted a splinter. "Wake the lads, I'm going to the town," and lighting a wax candle from the holy picture lamp, he crept with it into the storeroom under the floor. When he came back, there were fires alight, not at Dutlov's only, but at all the neighbours'. The lads had got up and were already making ready. The women were coming in and out with pails and tubs of milk. Ignat was getting one cart out, while the second son was greasing the other. The young wife was not wailing now, but was sitting in the hut on a bench, ready dressed, with a kerchief on her head, waiting till it should be time to start

for the town to say good-bye to her husband.

The old man seemed particularly severe. To no one did he say a single word; he put on his new long coat, fastened his sash, and with all Polikey's money in his bosom he went to see Yegor Mihalovitch.

"Don't you linger!" he shouted to Ignat, who was turning the wheel round on the greased axle of the tilted cart. "I'll come in a minute. Have everything ready!"

The bailiff was only just up and was drinking his tea; he was going himself to the town to deliver the recruits.

"What do you want?" he asked.

"I want, Yegor Mihalovitch, to buy off my lad. Graciously aid me! You said last night that you knew of a substitute in the town. Instruct me—we are all in the dark."

"Why, have you changed your mind?"

"Yes, Yegor Mihalovitch; I feel for him; he's my brother's son. However he may behave, I feel for him. Great sin has it brought about, this money! So graciously aid me, instruct me!" he said, bowing low.

As he always did on such occasions, Yegor Mihalovitch smacked his lips for a long while without speaking, with an air of profound thought. Then, having considered the matter, he wrote two notes and told him how and what to do in the town.

When Dutlov returned home, the young wife had already set off with Ignat, and the piebald pot-bellied mare stood at the gate all ready harnessed. Dutlov broke a switch out of the hedge, seated himself on the box, and set off. He drove the mare so violently that she was almost shaken to pieces and Dutlov did not look at her for fear of being moved by her plight. He was fretted by the fear of being somehow late, of Ilyushka's being sent off as a soldier, and the devil's money being left on his hands.

I will not attempt to describe all Dutlov's proceedings that morning; I will only say that he was particularly successful. The man for whom Yegor Mihalovitch had given him a letter had in readiness a volunteer who had already spent twenty-three roubles of his purchase-money, and had been passed by the medical board. The man, who was disposing of him, wanted four hundred silver roubles for him, while the purchaser, a tradesman, persisted in begging him to come down to three hundred. Dutlov concluded the bargain in a couple of words. "Three hundred and twenty-five will you take?" he said, holding out his hand with an expression by which it was obvious at once that he was ready to give more. The man drew back his hand and persisted in asking four hundred. "Won't you take three hundred and twenty-five?" repeated Dutlov, grasping the bargainer's right hand in his left and threatening to clap his right hand down on it. "Won't you? . . . Well God be with you!" he added suddenly bringing his hand down and turning away with a swing of his whole person. "It seems it was to be so; take the fifty then. Get out the discharge. Bring in the young fellow. And now for the earnest-money. Two red notes it will be eh?"

And Dutlov undid his sash and got out the money.

Though the man did not draw back

his hands he still seemed somehow not to agree; and without accepting the earnest-money, began talking about standing treat and something for the goodwill of the volunteer.

"Beware of sin," Dutlov repeated, thrusting the money upon him; "we must all die!" he repeated, in a tone so mild, edifying, and convincing, that the man said—

"So be it, then!" clapped hands together once more, and began praying. "God give luck!" he said.

They waked up the volunteer, who was still sleeping off his drinking-bout of the previous day. For some unknown reason they looked him carefully over, and all went off to the board. The volunteer was in good spirits; he asked for rum to clear his head after drinking, and Dutlov gave him some money to get some. His courage only failed him when they were entering the hall of the recruiting board. For a long while the elder man in his blue greatcoat, and the volunteer in his short, full-skirted coat, with lifted eyebrows and round eyes, were standing about in the entrance-hall; a long while they spent in whispering together here, asking for some direction, seeking some one, taking off their caps, and bowing to each copying-clerk in turn, and listening with an air of profundity to the decision delivered by the copying-clerk they knew personally. All hope of completing the business that day seemed abandoned; and the volunteer had begun to regain his cheerfulness and easy manners, when Dutlov caught sight of Yegor Mihalovitch, at once attached himself to him, and began imploring his aid, and bowing. Yegor Mihalovitch helped him to such good purpose, that by three o'clock the volunteer, to his great discomfort and surprise, had been brought before the board; and to the general satisfaction, as it seemed, of every one, from the sentry to the president, he was undressed, accepted, dressed, and allowed to depart. And five minutes later Dutlov had counted out the money, received the discharge; and taking leave of the volunteer and his patron, set off on his way to the lodgings where the recruits from Pokrovskoe were staying. Ilyushka and his young wife were sitting in the corner of the tavern kitchen; and as soon as the old man entered, they ceased talking, and stared at him with a look at once submissive and hostile. The old man—as always—prayed to God, unfastened his sash, took out a paper, and called into the hut his elder son Ignat and Ilyushka's mother, who was in the yard.

"Beware of sin, Ilyushka," said he, going up to his nephew. "Last night you said something to me. . . . Do you think I don't feel for you? I remember how my brother bade me care for you. If I had had the power, would I have let you go? God has brought me luck, and I have not grudged it you. Here is the paper," he said, laying the discharge on the table, and carefully spreading it out with his stiff, crooked fingers.

All the Pokrovskoe peasants, the innkeeper's workmen, and even a crowd of outsiders, came running into the hut from the yard. All guessed what was going on, but no one interrupted the old man's solemn discourse.

"Here it is, the paper! Four hundred roubles I have given for it. Don't reproach your uncle."

Ilyushka got up, but he was silent, not knowing what to say. His lips quivered with excitement; his old mother went up to him sobbing, and would have flung herself on his neck, but deliberately and peremptorily the old man held her back by the arm and went on speaking.

"You said a word to me yesterday," the old man repeated once more; "with that word you stabbed me to the heart. Your father, as he lay dying, gave you into my charge; you've been to me like my own son; and if I've wronged you in any way, well, we all live in sin. That's so, good Christian folk, eh?" He turned to the peasants standing round. "Here's your own mother too here and your young wife, and here is the discharge for you. God be with it, the money! And forgive me, for Christ's sake."

And turning up the skirt of his coat, he dropped deliberately on his knees, and bowed down at the feet of Ilyushka and his wife. In vain the young people tried to restrain him; not before he had touched the ground with his head did he get up; then, shaking himself, he sat down on the bench. Ilyushka's mother and wife howled with delight. Words of approval were heard in the crowd. "In the truth, in God's way, indeed!" said one. "What is money? You can't buy the lad for money!" said another. "What happiness!" said a third, "a righteous man, that's what he is!" Only the peasants who were to go as recruits said nothing, and slipped quietly out into the yard.

Two hours later the Dutlovs' two carts were driving out of the outskirts of the town. In the first cart, drawn by the piebald mare with the pinched-up stomach and sweating neck, sat the old man and Ignat. In the back of the cart rattled strings of pots and of fancy bread. In the second cart, which no one was driving, the young wife sat sedately and happily beside her mother-in-law, both with kerchiefs on their heads. The young wife was holding a flask under her apron. Ilyushka sat swaying to and fro on the front seat, with his back to the horse. With a flushed face he was bending forward nibbling at a roll, and talking incessantly. And the voices and the rumble of the cart on the pavement, and the snorting of the horses, all mingled into a general note of merriment. The horses, swishing their tails, moved at a more rapid trot as they recognised the way home. No one who walked or drove by them could help looking round at the merry family party.

Just as they drove out of the town the Dutlovs began to overtake a party of recruits. A group of them were standing in a ring round a tavern. One recruit wore his grey forage-cap pulled back on the nape of his neck; and with the unnatural expression given a man by the fore part of his head being shaven close, was jauntily strumming on the balalaica. Another, without a cap on his head, held a flask of vodka in one hand, while he danced in the middle of the ring. Ignat stopped the horse and got down to tighten the traces. All the Dutlovs stared with curiosity, approval, and amusement at the man who was dancing. The recruit seemed to see no one, but he was aware that the public admiring him had grown larger, and this gave him fresh energy and skill. He danced briskly. His brows were knitted, his flushed face

was rigid, his mouth wore a fixed smile, which had lost by now all meaning. It seemed as though all the energies of his soul were bent on moving one foot after the other with the utmost possible speed, now on the toe and now on the heel. Sometimes he would suddenly stop short, winking to the player of the balalaica, and the latter would begin striking all the strings more briskly than ever, and even tapping on the case with his knuckles. The recruit would keep standing still; but even when he stood still, he looked as if he were dancing all over. Suddenly he began moving slowly, shaking his shoulders, and all at once leaped into the air, threw up his heels as he went up, and with a wild shriek came down in a squatting position. The boys laughed, the women shook their heads, the men smiled approvingly. The old sergeant stood unmoved beside the dancer with an expression that seemed to say, "That seems a monstrous fine thing to you, but we know it all so well." The player on the balalaica was evidently tired; he looked round lazily, making a false chord. All of a sudden he tapped the case with his fingers, and the dance was over.

"Hi, Alyoha!" said the musician to the dancer, pointing to Dutlov; "yonder's your sponsor! . . ."

"Where? Ah, my dear good friend!" cried Alyoha; he was the recruit Dutlov had purchased as a substitute. With weary legs, stumbling forwards, and lifting a flask of vodka over his head, he came up to the cart. "Mishka, a glass!" he shouted. "Master! my dear good friend! This is a pleasure, really!" he cried, lurching tipsily against the cart, and he began offering vodka to the peasants and the women. The men took some, the women refused. "My dear soul, what present can I make you?" cried Alyoha, embracing the old woman.

A woman selling eatables was standing in the crowd. Alyoha caught sight of her, snatched her tray from her, and scattered its contents into the cart. "Never fear; I'll pa-a-ay, damn you!" he wailed in a lachrymose voice, and at once pulled out of his trousers a pouch with money in it, and flung it to Mishka.

He stood with his elbows on the cart and looked with wet eyes at the party sitting in it.

"Which is the mother?" he asked. "You, eh? I must make her an offering too."

He pondered an instant and felt in his pocket; then pulled out a new handkerchief folded up, took off the strip of linen he wore as a sash under his soldier's cloak, hurriedly untied a red kerchief from his neck, crumpled them all up together, and thrust them into the old woman's lap.

"There's an offering for you!" he said, in a voice which grew more and more subdued.

"What for? Thanks, my dear! Why, what a good-natured lad 'tis!" said the old woman, addressing old Dutlov, who had come up to their cart.

Alyoha sank into complete silence and stupefaction, and his head sank lower and lower, as though he were falling asleep.

"It's for you I'm going, for you I'm ruined!" he said. "That's why I give you presents too."

"I dare say he's got a mother too,"

said some one in the crowd. "Such a good-natured lad!"

Alyoha raised his head.

"I've a mother," he said, "and a father too. They've all cast me off. Listen, old mother," he added, taking Ilyushka's mother by the hand. "I've made you a present. You listen to me, for Christ's sake. Go to Vodnoe village, ask there for old Mother Nikonov —she's my own mother, d'ye see?—and tell that same old woman, Mother Nikonov—the third hut from the end, the one with the new well—tell her that Alyoha, your son . . . that is . . . Musician, strike up!" he shouted.

And he began dancing again, talking still, and flung the flask with the rest of the vodka on the ground.

Ignat got into the cart and was driving away.

"Good-bye, God bless you!" said the old woman, wrapping her cloak round her.

Alyoha stopped all at once.

"You go to the devil!" he shouted, shaking his clenched fist at them. "Your mother be . . . !"

"O Lord," said Ilyushka's mother, crossing herself.

Ignat urged on the mare, and the carts rattled on again. The recruit Alyoha remained standing in the middle of the road, and shaking his clenched fists, with a look of fury on his face, abused the peasants with all the violence he was capable of.

"What did you stop for? Go on! Devils, cannibals!" he shouted, "you won't escape me! . . . Devils, low clod-hoppers!"

At that word his voice broke, and as he stood, he fell flat on the ground.

Soon the Dutlovs got out into the open country, and looking back, saw no more of the crowd of recruits. After driving five versts further at a walking pace, Ignat got down from the cart, where his father had dropped asleep, and walked alongside Ilyushka's cart.

The two of them together emptied the flask of vodka they had brought from the town. Soon after, Ilyushka began singing; the women joined in with him. Ignat shouted gaily in tune with the song. A cheerful-looking posting-chaise came flying along to meet them. The driver shouted briskly to his horses as he passed the two festive carts; the postillion looked round with a wink at the flushed faces of the peasants and the women, swaying in time to their merry song in the cart.

Two Hussars

CHAPTER I

THE COUNT

IN the early years of the nineteenth century, in the days when there were as yet no railways nor macadamised roads, no gas nor stearine candles, no low sofas with springs nor unlacquered furniture, no disillusioned young men with eyeglasses nor liberal lady philosophers, no charming *dames aux caméllias* such as have become so numerous in our times: in those naïve days when people travelling from Moscow to Petersburg in their chariot or family coach took with them a complete commissariat of cooked provisions, drove for eight days and nights over the soft, dusty, or muddy road, and put their faith in Pozharsky cutlets, in Valdai bells, and dough rings; when in the long autumn evenings they burned guttering tallow candles to light up a family circle of twenty or thirty persons, and for balls stuck wax and spermaceti candles into candelabra; when furniture was arranged symmetrically; when our fathers were young not only from the absence of wrinkles and grey hair; when they fought duels over ladies, and, from the other end of the room, flew to pick up handkerchiefs dropped by accident or design; when our mothers wore short waists and huge sleeves, and settled family questions by the drawing of lots; when fascinating *dames aux caméllias* shunned the light of day —in those naïve days of masonic lodges, Martinistes, the Tugendbund, in the days of Miloradovitch, Davidov and Pushkin—in those days there was an assembly of the local gentry in the provincial town of K., and the elections of the representatives of the nobility were just over.

"Oh, very well, in the drawing-room then," said a young officer, in the greatcoat and forage-cap of a hussar. He had just got out of a travelling sledge, and was entering the best hotel in the town of K.

"The assembly, your Excellency, has been such an immense one," said the waiter, who had already succeeded in learning from the officer's servant that the hussar's name was Count Turbin, and so styled him "Your Excellency." 'The lady from Afremovo, with her daughters, promised to be leaving this evening; so if your honour will be pleased to take number eleven, when it is vacant," he said, stepping softly in front of the count along the corridor, and continually looking back.

In the public room, near the full-length portrait of the Emperor Alexander, which was black all over, several men were sitting at a little table over their champagne, in all probability representatives of the local gentry, and a little on one side were some travelling merchants in blue cloaks.

Entering the room and calling in Blücher, a huge grey dog he had brought with him, the count flung off his coat, which was still covered with frost about the collar, asked for vodka, and in his blue satin tunic sat down to the table and entered into conversation with the gentlemen. The latter, favourably disposed to the stranger at once by his fine and open demeanour, offered him a glass of champagne. The count tossed off at a draught a glass of vodka, and then he, too, ordered a bottle to regale his new acquaintances with. The sledge-driver came in to ask for something for vodka.

"Sashka!" shouted the count, "give him something."

The driver went out with Sashka and came back again, with money in his hand.

"Why, your 'Slency, didn't I do my best for your honour? Half a rouble you promised me, but he's given me a quarter."

"Sashka! give him a rouble!"

Sashka stared with a downcast expression at the driver's feet.

"That's enough for him," he said in a bass voice; "and besides, I've no more money left."

The count took out of his note-book all that was left in it—two five-rouble notes—and gave one to the driver, who kissed his hand and went out.

"See what we've come to," said the count, "the last five roubles."

"In true hussar style, count," said one of the gentlemen, smiling. His moustaches, his voice, and a certain swagger in his gait unmistakably betokened the retired cavalryman. "Are you intending to stay here long, count?"

"I must get some money, else I shouldn't be staying long. And there are no rooms either, damn them, in this cursed inn . . ."

"Permit me, count," replied the cavalryman, "won't you join me? I'm putting up here—number seven. If you won't object to sleeping there for a while. But you must stay three days with us. There's a ball this evening at the marshal's. How delighted he would be to see you!"

"Yes, indeed, count, pay us a little visit," put in another of the group, a handsome young man. "Why hurry away? It only comes once in three years, you know—the provincial election. You should at least have a look at our young ladies, count."

"Sashka! get out my linen; I'm going to the baths," said the count, getting up. "And then we'll see, may be, I might look in at the marshal's."

Then he called the waiter to speak

to him about something, to which the waiter responded, grinning, "All that can be arranged," and went out.

"Then, my good sir, I'll order my trunk to be moved into your room," the count shouted from behind the door.

"Do me the honour, most happy," answered the cavalry officer, running to the door. "Number seven—don't forget."

When his footsteps had passed out of hearing, the cavalry officer returned to his place, and sitting down closer to a government official, and looking him straight in the face with smiling eyes, he said—

"Yes, it's the very man."

"Oh?"

"I tell you, that's that very hussar, the duellist—Turbin, the notorious count. He recognised me, I bet you; he knew me. Why, we were drinking together for three weeks on end at Lebedyan when I was there getting remounts. A fine spree we got up there together. He's a gallant young fellow, eh?"

"He is. And so pleasant in his manners. You see nothing of all that— you know what I mean," answered the handsome young man. "How quickly we made friends. . . . He must be about five-and-twenty, not more, do you think?"

"No, he does not look that, but he's older. One must know him. Who was it eloped with Madame Migunov? It was he. It was he killed Sablin. He dropped Matynov out of window head first. He won three hundred thousand from Prince Nesterov. He's a desperate rake, you must know. A gambler, duellist, a regular lady-killer, but

a true hussar at heart. They've got a name for it, but if any one could understand what a real hussar means! Ah, that was a time!"

And the cavalry officer told a yarn of his revels in Lebedyan with the count, which had never taken place, and indeed never could have taken place. They never could, in the first place, because he had never set eyes on the count before, and had left the army two years before the count had entered the service; and secondly because the cavalry officer had never even served in the cavalry, but had been for four years the humblest cadet in the Byelevsky regiment, and had retired from the service immediately on being promoted to be an ensign. But ten years ago he had come into a legacy, and actually had visited Lebedyan, had squandered seven hundred roubles there in company with the remount officers, and had even ordered himself an Uhlan uniform with orange facings, with a view of entering an Uhlan regiment. This desire to enter the cavalry, and the three weeks spent with the officers at Lebedyan, had remained the brightest, happiest episode in his life, so that he had first translated the desire into an accomplished fact, then into a memory, and by now had himself a firm belief in his past career in the cavalry, though this did not prevent him from being a truly worthy man, full of kindliness and honesty.

"Yes, no one who hasn't been in the cavalry could ever understand fellows like us." He seated himself astride on a chair, and thrusting out his lower jaw talked away in a bass voice. "You ride at times at the head of your squadron; and under you a regular devil of a horse, prancing and rearing; you sit like the devil himself. The squadron commander rides up to inspect the troops. 'Lieutenant,' says he, 'if you please—it will be nothing without you —lead the squadron in parade order.' 'All right,' one says, and the thing is done. You look round you, shout to the whiskered fellows, your men. Ah, damn it, those were days!'"

The count came back, his face red and his hair wet from the bath and went straight to number seven, where the cavalry officer was already seated, in a dressing-gown, with a pipe, pondering with enjoyment and some trepidation over the good fortune that had fallen to his lot—of sharing a room with the notorious Turbin. "Why, if the fancy takes him, he'll seize me and strip me naked, drag me out beyond the town gates and sit me in the snow, or . . . smear me over with tar, or simply . . . no, he wouldn't treat a comrade like that . . ." he consoled himself by reflecting.

"Feed Blücher, Sashka!" shouted the count.

Sashka made his appearance. He had drunk a glass of vodka since his arrival and was rather drunk.

"You've given way to it already; been drinking, rascal! . . . Feed Blücher."

"He's not dying of hunger as 'tis; see how sleek he is!" answered Sashka, stroking the dog.

"Come, no talking! go along and feed him."

"All you care about is the dog's having enough, but if a man has a glass, you find fault."

"Ay, I'll beat you!" shouted the count in a voice that set the window panes shaking, and positively frightened the cavalry officer a little.

"You might inquire whether Sashka has had anything to eat to-day. Well, beat me, if your dog's dearer to you than your man," said Sashka. But at that moment he received such a terrible blow from the count's fist in his face that he fell down. Knocking his head against the wall and clutching his nose in his hand, he darted towards the door and staggered out on to a chest in the corridor.

"He has knocked my teeth out," growled Sashka, wiping his bloody nose with one hand, while with the other he scratched the back of Blücher, who was licking himself. "He's knocked out my teeth, Blushka, but still he's my count, and I could go through fire and water for him—that I could! For why? He's my count, do you see, Blushka? Do you want your dinner?"

After lying there a while, he got up, fed the dog, and, almost sober, went to wait on his count and offer him tea.

"You will really hurt my feelings," the cavalry officer began timidly, standing before the count, who was lying on his bed, scraping his feet against the wall. "I'm an old army man too, and a comrade, I may say; rather than you should borrow from any one else, I shall be most happy to put at your service two hundred roubles. I haven't that sum at this moment, only a hundred; but I will get it to-day. You really hurt my feelings, count!"

"Thanks, my dear fellow," said the count, slapping the cavalry officer on the shoulder and at once divining the nature of the relations that were bound to arise between them: "thanks! Well, we'll go to the ball then, if that's so.

But what are we going to do now? Tell me what there is to be seen in your town. Who are the pretty women, who are fond of a spree, and who are your card-players?"

The cavalry officer explained that there would be numbers of pretty women at the ball; that the newly elected police captain, Kolkov, was more given to dissipation than any one, though he had none of the real dash of a hussar about him, but was simply a good-natured fellow; that Ilyushka's band of gypsies had been singing in the town since the opening of the elections, Styoshka leading them, and that to-day *everybody* from the marshal's would go there to hear them. And the play was pretty good, he added. Luhnov, a wealthy visitor in the town, played cards, and Ilyin, a cornet of the Uhlans, staying in number eight, was losing heavily too. They were just beginning to play in his room. They played every evening. "And such a delightful young fellow, I must tell you, count, is that Ilyin; nothing stingy about him—he'll part with his last shirt."

"Then let's go and see him. Let's see what sort of people they are," said the count.

"By all means, by all means. They'll be awfully glad to see you."

CHAPTER II

THE CORNET

THE cornet of Uhlans, Ilyin, had not long been awake. On the previous evening he had sat down to play at eight o'clock, and had played for fifteen hours on end, till eleven o'clock in the morning. He had lost a great deal,

but exactly how much he did not know because he had had three thousand of his own money and fifteen thousand of government money which he had long ago mixed up with his own. And he was afraid to reckon up for fear of convincing himself of what he foresaw, that a good deal of the government money intrusted to him was missing. It was almost midday when he fell asleep, and he had slept that heavy dreamless sleep that only a very young man ever sleeps, and only after very heavy losses at cards. On waking up at six o'clock in the evening, at the very time when Count Turbin was entering the hotel, he saw cards all around him on the floor, chalk and smudged tables in the middle of the room, and recollected with horror the play of the preceding evening, and his last card, the knave, which had lost him five hundred roubles. But not yet quite believing in the actual state of things, he took his money from under the pillow and began counting it. He recognised several notes which had passed from hand to hand in "corners" and "transports" and recalled the whole course of his play. His own three thousand had all gone, and the government money was two and a half thousand short.

The Uhlan had been playing for four nights in succession.

He had come from Moscow where the sums of government money had been put into his charge. In K. he had been detained by the overseer of the posting station on the plea of the lack of horses, but in reality, in accordance with an understanding, he had long had with the proprietor of the hotel—to keep all visitors for a day for him. The Uhlan, a lively young fellow, who had only just received three thousand roubles from his parents in Moscow for his outfit for the regiment, was glad to spend a few days in the town of K. at the time of the provincial elections, and looked forward to enjoying himself thoroughly here. He was acquainted with a country gentleman of the neighbourhood with a family, and he had been meaning to go and see him, to flirt with his daughters, when the cavalry officer turned up and made the Uhlan's acquaintance. And the same evening, with no evil intent, he had introduced him to his acquaintance, Luhnov, and the other card-players in the public room. From that evening the Uhlan had been playing cards. He had not driven over to see his country friend, he had not even inquired about horses, he had not, in fact, left his room for four days.

After dressing and drinking tea, he went to the window. He longed to go out so as to shake off the haunting memories of the card-playing. He put on his greatcoat and went out into the street. The sun was already hidden behind the white houses with red roofs; twilight was coming on already. It was warm. Flakes of damp snow were falling softly into the dirty street. He suddenly felt it intolerably sad that he should have slept all through this day, which was just over.

"This day that has passed one can never recall," he thought.

"I have ruined my young life," he said to himself; not because he really thought he had ruined his young life— he was not indeed thinking about it at all—but the phrase happened to occur to his mind.

"What am I to do now?" he meditated. "Borrow from some one and go away." A lady walked along the pavement. "What a foolish-looking lady!" he thought inconsequently. "There's no one to borrow from. I've ruined my young life." He reached the shops. A merchant in a fox-lined cloak was standing at the door of his shop touting for customers. "If I hadn't taken up the eight, I should have made up what I'd lost." An old beggar-woman followed him whimpering. "There's no one to borrow from." A gentleman in a bearskin cloak drove by; a watchman stood still. "What could one do out of the ordinary? Take a shot at these people? No, it's a bore! I've ruined my young life. Ah, those are nice bridles hanging there with ornaments on them. I should like a drive in a sledge now with three horses—ah, the darlings! I'm going home. Luhnov will soon be coming, we shall begin playing." He went back and again counted over his money. No, he had not been mistaken the first time; again the government money was two and a half thousand roubles short. "I'll stake twenty-five on the first card, then a 'corner' on the second, then seven times the stake, then fifteen, thirty, sixty times—up to three thousand roubles. I'll buy the bridles and go away. He won't let me win, the scoundrel! I've ruined my young life." This was what was passing in the Uhlan's mind at the moment when Luhnov actually did come into his room.

"Well, have you been up long, Mihailo Vassilitch?" inquired Luhnov, deliberately taking his gold spectacles off his lean nose, and carefully wiping them on his red silk handkerchief.

"No; I'm only just up. I slept so well."

"There's some hussar come; he's staying with Zavalshevsky . . . have you heard about him?"

"No, I hadn't heard anything. How is it no one's here yet?"

"I believe they've gone to Pryahins's. They'll be here directly."

There did in fact come into the room shortly afterwards the garrison officer, who always accompanied Luhnov, a Greek merchant with a huge hooked nose of a cinnamon tint, and sunken, black eyes, a stout, puffy-looking land-owner and brandy-distiller, who gambled for whole nights at a stretch, always for half-rouble points. All were eager to begin playing; but the chief players made no reference to the subject; Luhnov, in particular, talked with extreme composure about a burglary in Moscow.

"Just imagine," he was saying, "Moscow a city of the foremost rank, the capital . . . and men go about at night with hooks, masquerading as devils, frighten silly people, rob travellers—and that's the end of it. What are the police thinking about? That's the puzzle."

The Uhlan listened attentively to the story of the robbery; but towards the end of it he got up and quietly ordered cards to be brought in. The stout land-owner was the first to express his feelings.

"Well, gentlemen, why waste the golden hours? If we mean business, let's get to business."

"Yes; you hauled in a good many half-roubles yesterday, so you like it!' said the Greek.

"Yes, it's time," said the garrison officer.

Ilyin looked towards Luhnov. Luhnov, looking him straight in the face, went on calmly with his account of the robbers with hooks.

"Shall we deal?" asked the Uhlan.

"Isn't it early?"

"Byelov!" called the Uhlan, blushing for some unknown reason, "bring me some dinner. . . . I've had nothing to eat yet, gentlemen. Bring champagne and bring us some cards."

At that moment the count and Zavalshevsky came into the room. It appeared that Turbin and Ilyin belonged to the same division. They made friends at once, drank champagne together, clinking their glasses, and in five minutes they were quite on intimate terms. The count seemed to take a great fancy to Ilyin. He smiled, continually looking at him, and rallied him on his youth.

"Ah, what a youngster for an Uhlan!" said he; "fine moustaches, fine moustaches, eh?"

The down on Ilyin's lip was perfectly white.

"Why, you were just going to play cards, I think?" said the count. "Well, I wish you good luck, Ilyin! You're a first-rate player, I expect!" he added, smiling.

"Yes, they're just going to begin," said Luhnov, tearing open a pack of cards, "and you, count, will you take a hand?"

"No; to-day I won't, or I should beat you all. When once I get started, I break any bank I have to do with. I've nothing to play with. I lost everything at the posting-station near Volotchok. I came across a fellow there, an infantry officer, with a lot of rings on his fingers, a cardsharper he must have been, and he completely cleaned me out."

"Did you stay long at the station then?" asked Ilyin.

"I spent twenty-two hours there. I shall remember that damned station! and, I dare say, the overseer won't forget my visit."

"Oh, why?"

"When I arrived, you know, out ran the overseer, a regular thievish, ruffianly-looking fellow. 'No horses,' said he; and my rule, I must tell you, is this: when there are no horses, I go straight into the overseer's room, not the public room, you know, but his private room, without taking off my cloak, and I order all the doors and windows to be thrown wide open, as though it were close with charcoal fumes. Well, and so I did there. And, you remember what the frost was like last month—twenty degrees of frost it was. The overseer began talking away. I gave him one in the face. Then an old woman, and a lot of wenches and females set up a squealing, snatched up their pots, and were for running out into the village. I stepped to the door. 'Fetch out the horses,' said I, 'and I'll go; I won't let you out else, I'll freeze you all out!'"

"That's a fine way of doing things!" said the puffy land-owner, going off into a guffaw; "that's how one freezes out beetles!"

"Only I didn't keep guard over them. I went out, and the overseer, with all the womenfolk bolted. I had one old woman only left as a hostage on the stove; she kept sneezing and praying to God. Then we opened negotiations: the overseer came forth, and from a distance tried to persuade me to let the old woman go, but I set Blücher on him—Blücher's a first-rate fellow with overseers. And so the blackguard didn't give me horses till next morning. Then this infantryman arrived. I went to the other room and began playing with him. You've seen Blücher . . . Blücher! Fugh! . . ."

Blücher ran in. The card-players gave him an affable reception, though they were obviously eager to get to quite other matters.

"But why aren't you playing, gentlemen? Please don't let me hinder you. I'm a chatterbox, I know," said Turbin, "and a good thing, too, whether you like it or no."

CHAPTER III

THE GAME

LUHNOV moved two candles nearer him, pulled out a huge brown pocketbook full of notes, and slowly, as though performing some mysterious rite, opened it on the table, took two hundred-rouble notes out of it, and laid them under the cards.

"The same as yesterday then—two hundred for the bank," he said, settling his spectacles straight, and tearing open a pack of cards.

"Very well," Ilyin said, not looking at him, but going on with his conversation with Turbin.

The game began. Luhnov dealt as precisely as a machine. At intervals he stopped in his play to mark the points with deliberate care, or glancing sternly over his spectacles, said in a weak voice, "Your lead." The fat land-owner talked louder than any one, making various remarks to himself aloud, bending the cards, and smudging them with his fat fingers. The garrison officer without a word wrote down his stake on a card in a fine hand, and bent down the corners under the table. The Greek sat beside the one who kept the bank, and his sunken black eyes kept careful watch on the game, as though in expectation of something. Zavalshevsky, standing at the table, was suddenly all excitement. He pulled out of his trouser-pocket a red note or a blue note, laid a card on it, clapped his open hand on it, called out, "The seven for luck!" bit his moustaches, shifted from one leg to the other, flushed, and was all over in a fidget, that lasted till the card was played. Ilyin was eating a plate of veal and cucumber, set on the horse-hair sofa beside him, and quickly rubbing his hands on his coat, he put down one card after another. Turbin, who sat from the first on the sofa, soon caught the position of affairs. Luhnov did not look at the Uhlan at all, and did not once address him; only from time to time his spectacles were turned for an instant towards the Uhlan's hands, but the greater number of the latter's cards were losing ones.

"Ah, I should like to beat that card," said Luhnov, of a card laid down by the fat landowner, who was playing for half-rouble stakes.

"You beat Ilyin's cards, but why beat mine?" observed the landowner.

And certainly Ilyin's cards were beaten oftener than the others. He nervously tore up the losing card under the table and with trembling hands chose another. Turbin got up from the sofa, and asked the Greek to let him sit beside the one who kept the bank. The Greek moved to another seat, and the count, sitting in his chair, began keeping an intent watch on Luhnov's hands, never taking his eyes off them.

"Ilyin!" he said suddenly, in his ordinary tone of voice, which, quite apart from any intention, drowned all other sounds, "why do you stick to the diamond? You don't know how to play."

"However one plays, it makes no difference!"

"Yes—you're bound to lose. Let me take a hand for you."

"No, excuse me, please; I'll play for myself. Play on your own account, if you want to."

"On my own account, I've said that I'm not going to; I should like to, for you. I don't like you to be losing."

"Well, it seems it's my fate!"

The count did not persist, and leaning on his elbows, he fell to watching Luhnov's hands intently again.

"A dirty business!" he said, all at once, loudly and deliberately.

Luhnov glanced at him.

"Dirty! dirty!" he exclaimed suddenly, speaking still more loudly, and looking Luhnov straight in the face.

The game went on.

"Not the right thing!" Turbin said again deliberately, just after Luhnov had beaten a high card of Ilyin's.

"What is it you don't like, count?" Luhnov inquired, with polite nonchalance.

"Why, that you give Ilyin his 'simples' and beat his 'corners.' That's what's wrong."

Luhnov faintly shrugged his shoulders, and lifted his eyebrows, as though to suggest that he should put it all down to luck, and went on playing.

"Blücher! fugh!" shouted the count, getting up—"*at* him," he added rapidly.

Blücher, brushing against the sofa and almost upsetting the garrison officer, jumped up, ran to his master and growled, looking round at every one, and wagging his tail, as though to ask, "Who's the offender? eh?"

Luhnov laid down his cards and pushed his chair back.

"One can't play like this," said he; "I particularly dislike dogs. How can one play when a whole pack of curs is brought into the room?"

"Especially those dogs; they're called leeches, I believe," agreed the garrison officer.

"Well are we going to play, Mihailo Vassilitch, or not?" said Luhnov to Ilyin.

"Don't hinder us, please, count!" Ilyin said to Turbin.

"Come here a minute," said Turbin, taking Ilyin by the arm, and he walked with him behind the screen.

From there the count's words were perfectly audible, for he spoke in his ordinary voice. And his voice could always be heard three rooms off.

"Why, are you mad? Don't you see that that gentleman in spectacles is a cardsharper of the first rank?"

"Oh, stop it, do! what nonsense!"

"Not stop it, but drop it, I tell you. Another time I might have cleaned you out myself; but somehow I feel sorry at seeing you done. And haven't you government money with you, too?"

"No; and what makes you suppose so?"

"Oh, my boy, I've been along that road myself, so I know all the cardsharper's tricks. I tell you the fellow in spectacles is a swindler. Drop it, please. I beg you to, as a comrade."

"Well, I'll only play one round and leave off."

"I know what one round means; well, we shall see then."

They went back. In one round, Ilyin played so many cards, and so many were beaten, that he lost heavily.

Turbin laid his hands in the middle of the table.

"Come, that's enough! Let's go."

"No, I can't; let me be, please," Ilyin said in a tone of annoyance, shuffling the bent cards and not looking at Turbin.

"Well, damn you! Lose away to a dead certainty if you want to, but I must go. Zavalshevsky! let's be off to the marshal's."

And they went away. No one spoke, and Luhnov did not deal till the sound of their steps and Blücher's paws had died away along the corridor.

"What a fellow!" said the landowner, laughing.

"Well, he won't hinder us now," added the garrison officer quickly, still speaking in a whisper.

And the game went on.

CHAPTER IV

THE QUARREL

THE musicians, serfs of the marshal's, standing at the buffet end of the room, which had been cleared expressly for the ball, had turned up the cuffs of their coats, and at the given signal were striking up with the old-fashioned polonaise "Alexander-Elisabeth." In the soft, brilliant light of the wax candles, couples began moving smoothly over the big parqueted hall: the governor, a general of Catherine's court, with a star, arm-in-arm with the thin wife of the marshal, the marshal arm-in-arm with the governor's wife, all the local grandees, in fact, in various combinations and permutations. At that moment, Zavalshevsky walked into the hall in a blue frockcoat with a huge collar and puffs on the shoulders, in stockings and dancing-shoes, diffusing a strong odour of the jasmine scent, with which his moustaches and handkerchief and the lapels of his coat were plentifully sprinkled. Besides him was the handsome hussar, in tight, blue riding-breeches and gold-embroidered, red tunic, on which hung the Vladimir cross and a medal of the year 1812. The count was not tall, but he had a very fine, elegant figure. His extremely bright, clear-blue eyes and rather long, dark-brown hair, curling in thick ringlets, gave a striking character to his handsome face. The count's presence at the ball was expected; the handsome young man who had seen him at the hotel had already brought the news of him to the marshal. The impression produced by his report was mixed, but on the whole not altogether agreeable.

"He might turn us into ridicule, the young whipper-snapper!" was the opinion of the elder ladies and the men. "What if he carries me off?" was more or less the reflection that occurred to the girls and young women.

As soon as the polonaise was over, and the couples parted with mutual bows, the ladies joining the ladies, and the men returning to the men, Zavalshevsky, proud and happy, led the count up to their hostess. The marshal's wife, with some inward trepidation lest this hussar should be guilty of some scandalous breach of the proprieties with her before every one, turned proudly and scornfully away, and said: "Delighted, I hope you will dance," and glanced distrustfully at him with an expression that said: "If you annoy a lady after this, you're a perfect scoundrel." The count, however, soon overcame this prejudice against him by his courtesy, his assiduity, and his handsome, good-humoured appearance, so that five minutes later the expression of the lady's countenance signified plainly to all around them: "I know how to manage this sort of gentleman; he saw at once to whom he was speaking. Now he'll be all attention to me the whole evening." At that point, however, the governor, who knew the count's father, approached him and very affably drew him aside and entered into conversation with him, which still further reassured the provincial public and raised its opinion of the count. Then Zavalshevsky took him to be introduced to his sister—a plump youthful little widow, whose large black eyes had been pinned on the count ever since he entered the room. The count invited the little widow to dance a waltz, which as it happened was being played at that moment. His skill in dancing completely won the favour of the assembly.

"Well, he's a first-rate dancer!" said a stout country lady, watching the legs in the blue riding-trousers as they darted about the ballroom, and mentally beating time to them: "one, two, three; one, two, three . . . first rate!"

"He does cut about, he does cut

about!" said another lady, a visitor to the town, who was considered not of the best breeding in local society; "how does he manage not to catch his spurs in anything! Wonderful, very clever!"

The count's dancing eclipsed the three best dancers in the province: a tall adjutant of the governor's, with white eyelashes, who was noted for the rapidity of his dancing and the close embrace in which he held his partner; a cavalry officer, distinguished for the graceful way in which he swung round in the waltz, and tapped lightly with his heels; and another gentleman, a civilian, of whom every one said, that though he had not much to boast of in the way of brains, he was a superb dancer, and the life of all the balls. The latter gentleman did in fact ask every lady to dance, taking them in order as they sat; he never ceased dancing for a minute from the beginning of the ball till the end, and only halted from time to time to wipe with his sopping cambric handkerchief, his exhausted, but beaming countenance. The count eclipsed them all, and danced with the three ladies of greatest consequence at the ball: a big lady, wealthy, handsome and stupid; a medium-sized lady, thin, and not over good-looking, but beautifully dressed; and a little lady, who was not pretty, but very intelligent. He danced with other ladies, too, with all the pretty ones, and they were numerous. But the little widow, Zavalshevsky's sister, the count liked best of them all; with her he danced a quadrille, an écossaise, and a mazurka. When they were sitting down in the quadrille he began paying her a great many compliments, comparing her with Venus, with Diana,

with a rose and with some other kind of flower. To all these civilities the little widow only responded by bending her white neck, dropping her eyes, gazing at her white muslin gown, or shifting her fan from one hand to the other. When she murmured: "Enough, count, you jest," and similar phrases, her rather deep voice had a ring of such naïve simplicity and comical silliness, that looking at her the idea really might well occur to any one that she was more a flower than a woman; and not a rose, but some rich, wild, rosy-white, scentless flower, growing alone in some distant land out of the virgin snows. This absence of all complexity, this naïveté in combination with her fresh beauty, made such a strange impression on the count that several times in the pauses in their conversation, when he gazed mutely into her eyes, or at the fine lines of her arms and neck, he felt such a strong desire to snatch her in his arms and kiss her vigorously, that he had to exercise serious self-control to keep himself in check. The little widow observed with gratification the impression she was making; but something in the count's behaviour began to agitate and alarm her, although with all his ingratiating attentiveness, the young hussar was, according to the standards of to-day, respectful almost to mawkishness. He flew to get her refreshment, picked up her handkerchief, pulled a chair out of the hands of a scrofulous-looking young landowner, who was also eager to be of service to her, in order to put it for her more quickly.

Noticing that the gallantry fashionable in those days had little effect on his partner, he tried to entertain her by telling her amusing anecdotes, and declared that at her bidding he would be ready to stand on his head on the spot, to crow like a cock, to jump out of window, or to throw himself into an ice-hole. This line was completely successful; the widow became more lively, went off into gushes of laughter, showing exquisite white teeth, and was perfectly satisfied with her cavalier. The count was more attracted by her every minute; so much so that by the end of the quadrille, he was genuinely in love with her.

After the quadrille, they were joined by a wealthy landowner's son, a young man of eighteen, not as yet in any branch of the service, who had long adored the widow; he was the same scrofulous youth from whom Turbin had carried off the chair. When he approached the widow, she gave him an exceedingly cold reception, and showed not a tenth part of the confusion of which she was sensible with the count.

"You're a pretty person!" she said to him, while she gazed at Turbin's back, and unconsciously considered how many yards of gold lace went to his coat; "you promised to fetch me to skate and to bring me some bonbons."

"But I did go, Anna Fyodorovna, and you were gone out; and I left the very best bonbons," said the young man, who, in spite of his tall figure, spoke in a shrill little voice.

"You always find excuses! I don't want your bonbons. Pray, don't imagine . . ."

"I see already, Anna Fyodorovna, how changed you are to me, and I know why. Only it's not right . . ." he added, but evidently could not conclude his speech from some violent emotion, which made his lips twitch very rapidly and queerly.

Anna Fyodorovna did not listen to him, but went on watching Turbin.

The marshal, the master of the house, a majestically portly, toothless old gentleman, went up to the count, and taking his arm, invited him to his study to smoke and have a drink, if he cared to. As soon as Turbin had gone, Anna Fyodorovna felt that there was positively nothing of interest in the ballroom, and taking her friend, a withered and elderly spinster lady, by the arm, she went with her into the dressing-room.

"Well, was he agreeable?" inquired the spinster.

"Only it's awful the way he pursues me," answered Anna Fyodorovna, going up to the looking-glass and looking at herself.

Her face was radiant; her eyes were laughing. She positively blushed at the sight of herself; and suddenly, mimicking the ballet-dancers she had seen during the present elections, she pirouetted round on one foot; then laughed her deep but charming laugh, and positively executed a little skip in the air, kicking up her heels.

"Fancy, only! he asked me for a keepsake," she told her friend; "but he will not get anythi-i-ing." She chanted the last word, and held up one finger, tightly covered with the kid glove that reached to her elbow.

In the study where the marshal had conducted Turbin there were various sorts of vodka, liqueurs, light refreshments, and champagne. Gentlemen sat or walked about in the tobacco smoke, discussing the elections.

"When all the noble gentry of our district have honoured him by election," said the newly appointed police captain, who had drunk heavily already, "he ought not to have disappointed local society; he never ought to have . . ."

The entrance of the count interrupted the conversation. Every one was introduced to him, and the police captain, in particular, clasped his hand a long while in both of his, and several times over begged him not to refuse to join their party after the ball at a new restaurant, where he was entertaining several gentlemen, and some gypsies were to sing. The count promised to be sure to come, and drank several glasses of champagne with him.

"Why don't you dance, gentlemen?" he asked, as a prelude to getting out of the room.

"We are not dancing men," answered the police captain, laughing; "we are more interested in the wine, count. And besides, they've all grown up under my eyes—the young ladies here, count. Though I do sometimes get through an écossaise, too, count. I can, count . . ."

"Well, come along, and get through it now, then," said Turbin; "let's enjoy ourselves before going to the gypsies."

"Yes; come along, gentlemen. Let us please our host." And three noblemen, who had been drinking in the study from the beginning of the ball, with flushed faces, put on their gloves —one a black pair, another silk knitted ones. They were just about to enter the ball-room with the count, when they were detained by the scrofulous youth, who, with a pale face, and hardly able to restrain his tears, went up to Turbin.

"You think, because you are a count, you are at liberty to push people as if you were at a bazaar," he said, breathing with difficulty. "Since that's ill-bred . . ." Involuntarily again his twitching lips arrested the flow of his words.

"What?" shouted Turbin, suddenly scowling. "What! . . . Boy!" he shouted, clutching him by the arms and squeezing them, so that the youth felt the blood rush to his head, not so much from anger as from terror. "Why, do you want to fight, eh? I'm at your service then."

Turbin had hardly let go the arm he was grasping so tightly, when a couple of noblemen seized the young man by his arms and dragged him away to a door in the rear.

"Why, have you lost your senses? You must have been drinking; wait till we tell your papa. What is the matter with you?" they said to him.

"No, I'm not drunk; but he pushes one, and doesn't apologise. He's a pig! that's what he is," wailed the youth, by now weeping outright.

Without heeding him, they got him away home.

"Let it be, count." The police captain and Zavalshevsky did their part meanwhile in soothing Turbin. "He's a mere babe; he's whipped still. Why, he's only sixteen; and what's come over him there's no making out. What madness possesses him? And his father's such a highly respected man—our candidate."

"Well, deuce take him, if he doesn't want to . . ."

And the count returned to the ball-

room, and just as before gaily danced
the écossaise with the little widow, and
laughed heartily as he looked at the
capers cut by the gentlemen who had
come with him from the study, and
broke into a roar that filled the ball-
room when the police captain slipped
and plumped down full length in the
middle of the dancers.

CHAPTER V

ANNA'S CARRIAGE

WHILE the count was away in the
study, Anna Fyodorovna went up to
her brother, and for some reason feeling
it necessary to affect to be very little
interested in the count, began questioning him. "What sort of hussar was it
that danced with me? Tell me,
brother." The cavalry officer explained
to his sister to the best of his powers
what a grand person the hussar in question was. He told her, too, that the
count was only stopping here because
he had had his money stolen on the
journey, and that he had himself lent
him a hundred roubles; but that, he
said, was too small a sum, and so,
could not his sister let him have two
hundred more. Zavalshevsky begged
her, however, to say nothing of this to
any one, especially not to the count.
Anna Fyodorovna promised to send her
brother the money the same day, and
to keep the matter a secret; but during the écossaise she was overcome by
a fearful longing to offer the count
herself as much money as he wanted.
She was a long while trying to speak;
she blushed, and at last, with an effort,
came to the point in this manner—

"My brother told me that you had
a misfortune, count, on your journey,

and have no money left. If you want
any, won't you borrow it from me?
I should be most delighted."

But as she uttered these words, Anna
Fyodorovna suddenly took fright, and
crimsoned. Every trace of good-
humour instantaneously vanished from
the count's face.

"Your brother's a fool!" he said
sharply. "You know that when a man
insults a man, they fight; but when a
woman insults a man, do you know
what's done then?"

Poor Anna Fyodorovna's neck and
ears were crimson with confusion. She
looked down and made no reply.

"A woman is kissed before every
one," the count said softly, bending
down to her ear. "You must let me
at least kiss your hand," he added slily,
after a long pause, touched by his partner's confusion.

"Ah, only not just now," Anna Fyodorovna articulated, with a deep sigh.

"When, then? I'm going early to-
morrow; and you owe me that."

"Well, but if so, it's impossible," said
Anna Fyodorovna, smiling.

"You only give me leave to find an
opportunity of seeing you to-night, so
as to kiss your hand. I will find it."

"But how can you find it?"

"That's not your affair. To see you
anything's possible for me; so that's
settled."

"Very well."

The écossaise was over. They danced
another mazurka, in which the count
performed wonders—catching handkerchiefs, dropping on one knee, and clank-
ing with his spurs in a peculiar way
after the Warsaw fashion—so that all
the old gentlemen left their game of
Boston to come and look on in the

ball-room; and the cavalry officer, reputed the best dancer, acknowledged himself surpassed. Then came supper; after it they danced "grandfather," and people began going home. During the whole time, the count had never taken his eyes off the little widow. He had spoken sincerely when he said he was ready to fling himself into an ice-hole for her sake. Whether it were caprice, or love, or obstinacy, that evening all his energies were concentrated on a single desire—to see her and to love her. As soon as he observed that Anna Fyodorovna was beginning to take leave of the hostess, he ran out to the footmen's waiting-room, and from there, without a cloak, he ran out of doors to where the carriages were standing.

"Anna Fyodorovna Zaytsov's carriage!" he shouted.

A high carriage with seats for four and lanterns, moved out from the rest, and drove up to the steps.

"Stop!" he shouted to the coachman running knee-deep in the snow up to the carriage.

"What do you want?" called back the coachman.

"I want to get into the carriage," answered the count, opening the door and trying to get in while the carriage was moving. "Stop, you devil! Fool!"

"Vaska, stop!" the coachman called to the postillion, and he pulled up the horses. "What are you getting into the wrong carriage for? This is a lady's carriage—Anna Fyodorovna's— and not your honour's."

"Hold your tongue, do, blockhead! Here's a rouble for you, and get down and shut the door," said the count. But as the coachman did not budge, he pulled up the carriage-steps himself,

opened the window, and somehow managed to slam the door to. In the carriage, as in all old carriages, especially those upholstered with yellow galoon, there was a smell of mildew and burnt bristles. The count's legs had been knee-deep in the thawing snow, and were terribly cold in his thin boots and riding-breeches; his whole body indeed was chilled by the winter frost. The coachman grumbled on the box, and seemed to be about to get down. But the count heard nothing and felt nothing. His face glowed, his heart beat violently. He gripped convulsively at the yellow strap, peered out of the side window, and his whole being was concentrated on the single emotion of anticipation. This anticipation did not last long. There was a shout from the steps—"Madame Zaytsov's carriage!" The coachman shook the reins, the carriage quivered on its high springs, the lighted windows of the house, one after the other, flew by the carriage window.

"Mind, if you tell the footman I'm here, fellow," said the count, poking his head out of the window in front to speak to the coachman, "I'll thrash you; but if you say nothing, another ten roubles."

He had hardly let go of the window, when the carriage jolted more violently again, and stopped. He huddled up in a corner, held his breath, even shut his eyes: he felt such dread that his passionate hopes would not be fulfilled. The door opened, one after another the steps were noisily let down; there was the rustle of a woman's dress, a scent of jasmine perfume was wafted into the stuffy carriage, rapid feet ran up the steps, and Anna Fyodorovna, cov--

ering the count's leg with the skirt of her open pelisse, sank on to the seat beside him, breathing hard but not uttering a word.

Whether she had seen him or not, no one could have said, not even Anna Fyodorovna herself. But when he took her by the arm and said, "Well, now I shall kiss your little hand," she showed very little alarm, made no reply, but let him have the arm, which he covered with kisses much higher up than the glove reached. The carriage drove off.

"Say something. You are not angry?" he said to her.

She shrank into her corner without a word; but all of a sudden she burst into tears, and of her own accord fell forward with her head on his breast.

CHAPTER VI

THE GYPSY GIRL

THE newly elected police captain with his party, the cavalry officer, and other noblemen had been a long while drinking and listening to the gypsies in the new restaurant, when the count joined them, wearing a blue cloth cloak lined with bearskin that had belonged to Anna Fyodorovna's late husband.

"Your excellency! we've been eagerly expecting you this long while," said a cross-eyed, dark gypsy, showing his gleaming teeth, as he met him in the entry and darted to take off his cloak. "We've not seen you since Lebedyan . . . Styoshka has been quite pining for you. . . ."

Styoshka, a graceful gypsy girl, with a brown face, brick-red cheeks, and deep, shining black eyes, shaded by long eyelashes, ran out, too, to meet him.

"Ah! little count! darling! heart of gold! this is a pleasure!" she murmured with a beaming smile.

Ilyushka himself ran out to meet him, affecting to be greatly delighted. The women, old and young, jumped up from their places, and surrounded their visitor. One claimed kinship with him as godfather to a child; another brotherhood through exchange of crosses. Turbin kissed all the gypsy girls on the lips; the older women and the men kissed him on the shoulder or the hand. The gentlemen of the party, too, were very much pleased at the count's arrival, the more so that the revelry having reached its zenith was by now getting a little flat. Every one was beginning to feel sated; the wine had lost its stimulating effect on the nerves, and was only cloying the stomach. Every one had performed by now all his stock of smart tricks, and every one was weary of gazing at the performances of the rest. All their songs had been sung, and were mixed up together in every one's head, leaving an impression of noise and dissipation. However queer or reckless a feat were performed, the idea had begun to occur to every one that there was nothing agreeable or amusing in it. The police captain, sprawling in an unseemly way on the floor at the feet of an old gypsy woman, kicked and shouted—

"Champagne! . . . the count has come! . . . champagne! . . . he has come! . . . here, champagne! . . . I'll make a bath of champagne, and I'm going to bathe in it. . . . Gentlemen of the nobility! I love the company of noble gentlemen. . . . Sty- oshka! sing 'The Path.'"

The cavalryman, too, was in an hilarious condition; but with him it took another form. He was sitting in a corner, on a sofa, very close to a tall, handsome gypsy woman, Lyubasha, and feeling that drunkenness had begun to dim his eyes, he kept blinking, shaking his head, and repeating the same words over and over again, as he tried in a whisper to persuade the gypsy to run away with him. Lyubasha, smiling, listened to him as though what he were saying were highly entertaining, though now and then she cast rather dejected glances at her husband, cross-eyed Sashka, who was standing behind a chair facing her. In response to the cavalry officer's declarations of love, she bent down to his ear, and asked him to buy her perfumes and ribbons, on the sly, so that the others should not see it.

"Hurrah!" shouted the cavalry officer when the count came in.

The handsome young man with an anxious countenance walked up and down the room, carefully steadying his steps, and humming airs out of the *Revolt in the Seraglio*.

An aged paterfamilias had been borne off to the gypsies by the urgent entreaties of the noble gentlemen, who had declared that everything would go amiss without him, and that they had better not go at all if he would not come. He was on a sofa, where he had lain down at once on arriving, and no one had taken any further notice of him. A government official of some sort, who was of the party, had taken off his coat, and was sitting on the table with his legs up; he ruffled up his hair,

intending thereby to signify that he was having a roaring time. As soon as the count came in, he unbuttoned the collar of his shirt, and squatted still higher on the table. The general gaiety in fact revived on the appearance of the count. The gypsies who had been wandering about the room sat down again in a ring.

The count seated Styoshka, the leading singer, on his knee, and ordered some more champagne.

Ilyushka stood with his guitar before the leading singer, and began to play the dance tunes, that is, a series of gypsy songs: "As I go along the street," "Ah, you hussar," "Dost thou hear and understand?" and so on in a certain order. Styoshka sang capitally. Her rich, supple contralto that came straight from her chest, her smiles as she sang, her laughing, passionate eyes, and her little feet, that unconsciously beat time to the song, her wild shriek at the beginning of the chorus, all set vibrating a responsive chord rarely stirred in the soul. It was evident that she was living wholly in the song as she sang it.

Ilyushka, smiling, accompanied her on the guitar, his back, his legs, his whole body working in harmony with the song, and intently, anxiously he nodded and lifted his head in time to it, with his eyes fastened on the singer, as though he were hearing her for the first time. Then at the last note of the singer he suddenly drew himself up, and proudly, resolutely, as though feeling superior to every one in the world, he kicked his guitar, turned it over, stamped, tossed his hair, and looked round at the chorus with knitted brows. His whole body began to dance in every fibre from his neck to his heels. . . . And twenty vigorous, powerful voices filled the air with sound, each trying to chime in more strangely and strikingly than the rest. The old women pranced up and down in their seats, grinning and waving their kerchiefs, and shrieked in time and in unison, one louder than another. The men singing bass stood behind their chairs, with their heads on one side and their necks strained.

When Styoshka took her high notes, Ilyushka brought the guitar nearer her, as though to support her, and the handsome young man screamed in an ecstasy that now "the A flat was coming."

When they played a dance tune, and Dunyasha tripped out, her shoulders and bosom quivering, and after turning round before the count, was floating away, Turbin leapt up, flung off his tunic, and in his red shirt gallantly stepped out, keeping time and step with her, and performing such feats with his legs that the gypsies looked at one another with smiles of approval.

The police captain sat cross-legged like a Turk, thumped himself in the chest with his fists, and shouted, "Vivi!" Then seizing the count by the legs, he began telling him that he had had two thousand roubles, but had only five hundred left, and that he could do anything he liked, if only the count would permit it. The old paterfamilias waked up and tried to get away, but they would not let him go. The handsome young man kept begging a gypsy girl to dance a waltz. The cavalry officer, pluming himself on his friendship with the count, got up from his corner. and embraced Turbin.

"Ah, my dear boy!" he said, "what did you run away from us for? Eh?" The count did not reply, evidently thinking of something else. "Where were you off to? Ah, you sly dog, I know where you were!"

This familiarity was, for some reason, not to Turbin's liking. Without a word or a smile, he stared the cavalry officer in the face, and all at once levelled upon him such a volley of coarse and terrible abuse that the cavalry officer, deeply mortified, could not make up his mind for a long while how to take this affront, as a joke or not. Finally he decided to take it as a joke, smiled, and went back to his gypsy, assuring her that he would certainly marry her after Easter. A second song was sung and a third, the gypsies danced once more, sang a special song in honour of their guests, and every one still seemed festive. Champagne flowed without stint, and the count drank a great deal. His eyes were veiled by a sort of dewy moisture, but he did not stagger; he danced better than ever, talked without faltering, and even sang capitally in the chorus, and took a second with Styoshka when she sang "Love's soft alarms." In the middle of a dance, the proprietor of the restaurant came in to beg the company to go home, as it was three o'clock in the morning.

The count seized the proprietor by the collar, and told him to dance the "squatting dance." The man refused. The count snatched up a bottle of champagne, and turning him wrong side up, with his legs in the air, told him to keep so, while amidst the laughter of the company he deliberately poured the whole bottle over him.

It was beginning to get light. Every one was pale and exhausted except the count.

"It's time I was starting for Moscow, though," he said all at once, getting up. "All come along to my hotel, lads. See me off . . . and we'll have some tea."

Every one consented, except the slumbering paterfamilias, who remained where he was. The rest crammed themselves into three sledges, that were standing at the entrance, and drove to the count's hotel.

CHAPTER VII

WILL YOU PLAY?

"PUT the horses in!" shouted the count, as he walked into the public room of the hotel with all his guests and the gypsies. "Sashka!—not Gypsy Sashka, but my man—tell the overseer that I'll beat him if the horses aren't good ones. And bring us some tea! Zavalshevsky, you look after the tea. I'm going to see Ilyin—I want to see what he's about," added Turbin, and he went along the passage to the Uhlan's room.

Ilyin had just finished playing, and had lost every kopeck he had. He was lying face downwards on a sofa with a torn horsehair covering, from which he pulled out the hairs one after another, put them in his mouth, bit at them, and spat them out. On the card-table, strewn with cards, stood two tallow candles, one of them burned down to the paper that had been twisted round it. Their dim light struggled feebly against the daylight that peeped in at the windows. There

was not an idea in the Uhlan's head; a sort of thick mist of gambling fever clouded all his mental faculties; he felt no remorse even. He tried once to think what he was to do now, how he could get away without a kopeck, how he was to pay back the fifteen thousand roubles of government money he had lost, what the commander of his regiment would say, what his mother would say, what his comrades would say—and such terror had come over him, and such disgust with himself, that he jumped up, anxious to find forgetfulness in something. He walked up and down his room, trying not to step except on the chinks between the boards of the flooring, and he began again going over the minutest details of the games he had played. He vividly recalled how he had imagined himself to be winning back his losses, had taken away the nine, had laid the king of spades on two thousand roubles, on the right had been dealt the queen, on the left the ace, on the right the king of diamonds—and everything had been lost; but if it had been the six on the right, and the king of diamonds on the left, then he would have won it all back, then he would have staked it all —doubles or quits—and have been fifteen thousand roubles to the good. Then he'd have bought himself a saddle horse from his regimental commander, and a pair of carriage horses, too, and a phaeton. And what else? Well, it would have been a splendid, splendid stroke of luck.

He lay down again on the sofa, and began gnawing the horsehair.

"Why are they singing songs in number seven?" he wondered; "no doubt some merry-making at Turbin's.

Shouldn't I go in and get thoroughly drunk?"

At that instant the count came in.

"Well, my boy, cleaned out, eh?" he roared.

"I'll pretend to be asleep," thought Ilyin, "or else I shall have to talk to him, and I really am sleepy."

But Turbin went up to him and stroked his head.

"Come, my dear fellow; cleaned out? lost everything? tell me."

Ilyin did not answer.

Turbin pulled him by the hand.

"Yes, I've lost. What is it to you?" muttered Ilyin in a voice of sleepy, careless annoyance, not changing his position.

"Everything."

"Well, yes. What does it matter? Everything. What is it to you?"

"Listen, tell me the truth, as a comrade," said the count, sympathetically disposed by the wine he had drunk, and still stroking his hair. "I like you, really. Tell me the truth; if you've lost government money, I'll make it all right, or else it will be too late. . . . Was it government money?"

Ilyin jumped up from the sofa.

"If you will have me tell you . . . don't speak to me, because . . . please don't speak to me . . . a bullet in my brains—that's all I've left to do!" he cried in genuine despair, and his head falling into his hand he burst into tears, although a minute before he had been quite serenely dreaming of the saddle horse.

"Come, come, why, what a girl you are! Who hasn't been through the same thing? There's no harm done; may be we can set it right yet. Wait here for me."

The count went out of the room.

"Where is that gentlman, Luhnov, staying?" he asked the corridor waiter.

The man offered to show the count his room. In spite of the footman's protesting that his master had only just come in and was undressing, the count went into the room. Luhnov was sitting in his dressing-gown, counting several bundles of notes that lay on the table before him. On the table stood a bottle of his favourite Rhine wine. In honour of his winnings, he was indulging himself with this treat. Luhnov gazed coldly and severely through his spectacles at the count, as though he did not recognise him.

"You seem not to know me," said the count, advancing with resolute steps to the table.

Luhnov recognised the count, and asked—

"What do you want?"

"I want a game of cards with you," said Turbin, seating himself on the sofa.

"Now?"

"Yes."

"Another time I shall be delighted, count, but just now I'm tired, and am just getting ready for bed. Will you take some wine? it's good wine."

"But I want to play now."

"I'm not inclined to play any more. Perhaps one of the other gentlemen will care to; but I will not, count! You must please, excuse me."

"Then you won't?"

Luhnov gave a shrug of the shoulders expressive of his regret at the impossibility of complying with the count's wishes.

"You will not on any consideration?"

Again the same shrug.

"But I most particularly beg you to . . . come, will you play?"

Silence.

"Will you play?" the count asked a second time; "mind now!"

The same silence and a rapid glance over the spectacles at the count's face, which had begun to look scowling.

"Will you play?" the count roared, bringing his hand down on the table, so that the bottle of Rhine wine toppled over and was spilt. "You won that unfairly, you know. Will you play? For the third time I ask you."

"I have told you I will not. This is really strange conduct, count! And quite improper to come and hold a knife to a man's throat," observed Luhnov, not raising his eyes.

There followed a silence of no long duration, in the course of which the count's face became paler and paler. Suddenly a terrible blow on the head stupefied Luhnov. He fell on the sofa, tried to get hold of the notes, and shrieked in a voice of shrill despair, which could never have been anticipated from his always composed and dignified appearance. Turbin gathered up the notes left lying on the table, pushed away the servant who came running in to his master's assistance, and walked with rapid steps out of the room.

"If you wish for satisfaction, I'm at your service. I shall be another half-hour in my room," added the count, turning at Luhnov's door.

"Robber! burglar!" came from within. "I'll bring him before a police-court!"

Ilyin, who had attached no significance whatever to the count's promise to make it all right, was still lying on the sofa in his room, and tears of despair were choking him. The count's friendliness and sympathy had broken through the strange medley of feelings, ideas, and memories that filled his soul, and had roused him to a sense of the reality, and that sense had not left him. His youth, so rich in hopes, honour, social esteem, dreams of love and friendship—all was lost for ever. The fount of tears was beginning to run dry, too calm a feeling of hopelessness took more and more possession of him, and the idea of suicide excited now no aversion or horror, and arrested his thoughts more and more frequently. At that point he heard the count's firm tread. Turbin's face still wore traces of wrath; his hands trembled slightly, but there was a gleam of kindly good-humour and self-satisfaction in his eyes.

"Here! I've won it back!" he said, flinging several bundles of notes on the table. "Count them. Are these all? And make haste and come into the public room. I'm just starting," he added, apparently not observing the intense emotion of joy and gratitude on the Uhlan's face; and, whistling a gypsy song, he walked out of the room.

CHAPTER VIII

TO THE TOWN!

SASHKA, tightly girt with a sash, announced that the horses were ready, but urged that they should go first to get the count's greatcoat, which was worth some three hundred roubles with its fur collar, and give back the filthy blue cloak to the scoundrel who had left it in exchange for the greatcoat at the marshal's. But Turbin said there was no need to look for the greatcoat, and went to his room to change his dress.

The cavalry officer sat speechless by his gypsy girl, and hiccupped incessantly. The police captain asked for vodka and invited the whole party to come at once to breakfast with him, promising that his wife would join them and dance with the gypsies herself. The handsome young man was arguing profoundly with Ilyushka that there was more soul in the pianoforte, and that one could not take A flat on the guitar. The government official was dejectedly drinking tea in a corner, and seemed in the light of day ashamed of his debauch. The gypsies were squabbling among themselves in their own tongue, and insisting on doing something more in honour of the gentlemen, which baroray (in Romany, count of prince, or more exactly, the great barin) would be angry. Altogether the revels had burnt down to their last embers.

"Come, one more song at parting, and march home," said the count, more fresh and gay and handsome than ever, as he came into the hall in his travelling dress.

The gypsies ranged themselves in a ring again, and were just beginning to sing, when Ilyin came in with a packet of notes, and called the count aside.

"I only had fifteen thousand roubles of government money, and you have given me sixteen thousand three hundred," he said; "these must be yours."

"Capital! give them here!"

Ilyin gave the count the notes, glancing timidly at him, opened his mouth, meaning to say something, but only blushed so that the tears came

into his eyes, then snatched the count's hand and began to squeeze it.

"Get along! Ilyushka!—listen—here's some money for you; only see me off with songs as far as the town gates." And he threw on to his guitar the thirteen hundred roubles Ilyin had brought him. But the hundred roubles the cavalry officer had lent the count on the previous day, he simply forgot about.

By now it was ten o'clock in the morning. The sun was above the house roofs, people were thronging the streets, tradesmen had long before opened their shops, noblemen and government clerks were driving about the streets, ladies were walking up and down the arcade of shops, when the whole procession of the gypsies, the police captain, the cavalry officer, the handsome young man, Ilyin, and the count in his blue bear-lined cloak came out on the hotel steps. It was a sunny day and thawing. Three sledges, each driving three horses abreast, with their tails tied up short, splashed through the sticky mud up to the steps, and all the festive company began to stow themselves away in them. The count, Ilyin, Styoshka, Ilyushka, and Sashka, the count's servant, were in the first sledge. Blüches was frantic, and wagging his tail barked at the shaft horse. The other gentlemen, together with the rest of the gypsies, got into the other sledges. As soon as they got out of the hotel yard, the sledges kept abreast and the gypsies struck up a song in chorus.

The three sledges drove through the whole town as far as the gates to the accompaniment of songs and bells.

forcing all the vehicles that met them right on to the pavement.

Great was the astonishment of the tradespeople and passers-by who did not know them—still greater that of those who did know them—when they saw the noble gentlemen driving in broad daylight along the streets accompanied by singing by gypsy girls, and drunken gypsies.

When they had driven out of the town gates, the three sledges stopped, and all began to take leave of the count.

Ilyin, who had drunk a good deal in honour of the occasion, and had been driving the horses all the time, suddenly became depressed, and began trying to persuade the count to remain another day. When he was convinced that this was impossible, he quite unexpectedly fell to kissing his new friend, and promised that when he got back he would ask to be exchanged into Turbin's regiment. The count was in particularly good spirits; the cavalry officer, who had towards morning dropped finally into addressing him as "thou," he shoved into a snowdrift; he set Blücher on the police captain, clasped Styoshka in his arms, and wanted to carry her off with him to Moscow. At last he jumped into the sledge, making Blücher sit beside him in spite of the dog's attempts to stand up in the middle. Sashka, too, mounted the box, after once more begging the cavalry officer to get the count's greatcoat back somehow and to send it after them. The count shouted "Off!" waved his forage-cap over his head, and whistled like a sledge-driver to his horses. The sledges drove away in different directions.

Far ahead nothing was to be seen but the plain of monotonous snow with the road, a dirty, yellowish streak, winding across it. The sun shone brightly, sparkling on the thawing snow and the thin crust of ice coating it, and pleasantly warmed the face and back. Steam rose in clouds from the sweating horses. The sledge bell tinkled. A peasant ran splashing with his soaked, plaited shoes across the sloppy road, and, tugging at his cord reins, hurriedly moved on one side with a loaded sledge that slipped quickly downhill. A stout, red peasant-woman, with a baby at her bosom inside her sheepskin, was sitting on another cart-load, slashing at her white nag with the ends of her reins. The count suddenly thought of Anna Fyodorovna.

"Back!" he shouted.

The driver did not at once understand.

"Turn back! drive to the town quickly!"

The sledge drove again past the town gates, and dashed smartly up to the wooden steps of Madame Zaytsov's house. The count ran rapidly up the steps, walked through the hall and the drawing-room; and finding the widow still asleep, took her in his arms, lifted her out of the bed, kissed her sleepy eyes and quickly ran away again. Anna Fyodorovna, half asleep, simply licked her lips, and wondered what had happened. The count jumped into the sledge, shouted to the driver, and without stopping again, without even thinking of Luhnov, of the little widow, or of Styoshka, musing only on what was awaiting him in Moscow, he left the town of K. for ever.

CHAPTER IX

LIZA

TWENTY years had passed. Much water, as they say, had flowed by since then; many people were dead, many had been born, many had grown up and reached maturity. Even more were the ideas that had been born and died; much that was good and much that was evil in the old time had passed away; much that was good in the young had grown up; and still more that was crude, grotesque, and new had come into God's world.

Count Fyodor Turbin had long since been killed in a duel with a foreigner, whom he had flogged with a dog-whip in the street. His son—as like him as one drop of water is like another—was a charming young man of three-and-twenty, an officer in the Guards. In his moral nature, young Count Turbin was not at all like his father. He had not the faintest shadow of the stormy, passionate, and, to speak frankly, dissolute propensities of the last generation. Together with intelligence, culture, and the gifted nature he inherited from his father, a love of decorum and comfort, a practical way of looking at men and circumstances, good sense and prudence, were his most marked characteristics. The young count had risen rapidly in the army; by the age of three-and-twenty he had been a lieutenant. . . . At the commencement of military operations he had decided that it would be advantageous, with a view to promotion, to exchange for active service, and had been transferred to a regiment of hussars as cavalry captain, and

had very soon after received a squadron.

In May, 1848, the S. regiment of hussars chanced to be passing through the K. province, and the very squadron that was commanded by young Count Turbin had to halt for the night at Morozovka, Anna Fyodorovna's estate. Anna Fyodorovna was living, but was by now so elderly that she no longer even regarded herself as young, which means a great deal for a woman. She had grown very fat, and that is said to make a woman look younger; but even in her white, plump contours thick, soft wrinkles were to be seen. She never visited the town now, and it was with difficulty that she clambered into her carriage. But she was just as good-natured, and there was no concealing the fact, now that there was no beauty to carry it off, that she was as silly as ever. With her lived her daughter, Liza, a Russian country beauty of three-and-twenty, and her brother, our old friend the cavalry officer, who with his easy good-nature had wasted all his little property and had found a refuge in his old age with Anna Fyodorovna. His hair was completely grey; his upper lip had sunk, but the moustache over it was carefully dyed black. Wrinkles covered not only his forehead and cheeks, but even his nose and neck, and his back was bent; but yet in his weak, crooked legs one could still see something of the bearing of the old cavalry officer.

In the small drawing-room of the old house, with its verandah door and windows opening on to an old-fashioned, star-shaped garden full of lime-trees, were sitting all the family and domestic circle of Anna Fyodorovna. She herself, a grey-headed woman, wearing a lilac, wadded jacket, sat on the sofa at a round table playing patience. Her old brother, in clean, white trousers and a blue coat, was settled near the window engaged in crocheting a strip of white braiding, an art which his niece had taught him, and he was very fond of practising as he was incapable of doing anything active now, and his eyesight was beginning to fail for reading the newspapers—his favourite occupation. Pimotchka, a girl Anna Fyodorovna had adopted and was bringing up, was learning a lesson near him under the guidance of Liza who was at the same time busy knitting on wooden pins a stocking of goat's wool for her uncle. The last rays of the setting sun threw always at that hour their slanting, broken patches of light through the lime-tree avenue on to the furthest window and the whatnot near it. It was so still in the room and the garden that they could hear the quick whir of a swallow's wings outside the window and Anna Fyodorovna's subdued sigh indoors, and the old man clearing his throat and crossing his legs.

"How is this played? Lizanka, do show me. I always forget," said Anna Fyodorovna, coming to a standstill in her game of patience.

Liza went up to her mother without stopping in her work and glanced at the cards.

"Ah, you have made a muddle of it, mamma, darling!" she said, changing the position of the cards; "that's how it ought to have been. Still it will do very well in the way you have hit on," she added, slipping a card off unseen by her mother.

"Oh, that's how you always deceive me! you say it is all right."

"No; really, it will succeed. It is all right."

"Well, well, you always spoil me! But isn't it tea-time?"

"I have told them to heat the samovar. I'll go and see after it in a minute. Will you have it brought in here? . . . Come, Pimotchka, make haste and finish your lesson, and let us have a run."

And Liza went out at the door.

"Lizotchka! Lizanka!" said her uncle looking intently at his crochet-hook; "I believe I've dropped a stitch again. Pick it up for me, darling!"

"In a minute, in a minute! I am only going to give out the sugar to be broken."

And three minutes later she ran back into the room, went up to her uncle, and pinched his ear.

"There, that's to teach you not to drop stitches," she said, laughing; "you haven't even crocheted to the end of your task."

"Come, that's enough; set it right, there seems to be a sort of little knot."

Liza took the crochet-hook, took a pin out of her kerchief, which blew open a little in the draught from the window, and picked up the stitch with the pin, pulled it through twice and gave the hook back to her uncle.

"Now kiss me for that," she said, offering him her rosy cheek as she pinned her kerchief again, "you are going to have rum to-day with your tea. It's Friday, you know." And she went back to the tea-room.

"Uncle, come and look; the hussars are coming!" her rich voice called from there.

Anna Fyodorovna went with her brother into the tea-room, from which the windows looked out on the village, to see the hussars passing. There was very little to be seen from the window; all that could be made out was a crowd of some sort moving through the dust.

"I'm sorry, though, sister," the uncle observed to Anna Fyodorovna, "that we're so cramped for room and the lodge isn't finished yet; we might have asked the officers to stay here. Officers of the hussars are always such gay, nice young fellows, you know; we might have seen a little of them any way."

"Well, I'd have been heartily pleased to do so, but you know yourself, brother, that we've no spare room. My bed-room, Liza's little room, the drawing-room, and this room of yours—that's all there is. Where could we put them, only think? Mihailo Matveyev has cleaned the village elder's cottage for them; he says it's clean, too."

"And we'd have picked out a young man for you among them, too, Lizotchka, a gallant hussar!" said her uncle.

"No, I don't want a hussar, I want an Uhlan; you were in the Uhlans, weren't you, uncle? I don't want to know those hussars; they're all such desperate fellows, they say."

And Liza blushed a little; but she laughed her mellow laugh again.

"Here comes Ustyushka running; we must ask her what she's seen," she said.

Anna Fyodorovna had Ustyushka sent for.

"You never can sit quietly at your work; what need had you to be running to stare at the soldiers?" said Anna Fyodorovna. "Come, tell us where the officers are being put up?"

"At Eremkin's cottage, madam. Two of them there are such handsome gentlemen; one's a count they do say."

"And what's his name?"

"Kazarov or Turbinov, I don't remember, I'm sorry."

"What a silly creature, can't even tell me anything. You might have found out the name."

"Well, shall I run now?"

"Oh, yes, I know you're always ready to do that! No, let Danilo go; tell him, brother, to go and inquire whether the officers are in want of anything; we must show them every civility; he's to say that his mistress sent him to inquire."

The old people settled down again in the tea-room, while Liza went to the maids' room to put the broken sugar back in the drawer. Ustyushka was talking there about the hussars.

"Mistress, darling, what a handsome fellow he was, that count!" she said; "simply a dark-browed cherub. There, if you'd a betrothed like that, it would make a fine couple!"

The other maids smiled approvingly; the old nurse sitting at the window with a stocking sighed and repeated some prayer, drawing deep, inward breaths.

"So I see you liked the hussars," said Liza; "but, I know you're always good at describing what you've seen. Take in some syrup, please, Ustyushka, to treat the hussars with."

And Liza, laughing, went out of the room with the sugar-basin.

"I should like to see what that hussar's like," she thought, "dark or fair. And, of course, he'd be glad, I dare say, to make our acquaintance. But he'll go away and never know that I was here and thought about him. And how many have passed by me like that! No one ever sees me but uncle and Ustyushka. However I do my hair, whatever sleeves I put on—there's no one to admire me," she thought, sighing as she looked at her plump, white hand. "He is sure to be tall, with large eyes and little, dark moustaches, most likely. No, twenty-two years have gone and no one has fallen in love with me, except Ivan Ignatitch, who's pock-marked. And four years ago I was better-looking than now, and so my girlhood has passed away giving no joy to any one. Ah, I'm an unlucky, unlucky country girl!"

Her mother's voice calling her to pour out the tea roused this country girl from her momentary melancholy. She gave her head a shake and went into the tea-room.

The best things always come by chance; and the more one tries to get them, the worse is the result. In the country people do not often try to give their children a good education, and so by chance they often give them an excellent one. It had been especially so with Liza. Anna Fyodorovna, with her limited intellect and her easy character, had not troubled herself about Liza's education. She had not had her taught music, nor that exceedingly useful language, French. But she had happened to bear her deceased husband a healthy, pretty child—a daughter. She had handed her over to nurses; had fed her, dressed her in cotton frocks and goat-skin slippers, sent her out for walks, and to pick mush-

rooms and berries; had her taught reading, writing, and arithmetic by a seminarist engaged for the purpose; and in Liza at sixteen she found, through no design of hers, a companion always gay and goodhearted, and a capable housekeeper to manage her house for her. Anna Fyodorovna's kindness of heart led her to adopt and bring up various girls, children of her serfs, and foundlings. Since she was ten years old Liza had begun looking after those protégées, teaching them, dressing them, taking them to church, and checking them when they were too mischievous. Then came her decrepit, good-natured uncle, who had to be waited on like a child. Then the servants and the peasants, who all came to their young mistress with their wants and their ailments. The latter she treated with elder-flower water, mint, and camphorated spirit. Then there was the management of the house, which insensibly had passed entirely into her hands. Then came the unsatisfied craving for love, which found an outlet only in nature and in religion. And Liza had happened to turn into a capable, good-humoured, cheerful, independent, pure, and deeply-religious woman. She had, it is true, her little pangs of vanity at the sight of neighbouring young ladies in fashionable hats from the town standing beside her in church. She was sometimes vexed to tears by her querulous old mother's whims. She had, too, her dreams of love in the most absurd and sometimes coarse forms. But the useful and necessary activity of her life dispelled them, and at twenty-two not a blemish, not a remorse, had marred the clear, serene soul of the developing girl, who was full of physical and moral beauty. Liza was of medium height, rather plump than thin; her eyes were brown and not large, with a very slight, dark shadow on the lower lid; she had long, fair hair. She had rather a loose, swaying gait—a duck's walk, as it is called. The expression of her face, when she was absorbed in what she was doing, and there was nothing special exciting her, told every one who watched it, as plainly as words: life is a sweet and joyful thing for one who has some one to love and a pure conscience. Even in moments of anger, embarrassment, agitation or distress, in tears, when her left brow scowled and her lips were set, in despite, it seemed, of her own wish, the dimples on her cheeks, the corners of her lips, the shining eyes, so used to smile and rejoice in life, fairly beamed with the light of an unsophisticated, kindly, upright heart.

CHAPTER X

THE SQUADRON

It was still hot, though the sun had set, when the squadron entered Morozovka. In front of them a brindled cow, that had strayed away from the herd, ran along the village street at a trot, looking back, lowing, stopping now and then, and never grasping that all she had to do was to move aside. The old peasants, the women and children, and the house-serfs flocked together on both sides of the street, eagerly staring at the hussars. In a thick cloud of dust the hussars rode in on their raven horses, snorting and clattering their hoofs. On the right of the squadron rode the two officers, sitting carelessly on their beautiful black horses. One was the commander, Count Turbin; the other, a very young man, only recently promoted from an ensign, Polozov.

A hussar in a white tunic came out of the best hut in the village, and taking off his forage-cap, went up to the officers.

"Where are the quarters set apart for us?" the count asked him.

"For your excellency," answered the quartermaster, with an alert movement of his whole figure, "here, at the elder's. I have had the hut cleaned. I inquired at the manor-house. They say they can't. The lady is so nasty."

"Oh, very well," said the count, dismounting at the elder's hut and straightening his legs. "Has my carriage come?"

"It has been pleased to arrive, your excellency!" replied the quartermaster, pointing with his cap to a leather-covered carriage that could be seen at the gates, and ran ahead into the entry of the hut, which was crowded with the peasant's family, come to stare at the officer. He upset one old woman, indeed, as he smartly opened the door into the freshly scrubbed hut, and stood aside to admit the count.

The hut was fairly large and roomy, but not perfectly clean. A German valet, dressed like a gentleman, stood in the hut. He had put up an iron bedstead, and was making the bed and unpacking the linen from a trunk.

"Foo! what disgusting quarters!" said the count crossly. "Dyadenko! couldn't you move us somewhere to some gentleman's house?"

"If your excellency bids me, I'll go

to the manor-house," answered Dyadenko, "but the little house isn't good
for much; it seems to be no better than
a cottage."

"Then there's no use in your going.
You can go." And the count, clasping
his hands behind his head, lay down
on the bed.

"Johann!" he shouted to his valet,
"you've made a lump in the middle of
the bed again! How is it you can't
make a bed properly?"

Johann would have smoothed it out.

"No, you needn't do it now . . .
Where's my dressing-gown?" he went
on in a dissatisfied voice.

The servant gave him his dressing-
gown.

Before putting it on, the count
looked at the skirt of the dressing-
gown.

"There it is; you've not taken out
those marks. Could any one do his
work worse than you do?" he added,
pulling the dressing-gown out of his
hands and putting it on. "Tell me,
do you do it on purpose? . . . Is
tea ready?"

"I hadn't time to see to it," answered
Johann.

"Fool!"

After that the count took the French
novel that had been put ready for him,
and for a good time he read it in
silence, while Johann went into the
outer room to blow up the samovar.
The count was unmistakably in a bad
temper—no doubt under the combined
influences of fatigue, a dusty face, a
tight uniform and an empty stomach.

"Johann!" he shouted again, "give
me an account of those ten roubles.
What did you buy in the town?"

The count looked at the account the

valet handed him and expressed dissatisfaction at the high price of the
purchases.

"Give me some rum with the tea."

"I didn't buy any rum," said Johann.

"Oh, indeed! how often have I told
you there must be rum!"

"I hadn't money enough."

"Why didn't Polozov buy some?
You should have got some from his
man."

"Cornet Polozov? I don't know.
His honour bought tea and sugar."

"Beast! . . . Go away! . . . No
one can put me out of patience as you
do . . . you know I always take rum
with my tea on the march."

"Here are two letters for you from
the staff," said the valet.

The count, lying on his bed, tore
open the letters and began reading
them. The cornet, who had been seeing the squadron to their quarters,
came in with a beaming face.

"Well, Turbin? It seems very nice
here. But I am tired, I must confess.
It has been hot."

"Oh, very nice! A nasty, stinking
hut and no rum, thanks to you; your
blockhead didn't buy any, nor that
fellow either. You might have told
them!"

And he went on reading. When he
had read to the end, he crumpled up
the letter and threw it on the floor.

"Why didn't you buy any rum?" the
cornet meanwhile was asking her servant in a whisper in the outer room.
"You had the money, hadn't you?"

"But why should we always buy
everything? As it is, I stand all the
expenses; while his German does
nothing but smoke his pipe."

The second letter was apparently not unpleasant, for the count smiled as he read it.

"From whom?" asked Polozov, running back into the room, and arranging a bed for himself on some boards near the stove.

"From Mina," the count answered good-humouredly, giving him the letter. "Would you like to read it? What a charming woman! . . . yes, really she's better than any of our young ladies. . . . See, what feeling and sense there is in that letter! One thing's bad—she asks for money."

"Yes, that's bad," answered the cornet.

"I promised her some, it's true; but what with the march here and everything . . . but if I'm in command of the squadron another three months, I'll send her some. I don't grudge it, really; charming creature! . . . eh?" he said, smiling, and watching the expression of Polozov's face as he read the letter.

"It's always illiterate, but sweet, and she seems really fond of you," answered the cornet.

"H'm! I should think so! It's only women like that who love truly when they do love."

"And from whom is the other letter?" inquired the cornet, handing back the letter he had read.

"Oh . . . that's a person, a miserable creature, to whom I lost money at cards, and this is the third time he's reminded me . . . I can't pay it now . . . a stupid letter!" answered the count, evidently mortified by the recollection of the letter.

Both officers were silent for some time after this conversation. The

cornet, who was unmistakably under the influence of the count, did not speak as he drank his tea, unable to make up his mind to start a topic. He glanced from time to time at the handsome, downcast face of Turbin, who was looking intently out of window.

"Oh, well, things may turn out capitally," the count said suddenly, looking with a cheerful shake of his head at Polozov. "If there's promotion this year in our regiment, in the line, and we get into action, too, I might get ahead of my old comrades in the Guards."

Their talk was still on the same subject over the second glass of tea, when old Danilo came in and gave Anna Fyodorovna's message. "And her honour bade me inquire, too, isn't your honour son of Count Fyodor Ivanovitch Turbin?" Danilo added on his own account, having found out the officer's surname, and still remembering the late count's visit to the town of K.: "Our lady, Anna Fyodorovna, was very well acquainted with him."

"He was my father; and tell your mistress that I am very grateful to her, that we need nothing; only say, we told you to ask if we couldn't get a room cleaner than this somewhere, in their house, or somewhere."

"Oh, why did you say that?" said Polozov, when Danilo had gone. "What does it matter? It's only one night, isn't it quite all right here?—and they will put themselves out."

"What next! we've had quite enough knocking about in smoky hovels, for my taste! . . . You're not a practical person, one can see that at once; why not profit by the chance, if, for one night at least, we can be lodged like human beings? It's quite the other way—they'll be awfully glad to have us. There's only one thing I dislike. If this lady really did know my father," the count said, showing his gleaming, white teeth in a smile—"I'm always ashamed in a way of my late papa; there's always some scandalous story or old debt cropping up. That's why I can't bear to meet these friends of my father's. Though, of course, the times were like that then," he added seriously.

"I never told you," said Polozov, "how I met a commander of an Uhlan brigade, Ilyin. He wanted very much to see you, and was extremely fond of your father."

"He's a wretched creature, I fancy, that Ilyin. And the point is that all these worthies, who declare they knew my father, so as to make up to me, tell me—as though they were delightful facts—stories about my father that I'm ashamed to listen to. It's a fact— I'm not led away by my feeling, but look at things dispassionately—that he was much too impulsive, and sometimes did things he shouldn't have done. It's all a question of time, though. In these days he would, very likely, have made a very successful man, for he had immense capacities, one must do him that justice."

A quarter of an hour later the servant returned with an invitation from his mistress for them to stay the night in her house.

CHAPTER XI

A PRETTY DAUGHTER

On learning that the officer of the hussars was the son of Count Fyodor Turbin, Anna Fyodorovna was thrown into a great flutter.

"Good gracious me! I shall be glad to see him! . . . Danilo, make haste and say your mistress invites them," she said, jumping up, and with rapid steps going to the maids' room. "Lizanska! Ustyushka! they must get ready your room, Liza. You must move into your uncle's; and you, brother! you must sleep in the drawing-room. For one night, it won't matter."

"Not a bit, sister! I can sleep on the floor."

"A handsome fellow, I bet, if he's like his father. I must have a look at him, the dear fellow. . . . You must see him, Liza! Ah, his father was handsome. . . . Where are you taking the table? leave it here!" cried Anna Fyodorovna, bustling about, "and bring in two bedsteads—you must get one from the bailiff's—and take the glass candlestick on the whatnot that brother made me a present of on my nameday, and put a stearine candle in it."

At last everything was ready. Regardless of her mother's interference, Liza arranged her room for the two officers in her own way. She got out the clean bed linen, fragrant with mignonette, and made the beds, told the maids to put a decanter of water and candles on a little table by the bedside; she lighted a perfumed paper in the maids' room, and moved her own belongings and her little bed into her uncle's room.

Anna Fyodorovna calmed down a little, settled herself again in her place, and even took up the cards again, but without dealing them she leaned on her fat elbow and fell to musing. "Time, ah, how time flies!" she repeated to herself in a whisper. "It doesn't seem long! I can see him now. Ah, he was a naughty man!" And tears came into her eyes. "Lizanka now . . . but still she's not what I was at her age . . . a good girl, but no, not the same! . . ."

"Lizanka, you'd better put on your *mousseline de laine* for the evening."

"But shall you really ask them in, mamma? Better not, really," answered Liza, who could not suppress her emotion at the idea of seeing the officers—"better not, mamma!"

She was really not so much eager to see them as frightened at some agitating happiness which seemed to be in store for her.

"Perhaps they want to make our acquaintance themselves, Lizotchka!" said Anna Fyodorovna, stroking her hair, and thinking, as she did so, "No, it's not hair such as I had at her age. . . . No, Lizotchka, how I could wish for you . . ." And she certainly did wish for something very much for her daughter; but marriage with the count she could hardly expect—such relations as she had had with his father, she could not desire for her— but for something of that sort she did very very much wish for her daughter. She longed, perhaps, to live over again in her daughter the emotions she had passed through with the count.

The old cavalry officer, too, was rather excited at the count's arrival. He went into his room and shut himself up there. A quarter of an hour later, he came out in a military coat and blue trousers, and with the expression of embarrassed satisfaction with which a girl puts on a ball-dress for the first time, he went into the room that had been assigned to the guests.

"I'll have a look at the hussars of these days, sister! The late count was a real hussar, truly. I'll have a look at them, I'll have a look at them."

The officers had by now arrived by the back stairs and reached the room allotted to them.

"Come, do you see," said the count, lying down just as he was in his dusty boots on the bed prepared for him, "isn't this better than a hut full of black beetles?"

"Better, of course it is, but it's putting oneself under obligations to one's hosts. . . ."

"What nonsense! One must be practical in everything. They're awfully pleased, not a doubt of it. . . . Boy," he shouted, "ask for something to hang over this window, or there will be a draught at night."

At that moment the old gentleman came in to make acquaintance with the officers. Though blushing a little, he did not, of course, omit to mention that he had been a comrade of the late count; that he had been so happy as to be on friendly terms with him, and even added that he had more than once been indebted to the count for his kindly offices in his favour. Whether he meant by the kindly offices of the count that he had not repaid him the hundred roubles he had borrowed, or that he had thrown him into a snowdrift, or that he had sworn at him, the old gentleman did not explain. The count was very civil to the old cavalry officer, and thanked him for putting them up.

"You must excuse its not being very

luxurious, count" — he had almost slipped out with "your excellency," he had got so out of the way of having to do with people of rank—"my sister's house is a small one. But we'll hang something up there immediately, and it will be all right!" added the old man, and on the pretext of seeing about a curtain, but principally to report as soon as possible on the officers, he withdrew scraping from the room.

The pretty maid, Ustyushka, came in to hang her mistress's shawl over the window. Her mistress had told her to ask also if the gentlemen would like some tea.

Their comfortable quarters evidently had a cheering effect on the count's spirits. He smiled and joked so good-humouredly with Ustyushka that the latter went the length of calling him a naughty man. He questioned her as to whether her young lady was pretty, and in answer to her inquiry about tea, said that they might certainly bring some tea, but that as their supper was not ready yet, what would be more to the point would be some vodka now, a snack of something to eat, and some sherry, if they had any.

The uncle was enthusiastic over the young count's courtesy and extolled the young generation of officers to the skies, saying that young men nowadays were incomparably superior to what young men used to be.

Anna Fyodorovna could not agree with this—better than Count Fyodor Ivanovitch no one had ever been—and at last, she was seriously vexed with him, remarking drily, "As for you, brother, whoever's civil to you last, you think he's the best. . . . We all know, of course, that people are cleverer

nowadays, but still Count Fyodor Ivanovitch danced the écossaise in such style and was such a pattern of courtesy that every one, one may say, was crazy about him; though he paid no attention to any one but me. So there were good people even in those old days, too."

At that moment, word was brought her of the request for vodka, light refreshments, and sherry.

"There, now, brother, how you do things! You always do everything wrong. We ought to have ordered supper for them," said Anna Fyodorovna. "Liza! look after it, darling."

Liza ran to the store-room for mush-rooms, and freshly churned butter, and ordered the cook to get beef collops.

"But what about the sherry? Have you any left, brother?"

"No, sister! I never had any."

"Never had any! why, what is it you drink with your tea?"

"That's rum, Anna Fyodorovna."

"Isn't it all the same? You give him that—it's just the same thing—rum. But wouldn't it be better to ask them in here, brother? You know all about them. They wouldn't take it amiss, surely?"

The cavalry officer declared that he would answer for it that the count would be too good-natured to refuse, and that he would bring him without fail. Anna Fyodorovna went for some unknown reason to put on her gros grain dress and a new cap, while Liza was so busy that she had not time to change the pink linen dress with full sleeves that she had on. She was, besides, extremely excited; it seemed to her that something stupendous was awaiting her, as though a lowering, black cloud were hanging over her soul. This count and hussar, who was so handsome, seemed to her some quite new kind of creature, beyond her comprehension, but magnificent. His character, his habits, his words,—all must be something extraordinary, such as she had never met. Everything he thought and said would be sure to be true and clever; everything he did must be honourable; his whole appearance would be splendid. She had no doubt about this. If instead of sherry and refreshments, he had asked for a bath of scented herbs and perfumes, she would not have been surprised, she would not have criticised him, and would have been firmly convinced that this must and should be so.

The count agreed at once when the cavalry officer communicated his sister's desire; he combed his hair, put on his coat and took his cigar-case.

"Come along," he said to Polozov.

"Really, we'd better not have come," answered the cornet; *"ils feront des frais pour nous recevoir."*

"Nonsense! it's a treat to them. Besides I've made investigations already; there's a pretty daughter. . . . Come along," said the count in French.

"Je vous en prie, messieurs!" said the cavalry officer; simply to give them to understand that he too knew French and was aware of what the officers were saying.

CHAPTER XII

HE!

LIZA flushed, and with downcast eyes affected to be absorbed in pouring out the tea, for she was afraid to look at the officers, when they came into the room. Anna Fyodorovna on the contrary jumped up hurriedly, bowed, and never taking her eyes off the count began to talk to him, at one moment expatiating on his extraordinary resemblance to his father, then introducing her daughter, then offering him tea, jams, or home-pressed fruits. The cornet was so retiring that no one paid him any attention, and he was very glad of it as, so far as good manners would permit, he was absorbed in scrutinising and minutely examining the beauty of Liza, who had evidently made a great impression on him. The old gentleman listened to his sister's conversation with the count, with the words ready on his tongue, waiting for a chance to begin upon his cavalry reminiscences. After tea, the count lighted his thick cigar, the smoke of which made Liza scarcely able to keep from coughing. He was very conversational and polite. At first he put in a few words in the intervals between Anna Fyodorovna's disconnected speeches, and finally obtained exclusive control of the conversation. One thing struck his listeners as rather strange. In his anecdotes he often made use of words which, though not regarded as reprehensible in the society he moved in, were here rather risky, and Anna Fyodorovna was a little alarmed, while Liza blushed up to her ears. But the count did not observe this, and was just as serenely polite and direct. Liza poured out the tea in silence, and instead of putting the glasses in the guests' hands, set them close beside them. She had not yet recovered from her agitation, and listened eagerly to the count's words. The absence of any special wittiness in his stories, the frequent hesitations in his speech, restored her composure a little. She did not hear from him any of the very clever things she had expected; she did not see that elegance in everything she had vaguely expected to find in him. By the time the third cup of tea was reached, after her timid eyes had met his eyes once, and he had not dropped them, but had with rather too much composure continued gazing at her and smiling, she felt even a little antagonistic to him, and quickly discovered that there was nothing striking about him, that he was not in fact distinguished in any way from all the men she had seen, that he was not worth being afraid of. His nails were long and clean, that was all, and he was not even particularly handsome. Liza promptly regained her serenity, not without an inward pang at parting from her daydream. Now only the eyes of the silent cornet, which she felt were fixed on her, disturbed her equanimity. "Perhaps it's not *he,* but *he!*" she thought.

CHAPTER XIII

TO-NIGHT!

AFTER tea, the old lady invited the guests into the other room, and settled herself in her own place.

"But wouldn't you like to rest, count?" she asked. "Then how shall we entertain our guests?" she continued on receiving a reply in the negative. "Do you play cards, count? Come, brother, you should make up a game of something to entertain them. . . ."

"But you play preference yourself, you know," answered the cavalry officer, "so let us have a game together. Will you play, count? and will you?"

The officers signified their readiness to do anything that seemed good to their obliging hosts.

Liza brought from her room her pack of cards, with which she used to try fortunes, to divine whether Anna Fyodorovna's cold would soon be over, whether her uncle would come back from town that day, when he was away, whether a neighbour would call, and so on. Those cards, though they had been in use for two months, were rather cleaner than the pack Anna Fyodorovna used for fortune-telling.

"Only you don't care to play for a small stake, perhaps?" inquired the uncle. "Anna Fyodorovna and I play for half kopeck stakes. . . . Even so she ruins us all."

"Oh, for what you fix, I shall be delighted," said the count.

"Well, for kopeck stakes—paper money! In honour of our dear guests let it be so; let them plunder me in my old age," said Anna Fyodorovna, seating herself at her ease in her arm-chair and smoothing out her cape.

"May be I shall win a whole silver rouble from them," thought Anna Fyodorovna, who had acquired a slight weakness for gambling in her old age.

"If you like I will teach you to play with 'honours,'" said the count, "and with 'misery.' That's very amusing."

They were all much pleased with the new Petersburg way of playing the game. The uncle declared, indeed, that he knew it, and that it was just the same thing as in Boston, only he had forgotten it a little. Anna Foyodorovna could make nothing of it, and she was so long unable to understand it, that she felt obliged at last to smile and nod her head approvingly, declaring that now she understood it, and it was all perfectly clear to her. There was a good deal of laughter in the middle of the game when Anna Fyodorovna called "misery" with the ace and king in her hand, and made six. She began, indeed, to lose her head, smiled timidly, and hurriedly admitted that she was not yet quite accustomed to the new way of playing. The points she lost were reckoned against her, however, and numerous they were, too, especially as the count, being used to play for high stakes, played carefully, kept an exact count, and would not grasp the significance of the kicks the cornet gave him under the table, and the glaring blunders he made in his play.

Liza brought in some more pressed fruit, three sorts of preserves, and apples kept in a special sort of syrup. She stood behind her mother, watching the game and occasionally looking at the officers, and particularly at the delicate, pink, carefully-trimmed nails and white hands of the count, as they deftly, confidently, and gracefully flung down cards and picked up tricks.

Again Anna Fyodorovna, in a kind of frenzy, trying to outdo the others, called as high as seven, failed to make even three, and on her brother's demanding her score, she made a grotesque blunder in her reckoning of it, was in a great flutter, and quite lost her head.

"Never mind, mamma, you'll win it back again!" said Liza with a smile, trying to get her mother out of a ridiculous position. "You'll score off uncle; then it'll be his turn."

"If only you would help me, Lizotchka!" said Anna Fyodorovna, looking in a scared way at her daughter. "I don't know how it is . . ."

"But I don't know how to play that way, either," answered Liza, mentally reckoning up her mother's losses. "And you're losing so much, mamma! you won't have anything left for Pimotchka's new frock," she added as a joke.

"Yes, playing in this way one may easily lose as much as ten silver roubles," said the cornet, looking at Liza, and eager to enter into conversation with her.

"Why, aren't we playing for paper money?" inquired Anna Fyodorovna, looking round at the whole party.

"I don't know how it is, but I don't understand reckoning by paper money," said the count. "How do you do it? What does it mean, really, a paper rouble?"

"Oh, but nowadays no one reckons by paper roubles," chimed in the uncle, who was winning.

The old lady ordered some effervescing drink, drank two glasses herself, and flushing very red, seemed to become quite reckless. One lock of her grey hair, indeed, strayed from under her cap, and she did not put it back. She probably felt that she was losing millions, and was completely ruined. More and more frequently the cornet kicked the count under the table. The count noted down the old lady's losses. At last the game was over. In vain Anna Fyodorovna tried to cheat in adding up her losses, and to pretend she had made a mistake in the reckoning; in vain she protested her horror at the magnitude of her loss; at the end of the reckoning it was unmistakably clear that she had lost nine hundred and twenty points. "Does that make nine roubles in paper money?" Anna Fyodorovna asked several times; and she did not grasp all the enormity of her loss till her brother, to her horror, explained that she had lost thirty-two roubles and a half in paper, and that she really must pay it all. The count did not even count his winnings, but as soon as the game was over got up and went to the window, where Liza was setting various dishes and putting some mushrooms out of a jar on to a plate for supper. Quite calmly and directly he did what the cornet had been longing to do all the evening and had not been able to do—he began to talk to Liza about the weather.

The cornet, meanwhile, was placed in a very unpleasant position. When the count, and still more Liza, who had been keeping her mother in good-humour, had left Anna Fyodorovna's side, she became openly furious.

"How annoying it is, though, that we should have plundered you like this!" said Polozov, in order to say something. "It's simply shameful!"

"And bringing in misery and honours, or whatever they are, too! I can't make head or tail of them. Well, in paper roubles, then, how much does it all come to?" she asked.

"Thirty-two roubles, thirty-two and a half," repeated the cavalry officer, who, having won something, was in a jocose humour. "Pay up the money, sister . . . pay it up."

"Yes, I will pay all; only you won't catch me again, no! In all my life, I shall never win all that back."

And Anna Fyodorovna trundled hurriedly to her room, and came back bringing nine rouble notes. It was only

upon the old gentleman insisting on it that she paid up all her debts.

Polozov was in some trepidation lest Anna Fyodorovna might fly out at him if he addressed her. In silence he moved quietly away from her and joined the count and Liza, who were talking at the open window.

In the room, on the table laid for supper, stood two tallow candles. Their light flickered now and then in the fresh warm air of the May night. In the window, open on the garden, it was light too, but the light there was quite different from the light within the room. An almost full moon, with no shade of gold left in it, was sailing above the treetops, throwing brighter and brighter light on the delicate, white clouds that at times obscured it. Frogs croaked in chorus about the pond, part of which could be seen through the avenue, all silvery in the moonlight. In the fragrant lilac bush just under the window the wet flowers swung slowly to and fro, and birds faintly stirred and twittered.

"What exquisite weather!" said the count, going up to Liza and sitting down in the low window. "I suppose you do a great deal of walking?"

"Yes," answered Liza, feeling somehow not the slightest embarrassment now in conversation with the count; "every morning at seven o'clock I go out to see after things on the estate, and then I walk a little with Pimotchka —mamma's ward."

"How pleasant a country life is!" said the count, sticking an eyeglass in his eye, and looking now at the garden and now at Liza. "And on moonlight nights don't you sometimes take walks?"

"No. Two years ago, though, uncle

and I used to go a walk every night when there was a moon. He had a strange sort of complaint—he suffered from sleeplessness. Whenever there was a full moon, he could not sleep. His room—you see, that one—looks straight into the garden, and the window is a low one; so the moonlight falls straight on it."

"How strange!" observed the count; "but that's your room, surely, isn't it?"

"No, I'm only sleeping there for to-night. You have my room."

"Is it possible? . . . O heavens! I shall never forgive myself for inconveniencing you!" said the count, letting his eyeglass drop out in token of the sincerity of his feeling; "if I had only known I was disturbing you."

"Disturbing me! On the contrary, I'm very glad; uncle's room is so charming and bright, with a little low window. I shall sit there comfortably till I go to sleep, or creep out into the garden for a walk in the night."

"What a delightful girl!" thought the count, sticking the eyeglass in again, staring at her, and moving as though to settle himself in the window, he tried to touch her foot with his. "And how cunningly she let me know I could see her in the garden at the window, if I care to!" Liza, indeed, lost a large part of her charm in his eyes, so easy seemed her conquest.

"And what happiness it must be," he said, gazing pensively into the dark avenue, "to spend such a night in a garden with some one one loves."

Liza was somewhat disconcerted by these words, and by the repetition of the apparently accidental contact of his foot. Without thinking, she said something simply to cover her embarrassment. She said, "Yes, it is delightful walking by moonlight." She felt vaguely annoyed. She tied up the jar from which she had taken the mushrooms, and was about to retreat from the window, when the cornet came up to them, and she felt a desire to find out what sort of man he was.

"What a delightful night!" he said.

"They talk about nothing but the weather," thought Liza.

"What a marvellous view!" the cornet went on; "but I dare say you are tired of it," he added, with a strange propensity he had for saying disagreeable things to people who attracted him.

"Why should you think so? The same thing to eat always, or the same dress one may get tired of, but one never tires of a beautiful garden when one is fond of walking, especially when the moon rises a little higher. From uncle's room one can see the whole pond. I shall look at it to-night."

"But you have no nightingales, I think?" queried the count, highly displeased at Polozov's coming and hindering him from arriving at a more definite understanding about meeting her.

"No; we always used to have them; but last year the bird-catchers caught one. This year—last week, in fact—one was singing beautifully, but the constable came with a bell and frightened it away. The year before last, uncle and I used to sit in the thick avenue, and listen to them for two hours at a time."

"What is this chatterbox telling you?" said her uncle, approaching the group. "Will you please to take some supper?"

After supper, in the course of which the count succeeded in somewhat softening the ill-humour of his hostess, the officers took leave of their host, and went off to their room. The count shook hands with the uncle, and to Anna Fyodorovna's astonishment merely shook her hand too, without kissing it. He even shook hands with Liza, looking straight into her face as he did so, and faintly smiling with his agreeable smile. His expression embarrassed the girl again.

"He's very handsome," she thought, "only too much taken up with himself."

CHAPTER XIV

LIZA'S THOUGHTS

"COME, aren't you ashamed?" said Polozov when the officers had returned to their room: "I tried to lose on purpose, and nudged you under the table. I wonder you're not ashamed of yourself; why, the old lady was quite distressed."

The count burst into a tremendous roar of laughter.

"She's a killing old lady; how offended she was!"

And he laughed again with such enjoyment that even Johann, who was standing beside him, looked down and faintly smiled aside.

"And the son of the old friend of the family too! . . . ha, ha, ha!" the count went on laughing.

"No, really, it was too bad. I felt positively sorry for her," said the cornet.

"What nonsense! How young you are! What, would you have me lose? Why should I lose? I used to lose too when I couldn't play properly. Ten roubles will come in useful, my boy. One must look at life from a practical point of view or you'll always be one of the fools."

Polozov did not reply; he wanted indeed to be alone to think of Liza, who seemed to him a wonderfully pure and noble creature. He undressed and lay down in the soft, clean bed that had been prepared for him.

"What nonsense all the honours and glories of war are!" he thought, looking at the window curtained with the shawl, through which stole the pale beams of the moon. "This is happiness—to live in some quiet retreat with a sweet, clever, simple wife, that is true, enduring happiness!"

But for some reason he did not communicate these dreams to his friend, and did not even mention the country girl, though he felt sure that the count too was thinking about her.

"What! aren't you undressing?" he asked the count, who was walking up and down the room.

"I don't feel sleepy yet. Put out the candle if you like; I'll go to bed without it."

And he went on pacing up and down.

"Doesn't feel sleepy yet, repeated Polozov, who after that evening felt more than ever dissatisfied with the count's sway over him, and disposed to revolt against it. "I can fancy," he reflected, mentally addressing Turbin, "the ideas that are passing through your well-brushed head at this moment! I saw how much you liked her. But you're not capable of understanding that simple, truthful nature; you need a Mina, you want a colonel's epaulettes. I'll ask him, though, what he thought of her."

And Polozov turned towards him, but changed his mind; he felt that he would not be able to contend against the count, if his view of Liza were not what he supposed; that he would not be strong enough to hold out against agreeing with him even, so accustomed had he become to submitting to his influence, though it was growing every day more irksome and unjustifiable to him.

"Where are you going?" he asked, when the count put on his forage-cap, and went towards the door.

"I'm going to the stable to have a look whether everything's as it should be."

"Queer!" thought the cornet; but he put out the candle, and, trying to shake off the absurdly jealous and hostile feeling towards his former friend that would obtrude itself upon his mind, he turned over on the other side.

Meanwhile Anna Fyodorovna had also retired to her room, after saying good night as usual and affectionately kissing and signing with the cross her brother, her daughter, and her ward. It was long since the old lady had experienced in one day such violent emotions that she could not say her prayers calmly. She could not get out of her head the melancholy and vivid picture of the dead count and of the young dandy who had so ruthlessly despoiled her. After undressing, however, and drinking half a glass of rye-beer, which had been put ready for her on a table by her bedside, she got into bed as usual. Her favourite cat crept softly into the room. Anna Fyodorovna called to her, and began stroking her, listening to her purring, and still she could not go to sleep.

"It's the cat that prevents me," she thought, and she drove her away. The cat dropped softly to the floor, slowly shaking its fluffy tail, and jumped on the low stove; but the maid who slept on the floor in the room brought her felt mat in to lay it there, and proceeded to light the lamp before the holy picture and put out the candles. At last the girl was snoring; but still Anna Fyodorovna could not go to sleep, and could not calm her heated imagination. The face of the hussar simply stood before her when she closed her eyes, and seemed to appear in various strange shapes in the room when with open eyes she looked in the dim light of the lamp at the chest of drawers, at the table, at a white dress hanging up. First she felt too hot on the feather bed, then the clock ticking on the table was intolerable, and she could not stand the maid's snoring. She waked her up, and told her to give over snoring. Again, thoughts of her daughter, of the old, and of the young count, and of preference were strangely mingled in her brain. At one moment she saw herself waltzing with the old count, saw her plump, white shoulders, felt kisses on them, and she saw her daughter in the young count's arms. Again Ustyushka began to snore. . . .

"No, there's something amiss nowadays; people aren't the same. He was ready to go through fire for my sake. Yes, and he had good reason too; while this fellow, I'll warrant, has gone to sleep like a simpleton, pleased at what he has won, and no thought of making love. Now he said on his knees, 'What will you have me do? I'd kill myself on the spot if you will.' And he would have killed himself if I'd said so."

All of a sudden there was the sound

of bare feet in the corridor, and Liza, with only a kerchief thrown over her, ran into the room all pale and trembling, and almost fell on her mother's bed. . . .

After saying good night to her mother, Liza had gone alone to her uncle's former room. Putting on a white dressing-jacket, and wrapping a kerchief about her thick, long hair, she put out the candle, raised the window, and sat down with her feet upon a chair, fixing her dreamy eyes on the pond, which was now all a-glitter with silver brilliance.

All her habitual pursuits and interests suddenly appeared to her in quite a new light. Her capricious old mother, whom she had loved without criticising, her love for whom was part of her very soul; her feeble but genial uncle, the servants, the peasants, who adored their young mistress, the milch cows and the calves, and all nature about her—that had so many times died away and quickened again to life—in the midst of which she had grown up with love for others and from others; all that had given her such quiet, sweet peace at heart; it all seemed suddenly not *the real thing;* it all seemed *dreary, useless.* It seemed as though some one were saying to her, "Little fool! little fool! for twenty years you have been wasting time, doing this and that for people, and never knowing the meaning of life and happiness!" Gazing into the depths of the still, moonlit garden, she thought this more intensely, far more intensely, than she had ever thought it before. And what had led her to such reflections? Certainly not that she had suddenly fallen in love with the count, as might have been imagined. On the

contrary she did not like him. The cornet would sooner have made an impression on her; but he was plain, poor man, and silent. She had unconsciously forgotten him, and with anger and annoyance recalled the image of the count. "No, not the real thing," she said to herself. Her ideal was so exquisite! It was the ideal figure that, on a night like this, amid nature like this, might be loved without jarring on its beauty, the ideal that had never been cut down to fit in with the coarseness of fact.

At first her solitary life and the absence of people who might have engaged her attention had kept whole and untroubled in her heart all that force of love which Providence has implanted in the soul of every one of us alike; and now she had too long lived in the mournful happiness of feeling in herself that vague force, unveiling at times the mysterious treasure store of her heart, and gloating over the contemplation of its riches—too long to lavish heedlessly all its wealth on a chance comer. God grant she might find joy in that meagre happiness to the grave. Who knows whether it be not a better and a keener joy, whether, indeed, it be not the only real and possible joy?

"Merciful God!" she thought, "can I have missed youth and happiness altogether, and will it not come now? Will it never come? Can it be true?" And she gazed up into the vast, clear sky near the moon, covered with billowy clouds, which floated towards the moon, hiding the stars. "If that topmost white cloud reaches the moon, it means that it is true," she thought. A misty, smoky streak flitted over the lower half of the bright disc, and gradually the light grew dimmer on the grass, on the tops of the lime-trees, on the pond; the black shadows of the trees were less marked; and like a repetition of the dark shadow cast over nature, a faint breeze fluttered over the leaves, and wafted to the window the dewy fragrance of leaves, of wet earth, and flowering lilac. "No, it's not true," she comforted herself; "if the nightingale sings to-night, it means that what I am thinking is all nonsense, and I must not despair," she thought. And for a long while she sat on in silence, as it were expecting some one, though it all grew light and living again, and again, several times, clouds floated across the moon and all was darkened. She had begun to doze, sitting in the window, when a nightingale waked her with its repeated trill, that rang out clear from below, near the pond. The country girl opened her eyes. Again, with fresh joy, all her soul was renewed by that mysterious union with nature, which lay, so serene and bright, unfolded before her. She leaned on her elbows. A sort of aching, sweet melancholy weighed on her bosom, and tears of pure, large love, craving satisfaction—good, comforting tears—came into her eyes. She folded her arms on the window-sill, and laid her head on them. Her favourite prayer came spontaneously into her soul, and she sank into a doze with wet eyes.

The touch of a hand roused her; she waked up. But the touch was gentle and pleasant; the hand pressed her hand more tightly. Suddenly she came to a sense of reality, cried out, jumped up, and telling herself that it could not be the count she recognised standing under the window, in the full moonlight, she ran out of the room.

CHAPTER XV

THE STORY

IT really was the count. When he heard the girl's cry and the grumbling utterance of the watchman behind the fence, roused by her cry, he rushed headlong, with the sensation of a caught thief, and ran through the wet, dewy grass into the thickest part of the garden. "Ah, I'm a fool!" he repeated unconsciously; "I frightened her. I ought to have been gentler, to have waked her with words. Ah, I'm an awkward ass!" He stood still, and listened; the watchman went through the little gate into the garden, trailing his stick along the sandy path; he had to hide. He went down towards the pond; frogs plopped hurriedly from under his feet into the water, making him start. Here he squatted down on his heels, and in spite of his soaking feet, began going over all he had done: how he had crept over the fence, looked for her window, and at last seen a white shadow; how, listening to the slightest rustle, he had several times approached and retreated from the window; how it had seemed to him at one moment certain that she was expecting him, and vexed at his tardiness; at the next, that it was impossible she could have brought herself so readily to arrange such an interview; how at last, assuming that she was only pretending to be asleep, from the bashfulness of a provincial young lady, he had gone resolutely up to her and saw her attitude distinctly; but then he had for some reason suddenly darted headlong back, and it was only through shame at his own cowardice that he went boldly up to her and touched her hand. The watchman again cleared his throat, and came out of the garden, making the gate creak. The window of the young lady's room shut with a slam, and was fastened with a shutter from within. It was horribly irritating to the count to see this. He would have given a great deal simply to be able to begin the whole affair over again from the beginning; that time he would not have acted so stupidly. "An exquisite girl! so fresh! simply charming! and to make such a mess of it! Silly ass I am!" He was not sleepy, moreover, and with the determined steps of a thoroughly irritated man, he walked at random along the paths of the close lime-tree avenue.

And then to him, too, the night brought its peace-giving offerings of soothing melancholy and yearning for love. The clayey path, with here and there a tuft of grass or a dry twig, was lighted in circular patches by the straight, pale moonbeams shining through the thick foliage of the lime-trees. A crooked branch was lit up on one side, looking as though overgrown with white lichen. The silvery leaves whispered at intervals. In the house all lights were out, all sounds were hushed. Only the nightingale seemed to fill all the fathomless, silent stretches of light. "Heavens! what a night! what a marvellous night!" thought the count, drinking in the fragrant freshness of the garden. "I feel, somehow sad; as it were dissatisfied with myself and others, and dissatisfied with the whole of life. A delightful, sweet girl! Perhaps she was really offended." There

his musing changed; he pictured himself in that garden with the provincial lady in the most various and strange circumstances; then the part of the young lady was filled by his complaisant Mina. "What a fool I was! I ought simply to have put my arms round her waist and kissed her"; and with this regretful reflection the count went back to his room.

The cornet was not yet asleep. He turned over in bed at once, and faced the count.

"You're not asleep?" inquired the count.

"No."

"Shall I tell you what's happened?"

"Well?"

"No, better not tell you—yes, I will though. Move your legs."

And recovering from his annoyance at the intrigue he had so mismanaged, the count sat down on the edge of his friend's bed, smiling eagerly.

"Only fancy! that young lady, do you know, arranged a rendezvous with me?"

"What do you say?" cried Polozov, jumping out of bed.

"Come, listen."

"But how? when? Impossible!"

"Why, while you were reckoning the points of the preference, she told me she should be sitting to-night at her window, and that one could get in at her window. You see what it is to be a practical man. While you were reckoning up with the old lady, I put up this little job. Why, you heard it, in fact; she said in your presence she should sit at her window and look at the pond."

"But she said that by chance."

"That's just what I don't know; whether it was on purpose or not that she said that. Perhaps she really did not mean it straight off; only it looked like it. A wretched mess it's turned out! I acted like a perfect fool!" he added, smiling contemptuously at himself.

"But how? Where have you been?"

The count described everything just as it had happened, only omitting his hesitations and reiterated retreats.

"I spoilt it all myself; I ought to have been bolder. She screamed, and ran away from the window."

"So she screamed and ran away?" said the cornet, with an awkward smile, responding to the smile of the count, which had so long had such a powerful influence over him.

"Yes. Well, now it's time to go to sleep."

The cornet turned over again, with his back towards the door, and lay in silence for ten minutes. God knows what was passing in his soul; but when he turned over again, his face expressed suffering and determination.

"Count Turbin!" he said, in a jerky voice.

"What is it? Are you talking in your sleep?" the count responded tranquilly. "What is it, Cornet Polozov?"

"Count Turbin, you're a blackguard!" cried Polozov, and he jumped out of bed.

CHAPTER XVI

RESULT

NEXT morning the squadron moved on. The officers did not see their hosts again, and did not take leave of them. They did not speak to one another either. On reaching their first halt, a duel was proposed: but Captain Schultz, a very good fellow with a capital riding-seat, a regimental favorite and the count's second, smoothly suppressed the affair and no one ever knew of it. Turbin and Polozov, not as friendly as before still notice each other at celebrations and dinners.

Anna Karenine

PART I

CHAPTER I

THE HOUSEHOLD OF OBLOWSKY

A SHADOW had fallen upon the Oblowsky household. The princess had learned of her husband's "affairs" with the French governess of her children, and had declared that she would no longer live under the same roof with him. The wife remained in her private apartments all day, the husband absented himself, and their children, free from all restraint, wandered from room to room, puzzled as to the cause of the sudden release from their tasks. Even the servants felt the influence of coming trouble, and, one by one, gave notice of their departure.

The climax had come about a few nights before, when the Prince Stépane Archadievitch Oblowsky, returning from the theater, full of gayety and high spirits, had sought his wife in vain. She was neither in the salon nor in her boudoir, but was finally discovered by him sitting in her bedroom with the letter, which had told her all, in her hands. There she sat, an expression of despair, of terror, and of indignation on her face.

"What is the meaning of this?" she asked, holding out the venomous sheet.

Stépane was dumfounded. Instead of defending himself, or denying the anonymous charge, or even of asking pardon and forgiveness, he allowed a cynical smile to pass across his lips, and said nothing.

His wife burst forth into a torrent of reproach and bitter upbraiding, and then fled from the room. From that moment she had refused to see him.

CHAPTER II

MATRONA'S MESSAGE

ONE morning, three days later, Stépane rose from his bed, and having donned his dressing-gown, summoned his valet.

Matvei, an old servant of the family, entered the room with a telegram in his hand. Stépane hurriedly opened it.

"Matvei," he said, "my sister, Anna Arcadievna, will arrive to-morrow."

"Thank goodness, sir," said the old and privileged servitor, who, in the coming of his master's sister, foresaw the only means of a reconciliation. "Will she be alone, or is her husband coming?" he added.

"Alone. See that her rooms are made ready, and show this telegram to your mistress."

The old valet left the room, but returned before Stépane had proceeded far in his toilet, with the telegram still in his hand.

"My mistress says that she is about to leave your house; and, as regards this message, you are to do as seems best to you."

Stépane stood silent for a few moments. Then a slight smile passed across his face.

"And what do you think of it all, Matvei?" he said.

"I think, sir, that it will arrange itself."

"Arrange itself?"

"Without a doubt, sir."

"You think so? Ah! who is there?" asked Stépane, as a light knock sounded on the door.

"It is I, sir," said a firm but pleasant voice; and Matrona Philomonovna, his children's nurse, entered the room.

"What is it, Matrona?" asked Stépane. "What do you want of me?"

"I want you, sir, to go to madame and ask her pardon. She is broken-hearted, and it is pitiable to see her. And then, too, sir, you must think of the children."

"But she will not admit me—"

"You can at least try, sir; and it is your duty."

"Very well, Matrona; I will try. You may go now. Matvei, give me my things; I will finish dressing;" and this the old servant did with a satisfaction that could not be concealed.

CHAPTER III

RELIEF

DARIA ALEXANDROVNA, dressed in a simple morning-robe, looking pale and haggard, her beautiful eyes bedimmed from excess of grief and weeping, was seated before an open desk, hurriedly turning over the contents of its drawers. For three days she had been struggling between two inclinations—the one, to fly for refuge to her mother; the other, to do her duty and remain by her children. The desire to punish and humiliate the husband who had deceived her was almost uncontrollable. But then came the thought of her little ones, so dearly loved, and so innocent. She must consider them before herself.

The door opened, and intuitively she felt that her husband had entered the room. She hastily pushed to the open drawers, and raised a face to him on which, in place of the severe and scornful look she would fain have assumed, only doubt and suffering were to be seen.

"Dolly," he said in a quiet, humble tone.

She threw a hurried glance at him as he stood there looking young, handsome, and without a care.

"He is happy and content," she thought to herself. "While as for me—" and her mouth twitched nervously.

"What do you wish?" she asked, coldly.

"Dolly," he repeated in a low voice, "Anna arrives tomorrow."

"That is of no interest to me. I can not receive her."

"But you must, Dolly. It is necessary."

"Go away! go away!" she cried in a broken, grief-laden voice, without looking at him.

Calm as he had been, Stépane, now that he saw his wife's face so completely overshadowed with grief, and heard the sorrow in her tones, felt a lump rise within his throat, and his eyes filled with tears.

"What have I done, Dolly?" he said. "In Heaven's name, what have I done? Can you not forgive me? Can you not consider the nine years of our married life? And if, in a moment of impulse and temptation—"

She turned suddenly upon him, her face again contracted into hard and bitter lines.

"Leave me!" she cried again. "Go away! Don't speak to me of your impulses and your temptations!"

She strove to rise, as if to leave the room, but fell back sobbing in her chair.

"Dolly," he said, almost himself in tears, "for God's sake, think of the children! They are not to blame. It is I, and I alone—I know it, and I ask you now what I can do to earn your forgiveness?"

There was a moment's silence, and then she said:

"You speak of the children—you, who have only looked upon them as pets and playthings. But to me they are all the world—everything, do you understand? And now the doubt is killing me whether I should take them away with me or leave them with their father, who is nothing but a debauchee! After what has passed, it would be impossible for us to live together again. My husband—their father"—she added, her voice rising—"engaged in a *liaison* with—"

"What would you have me do?" interrupted Stépane, with bowed head and shamefaced look.

"You disgust me!" she cried, her feelings overcoming her. "Your tears are simple pretense. You have never loved me. You have neither heart nor honor. Henceforth, to me, you are a stranger!" and as she spoke the word her voice was full of bitter, implacable anger.

He gazed at her, surprised and half frightened. He could not understand how his pity had incensed his wife—a woman.

At this moment the voice of one of the children was heard crying in the adjoining room. A sudden change came over her face. For one moment she hesitated, then rose and hurriedly moved toward the door.

"Dolly, one word!" he said, following her.

She turned upon him.

"If you follow me, I will call the servants, and the children shall know you for the coward you are! To-day I leave you forever!"

She went out and closed the door violently behind her.

Stépane remained for a few moments, lost in thought, and then, with a sigh, quietly left the room and returned to his own apartments.

"Matvei," he called, "see that the little salon is prepared for my sister Anna Arcadievna."

A few minutes later he had left the house.

The Princess Dolly, having quieted the children, returned to her own room. She heard the noise of her husband's carriage as he drove away.

Resuming her former seat, she clasped her hands across her forehead as if to aid her thoughts and memory.

"He has gone!" she said to herself. "Is he still deceiving me—why did I not ask him plainly? No! we could never live together again; and yet, to live as two strangers beneath one roof! It is too cruel! How I have loved him! And, my God! how I still love him! Perhaps it is my fault for having loved him so much—"

Her thoughts were interrupted by Matrona Philomonovna, who entered the room to ask some questions regarding the care of the children. The distraction served to relieve the mind of the princess from the terrible strain left by the recent interview and her own jealous grief.

CHAPTER IV

STEPANE

In the society of St. Petersburg and Moscow there was no more popular young man than Stépane Archadievitch. Handsome, of ever-cheerful and good-natured disposition, he could claim as a friend almost every one with whom he came in social contact. Through the influence of Alexis Karénine, the husband of his sister Anna, himself a leading member of the imperial ministry, Stépane had obtained the office of president of one of the tribunals of Moscow. During the three years in which he had now held the position, he had gained the respect and esteem of all with whom his official duties brought him in contact—superiors, colleagues, and inferiors.

On this morning, when he reached his bureau, he was soon immersed in official affairs with the other members of the Council. At the end of a two-hours' session, he was informed that a stranger wished to see him and was waiting in Stépane's own private office.

"Ah, Levine!" he cried, with a smile of welcome, as he entered the room. "What good wind has blown you here? How long have you been waiting?"

"I have just arrived in Moscow," answered the other, "and came at once to see you."

"And none could be more welcome," said Stépane, heartily. "But you have not told me what has induced you to leave the country and visit us poor dwellers in the city."

"I will tell you all my news later on—"

"Which means," interrupted Stépane, "that you will dine with me this afternoon. I can not ask you to my house, as my wife is not well, but I shall be at liberty at three o'clock, and we will dine together at Gourive's."

"With pleasure," answered Levine; "and now, can you tell me one thing"—and here he blushed and stammered like a boy—"the Cherbatzkys, are they in town?"

Stépane smiled. He had known for some time that Levine was deeply in love with his own sister-in-law, Kitty.

"Ah! I understand," he said, with a laugh. "I think you will find them in the Zoölogical Gardens between four and five. Kitty is learning to skate, you know. I will meet you there myself, and then we can go off to dinner. Now, don't forget our appointment, and don't let me hear that you have suddenly rushed off to your beloved estates in Karasink."

"No, no; I will be there. Till then, *au revoir!*"

CHAPTER V

TO MOSCOW

When Oblowsky had first asked him the reason of his visit to Moscow, Levine had blushed and purposely avoided answering. He could not well blurt out: "I have come to ask the hand of your sister-in-law," and yet this was the one and only reason of his coming.

Between the two families of Levine and Cherbatzky a close and warm friendship had long existed. Constantin Levine himself had been at the Moscow University with the young Prince Cherbatzky, the brother of Dolly and Kitty, and had been looked upon almost as a member of the family by the whole Cherbatzky household. His own parents were both dead, and his only female relative was a sister much older than himself. His girl acquaintance was practically confined to the three daughters of the Prince and Princess Cherbatzky. His first love had been Dolly, the eldest girl —a romance which was soon cut short by her marriage with Oblowsky. It was then clearly his duty to transfer his affections to the next sister, Nathalie—an arrangement which was, unfortunately, nipped in the bud by her wedding the famous diplomat, Loof. Kitty was then still a child. The young Prince Cherbatzky, who, on leaving the university had entered the navy, was drowned while cruising in the Baltic, and Levine's relations with the family became less intimate. He spent a year in the country upon his own estates, but immediately upon his return to Moscow he visited the Cherbatzkys, and it was soon made clear to him which one of the three daughters was destined to be his fate.

To all outward appearances there could be no possible obstacle to his asking the hand of the young princess in marriage. A man of thirty-two, of good family, possessing a more than handsome fortune—a better match could hardly have been desired. But Levine was too deeply in love. To him, Kitty appeared a superior creature, almost an ideal, far beyond his own unworthy aspirations. After spending two months in Moscow, during which he saw her every day, he suddenly determined that such a marriage was impossible for him, and returned to the country. What was he,

he argued, but a farmer?—a farmer on an immense scale, it is true, but still a raiser of cattle and a tiller of the soil. His former friends and school-fellows held high positions in the army, were imperial aids-de-camp, learned and distinguished professors, directors of banks and railroads, or prominent officials like Oblowsky. And yet, in spite of such self-arguing, after a few months spent at his country home, his feelings toward Kitty proved too much for his cold calculations. He felt that he must put it to the test. After all, he could only be refused, and his lot would be none the worse than it was now. He set out for Moscow once more, determined to learn his fate.

CHAPTER VI

HIS ANSWER

On leaving Oblowsky, Levine turned his steps toward the house of his half-brother, Serge Ivanitch Kosnichef. He was received by him in the cold but pointedly polite manner which was his chief characteristic.

"I am glad to see you," said Serge Ivanitch. "Are you going to stay any length of time? How are your affairs?"

Levine knew that his elder brother took but little interest in agriculture and such questions as the price of wheat and cereals, and that in assuming even a show of interest he was making a large concession to politeness. He himself had no wish to talk upon such topics; he had rather come to speak of his own projects in regard to marriage, and to ask his brother's advice. Now that he was there, however, he felt that he could not turn the conversation on what lay uppermost in his mind.

"Were you aware," said Serge Ivanitch, "that our brother Nicolas is in the city again?"

Nicolas was an elder brother of Levine, and, consequently, a half-brother of Serge Ivanitch. He was an eccentric character, of somewhat doubtful reputation, who had already eaten into the greater part of his fortune, and lived regardless of the thoughts and censures of the world.

"What do you say?" cried Levine, excitedly. "Nicolas here? How do you know it?"

"Prokofi saw him in the street."

"Here—in Moscow? Where is he?" and Levine rose as if he wished to set out at once in search of him.

"I am sorry I told you," said Serge, shaking his head, as he noticed the other's emotion. "I sent some one to find out where he lived and to give him a letter. Here is his answer."

And Serge held out a paper, which he had taken from his desk. Levine read in a well-known handwriting:

"I humbly beg to be left alone and in peace. It is all that I have to ask of my dear brothers.

"NICOLAS LEVINE."

Constantin remained standing before his brother Serge, with his head bent down.

"It is plain that he wishes to offend me," said Serge; "but that he can not do. I wished from my heart to do all I could for him, should he need assistance."

"Yes, yes," agreed Levine, "I know that, and I at least appreciate your conduct toward him. But I myself must go and see him."

"Do so, if you wish," said Serge; "but I should not advise you to go. It is not that I am afraid of his causing trouble

between you and myself, but simply on your own account. You can do nothing for him or with him."

"Perhaps not; but I shall feel easier in my mind."

"I can not quite understand you," said Serge. "All I know is that since our brother's latest escapade—and you know what that is—I feel more tolerant toward the scamps and sinners of this world."

"Alas! yes, it is frightful!" replied Levine.

Having learned the address of his brother Nicolas from Serge's servant, he left the house, meaning to make the visit at once. He changed his mind, however, and determined to postpone it until he had first decided the question which had brought him to Moscow.

CHAPTER VII

AU REVOIR!

TOWARD four o'clock Levine dismounted from his isvostchik at the gate entrance to the Gardens, and, with beating heart, made his way toward the lake on which the skaters thronged. He knew that *she* was there, for he had seen the Cherbatzky carriage standing at the gate.

As he walked along, he reasoned with himself and his foolish nervousness. "Be calm! Why excite yourself, you imbecile! What is it you wish?" But the more he strove against it, the more nervous he became.

As he came to the edge of the crowded sheet of ice, young Nicolas Cherbatzky, a boy cousin of Kitty's, caught sight of him. "Ah!" he cried, "here he is—the best skater in Russia! Have you been here long? Put on your skates; the ice is in splendid condition!"

"I have no skates," answered Levine; and the next moment, Kitty, her beautiful young face aglow with the healthy exercise, and her golden hair glistening in the bright winter sunlight, glided up and leaned upon her young cousin's arm for support.

"When did you arrive in town?" she asked, as she held out her hand to Levine in cordial greeting.

"A short time ago—yesterday—no, to-day I mean," he stammered in another access of nervousness. "I was coming to call upon you"—and, as he recollected the object of his visit, the blood mounted to his face—"I had no idea that you skated—and so well, too."

She glanced at him, as if trying to discover the cause of his embarrassment.

"Thanks for the compliment," she said. "Coming from such a skater as yourself, it is doubly precious;" and she brushed away, with her little glove of fur, some particles of ice which had gathered on her muff.

"I used to be passionately fond of it," he said.

"Then why not put on some skates and let us skate together?"

"I will, indeed, at once," he said, and rushed off, delighted, to procure a pair.

He could hardly restrain his impatience while the skates were being fixed to his feet. The prospect of skating with *her* was almost too much for him.

Soon he was gliding on the ice toward Kitty who greeted him with a smile. She gave him her hand, and together they skated side by side, the grasp of her little fingers growing stronger as their pace increased.

"I shall learn quickly with you," she said. "I don't know why, but you seem to give me confidence, which is everything when one is learning.

"And you, too, give me confidence," he said; and then stopped short as he noticed a slight cloud pass over her face, and the smile fade from her eyes. Her forehead wrinkled in a little frown.

"What is the matter?" he said; "though, perhaps, I have no right to ask."

"Why not?" she replied in a cold tone; and then, suddenly: "But you have not seen Mademoiselle Linon yet?" and she led him toward the elderly governess, who sat patiently and good-naturedly watching her young charge from the bank.

The good soul received Levine with a friendly smile and warm welcome.

"Are we not growing?" she asked, nodding her head toward Kitty. "Do you remember how we used to call her the Tiny Bear of the old nursery story?"

Levine laughed as his memory traveled back to the old days of ten years before.

"Now go on with your skating," she added. "Don't you think our Kitty is learning quickly?"

When Levine rejoined her, he noticed that the cloud had passed from Kitty's face. She led the conversation to his own life and doings.

"Do you not grow tired of the country?" she asked.

"No, I am too busy," he answered, in the calm tone which he had resolved to assume.

"And for how long are you going to stay here?"

"I have no idea—not the least."

"No idea? Is not that rather strange?" said the girl.

"No; for it depends entirely upon you!"

The moment the words had left his mouth, he could have bitten out his tongue.

Kitty said nothing, but turned and skated rapidly toward the little club-house, for the purpose of taking off her skates.

"Is it my own fault?" she thought to herself. "Have I encouraged him? I know that I do not love him, but still I always enjoy being with him. He is so good and kind. But why—why did he say that?"

Levine, seeing that Kitty had now joined her mother, removed his own skates and hurried toward them.

"I am very glad to see you," said the princess. "We still receive, you know, on Thursdays."

"This evening, perhaps?" he asked.

"We shall be charmed to see you," she answered, coldly.

Her mother's tone distressed Kitty somewhat, for she felt sure Levine must notice it. She turned toward him with a bright smile: "*Au revoir*, then!" she cried.

As the carriage containing the ladies drove away, Levine turned and caught sight of Stépane entering the Gardens. The sound of Kitty's voice and her last words—"*Au revoir*"—were in his ears as he joined his friend.

"If you are ready, we will go at once," said Stépane. "I am glad you have kept your isvostchik, for I sent my carriage home."

During the drive few words passed between them. Levine's thoughts were full of Kitty. At moments he would recall her manner toward him after his incautious speech, and a feeling of deep depression came over him. Then, the next instant, he would see again the bright look she gave him on parting, and hear again the words which seemed to bring him hope—"*Au revoir!*"

CHAPTER VIII

WRONSKY

TOWARD the end of the dinner at which Levine was entertained by Stépane, the two friends felt that the time had come for an interchange of the thoughts with which they were both oppressed.

"And now," said Stépane, as he lighted a cigar and settled back in his seat, "tell me what has brought you to Moscow."

"Have you not already guessed?" asked Levine, looking fixedly at him.

"I have guessed it, certainly; but it was not for me to be the first to speak."

"Well, and what have you to say?" asked Levine, with a slight tremble in his voice. "What is your own opinion?"

Stépane slowly emptied his glass, and, returning the other's look, said:

"Simply that there is nothing I would desire more—absolutely nothing."

"But are you sure we are alluding to the same thing?" said Levine, nervously. "Do you think it could possibly be?"

"Why not?"

"Tell me frankly. Say everything that is in your thoughts. Am I not sure to be refused?"

"Why should you be?" said Stépane, unable to repress a smile at his friend's emotion.

"It would be terrible—both for me and for her."

"Oh, I see nothing terrible about it, so far as she is concerned. A young girl should be—and generally is—flattered at being asked in marriage."

"Ordinary girls, perhaps; but not she."

Stépane again smiled. He knew well that in Levine's mind all the women in the world were practically of another planet to that on which Kitty had been born.

"To me," continued Levine, "it is simply a question of life or death. I have never spoken of it, nor could I ever speak of it to any one save yourself. We are, I know, two men of totally different character and nature. It is that, I think, which binds us together. In Heaven's name, be honest and sincere with me."

"I will tell you not only what I myself think," said Stépane, "but I will tell you more. My wife, who, I think you will own, is an exceptional woman"—and as he thought of their present relations, he could not keep back a sigh—"my wife has the gift of what I will call 'second sight.' She sees all that is passing in the hearts of others, and more especially where love and marriage are concerned. I could tell you many instances where her prognostications have turned out correct against the opinion of every one else. Well, my wife is on your side."

"What do you mean?"

"I mean that not only does she herself esteem you most highly, but she is positive that Kitty will one day be your wife."

When he heard these words, Levine's face suddenly brightened.

"She said that?" he cried. "I always looked upon your wife as an angel. It is enough for me," he added, rising from the table.

"Sit down and calm yourself," said Stépane; but it was not until he had paced excitedly up and down the little room several times that Levine could sufficiently control his feelings.

"You must understand," he exclaimed, "that it is almost more than love that I feel for her. Should the happiness I have dared to dream of come to me, it would be beyond mere human happiness. My whole existence is wrapped up in this. I must decide it, one way or the other."

He drained the glass of wine before him, and for some moments there was silence between the two friends.

"There is one other thing I must tell you," said Stépane, at length. "Do you know Wronsky?"

"No. Why?"

"He is your rival."

"Who is this Wronsky?" asked Levine, over whose face the shadow had suddenly fallen again.

"He is a son of Count Cyrille Wronsky, and one of the best known among the *jeunesse dorée* of St. Petersburg. I knew him at Iver, when I was in the service. His regiment was also stationed there. He is immensely rich, good-looking, aid-de-camp to the emperor, well connected, and, above all, a good fellow. From what I could see, he is even more, for he is exceptionally well educated and clever. In fact, he is a man who is bound to make his mark."

Levine's face grew dark, and he remained perfectly silent.

"He appeared on the scene shortly after you last left here," continued the other. "They say he is most decidedly *épris* with Kitty, and her mother, you know—"

"Pardon me," interrupted Levine, "but I know nothing." At that moment the thought of his brother Nicolas flashed across his mind.

"Well," said Stépane, laying a friendly hand upon the other's arm, "I have told you all I know, and I can only repeat that, in spite of everything, the chances seem to me to be in your favor."

Levine grew pale, and leaned back in his chair.

"Why," he asked, "do you never come to stay with me and have some shooting or hunting? Come this spring."

In his heart he was sorry now that he had brought about the conversation with Stépane. His very soul was now up in arms at the thought of his rival, this well-favored young officer from St. Petersburg. Stépane could easily read what was passing in his mind, and he made haste to answer:

"I will come to you some of these days; but, my friend, I will only now remind you that this world circles around, and is controlled by, the women. My own trouble is serious—very serious —and caused entirely by women. It is now my turn to ask you to give your advice, freely and frankly," he added, lighting a fresh cigar.

"Concerning what?"

"This—supposing you were married, that you dearly loved your wife, and yet became entangled with some other woman."

"Excuse me; I can not understand such a supposition. To me it is as if, on leaving this dinner-table, I stopped at the first baker's shop and stole a loaf of bread from his counter."

A bright gleam of fun flashed across Stépane's eyes.

"Well, and why not? It is very hard sometimes, you know, to resist the enticing odor of a freshly baked loaf."

Levine took no notice of the pleasantry.

"Joking apart," continued Stépane, "supposing that a charming, modest, and lovable woman had sacrificed everything for you; that without you she would be in poverty and cut off from the world, should you, now that the mischief is done, abandon her? Should you not, even if it were to cost your own family some pain and grief, have some pity for her, soften the separation, and think for a moment of *her* future?"

"Pardon me once more; but, as you are well aware, for me the world contains only two classes of women, or, rather, it contains women and—well, I need not use the word. I have never met, nor do I believe in, the repentant Magdalen. To me a fallen woman is, and will always be, repugnant."

"And the Saviour—what was His thought?"

"Leave that argument alone. He would never have spoken the words He did had He known the mischief they would do. I repeat, I have the same disgust for fallen women that you probably have for, let us say, spiders. There is no more need for you to study and analyze the habits and doings of these loathy insects than there is for me to study those other creatures."

"You are begging the question. What should one do? That is what I asked."

"One should *not* steal the loaf of fresh bread."

Stépane commenced to laugh.

"You moralist! You do not understand the situation. Here are two women: the one lays claim to her rights, which consist of the love you can no longer give her; the other, sacrifices everything, and asks for nothing in return. What should one do in such a case? Is it not a terrible drama?"

"If I must say what I really think, I will tell you that I have no belief in this drama. To my mind, love, the two different loves of which, you remember, Plato speaks in his 'Banquet,' serve as a touchstone for men. Some understand but one of these two loves, others are ignorant even of that. Those who do not comprehend platonic love have no excuse for speaking of a 'drama.' In platonic love all is clear and pure, because—" He stopped as he suddenly remembered his own transgressions and inward struggles; then, as if restraining himself, he added: "After all, perhaps you are right. As for me, I know nothing about it, absolutely nothing."

"You are a man of the most perfect consistency," said Stépane. "It is at once your best quality and your worst fault. You would have it that love and conjugal life have but the one end in common."

Levine made no response; it is doubtful if he heard the other's words; his thoughts were all turned upon what touched himself.

The feeling came to both men that, so far from the dinner having united them in closer friendship, it had, in some way, brought about a breach between them. Each thought of his own cares and gave no thought to the troubles of his friend. The strain was relieved by Stépane, who called for the bill, and, passing into the public room, was soon engaged in light and cheerful conversation with some friend he chanced to see. Levine returned to his own rooms in order to dress before repairing to the Cherbatzky mansion to learn his fate.

CHAPTER IX

FORGIVE ME!

THE Princess Kitty Cherbatzky had now passed her eighteenth birthday. The present winter was her first season in the world of society, and the admiration she had already met with even surpassed what had fallen to the lot of her two other sisters. Two suitors for her hand she could at least lay claim to—Levine, and, after his departure from Moscow, the young Count Wronsky.

Levine's frequent visits and his evident love for their daughter had been the subject of many serious conversations between the prince and princess. The former was altogether on his side, and declared that he wished no better match for Kitty. The princess held other views. Kitty, she said, was yet too young to think of marriage, nor, to her mind, were Levine's attentions serious. These were merely her words; in her inmost heart she was counting upon a more brilliant alliance. Needless to say, when the young man had left Moscow she was much elated.

"You see, I was right in my estimate of him," she said, with an air of satisfaction to her husband; and her contentment was increased when Wronsky appeared upon the scene as an evident lover.

She had never understood Levine's character; his brusqueness and occasional awkwardness she attributed to pride and what she called the savage life of the country, among his beasts and peasants. During the six weeks in which he had almost daily visited the house, his manner, she maintained, was that of a man who was hesitating, observing, and constantly asking himself whether the honor he was about to confer upon the girl and her family was not too great.

Wronsky, on the other hand, exactly suited her requirements. He was rich, intelligent, and of excellent birth; a brilliant career, either at court or in the army, awaited him, and, above all, he was most charming. What better could she ask for her daughter? And yet, at times, throughout the winter, she was tormented by bitter doubts and misgivings.

After dinner, on the evening of Levine's return to Moscow, Kitty mounted to her room to prepare her toilet for the evening. As she descended to the salon, a servant announced:

"Constantin-Dmitrievitch Levine!"

Her mother was still in her own apartments, and the prince in his study.

"He has come," thought Kitty, and the blood coursed through her veins. She knew, without a doubt, that the object of Constantin's visit was to declare himself. At last the situation was clear to her—it would be necessary for her to wound a man whom she liked, and to wound him cruelly. But there was no other course open; it must be done.

"Must I see him alone?" she thought to herself, "and must I tell him what is not true—that I do not like him? What shall I say? I can not tell him that I love another!"

As he entered the room, looking tall, strong, and manly in spite of his evident timidity, she could not help throwing a glance at him as if to implore his protection.

"I have come rather too early," he said, looking around the empty room.

"Oh, no," said Kitty, seating herself near a table.

"It is precisely what I was hoping for, to find you alone," he continued, still standing before her.

"My mother will be here presently. She was rather fatigued this evening."

Levine turned a glance upon her which made her blush and tremble. "I told you," he said, "this afternoon, that I did not know how long I should remain here—that it depended upon yourself."

Kitty lowered her head; there was nothing she could say.

"Yes," he continued, "it depends upon you. What I came here for was—was to ask you to be my wife!"

He said no more, but stood and gazed at her.

Kitty did not raise her head; she could hardly breathe; a glow of happiness filled her heart. She had not thought that a declaration from him could affect her thus. But the impression lasted for a moment only. She remembered Wronsky, and, raising her eyes, in which there was a look of tearful sincerity, to Levine's face, she answered, quickly and in a low tone:

"It can not be—forgive me."

A moment before she had been near him, and, as he felt, necessary to his very life; now she was far from him, and they were worse than strangers.

"It could not have been otherwise," he said, and, bowing to her, was about to leave the room.

CHAPTER X

THE LAST VIEW

At that moment the princess entered the room. A look of fear passed across her face as she saw the two young people alone and evidently moved. Levine bowed, without speaking. Kitty did not raise her eyes.

"Thank God, she has refused him!" thought the mother, and her face was wreathed in smiles.

She sat down by Levine and questioned him about the country, and before many minutes had elapsed the Countess Nordstone was announced.

The countess was a friend of Kitty's, a few months married, a small, thin-featured, nervous little woman, whose one aim now was to see her young friend also enter the conjugal estate. Wronsky was her favorite. Levine she had never liked; and her greatest pleasure, when they met, was to exercise all her arts in teasing and mocking him.

"I know he looks down upon me from the height of his wonderful cleverness," she would say of him. "I am far beneath his condescension, and I am glad of it."

She was partially right, for Levine did actually dislike and distrust her. Her shallowness and disdainful indifference toward all things serious repelled him. She at once attacked him.

"Ah, Constantin-Dmitrich! So you have returned to this wicked Babylon of ours"—he had once incautiously used the word when speaking of life in Moscow. "Has Babylon been converted, or is it you that are corrupted?" she added, with a mocking smile and a glance at Kitty.

"I am flattered, countess, that you should have treasured up my words," answered Levine. "They must certainly have impressed you."

"Yes, indeed, I take note of everything. Well, Kitty have you skated to-day?" and she began to talk with her friend.

Left momentarily to himself, Levine would have escaped; but the princess, noticing it, turned to him and asked:

"How long do you remain in Moscow? Are you not a justice of the peace in your own district? Your duties, I suppose, forbid a long absence?"

"No, princess; I resigned a short time ago. I shall be here for some days."

As he spoke, several other visitors entered the salon, among them a young officer.

"This must be Wronsky," Levine said to himself, and quickly looked at Kitty. In a moment he understood that she was in love as surely as if she herself had told it. Levine was not one of those men unable to do justice to the claims physical or otherwise, of a rival. He owned at once to himself that in appearance Wronsky was all that a woman could desire. Tall, well-proportioned, with handsome, sunburned face, he looked, as he stood there in his uniform, a gallant soldier, from his closel cut dark hair downward to his feet. As he greeted Kitty in her turn, Levine thought he could detect an expression of happiness and triumph in the young soldier's face.

"Let me introduce you," said the princess, bringing the two men together. "Constantin-Dmitrich Levine — the Count Alexis-Kirilovitch Wronsky."

They greeted each other cordially.

"I had hoped to have met you earlier in the winter," said Wronsky, "but you left suddenly for the country."

"Constantin-Dmitrich distrusts and flies from the city and its inhabitants," put in the Countess Nordstone, who was standing near.

Wronsky looked from one to the other, and smiled.

"Then you always live in the country?" he asked. "Is it not rather dull in winter time?"

"Not when one is occupied," answered Levine, curtly. "And even in town it is possible to be dull."

"That is true," said Wronsky; "and,

now that I think of it, I never longed for the country—the real Russian country, I mean—so much as during one winter I spent with my mother at Nice. And Nice, you know, can not be accused of being a dull place."

And so the conversation went on, never flagging for an instant, and rendering it impossible for poor Levine to make his adieus and escape.

After some time the prince came in, and, having saluted the ladies present, turned to Levine.

"Ah!" he cried in a warm and friendly tone, "I did not know that you were here. When did you come? I am more than glad to see you."

He held his arm and talked to him, taking no notice of Wronsky, who stood quietly by.

Kitty noticed everything, and thought how hard her father's cordial greeting must be to Levine after her own rejection of him. Wronsky at last approached her and commenced to talk of a ball which was to be given at a great house during the ensuing week.

"I hope you will be there," Levine heard him say to her.

As soon as the prince released him, Levine saw that the moment had come when he might make his adieus. His last impression, as he left the house, was of Kitty's smiling and happy face as she chatted with Wronsky about the coming ball.

CHAPTER XI

SLEEP

WRONSKY had never known the charms and advantages of domestic life. His mother, a woman of the world, whose youth had been a brilliant one, had. during her married life, and, to a greater degree, during her widowhood, made her name notorious by the frequency of her *affaires*. His father had died soon after the young count's birth, whose education had been intrusted to a succession of governors and tutors.

On finishing, with much distinction, his military studies, he had taken his place as a household officer among the highest in St. Petersburg. His life there was a constant round of official duties and social gayeties. It was at Moscow that, for the first time, he experienced the influence of true womanly society, and found himself in frequent and familiar contact with a young, charming, and innocent girl. The contrast between his life there, and the false, luxurious existence of St. Petersburg, delighted him. He saw Kitty nearly every day, and there gradually grew to exist between them an indefinable yet very certain tie. In his own mind, however, the idea of marriage had never entered; her society was simply a new pleasure to him, and one which he saw no harm in enjoying as such, and nothing more. Had he been told that, by not announcing himself, he was causing Kitty much grief, he would have disbelieved the words. Why should marriage take the place of and spoil this delightful intimacy? To him the life of a married man was something strange, almost ridiculous.

Although he was unaware of what was expected of him by the Cherbatzky family, Wronsky left the house on this particular evening conscious that the tie between himself and Kitty had been drawn closer. As he thought of her, her innocence and purity, a glow of satisfaction pervaded him, and he felt that his intercourse with her made of himself a better man. As proof of this, he found it difficult to decide where and in pursuit of what pleasure and excitement he should finish the evening. At the club, with a game of cards and a friendly bottle of champagne? No. At the Château des Heurs, where he was sure of finding Oblowsky watching the deviltries of the can-can? No; the idea, as he thought of the house he had just left, was distasteful to him. He would return quietly to his own hotel. And so, after enjoying as good a supper as Dussaux could provide, he retired to his own room, and was soon enjoying the sleep of a young and healthy man to whom care and trouble are unknown names.

CHAPTER XII

MY HOPE

THE next morning, toward eleven o'clock, Wronsky betook himself to the railway-station to meet the train by which his mother was to arrive. Upon the platform the first person he saw was Oblowsky, who was there for the similar purpose of meeting his sister Anna.

"What brings you here?" he asked, as they greeted each other.

"To meet a very charming woman."

"Ah! indeed."

"*Honi soit qui mal y pense!* The charming woman is my sister Anna—Madame Karénine—you know her, I suppose?"

"I think I have met her," said Wronsky, somewhat doubtfully. The name of Karénine seemed to recall to him some tiresome and affected person.

"At least you know my famous brother-in-law, Alexis Alexandrovitch? He is known the world over."

"Yes, by reputation and by sight only. These wise and scientific men are far above poor me."

In addition to the pleasure which all his friends and acquaintances found in Stépane's society, Wronsky, just at present, felt additionally attracted to him, through his connection with the Cherbatzkys. He took his arm, and they strolled together along the platform.

"Tell me," said Stépane, "did you meet my friend Levine last night?"

"Yes; but he left the house quite early."

"He is a good fellow, is he not?" continued Stépane.

"Well," answered Wronsky, "I don't know why it is so, but all Moscow people—present company, of course, excepted—seem to me to be over-impressed with a sense of their own importance—rather overbearing, in fact, and as if they were always anxious to teach you something."

"Perhaps there is some truth in your accusation," said Stépane, with a laugh. "But I think in this case you are a little unjust. Levine is a very nervous man, at times possibly rather disagreeable in his manner; but, on the other hand, no one can be more charming than he when he wishes. Just at present," he added, significantly, "there are reasons why he should be either very happy or intensely unhappy."

"You mean," said the other, quickly, "that he has proposed for your sister-in-law?"

"It is probable," answered Stépane; "he has been in love with her for a long time."

"Ah!" said Wronsky, reflectively,

quickening his pace. "I thought so; but here is the train coming in."

The train steamed slowly up to the platform, and disgorged its load of travelers. The conductor approached the young men. "The Countess Wronsky is in that carriage," he said, pointing it out.

The words recalled Wronsky to himself, and he hastily thought of the coming meeting with his mother. Though on the best of terms with her, he had neither love nor any great respect for his mother. Perhaps on this account, his outward manner and behavior to her, when they were together, were marked by a consideration and respect almost exaggerated in degree.

Wronsky followed the conductor. As he reached the compartment where his mother was, he was forced to draw aside and leave a clear passage for a lady, who at that moment descended from it. For some reason, not on account of her beauty, or the grace and elegance of her movements, he turned his head and met her eyes—beautiful gray eyes—in whose depths he seemed to see a friendly and pleased look. The interchange of glance was but for an instant, and the next moment Wronsky had entered the compartment. His mother, an elderly woman, still preserving traces of great beauty, and dressed in the very height of fashion, rose from her seat, handed her traveling-bag to the maid who accompanied her, and extended her hand toward her son.

"You received my telegram?" she asked. "You are well, I hope?"

He sat down by her side and was questioning her about her journey, when the lady whom he had met at the carriage door entered it again.

"Have you found your brother?" asked Madame Wronsky.

At once Wronsky recognized Madame Karénine.

"Your brother is on the platform," he said, rising from his seat. "Will you pardon me, madame, for not having recognized you. I have so seldom had the honor of meeting you."

"Certainly," she answered, with a pleasant smile. "I knew you at once, though, for your mother has spoken to me so much about you during our journey. But where is my brother?"

Wronsky jumped from the carriage, and called to him across the crowd.

At the moment Madame Karénine herself caught sight of Stépane, and leaving the carriage, walked quickly to him, and passing her arm around his neck, gave him a warm and loving embrace.

Wronsky stood and watched them, a little smile upon his lips.

"Well, countess," said Madame Karénine, returning once more to the carriage for her traveling articles, "you have found your son, and I, my brother. I have inflicted all my own history upon you, during the journey, and have nothing else to say but to ask forgiveness."

"Your company and conversation, my dear, have been most charming. As for your little boy at home, don't be uneasy about him. It is impossible but that you must sometimes be separated. Anna Arcadievna," explained the countess to her son, "has a little boy eight years of age. She has never left him before, and is fretting about him."

"We have both been talking about our sons," said Madame Karénine, her face lighting up with her strange, caressing smile. "I of my little fellow, and the countess of you."

"The latter a most tiresome topic, I should think," said Wronsky, with a laugh.

They left the carriage and stood for a moment on the platform. Suddenly there was a commotion, and a crowd of people were seen to rush toward the end of the train. Some accident, it was evident, had occurred. Wronsky and Stépane made inquiries as to what had happened. An unfortunate man, not hearing, for some reason or another, the approach of an engine, had been struck down upon the rails and killed.

Stépane and Wronsky were among those who viewed the body. When they returned: "It was a frightful sight," said the former to the ladies. "If you could only have seen it, Anna—it was horrible!"

Wronsky was silent, his handsome face serious, but absolutely unmoved.

"And his wife was there," continued Stépane. "She threw herself upon the body, and would not let them raise her. There were some who knew him, and said that he leaves a large family quite unprovided for."

"Could not something be done for the poor woman?" asked Madame Karénine in an agitated tone.

Wronsky turned and looked at her for an instant.

"I will return in a moment," he said to his mother, and walked rapidly away.

When, after some minutes, he rejoined them, Stépane was discussing the merits of a new singer with the countess, who was evidently impatient to be gone.

"Let us go," said Wronsky, and walked in front with his mother, while Madame Karénine and her brother followed. The station-master came running up. "I am told," he said to Wronsky, "that you have left two hundred roubles with my deputy. Will you tell me, monsieur, how you wish the money to be used?"

"It is for the widow, of course," said Wronsky, with an impatient gesture. "How can you ask such a question?"

"Did you do that?" cried Stépane, from behind, and, as he pressed his sister's arm, he said in a low tone: "Is he not a good fellow?"

As he and Anna reached the exit from the station, the Wronskys' carriage was driving away. Small groups of persons were talking of the accident on all sides. When Madame Karénine had entered their carriage, her brother noticed that her lips were trembling, and that it was with difficulty she kept back the tears.

"What is the matter, Anna?" he asked, as they drove away.

"It is a bad omen," she said, "just upon my arrival."

"Nonsense!" replied her brother. "You are here yourself, safe and sound. You can not tell what hopes I have built upon your visit."

"Have you known Wronsky for long?" she asked.

"Yes; we are in hopes of a match between him and Kitty, you know."

"Indeed?" said Anna, quietly. "Now, let us talk about yourself," she added, as if trying to shake off her thoughts. "I received your letter, and here I am."

"Yes, as I tell you, my whole hope is in you."

"Tell me everything, then."

Stépane commenced the story of his domestic trouble. When they arrived at the house, he escorted her to the door, pressed her hand, and with a sigh, returned to his official duties.

CHAPTER XIII

ANNA'S HELP

WHEN Anna entered the house, Dolly was seated in her little salon reading in French with her little son, a well-grown boy with a mass of golden hair, his features the very image of his father's.

In her mind she was ill at ease. Although she had told her husband that his sister's visit would make no difference to herself, she was none the less nervous as to how she should receive her. She could not forget that Anna was one of the leaders of society in St. Petersburg, the wife of a high official.

"After all," she thought, "Anna is not to blame. She and I have always been good friends. Why should I not receive her—provided she does not interfere in this trouble or try to console me? Resignation and Christian consolation, I know what it all means!"

Every minute she had been expecting the arrival of her sister-in-law, and following the slowly moving hands of the little clock. So absorbed did she become in her thoughts, that she did not hear the ringing of the bell when Anna actually did arrive, and her first intimation was the opening of her boudoir door.

"You have arrived already?" she cried, advancing toward Anna, and embracing her.

"Dolly, I am so glad to see you again!"

"And I, too, am very glad," said Dolly with a poor attempt to smile, seeking to read in the other's face how much she already knew. "She knows everything," was her thought, as she remarked the compassionate look on Anna's face.

"Come," she added, aloud; "let me take you to your room."

She strove to defer the inevitable moment of explanation.

"And is this Grisha?" exclaimed Anna, kissing the child, but keeping her eyes bent upon Dolly. "What a big lad he has grown!" Then she added, with a little blush: "Won't you let me rest here a little?"

She removed her cloak and hat, and gave some little touches to her glorious black hair.

"How well and happy you look!" said Dolly, half enviously.

"I? Yes, indeed, I am very well—and here is Tania"—as the little girl came running into the room—"just the same age as my own little Serge. You must show me all the children," she added, evidently remembering every little detail concerning them.

Dolly was touched. "Yes, you shall see them; but Wasia, I am afraid, is asleep."

Having visited the nursery, they returned to the salon, where coffee was served.

"Dolly," said Anna, suddenly, "he has told me everything."

Dolly looked at her coldly, waiting for the expected platitudes and words of sympathy, but none came.

"Dolly, my dear, I do not wish to defend him, nor to try and console you. It is impossible; but, dear, I am grieved, grieved to the bottom of my heart."

The tears stood in her eyes. She moved her seat and sat down beside her sister-in-law, with one arm about her waist. Dolly did not repulse her.

"No one could console me," she said. "Everything is over for me."

Anna carried the thin little hand to her lips, and gently kissed it. "But, Dolly, what is to be done? How shall we get away from this dreadful state of affairs?"

"All is over; there is nothing left for me to do," answered Dolly. "What I feel most is that I am bound to him by our children. I can not leave them, nor can I live with him. The very sight of him is torture to me!"

"Dolly, dear, he, as I tell you, has spoken; now let me hear all you have to say. Tell me everything." And Dolly could see that her eyes were full of affection and true sympathy.

"Very well; but I must tell you all, from the very beginning. You know all about my marriage. My mother's education had left me as innocent and ignorant on some matters as a child. I knew nothing of the world. They say that, as a rule, husbands tell their whole past to their wives; but Stiva"—the familiar name had passed her lips despite herself—"Stépane Archadievitch, I mean—told me nothing. You may not believe it, but at the time I did not suppose he had ever paid attention to another woman than myself. For eight years this belief stayed with me. Not only was I unsuspicious of infidelity, but I did not even think such a thing was possible. With such ideas, you can imagine what it was for me to learn of this horror, this baseness. Confident in my own happiness," continued Dolly, striving to keep back her sobs, "to receive a letter which he had written—a letter from him to his mistress, the

governess of my little children! It was too cruel."

She hid her face for some moments in her handkerchief.

"I might perhaps have understood a sudden temptation," she continued; "but this deceit, this constant scheming to deceive me—and for whom! It is awful! You can not understand it!"

"Ah! yes, my poor Dolly, I can understand it," said Anna, pressing her hand. "And he, dear, has suffered too. He is full of remorse. I could not look at him without feeling a great pity for him. He has always been proud; now he is humiliated. What touched me most"—Anna surely knew what would most touch the wife and mother—"was his suffering on the children's account, and that he feels that he has wounded, almost killed, you whom he loves—yes, loves more than all the world," she added, quickly, as Dolly would have interrupted her. "'She will never forgive me—never!' he is constantly saying."

Dolly listened attentively, not looking at her sister-in-law.

"I can understand that he suffers," she said. "It is only right that the guilty should suffer more than the innocent. But how can I forgive him? How can I be his wife after—after *her?* Life with him would hereafter be as great a torture as my love was formerly a happiness." Her voice was choked by her sobs. When she could speak again, her thoughts centered on what seemed to her the greatest injury: "She is young—and handsome. By whom have my looks and my youth been sacrificed? By him and by his children! I have served my turn—all that is good in me has been used up in his service. Now, a creature, fresher and younger than I, is more agreeable to him. They have discussed me together. Worse than that, they have passed me over in contemptuous silence!" and her looks were alive with jealousy. "What can he say to me now? How could I believe anything he said? No, all is over. Listen! When you came, I was trying to teach Grisha his lessons. Formerly this was my greatest pleasure; now it is a torment! Why should I give myself this care? Why have I any children? In place of the love and tenderness I used to have, there is now hatred—yes, hatred! I could kill him, and—"

"Dolly, dear, I can understand all that; but do not needlessly torture yourself. You are too agitated, too much hurt to see things in their proper light."

Dolly grew calmer, and for some moments both were silent.

"What am I to do?" at last she said. "Think, Anna, and advise me. I can see no way out of it."

Nor, indeed, could Anna; but her heart responded to every word, to every sad look of her sister-in-law.

"This is what I think," she said: "I am his sister, and I know his character so well. He is easily tempted, and he forgets himself as quickly as he afterward repents. As a matter of fact, he hardly realizes what he has done. When he spoke to me, I will frankly own that I did not comprehend the extent of the evil. I saw only one thing—the disruption of your family—and that grieved me sorely. Now that I have had this talk with you, woman to woman, I see things differently. I can not tell you how your suffering pains me. But, Dolly, dear, there is one point on which I am still ignorant, and that is, the ex-

tent of your love for him. Do you love him enough to forgive him? If you do, then pardon him."

"No," commenced Dolly; but Anna interrupted her.

"I know the world better than you, dear; and I know the characters of such men as Stiva. You say that he and she have talked together of you. Do not believe it. Such men as he can prove unfaithful, but their wives and their domestic life always remain as something sacred. Between such women as this one and their own family they draw a line of demarkation which is never passed. Why this should be I do not know, but so it is."

"But he has loved her, and—and caressed her."

"Listen, Dolly. I saw Stiva when he first fell in love with you. I remember how he used to speak to me of you, and how his admiration for you grew from day to day. Among ourselves it was a joke to hear him say on every possible occasion, 'Dolly is such a wonderful woman!' As such, you will always remain to him. This has only been a chance entanglement."

"But if it should be renewed?"

"That is impossible."

"Would you yourself have forgiven him?"

"That I do not know, and therefore can not say. "Yes," she added, after a moment's pause, as if she had weighed the question—"yes, I would. I might not, perhaps, feel the same toward him, but I should forgive him, and to such an extent that the past would be forgotten."

"That," said Dolly, quickly, "would be a matter of course, or the forgiveness would be worth nothing. Come," she said, rising from her seat; "let me show you your room," and she linked her arm in that of her sister-in-law. "Dear Anna," she said, "how glad I am that you came to me. I suffer less, far less, now."

CHAPTER XIV

KITTY'S SURPRISE

ANNA passed the whole day in her brother's house, receiving none of the visitors who called on hearing of her arrival in Moscow. The morning was spent with Dolly and her children. To Stépane she sent a note, bidding him dine at the house. "Come," she wrote; "I trust matters will go well."

He followed her advice and dined at home. The conversation at the table was general, and Dolly's manner, though cold, was in marked contrast with her previous behavior since the discovery of her wrong.

After dinner, Kitty arrived. She had but a slight acquaintance with Anna, and was astonished that this great lady from St. Petersburg should be received so quietly and unceremoniously. She felt attracted toward her, and Anna, on her part, was charmed with Kitty's youth and beauty, and treated her as an elder woman treats a young one, whom she is prepared to esteem and love. Her manner was more like that of a girl of twenty than a woman and the mother of a family. Simple and sincere as she was, she seemed to others a woman far superior to most of those with whom they came in contact. When dinner was over, Anna approached her brother, who was smoking his cigar. Dolly had retired to her own room.

"Stiva," said Anna, pointing to the door through which the wife had gone, "go to her, and may Heaven help you!"

He understood, and, throwing away his cigar, followed his wife.

Anna sat down, surrounded by the children, who by this time were her devoted admirers.

"Now," she said, addressing Kitty, "tell me about this grand ball. When does it take place?"

"Next week," answered the young girl. "It ought to be splendid, for it is at a good house. Have you not noticed how dances and balls differ according to the house where they are given?"

"Well, dear, for my part, they are all much the same now. It is only a question of their being more or less tiresome."

"How can you find them tiresome?" said Kitty, wonderingly. "Surely, you are always—how shall I say it?—the belle?"

The abruptness of the remark caused Anna to blush—a little weakness she was very prone to. "Oh, no! Not now," she said; "and if I were, it would make little difference."

"Shall you go to this one?" asked Kitty.

"I fear that I must, if I remain in Moscow."

"I should so like to see you there," said the girl.

"Well, that will be one consolation to me, if I find that I must go. But I think I can guess why you wish me to be there. You expect something important to happen on that evening."

"How do you know it? It—it is true."

"Ah! my dear, I have been a girl myself, and passed through it all."

Kitty smiled as she heard Anna's

words. "What has she passed through?" she thought. "How I would like to know what her romance was!" and she remembered what she had been told of Anna's prosaic and unromantic marriage.

"I am very well informed, I can assure you," continued Anna. "Stiva has told me, and I met Wronsky on my arrival this morning. I was very pleased with him."

"Ah! was he at the station?" asked Kitty, blushing. "And what did Stiva tell you?"

"Merely some gossip. I traveled all yesterday with the Countess Wronsky, and all her conversation was of this wonderful son of hers. He is her favorite, and she is prejudiced in his favor, I suppose; but she told me of many things which prove his brave and chivalrous nature. In a word, he is a sort of hero," added Anna, smiling, as she thought of his gift to the unfortunate widow at the railway-station. "The countess asked me to call on her," she continued, "and I shall do so to-morrow. Stiva is a long time with Dolly; but I am glad of it—it is a good sign," she added, so abruptly as to arouse Kitty's astonishment; and she turned to the children and commenced to play with them.

CHAPTER XV

CURIOSITY

JUST at the moment that tea was served, Dolly came out from her room. Stépane had made his exit by another door.

"I am afraid that you may find your room too cold," said Dolly to Anna. "Let me have it changed to one on this floor."

"I assure you," replied Anna, "that I can sleep anywhere, and always very soundly."

"What is the matter?" asked Stépane, entering the room and addressing his wife.

There was nothing in his voice to indicate a reconciliation.

"I want Anna to occupy another room, and if so, I must see to it myself," answered Dolly.

The coldness of her tone somewhat alarmed Anna.

"Don't you bother about it, Dolly," said Stépane; "I will arrange it."

"I know what that means," Dolly said, with a mocking laugh. "You will give the order to Matvei, then you will go out, and the whole thing will be forgotten."

"Thank God!" said Anna to herself, "they are reconciled!" and going up to Dolly, she kissed her tenderly.

"I don't know why you should always suspect Matvei and myself," laughed Stépane.

Throughout the remainder of the evening, Dolly's manner toward her husband was slightly ironical, while he himself was all gayety and cheerfulness, though somewhat subdued, as if to show that the forgiveness could not banish the offense from his own mind.

Toward ten o'clock, while the conversation round the tea-table was still brisk and lively, a little incident occurred.

They were talking of some mutual friend in St. Petersburg, and Anna, recollecting that she had his photograph in her album, left the room to fetch it from her own apartment. As she reached the staircase, there was a ring at the street bell.

"Who can that be?" said Dolly.

"It is too early for them to have sent from home for me," remarked Kitty, "and too late for any visitor."

"Probably some message or papers for me," said Stépane.

Anna was standing at the foot of the stairs, the hall-light throwing its glow around her. A servant opened the door, and in the visitor Anna was astonished to recognize Wronsky. A strange sensation of joy and affright passed through her heart. Wronsky stood upon the threshold, without removing his cloak, and sought for something in one of his pockets. He suddenly raised his eyes, and as they met those of Anna, who had now ascended a few stairs, an expression of confusion passed across his face.

She made a slight bow to him, and passed upstairs as she heard Stépane's voice calling to Wronsky to come in. The latter's refusal, however, reached her ears.

When she came down again with the album, Wronsky had gone, and Stépane was explaining the object of his call. It was to tell the exact hour of a dinner which was to be given the next day to some celebrity who was passing through Moscow.

"What a curious fellow he is! I could not persuade him to come in."

Kitty blushed. She thought she knew the reason of this sudden bashfulness on Wronsky's part.

"He has been to the house," she said to herself, "and finding no one at home, guessed that I was here. He would not come in because of Anna being here and the lateness of the hour."

They all commenced to examine Anna's album, and the subject was dropped; nevertheless, each of them was more or less puzzled at the visit on such a trifling excuse—none more than Anna, to whom it seemed a curious, if not a displeasing, occurrence.

CHAPTER XVI

THE BALL

THE ball had hardly commenced, when Kitty and her mother ascended the brilliantly lighted staircase, with its double row of powdered lackeys in gorgeous livery.

Kitty was looking her very best. Even she herself was aware of this in her innermost mind. Never had she so clearly felt the power of her own beauty, and as she surveyed herself in a long mirror before entering the ball-room, a glow of self-satisfaction passed through the young girl's frame.

Hardly had she entered the room than she was greeted by the famous leader of cotillons and general master-of-ceremonies, the dandy, Georges Korsunsky.

"You have done well to come early," he said. "I can not understand those people who make a rule of arriving when a ball is half over;" and, almost without being formally asked by him, she found herself being whirled away in the mazes of the dance.

"It is less than no exertion to dance with you," he said. "You have the perfection of lightness and precision. It is charming!"

Kitty smiled at this praise from one who was an undisputed authority, and glanced over his shoulder and around the room in search of her most intimate friends. At last she saw them in a corner of the room—Lydia, the beautiful wife of her present partner, Korsunsky; her brother-in-law Stépane, standing side by side with his sister Anna; and then—*him* for whom she looked most of all. She had not met him since the evening on which she had refused Levine, and now she thought that his eyes were seeking hers.

"Will you take me to Madame Karénine?" she asked her partner.

"Certainly, whenever you command;" and a few turns brought them to where the little group was standing.

Anna's costume was of black velvet, cut low enough to show her symmetrical neck and the beauty of her white and well-formed arms. She wore little or no jewelry save a necklace and tiara of marvelous pearls.

"A waltz with you, Anna Arcadievna!" cried Korsunsky, as he joined the group.

"Thanks; but I do not dance if I can avoid it."

"You can not avoid it to-night."

At this moment Wronsky approached.

"Well," said Anna, quickly, and paying no attention to Wronsky's salutation, "in that case, I suppose I must yield;" and she moved away on Korsunsky's arm.

"Why did she do that?" thought Kitty, who had remarked the evident intention with which Anna slighted Wronsky.

He himself gave up Kitty and said some words of regret at not having seen her for so long. She, as he spoke, was watching Anna dancing, astonished that he did not at once ask her to dance. At last, with a certain hesitation, he invited her, and as his arm encircled her, Kitty was well aware that the look she gave him was one full of love and tenderness. It was many years before she could recall the occasion, and

the betrayal of her own feelings, without a sensation of bitter grief and shame at her heart. When they had made a few turns, the music ceased, and Kitty returned to her mother's side. She was chatting with the Countess Nordstone when Wronsky again came to seek her for a square dance. It was not, however, to such dances that Kitty had been looking forward with a beating of her heart, but to the cotillon. It was then, she felt certain, that everything would be decided. Although he had not yet asked her, she had so far relied upon it as to refuse half a dozen other invitations.

The ball went on, and the last quadrille was reached. To Kitty the evening had been an enchanted one, full of the scent of flowers, sweet sounds, and joyous motion. During this last quadrille, which she danced with a somewhat tiresome young adorer, she found herself *vis-à-vis* to Wronsky and Anna. Kitty could not fail to see that Anna's whole manner and appearance had altered since the commencement of the evening. She looked excited, and as if intoxicated with success. "Who is the cause of it?" Kitty asked herself. "Is it from one conquest, or several?" She hardly listened to her partner's conversation, or the noisy directions of Korsunsky, who was directing the quadrille; her whole attention was given to the couple opposite her.

"No," she thought again, "it is not the admiration of the crowd which has caused her to change. It is one man. Who is it? Can it be—*he?*"

At each remark of Wronsky's, Anna's eyes would lighten up and a smile of happiness rise to her lips. She seemed as if struggling to conceal this happiness, but without success; it was too strong for her.

Then Kitty looked at him and her heart stood still with fear. The same look was on his face as upon Anna's. Where was his usual *sang-froid*, the calmness and repose of feature? As he spoke to his partner, bending his head as if in humble worship, there was a look of passion in his eyes. "I would save my heart from you," it seemed to say, "but how can I? It is impossible!"

And yet, what little of their conversation Kitty could hear in the movements of the dance was trivial and commonplace enough.

Poor child! The whole fabric had fallen, and her innocent young heart was in a turmoil. With an effort she forced herself to answer her partner's questions, and even to smile.

The quadrille was over, and they were arranging the chairs for the cotillon. Despair seized upon Kitty; she, in spite of her many offers, was without a partner. She would have told her mother that she was suffering and wished to be taken from the ball, but her strength failed her; she felt crushed and broken. She hurried to a small boudoir where no one was, and threw herself upon a sofa, intense despair at her heart.

"Perhaps I am mistaken," she thought. "Surely, it can not be!"

"What is the matter, Kitty?" asked the Countess Nordstone, entering the room. Kitty rose hurriedly, with trembling lips. "Why are you not joining in the cotillon?"

"I do not wish to," Kitty answered in a half-broken voice.

"He asked her to be his partner in my presence," said the countess, knowing well the cause of the girl's trouble.

"She said to him, 'Are you not dancing it with the Princess Cherbatzky?'"

"It does not matter to me," said Kitty. The countess could not tell that, shortly before, the girl had sacrificed a man whom perhaps she might have loved to this false and ungrateful suitor.

The countess went to find Korsunsky, and begged him to invite Kitty for the cotillon.

Fortunately for Kitty, her partner's duties in directing the dance saved her from the effort of conversation. Wronsky and Anna were again almost opposite her.

In spite of the crowd, it seemed as if they two were alone, unconscious of all save themselves. On Wronsky's usually placid face Kitty again remarked the expression of humility and half fear such as one sees in the eyes of an intelligent dog.

If Anna smiled, his smile answered hers; if she, for a moment, became pensive, he, in turn, was serious. In her costume of black, with flushed cheeks and sparkling eyes, she looked even more charming than on her entrance to the ball-room; but to Kitty's eyes there was something in her attractiveness which was almost terrible and cruel-looking.

A movement of the dance brought them together. Anna pressed the girl's hands and looked at her with half-closed eyes; but when she saw the expression of grief and surprise in Kitty's face, she turned quickly away and spoke to her nearest neighbor in an excited, animated tone. When the dance was over, Anna commenced to make her adieus, refusing the host's persuasion to remain to supper.

"No, I can not stop," she said, with

a smile, but with the evident intention of being firm in her refusal. "I have danced more at this one ball, here in Moscow, than during the whole winter at St. Petersburg;" and she turned to Wronsky, who was standing near. "I need some rest, too, before my journey," she added.

"And you go, for certain, to-morrow?" he asked.

"Yes, I think so," answered Anna, as if astonished at the boldness of the question.

Again refusing all entreaties to remain, Anna left the ball-room.

CHAPTER XVII

LEVINE'S HOUSE

THE morning after his interview with Kitty, Levine left Moscow, and toward evening had arrived at his own home. During the journey, he had conversed with his fellow-passengers on every conceivable topic; but, all the time, he felt as if in a dream, and as if some great misfortune had overtaken him. When, however, on reaching his own station and seeing his coachman, Ignace, wrapped in heavy furs, patiently waiting for him; when, as they drove away, the old servant poured forth a string of home news and domestic happenings, telling of the arrival of Simon, the head steward; how Pava, Levine's most valuable and best-bred cow, had calved the day before, Constantin's ideas marshaled themselves in order, and a portion of his discontent seemed to be lifted away. He ceased to regret his own individuality and to wish that he was some one else than himself, and in place of the regret there came a determination to prove himself a better and

more useful man than he had hitherto been.

Levine's house was an old-fashioned and roomy mansion. In his eyes, it was the dearest spot in all the world. His father and mother had lived and died there—lived what seemed to him the very ideal of existence, and one which his great envy was to follow. The memory of his mother was something sacred; he longed for a wife who should follow in her very footsteps. For him there could be no love apart from marriage. He went still further— he thought first of the family which might be given him, and then of the wife who might bear them.

When he entered the little sitting-room, where, as a rule, his tea was served, and was seated, with a book, in his own chair, while Agatha Mikhiloona brought him his cup, addressing him as "Mon Petit Père," he felt that, in spite of what had recently occurred, his former dreams of domestic life were not dispelled, and that he could not exist without them.

Agatha told him all the gossip and trivial details of the household, and, as he listened, his thoughts went far afield, picturing the life it would be possible for him to lead with a wife of tastes in sympathy with his own. He thought of what had occurred in Moscow. "I can do no more," he said to himself; "even if things can never be quite the same, I must not be influenced by what has passed, but must try to improve my life to raise it to a higher level." As he was pondering over past and future, his old and faithful dog, Laska, bounded into the room, overjoyed to see his master again, and seeming to bring with him the odor of the fresh and frosty air outside. The dog ran to him with furious wagging of the tail, and laid his head upon Levine's knee, awaiting the caress which he knew was sure to come.

"He can do everything but speak," said old Agatha. "He understands that his master has come home and is feeling sad."

"Why sad?" asked Levine.

"Can I not see it, Petit Père? It is time that I should be able to read my master's feelings, for have I not grown up with them? If one's health is good, and one's conscience pure, nothing else can signify."

Levine looked at her attentively, astonished that she should have been able to read his thoughts.

"Shall I fill your cup again?" she asked, moving toward the table.

Laska remained motionless, with his head in Levine's lap, who patted him affectionately. Then the dog moved away, and, stretching himself at his master's feet, composed himself to sleep in canine fashion, with eye and ear constantly on the alert. Levine looked down at him and smiled.

"I, too," he said, "will go and rest. Everything will arrange itself in time."

CHAPTER XVIII

AS A GENTLEMAN

THE morning after the ball, Anna Arcadievna telegraphed to her husband in St. Petersburg that she would leave Moscow that day.

Dolly parted from her with affectionate regret, while Stépane, who accompanied her to the station, was profuse in his expressions of gratitude for the reconciliation she had brought about. "I shall never forget it, Anna," he said, "and, as in the past, shall always look upon you as the best friend a brother ever had."

"I can not understand why," said Anna, kissing him, while the tears came to her eyes.

"You do understand, and you have always understood," answered Stépane. "Good-bye, dear."

"Thank God, it is all over!" was Anna's thought, as she threw herself back in the seat which her maid had procured for her. "To-morrow I shall see Serge and Alexis Alexandrovitch again, and life will go on as before."

As she settled herself for the journey, some ladies, fellow-passengers, entered into conversation with her, and spoke of the intense cold. Anna answered politely but very briefly; and when the maid had affixed her little reading-lamp to the cushion of her seat, she commenced to read an English novel. She had difficulty in keeping her thoughts upon the book before her; every little trifle distracted her attention—the snow beating against the windows; the passage of the conductor through the train, his beard glistening with frozen moisture; the conversation of those around her. She reviewed in her mind the events which had transpired during her stay in Moscow. She thought of Wronsky and their sudden friendship, of his looks, respectful but full of admiration; and, on the whole, she found her reflections pleasant and agreeable. As night drew on, the book fell from her hands, and she fell into a sort of waking slumber. The people and objects in the carriage assumed grotesque and indistinct shapes, puzzling and amusing her at the same time. Suddenly, just as consciousness seemed leaving her, she started and quickly raised herself in her seat. A man, covered from head to foot with snow, stood at the door calling out the name of some station, and Anna noticed that the train had come to a standstill.

"Does madame wish to go outside?" asked Annouchka, the maid; "we stop here for some minutes."

"Yes," said Anna. "I would like some fresh air—it is so warm in here."

She opened the door and stepped out upon the snow-covered platform of the station.

The snow was still falling heavily, blown about by a cold and piercing wind. Passengers were walking hurriedly up and down, some rushing to and from the telegraph-office and refreshment-room, others trying to enjoy their cigar or cigarette. As Anna stood looking on the busy scene, a tall figure, wrapped in a military cloak, approached her. In a moment she recognized Wronsky. He raised his cap, and, in a respectful tone, asked her if he could be of any service. Anna looked at him, and for a few seconds could not answer; she experienced a sudden feeling of pride and joy. It was useless to ask him why he was there; she knew too well what his answer would be.

"I did not know you were coming to St. Petersburg," she said, struggling to hide the pleasure in her looks. "May I ask why?"

"Why?" he repeated, looking fixedly into her face. "You know very well that it is because I must be where you are. There could be no other reason."

She was silent; but he could read her thoughts and her inward struggle.

"Forgive me if what I have said displeases you," he said in a low tone, but one which showed no want of resolution or decision.

"What you said was certainly not right," she replied, "and, as a gentleman, you will forget it as I myself shall."

"I shall not forget it, any more than I can forget you—"

"Enough, enough!" she cried, trying to force a look of severity into her face, and turning to re-enter the carriage. She stood by the door for some moments, as if about to rebuke him still further; but the words would not come to her, and she entered the carriage and once more took her seat.

When the train moved on, she found that sleep was out of the question; her nerves were overstrained, and the same feeling of troublous joy came back to her. Toward morning she sunk into a light doze, from which she did not awaken until the train was gliding into the station at St. Petersburg. Her first conscious thought was of the home to which she was returning, of her husband and her son. As she left the carriage, the first face she saw was that of her husband, and a strange sensation came over her at the sight of his cold but distinguished looking features.

Karénine advanced toward his wife with his usual ironical smile upon his lips. His look annoyed Anna. She felt a sudden discontent, not only with herself, but with the hypocrisy which now, for the first time, she recognized in her relations with her husband.

"You see what an affectionate husband I am," he said in his gentle, slightly mocking voice; "as affectionate as during the first year of our married life. I have been burning with desire to see you again."

"How is Serge?" she asked, abruptly.

"And that is how you quench the flame," he said. "Serge is well—very well."

At this moment Wronsky approached her. He had spent a no less troubled night than Anna herself. Their short interview during the journey had told him even more than he had wished to know. When he took his own seat in the train again, his mind was full of the future and its possibilities which his imagination painted.

When they arrived at St. Petersburg, he stood near the door of his carriage to see her pass. "She may perhaps say a word or two to me, or least give me a look, a smile," he thought. But his eyes fell upon the husband, and Wronsky, for the first time, realized that this husband was an essential part of Anna's life. Aware as he was that she was married, the existence of her husband had never entered his mind, nor troubled him for one moment. But now he was there, before his eyes, holding Anna's hand in the manner of one whose property it was. The sight of Karénine irritated him; it was as if some parched and thirsty man had come upon a spring of clear, cold water, only to discover that it had been polluted by some dog or unclean animal. Wronsky gave his valet some instructions concerning his luggage, and walked toward Anna. As he watched her face, he said to himself: "No, she does not love him, and never could love him."

"Did you pass the night well?" he asked, saluting her.

"Thanks; yes, very well," she answered. Tired as her looks were, there was an expression in her eyes, as they met his own, which filled Wronsky with delight. Karénine was looking at him with an air of slight impatience. "Count Wronsky," said Anna, introducing him.

"Ah! I think we must have met before," said Karénine, indifferently, as they shook hands. "You were fortunate, Anna," he continued, "in traveling one way with the mother, and the return journey with the son. I suppose you have been on leave, Count Wronsky?" and without waiting for an answer, turned again to his wife with some trivial question.

Accepting the evident hint that Karénine wished to be alone with his wife, Wronsky took his leave.

"I hope to have the honor of calling on you," he said, addressing Anna.

It was Karénine himself who answered in his cold, indifferent tone:

"We shall be most happy. We receive on Mondays."

CHAPTER XIX

GLADNESS ABSENT

THE first to greet Anna on her entering the house was her little son Serge. He came bounding down the staircase, crying out: "Mamma! mamma!" in a transport of joy, and threw his arms about her neck.

"I told you it must be my mamma when we heard the bell," he said to his governess, who followed him. "I was quite sure it was she."

But the sight of the son, even as of the father, caused Anna to feel a strange disappointment, a sort of disillusion. He was a graceful, handsome lad to look at—and yet this new and unaccustomed feeling came upon her.

She returned his caresses, and answered his prattling, childish questions, while she unpacked the presents which

Dolly and his little cousins had sent him. She told him of the little girl Tania, just his own age, who was now able to read to her younger brothers and sisters.

"Is she nicer than I am?" asked the boy.

"No, dear, not to me. To me you are the best in the whole world."

"I was sure of it," said the child, with a loving smile.

Karénine returned from his official duties at the ministry toward four o'clock, going straight to his library to examine and sign a batch of documents which his secretary had arranged for him.

At five o'clock he entered the salon, where Anna was already entertaining a few guests invited to dinner, in his evening dress and one or two decorations pinned to his coat. Punctuality was his one rule. "No laziness, and no rash haste" his motto. During dinner, save for a few questions by the husband to the wife as to her doings in Moscow, the conversation was general, and chiefly on topics of St. Petersburg society.

When dinner was over, he remained talking with his guests for a half hour, and then left to attend a meeting of the council. Anna had received an invitation for the evening, from the Princess Betsy Tverskoï, but decided neither to go there nor to their own box at the theater. When the guests had gone, she devoted her evening to her little son, putting him to bed with her own hands, and not leaving him until his eyes were closed in childish slumber.

Precisely at half past nine Karénine returned and entered the salon.

"You have come at last?" she said, extending her hand.

He kissed it, and sat down by her side.

"Your visit to Moscow was successful?" he asked.

"Perfectly," she answered; and gave him a full account of all her doings, and of the reconciliation.

"I can make no excuses for such a man," said Karénine in a severe tone, alluding to Stépane, "even though he is your own brother."

Anna smiled. She knew that it was not in his nature to allow relationship to influence his judgment, and she respected him for it.

"Still," he continued, "I am glad you were able to arrange matters, and still more glad to see you home again. Did you not wish to go out to-night?" he asked, as he rose to return to his library.

"No, not at all," she answered. "What book are you reading now?"

"The 'Poésie des Enfers,' by the Duc de Lille, a most remarkable book," he answered, with enthusiasm.

She smiled again, and, taking his arm, walked to the library with him.

"Well, good-night," she said, as they reached the room where his favorite chair and reading-lamp and carafe of water were all arranged for him. "I must go and write a few lines to Moscow, to tell them of my safe return."

"He is a good man, and an honest and loyal one," said Anna to herself, as she entered her boudoir; but on her face there was no smile such as she had worn in the ballroom at Moscow, and the glad light was absent from her eyes.

PART II

CHAPTER I

SICKNESS

TOWARD the end of the winter, the Cherbatzkys deemed it expedient to call a consultation of physicians in regard to their daughter Kitty's health. For some weeks she had been growing thinner and paler every day, nor had such remedies as the family doctor prescribed the least effect in bringing her back to health. The result of the consultation, at the head of which was the leading specialist of Moscow, was that she must have immediate change of air and scene, and must go abroad.

As soon as the doctors had left the house, the prince entered the room where his wife and daughters—for Dolly had come to support her sister during the ordeal of examination—were discussing future plans.

Dolly herself was far from well or happy; a change for the worse had come upon her life. She felt constantly humiliated by the renewal of her former relations with Stépane. The reconciliation which had been effected by Anna had been of little use. The husband absented himself as much as ever from the house, and the suspicions which Dolly could not drive out of her mind tortured her beyond endurance. Some of her children, too, were suffering from a sickness, childish but severe, and her whole horizon seemed very dark.

"What has been decided?" asked the prince. "You are to go abroad? And what is to become of me?"

"I think, Alexander," said the princess, "you had better remain here."

"As you think best."

"Why should not papa come with us?" asked Kitty. "It would be much pleasanter, both for himself and us."

The prince went over to her and lovingly stroked her hair. She lifted her face and smiled at him, though as if with an effort. It seemed to her that her father understood her better than any one; and, to him, she was his youngest and best-loved child.

"Kitty," he said, "I can tell you what you must do. Some fine morning you must wake up and say to yourself, 'I am quite well and happy. Why should I not take one of the old walks with papa in the bright sunlight and frosty air?'"

At these simple words, Kitty trembled with emotion. "He understands everything," she thought, "and means that, however greatly I may have been humiliated, I should do my best to struggle against it, and overcome it;" and she ran from the room.

"Alexander, you are cruel!" said the princess. "Can you not see that the poor girl is suffering, and that any allusion to the cause of her grief pains her beyond endurance?" and they both knew that she was alluding to Wronsky. "I can not understand why there should be no law to punish such vile conduct."

The prince rose and moved toward the door, then stopped, as if he felt that he must speak. "There are laws to punish most offenses, Ma Petite Mère, but since you have opened the subject, I must tell you that I think you yourself are greatly to blame for this affair. Old as I am, I would have undertaken to bring him to task had it not been that you were the one to invite him to this house." It was seldom that the prince spoke so sternly, and his wife could not keep back her tears. "Don't cry," he said in a gentler voice; "I know it is hard for you also. Perhaps God will take pity on us all;" and raising her hand to his lips, he left the room.

Within a few days, while Lent was still in progress, the Cherbatzkys left Moscow and went abroad.

CHAPTER II

PERSECUTIONS

THE highest society of St. Petersburg is limited to a narrow circle as regards perfect intimacy. The well-born families may all know and visit each other, but there are certain definite subdivisions.

Anna Karénine was a privileged member of at least three different circles in the great world. First, there was the ministerial and official circle, composed of her husband's colleagues and subordinates.

The second was the more social one which had contributed to the career of Alexis Karénine. Of this, the Countess Lydia Ivanovna was the pivot, and it was mainly composed of learned, scientific, and prominent men, and of elderly, well-born, charitable women. Some one, in jest, had once christened it "the *conscience* of St Petersburg."

The third set with which Anna had intimate relations, was that of society *par excellence;* the world which occupied itself with balls, dinners, brilliant toilets, and gayeties of every sort. The tie which bound Anna to this world of pleasure was the Princess Betsy Tverskoï, the wife of one of her cousins, possessed of an enormous income. "When I am old and ugly," said Betsy, when discussing the princess and her associates, "I will apply for admittance to this 'asylum for aged people'—not before."

Hitherto, Anna had rather avoided the society of which the Princess Tverskoï was an acknowledged leader, but since her return from Moscow, everything had changed. She neglected her more staid and quiet friends for the more pronounced world of fashion. It was there that she experienced the troublous joy of meeting Wronsky. They met, most often, at the house of the Princess Betsy, who was herself a Wronsky, and the younger soldier found frequent opportunities of expressing his love for Anna. She, on her part, made no actual response or advance, but, in her heart, the same feeling was ever present which he had experienced at their meeting on the train. Her joy was visible in her eyes, her smile, her every glance; and, do what she would she could not conceal it.

For a long time Anna tried to flatter herself that Wronsky's attentions—persecutions, she called them—were displeasing to her; but the truth became only too clear to her one evening, when on going to a house where she had felt sure of meeting him, she found that he was not present. Then, at last, she was forced to own that he was now the dominating interest in her life.

One night, from his seat at the opera, Wronsky perceived the Princess Betsy in her box, and, without waiting for the *entr'acte*, joined her.

"Why did you not come to dinner?" she asked him. Then lowering her voice: "I do envy the second-sight which you lovers are gifted with—*she* was not there; but come after the opera."

Wronsky looked at her inquiringly; but Betsy merely made a little movement of her head, and continued, "Where has all your old gayety vanished to? You are *épris*, my friend."

"That's is all I desire," answered Wronsky, smiling. "If I have any fault to find, it is that I am not sufficiently so. I am even beginning to lose hope."

"What hope are you entitled to have?" said Betsy in defense of her absent friend; but her eyes told only too plainly how well she understood.

"None," he answered, laughing, and showing his perfect teeth. "Excuse me," he added, taking the operaglass from her hands and looking across the house; "I am afraid of making myself ridiculous."

He knew very well that in Betsy's eyes and those of her world, he ran no such risk. There might be a chance of ridicule were he hopelessly in love with a young girl or an unmarried woman, but in risking everything to seduce a married woman there was small chance of being laughed at.

CHAPTER III

FORBIDDEN

THE Princess Betsy left the theater before the end of the last act. Hardly had she reached her own boudoir and made some little alterations in her toilet than the carriages of her guests began to roll past the large gates of the palace, and discharge their occupants at the door, which was noiselessly opened to them by a gigantic Swiss lackey. The mistress of the house received her friends in the large salon, its walls hung with somber-colored draperies and tapestry, its floor covered with a luxuriously thick carpet. Upon a table, with a cloth of spotless white, and lighted by numerous wax candles, stood a silver samovar and tea service of most delicate porcelain.

After a time the princess removed her gloves and sat down before the samovar, while the footmen glided about the room serving the cups of fragrant tea.

Wronsky had already arrived, and was standing by her side when Anna entered the room. She crossed toward the mistress of the house with a light and rapid step, and greeted her; then turned to Wronsky.

"I received a letter from Moscow to-day," she said. "They write me that Kitty Cherbatzky is very ill."

"Indeed?" said Wronsky, gravely.

Anna looked fixedly at him.

"Is it such a matter of indifference to you?" she asked.

"On the contrary, I am deeply grieved. What are the particulars, if I may ask?"

Anna approached Betsy.

"Will you give me a cup of tea?" she said.

As Betsy poured out the tea, Wronsky came up to Anna.

"What have they written?" he asked again.

"I have often thought that what they

call nobility of action in men is a mere empty phrase. I have several times felt tempted to tell you this," she added, moving away to a table on which a number of photographs were lying.

"I can not quite understand your words," he said, relieving her of the empty cup.

She glanced at the sofa near her, and they both sat down.

"Yes, I have often wanted to say it," she continued, without looking at him. "You have behaved badly, very badly."

"Do you not suppose that I am aware of it? But whose fault is it? Who is responsible?"

"Why do you ask me that?" she said in a severe tone.

"You know only too well," he answered, meeting her look without lowering his eyes.

She was conquered. "It only proves that you have no heart," she said; but her eyes expressed the very contrary.

"What you have just spoken of was a mistake—it was not love."

"Have I not forbidden you to use that wretched word?" said Anna, trembling; and as the word "forbidden" passed her lips she saw that it implied some claim upon him, some rights to his obedience. "For a long time I have been wishing to talk to you," she continued in a firm tone, though her cheeks were dyed with crimson. "I came here to-night for that purpose, knowing that I should meet you. This must all come to an end. No one has ever before caused me to blush; but you have, and you have caused me grief, too."

He looked at her, struck with the unusual beauty of her face

"What would you have me do?" he asked, simply and seriously.

"I would have you go to Moscow and ask Kitty's pardon."

"You do *not* wish it!" he exclaimed, for he plainly saw that her words and her desire were at variance.

"If you loved me as you say you do," she murmured, "you would take care that I was at peace."

Wronsky's whole face lightened up

"Do you not know," he exclaimed, "that you are everything to me? But I myself do not know what peace of mind means, nor can I give it you. I can give you my whole being, my whole love, yes; but I can not separate you from myself in my own thoughts. To my eyes, you and I are one. I can foresee no peace of mind in the future either for you or for myself. I can see one of two things only—despair or happiness—and what happiness!" he added, almost inaudibly.

Her whole intelligence asserted itself and showed her what answer it was her duty to make; but, instead of speaking she looked at him with eyes full of love and remained silent.

"My God!" he thought, while his brain seemed to reel with joy, "at the moment when I was despairing, when all seemed hopeless, love has come She loves me—her looks avow it!"

"Let us be good friends, and never speak to me like this again," were her words; but her looks spoke differently

"We can never be *friends*—you know it well yourself. We must either be the happiest or the most wretched of mortals. It rests with you to decide which."

She would have spoken, but he interrupted her:

"All that I ask is the right to hope and suffer as I do at this moment. I it can never be, bid me to disappear, and I will disappear. You shall never again be troubled with a presence which is odious to you."

"I do not wish to send you away."

"Then let there be no change. Leave things as they are," he said in a trembling voice. "But—there is your husband."

As a fact, Karénine at that moment entered the room, with his usual calm air and awkward step.

He approached the mistress of the house, throwing a passing glance on Anna and Wronsky; then taking a seat near the tea-table, he looked round the assembly, and said, with the mocking smile upon his lips:

"Princess, your rambouillet is complete. You have all the Graces and the Muses."

But the Princess Betsy, who abominated his sneering manner, was quick to meet his attack, and at once challenged him to a discussion on some public affair. Wronsky and Anna retained their seats near the little table.

"This affaire is becoming somewhat tiresome," said one guest in a low tone to her next neighbor.

"What did I tell you?" replied the other.

Nor were they the only ones to notice and criticise. The eyes of most of those present were from time to time turned upon the two who sat apart. Karénine, apparently, was the only one who remained obstinately blind and inwrapped in his own conversation.

At last the Princess Betsy, noticing the bad effect produced upon her guests, cut short her conversation with Karénine, and crossed the room to where Anna sat.

"I am always," she said, "so much struck with your husband's terse and clear language when discussing anything. He makes the most formidable questions appear quite simple."

"Oh, yes," said Anna, hardly hearing the princess's words, and radiant with happiness. She rose and joined in the general conversation.

When half an hour had passed, Karénine proposed to his wife that they should return home; but she, almost without looking at him, declared that she wished to remain to supper. He made his own adieus and left.

It was much later when Wronsky conducted Anna to her own carriage, which was still in waiting, the servants and horses almost frozen with the cold.

"Remember," said Wronsky, "though you have made no promise, it is more than friendship that I want. As for me, the only happiness of my life is contained in that word which you disliked so much—love!"

"Love!" she repeated, softly, to herself. "The use of the word displeases me because, in my mind, it means so much—more than you can ever imagine. *Au revoir*," she added, giving him one glance as the carriage rolled away. Her look, the clasp of her hand, set Wronsky's brain in a whirl. He kissed the spot her fingers had touched, and went toward his own home, convinced that this evening had brought him near the realization of his dream.

CHAPTER IV

ALEXIS KARENINE

On finding his wife engaged in a marked *tête-à-tête* conversation with Wronsky, Alexis Karénine had felt little or no annoyance; but when he subsequently perceived that the two were the subjects of half-whispered conversation throughout the room, he determined to give Anna some sort of warning.

On reaching the house, he went, as usual, to his library and commenced to read an abstruse article on papism which he had received that day. From time to time he passed his hand across his forehead, as if to brush away some thought which troubled him. At the accustomed hour he closed his book and returned to make his toilet for the night. Anna had not yet returned. Finding that his mind was stirred beyond its wont, Karénine commenced to walk up and down the length of the rooms, which were connected with each other, and to let his thoughts wander as they willed.

He was not jealous. A husband, in his eyes, insulted his wife by displaying jealousy. Strange to say, the one question which he never for a moment thought of putting to himself was—why should he feel confident that she would always love and be faithful to him? Having never known suspicion or doubt, his trust was still entire. But, for some reason he could not explain, even to himself, he felt at this moment like a man walking tranquilly across a bridge between two precipices and feeling the bridge sink suddenly beneath his feet.

Without thinking of undressing, he continued his promenade of the dimly lighted rooms, turning his steps in his wife's boudoir full of its little ornaments and feminine luxuries. More than once he stopped short and said to himself: "Yes, it must be put a stop to, definitely and at once; but what shall I say? What reason shall I put forward? I know absolutely nothing save that she was talking confidentially and for a long time with the young man. To show myself jealous would be to humiliate both of us." Then, with greater insistency the thought would come: "It must be cut short. Others, if not I myself, have noticed and remarked upon it." He seated himself in her boudoir and endeavored to think out his plan of action. "I must impress certain things upon her mind," he said to himself. "First, the meaning and importance of public opinion; secondly, the religious obligations which marriage brings; thirdly, the evil which might react upon her young son; and fourthly, the possible harm to herself."

The noise of carriage-wheels reached his ears, and soon he heard Anna's footsteps as she slowly mounted the staircase.

She entered the room, toying with the gloves she had just removed. There was a strange light in her face, but not one of joy. When she saw her husband, she raised her head and smiled, as if waking from some dream.

"Not in bed?" she said. "What a wonder!" and she passed through to her own dressing-room, calling out to him: "It is very late, Alexis."

"Anna, I wish to talk with you."

"With me?" she said in an astonished tone, re-entering the room and looking at her husband. "About what? Well"—sitting down—"let us talk."

"Anna, I want you to be upon your guard."

"Upon my guard? Why?"

Her tone and looks were both simple and natural.

"She will be candid with me," he thought, "and we can both speak openly."

"I wish to put you on your guard,"

he continued, "against the interpretation the world will put upon what is simply imprudence and frivolity on your part. Your animated conversation tonight with Count Wronsky"—he pronounced the name slowly and firmly—"attracted great attention."

As he spoke, he looked into her smiling but impenetrable eyes, and in a moment full of terror it flashed upon him that his words would be useless and in vain.

"It is always so with you," she replied, as if hardly conscious of the words he had used. "At times you are displeased because I am dull; at others, because I amuse myself; to-night I enjoyed myself, and that annoys you."

Karénine trembled and fidgeted about in his seat.

"Please keep still," she added, irritably. "I am very nervous to-night."

"Anna, can it be yourself who is speaking?" he said, making an effort to control himself.

"What is it all about? she insisted. "What do you wish me to do?"

"What I would say to you is this," he answered in a cold, quiet tone; "and I must ask you to hear me to the end. As you may know, I look upon jealousy as a hurtful and humiliating sentiment, of which I hope never to be guilty; but there are certain social barriers which can not be overstepped with safety. Judging from the impression you seem to have given to-night—not to myself, but to the others who were present—you have not been very careful of yourself."

"Perhaps not," said Anna, with a shrug of her shoulders. "That is just like him," she thought; "he simply cares about what others think." "You are not well, Alexis," she continued, rising

to leave the room; but he stood before her and stopped her, with a sterner expression on his face than she had ever seen before. "Well," she said in a calm, mocking tone, "I am listening, I am even interested, because I want to learn what it all means."

Her own calmness, and the ease with which the words came to her, surprised herself.

"I have no right," continued Karénine, "to inquire into your feelings. It would be useless, and even dangerous. If we search too deeply into our souls, we may chance upon something which had better have remained hidden. Your own conscience is responsible for your feelings, but, between you and myself and God, I am obliged to remind you of your duties. Our lives have been joined together, not by men, but by Him. Only sin can break the tie—a sin which brings its own punishment."

"I do not understand what you are talking about, and I am very tired and sleepy," said Anna, drawing the jeweled fastenings from her hair.

"Anna, in Heaven's name, do not speak so!" he said, quietly. "Perhaps I have been mistaken; but, believe me, what I say is as much for your own sake as for mine. I am your husband, and I love you."

For an instant Anna's face softened, and the mocking expression left her eyes; but the word "love" irritated her beyond endurance. "Does he know what love means?" she thought. "If he had not heard the word used he would have ignored it."

"Alexis, I really do not understand you. Please explain yourself clearly."

"I will. Though I love you, it is not for myself that I speak. but rather for yourself and our son. It is possible, 1 repeat, that my words seem empty and out of place to you—and perhaps I am in error. In that case, I must ask your pardon; but if you yourself feel that there is any foundation, even the slightest, for my remarks, I beg you to reflect over them, and to open your heart to me."

Without being conscious of it, Karénine was using arguments directly opposite to those he had prepared.

"I have no such confidences to give," she said, quickly, suppressing a smile with difficulty; "and it really is time to think of sleep."

Alexis Karénine sighed, and, without a word, walked away to his own room.

Anna remained some time, thinking, almost hoping, that he would return and say no more. At last he passed away from her thoughts, and the image of another filled her heart with a great joy. "It is too late," she thought, "too late!"

CHAPTER V

LATER!

FROM that night the relations between Alexis Karénine and his wife were entirely changed. Outwardly, however, their lives continued the same. Anna went much into the world of society, especially to the house of the Princess Betsy, where she was always sure of meeting Wronsky. Karénine was well aware of it, but powerless to prevent it. The slightest remonstrance on his part was met by Anna with an absolutely impenetrable smile. He, who knew himself to be so strong in the important affairs of state, here felt himself powerless. He remained awaiting the final blow, patiently and resigned as an ox at

the slaughter-house. Time and again he resolved to try once more the effect of kindness, tenderness, and affectionate reasoning in restoring Anna to her wonted being; but, on each occasion, he was overcome by the same spirit of evil obstinacy which mastered her, and found himself speaking words far removed from those he had intended.

That which, for a whole year, had been the one end and aim of Wronsky's life, and to Anna a dream, as enchanting as it had seemed improbable and terrible, had come to pass.

Pale and trembling himself, he stood by her side, entreating her to be calm, in words he was unconscious of.

"Anna! Anna!" he said in a voice full of emotion. "Anna! for Heaven's sake, be calm!"

But the higher his voice, the lower she bent her head—the head which, until now, had been so erect and proud, and now was so humiliated. She would have fallen to the ground had he not supported her.

"Oh, forgive me!" she sobbed, pressing his hand against her breast. To herself she was now so culpable and sinning that she felt herself compelled to ask pardon of some one, and it was to him she turned for forgiveness, having now no one else in the world but him.

As for Wronsky, he felt like an assassin standing above the lifeless body of his victim. The sacrifice which had been offered up by them was their love, the first phase of their love. There was something terrible and odious in the thought of what they had paid as the price of their shame.

The feeling of moral degradation which ingulfed Anna was not shared by Wronsky. Whatever might be the murderer's horror as he views his victim's corpse, it must be concealed and the fruits of the crime enjoyed. In the same spirit that he might have fallen on the dead body and torn it to pieces in his rage, he now covered this woman's face and neck with kisses. She held his hand and did not move; she had bought the kisses with her honor, the hand was that of her accomplice, and belonged to her forever. She raised it to her own lips and kissed it. Wronsky fell upon his knees and strove to see the face which she kept concealed. At last she rose with an effort and gently put him away. "All is over now," she said. "I have nothing left to me but you. Remember that!"

"How could I forget what is my whole life! For an instant of such happiness—"

"What happiness!" she cried, with an accent of terror and disgust so strong that is was communicated to him. "Not a word—not another word!"

She rose from her seat again, and moved away.

"Not another word!" she repeated, with a strange expression of despair, and quickly passed from the room.

As the meaning of this new existence dawned upon her, Anna felt the impossibility of expressing her shame, her fear, the joy which she experienced. Rather than allow trifling and insufficient words to pass her lips, she preferred to remain silent. And yet, later on, the words which might have adequately told her feelings, would not come to her; even her thoughts could not translate the impressions of her soul. "No," she said to herself, "I can not think of it all now; later, perhaps, when I am calmer." But the calmness did not come. Each time that she thought of what had taken place.

of what was still to happen, of what she herself would become, she was terrified, and strove to throw away such thoughts. "Later," she kept repeating to herself—"later on, when I am calmer."

CHAPTER VI

GOOD-NIGHT, KOSTIA!

One bright day in early spring, some weeks after his return from Moscow, Levine had ridden to visit a distant portion of his estates and transact some business with his local agent.

As he approached the house again, he saw a carriage, evidently from the neighboring railway-station, draw up to the door, and its occupant, wrapped in a fur cloak, descend. He hurried forward, puzzled as to who the visitor might be, and, much to his astonishment, recognized his friend Stépane Archadievitch.

"How glad I am to see you!" he cried, as they shook hands; and his first thought was: "Now I shall learn for certain if *she* is married."

"You hardly expected me," said Stépane, looking the very picture of health and self-content. "I have come for three objects—to see you; to have a day's shooting; and to sell some of my timber to a neighbor of yours."

"No matter what has brought you, I am delighted to see you," said Levine; and, taking Stépane by the arm, he led him to the room which he set apart for the reception of such visitors. During luncheon, Stépane descanted on the beauty of Levine's home and its surroundings.

"You are a lucky man," he said, "for you possess all that you care for or desire—horses, dogs, abundance of game, broad acres, and good crops. What more can a man want?"

"My luck, perhaps, consists in being able to appreciate what I have, and in not being too envious of what I do not possess," answered Levine, whose thoughts, at the moment, were of Kitty.

Stépane understood him, but said nothing. Levine, much as he wished for news on the subject, could not yet bring himself to make inquiries concerning the Cherbatzkys.

"And how are your affairs?" he asked.

Stépane's face brightened.

"If you remember," he replied, "you have no patience with any one who, on the top of a good meal, takes a fancy to fresh bread, while I will not admit that it is possible to live without love. In any case, I, for one, can not, and I find much pleasure and little wrong in it."

"What! Is there some fresh object?" asked Levine.

"Yes, my friend. The sort of woman that, as a rule, one sees only in dreams—you know the type of the women of Ossian. They are very seldom found in actual life, and when they are—well, one has much to study."

"That is no hardship, I suppose."

"Oh, no; I forget exactly who it was, but some great man has said that true happiness consists in seeking the truth, not in finding it."

Levine said nothing. To him the foibles of his friend were incomprehensible.

After luncheon, the two friends took their guns and, with the dogs, sallied forth in search of game.

The sport was excellent, and as evening drew on, they turned toward home with well-filled bags.

They walked slowly and some little distance apart, for there was still light enough for a chance shot. "Stiva," Levine called out suddenly, "you have not told me if your sister-in-law is already married, or if she is about to be." He felt so calm and secure of himself that nothing he might hear, he thought, could move him; but Stépane's reply quickly dispelled this illusion:

"She is neither married," he said, "nor has she any intention of marriage. She has been very ill, and the doctors have ordered her abroad. They have even feared for her life."

"What do you say?" cried Levine. Ill! But what is it?"

"How—"

At that moment a shrill note and the rushing of wings met their ears. Levine was the first to fire, and in a few moments, Laska, the dog, ran back with the dead bird in his mouth.

The subject of Kitty's health was not again alluded to until they reached the house, when Stépane gave his host all particulars. As he listened, Levine was conscious that though he might not avow it, he was still possessed of hope, nor could he help a slight feeling of satisfaction at the thought that she too, had suffered even as had he. But when Stépane would have gone into particulars concerning Wronsky's conduct, Levine interrupted him. "I have no right," he said, "to learn these family secrets, nor do they interest me."

Stépane, who had marked the other's sudden change from gayety to sadness, smiled quietly, but said nothing more.

During the remainder of the evening, Levine was somewhat *distrait* and out of sorts. There was still one question which he wished to ask Stépane, and yet he could not bring himself to frame it. Stépane, for his part, pleased with himself for his afternoon's sport, and experiencing the satisfaction of a health-ily tired man who has recruited himself with an excellent dinner, was content to enjoy his cigar in peace and quiet. It was not until he had escorted his guest to his bed-chamber before retiring that Levine at last spoke.

"And Wronsky—where is he now?" he asked, abruptly.

"Wronsky?" said Stépane, stifling a slight yawn. "He is in St. Petersburg. He left Moscow soon after you did, and has not been there since. Do you know, Kostia," he continued, as he laz-ily removed his coat, "if you care to hear what I think, you yourself are partly to blame for what has happened. You took sudden fright at a rival, al-though, as I tell you once more, it was by no means certain whose chances were the better. You were certainly the first in the field, and—" He was interrupted by a yawn which he could not suppress.

"Does he, or does he not, know how far I went?" asked Levine of himself, watching his friend's face; but though he blushed slightly, he said nothing.

"If," Stépane resumed, "she expressed some preference for the other man, it was simply a superficial feeling, the attrac-tion of his aristocratic and high posi-tion in the world—advantages which her mother was only too ready to dilate upon."

Levine frowned. The pain of his refusal came back to him fresh and dis-tinct.

"One moment," he interrupted. "You speak of aristocracy—will you tell me in what Wronsky's aristocracy consists, and how it can account for her repulsing me? You look upon him as an aristo-crat. I do not agree with you. A man whose father rose from the gutter through intrigue, whose mother has had a *liaison* with God knows whom! Oh, no! The true aristocrats, in my mind, are those men who can show three or four generations of honest and upright ances-tors, who belong to the most highly cultured classes—I do not say intel-lectual, that is another question—who have never toadied to any one, and who have never asked a favor of any man; such, in short, as my own father and grandfather. I appreciate what they have bequeathed to me, and what gives me work to do, and I say to you that it is we who are the aristocrats, not those who live at the expense of those in power, and who can be bought at any time for twenty kopecks!"

"I entirely agree with you," said Stépane, laughing at the other's words, and the evident sincerity in which he spoke them. "Perhaps you are a little unjust as regards Wronsky; but that is neither here nor there. I tell you frank-ly: were I in your place, I would go to Moscow and—"

"No. I don't know if you are aware of what actually happened, and, so far as that goes, it matters little to me. I proposed to Catherine Alexandrovna, and was refused in such a manner as to cause me much pain and humiliation."

"Why? What folly on her part!"

"We will say no more about it. You must forgive me for having kept any-thing back from you. Now everything is explained."

And taking up his candle from the table, he added, holding out his hand to his friend:

"You would not wish me to go now, Stiva, I am sure; and I am also sure that you will not let it cause any restraint or ill-feeling between us."

"Most certainly not. I am only too glad that we have had this explanation. Good-night, Kostia, good-night!"

CHAPTER VII

ENCEINTE

WRONSKY, although entirely absorbed by his passion, had made no outward change in his daily life. He was careful to preserve his relations in the two worlds wherein he had hitherto existed —the social and the military worlds. It need hardly be said that he was not the kind of man to talk about his love affairs. Never—no matter in what company, nor how much wine he might have consumed—did he allow a word to pass his lips, nor would he permit the slightest allusion to be made to them in his presence. Yet this passion was his whole existence. For one thing he was especially envied by his younger associates—the high position in society of Madame Karénine; but this very fact, perhaps, was what weighed most heavily upon his mind.

As for the women, most of the younger ones, being jealous of Anna, were secretly delighted to see their predictions verified. Formerly they had been wearied with hearing her spoken of as a model of rectitude and morality, and now each one of them was holding in reserve the mud with which they would sooner or later bespatter her. The more elderly of her acquaintances, and those of the highest rank, saw with regret the brewing of an immense scandal.

At first Wronsky's mother had heard with a certain satisfaction of her son's *liaison*; nothing, from her point of view, was so well fitted to "form" a young man as an *affaire* with a woman of high birth and station. She experienced, too, no little pleasure in discovering that, after all, Anna was much like the other women of her own set. But this condoning view taken by the countess was altogether changed when she learned that her son, in order to remain near Madame Karénine, had refused a military exchange which would have materially advanced his career. Now she felt prepared to see him commit any foolishness at any moment. Since his sudden departure from Moscow, so soon after her own arrival there, she had not seen him, and finally sent word to him through his elder brother, who was also displeased with the *liaison*, that she desired a visit from him.

In addition to his liking for society and for army life, Wronsky had one great passion, and that was for horses. Some regimental races were shortly to take place. He subscribed to one race —a steeple-chase—and entered a purchase he had recently made—an English thorough-bred mare. In spite of his absorption in his love, the idea of racing was still attractive to him. He felt, indeed, that some such excitement was necessary to counteract the violent emotions of his passion for Anna.

The morning of the day on which the races were to take place arrived, and Wronsky's thoughts were full of the rendezvous which Anna had given him for an hour when the races should be over. For three days he had not seen her, and, hearing that her husband had just returned to St. Petersburg from abroad, he was troubled in his mind as to whether she would be able to keep the appointment. As he sat at his breakfast he determined that he would call upon her at all risks, and so assure himself.

"I will simply say," he thought to himself, "that I am charged with a message from Betsy as to their meeting on the race-course. Yes, I am determined; I will take the risk."

Anna was now staying at a country residence of her husband's, some few miles from the city; and Wronsky, having hired a private carriage, set out at once.

He dismounted some short distance from the house, so as to attract as little attention as possible, and entered the grounds on foot.

"Has your master arrived?" he asked a gardener.

"Not yet, sir; but madame is at home, I think. If you will ring at the gate they will open to you."

"No; I prefer entering by the garden."

Knowing that Anna was alone, he wished to surprise her, for he knew that she would not expect him on account of the coming races. He walked quietly along a small path which led to the house, raising his sword with one hand so that its clatter should not be heard.

Anna was sitting alone upon the terrace, awaiting the return of her young son Serge from his morning walk. She did not hear Wronsky's approach. She sat, resting her head upon her jeweled hands, lost in reverie and apparent sadness. The beauty of her face and figure struck Wronsky—as, indeed, they did each time he saw her.

"What is the matter?" he asked. "Are you ill?"

"No; I am very well," she answered, rising, and pressing the hand he held out to her. "I did not expect you."

"Your hands—how cold they are!"

"You startled me a little. I was alone, waiting for Serge to come back from his walk."

In spite of her assumed calm, her lips were trembling.

"You must forgive me for coming; but I could not pass the whole day without seeing you."

"There is nothing to forgive; it only makes me too happy."

"But you are ill—or feeling sad?" he said, still holding her hand as he leaned over her. "What were you thinking of?"

"The same thing that I am always thinking of," she answered, with a little smile. She spoke truly; at any hour or minute of the day, had she been asked of what her thoughts were, the true answer would have been of her happiness and her misfortune. At the very moment of his coming she had been wondering to herself how others, such as the Princess Betsy, could accept so lightly the burden of their own *liaisons;* her own she found a cruel burden.

They spoke of the races, and Wronsky strove to raise her spirits by giving her a full account of the race he was to ride in, and his hopes of winning it.

"Shall I, or shall I not, tell him?" she asked herself, covering him with her caressing glance. "He seems so happy and so full of the sport before him, perhaps he would not understand the importance of what has happened."

"You have not yet told me of what you were thinking when I came," he said, interrupting her thoughts. "Tell me, please."

Still she made no answer. In her

beautiful eyes was a look of questioning; her hands idly played with a leaf she had plucked from a bush near by.

Wronsky's own face was full of passionate worship and devotion. "I am sure something has happened. How can you expect me to bear the thought of your having a grief which I do not share? Speak, for God's sake!" he repeated in a beseeching tone.

"If he does not see the importance of what I have to say," she thought, "I could never forgive him. Perhaps it would be better for me to run no risk."

"What is it?" he asked again.

"Must I tell you?"

"Yes, yes!"

"I am *enceinte*," she whispered, gently.

The leaf which she held between her fingers trembled still more, but her eyes did not leave his; she sought to read in his face how her words affected him.

He grew suddenly pale, and appeared as if about to speak; but no words came. He lowered his head, and allowed the hand which he had held between his own to drop.

"Yes, he understands all that it means," she thought, and, in her turn, took his hand.

But she erred in thinking that he felt as she herself did. Hearing this news, a strange feeling of horror came upon him, and he understood that the crisis had arrived. Henceforth it would be impossible to further deceive the husband, and they must extricate themselves, no matter at what price, from this odious and unbearable condition of affairs.

When, at last, he made answer, his words were:

"Neither you nor I have looked upon our *liaison* and love for each other as a transient happiness. Now our future is fixed; we must put an end to the lying deceit in which we have been living —it is absolutely necessary."

"Put an end to it? How can we do so, Alexis?" she asked, quietly.

"You must leave your husband, and our existence must be united."

"Is it not already united?" she said in a low tone.

"No—not completely."

"But what shall we do, Alexis? Tell me," she said in a sad almost ironical tone, thinking of her own inextricable situation. "Am I not his wife?"

"However difficult the situation, there is always some way of solving it if one acts decisively. Anything would be better than the life you are at present leading. Can I not see how everything is torture to you—your husband, your son, the world—everything!"

"Not my husband,' she said, with a smile. "I no longer know him; I never think of him; I ignore his very existence."

"That is not so. I know you too well. You torment yourself on his account."

"But he knows nothing," she replied; and suddenly her whole face, even her neck, became suffused with a deep blush and the tears started to her eyes. "Do not let us speak of him."

It was not the first time that Wronsky had been struck with the difficulty of making her understand her own position. More than once it had seemed to him as if she were influenced by sentiments which she either could not or would not explain, and that in place of the real Anna there appeared a strange, mysterious being, unintelligible, almost repulsive to him.

Now the time had come when he would speak plainly.

"Whether he knows or does not know, is immaterial," he said in a quiet, firm tone. "We can not, *you* certainly can not, remain in this situation—now, least of any time."

"What ought we to do, then, in your opinion?" Anna asked, with the same touch of irony. She who had been so fearful of his receiving her news too lightly was now inclined to find fault with the energetic resolution he displayed.

"Acknowledge everything and leave him."

"Supposing I were to do so, do you know what the result would be? I will tell you," and her eyes, so tender a few moments ago, were filled with a wicked light. " 'Ah! you love another and have been guilty of a criminal *liaison?*' " she said, imitating exactly her husband's voice and speech. " 'I warned you, some time ago, what the consequences would be, from the point of view of religion, of society, and of family ties. You would not listen to me, and now—now I will not bring shame upon my own name and that of—' " She was about to say "my son," but stopped short, at the thought of Serge. "In a word, he would tell me that he refused to give me my liberty, but would take measures to avoid a scandal. He is not a man, he is a machine—and a cruel one, too, when he chooses to be."

"But, Anna," said Wronsky, quietly, hoping to convince and, at the same time, to calm her, "it would be better to avow everything at once, and then we shall know how to act."

"We should have to run away."

"And why not? It is impossible to live on like this. It is not a question of myself, but of you, who are suffering."

"To fly, and to openly become your mistress!" she said in a bitter tone.

"Anna!" he cried, pained beyond hearing at her words.

"Yes, your mistress; and to lose—everything!" She would have said—her son—but again the word refused to come.

Wronsky was incapable of understanding that her strong and loyal nature accepted the false situation in which she found herself without seeking for release. When Anna pictured to herself what the life of her child would be when she had left the father, the horror of the thought overcame her.

"I beg you," she said, her voice again tender and sincere, "do not again speak of this."

"But, Anna—"

"No, no; let me think the situation over. I understand all its baseness and horror; but it is not so easy to change everything as you imagine. Have confidence in me, and do not speak of it again. You promise me?"

"I promise everything; but how can you expect me to be at ease after what you have told me? How can I be calm when you are in such distress?"

"I?" she repeated. "Well, it is true; but it will all pass away if you will speak no more of it. I know," she added, "how your loyal nature suffers from this deceit. I often tell myself that you have sacrificed your whole life for my sake."

"That is just it. I can never forgive myself for having made you unhappy."

"I—unhappy?" she said, rising, and looking on him with eyes full of love. "Why, I am like a starving beggar to whom food has been given, and who forgets his rags and the bitter cold. Unhappy! No; there is my happiness;" and the voice of little Serge was heard as he came across the garden toward the house.

Anna quickly approached Wronsky, and taking his head in her two hands, brought down his face to hers, and kissed him tenderly on the lips and eyes; then she pushed him gently from her and walked quickly toward the house.

CHAPTER VIII

THE VICTIM

THE parade in front of the grand stand, and the preliminary canter of the horses engaged in the great steeplechase were over, and the competitors had reached the starting-post in readiness for the race.

Three times had there been a false start. The colonel of the regiment, who held the starter's flag, was becoming impatient at the delay; but when it fell for the fourth time, the horses broke away in even rank.

"They are off! Here they come!" was the cry from the crowded stand, and each spectator pressed forward in eagerness to catch sight of the field.

Frou-Frou, Wronsky's mare, fractious and nervous, lost considerable ground at the start, but Wronsky soon steadied her and swept by those in front of him until he was only headed by the favorite, Gladiator, ridden by an officer named Maholine, whom he intensely disliked, and the good-looking English mare Diana, carrying Prince Kouzlof. For the first few minutes he had small control over his mount. Gladiator and Diana took the first water-jump with an easy bound, Frou-Frou following them as if borne on wings. At the next jump, which was

cleared by Gladiator in the same ea y fashion, Diana and her rider fell, and it was by a miracle that Wronsky saved himself from jumping on to the struggling man and horse. Then he obtained full mastery over the mare, and eld her back behind Maholine, nursing her for the grand effort of the jump in front of the grand stand. At this point the emperor, his staff, and the crowd of fashionables were viewing the race. As they approached it, Wronsky could see nothing but the horse and rider in front of him, and through the din of shouts and applause the only sound which reached his ears was the clatter of Gladiator's hoofs. Maholine cleared the jump and disappeared beyond it. Frou-Frou, in her excitement, jumped too soon, and struck the topmost fence-fail, though without losing ground. When once more on the level, Frou-Frou seemed to put her best effort forward, and rapidly overhauling Gladiator, was soon at his neck. Then in a few strides she passed him, though Wronsky, as he flashed by, caught sight of a satisfied smile on Maholine's face, and knew that the latter, content to take the second place, was pressing him closely in the rear.

The next two obstacles, a ditch and a fence, were safely passed, and, to Wronsky's delight, Frou-Frou drew considerably ahead of the rival behind her.

Wronsky was filled with delight; now he felt sure of winning. He would have turned in his saddle and looked round, but dared not relax his attention for a single instant. The next jump was the hardest of all—a stone wall, or "Irish" fence. "Once over that," he thought, "and we are sure to win." As they approached it, he noticed that the mare seemed to hesitate for a moment. He felt her mouth with the reins, and knew at once that she was prepared for what was expected of her. He gave her her head, and without an effort she cleared he obstacle without any difficulty, landing far on the other side, and keeping her stride.

"Bravo, Wronsky!" he heard some one cry; and he could distinguish the voice of a friend, Yashvine, who stood, with a large crowd, about the jump. His thoughts went back to Gladiator, who had safely cleared the fence, and was close behind him.

But one more jump remained—a hedge with a broad ditch beyond. Eager to increase his lead, Wronsky began to push the mare. She was almost exhausted; her breath was coming in short gasps, and the sweat poured from her neck and shoulders. They were over the jump almost before he knew it, Frou-Frou skimming over it like a bird; but before they touched the ground, he felt, to his horror, that he had lost his seat. What had happened? He could not tell, save that it was something terrible. Maholine passed him like a flash. Wronsky's foot touched the ground, and he felt the mare sink under him. He had barely time to remove his feet from the stirrups when she sunk completely down, making futile efforts to regain her feet; though Wronsky did not know it until later, by his false movement in the saddle as they took the jump, the mare had strained her back. He saw only one thing— Gladiator galloping away in the distance —while Frou-Frou lay upon the ground before him, breathing in short, hard gasps. Again and again, in answer to Wronsky's words and blows, she strove to rise; but all in vain.

"My God!" thought Wronsky, in despair, "what have I done? what have I done?" and a great humiliation came over him. A surgeon and a crowd of others ran toward him: but, almost to his disgust, he himself was safe and sound of limb.

The mare's spine was broken; she must be shot, was the verdict. Without a word or any answer to the many inquiries poured upon him, Wronsky walked away. He was in despair. For the first time in his life he was the victim of an accident for which he could bring no remedy, and for which he alone was to blame.

His friend Yashvine ran after him and led him to his dressing-room. After some time he became calmer and regained his self-possession, but for many a day the recollection of the race was one of his most painful and cruel memories.

CHAPTER IX

EXTERNAL RELATIONS

THE relations between Karénine and his wife remained outwardly the same— to the eyes of those about him he seemed even more attentive than before.

When spring came he had made a short trip abroad, as was his usual custom, leaving Anna installed at their country house.

Since their conversation after the Princess Tverskoï's reception, there had been no further allusion to the subject, but his manner toward Anna became much colder, his usual tone more sarcastic even than before. "You would not confide in me when I invited it," he seemed to imply, "now it is for you to come to me of your own self." He could not see the absurdity of his conduct— perhaps because the situation was too terrible for him to analyze. He preferred to bury his affection for his wife and his son at the bottom of his soul, as in a sealed cabinet; and toward the boy, too, his attitude was cold and unloving. He would not allow himself to reflect, and he did not reflect; but in spite of all, though he was without actual proof, he felt that he was being deceived, and suffered deeply.

Since his return from abroad to St. Petersburg he had visited his wife once or twice at their country-seat, but his official duties would not permit him to permanently reside there. On the day of the races he determined to leave the city early, go to Peterhof, and from there, with his wife, to the race-course.

Anna was standing before the mirror in her own room, completing her toilet, when the noise of wheels upon the graveled path reached her ears.

"It is rather early for Betsy to have come," she thought; and, looking out of the window, saw that the visitor was her husband.

"How awkward!" she said to herself. "Can he have come to stay?"

She thought of her next appointment with Wronsky, and the results which might be brought about by her husband's visit. Entirely dominated by the spirit of deceit which had lately come upon her, she hurriedly descended the stairs to receive him, and commenced to speak, scarce knowing what she said.

"How nice of you to come!" she said, with a smile, extending her hand to Karénine. "I trust you are going to remain all night." For her life she could not have suppressed these words. "Of course you will come to the races. How sorry I am that I promised to go with Betsy!"

Karénine made a slight grimace at the mention of the name.

"Oh, I would not dream of separating the two inseparables," he said in a mocking tone. "The doctor has ordered me to take exercise. I will walk part of the way at least."

"But there is no hurry," said Anna. "Will you have some tea?" and she rang the bell. "And how is your health?" she asked, speaking simply and naturally, though somewhat quickly. "You are not looking quite yourself."

"No; the doctor called on me this morning, taking up a full hour of my time. My health, you see, is so precious!"

"What did he say?" and she commenced to question him about his health and his official work, pressing him to take rest, and to settle in the country for a time. There was nothing out of the common in this conversation, and yet, when Anna recalled it later, the memory caused her actual pain.

"It is getting late," she said, at last, looking at her watch. "I wonder why Betsy does not come?"

"By the way," said Karénine, "I have brought you some money. I am sure you must need some; one can not support the household on nightingale's songs!"

"No—yes—I certainly do need some," said Anna, blushing to the roots of her hair. "But you will come back after the races?"

"Oh, yes," he answered. "And here comes the glory of Peterhof, the Princess Tverskoï!" he added as he saw the English victoria coming up the drive. "What elegance! How charming! Well, I will set out myself."

The princess did not leave her carriage.

"I must go now," said Anna. "Good-bye"—giving her hand again to her husband—"I am so glad you have come."

Karénine bent and kissed the hand.

"Au revoir!" she cried, going from the room with a bright and joyous air. But no sooner had the door closed upon her than a shudder of repugnance passed over her as she felt the kiss upon her hand.

CHAPTER X

THE RACE-COURSE

WHEN Karénine appeared upon the race-course, Anna was already seated by the Princess Betsy's side in the portion of the grand stand reserved for the officers and their friends. She saw her husband while he was yet some distance away, and followed him with her eyes as he threaded his way among the crowd of fashionables. As he approached the stand, he exchanged salutations on all sides, varying his cordiality and greeting in accordance with the rank of those he addressed.

"He thinks of nothing," she said to herself, "but his own ambition and political success; his elevated views upon morals and religion are nothing but the means to an end—nothing more."

She could see that he was in search of her but had not yet seen her, and she herself made no sign of having discovered his presence.

"Alexis Alexandrovitch," cried the Princess Betsy, "do you not see your wife? She is here."

His usual cold smile crossed his lips.

"It is so brilliant here," he said, approaching them, "that one's eyes are dazzled and blinded."

He smiled at Anna as a husband does who has but just left his wife, and saluted Betsy and the men and women round about her, most of whom he was acquainted with. A great general was standing near the balcony. Karénine greeted him, and they commenced a short discussion on the merits of horse-racing as an amusement. His harsh and measured tones sounded disagreeably on Anna's ears.

When the time for the steeple-chase came she leaned forward and gave her whole attention to watching Wronsky. She saw him exchange some last words with his trainer, and then mount his horse, and, in her nervousness, her husband's voice sounded odious to her. "I am a lost and wicked woman," she thought; "but I hate deceit—to me it is unbearable, while *he* thrives upon it. He sees everything and knows what is going on—how he can talk and act with such tranquillity! If he killed me, or killed Wronsky, one might respect him; but no, he prefers this acting and pretense, and to observe the proprieties." She did not understand her husband, nor could she know that his volubility, which irritated her so acutely, was simply the outcome of his inward agitation. He sought some means to stifle the ideas which oppressed him in his wife's presence, and to deafen his ears to the repeated sound of Wronsky's name on the lips of those around him.

"Princess, a bet with you!" cried a voice, addressing Betsy. It was Stépane Arcadievitch. "Whom will you back?"

"Anna and I are backing Kouzlof," she answered.

"I will back Wronsky for a pair of gloves."

"Agreed—done!"

The next moment the starting flag was seen to fall and conversation ceased.

Alexis Karénine stood silently and

watched, not the horses and their gayly colored riders, but his wife's face. Pale and serious, Anna watched the race intently. She nervously grasped the fan in her hand, and hardly seemed to breathe. Her husband could read only too clearly that which he would fain have ignored. When Kouzlof fell there was a general movement of excitement and sympathy, but the triumphant look on Anna's face showed that her thoughts were undisturbed by the accident, and so it was when a second rider had a more dangerous fall and many thought that he was killed, her face showed no emotion.

But when it came to Wronsky's turn, as has been described, amid the general excitement Anna's cry of horror was almost unnoticed. Her face, however, expressed only too plainly the agitation which decorum compelled her to conceal. She strove to rise, and, turning toward Betsy, exclaimed, "Let us go! let us go!"

But the princess did not hear. She was questioning an officer who stood near.

Karénine came toward his wife and offered her his arm.

"Let us go, if you wish it," he said; but Anna turned away as though she had not seen him, and listened to what was being said to Betsy.

"They say he has broken his leg; but that is absurd."

Paying no heed to her husband, Anna continued to look through her field-glass toward the spot where Wronsky had fallen; the distance and the crowd around him were so great she could distinguish nothing. She lowered her glass and was about to move away when an officer galloped up to make a report to the emperor.

"Stiva! Stiva!" she cried, catching sight of her brother; but her cry did not reach him.

"I am offering you my arm, if you desire to go," repeated Karénine, as he touched her hand.

Anna shrunk back with a movement of repulsion, and answered, without looking at him:

"No, no; leave me! I will stay here!"

Another officer had ridden across the field from the jump, and was telling Betsy that the rider was safe and sound, though the horse's back was broken.

At this news, Anna sunk back and hid her face behind her fan. Karénine could see that not only was she in tears, but that she could not repress the sobs which convulsed her frame. He placed himself in front of her to shield her from the curiosity of the crowd, and to allow her time to recover herself.

"For the third time, I offer you my arm," he said, after some moments, turning round to her.

Anna looked at him, not knowing what to say, when Betsy came to her rescue.

"No, no, Alexis; I brought Anna here, and will take her home."

"Excuse me, princess," he answered, smiling politely, and looking her full in the face, "but I see that Anna is suffering, and I wish to take her away myself."

Anna, frightened into submission, rose and took her husband's arm.

"I will send you news," whispered the Princess Betsy.

Karénine and Anna left the pavilion, he talking naturally to the acquaintances they chanced to meet, and she obliged to listen and to answer as one in a dream.

"Is he hurt? Or was what that man

said true?" she thought. "Will he come to me? Shall I see him to-night?"

Silently they entered the carriage and were soon driven beyond the crowd. In spite of all that he had seen, Karénine would not yet allow himself to judge his wife. In his mind, outward appearances were of small importance. He felt that he must say something; but when the words did come, they were the opposite of what he would have said.

"How fond we all are of seeing these cruel sights! I have often remarked—"

"I beg your pardon, I don't understand," interrupted Anna in a tone which irritated and displeased him.

"I wish to say," he went on, "that your behavior today has been hardly correct."

"In what?" she asked, turning quickly toward him and looking him in the face, no longer with the false cheerfulness under which she was wont to hide her feelings, but with an assurance which ill concealed her affright.

"I will tell you," he said, raising the window of the carriage.

"What have you seen that was not correct?" she repeated.

"The distress you openly showed when one of the riders fell."

He awaited her answer; but she was silent and looked straight before her.

"I have already begged you to conduct yourself before the world in such a manner as to protect yourself from gossiping tongues. There was a time when I used the relations which should exist between us as an argument; I do not do so now. It is now a single question of outward facts. You have not behaved with propriety, and I desire that it shall not happen again."

His words hardly reached Anna's ears.

Her thoughts were still of Wronsky, and whether he could have been seriously hurt. It was hard to believe that he was uninjured, when the horse's back was broken. She glanced at Karénine with an ironical smile, and made no answer. The smile caused him to fall into a strange error.

"She is smiling at my suspicions," he thought. "She is going to tell me, as before, that they are absurd and without the least foundation."

The intense desire, perhaps, was the father to the thought. So great was his dread of having his fears confirmed that he was willing and prepared to believe anything.

"Perhaps I have been deceived," he said. "In that case, I must ask your pardon."

"No," she said, quietly, with one desperate glance at the impassive figure of her husband. "You have not been deceived. I was distressed, and am so still. I have heard what you said. I have been thinking only of him. I love him— I am his mistress; I can not tolerate you; I fear you and I hate you. Do with me whatever you will;" and, sinking back in her seat, she covered her face with her hands and burst into sobs.

Alexis Karénine did not move, nor did he change the direction of his looks, but the grave expression of his features became fixed as if in the rigidity of death, and so remained during the remainder of the drive. As they approached the house, he turned to Anna, and said:

"Let us understand each other. I insist that until I shall have taken the necessary measures"—and here his voice trembled—"to protect my honor, measures of which you shall be informed, I insist that appearances and decency shall be preserved."

He left the carriage and helped Anna to alight; in front of the servants, he pressed her hand, entered the carriage again, and was driven to St. Petersburg.

Hardly had he gone, when a messenger from Betsy arrived with a note:

"I have sent to him for news. He writes me that he is well and uninjured, but in despair."

"Then he *will* come," was Anna's thought. "I have done well in acknowledging everything."

She looked at her watch. There were yet some hours before he could arrive. The memory of their last meeting caused her heart to beat.

"My God!" she said to herself, "how I love him! My husband! Ah, yes! Well, so much the beter; all is now over between us."

CHAPTER XI

HIS WEAKNESS

No one, not even those most intimate with him, would have suspected that Alexis Karénine, this cold and reasoning man, was prone to a weakness in absolute contradiction to the general tendency of his nature. He could not see a child or woman weep without losing all his sangfroid; the sight of their tears troubled and moved him to such a degree as to counteract all his other faculties.

When Anna, during their return from the races, had acknowledged her *liaison* with Wronsky, and, covering her face, had burst into tears, Karénine was unable to suppress a certain amount of pity. It was to conceal this weakness the more surely that he preserved the look of fixed rigidity upon his face. It was with an effort that, on leaving his wife, he displayed his customary politeness toward her. Her words had confirmed his worst suspicions, and she had increased his sense of injury by her tears. As he sat alone in his carriage, he almost experienced a feeling of relief. It seemed to him that now his doubts, his jealousy, his compassion, were all gone. He had experienced the terrible suffering of doubt, but now it was all over.

"She is a lost woman," he said to himself, "heartless, and without honor or religious feeling. I have always known it, but, in pity, strove to blind my own eyes. I have committed a great error in joining my life to hers; but I am not to be blamed for the mistake, nor should I suffer for it. It is she who is to blame. Why should I be unhappy because my wife has committed a fault? I am not the first nor the last to find himself in such a situation;" and he recalled in his mind the names of several of his acquaintances and contemporaries who had been betrayed by their own wives. "Well," he thought, "after all those it is now my turn. The most important thing is to preserve my presence of mind and decide as to a future course." Naturally, his first idea was the advisability of a duel. He had always, from his youth upward, entertained a horror of this mode of settling wrongs. "If our society," he argued to himself, "were not still in a state of semi-savagery, the duel would not be tolerated. It is not, in England and many other countries. And to what would it lead, supposing I were to challenge him? Even were I to kill him, it could not re-establish my relations with my wife and son. Would it be honest on my part to challenge him, knowing, as I do, that my friends would not allow the risking of a life which at least is useful to the country? I should have the air of an impostor. No; my sole aim should be to keep my own reputation unsullied and suffer nothing to impede my career."

Always important in his eyes, the "service of the state" now seemed everything to him.

The idea of a duel, discarded, there remained—divorce; and among the many instances which Karénine now called to mind he could remember none in which the end had been satisfactory. In each case the guilty party was the one to profit by the ability to establish new ties. Divorce broke off all relations between the husband and the wife, and left her to her lover. The actual proof which the law so brutally demands, he felt that it would be impossible for him to furnish. His enemies, too, would make profit by calumniating his name and smirching his reputation, and his aim, which was to extricate himself as quietly as possible from this crisis, would by no means be attained. "No, no," he cried, moving nervously about the carriage, "it is impossible! Impossible! I can not be made unhappy, and they have no right to be happy."

Having reviewed in his mind the objections to the duel, to divorce, or to separation, Karénine convinced himself that his only plan was to guard his wife in concealing her fault from the world, to employ every imaginable means to break off her *liaison* with Wronsky, and—though this last he would not acknowledge to himself—to punish the guilty woman. "I will explain to her fully what she has done and in what position she has placed the family, and consent to

keep her on the express condition that she ceases every relation with her lover. The time may come—for time solves most difficulties—when our former relations shall be re-established between us; she herself must go through much suffering; but why should I, who am entirely blameless, be made to suffer?"

When, having arrived at St. Petersburg, he found himself in the seclusion of his own library, Karénine, after nervously pacing the room for some time, sat down and wrote the following letter to his wife:

"At our last interview I expressed my intention of informing you as to my decision in regard to the subject of our conversation. After deep and serious reflection, I now fulfill my promise. My decision is this: Whatever your conduct may have been, I can not recognize my own right to break the ties consecrated by a supreme power. The family name must not be exposed to the effects of a caprice, of an arbitrary act, even though it may have consisted in a crime on the part of one of us, and our social life must remain the same. This should be so, on my account, on yours, and on that of your son. I am convinced that you have repented, that you are still repentant, and that you will assist me in destroying, while it is in the germ, the cause of our disagreement and in forgetting the past. Should you not do so, you can understand what the future will be for you and your son. I hope to talk more fully at our next meeting. As the summer is now nearly at an end, you will oblige me by returning to town as soon as possible—by Tuesday next at latest. I will see that all arrangements for your moving are attended to. I must beg you

to notice that I attach particular importance to what you have placed it in my
power to demand.   A. KARENINE.

"P. S.—I inclose, with this letter, sufficient money to meet your requirements."

He sealed the letter carefully and
methodically and rang the bell.

"Give this letter," he said to the servant, "to the courier, and tell him to
carry it to your mistress tomorrow."

CHAPTER XII

DECEPTION FOREVER

THOUGH Anna, in speaking with
Wronsky, had refused to admit that their
position was false and dishonorable, she
none the less felt at the bottom of her
heart that he was right. She was eager
to escape from such a deplorable existence, and when, impelled by her emotion,
she had avowed everything to her husband, she experienced a great relief.
After his departure she kept repeating
to herself that, at least, everything was
now explained, and that there would be
no further necessity for lying and deceit.
If her situation was still evil, it was no
longer equivocal. And yet, when
Wronsky came that night to see her, she
said nothing to him of her confession to
her husband, nor gave him any warning
that they must decide on a new future.

The next morning, when she awoke, her
first thought was of the words she had
spoken to her husband. They now appeared so odious, in their strange bru-
tality, that she could not understand how
she had found the courage to pronounce
them.

What would the result be?

Her husband had left her without any
rejoinder.

"I have seen Wronsky since then," she
thought, "and have said nothing to him.
When he left me I felt inclined to call
him back, but thought of his astonishment at my not having told him at once.
Why did I not?"

She blushed vividly, for she well knew
that what had kept her silent was—
shame. Now, her situation, which, the
previous evening had seemed lightened,
was darker and more inestimable than
ever. All sorts of foolish fears as to what
her husband might do seized upon her.

Wronsky, she thought, no longer loved
her as much as formerly, and was beginning to tire of her. Was she the one
to force herself upon him? And there
was a bitter feeling in her heart against
him. Her confession to her husband
seemed to her to have been made before
all the world, to have been heard by
every one. How could she face her own
household, even?

She would not go down-stairs, but remained in her own room. "There is
nothing to be gained by thinking," she
said to herself. "I must go away. But
where, when, and with whom? To-morrow, by the evening train?"

Yes, she would go, and take Serge
and her maid, Annouchka, with her. But
first she must write to both men, and she
sat down at the table to write to her
husband.

"After what has passed, I can no
longer live with you. I am going away,
and take my son with me. I know nothing of the law, and so am ignorant as to
which of us he should remain with; but
I take him because I could not live without him. Be generous; let me keep him!"

Up to the last words she had written
quickly and naturally; but the appeal
to a generosity with which she did not

credit her husband, and the necessity for framing some words of farewell, stayed her pen.

"I can not speak," she resumed, "of my fault and my repentance; it is on that account—"

She stopped again, unable to find words to express her thought.

"No," she said, "I will say nothing more;" and tearing up the paper, wrote another note, making no appeal to his generosity.

Her second letter was for Wronsky. "I have told my husband *everything,*" she wrote, then stopped, unable to proceed. The words seemed so brutal, so entirely unfeminine. Besides, what had she to say to him. And this note, too, she tore into a thousand pieces. Better remain silent, she thought, closing her writing-desk; and then, summoning the governess and her maid, she told them of her departure for Moscow that evening and bid them make all preparations.

While attending to the little details of her own packing, Anna, in a slight measure, forgot her troubles. Her maid, who was in the room, called her attention to the noise of a carriage approaching the house. From the window she saw her husband's courier at the front entrance.

"Go and see what it is," she said to Annouchka, and with her hands folded in her lap, sat waiting in her chair. A servant brought her a packet addressed in Karénine's own hand. "The courier has orders to wait for an answer," he said.

"Very well," she answered; and as soon as he had gone she tore open the envelope with a trembling hand. Some bank-notes fell from the cover; but she had only thoughts for the letter itself,

which, in her impatience, she commenced to read from the end.

"I will see that all arrangements for your moving are attended to. . . . I attach particular importance to what you have placed it in my power to demand."

And then she read it through from the beginning to the end. When she had finished, she felt quite cold, and crushed by some terrible and unexpected misfortune.

That morning she had regretted her confession, and would have recalled her words if possible. Here was a letter written as though they had never been uttered, giving her all that she desired, and containing some lines which seemed worse to her than she could have imagined.

"He is right—right!" she exclaimed. "Is he not always right, always Christianlike and magnanimous? Oh, what a mean and contemptible man he is; and no one but myself understands or will understand him, and I can explain nothing. 'He is a religious man,' they say, 'a moral, honest, and intelligent man'; but they can not see what I see; they do not know that for eight years he has oppressed my life, stifled all that was alive in me. Has he ever looked upon me as a woman of flesh and blood, one who had need of being loved? No one knows how he has insulted me at every step, only to feel more satisfied with himself. Have I not tried my best to love him, and, when unsuccessful, have I not wrapped myself in my son? But the time came when I found that I could no longer deceive myself. It is not my fault if God has made me so—I must breathe and love. And now? If he would kill us both, one could pardon him; but no, he—can I not guess what he will do? He will continue, confident and strong in his own rights, and I, poor wretch, will be still further lost. 'You can understand what the future will be for you and your son.' That is a threat to take away my boy, an act which I suppose the absurd laws authorize. I can see, though, why he says it. He knows that I will never abandon the child; that I could not live without him; and that, if I did abandon him, I should fall among the ranks of the lowest women. He knows that nothing could make me do that. 'Our life must remain the same.' It was torture before; now it is far worse. He knows that I can never repent or give my love to him, and that what he insists upon can only result in falseness and deceit. But he must prolong my torture; he swims in deceit as a fish does in the water. I will not give him this joy. I will break through the tissue of falsehood which surrounds me. My God! I will break through everything—everything!"

She approached the table as if to write another letter, but at the bottom of her soul she knew that she was powerless to change anything or to escape from the situation, however false, in which she found herself. She sat before the table, her head bent upon her arms, and commenced to cry like a child, the sobs bursting from her bosom.

She knew that it would never be her lot to love openly and in freedom; that she must always remain the woman to be blamed, always be in fear of detection and surprise, deceiving her husband for a man whose life she could never be a part. All this she knew, and yet, her destiny was too terrible for her to face; she must go blindly on.

The footstep of a servant startled her. She concealed her face, pretending that she was writing.

"The courier wishes to know if the answer is ready, madame."

"Yes; wait," she said, and wrote:

"I have received your letter.
                                      "ANNA."

"Give him this, and tell Annouchka that we do not go to Moscow to-night."

CHAPTER XIII

CONFESSION

WRONSKY received a line from Anna, bidding him come to her at five o'clock that evening. Hiring a carriage, he ordered the coachman to drive at a good pace, and stretching himself at full length upon the seats, gave himself up to his own thoughts. They were not unpleasant. A smile came to his lips as he thought of the coming meeting with Anna. It was a cool, clear day in August, and the evening air seemed to invigorate him, and to stimulate his every sense. The sun was sinking toward the horizon, and the little details of country life which betokened the close of a day, pleased him as he looked out from the carriage window.

He bid the coachman, as usual, to wait outside the avenue, and passed on foot through the gates. No sooner had he entered the park than he saw Anna advancing toward him, her face covered with a thick veil. He quickened his pace, his heart beating with delight at sight of her, and they were soon face to face. She seized his hand.

"You must not be angry with me for asking you to come; it was absolutely necessary for me to see you," she said, and there was something in her face which repressed Wronsky's joy.

"I—angry with you?" he exclaimed in astonishment.

"Come; I want to talk to you," she said, passing her arm through his.

He saw at once that something new and unexpected had occurred, and that their talk was not to be altogether a pleasant one.

"What is it?" he asked, seeking to read her face.

She made a few steps in silence and then suddenly stopped.

"I did not tell you last night," she commenced, speaking rapidly but as if with an effort, "that, as I returned from the races with Alexis Alexandrovitch, I told him everything, told him that I could no longer be his wife—everything, in fact."

He listened, bending toward her as if he would have softened the bitterness of this confidence; but as soon as she had spoken, she drew herself erect and her face bore a proud and stern expression.

"Yes, yes," he said; "it was a thousand times better. I know what you must have been suffering."

But she did not listen to his words; she was trying to read her lover's thoughts. How was she to know that his looks, on hearing this news, were controlled by what at once suggested itself—the duel, which, in his mind, was now inevitable? No, Anna never for a moment dreamed of this, and her reading of his face was a very different one.

Since reading her husband's letter she felt that all must remain as before; that she would never have the strength to sacrifice her position in the world, or her little son, for the sake of her lover. Nevertheless, she had attached a great importance to this interview with Wronsky, and hoped that it might bring about some change in their situation. If, at the first moment and without hesitation, he had said: "Leave everything and come with me," she would even have abandoned her child. But he made no such move, and it seemed to her that he was annoyed and displeased.

"Oh, no, I have not suffered," she said in a tone of irritation. "Look at this," and she drew from her glove her husband's letter.

"I understand! I understand!" interrupted Wronsky, taking the letter, though without reading it, and striving to calm Anna. "This was all that I desired in order to devote my whole life to your happiness."

"Why say that? How could I doubt it?" she said. "If I did doubt—" and she paused for a few moments. "I repeat," she began again, "throughout this whole affair I have never doubted you. But read what he has written to me."

As he read the letter, the same impression came back to Wronsky that he had had on hearing of Anna's rupture with her husband. He foresaw the provocation and subsequent challenge he would receive, and himself face to face with his adversary, calm and cold, discharging his weapon in the air and awaiting the other's fire.

When he had finished reading he looked at her with an expression of indecision in his eyes. She concluded that he had reflected, and, no matter what his words might be, that they would not express his real thoughts; her last hope vanished.

"You see what sort of a man he is," she said in a trembling voice.

"Pardon me," said Wronsky, seeing the difficulty of expressing his thoughts.

"This does not alter anything; it is impossible, whatever he may think, for things to remain as they are."

"And why?" asked Anna in a strangely altered voice. His answer would mean little to her; she felt that her fate was decided.

What Wronsky wished to say was that the duel, which he himself deemed inevitable, would change everything; but his actual words were quite different.

"This can not continue. I hope, now, that you will consent to leave him, and that you will permit me"—here he blushed and hesitated—"to arrange for our life together. To-morrow—"

She did not allow him to finish.

"And my child? You see what he has written? I should have to leave him. I can not, nor do I wish it."

"But, in Heaven's name, would it not be better to leave your son than to remain in this humiliating position?"

"For whom is it humiliating?"

"For all; but for you especially."

"Humiliating! Do not say that; the word implies nothing to me," she said, her voice still low and trembling. "Do you not understand that from the day I first commenced to love you life itself was changed for me. In my eyes, nothing exists outside your love. If I can always have it, I shall stand on a height where nothing can reach me. I am proud of my position because—" She could not finish her sentence; the tears of shame and despair stifled her voice.

He also was deeply affected, and for the first time in his life felt as if the tears would come, though hardly knowing what moved him; whether it was pity for her whom he was powerless to aid and whose trouble he had caused, or the consciousness that he himself had committed a grievous and bad action.

"Then a divorce would be impossible?" he said in a quiet tone. She bent her head without replying. "Could you not leave him and take the child with you?"

"Yes; but everything depends upon him now. I must go back to him," she said in a dry tone. Her presentiment was verified; everything must remain as in the past.

"I shall be in St. Petersburg on Tuesday," he said, "and we will decide then."

"Yes," she answered; "but do not speak of that." She bid him farewell and they parted.

CHAPTER XIV

SILENCE

WHEN Karénine awoke on the Tuesday morning, his first thought was of a triumph he had won in the Council the previous evening. When he commenced his labors for the day, he was so completely absorbed in his work that he forgot it was the date which he had appointed for his wife's return to St. Petersburg. He was, therefore, disagreeably surprised when a servant informed him of her arrival. He could not, at that moment, receive her in person, for he was engaged with the chief of his staff on business of importance.

Having advised him of her arrival, Anna went straight to her own apartments, and, while superintending the unpacking of her things, expected each moment to hear her husband announced. An hour passed, and yet he did not appear. Anna, impatient, passed into the dining-room, which adjoined his library, and gave some orders to the servants in a voice loud enough to penetrate the sanctum where he sat. Still there was no sign of him, and presently she heard him conducting his subordinate to the front door. She knew that, after that, his invariable custom was to leave the house for a time; and, intent upon seeing him and deciding the future, she determined to enter his study.

Karénine was sitting at a table in full official uniform, as if on the point of starting out, and looking straight before him with a look of sadness in his eyes. She saw him before he noticed her entrance, and knew that his thoughts were of her. When he did perceive her he moved nervously in his seat, and then, rising abruptly, walked forward to meet her, looking over her head, as if to avoid her eyes. He took her hand and invited her to sit down.

"I am glad to see you home again," he simply said, for no other words would come to him.

Nor, for her part, was Anna able to speak to him as she had planned. She could only keep silent and pity him.

"And Serge—is he well?" said Karénine at last; and then, without waiting for an answer, "I shall not dine at home; I must go out at once."

"I had wished to go to Moscow," said Anna.

"No, it was much, very much better for you to return here," he replied; and again there was silence for some moments.

Anna was the first to break it.

"Alexis Alexandrovitch," she said, looking straight into his face, "I am a wicked and guilty woman; but I still remain what I was—what I confessed to you that I was—and I have come to tell you that I can not change."

"I do not ask you about that," he replied, also in a decided tone, his face full of anger and dislike. "I supposed it was so; but what I wrote to you I now repeat. I am not obliged to acknowledge it, and I wish to ignore it. I will know nothing so long as the world is kept in ignorance and my name is not dishonored. That is why I have informed you that our relations toward each other must outwardly remain the same as they have heretofore been. I shall only allow my honor to be smirched in case you compromise yourself."

"But our relations can not remain as they were," said Anna, timidly, and with a frightened glance at him.

Finding him so calm in his manner, his voice and look unchanged, all the pity for him that had sprung up within her disappeared, and a feeling of repulsion took its place. Of one thing only was she afraid—her own inability to express sufficiently clearly what their future relations must be.

"I can not be your wife when I—"

Karénine interrupted her with a cold and bitter smile.

"The sort of life which you have lately been pleased to adopt influences your understanding. I have too much respect for the past and too great a distrust of the present to warrant the interpretation which you put upon my words."

Anna sighed and bent her head.

"Still," he continued, "I can hardly understand how you, having found nothing blamable in announcing your infidelity to your husband, should have any scruples concerning your duties as a wife."

"Alexis Alexandrovitch, what do you demand of me?"

"I demand that you shall not see this

man again. I demand that you shall so conduct yourself that neither the outside world nor our own families shall be able to accuse you of anything. It seems to me that this is very little to demand. Now, I have nothing further to say. I must go, and, as I told you, shall not dine at home."

He rose and walked toward the door. Anna rose also. He bowed to her without a word, making room for her to pass out first.

Anna Karénine

PART III

CHAPTER I

THE KARENINES' LIFE

THE Karénines continued to live under the same roof, to meet each other every day, and yet were virtual strangers. The husband constantly showed himself in his wife's company before the servants, so as to avoid their gossip, but he rarely dined at home. Wronsky never appeared at the house. Anna met him at other places, and Karénine knew it.

All three found the situation intolerable, nor could they have submitted to it had each not thought it merely temporary. Karénine was waiting for the entanglement to die out, by a natural death, before his own honor had been openly sullied. Anna, the cause of all the evil, and the one who suffered most from it, lived in the conviction of an approaching crisis. As for Wronsky, he had ended by thinking as she did.

One afternoon Wronsky returned to his rooms, fatigued and out of sorts. He had been deputed by the highest authorities to act as cicerone to a foreign prince who was visiting St. Petersburg. The prince was a man whose tastes and inclinations were confined to gayety and dissipation when absent from his own country, and Wronsky had been forced for some days to conduct his royal protegé from one gilded

pleasure to another—an occupation, at the present time, most distasteful to him.

He found a note from Anna.

"I am unwell and very unhappy," she wrote. "I can not leave the house, and must see you. Come to me this evening. Alexis Alexandrovitch will be at the Council from seven o'clock until ten."

Knowing, as he did, the strict injunctions Karénine had laid upon his wife, this invitation, in direct defiance of them, seemed strange to Wronsky, but yet he decided to go to her.

He lay down to rest himself, and, tired out, was soon asleep. It was quite dark when he awoke with a sudden start, and looking at his watch, he saw that it was not far from nine o'clock. He called his valet, dressed with great haste, and hurried toward the Karénine mansion.

As he approached the house, he saw that Anna's carriage was standing before the door. "She was going to my rooms," he thought; "it would have been far better." He mounted the steps and rang. The door was immediately opened by the Swiss footman, and before he had time to open his mouth, Karénine, who was leaving the house, almost ran into his arms. He was in full evening dress; he looked straight into Wronsky's eyes, who could see the worn and sad look in his face, raised his hat slightly, and passed down the steps to the carriage.

"What a situation!" thought Wronsky, entering the anteroom, his eyes full of anger. "It makes it seem as if I came here, to his own house, to deceive him, and I am far from wishing to do that."

He entered the salon where Anna was awaiting him. "No," she cried, as she saw him, "it can not go on like this!" and he noticed that her voice was full of tears.

"What is the matter, Anna, dear?" he asked.

"The matter is that I have been waiting for you, in torture, for two whole hours. But I must not quarrel with you. I am sure you had some good excuse. No, I won't scold you any more." She laid her hands upon his shoulders and looked into his face with her deep and tender eyes, as if she would have read his innermost thoughts. Then, after some moments, she led him to a seat. "You must have met *him*," she said. "It is your punishment for coming so late."

"How did it happen? Was he not to be at the Council?"

"He had been there, but returned for some reason which I am ignorant of. Never mind; we will speak no more of it. And so the prince has gone?"

"Yes, thank Heaven! You have no idea what a week it has been for me."

"Why so? Have you not been leading the life that all you young men are fond of? It is the neglected woman who is to be pitied, especially when, as in my case, she knows only what you choose to tell her of your doings. How can I be sure that even what you do tell me is true?"

"Anna! Do you not trust me? Have I ever concealed anything from you?"

"No, you are right," she answered, trying to drown her jealous fears; "but if you only knew how I suffer! But I do trust you—I do trust you!"

Anna's fits of jealousy were becoming more and more frequent; and such scenes as this, though proof of her great love for him, had a thrilling influence upon him. How often had he not only declared that his only happiness consisted in his love, and now, when he knew that he was loved, as only a man can be by a woman who has sacrificed everything for him, his happiness seemed more remote than when they had both left Moscow.

"This demon," she went on, alluding to her own jealousy, "is sometimes too strong for me. You can not imagine what I have suffered while waiting for you. When you are with me I feel sure of you, but when you are away from me—" She stopped, as if wishing to let the subject drop. "You came face to face with *him*, you say? And I suppose he saluted like this"—she lengthened her face, half closed her eyes, and changed the whole expression of her features so completely that Wronsky could almost fancy he saw Karénine. He smiled, and Anna, too, commenced to laugh, the clear and ringing laughter which was one of her greatest charms.

"I can not understand him," said Wronsky. "After your avowal in the country, I fully expected him to call me out. One can see that he is suffering."

"He suffering!" she said, with an ironical smile. "He is very happy."

"But why should we all torture ourselves when everything could be arranged?"

"That would not suit him. Oh, I know his nature well; he is made up of deceit. How else could he live with me, the wife who has been false to him, and speak to me as he does?" And she imitated his manner of saying "Now, my dear Anna—" "Had I been in his place, I would have torn the woman to pieces. He is not a man, he is a ministerial machine. He does not understand that he is nothing to me. No, we will not talk about him!"

"You are unjust, dear," said Wronsky, trying to calm her; "but, as you say, we will not speak of him any more. About yourself now: what does the doctor say? You told me in your note that you were unwell. When will *that* take place?"

The mocking smile which had been on Anna's face gave way to an expression full of sadness.

"Soon," she said, "soon. You have said that our position is dreadful and that we must escape from it. What would I not give to be able to love you openly and freely! I should no longer weary you with my jealousy; but soon all will be changed, though not in the way we have thought of."

Her tears stopped her from saying more. She laid her white hand on Wronsky's arm.

"I don't understand you," he said—though he did, only too well.

"You asked me when *that* will take place. Soon—and I shall not live through it"—she spoke hurriedly—"I know it, I am positive of it. I shall

die, and be very glad to die and to relieve you both of myself."

The tears were running down her cheeks. Wronsky kissed her hands, and sought, in calming her, to hide his own emotion.

"It will be better so," she said, pressing his hands convulsively.

"What foolishness!" exclaimed Wronsky, raising his head and recovering his self-possession. "How absurd!"

"No, it is true."

"What is true?"

"That I shall die. I know it—I have seen it in a dream; but let us talk of something else," she said, rising. "I will ring for tea, and we will have a pleasant chat, for your time is growing short."

She stopped suddenly as she gained her feet, and all at once a wonderfully sweet and serious expression came into her face. Wronsky saw it, yet could know nothing of the cause of this sudden transfiguration. In herself she had just felt the first movement of the new life she was soon to give birth to.

CHAPTER II

LEAVE ME SERGE!

AFTER meeting Wronsky at the door of his own house, Karénine, as he had planned to do, betook himself to the Italian opera. He heard two acts, spoke to those of his acquaintances who greeted him, and then returned home.

Instead of at once retiring, as was his rule, he passed up and down his room until the small hours of the morning. His anger would have prevented him from sleeping, for he could not pardon his wife for having broken the only condition he had imposed upon her—that she should not receive her lover in her own house. As she had seen fit to do so, he would punish her, would put his threat into execution, apply for a divorce and take away her son from her. It would be no easy matter, but he would keep his word. When he was in bed he could not sleep, and his state of mind was still more exasperated when at last he rose, hurriedly dressed himself, and proceeded to his wife's apartments.

Anna, who at least believed that she was familiar with his every mood, was startled when she saw him enter the room, his face sternly set, his lips compressed, and a fixed look of sadness in his eyes. He had never outwardly shown so much decision. He made no greeting, but walked straight to her writing-desk and opened it.

"What do you want?" she cried.

"Your lover's letters."

"They are not there," she said, and made an effort to close the desk; but he roughly pushed her hand aside and seized the portfolio in which Anna kept her more important papers.

"Sit down; I wish to speak to you," he said, pressing the portfolio tightly underneath his arm.

She looked at him in fear and astonishment.

"Did I not forbid you to receive your lover in this house?"

"I wanted to see him to—" She paused; the explanation was not an easy one to make.

"I do not wish to go into details, nor to know why a woman has need of seeing her lover."

"I merely wanted—" she began, emboldened by her husband's plain words; but again she hesitated. "Can you not see how easy it is for you to wound and hurt me?"

"One can only wound an honest man or an honest woman. To call a person a thief who *is* a thief is merely stating a fact."

"You are showing a cruelty of which even I did not think you capable."

"Indeed? So you consider a husband, who allows his wife her full liberty so long as she maintains a respect for decency, cruel?"

"It is worse than cruelty, it is cowardice!" exclaimed Anna, rising to leave the room.

"No," he cried in a harsh voice, forcing her to her seat and holding her arm, "I have not finished. You speak of cowardice. Should not that word be applied to her who abandons her son and husband for a lover, yet still eats that husband's bread?"

Anna lowered her head. The justice of his words crushed her. She answered quietly: "You can not judge my behavior more severely than I do myself. But why speak of it now?"

"Why?" he exclaimed, his anger increasing. "Simply to let you know that since you can not respect my wish, I am about to take the necessary steps to put an end to this condition of affairs."

"Soon, very soon, it will put an end to itself," said Anna, her eyes filling with tears at the thought of the death which seemed to her so near and so desirable.

"Sooner than you and your lover imagine. Ah, yes; you look for satisfaction in sensual passion—"

"Alexis Alexandrovitch!" she cried.

"It is ungenerous, unmanly to strike one who is already on the ground."

"Ah! you think only of yourself. The sufferings of the man who has been your husband do not concern you in the least. What matter if his whole life be ruined, his—" But the words refused to come, so great was his agitation.

For the first time, though it was but for an instant, Anna understood her husband's sufferings and pitied him. But what could she say or do but lower her head in silence? He also was silent for a space, and then commenced in a severe tone:

"I came to tell you—"

"I can not change," she murmured, interrupting him.

—"I came to tell you," he went on, "that I am going to Moscow, and that I shall not enter this house again. You will learn everything which I have determined upon from the lawyer to whom I shall intrust the proceedings for divorce. My son," he added, suddenly remembering what he wished to say concerning the boy, "will go to some of my own relations."

"You are simply taking him away to make me suffer," she stammered, raising her eyes to him. "You do not care for him—leave him with me!"

"It is true that the repulsion with which you have inspired me reacts upon my son; but, nevertheless, I shall look after him. Adieu."

He would have left the room, but she held him back.

"Alexis, leave me Serge," she said again; "it is all I ask of you. Leave him to me for my own deliverance—"

Karénine's face flushed; he shook off the arm which held him, and left the room without answering a word.

CHAPTER III

THE LAWYER'S OFFICE

THE reception-room of the noted lawyer to whose office Karénine at once betook himself, was crowded with clients waiting their turn for admittance to the inner private office.

He handed his card to a clerk who, without looking at it, informed Karénine that his employer was engaged, and was likely to be for some time.

"Have the goodness to take my card to him," said Karénine, with dignity.

Within a few moments, the door of the private office opened and the lawyer himself appeared.

"Will you come in?" he said, holding the door for Karénine to pass through. He showed him to a seat, and then himself sat down at his desk and turned his chair so as to face his visitor.

"Before commencing to explain my business," said Karénine, "I must impress upon you the necessity for allowing it to remain a secret between us."

An almost imperceptible smile passed the lawyer's lips.

"If I were not capable of preserving secrecy," he said, "I should not occupy my position as a lawyer."

Karénine glanced into the other's intelligent gray eyes, and jumped to the conclusion that he already knew all.

"You know my name?" he asked.

"I know the services you have done for Russia," said the man of law, with a slight bow.

Karénine sighed. It was difficult for him to speak; but when once he had commenced, his voice was clear and steady, and, at the proper time, emphatic.

"I have the misfortune," he began,

"to be a husband who has been wronged. I wish to sever, by a legal divorce, the ties between myself and my wife, and, more especially, to separate my son from his mother."

The lawyer strove to throw a serious look into his gray eyes; but Karénine could see that they were full of satisfaction at the thought of such a *cause célèbre* of professional interest and enthusiasm.

"You wish assistance in procuring a divorce?"

"Precisely; but I must warn you that I have laid down certain conditions to myself, and should abandon the idea of a divorce if they can not be complied with."

"I understand you perfectly," said the other, lowering his eyes that Karénine might not read his satisfaction.

"I am fairly well acquainted with the general laws of divorce," continued Karénine, "but wish to learn the different forms most commonly practiced."

"In a word, you wish to know the different ways of obtaining a legal divorce," said the lawyer; and receiving an affirmative sign from his client, he went on: "A divorce, according to our laws, is possible, as you doubtless are aware, under these three conditions: a physical defect or incapacity of one of the two parties; desertion and abandonment by one or other for the space of five years; and"—pronouncing the word in a satisfied tone—"adultery. There is the theoretical side of the question; but I think that, in honoring me with your consultation, you have wished to learn about the practical side. As I am sure that neither of the first two conditions which I have named exist—"

Karénine made a slight movement with his head.

—"There remains," went on the lawyer, "the act of adultery by one of the two; and unless he or she is willing to acknowledge the guilt, proof the most positive is necessary."

The lawyer paused, as if to allow his client time to choose between the two alternatives. After a moment, as Karénine said nothing, he continued:

"In my opinion, the simplest and most reasonable course is the acknowledgment of adultery by mutual consent. I should not speak so openly to every one; but, if I am not mistaken, we understand each other."

Karénine was so troubled that the last words of the lawyer barely reached his ears. His astonishment was so patent that the other came to his rescue.

"I am, of course, supposing that the married parties find it impossible to live with one another. If both consent to a divorce, the details and formalities are of slight importance. It is the simplest and surest method."

This time Karénine clearly understood; but his religious feelings were opposed to such a measure.

"In the present case this method is out of the question," he said. "Can such proof as correspondence establish adultery, even if indirectly? I have some in my possession."

The lawyer closed his lips with a little expression of pity and disdain.

"Proofs," he said, "require witnesses. If you do me the honor to intrust this affair to me, I must be allowed to choose my own measures."

Karénine, his face very pale, rose from his seat.

"I will write to you when I have

made my decision," he said, leaning with one hand on the table before him; "and since I can conclude, from what you say, that a divorce is possible, I shall be obliged if you will let me know your terms."

"Everything is possible provided you allow me entire freedom of action," replied the lawyer, evading the last question. "When may I count on hearing from you?"

"Within eight days. You can then inform me whether you will undertake the case, and on what terms."

"Certainly," said the lawyer, and conducted him to the door with great respect.

That same day Karénine made application in the highest quarters for permission to go abroad, ostensibly with the object of studying for himself some questions which had reference to certain foreign governments. Having obtained the necessary leave, he left St. Petersburg, and, having to pass through Moscow, determined to remain there for a few days.

CHAPTER IV

AT FIVE O'CLOCK

THE morning after his arrival at Moscow, as Karénine was leaving his hotel for the purpose of calling upon the governor-general, he heard some one call him from a passing carriage. It was Stépane Arcadievitch, accompanied by Dolly and two of her children. Stépane was dressed in the very height of fashion, as handsome, gay, and cheerful as ever.

Karénine had no wish to meet any of his Moscow's friends, least of all the brother of his wife. He would have bowed and passed on, but Oblowsky jumped from the carriage and rushed up to him with the usual effusive greeting.

"When did you arrive? Why did you not let us know you were coming? I saw your name last night among the list of arrivals at Dusseaux's, and was going to look you up."

"My time here is very short, and I am also very busy," said Karénine, dryly.

"Come and speak to my wife. She is anxious to see you."

They passed to Oblowsky's carriage.

"What has happened, Alexis Alexandrovitch, that you should avoid us?" asked Dolly, smiling. "How is dear Anna?"

Karénine murmured some words in an indistinct tone, and after a few moments' conversation would have excused himself, but Stépane stopped him.

"Do you know what you have to do?" he said. "You must come and dine with us to-morrow. Kosnichef and Pestzof will be there, so that you will hear the pith of our Moscow news."

"Do come," said Dolly. "We will dine at any hour that suits you—five or six, just as you please."

Karénine again answered in a voice which hardly reached their ears, and, raising his hat, walked quietly away to his own carriage.

"What a curious fellow!" said Stépane, following him with his eyes.

Some weeks previous to this, the Prince and Princess Cherbatzsky had returned to Moscow from abroad, bringing their daughter Kitty with them, almost completely restored to health. There was no outward sign of the grief and subsequent sickness which she had gone through, save that she seemed to have lost much of her former girlishness and childish spirits, and to have changed from an ignorant and innocent girl into a woman who now knew the world and something of its sufferings and trials. Time and her own thoughts had served to convince her that Wronsky's sudden desertion—which, at the time, seemed utterly unbearable—had doubtless been for the best, so far as she herself was concerned; and now, though even yet it was painful to look back to what had happened, she was able to enjoy life as of old, and to constitute herself the light and happiness of her father's household. Perhaps her saddest moments were those in which she thought of Constantin Levine and her abrupt dismissal of him. She had heard but little and seen nothing of him through all the months which had intervened since that winter's day on which he stood before her in her mother's drawing-room and accepted his rejection with much dignity and bravery, aggravated, as it was, by the presence of the man whom he was justified in regarding his successful "rival."

As for Levine, he, too, during these months, had altered much. Time had dulled the pain of his disappointment, and though thoughts of Kitty were constantly in his mind, he was able to take his own share in the duties and interests of life. Most of the time he had spent at his own country home; but he had also made one or two journeys to distant parts of the country and had benefited by the complete change of surroundings which such travel brought with it. He had steadfastly refused the many invitations his friend Stépane had sent him to visit them in Moscow. Of what use was it, he thought, to revive the old sorrow and run the risk of again reopening the wound his pride and love had sustained by again seeing and meeting Kitty? Had he known how often her thoughts were of him, and the regret with which she looked back upon her share in his past, he might have conquered his sensitiveness and again appeared upon the scene of his defeat; but Levine was essentially a proud man —that he had been once refused was sufficient for him.

In his eyes such a refusal was definite, sad and regrettable though it might be; and so, burying the past to the best of his ability in the duties and cares of his life as a land-owner and proprietor, he had given himself up to the improvement of his estates and in the condition of those who were his tenants and, in his eyes, dependent on him. Within the past few weeks he had made a short trip abroad, and, being obliged to pass through Moscow on his return, had determined to break his journey by a few days' sojourn in the city before returning to his own estates. He had arrived on the same day as Karénine, and was also making Dusseaux's his head-quarters.

It need hardly be said that Levine's first visitor was Stépane Arcadievitch.

The greeting between these two friends, of such different natures, was very warm.

"Take off your cloak and sit down," said Levine.

"I have not a moment to spare. I merely dropped in for a second," answered Stépane, who, nevertheless, proceeded to loosen his coat, then, after a short time, to remove it altogether, and finally to remain for a whole hour chatting with Levine on sport and other matters.

"Tell me what you have done while you were abroad; where have you been?" he asked.

"I have been in Germany, in France, and in England, but simply visiting the manufacturing centers, not the capitals and larger cities. I was very much interested, too."

"Yes, yes; I know how interested you are in all labor questions."

"Not so much, perhaps, where our own country is concerned as in the relations between land-owners and their peasantry;" and he commenced a somewhat lengthy dissertation on his own views and those of his opponents.

"Don't go yet," he said as Stépane rose from his seat; "I am probably leaving to-morrow, and have seen nothing of you as yet."

"Ah! that reminds me of the most important thing I had to say," exclaimed Stépane. "We expect you to dine with us to-morrow, and will take no refusal. My brother-in-law, Karénine, and one or two others will be there."

"Is he here?" asked Levine, more anxious, however, for news of Kitty.

He knew that she had been visiting at St. Petersburg recently, but had no idea whether she had yet returned. Stépane did not enlighten him.

"Whether she is likely to be present or not," thought Levine, "I will accept."

"May we count upon you?" asked Stépane.

"Certainly. I will come with pleasure."

"Good! At five o'clock, then, and without any ceremony."

And Stépane rushed off to his next appointment—a luncheon—with a new chief of his department who was passing through Moscow on a tour of inspection.

CHAPTER V

MY PROMISE

THAT same afternoon Stépane Oblowsky called upon Karénine at his hotel. He was anxious to obtain a decided acceptance or refusal of his invitation to dinner which Karénine's answer at their first meeting had somewhat left in doubt.

During the morning, Karénine had been occupied with official business, including the reception of a deputation from local bodies. The earlier part of the afternoon he devoted to his own affairs, chief among which was the promised letter to his lawyer.

He wrote, giving the lawyer full powers to proceed, and inclosing three letters from Wronsky to Anna, and one from her to her lover—these he had found in her portfolio. As he was closing the letter, he heard Stépane's voice asking to be announced.

"So much the worse," thought Karénine, "or perhaps I should say, so much the better. I will tell him what I have just done, and he will then understand that I can not dine with him."

"I am glad to see you again," said Stépane, heartily, as he entered the room. "I hope—"

"It will be impossible for me to come to you," interrupted Karénine, dryly, and receiving his brother-in-law standing.

Considering his determination as regarded a divorce, he thought it only right to be formal and distant toward the brother of his wife. He forgot Stépane's irrepressible good nature and suavity.

"Why so?" the latter asked. "You can not mean it. You promised us, and we are counting upon you."

"It is impossible. The relations between our two families are about to be broken."

"How—and why?" asked Oblowsky, smiling.

"Because I am applying for a divorce from my wife—your sister. I should have—"

He did not complete the sentence. Contrary to what he had expected, his brother-in-law, with a startled exclamation, sunk into a chair.

"Alexis Alexandrovitch, it is impossible!" he cried in a voice of grief.

"It is, nevertheless, true."

"Pardon me. I can not believe it!"

Karénine himself sat down. He felt that his words had not produced the effect he had desired, and that the most categorical explanation would not change his brother-in-law's relations toward himself.

"It is a cruel necessity; but I am forced to apply for the divorce," he said.

"What am I to say? Knowing you to be an upright man, and Anna as an exceptionable woman—excuse me, but nothing could change my opinion of her —I can not believe this. There is some grievous mistake."

"Ah! if it were only a mistake!"

"Permit me—but I understand. One thing I beg of you, do not act in haste."

"I have done nothing hastily," replied Karénine, coldly. "In a case like this,

one can not ask the advice of others. I am decided."

"It is frightful!" said Stépane, with what was almost a groan. "I implore you if, as I suppose, matters have not yet gone too far, to do nothing until you have talked with my wife. She loves Anna as a sister; yes, loves her, and she is a woman of great common sense. If only out of friendship for me, first talk with her."

Karénine was silent and reflected. Stépane respected his silence and watched him with sympathy.

"Why not come and dine with us?" he said at last. "This once, at least. My wife expects you. Come! I ask you again, come and speak with her."

"If you wish it so strongly, I will come," said Karénine, with a sigh; and then, making a great effort, he changed the conversation and brought it to bear upon Stépane's own affairs, his new chief, and other matters which he knew were of interest to the younger man.

Stépane looked at his watch.

"Heavens!" he cried, "it is past four, and I have another call to make. It is settled, then? You come to dinner? You would grieve both my wife and myself very much by refusing."

"As I have promised, I will come," answered Karénine in a melancholy tone, conducting his brother-in-law to the door.

"Thanks. I trust you will not regret it;" and taking his cloak from the servant, Stépane hurried from the hotel.

CHAPTER VI

THE GUESTS

AT five o'clock the Oblowskys' guests had assembled. In addition to Kosnichef and Pestzof there were the old Prince Cherbatzky, Karénine, Kitty, and her young cousin. Levine was the last to come, and Stépane met him in the hall.

"Am I late?" he asked. "You have a number of guests, I see. Who are they?" he added, nervously.

"No one but family friends. Kitty is here," said Stépane. "Come; I want to introduce you to Karénine."

Now that he knew he was about to meet Kitty for the first time since that fatal evening, Levine's courage left him.

"Present me to Karénine, I beg," he said; and entered the salon with a beating heart and the courage of despair.

She saw him at once, and so great was her joy that while he was greeting her sister Dolly, the tears welled to her eyes. Levine and Dolly both noticed it. Blushing and growing pale in turn, she was so distressed that her lips trembled. Levine approached her; she held out to him a cold little hand with a smile which might have passed for calm had it not been for the tearful brilliancy of her eyes.

"It is a long time since we have seen you," she forced herself to say, and for a few moments they talked of commonplaces.

Stépane came up to Levine to lead him to where Karénine was standing, and the introduction took place. When they entered the dining-room, Stépane, as if by accident, seated all his guests with the exception of Levine and Kitty. Then, as if suddenly recollecting their existence, he placed them side by side in the only remaining seats. Throughout the dinner, though they spoke but little to each other, their happiness was complete. Each felt drawn toward the

other by some mysterious tie, and as if just entering upon a new world inhabited only by themselves.

When the ladies had left the dining-room, Stépane passed round the cigars, and the usual after-dinner talk among the men commenced; but Karénine, who did not smoke, soon excused himself and passed to the salon. Dolly, who was evidently waiting for him, sat alone in a quiet corner of the room.

"How glad I am that you came!" she said. "I want so much to talk to you. Let us sit here."

Karénine, with an air of polite indifference, sat down by her.

"I am glad myself," he said, "to have the opportunity of seeing you, for I leave here to-morrow."

Dolly, who, in herself, was convinced of Anna's innocence, grew pale with agitation as she saw the calm indifference of this man who was about to put away his wife from him.

"Alexis Alexandrovitch," she said, summoning all her strength and courage, "I asked you for news of Anna and you have told me nothing. How is she?"

"I think that she is well, Daria Alexandrovna," he answered, without looking at her.

"Forgive me if I seem to go beyond my rights in what I say; but I love Anna as if she were my own sister. Tell me, I beg of you, what has passed between you and of what you accuse her?"

Karénine frowned and looked straight before him.

"Your husband has doubtless told you of the reasons which cause me to bring about this rupture with Anna Arcadievna."

"I do not believe it, and I never will believe it!" exclaimed Dolly, pressing her hands tightly together. At that moment the rest of the men entered the room. She rose quickly from her seat, and laying her hand upon Karénine's arm, said: "Will you come with me where we shall not be disturbed?"

Karénine, who was commencing to share her emotion, obeyed, and followed Dolly into a little room used by her children as their school-room. It was quite empty, and they sat down before the plain little table at which the infantile brains were wont to puzzle over their daily tasks.

"I repeat, I believe nothing of it!" said Dolly, striving to meet his eyes.

"Can *facts* be contradicted?" he asked, laying emphasis upon the word.

"But what fault has she committed? Of what do you accuse her?"

"She has failed in her duties and betrayed her husband—that is what she has done."

"No, no; it is impossible! No; thank God, you are deceiving yourself!" cried Dolly, pressing her two hands to her forehead.

Karénine smiled bitterly. He felt anxious to prove to her, and to himself also, that his conviction was correct. This warm championship of his wife brought back all the pain of his wound, and although doubt was no longer possible to him, he answered, less coldly:

"It is impossible to be mistaken when a wife herself comes and declares to her husband that eight years of married life and a son are to count for nothing; that she wishes to commence a new life."

"Anna and sin! How can one associate the two? How can one believe—"

"Daria Alexandrovna," he exclaimed, angrily, "I would give anything to be able still to doubt. The doubt itself was cruel, the present certainty is still more cruel. When I merely had doubts, I could still hope. Now I have no hope and many more doubts. I am even prejudiced against my son. I ask myself if he is mine. I am a most unhappy man?"

Dolly, though she could not see his face, knew that what he said was true, and her pity for him was great.

"My God! it is terrible! But you are firmly decided upon a divorce?"

"I have taken this last step because there is none other left to me. The most grievous part of such a misfortune is that the burden can not be carried as in other misfortunes," he added, reading Dolly's own thoughts. "One can not remain humiliated."

"I understand—perfectly," replied Dolly, lowering her head. She was silent. Her own domestic griefs came back to her memory; but suddenly she clasped her hands together with a gesture of supplication, and raising her eyes courageously to Karénine's, she said: "But stay! You are a Christian. Think of what she will become if you abandon her."

"I have thought of it—thought deeply over it. When, with her own lips, she told me of her dishonor, I gave her the chance to re-establish herself—I sought to save her. And what has she done? She has utterly disregarded all sense of decency and respectability. One can rescue a fellow-being from death who is unwilling to die; but with a nature so corrupt as to find happiness in its own degradation, what is to be done?" The memory of his last interview with his wife came back to him, and his manner again became cold and stern. "I am deeply grateful to you for your sympathy," he said, rising from his seat. "Now I am forced to leave you."

"One moment! You should not lose her—listen to my own experience. I also am married, and my husband deceived me. In my jealousy and indignation, I, too, wished to leave him; but I paused and reflected. And who was it that saved me? Anna. And now we are united again, my husband saw the wrong he had done me and I forgave him. You also must forgive."

Though Karénine listened to her words, they had no effect upon him, for the same anger was still burning in his heart which had decided him upon divorce. He made answer in a harsh, firm voice:

"I can not—and I do not wish to forgive. It would be an unjust act. I have done everything for this woman, and she has willfully dragged me through the mire. I do not think I am a bad-hearted man, and I am not given to hatred; but her I hate with all the strength of my soul, and I will not forgive her. The wrong she has done me is too great."

His voice was fairly trembling with anger.

"Love those who hate you," murmured Dolly, half in shame.

Karénine smiled. He knew the text, but it did not apply to his own position.

"You can love those who hate you, but not those whom you yourself hate. Forgive me for having troubled you," he said. "Each of us has his own sorrow;" and recovering command over himself, he quietly bid Dolly good-night and took his departure.

CHAPTER VII

AVOWAL

LEVINE had difficulty in restraining the temptation to follow Kitty to the salon when she left the dinner-table, but he was fearful of displeasing her by any too pronounced attention. He remained with the other men, joining in the general conversation, but his thoughts were with Kitty in the adjoining room.

At last the cigars were finished and a move made to the salon. Even as he entered the room, Levine felt that Kitty's eyes were singling him out from among the other men, and he saw that a glad smile was upon her face.

"I was in hopes of finding you at the piano," he said, "ready to delight us with some music. It is what a poor country bachelor like myself misses most of all."

"No," she answered, "I was waiting and wondering how long you would stay in the dining-room, occupied with stupid discussions. What pleasure can men find in arguing? It never convinces any one."

"Very, very true," he said; and seated himself at the small table where she sat.

Kitty had taken up a pencil and was idly scribbling on a piece of paper. It helped her, in a measure, to conceal the nervousness she felt, for now that Levine had come to her, her heart was beating furiously. They were both silent for some time. Levine was watching her face and thinking to himself how impossible it would now be for him to live without her.

"See what a lot of paper I have

wasted with my scribbling," she said at last, and rose as if to move away.

"Stay, one moment!" exclaimed Levine, an idea suddenly entering his head. "There is something I have long wanted to ask you."

There was a little troubled look in her eyes as she sat down again. "Ask it," she said in a low tone.

"I will do so in this way," Levine replied, taking the pencil which she had been using, and writing on a piece of paper. "Here is my question," he said, handing her the sheet on which he had written these letters: *w. y. s. t. i. w. i. d. y. m. t. o. f. a.*: they were the first letters of the words, "When you said that it was impossible, did you mean *then* or for *always?*"

Levine had little hope that she would be able to decipher his mysterious screed, yet he watched her as she glanced at it as if his whole life depended on the result.

Kitty bent over the paper and studied it with knit brows, then, as if its meaning suddenly dawned upon her, she raised her eyes to Levine's. "I understand," she said, blushing.

"What word does that stand for?" he asked, pointing to the *i.* of the word "impossible."

"For *impossible*," she answered; "but the word was not the right one."

She took the pencil from his hand, and, in her turn, wrote: *"a. t. t. i. c. m. n. o. a."*

Dolly, from her seat across the room, could see her sister with the pencil in her fingers, a timid and yet happy smile upon her lips, her eyes shining with a bright light as she raised them to Levine's face. It softened the sorrow her conversation with Karénine had left

in her heart. She saw Levine radiant with joy—he had understood Kitty's answer: *"At that time I could make no other answer."*

He looked questioningly into her eyes. "You meant *then* only?"

"Yes," answered the girl, with a smile. "And now?" he asked.

"You shall read what I will own to you is my one great wish," and she wrote the first letters of the words, "That you have been able to forgive and forget."

With trembling fingers, he traced his own reply:

"I have never for a moment ceased to love you!"

Kitty looked at him, and her lips trembled.

"I understand," she murmured.

"Are you playing at being Levine's secretary?" said Prince Cherbatzky, approaching the two young people. "If you are coming to the theater with me, my dear, it is time for us to go."

Levine rose and escorted Kitty to the door. All doubts were now at rest. Kitty had acknowledged that she loved him, and had given him permission to speak to her parents the next day.

CHAPTER VIII

CONGRATULATIONS

WHEN Kitty had gone, the one attraction of the evening, so far as he was concerned, seemed to Levine to have disappeared. He felt a strong desire to be alone and able to give himself entirely to his own thoughts, and, before long, he succeeded in making his excuses and at the same time his escape from his friend's house.

He counted the hours which must

elapse before he could with any sense of propriety present himself at the Cherbatzky mansion. Sleep, he felt, was out of the question, his nerves were too highly strung, nor was he willing to allow Kitty's sweet face to disappear from his thoughts even during the few hours of necessary sleep. In spite of the coldness of the night air, he sat by the open window of his room at the hotel and gave himself up to his own reflections. Hour after hour passed away, but it was still quite early in the morning when, having refreshed himself with a plunge into cold water, he changed his dress and sallied forth into the streets, toward the house which sheltered *her*. Though he had neither slept nor broken his fast, he still felt buoyant and excited. After walking about the streets for several hours he returned to his hotel, by this time sufficiently calm to sit down and patiently await midday. When noon came he called an isvostchik from those in front of the hotel and set out to learn his fate.

When he reached the entrance to the Cherbatzky palace, the huge Swiss on duty at the door recognized him with what seemed to Levine a knowing smile.

"It is a long time since you were here, Constantin Dmitrich!"

Far from the familiarity annoying him, Levine felt a glow of satisfaction at the good fellow's greeting. The latter insisted on removing the visitor's hat and cloak with his own hands, and ushered him into the large hall.

"To whom shall I announce monsieur?" asked a footman; and it seemed to Levine that he, too, knew everything.

"To the prince and princess," he answered.

The first member of the household that he met was the French governess, Mademoiselle Linon. The good old lady's eyes fairly shone through her gold-rimmed spectacles as she greeted the young man with genuine warmth; but before they had interchanged many words, the rustle of a dress was heard near the door and the sound of a light footstep. The governess disappeared—how or where Levine had no eyes to notice. Kitty had entered the room, and coming up to him with rapid steps, her eyes brimming over with happiness, she laid her hands upon his shoulders. In another moment he was holding her in his arms. She, too, had spent a sleepless yet happy night, and had counted the minutes throughout the morning to the time that she might expect him.

Few words passed between them. Their joy kept them silent.

"Come and find my mother," she said at last, taking his hand.

He lifted hers to his lips and kissed it.

"Can this be true?" he asked in a broken voice. "I can hardly believe that you love me."

She smiled at his doubt and hesitation.

"Yes, it is true," she said, gently. "and I am very happy."

Still holding his hand, she led him into the large salon where her mother sat. The princess, as she saw them enter, rose from her seat, half weeping and half laughing. Then, with sudden energy, she advanced toward Levine and embraced him.

"So it is all settled?" she said through her tears. "I am very, very glad. You must love her very dearly. Kitty, dear, I am very happy."

"You have certainly lost no time," said the prince, who had just entered the room. He strove to appear calm, but Levine could see that his eyes, too, were full of tears. "I have always wished it," he went on; "and when this little goose was foolish enough to think—"

"Papa!" cried Kitty, closing his mouth with her little hand.

"Very well," the prince said, "I will say no more, only that I, too, am very— Heavens, what an old fool I am!" and taking his daughter in his arms, he kissed her tenderly.

After some minutes the emotion which each of the four experienced had sufficiently calmed down to allow of a more practical discussion of the future. It was a welcome means of relieving their feelings, for each of them, during the first moments, had experienced a strange impression as if he or she had, during the past, been in some way to blame.

The princess was the first to speak.

"And when shall it be? We must announce the marriage and arrange the betrothal. What do you say, Alexander?" to her husband.

"There is the one who has most right to decide," answered the prince, designating Levine.

"When?" said the latter, blushing. "To-morrow, if my wishes are consulted—the betrothal to-day, the marriage to-morrow."

"Come, come, my dear boy, that is absurd!"

"Well, then, let us say—in eight days."

"That, too, is out of the question," said the princess, smiling at the lover's impatience. "Think of the *trousseau.*"

"Must there be a *trousseau,* and all that sort of thing?" said Levine to himself in affright. "Well, after all, neither the *trousseau,* nor the betrothal, nor anything, in fact, can spoil my happiness." He glanced at Kitty and thought that he could read in her face an approval of her mother's words. "Well, I suppose my ignorance is to blame," he said, aloud. "I merely spoke from my own wishes."

"We will think it over," said the princess, "before deciding. In the meantime, we can announce the engagement."

She approached her husband's chair, and, bending over, kissed him in silence. He rose from his chair, passed his arm around her waist, and the father and mother left the room together.

When the door had closed upon them, Levine, who by this time had recovered his self-possession, sat down by Kitty and held her hand in his. His heart was full of many things he wished to say, but he had difficulty in finding the proper words.

"I see now," he said, "that in my innermost mind I have always known that this would be, though I could never bring myself to cherish an actual hope."

"And I also knew," said Kitty, "that even when I threw away my own happiness, it was you that I loved. I was carried away by some foolish impulse. Now, what I have to ask you is this: Can you forget the past?"

"Perhaps," said Levine, "it has been all for the best. I, too, ought to ask for your forgiveness."

Their conversation was interrupted by the entrance of Mademoiselle Linon, who came to congratulate her favorite pupil, a tender smile upon her kind and honest face. She was followed by the older and more privileged of the family servants, each anxious to say a few kindly words to their young mistress and her lover.

So quickly had the news traveled that, before long, a big stream of relations and friends passed into the Cherbatzky palace, full of congratulations and good wishes. Among them was the Countess Nordstone. She had always protested that her friend should look higher for a husband, but there was something in Kitty's face which told her that the girl's choice was fixed and irrevocable, and from that time Kitty and her future husband had no more enthusiastic supporter than the Countess Nordstone.

CHAPTER IX

SOBS OF A MAN

WHEN he found himself once more alone, and in his own room, Karénine recalled, one by one, the events and conversations of the evening. By Dolly's words he had been especially affected. He smiled within himself at the idea of her applying biblical precepts to his case. It seemed to him an inconsistency truly feminine.

He ordered tea to be served, and then, taking a railway guide, commenced to map out his tour of inspection.

At this moment a servant brought him two telegrams. Karénine laid down the guide and opened them. The first announced the appointment of a political rival to an office which he himself had hoped to fill. He reddened with anger, and, throwing the dispatch to the ground, paced up and down the

room. "Those whom the gods wish to destroy, they first make mad!" he quoted to himself, applying the words to those who had supported his rival's nomination. His eyes fell upon the second message. "Some more news of a similar kind," he thought as he opened it. The one word "Anna" danced before his eyes. It was from his wife! "I am dying. I implore you to come to me. I shall die more easy if I have your forgiveness," it ran.

He read the words with a contemptuous smile and cast the paper from him. "Some new trick," was his first thought; "she is capable of any deceit. She should be on the point of her confinement; but what can be her aim? To render their child legitimate? to compromise me? to stop the divorce? The message says, 'I am dying.'" He read it once again, and this time its real meaning seemed to strike him. "If it is true, if suffering and the approach of death have brought her to repentance, and if, for fear of her deceiving me I should refuse to go to her, it would be not only cruel but wicked, and I could never forgive myself."

"Pierre," he called to his servant, "order a carriage. I am going to St. Petersburg."

He decided that he would see his wife. He would leave her at once if he found that her illness was feigned or exaggerated; if not, or if he arrived too late, he would at least follow out her last wishes.

The next morning Karénine arrived in St. Petersburg, tired with the night's travel. Do what he would, he could not drive from his brain the idea that this death, if it did occur, would cut short all his present difficulties. When he reached his house, he saw that a carriage and an isvostchik were drawn up before the door, their drivers both asleep on their boxes. As he mounted the steps, a momentary indecision came over him, but he nerved himself. "If she has deceived me," he thought, "I will keep quite calm and go away again. If she has spoken the truth, I will do all that propriety demands."

The door was opened by a footman in plain clothes whose appearance betokened that he had been up all night.

"How is your mistress?"

"Madame was safely confined last night," the man answered.

Karénine stopped short, and felt that every drop of blood had left his face. He realized now how much he had desired this death.

"And her health?"

"Madame is very weak. There has been a consultation. The doctor is here now," was the answer.

"Take my things," said Karénine, shortly, slightly relieved that all danger was not over.

He entered the ante-chamber. A military cloak was hanging there. Karénine noticed it and asked:

"Who is here?"

"The doctor, the nurse, and Count Wronsky."

Karénine passed through the rooms. The salon was empty. The nurse came out from his wife's boudoir, and with the familiarity which the approach of death brings with it, took him by the hand and led him toward the bedroom.

"Thank God you have come!" she said. "She speaks of nothing but you—always of you!"

"Bring some ice at once," came from the bedroom in the doctor's imperative voice.

Seated on a low chair in the boudoir, his face covered with his hands, through whose fingers the tears forced their way, was Alexis Wronsky. At the doctor's words he uncovered his face and saw that Karénine was before him. He sunk back in the chair and again concealed his features, as if in complete despair; then, with an effort, he raised himself, and said:

"She is dying. The doctors say that there is no hope. You are the master here. But grant me permission to remain. I will conform to your slightest wish."

As he saw Wronsky weep, Karénine felt the compassion which always seized him at the sight of the suffering of others. He turned away without making a reply, and walked to the bedroom door.

Anna's voice could be heard speaking rapidly in distinct and lively tones. Karénine passed in and approached her bed. Her face was turned toward him, the cheeks flushed, the eyes shining with feverish brilliancy, her small white hands nervously clutched and played with the coverlid of her bed. At the first glance she seemed herself, and in the highest spirits. The words came clearly and perfectly accentuated from her lips:

"Alexis—I mean Alexis Alexandrovitch—is it not strange and cruel that they should *both* be called Alexis—Alexis would not refuse me, he would have forgiven me—why has he not come? He is a good man, he does not know himself how good he is. My God! my God! how I suffer! Give me some water, quickly! But I suppose it is not good for *her*—for my little daughter! Give her to a nurse, then—I will consent. Perhaps it will be better. When he comes, he would not like to see her. Take her away."

"He has come—he is here," said the nurse, trying to attract Anna's attention to Karénine.

"What nonsense!" continued Anna, still not seeing him.

"Give me the little one; give her to me. He has not arrived yet. You say he will not forgive me because you don't understand him. Nobody does—except myself. His eyes—Serge has got his eyes; that is why I can not bear to see him any more. Has Serge had his dinner yet? I am sure they are neglecting him. *He* would never forget him. Put Serge's little bed in the corner of the room, and Marietta must sleep near him."

Suddenly she paused. A look of fear came into her face, and she raised her arms above her head as if to ward off a blow—she had recognized her husband.

"No, no," she said, quickly; "I am not afraid of him, I am only afraid of death. Alexis, come near to me. I must be quick, for time is short, and I have only a few minutes to live. The fever will come back again and I shall not be able to understand anything. Now I do understand, I understand everything and see everything."

Karénine's face was full of suffering. He tried to speak, but his lips trembled and he could not control his voice. He took her hand between his own, and each time that he turned his eyes to hers he saw that they were fixed upon him with a sweet and humble expression he had **never seen** before.

"Wait—you do not know—" She paused, seeking to collect her ideas. "Oh, yes, yes; this is what I wanted to say. Don't be astonished. I myself am always the same, but there is another being in me of whom I am afraid. It is she who loved him, while I myself could not forget what I used to be. Now I am altogether myself, not the other one. I am dying—I know it—ask the doctor. There are terrible weights upon my feet, my hands, and my very fingers: but it will soon be over. There is only one thing I must have—your forgiveness—you must forgive me entirely. I have sinned and am to blame; but I have heard—was there not some holy martyr who was even worse than I have been—I forget her name. No, you can not forgive me. I know it is impossible. Go, go; you are too perfect!"

She held him with one burning hand and pushed him from her with the other.

Karénine's emotion now overpowered him. He had never acknowledged that the Christian law, by which he guided his life, commanded him to pardon and love his enemies, and yet now his heart was filled with love and forgiveness! He knelt down by the bedside, and hiding his face in the coverlids, sobbed like a child. Anna leaned toward him, put one hot, feverish arm around his head, and raising her eyes, said, almost defiantly:

"There, I knew it well! Good-bye, now, good-bye to every one—see, they have come back again! Why don't they go away? Take these furs away!"

The doctor gently lowered her to the pillow and covered her arms. She made no resistance, but looked straight before her with burning eyes.

"Remember that I only asked for your forgiveness—nothing more. Why does *he* not come?" she asked, quickly glancing at the door. "Come! Come here! Give him your hand."

Wronsky came to the bedside and still hid his face between his hands.

"Uncover your face," she said, "and look at him. He is a saint. Uncover your face, I say! Alexis"—to her husband—"make him draw his hands away. I want to see his face."

Karénine took Wronsky's hands and gently drew them from before the face distorted with suffering and humiliation.

"Give him your hand," said Anna. "Forgive him."

Karénine, his own tears falling, held out his hand.

"Thank God! Thank God!" she said, "now all is right. I will stretch my limbs a little—it gives me ease. There, that is good. How ugly those flowers are"—pointing to the pattern of the hangings—"they are not like violets at all. Oh, my God! When will this be over? Give me some morphine, doctor—some morphine! Oh, God!" and she threw herself about the bed in a convulsion of pain.

The doctors were fearful of the worst. For the whole day she remained unconscious and delirious. Toward midnight her pulse almost ceased to beat, and they looked for the end each moment.

Wronsky went to his own home, but came early in the morning to hear the news and sat in the little ante-chamber.

Karénine led him to his wife's boudoir. "Remain here," he said; "perhaps she may ask for you."

So another day passed, and on the third the doctors commenced to have some hope—her vitality was so strong. On that morning, Karénine entered the boudoir where Wronsky was, and, closing the door, sat down and faced him.

"Alexis Alexandrovitch," said Wronsky, feeling that an explanation was at hand, "I am incapable of speaking or of understanding. Have pity on me! However great your own suffering, believe me, mine is still more terrible."

He would have risen, but Karénine detained him.

"You must listen to me," he said; "it is necessary. I must explain to you the nature of the feelings by which I am guided, and by which I shall still be guided, so that you may fall into no error through me. You are aware that I had decided upon obtaining a divorce, and had taken the first steps toward it. I will not hide from you that at first I hesitated, possessed as I was with a desire for revenge. When I received her message, this desire still existed—I will go even further, and say that I wished for her death"—he paused for a moment, anxious to express his meaning clearly—"but I have seen her again. I have forgiven her, and without any restriction. The satisfaction of being able to forgive has seemed to show me my duty still more clearly. Now, I only ask of God this one thing—to let me still have the joy of forgiving." The tears filled his eyes. Wronsky was struck by his calm and steadfast look. "That is how I am situated," he continued. "It is in your power to drag me through the mud and make me the laughing stock of the whole world; but I shall not abandon Anna on that account, nor shall I reproach her. I can see clearly and precisely what my duty is. It is to remain with her, and I shall remain. If you wish to see her, you shall be informed of her condition; but I think that, for the present at least, it would be better for you to withdraw."

Karénine rose, his voice stifled with sobs.

Wronsky rose also, and stood with downcast face and bent body. It was not in his nature to understand sentiments of this kind, and yet he felt that he was in the presence of one whose ideas were of a standard far beyond the conception of such a one as himself.

CHAPTER X

HER FACE

WHEN Wronsky left the house after this interview, he stood upon the steps, asking himself where he was and whither he was going; he felt humiliated and confused, as if he had just lost the path along which he had been walking proudly and contentedly. The rules according to which he had hitherto lived, seemed false and full of deception. The betrayed husband, whom he had so far looked upon as an obstacle in his way, had raised himself to a height which compelled respect, and now appeared honest, high-minded, and generous, while he himself was a mean and spiritless creature.

What caused him the most acute unhappiness was the thought of losing Anna forever. His passion, which had momentarily cooled, now awoke, more violent than ever. He was to lose her at the moment when he had learned to know and love her to a degree beyond

what he had thought possible. He recalled with horror the time when Karénine had forced him to uncover his face.

When he reached his room, he threw himself upon a sofa, utterly worn out with the past three nights of sleeplessness; the strange events of the past few days came back to his mind one by one.

"If I could but go to sleep and forget!" he sighed; and, indeed, in a few moments, felt that sleep was coming over him. Suddenly he found himself upon his knees, beside the sofa, and wide awake. These words were ringing in his ears: "It is in your power to drag me through the mud," the words which Karénine had used; and then he saw Anna's face, flushed with fever, her eyes looking tenderly, not upon *him*, but upon her husband, and he pictured his own foolish and absurd appearance.

"To sleep—and forget!" he kept repeating, throwing himself again upon the sofa and closing his eyes. "I can not. It is impossible!" he groaned. "How can I blot out this memory? I can not exist like this!" But still there sounded in his ears the words of Anna: "Uncover his face!" "What is happening? Am I going mad?" he asked himself. "Mad? Why, madmen find refuge in suicide! No, no; I must go to sleep!" Of a sudden he sat up, trembling all over. "All is over now; there is nothing left for me to do"; and then, in his imagination, he saw his life as it might have been had Anna not entered into it. His old ambitions —his military life, the friends and comrades who had passed by him in their career, the good opinion of the imperial circle—all were gone; there was nothing left.

He jumped to his feet, unloosened his coat and collar so that he might breathe more easily, and commenced to pace up and down the room. "This is how one goes mad," he thought; "how one first thinks of suicide—to escape from shame!"

He walked to the door and closed it securely; then with fixed look and compressed lips he approached the table, took up a revolver, raised the trigger, and reflected. For two whole minutes he remained motionless, the weapon in his hand, his head bent down, his mind turning upon the same train of thought —his lost happiness, his ruined future, and his present shame.

Then he pressed the revolver against his left side, and fired. He felt a violent shock, and fell, without hearing the report. The pistol fell from his grasp, the room and all its furniture seemed to go round and round, and he felt that he was losing consciousness. The hurrying steps of his servant aroused him. With an effort he understood that he was lying stretched upon the ground, his hands and the tigerskin on which he lay bespattered with blood.

"What a fool I am! I have missed!" he murmured, raising himself upon one arm and groping for the pistol. His head commenced to swim round again, and once more he fell, bathed in his own blood.

His valet entered the room, saw the figure of his master stretched before him, and, frightened, rushed away to summon help.

In an hour's time he lay in his bed, three surgeons examining his wound, and his sister-in-law, Maria, watching over him as nurse.

CHAPTER XI

BETSY'S ARRIVAL

WHEN Karénine had granted his forgiveness to his wife, whom at the time he supposed to be close on death, he had not thought how matters might turn out in the event of her recovery. By her bedside, for the first time in his life, he had allowed his pity to go out freely and without constraint toward another who was suffering; heretofore he had looked upon this as a weakness, and had resolutely fought against it. Remorse at having wished for her death, the pity with which she inspired him, and, most of all, the happiness he found in the ability to forgive, had changed his grief into a profound peace, his sufferings into joy.

He had forgiven his wife and he pitied her. Since being a witness to Wronsky's despair, he pitied him also. Toward his son, whom he blamed himself for having neglected, he was now all kindness, while as for the little babygirl, what was at first pity soon developed into tenderness when he saw the weak and helpless little creature almost neglected during the mother's illness; he busied himself in caring for her, and soon became devotedly attached to her.

But it was soon apparent that his new relations with his wife lacked naturalness and stability. When the weakness caused by the nearness of death had passed away, Karénine noticed that Anna seemed afraid of him, uneasy in his presence, and unable to look him in the face.

It was as if she, too, were conscious of the instability of their present position toward each other, and simply waiting for some move or further explanation on his part.

One day, toward the end of February, when Karénine returned home from the ministry, he noticed a strange footman standing in the hall, holding a thick cloak of fur.

"Who is here?" he asked.

"The Princess Elizabeth Tverskoï," answered the lackey.

Betsy's presence in his house was far from agreeable to Karénine; she was connected, in his mind, with too many unhappy memories. He went straight to the apartments devoted to the children.

Serge was sitting with the English governess, busily employed upon his lessons. His father greeted him with some affectionate words, patting him on the head as he spoke to him. He was anxious to see his wife, but did not wish to meet the Princess Betsy. However, he knew that Anna would be astonished if he did not go to her at once, and so, putting his own inclinations aside, he walked toward the door of her room. It was partially open, and as he approached, the noise of his footsteps drowned by the thick carpet, he heard Betsy say:

"If he were not going away, I could understand your refusing to see him, and your husband's objection."

"It is not a question of my husband, but of myself alone. Please say no more about it," was Anna's answer in moved tones.

"Surely you must have some wish

to see him—the man who has almost died for you—"

"It is exactly on that account that I do not wish to see him."

Karénine stopped, feeling like a guilty man. He would have turned back had not the thought struck him that such a course would be unworthy of him. The voices were now silent, and he entered the room.

Anna, in a gray peignoir, her black hair cut quite short, was sitting in an invalid's chair. As usual, at the sight of her husband, all animation left her face; she bent her head and threw an uneasy glance toward Betsy. The latter, dressed, as usual, in the very height of fashion, greeted Karénine with an ironical smile.

"Ah!" she said, with an air of astonishment, "I am charmed to meet you in your own house. You never show yourself elsewhere nowadays; and, indeed, I have not seen you since Anna was taken ill. I have heard of all your troubles from other people, though. You are certainly a model of a husband."

Karénine greeted her coldly though politely, and, taking his wife's hand, questioned her about her health.

"I seemed to be rather better," she said, avoiding his look.

"Still, I think you are feverish," he said.

"We have been talking too much," interrupted Betsy. "It is dreadfully selfish on my part, and I must run away."

She rose; but Anna, into whose face the blood had rushed, held her by the arm and detained her.

"No, please don't go just yet," she exclaimed. Then, turning to her husband: "I may as well tell you now, for I wish to hide nothing from you. Betsy tells me that Count Wronsky wishes to come and say good-bye before his departure for Tashkend." She spoke quickly, still without raising her eyes to his face. "I have told her," she added, "that I can not receive him."

"What you said, dear, was that it depended upon Alexis Alexandrovitch," corrected Betsy.

"No, I can not receive him; it would be—" Anna paused, questioning her husband with a look; but he had turned away his head. "In a word, I do not wish to."

Karénine advanced and took her hand. She would have withdrawn it, but mastered herself and let him take it in his own.

"I thank you for your confidence," he began; then, looking at the princess, he stopped. In her presence it was impossible for him to express any generous sentiment.

"Well, good-bye, dear," said Betsy; and kissing Anna, she left the room escorted by Karénine.

When they reached the boudoir, Betsy stopped short, and, pressing Karénine's hand significantly, said:

"Alexis Alexandrovitch, I know you to be a truly generous man, and my esteem and liking for you are so great that I venture on one word of advice, though it is, perhaps, no business of mine. It is this: Alexis Wronsky is the soul of honor, and he is just setting out for Tashkend."

"I am much obliged to you both for your sympathy and your advice, princess. All I have to say is, that if my wife is able or wishes to receive any one she will decide for herself."

He spoke gravely and with dignity, though the ironical smile with which Betsy received his words showed him how unable she was to appreciate it.

CHAPTER XII

WHAT TO DO?

HAVING taken leave of the Princess Betsy, Karénine returned to his wife's room. She rose in her chair, at his entrance, with a startled look, and he could see that she had been crying.

"I am much obliged to you for your confidence," he said again in a quiet tone; "and I agree with you that, when once he has gone away, there is no necessity for you to receive Count Wronsky."

"What is the use of mentioning it again?" asked Anna, peevishly, "after I have already said so myself"; but her thought was: "No necessity for a man who has tried to kill himself to bid good-bye to the woman he loves, and who, for her part, can not live without him!" "Let us say no more about it," she added, more calmly.

"I left you at full liberty to decide for yourself," he recommenced. "The Princess Tverskoï certainly interferes in family matters of a painful nature, and which—"

"I know nothing about that," interrupted Anna. "I only know that she is sincerely fond of me."

Karénine sighed and said no more on the subject.

Anna played nervously with her handkerchief, and looked at him from time to time with the dislike which she could not suppress. Her only wish was to be relieved of his presence.

"I am going to see the doctor," said Karénine at last.

"What for? I am doing well."

"On the baby's account. She is fretting very much, I hear, and I have no great confidence in the wet nurse."

"Why did you not let me nourish her myself when I begged you all to? I could at least have tried. In spite of everything"—Karénine well understood the meaning of her words, "in spite of everything"—"she is a child, and should not be allowed to die." She rang the bell and ordered that the baby should be brought to her. "When I wished to nourish her you would not let me, and now you reproach me for not having done so."

"I reproach you for nothing—"

"Yes, you do. My God! why did I not die! But," she added, struggling to control herself, "forgive me; I am nervous and talking unjustly. Leave me, please!"

Karénine left the room. "This can not last," he thought as he closed the door.

He had never yet been so forcibly impressed with the impossibility of keeping up such a state of affairs in the eyes of the world, nor had his wife's dislike been made so plain to him. It seemed to him that the world and his wife demanded of him something which he could not even understand, but which was reawakening the feeling of hatred in his heart and nullifying the victory he had lately gained over himself. His one thought was of a course of action which would save Anna from a degrading and shameful future; but he felt the unevenness of the struggle and his own powerlessness, and dreaded lest he eventually be forced to do the evil thing which the world seemed to expect of him.

CHAPTER XIII

TWO MISSIONS

STEPANE OBLOWSKY had arrived in St. Petersburg with two missions—to see for himself his sister's condition, and assist as far as possible in arranging her troubles, and also to express his thanks in the proper quarter for his appointment as chamberlain—an honour which had recently been conferred upon him.

His first visit to Anna was made soon after her husband had left her, after their last interview, and she was still in tears. In spite of his natural buoyancy and cheerful spirits, Stépane was shocked to see the change in his sister, and the marked sadness of her face.

"Everything is going badly," she said in answer to his affectionate inquiries. "Day and night, the past and the future—everything is wrong."

"You see things too darkly," he replied. "You must take courage and look life in the face. It is hard, I know; but—"

"I have heard of certain women," interrupted Anna, "who love those whom they are deceiving. For myself, I hate him because of his very generosity and goodness. I can not live with him! Understand me; it is some physical weakness over which I have no control; but I can not live with him any longer. What am I to do? I thought that I had been as unhappy as it was possible to be; but this passes all that I had ever imagined. Though

I know him to be a good man, perfect, and recognize my own inferiority, I, nevertheless, hate him!"

"You are still weak and nervous," her brother said, "and inclined to exaggerate everything. Things are not so very terrible." And in the face of such despair, Stépane Arcadievitch was able to smile with such a kindly and good-hearted expression that Anna felt somewhat comforted.

"No, Stiva," she said; "I am a lost woman—a lost woman! I am worse, in fact, for I can not yet say that all is over. I feel, alas! the very contrary. The cord is tightly stretched and must soon break. But the end has not yet come. When it does, it will be terrible!"

"No, no; the cord can very easily be slackened. There is no situation without some exit."

"I have thought and thought, and can see only one."

He knew, without further words, that she meant—death.

"Now, listen to me," he said. "You can not judge of your own position as I can. Let me give you my advice, frankly and freely. I will take things from the commencement. You married a man twenty years older than yourself, and you married without love, or at least without then knowing what love was. It was a mistake, I grant—"

"A terrible mistake!" said Anna.

"But, I repeat, it is done—an accomplished fact. You then had the unhappiness to fall in love with another than your husband—that also was unfortunate, but equally a fact. Your husband discovered it and pardoned it." He paused between each sentence to allow her to make an answer, but she remained silent. "Now, the question resolves itself into this: Can you continue to live with your husband? Do you wish it? Does he wish it?"

"I know nothing—nothing at all."

"You have just told me that you can not endure him."

"No, I have not said so. I deny it; I know nothing, and can understand nothing."

"But let me—"

"You can not understand. I am hanging head foremost over a precipice, and *ought* not try and save myself. I *can not* do so."

"Well, *we* will save you from falling and hurting yourself. I understand you. I can see that you are unwilling to express your real feelings and desires."

"I desire nothing, nothing, except that this should all be over."

"Do you suppose he does not perceive that? Do you think he, too, is not suffering? And what can result from all this self-torture? Divorce, on the other hand, would solve everything."

It had not been easy for Stépane to lead up to the desired climax. He watched Anna closely to see its effect upon herself.

She shook her head without replying, but her face was lighted up for an instant with a look which clearly told how entrancing such a prospect was to her.

"I shall be so glad to do all I can to arrange it," said Stépane, smiling with confidence. "Now, say no more. I will do my best. I will go and see him." Anna looked at him with brilliant and pensive eyes, but still made no reply.

CHAPTER XIV

GOD'S WILL

STEPANE ARCADIEVITCH entered his brother-in-law's office with what, for him, was an unusually solemn face.

Karénine, his hands behind his back, was walking up and down the room, his thoughts, indeed, occupied by the same subject as his visitor's.

"I am not disturbing you, I hope," said Stépane, troubled at the expression of the other's face. "I want to talk with you on a very important matter."

Karénine bent his head and waited for him to continue.

"I wish to speak to you," Stépane went on, "about my sister, and about the position in which you are both, at present, placed."

A sad smile came upon Karénine's face. He made no direct reply to Stépane's words, but taking from his desk a letter which he had commenced to write, held it toward him.

"It is my thought every moment," he said. "Here is what I have tried to say to her, thinking that possibly I might express myself better in writing, as my presence seems only to irritate her."

Stépane, somewhat bewildered, took up the paper and read:

"I am well aware how my presence oppresses you, painful though it may be to me to know it. I acknowledge it and feel that it could not well be otherwise. I do not reproach you at all. God is my witness that during your illness I resolved to forget the past and commence a new life. I do not regret, and shall never regret, what I did then—it was your recovery, the recovery of your soul, that I desired. I have been unsuccessful. Tell me yourself what will bring you rest and happiness, and I promise, in advance, to abide by the sense of justice which I am sure will guide you."

Stépane handed the letter back without a word. Karénine's lips were trembling convulsively.

"What does she herself wish? That is what I want to know."

"I am afraid she hardly knows," answered Stépane. "She is unable to judge for herself. She has been crushed, literally crushed, by your generosity and forbearance. Should she read your letter she will not be able to answer it. It will only humiliate her still more."

"Then what is to be done? How am I to know what she wishes?"

"If you will permit me to offer my advice, it is that you should clearly and concisely point out the measures you think needful to solve the situation."

"But how?" said Karénine, passing his hand over his eyes. "I can see no possible solution."

"Every difficulty has one," said Oblowsky, rising, and coming to the point. "You spoke some time ago about divorce. If you are convinced that all chance of mutual happiness has gone—"

"There are different degrees of happiness. Supposing that I do consent to everything, no matter what, how are we to escape from this trouble?"

When Stépane answered, there was the same calm and soothing smile upon his face which had done much to comfort Anna, and now, in turn, it had a similar effect upon her husband.

"She will never say what it is that she wishes. Her secret longing, though, is to break the bonds which bind her to cruel memories. In my opinion, it is indispensable that your mutual relations should be made perfectly clear, and that can only be done by your both regaining your liberty."

"By divorce?" interrupted Karénine in a tone of disgust.

"Yes, divorce, in my opinion," repeated Stépane, blushing. "From every point of view it is the most sensible course for two married people who find themselves in your position. When living together has become intolerable, what is to be done?"

Karénine gave a deep sigh and covered his eyes with his hand.

"There is only one point to be considered," continued Oblowsky, "and that is whether one of the two wishes to marry again. If not, it is very simple."

Overcome with emotion, Karénine murmured some unintelligible words. What seemed so simple to Stépane, he had turned over in his thoughts a thousand times, and so far from finding it simple, he deemed it impossible. His own dignity, his respect for religion, would be violated, and, what was still worse, the woman whom he had loved and had once pardoned, would be condemned to dishonor. What would become of their son? He could not possibly be left with his mother; what sort of bringing up could he receive? But, above all, was the one idea that, by consenting to a divorce, he would be dooming Anna to destruction. Once

divorced, she would unite herself to Wronsky by ties that would be both illicit and illegal—for marriage, according to Church law, could be dissolved by death alone.

He would not admit the truth of a single one of Stépane's arguments; he could refute them a hundred times over; and yet, as he listened to them, he knew that they were simply the manifestation of the irresistible force which governed his life and to which he would end by submitting.

"It only remains for us to know the conditions under which you will consent to a divorce," said Stépane, "for she will never dare to ask anything of you, and will leave herself entirely in your hands."

"My God! my God! Why should all this come upon me?" thought Karénine, burying his face in his hands.

"I can understand your being moved like this," said Oblowsky; "but if you reflect—"

"If one smites you on the left cheek, offer him the right; if he robs you of your cloak, give him your coat also," said Karénine, bitterly, to himself.

"Yes, yes," he exclaimed, aloud, "I will take all the shame upon myself— I will even give up my son. Do what you wish!" and turning from his brother-in-law, he seated himself by the window and said no more.

"Alexis Alexandrovitch, you may be sure she will appreciate your generosity. Without a doubt it is the will of God"; and then, feeling that he had said something foolish, Stépane broke off and smiled.

Karénine would have answered; but the tears still hindered him.

CHAPTER XV

ABROAD

THOUGH the bullet had not reached his heart—the spot at which he had aimed—Wronsky's wound was a dangerous one, and for days he hung between life and death.

When the crisis was safely passed and he could converse, he called his sister-in-law, Maria, who had nursed him tenderly, to his bedside.

"Maria," he said, very seriously, "I shot myself accidentally—tell everybody so; it would seem so ridiculous; they must not think or say that I did it purposely."

"None has said so," she answered; and then with a smile she added: "I hope, though, that you will leave off shooting yourself accidentally."

"Perhaps it would have been better," began Wronsky, and then he stopped. Now that he was out of danger, he felt as if he had been freed from much of his unhappiness—as if, in fact, his shame and humiliation had been washed away. Henceforth he would be able to think calmly of Karénine and recognize his grandeur of soul without himself feeling abased. He could take up his life once more and again look people in the face. One thing, however, he could not tear from his heart—regret at the loss of Anna, even though he had determined to come no more between the repentant wife and her husband.

His recovery was speedy, and one of his first acts was to accept the offer of a mission to Tashkend.

As the moment of his departure drew near, the sacrifice he was about to make to duty seemed more and more cruel, and the pain was increased by the refusal of Anna to see him before he left.

When, however, his cousin Betsy hastened to his apartments, and informed him that Stépane Oblowsky had obtained Karénine's consent to a divorce, he felt that nothing hindered him now from seeing Anna.

He hurried to the house, rushed upstairs without waiting to be announced, and entering Anna's room, took her in his arms and covered her face and neck with kisses. Anna had expected that he would come to her, and had thought deeply over what she would say to him; but now that he was here she had no time to speak—his passion carried her away. She would have tried to calm him and herself, too, but it was impossible. Her lips trembled, and for a time she could not speak.

"Yes, you have conquered me," she said at last. "I am altogether yours," and she pressed his hand to her bosom.

"So it should be, and always shall be, as long as we live," he said. "We will forget everything in our happiness. If anything were needed to increase our love, the terrible past would suffice"; and taking her hand in one of his, with the other he caressed her pale face and her hair, whose locks had been shorn so short.

"I can hardly recognize you with your hair cut short," he said. "You make a splendid boy. But how pale you are!"

"Yes, I am still very weak," she answered, her lips again trembling.

"We will go to Italy and build your health up again."

"Is it possible," she said, looking into his eyes, "that we shall be alone together, like husband and wife?"

"I am only surprised that we have not been so hitherto."

"Stiva tells me that *he* consents to everything," said Anna; "but I will not accept his generosity. I no longer wish for a divorce, but only for some decision as regards Serge."

How, in this, the first moment of their reunion, she could think of her son and of divorce at the same time, was beyond Wronsky's comprehension.

"Don't speak of that; don't even think about it," he said, turning her hand over and over in his own, as if to withdraw her attention to himself; but she looked beyond him and appeared as if she did not hear his words.

"Ah! why did I not die—it would have been far better!" and the tears filled her eyes.

At one time Wronsky would have deemed it impossible to withdraw from the dangerous but much-coveted mission to Tashkend. Now, without hesitation or delay, he refused it; and, seeing that his refusal would be received with displeasure in the highest quarters, he also handed in his resignation.

A month later Karénine was alone, with his son, in his own house, and Anna went abroad with Wronsky, having refused the proffered divorce.

PART IV

CHAPTER I

MARRIAGE

WITHIN six weeks of the announcement of their betrothal, the marriage of Constantin Levine and the Princess Kitty Cherbatzky took place.

The whole fashionable world of Moscow was present at the ceremony, which was celebrated with all the religious pomp and outward observance that the ritual of the Church allowed.

For many days prior to the wedding Levine had been in a state of nervousness and agitation common to men of his peculiar nature. For himself, he would have preferred a quieter and less ostentatious celebration of the service, but this by no means met the views of the Prince and Princess Cherbatzky, who saw no reason why the affair should not be held on a scale commensurate with the social position of both parties. Nor was Kitty herself unwilling to have her one great day of triumph in the eyes of all the world, and in like manner to the sisters who had preceded her in their entrance into married life. The greater part of the service, with all its forms and peculiar ceremonies, seemed to Levine like a dream. Only here and there did the words of the archdeacon and assisting priests reach his ears.

"I unite thee, Constantin, servant of God, to Catherine, servant of God," and then, as he passed the large ring upon Kitty's slender finger, the same formula was repeated by the priest to her.

The tears came to his eyes; a lump seemed to rise in his throat. All his former ideas of marriage and married life were mixed up in his brain in dire confusion. And Kitty, too, could scarce hear or comprehend the utterance of the many prayers and exhortations. As the ceremony progressed, her heart was filled with a triumphant joy which prevented her from fixing her attention upon what was going on.

At one period, when the priest instructed them both to advance and stand upon a small piece of carpet in front of him, all those around them were curious to see whose foot should be the first to press the carpet, and so, according to the old superstition, determine whether he or she were in future life to be the real master or mistress.

But in spite of the audible remarks made by those about them, neither Kitty nor Levine recalled the familiar tradition.

Then, as if in disjointed sentences, they heard the priest's voice as he prayed to the Almighty, "that husband and wife may have the gift of wisdom and be blessed with numerous progeny," and then the words, "for the woman must leave her father and her mother and become as one with her husband," and the supplication, "bless them even as Thou didst bless Isaac and Rebecca, Moses and Sephora, and let them behold their children unto the third and fourth generation!"

When the priest held out the marriage crowns, and Prince Cherbatzky, with trembling hand, placed the one which was destined for the bride on Kitty's head, Levine turned his eyes to her and saw the joyous smile upon her face as, with her own fingers, she assisted her father. He was struck with her look of intense happiness, and, from that moment, himself felt reassured and inexpressibly content.

They listened patiently to the priest's final words of advice and exhortation; they drank together the wine and water which he blessed for them, and followed him as he bid them walk around the pulpit with one of their hands in each of his.

At last came the time when the priest, with a smile, exclaimed: "And now embrace your wife; and you"—turning to Kitty—"your husband."

Levine left the church, his young wife upon his arm, with a new and strange sensation within him. He felt that now, and for the first time, they had come together and were one.

The same evening the newly married pair left Moscow for their country home.

CHAPTER II

AFTER THREE MONTHS

WRONSKY and Anna had now been traveling together for three months. They had visited in turn Venice, Rome, and Naples, and had arrived at a small Italian town where they had planned to stay for some time.

Wronsky, who, immediately on their arrival, had entered into negotiations with the agent for the tenancy of a villa in the neighborhood, was informed by the proprietor of the hotel that a Russian gentleman had called upon him in his absence, and would return later.

While Wronsky was speculating as to who the visitor might be, the latter entered the hotel. It was his former friend and fellow-student, Golinitchef. Though, during the past few years, they had seen little of each other, their greeting was warm and cordial.

There can be little doubt that Wronsky's pleasure at the meeting was largely caused by the feeling of loneliness and *ennui* he had lately suffered from.

"I am more than glad to see you," he said, with a smile.

"I saw your name among the arrivals," said the other, "but could hardly believe that it was you. I am pleased to meet you."

"And what brings you here?" asked Wronsky.

"I have been here for more than a year. I am hard at work."

"Indeed?" said Wronsky, with interest. "Let us go inside. You know Madame Karénine, I think? We are traveling together, as I suppose you know"; and as he spoke he watched the other's face.

"No," answered Golinitchef, with what was perhaps an excusable falsehood, "I was not aware of it. And how long have you yourself been here?"

"For the past three days," said Wronsky, still watching his friend's face. "He is an intelligent and sensible man," was his thought, "who can see things in their proper light. I can safely introduce him to Anna."

Since they had been together, every chance meeting of this kind caused Wronsky the same doubt and hesitation. As a rule, the men whom they had come across had seemed to understand the situation in what Wronsky called "the proper light," though, had he been asked, he would have found it difficult to exactly define his own meaning. The fact was that they did not wish to know or understand more than they could see, and simply behaved as men of the world accustomed to face such delicate situations.

The entrance of the two men into the room brought a quick blush to Anna's face, which the new-comer noticed and was pleased by. He had never met Anna, and was much struck by her beauty and the simplicity of her manner. He was charmed, too, with the openness with which she seemed to meet the situation, calling Wronsky by his first name and speaking without hesitation of their intention to establish themselves at the villa, which was dignified by the name of palace. Still, he had known Karénine, and could not quite understand how Anna, having deserted her husband and her son, and having lost her own good name, could be so gay and happy.

"Your 'palace' is mentioned in all the guide books," he said. "You will find a superb Tutorial there—a magnificent specimen of his latest style."

"I propose," said Wronsky, addressing Anna, "that we go and see it. The weather is splendid."

"Gladly," she replied. "I will go and put on my hat."

She could read in Wronsky's face that he was satisfied with her reception of his friend, and she answered him with a little quick and gracious smile.

When she had left the room, the two men felt some slight restraint: Golinitchef, as one who wished to express his admiration, yet did not venture to do so; Wronsky, as one who desired the complimeⁿt, yet had rather it were not expressed.

"So you have settled down here?" said Wronsky, forcing himself to open conversation. "Are you still devoted to the same studies?"

"Yes," answered Golinitchef, highly gratified by the question. "I am writing the second part of 'The Two Origins,' or, rather, to be more exact, I am busy collecting and preparing the material. It will be a much larger work than the first part"; and he commenced a long dissertation on his literary offspring.

So intent was he upon his subject that he did not even notice Anna's re-entrance. Dressed in out-door costume, with her sunshade in her hand, she stood quietly near the two men; and to look upon her face and perfect figure was an immense relief to Wronsky, who was commencing to feel bored by his friend's careless flow of words.

It cost Golinitchef no little effort to break away from his one pet hobby; but Anna skillfully led the conversation into another channel, and in a lively discussion on painting and works of art, they finally arrived at the palace.

"One thing in particular pleases me in our new quarters," said Anna, as they entered the villa. "You will have a splendid studio."

"And do you paint?" asked Golinitchef, quickly, turning to Wronsky.

"I used at one time," said the latter, with a modest blush, "and am now returning to my old love."

"He has real talent!" cried Anna, joyously. "I am no judge myself, but have heard true critics and connoiseurs say so."

CHAPTER III

THE START OF THE PORTRAIT

THE early period of her moral freedom and return to health was, for Anna, one of unalloyed joy. The idea of the evil she had wrought did not in any way imbitter her existence. Did she not owe to it a happiness great enough to blot out all remorse? The events which had followed her illness, from the time of her reconciliation with Karénine until her departure from under his roof, appeared to her as a nightmare, from which she had been freed by her travel with Wronsky. Why look back at it?

"After all," she said to herself, "though I have done this man a fatal and inevitable wrong, I will not profit by his misfortune. If I have caused him suffering, I also will suffer; I renounce all that I have loved and esteemed in the world—my son and my reputation. Since I have sinned, I deserve neither happiness nor the freedom of divorce, and I accept the shame as well as the grief and separation."

Sincere as she may have thought herself, Anna had not really known either suffering nor shame. During their travels both she and Wronsky had avoided all meetings which might have placed them in a false position, and those persons whom they had met had understood, or pretended to understand, their position toward each other. As for the separation from her boy, it no longer caused her suffering. She was passionately attached to her little daughter, and thought but seldom of Serge.

The more she saw of Wronsky, the

dearer he became to her. His presence was always new and enchanting to her. Every trait of his character seemed perfect to her, his words and ideas truly grand and noble. This excessive admiration frightened even herself, and she dared not avow it to him. By acknowledging her own inferiority, she might be opening a breach between them, and there could be no more terrible thought for her than the loss of his love. This fear, however, was in no way justified by Wronsky's own conduct. He never manifested the slightest regret at having sacrificed to his passion a career which promised to be most brilliant; he had never been more respectful in his treatment of her, more fearful lest her position cause her suffering. Her slightest wish was law to him, and he thought of nothing but of following out her smallest desires. Indeed, the finding herself the object of such unceasing care caused a sense of weariness to come over her at times.

As for Wronsky, in spite of the complete fulfillment of his desires, he was not entirely happy. The eternal mistake of those who expect to find satisfaction in the accomplishment of their wishes was his. He had found that he had gained but a portion of the expected happiness. At times, since his actions and his love had become free, his happiness did appear complete; but then, inevitably, a certain sadness would fall upon him. Without knowing it, he was continually seeking some new aim to his desires, and mistook passing caprices for serious aspirations. The life of constant travel, far away from his old life and associations in St. Petersburg, oppressed him; nor could he allow himself to think of finding such distraction as he had done when traveling in former days. On one occasion his proposal to sup with some old friends whom he chanced to meet threw Anna into a state of veritable despair. As a starved animal rushes upon some food he has chanced to come across, so Wronsky unconsciously threw himself upon such distractions as painting, reading, and political study could afford. When quite a youth he had shown a decided taste for art, which he now revived as something with which to occupy and stimulate his mind. The French school of art had most charm for him, and, governing himself by its lines, he commenced to work upon a portrait of Anna. She was in Italian costume, and all those who saw the picture appeared as highly pleased with it as the artist himself.

CHAPTER IV

FOR SALE

At first the novelty of his life in the palace, with its old-fashioned furniture, rare works of art, and wealth of antiques and tapestries, was highly pleasing to Wronsky. He had formed the acquaintance of an Italian artist, under whose tuition he commenced to study from nature, and soon, even in his outward appearance and dress, he assumed the rôle of the amateur painter and artist.

"Do you know anything of this man —Mikhaïlof?" he asked, one morning, as Golinitchef entered the study. He held out to him a newspaper in which mention was made of a great picture just completed by an artist named Mikhaïlof, who was said to be living in poor circumstances in that very town.

"I do not know him," answered Golinitchef as he read the article. "He possesses a certain amount of talent, but his conceptions are absolutely false. They are, without exception, conceptions of Christ or other religious characters, according to the ideas of Ivanof, Strauss, and Renan."

"What is the subject of this particular picture?"

"'Christ before Pilate.' He portrays Christ as a Jew of the newest and most realistic school"; and Golinitchef started upon one of his accustomed voluminous dissertations.

"Is it true that this Mikhaïlof is in want?" asked Wronsky, interrupting him. The thought flashed upon him that here might be an opportunity for him to appear in the rôle of Mæcenas and patron of a true but needy artist. "We might get him to paint Anna Arcadievna's portrait."

"Why mine?" she asked. "I have your portrait, and want no other. Let us, rather, have one painted of Anny" —for so she called her little girl.

"And you say you know him?" asked Wronsky again of Golinitchef.

"I have met him. He is an original character, without any education, a free-thinker, full of atheism, materialism, and the negation of everything— a regular savage, in fact. The son of a small hotel keeper in Moscow, he received little or no education. He entered the Academy with a certain amount of reputation—for he is no fool—and set himself up as an instructor of every one else."

"Why should we not call upon him and see him for ourselves?" suggested

Anna. The two men acquiesced, and, an hour later, they drove up to the small house which was pointed out as Mikhaïlof's, and sent up their cards.

The artist was sitting before the easel hard at work when the visitors' cards were brought to him. The next moment they themselves were ushered in.

Anna and Wronsky, already disenchanted by Golinitchef's description of Mikhaïlof, had this feeling disagreeably emphasized by the appearance of himself and his surroundings. He was of short stature and insignificant bearing, and his shabby clothes and general appearance of vulgarity were too much for the air of importance and dignity which he strove to assume.

He strove to read at a glance the character and station in life of his visitors. Wronsky and Anna, he presumed, were Russian tourists of distinction, rich maybe, but ignorant on all questions of art. Golinitchef's face he remembered, but could not for the moment determine when or under what circumstances he had met him.

"They have, without a doubt," he said to himself, "been visiting all the old and famous galleries, and now, having run the gauntlet of the German imposters and English pre-Raphaelites, they are honoring me with a visit, so as to authorize them in saying that they have completed the list."

He was well acquainted with the ways of *dilettantes* visiting the studios of modern painters, and how prone they are to be convinced that modern art merely serves to prove the incontestable superiority of the older masters.

And yet, in spite of his conviction that these rich and high-born Russians could not be aught else than imbeciles and fools, he displayed his sketches and uncovered his one large canvas with a nervous and shaking hand.

"This," he said, disclosing the picture, "is 'Christ before Pilate'—the subject being taken from the twenty-seventh chapter of St. Matthew's Gospel."

His lips were trembling with emotion. He stood behind his visitors and viewed the picture critically, as if he were one of their party. In spite of himself, he was anxiously awaiting the verdict of these three people whom, a few moments ago, he had affected to despise.

The silence which they kept was unbearable to him, and, to conceal his anxiety, he addressed Golinitchef.

"I think I have had the honor of meeting you before," he said, his eyes still fixed upon the faces of Anna and Wronsky.

"Certainly. We met, if you remember, at Rossi's house, the evening when the young Italian actress—'the new Rachel,' as they style her—recited," answered Golinitchef, lightly; and then, seeing that Mikhaïlof was waiting for some word of praise, he added:

"You have made great progress with your picture since last I saw it; and now, as I was then, I am very much impressed with your figure of Pilate. It represents a man of good intentions but of weak mind, a man who has no conception of the importance of his own action. It seems to me, though—"

He was interrupted by a fit of coughing on Mikhaïlof's part, who took this means of concealing his inability to find words with which to reply to the other's criticism. Little as he would have acknowledged it, even those few words

from his visitor filled him with joy. In one short moment he was lifted from self-abasement to enthusiasm.

Wronsky and Anna, meanwhile, were exchanging their opinions in low tones, fearful of expressing some criticism whose ignorance might offend the artist's ears. Mikhaïlof, however, thought that he could read a favorable verdict in their faces, and approached them.

"What an admirable expression the Christ has!" said Anna, thinking that praise of the central figure could not fail to gratify the artist. "One feels that he is pitying Pilate," she added.

"And how beautifully painted!" said Golinitchef. "What an air of divinity surrounds the figure!" He was not unwilling to imply a disapproval of the realistic Christ the artist had had in view.

"Yes, it is a strong work," said Wronsky. "Those figures in the background stand out in wonderful relief. You can see the cunning of the skilled hand," he added, turning to Golinitchef.

But his remark annoyed Mikhaïlof, on whose face there came a frown of discontent. He could not understand the epithet of cunning, and had always been opposed to the application of praise for technical skill toward the intrinsic merit of a work.

"The only criticism I would dare to make—" began Golinitchef.

"Make it, pray," interrupted Mikhaïlof, smiling.

"It is," said the other, "that you have painted God in man's form and not a man fashioned in God's image. Of course I know that such was your intention."

"I can only depict Christ as I myself

understand Hiim," said Mikhaïlof, gloomily.

Anna and Wronsky, fearing lest a bitter and tedious discussion might ensue, moved away from the easel and commenced to make a tour of the studio. They stopped in front of a small picture.

"What a gem! How charming!" they said with one voice.

Mikhaïlof wondered what had pleased them. He had completely forgotten the picture, which had been painted some three years before, and had only been lately brought forth at the request of some would-be purchaser.

"It is nothing—an old study," he said, carelessly.

"But a very excellent one," said Golinitchef, sincerely.

It was a simple sketch. Two children, beneath the shade of a leafy tree, fishing with rustic rod and line in the waters of a placid stream. The elder of the two seemed all intent on the sport; the younger, leaning on one elbow, and careless of his rod, gazed on the water with pensive eyes. Of what were his thoughts? was one's first impression.

Mikhaïlof would have led his visitor to another and more pretentious picture, but Wronsky unconsciously gave offense by asking if the study were for sale. The question of money seemed out of place and ill-timed to the sensitive artist. He answered, with a slight frown:

"It is offered for sale."

Before leaving the studio, Wronsky had bought the picture and had arranged with Mikhaïlof that he should paint Anna's portrait.

CHAPTER V

ENVY

MIKHAÏLOF came to the palace upon the day appointed and commenced his picture of Anna. At the fifth sitting it had assumed a likeness of her which surprised Wronsky.

"I made innumerable efforts, one after another," he said, speaking of the portrait he himself had painted, "and with small success. He has only to look once at her to catch the likeness. There lies the difference between one who understands his art and one who does not."

"It will come to you with time and practice," said Golinitchef, consolingly. for in his eyes Wronsky had decided talent, and was bound, sooner or later, to make a name for himself as an artist.

Away from his own studio, Mikhaïlof appeared a different man. When visiting the palace he was respectful without humility, and careful to avoid all intimacy with people whom he at heart did not care for. He would always address Wronsky as "your excellency," and, in spite of Anna's frequent invitations, could not be induced to dine with them, or to appear at the palace save for the appointed sittings. Anna was more kind to him in her manner than the others were; Wronsky treated him with marked politeness, and constantly asked for his criticism on his own efforts; Golinitchef lost no opportunity of endeavoring to inculcate in him his own particular views on art. But Mikhaïlof remained as cold and repellant as ever. Even with Anna he refrained as much as possible from conversation; while, to Wronsky's questioning, he maintained an obstinate silence, and took no trouble to conceal the weariness which Golinitchef's discourses caused him.

The ill-concealed hostility soon produced a general feeling of discomfort, and the feeling of relief was general when the sittings in due time came to an end, and the artist's visits to the palace ceased. His portrait, now that it was finished, was an admirable work of art.

Golinitchef was the first one to express the opinion that the painter was envious of Wronsky.

"What makes him furious," he said, "is to see a man rich, well-born, and generally fortunate, attain without much trouble a position in art as good as, if not better, than his own. He has consecrated his whole life to painting; but you possess a culture of spirit which such a man as Mikhaïlof can never hope to attain to." With all of which, it must be owned, Wronsky was very far from disagreeing, try as he might to fight the artist's battles behind his back.

The latter, for his part, was happy at being delivered from Golinitchef's discourses and Wronsky's pictures. He could not prevent these amateurs from puerile attempts to fathom his own art, and yet, mixed with the amusement it afforded him, was a large amount of indignation. Wronsky's work produced a curious effect upon him; it caused him actual annoyance; it was ridiculous and pitiable.

Wronsky's infatuation for painting was of short duration. He was possessed of sufficient artistic instinct to recognize his own faults, and to see that the further he advanced the more marked they became. The discovery did not disturb his equanimity; he simply laid down his brush and abandoned painting without seeking to justify himself or explain the cause.

But life without any special occupation in a small Italian town became intolerable; he grew tired of the palace, of Golinitchef's perpetual society, of his Italian teacher, and the few travelers he occasionally met; he felt that he must change his present existence.

Anna was much surprised at his abrupt disenchantment, but consented very willingly to return to Russia. Wronsky was desirous of passing through St. Petersburg to transact some business which required his presence, and Anna hoped to be able to see her son. The summer they would spend in the country, upon the Wronsky family estate.

CHAPTER VI

TEARS

LEVINE had now been married for about three months. He was happy, though in a different fashion from what he had imagined, and, in spite of certain unforeseen delights, he was met at each step by some disillusion. Married life was very different from what he had anticipated. Formerly, when a mere youth, he had often smiled inwardly at what he looked upon as the small miseries of conjugal life—quarrels, jealousies, and unworthy preoccupations. His own condition, he thought, should never allow of such things, and he would prove an exception to the generality of husbands. And yet, here were these same smallnesses, these indefinable trifles which were able to disturb the current of life. Like mos other men, he had imagined that his love would be completely satisfied in marriage; that it would bring him rest after his work; that his wife would be content to be worshiped and adored; and, in so thinking, he had totally ignored the fact that she also could claim some rights by reason of her own personality. Great was his surprise to discover that the innocent and charming Kitty was capable of forming an opinion for herself, and that, not only where domestic matters were concerned, but on broader questions and the more important topics of the day.

Their small and unimportant quarrels were a matter of surprise to him. He had never supposed that, even for a few moments, their relations toward each other could be anything but tender and affectionate; and here, even in the first days of marriage, disputes were not uncommon. Kitty would declare that he thought only of himself, and would close all argument by a furious burst of tears.

The reconciliation always followed very soon. Kitty, though she would not acknowledge it, felt that it was she who had been in the wrong, and would lavish such tenderness upon her husband as to increase, if possible, their mutual love. And yet these constant scenes had an effect upon both of them, and the first few months of the married life from which Levine had expected so much were by no means devoid of painful memories.

One evening, when Levine returned home from a visit to an outlying farm, and joined his wife in her own sitting-room, he found her reading a letter which had just arrived from her sister Dolly.

"Here is a letter for you," she said, holding out an envelope addressed in a strange handwriting. "I think it must be from—from that woman—your brother's—but I did not open it. Dolly sends me such a nice letter; she took little Grisha and Tania to a children's ball at the Sarinatzkys'."

But Levine was not listening. He had taken the letter, which he saw was from Marie Nicolaevna, the former mistress of his eccentric brother Nicolas, and glanced at it. It was the second communication he had lately received from her. The first told him that Nicolas had driven her away from him for no fault of hers, adding, with touching sincerity, that she herself wished for no assistance, but was solely anxious on his account. The second was different in tone. She had rejoined Nicolas, and set out, in his company, for a provincial town where he had received some official appointment; shortly, however, after arriving there he had quarreled with one of his chiefs, thrown up his appointment, and returned to Moscow. On the way he had been taken suddenly and dangerously ill. "He is constantly asking for you," the letter said, "and we have no more money left."

Kitty noticed that her husband was affected by what he was reading. "What has happened?" she asked.

"She writes that my brother Nicolas is dying. I must go to him."

Kitty's whole countenance was changed. The doings of her little nieces vanished from her mind.

"When shall you start?" she asked.

"To-morrow."

"Can I go with you?"

"Kitty! what an idea!" he exclaimed, almost reproachfully.

"And what is there strange in the idea?" asked Kitty, hurt at seeing her proposition received in this manner. "Why should I not accompany you? I shall not be in your way—"

"I myself am merely going because my brother is dying. What could you do there?" said Levine; and he thought: "At a moment like this, so serious for me, she only thinks of the dullness of being left alone." "It is out of the question," he added, aloud.

His tone wounded Kitty still more.

"I tell you," she said, angrily, "that if you go I go also. I should like to know why it is out of the question. What reason have you for saying so?"

"Because God only knows in what wretched way-side inn I may find him," said Levine, striving to retain his calmness. "I am not even sure of the proper route to take. You would only hinder me."

"Not at all. I need nothing. Where you go I can go."

"You appear to forget this woman—a woman with whom you can not come in contact."

"And why? I have nothing to do with her history," said Kitty. "It is no business of mine. I only know that my husband's brother is dying; that my husband is going to him, and that I accompany him so that—"

"Kitty, do not be unreasonable. Think how it must vex me to see that when I am in such grief your only thought is not to be left alone. If you are afraid of being dull, you can go to Moscow while I am away."

"That is like you!" cried Kitty, with tears of anger in her eyes. "You al-ways credit me with mean thoughts like that. I am not so weak and foolish; I feel that it is my duty to be with my husband at such a time, and you purposely wound me by pretending to misunderstand me."

"This is simple slavery!" cried Levine, rising from the table, no longer able to control himself. The words were hardly out of his mouth, when he perceived the injustice of them.

"Why did you marry me, then, if you already repent it?" and Kitty rushed from the room.

When he joined her, she was crying bitterly.

He strove to find words, not to persuade her, but to calm her; she would not listen, nor admit the truth of any of his arguments. He bent over her and kissed the hand she unwillingly let him hold, and still she kept silence. But when, at last, he took her face between his hands and spoke some loving words, she softened. The tears flowed again and the reconciliation was made.

They decided to set out together. Levine assured her that he was well aware her only object was to be of use to him, and that no awkwardness would arise from the presence of Marie Nicolaevna; but, at the bottom of his heart, he was annoyed with himself and with his wife. It was strange that he, who at one time could not credit his own happiness in being loved by her, now almost felt that it was possible to be too well loved. He looked forward with dread to the inevitable meeting of his wife and his brother's mistress; the idea of seeing them together in the same room filled him with horror and disgust.

CHAPTER VII

DYING

THE provincial hotel where Nicolas Levine lay dying was even worse than Constantin had anticipated. It was a small, shabby, and ill-kept house, and its general appearance of dirt and discomfort affected him most painfully. The best rooms, such as they were, were occupied, and Levine and Kitty had to content themselves with a small, ill-furnished apartment, and the promise of better ones as soon as they should be vacated.

Levine, at his wife's request, left her to look after all arrangements and hurried to his brother's room. As he reached the door, he found himself face to face with Marie Nicolaevna, whom he had already met at his brother's house in Moscow.

"Well, how is he?" he asked.

"Very, very ill. He can not leave his bed, and asks continually for you. Is—is your wife with you?"

Levine, as he told her, fully expected that the news would render her confused; but she said quite naturally:

"Well, I will go down-stairs. He will be very glad to see you—and her also."

Before she could leave the room, the door of Kitty's room opened and she herself appeared. Seeing the position his wife was placed in, Levine blushed, and Marie Nicolaevna also; she leaned against the wall of the passage and nervously twisted her hands in her shawl, almost ready to cry. Levine noticed the momentary glance of curiosity which Kitty threw at Marie Nicolaevna.

"Well, what is it?" she asked her husband.

"We must not stand talking in the passage," he said, irritably.

"Then let us go in—or, rather, do you go alone. I will wait in our own room," replied Kitty, as Marie Nicolaevna retreated down-stairs.

Levine entered his brother's room.

It was a small and stuffy room, badly furnished, unclean, and with great cracks in the plaster of the walls. Upon the tumble-down bed, barely covered with the dirty bed-linen, lay a body which at first sight seemed a corpse, so thin, emaciated, and washed away was it.

"Can this be my brother Nicolas?" thought Levine; but a second glance at the features, worn as they were, at once dispelled all doubt.

He took his brother's hand; the latter smiled, but so feebly as barely to change his features.

"You did not expect to find me like this," he said, feebly.

"Yes—no," answered Levine, confused. "Why did you not let me know sooner? I could not discover in what part of the country you were."

His brother said nothing, but continued to look at him, and Levine's embarrassment increased. He spoke of his wife having accompanied him, at which a look of satisfaction came upon the sick man's face. Then there was silence for a few moments, which Levine broke by saying that he would go for his wife. He was only too glad of an excuse to escape for a few seconds, and relieve his over-strained nerves.

But when once outside the room, he regretted that he had promised to bring his wife, and determined to persuade her that the visit would be useless. "Why should she be pained?" he asked himself.

"Well, what is the matter?" asked Kitty, alarmed at the expression of his face.

"It is awful! Why—why did you come with me?"

Kitty was silent for an instant, and then, taking her husband's arm, she said in a gentle voice:

"Kostia, take me to him. It will be better for both of us. Take me to him and leave me with him. Can you not understand that it is much harder for me to witness your suffering, without having seen the cause? Perhaps I can be useful to him, and to you also. I beg of you to let me go," and there was deep entreaty in her voice.

Levine silently consented, and they left the room. He had, for the moment, forgotten Marie Nicolaevna's existence.

Kitty walked lightly by her husband's side, her face full of courage and affection. When they entered the sick-chamber, she advanced to the opposite side of the bed so as not to cause the invalid to turn his head. She placed her young, fresh hand in that of the dying man, and began to speak with gentle animation.

"I am your sister," she said, "though you have never seen me, and, perhaps, have hardly heard of me; but a day never passes that Kostia does not remember you and distress himself at receiving no news of you."

The sick man's face was lighted up for an instant by a smile; but it soon faded, and the former expression of pain and suffering returned.

"I am afraid you are not very comfortable here," continued Kitty, avoiding his fixed look, and glancing round the room. "We must get another room for him, and one near it for ourselves," she said to her husband.

From that moment Kitty took entire charge of the sick man. As for Levine, unused to the ministrations of a sick-room, overcome by its atmosphere, the complaints of the invalid, and the thousand other little disagreeables of severe illness, he was practically useless, and wandered in and out of his brother's room, unhappy in his presence, still more unhappy when away from him.

Kitty dispatched her husband to seek a new doctor, and during his absence effected a complete change in the sick-room. When Levine returned with the physician, he could hardly recognize the room or its principal occupant. The air was fresh and sweet, scented with some aromatic perfume; the bed and all its linen was clean and new, and Nicolas himself, supported by soft pillows, was washed and reclothed, and, sick though he might be, looking a different man. On every side were traces of the handiwork of Kitty herself, her maid, and Marie Nicolaevna.

The doctor whom Levine had brought with him made a careful examination, shook his head ominously, but without expressing his opinion at the moment, wrote out a prescription, and gave some general directions as to diet and treatment. When he had gone, Nicolas said something to his brother, who was only able to catch the one word "Katia," which he saw at once was the other's affectionate term for his sister-in-law. He called her to the bedside.

"I feel much better now," the sick man murmured, "and it is entirely owing to you." He took her hand and made a motion as if he would have kissed it, but seemed to fear her displeasure, and contented himself with caressing it. "Let me turn upon my left side," he went on, "and then you must all go and get some sleep."

Kitty alone understood his words. With her husband's assistance she changed his position on the bed, rearranged his pillows, and made him comfortable. He now took his brother's hand in his, and Levine, not trusting himself to look, could feel that he had raised it to his hot and feverish lips. He feared that the sobs would rise to his own throat and choke his utterance; so, without a word, he hurriedly turned away and left the room.

CHAPTER VIII

THE LAST SMILE

"Do you think that his recovery is possible?" asked Levine of his wife when they were alone.

Late as it was, he felt that he could neither eat, nor sleep, nor remain still for any length of time. The wonderful ease with which this young girl—his wife—had adapted herself to the needs of the sick chamber; the tender care with which she had treated his brother, anticipating his every want, cheering and consoling him; and in addition to all this, the attention she found time to bestow upon himself and his own comfort in a strange hotel, had impressed Levine to a marked degree, and made him the more conscious of his weakness and want of nerve, strong man though he might be.

"I asked the doctor," said Kitty, replying to her husband's question, "and he says he can not live more than three days

at most. However, one can never tell. I am so glad I was able to induce him to receive extreme unction to-morrow."

It was seldom that the subject of religion was mentioned between the young husband and wife. Kitty was well aware of Constantin's views on such questions, or, perhaps, it would be more correct to say his want of them. She had determined to leave everything to time; and though, since her marriage, she continued her own religious duties with her accustomed enthusiasm and regularity, she abstained from all comment upon the difference of their opinions. She knew that at heart he was a good man and a good Christian—perhaps a better Christian than herself, she often thought.

"Yes," said Levine, "this woman—Marie Nicolaevna—would never have been able to persuade him. I will own to you that I am very, very glad you came with me. You have changed disorder into order, discomfort into comfort." He took her hand and pressed it, and she could read contrition in his eyes.

"You could not have borne it alone," she said, striving to hide the blush of happiness on her cheeks. "I learned a great deal about sickness when I was abroad last year. I was an invalid myself, you know."

The sacrament was administered to Nicolas next day, and he received it with strange fervor, his face full of passionate supplication and hope as he gazed upon the holy image. Levine, as he stood near and watched him, was filled with troubled thoughts and doubts.

"God, if Thou dost exist," he said to himself, "heal this, my brother, and Thou wilt save us both!"

The sick man's condition seemed wonderfully improved after the religious ceremony. He was even able to sit up and take some solid food; but after that he fell into a short sleep, from which he woke with a return of all the worst symptoms, and exhausted by a succession of terrible fits of coughing.

Levine sat by his bedside, holding his hand, throughout the night. Once or twice, when he thought that Nicolas was sleeping calmly, he tried to rise and steal quietly away, but always the sick man would move uneasily and whisper in a troubled voice, "Don't leave me; don't go away." It was not until day came that Levine was able to obtain any sleep.

His condition remained almost unchanged for the three following days. It was now plain to every one, even to the dying man himself, that recovery was hopeless. His sufferings became intense, and each one of those by his bedside was secretly longing for the moment when release should come.

Kitty herself had given way at last, and was forced to submit herself to the doctor's advice and care; he ordered complete rest and quiet, but she was obstinate in her refusal to keep entirely away from the sick-room, and persisted in at least sitting by the bedside and occupying herself with embroidery or other work.

Toward evening, on the fifth day, Nicolas became so weak as to be unable to move his arms; his face took a fixed expression which did not change in the least even when his brother or sister-in-law bent over him—it was doubtful whether he could still see them. Kitty sent for the priest once more, to recite the prayers for those in their last anguish.

Nicolas gave no sign of life beyond, when the prayers were over, uttering a slight sigh and opening once his eyes. The priest laid the cross upon his cold forehead, and laying his hand upon that of the dying man, said quietly, "It is over."

Then Nicolas's lips trembled slightly, his chest heaved, and in the stillness of the room the words were heard: "Not yet—soon—"

The next instant his face was lightened up, a smile passed on to his lips, and all was over.

* * * * * * *

Levine's grief was bitter. At times it seemed as if but for his wife's presence he would have given way entirely to his despair. This death had filled his whole being with terror, but a terror which made clear to him his need of living and loving.

Hardly had he witnessed the accomplishment of one mystery—that of death —than a new miracle even more strange was presented to him—that of life. The doctor announced that Kitty was *enceinte*.

CHAPTER IX

CONDITIONS

WHEN Karénine, through the offices of Oblowsky and the Princess Betsy, learned that every one, and Anna most of all, expected him to relieve his wife of his presence, he was intensely troubled. Incapable for the time being of acting on his own responsibility, he ended by accepting all that was proposed to him.

He hardly realized the true meaning of it until the day after Anna's departure, when the English governess came to him to ask whether she should for the future dine with him down-stairs, or, as formerly, in the school-room. For the first few days, he continued to hold his receptions, to repair to the meetings of the Council, and to dine at home, as had always been his custom; his one effort was to appear calm and indifferent. He answered all the questions put to him by the servants in regard to future arrangements, as if their mistress's departure was a matter of course, and in no way extraordinary. The effort lasted over two days; on the third, the strain became too great. He felt that his courage was not great enough for such a struggle; he ordered his carriage, and from that time either dined away from home or in the strictest privacy.

Karénine had lost his mother when he was but ten years of age; his father he had never known, and his brother and himself were left orphans with a moderate fortune between them, their education and bringing up being undertaken by an uncle, a man of influence and in high favor at Court. On completing his studies at the Gymnase and the University, Karénine, thanks to this same uncle, found a brilliant opening for an administrative career. He devoted himself entirely to his work, and possessed no intimate friends save only his brother, and he indeed left Russia for an indefinite mission abroad soon after the marriage of Alexis.

It was during his tenancy of a provincial governorship that Karénine became acquainted with Anna's aunt—a woman of great wealth—who schemed and planned for the marriage of her niece to the newly appointed governor.

At last there came a day when Alexis Alexandrovitch recognized that he must either ask the girl's hand in marriage or resign his office. For some time he hesitated, and might eventually have chosen the less risky course had not a friend of Anna's relative pointed out to him that, by his marked attentions, he had compromised the girl, and, as a man of honor, should declare himself.

He did so; and from that moment, first upon his finances and then upon his wife, he showered the entire amount of affection his nature was capable of.

His attachment for her sufficed to him in place of any other intimacies. He had numerous relations, a large acquaintance among the most prominent and influential people, was always ready to entertain socially, or be entertained; but that was the limit of his cordiality.

The only intimates that he had in St. Petersburg were the chief of his own cabinet and his physician. The former, Michel Wassilievitch Sludine, a brave gentleman, simple, honest, and intelligent, was full of sympathy for him. But the traditions and unwritten laws of public service placed a barrier between them which prevented all confidence. Many a time, after they had transacted some business together, Karénine was sorely tempted to open his heart to his subordinate; but when the moment came, he felt that his lips must remain closed on that one topic, and in place of the confidence he longed for, he would close the interview with some cut and dried formula of official routine.

The doctor, whose goodness of heart was equally well known to Karénine, was a very busy man, and it seemed as if by some tacit but well-recognized understanding, that this one subject was to remain tabooed.

As for his ordinary friends, and chief among them the Countess Lydia, Karénine never for a moment dreamed of unbosoming himself to them. He was almost afraid of women, and did his best, as a rule, to shun them.

CHAPTER X

LYDIA

BUT if Karénine, in reviewing his possible confidants, had omitted to think of the Countess Lydia, she, for her part, thought much of him.

Her first visit to him was made at the moment when he sat with his head bowed between his hands, overwhelmed by his despair. She entered his library without waiting to be announced, her bosom heaving with emotion and agitation.

"Alexis Alexandrovitch, my friend!" she exclaimed, "I know all!" and she pressed his hand in hers, looking in his face with her beautiful, deep eyes.

He rose in some confusion, and placed a chair for her.

"Be seated, countess," he said, with trembling lips. "I am suffering too much to receive visitors."

"My dear friend!" she simply repeated; but he could see that the tears were very near her eyes. He raised her hand to his lips and kissed it.

"I am utterly broken down," he continued; "weak and powerless. It is not my loss that I feel so much as my shame in the eyes of the world. If you could only know all the details! A man's strength has its limits, countess, and the limits of mine have been reached. Every action of my day brings to my mind my solitary situation. Servants, governess, household accounts, all serve to constantly remind me. Yesterday, at dinner, I could not bear my little son's looks—he is afraid of me."

"I understand, my friend, I understand everything," said the countess. "I can not hope to bring you any real help or consolation; but I have come to offer you my services, to try and relieve you from these wretched little cares and anxieties which should not be allowed to trouble you. A woman's hand is needed here; let me offer you mine."

Karénine was silent, and merely pressed her hand.

"We will both occupy ourselves with little Serge," she went on. "I have had little experience with children, but sufficient to be able to assist you. You must not thank me—it is not I who do it—"

"Not thank you!"

"No, my friend," replied the countess, whose one weakness was for religion and religious motives in all her acts; "you must thank Him to whom you must pray. In Him alone can we find true peace, consolation, and love!"

Though at another time such expressions might have seemed superfluous and have displeased him, Karénine, in his present distress, was inclined to make allowances, to recognize the meaning rather than the words.

"I am more than grateful to you for your words and your promises," he said.

The countess again took his hand in hers.

"Now I am going to commence at once," she said, wiping from her cheek the traces of her tears. "I am going to see Serge. I shall appeal to you in every serious matter."

She rose and went to the child's nursery. There, while her tears fell upon the boy's cheeks, she told him that his father was a saint, and that his mother was dead. From that time she fulfilled her promise, and relieved Karénine from most of his domestic anxieties. She had not exaggerated, however, in speaking of her own inexperience, and the more important direction of the household affairs soon passed into the hands of Karénine's *valet de chambre*, Kornei. The countess, however, was quite content; her chief aim was the consolation of Karénine himself and his conversion to her own pronounced religious views. She meant that her affection and esteem should prove a moral support for him, and, despite her methods, her end was by no means unsuccessful.

CHAPTER XI

AT TEA

THE Countess Lydia had been married when still a young girl. Her husband was a young man of great wealth, excellent family, and dissipated to an exceptional degree.

Two months after their marriage he left her, responding to her effusive tenderness with an ironical, almost diabolical smile, the meaning of which was hard to fathom. The count's good nature was known to every one, and Lydia, romantic as she was, had never laid herself open to the world's criticism. Since then husband and wife, though not legally separated, had lived apart from each other, the count's invariable greeting to her being the same mysterious, bitter smile.

Having long ago removed her husband from the list of her adorers, the countess had so far made a point of never being without a favorite—sometimes, indeed, she had several simultaneously—and, whether it were man or woman, the one qualification she insisted on was, that he or she should be in some way known to fame. At different times it had been

some prince or princess newly allied to the imperial family; at others her favor had been bestowed upon a metropolitan, a grand vicar, a noted journalist, a celebrated doctor, an English missionary and many others in rapid succession, the last of whom was Karénine. Her feelings toward him soon merged from mere interest into affection; she felt that she had liked none so well as him. More than once she found herself thinking of what might have been had they both been free.

For several days the countess had been much perturbed in mind. She had heard of the return of Wronsky and Anna to St. Petersburg, and was sorely puzzled as to how she could most surely spare Karénine the pain of seeing his wife again.

The next news that reached her was that the guilty couple, having attended to their affairs, were about to leave the city the next day, and she was just commencing to feel reassured, when a note was brought to her, whose address she recognized as in the handwriting of Anna.

"Who brought this?" she asked.

"A messenger from the hotel," was the reply.

For some time the countess sat without the courage to open the letter. When she grew calmer she tore open the envelope and read:

"MADAME LA COUNTESS,—The sentiments of Christianity with which I know your heart to be filled give me the courage to address you. I am unfortunate enough to be separated from my son, and ask your permission to see him once before my departure. My reason for not addressing myself directly to Alexis Alexandrovitch is that this generous man may be spared the pain of being troubled with my affairs. Knowing your friendship for him, I have thought that you would understand me in this. Will you send Serge to see me?—or, should you prefer it, I will come at any hour and to any place you may think best. When I think of the nobleness of character of her who must decide this, a refusal seems to me impossible. You can not imagine how I am longing to see my child again, nor the gratitude I shall forever feel toward you for lending me your support in this matter.   ANNA."

The whole contents of the note irritated the Countess Lydia beyond expression, more especially the allusions to Karénine's nobility of mind, and the general tone of easiness with which it was worded.

"Say that there is no answer," she said to the servant; and sitting down at the table, she wrote to Karénine, begging him to come to her as soon as possible, as she had something of importance to consult with him about.

It was rarely that a day passed in which the countess did not send Karénine two or three notes or messages. She enjoyed the little mystery, and the suggestion of familiarity which this means of communicating with him implied.

When Karénine entered the Countess Lydia's boudoir, she was seated at a table on which tea had been prepared, and was evidently anxiously awaiting him.

"At last!" she exclaimed, rising to greet him. "Now we can be alone and quiet here while we take our tea." Then she added: "I have received a note from *her*. She is in here in St. Petersburg"; and with a blush upon her face, she held out Anna's letter.

He read it, and was silent for some time.

"I do not think that I have the right to refuse her," he said at last.

"My dear friend, you can see no bad in anything."

"On the contrary, I find bad in everything. But would it be just?" and his look expressed his indecision, his desire for another's advice, for some one to lean upon.

"There are limits to everything," said the countess, firmly. "I can understand immorality; but what I can not understand is such wanton cruelty. And toward whom? Toward you! How can she remain in the same place where you are? One is never too old to learn; and every day I learn more and more of your goodness and her baseness."

"Who shall be the one to cast the first stone?" said Karénine. "Having once pardoned her, can I refuse her the one need of her heart, her love for the child?"

"But is this love? Is it all sincere? You have forgiven her, and will do so still further, I hope. But are we justified in troubling the mind of this poor little child? He believes her to be dead; he prays for her and asks God's pardon for her. What would he think now?"

"I have not looked at it in that light," said Karénine, feeling the justice of her reasoning.

The countess covered her face with her hands, and was silent for some moments.

"If you ask my advice," she said, at last, slowly, "you will not grant this permission. Can I not see how you suffer, how your wound still bleeds? Even supposing you put aside your own feelings, what will it lead to? You will be bringing new suffering and new trouble to the child. If she had any feelings of humanity left, she would be the first to acknowledge this. No; I should be firm in your place; and if you will authorize me, I will answer her."

Alexis Alexandrovitch consented, and the countess wrote as follows:

"MADAME,—Such a meeting could not take place without causing your son to ask questions concerning matters which it were better he should never know of.

"On these grounds you will understand that your husband's refusal is made in all Christian charity.

"I pray that the Almighty may be merciful to you.

"COUNTESS LYDIA."

The effect of this reply produced the effect which the countess resolutely conceded from herself—it wounded Anna to the very bottom of her soul. Karénine, on his part, returned home troubled in his mind, unable to attend to his usual occupations, nor to find peace within himself.

He could not drive out from his mind the cruel reminiscences of the past. He recalled Anna's first confession. Why had he not compelled her to respect the conditions and decencies of her world? Why—and this thought troubled him most of all—why had he not challenged Wronsky? His first letter to his wife, his usual forgiveness, the care he bestowed upon her infant, all came back to his memory and filled his heart with shame and confusion.

"But in what have I myself been to blame?" he asked himself. It cost him a terrible effort to drive away these thoughts and to remember the line of conduct he had laid down for himself—

peace and charity toward all. His present suffering made any future reward seem like some empty dream. Happily the struggle did not last long. Karénine gradually recovered his calmness and the elevation of his spirit, thanks to which he was able, in some measure, to forget.

CHAPTER XII

ST. PETERSBURG

WRONSKY and Anna were staying at one of the principal hotels of St. Petersburg.

On the first day of his arrival, Wronsky went to his brother's house, and there met his mother, whom some business had brought to St. Petersburg. Both she and his sister-in-law, Maria, received him as usual, questioned him about his travels, gossiped about their mutual friends, but made no allusion whatever to Anna. His brother, calling on him the next day, was the first to speak of her. Alexis took the opportunity of explaining to him that he regarded his *liaison* with Madame Karénine as a virtual marriage and that he desired his mother and sister-in-law to clearly understand his intentions.

"The world may not approve it," he added, "but that is a matter of indifference to me. If my own family, however, wish to remain on good terms with me, they must receive her as my wife."

His brother, who always paid great deference to his younger brother's opinions, did not attempt any solution of this knotty question, and called upon Anna in company with Alexis.

In spite of his knowledge of the world, Wronsky had fallen into a strange error. He who better than most others, should have understood that Society's doors would be forever closed to them, imagined, through some strange process of reasoning, that public opinion would lay aside all old-fashioned prejudices, and receive him on his own terms. "In any case," he said to himself, "even if the official world is critical, our own relations and friends will understand things for what they are."

One of the first women of the fashionable world whom he met was his cousin, the Princess Betsy.

"At last!" she cried in a glad tone; "and Anna, how is she? Where are you staying? How commonplace and dull St. Petersburg must seem to you after your travels? And the divorce—is it all arranged?"

Her enthusiasm, Wronsky noticed, visibly decreased when she heard that no divorce had as yet been obtained.

"I know they blame me," she said; "but I am coming to see Anna. You will not remain here for long, I suppose?" As a matter of fact, she called upon Anna that same day, but her tone had now completely changed. She seemed to wish to call attention to the fact that her visit to Anna was an astonishing proof of friendship. After chattering for ten minutes, she rose and said, as she took her leave: "You have told me nothing about the divorce. Of course I myself am not foolishly prejudiced, but I warn you that others may have different views, and will be correspondingly chilly in their manner. It could be so easily arranged, too! You leave Thursday, you say? I am sorry we shall not see more of you."

Betsy's tone had opened Wronsky's eyes in some degree to the reception which awaited them. He wished, however, to make another experiment with his own family. He was very sure that his mother, in spite of her attractions to-ward Anna when they first met, would now be inexorable toward one whom she deemed had ruined her son's career; but he rested great hopes on Maria, his sister-in-law. She, for certain, would have no stone to fling at Anna, and would come to see her as a matter of course.

The next day he called on her, and, finding her alone, stated his case.

"You know, Alexis, how much I think of you," she answered, "and how devoted I am to your interests; but what has sorely grieved me is the impossibility of my being of any service to Anna. Do not imagine for one moment that I allow myself to judge her; I might, perhaps, have acted just as she has, had I been in her place. I do not wish to go into any details," she said, nervously, noticing the cloud upon his brow; "but it is sometimes absolutely necessary to call things by their right name. You would have me call upon her so that, in turn, I could receive her in my own house and reinstate her in society. I simply *can not* do so. My daughters are growing up; I am forced, if only on my husband's account, to go into society. Supposing that I did visit Anna Arcadievna, I should still be unable to invite her to my house for fear lest she should meet some one holding different views from my own. Would it not simply wound her? It is not in my power to raise her up—"

"I do not for one moment admit that she has fallen," interrupted Wronsky, rising from his seat; "nor would I think of comparing her to scores of women whom you receive."

He was sure that his sister-in-law would not yield.

"Alexis, please do not be angry; it is not my fault," said Maria, with an attempt to smile.

"I do not blame you," he replied; "but my trouble is now doubled. I regret that our friendship should be broken off, or, at least, strained; but you must surely understand that it is inevitable."

With these words he left her; and being now convinced of the hopelessness of any further attempts, he determined to look upon himself as one in a strange place, and to run no risk of additional repulses.

In addition to all this, Anna's own bearing annoyed him. He now saw in her some strange moral disposition which he himself could not fathom; she was affectionate and cold in turn, but constantly irritable and mysterious in her manner. There was plainly something on her mind which troubled her, and instead of perceiving how her conduct at times caused Wronsky suffering, she appeared to be simply preoccupied in concealing her own cares and perfectly indifferent to aught else.

CHAPTER XIII

MY DARLING BOY!

THE one thought which filled Anna's mind on her return to St. Petersburg was to see her son. "It was a simple and natural thing," she thought, "to see one's own child when living in the same town with him." But as the time passed on, the difficulty of obtaining such an interview seemed to increase.

How was she to act? She could not call at her husband's house and run the risk of being refused admission, nor could she bring herself to write to Karénine. The old nurse who formerly had charge of Serge, and who would have assisted the mother, had left the house. After two days of doubt and indecision, Anna decided to write to the Countess Lydia.

To see the messenger return without an answer was a cruel disappointment to her. She felt wounded and humiliated, even though she was forced to admit that the countess had reason on her side.

She had no one in whom to confide, and this, perhaps, was worst of all. She knew that Wronsky would not understand; that he would treat the matter as one of no great importance, and that his want of sympathy would enrage her. The greatest fear she had was lest she should sometimes grow to hate him. She would say nothing to him of her plans to see her child.

At last she decided to write directly to her husband.

At the very moment she was commencing the letter, the Countess Lydia's answer was brought to her. Silence she could have borne, but the animosity, the irony which she was able to read between the lines of this note, revolted her.

"What cruelty! what hypocrisy!" she thought. "They wish to wound me and to torture the child. I will not let them do it. She is far worse than I—I, at least, am not a liar!"

The next morning early, Anna stepped from a carriage, and rang the bell of her former home. On the way, she had bought a large box of his favorite sweetmeats for the child, and in her hand she held sufficient money with which to bribe the servants, if necessary; her face was covered with a heavy veil.

The door was opened by a young footman whose face was strange to her.

"Whom do you wish to see, madame?" he asked.

"I come—I come from Prince Skaradoumof, to see Serge Alexeitch."

"He has not yet risen, madame," said the man, noticing her agitation, and striving to see her features through the veil which hid them.

She pressed some money in his hand.

"If your excellence will enter, I will go and see," he said. "I will inform his tutor."

He mounted the staircase, and Anna, with silent footsteps, followed him. Even now, through the quiet of the house, she could hear the boy's prattling voice.

"Let me go to him," she said, quickly. "I know the way."

She pushed her way into the room, and in a second was beside the little cot on which her son was lying.

"Serge! My darling boy!" she exclaimed in a voice choked with tears, as she passed her arms around the little white-robed body.

"Mamma! mamma!" he cried, nestling in her arms and gazing up at her with childish eyes still full of sleep.

The thought flashed across Anna that the boy was not as she had left him. He seemed older, and to have lost much of his childish plumpness; his limbs were so much larger than those of her Serge; but yet it was he himself, the dear little face, the eyes, the lips; it was her own little Serge!

"I knew you would come," he said, striving to open his sleepy eyes as wide as possible. "It is my birthday. I will get up at once."

Anna devoured him with her eyes, she pressed him still closer to her heart, and her tears now hindered her from speaking.

"Why do you cry, mamma?" he asked, now wide awake. "Why do you cry?" and his own tears were near.

"I—I will not cry any more, darling—it is from joy. It is so long since I have seen you. It is all over now," she said, stifling her tears. "Now you must get up and dress;" and without letting go his little hand, she sat on a chair beside the bed. "How do you manage to dress yourself without me? How—"

"Wassili Loukitch helps me. But you haven't seen him, have you? He will be here presently. But see; you are sitting upon my clothes!" and the child commenced to laugh.

Anna looked at him and smiled herself.

"Mamma, dearest!" he cried, throwing himself once more into her arms as he saw her smile.

"What did you think had become of me?" she asked. "Did you think that I was dead?"

"No; I never believed it."

"You did not believe it?"

"No; I knew very well it wasn't true;" and taking the hand which was stroking his head, he pressed the palm against his little mouth and kissed it over and over again.

"Koutia, dear," she murmured, using the name she had given him when he was a baby, "you will not forget me; you will not forget your—"

She could not finish.

There was so much she had come prepared to say to him, and now she could find no words. But Serge understood everything. He felt that his mother loved him, and that she was unhappy; he knew that his father was concerned in it, and that he—his father—must not meet his mother. What he could not understand was the expression of affright and shame on his mother's face. Of what was she afraid, and why did she blush? He would have liked to ask her, but dared not, for he knew it would be adding to her grief.

He pressed himself against her and murmured:

"Don't go yet, mamma. *He* will not be here for some time."

His mother held him from her for one moment to try and read from his face whether he knew what he was saying. The child's expression told her that he had spoken of his father.

"Serge, my boy," she said, "you must love him. He is better than I am, and I have been to blame toward him. When you are older, you will know."

"None is better than you," cried the child, throwing his trembling little arms about her neck.

"My dearest! my dearest!" exclaimed Anna, herself now weeping.

At this moment the door opened, and the tutor, Wassili Loukitch, entered the room. Serge fell upon his bed sobbing, and covered his face with his hands. Anna drew the hands aside, and having kissed the little, tear-stained cheeks, quickly left the room.

In the passage she came face to face with her husband. He stood still at sight of her and bent his head.

Though, a moment before, Anna had said that he was better than she, the one rapid glance that she directed toward him was full of hatred, distrust, and jealousy on her son's account. She lowered her veil and almost ran from the house. When she regained her carriage, she saw that in her haste she had left upon the seat the sweetmeats chosen with such sad and loving care for the child she had just parted from.

CHAPTER XIV

SOON

ANNA, although she had prepared her-self beforehand, had not expected that the sight of her son would cause her such great emotion. When she was once more in her rooms at the hotel, she asked herself why she had gone. "All is over now," she said to herself; "I am quite alone!" and sinking into a chair, she abandoned herself to a succession of sad thoughts and remembrances.

The Italian nurse entered the room, carrying her little daughter, dressed to go out. The child, seeing its mother, smiled and beat the air with its little hands, stretching them out toward Anna.

She took the infant upon her lap, fondling it, and kissing the dimpled fingers; but even the sight of this, her little daughter, merely recalled to her her great love for Serge.

In former days all her tenderness had been lavished upon him, the child of a man whom she had never loved; and her little daughter, born under such sad conditions, had never received a hundredth part of the care which had been bestowed upon Serge. Having given the child back to its nurse and seen them set out for their walk, Anna opened a locket which contained a portrait of Serge at the same age as the little girl; then she opened an album and took from it all the other portraits she could find of him.

As she was closing the book, her eyes fell upon a photograph of Wronsky taken when they were in Rome.

"There he is," she said to herself, and suddenly called to mind that he was the author of all her sufferings. During the whole morning she had not thought of him, but the sight of his picture filled her heart with love.

"Where is he? Why does he leave me here alone with my grief?" she asked herself, bitterly, forgetting that she had carefully concealed from him the visit to her son. She immediately sent a message to his room, asking him to come to her, and waited for him, her heart beating in anticipation of the tender words with which he would console her. The servant returned to say that Wronsky was entertaining friends, but wished to know if she would receive him with Prince Yashvine, who had just arrived in St. Petersburg. "He does not care to come alone," she thought, "though I have not seen him since yesterday, before dinner. I can say nothing to him, as Yashvine will be with him." And then came the cruel thought: "If he should have ceased to love me!"

She reviewed in her memory several incidents of the past few days, and found what she thought was confirmation of this terrible idea. The previous evening he had not dined with her—he had passed the night in his own room, or, at least, not in hers—and now, as if fearing a tête-à-tête, he was coming to her accompanied by a friend. "But it is his duty," she said to herself, "to confess it to me, and mine to find out for myself. If it be true, I know well what to do." She rang for her maid, and changed her costume with more than her usual care.

When she entered her sitting-room again, the first person that she noticed was Prince Yashvine examining the portraits of Serge which she had left upon the table.

"We are old acquaintances," she said, advancing to the prince, a man of gigantic stature, and laying her small hand in his tremendous palm. "We met at the races last year, I think;" and with a rapid movement she gathered up the photographs from the table and handed them to Wronsky. "Was this year's meeting successful?" she continued. "We saw the races at Rome, on the Corso. But I know you take no interest in foreign life. Though we have met so seldom, I think I know your tastes."

"I regret to hear it, for I fear they are generally bad," said Yashvine, gnawing his long mustache.

After a few minutes' conversation, the prince, noticing that Wronsky was looking at his watch, rose to take his leave, and asked Anna if she intended to remain in St. Petersburg for any length of time.

"I think not," she answered, with a troubled look at Wronsky.

"Then we may not meet again," said Yashvine; and turning to Wronsky: "Where do you dine to-night?"

"Come and dine with me," said Anna, quickly, and with a slight blush. "The dinner here, perhaps, is not very good; but you can see for yourself, and I know how glad Alexis will be of your company."

"I shall be delighted," said Yashvine, with evident sincerity. "It is *au revoir*, then?" and left the room.

"Are you going also?" Anna asked Wronsky.

"I am late already. Go on; I will follow you," he called to his friend.

She took his hand, and looking in his face, tried to speak to him of what she had been thinking.

"I have something to ask you," she said, pressing his hand against her cheek. "Was I wrong to invite him to dinner?"

"You were perfectly right," answered Wronsky, with a quiet smile.

"Alexis, you have not changed in your feelings toward me?" she asked, still holding his hand between her own. "I can not stay here any longer. When do we leave?"

"Oh, soon. You have no idea how unpleasant being here is to me also," and he drew his hand away.

"Well, go if you must," she said in a wounded tone, and walked quickly into her private room.

CHAPTER XV

IRRITATION

WHEN Wronsky returned to the hotel, Anna was not there. He was informed that she had gone out with a lady. The fact of her having gone out without leaving any message, joined to her recent agitation and the tone in which she had spoken to him, set Wronsky thinking. He decided to wait for her and ask an explanation.

Anna was not alone when she came back. One of her aunts—an old maid, the Princess Oblowsky—had been shopping with her, and, as if unconscious of Wronsky's uneasiness of manner, Anna began to give a humorous account of all that they had seen and done. The expression of her eyes, however, and her nervous movement told him that she herself was also far from easy.

They were on the point of sitting down to dinner, which was laid for four, when Toushkewitch, an intimate friend of the Princess Tverskoï, was announced. He was the bearer of a message from Betsy to Anna. Betsy sent her excuses for not being able to call and say good-bye, and begged that Anna would come and see her between eight and nine, as she herself was indisposed. Wronsky looked at Anna, to see how she would take the invitation—evidently given for an hour when she would not be likely to meet any one else—but Anna seemed not to notice it.

"I am very sorry," she said, with an almost imperceptible smile, "but I shall not be free at that hour."

"The princess will regret it exceedingly, I am sure."

"And I also," said Anna.

"Perhaps you are going to hear Patti?" asked Toushkewitch.

"Patti? You have given me an idea—I would certainly go if I could get a box."

"I think I can get one for you," said Toushkewitch.

"I should be very much obliged," replied Anna; "but will you not stay and dine with us?"

Wronsky shrugged his shoulders. He could not understand her. Why had she brought the old princess with her? why asked Toushkewitch to dinner? and, more especially, why did she wish for a box? Could she, in her position, think of going to the opera on a subscription night? The whole of St. Petersburg would be there. He looked at her questioningly, but she was careful to avoid his eye.

After dinner, through the whole of which Anna had been exceptionally gay and lively, Toushkewitch went away to obtain the box, while Yashvine and Wronsky repaired to the latter's rooms for their cigars. After some time Wronsky returned to Anna's apartments and found her in full evening dress.

"Are you really going to the opera?" he asked.

"Why ask the question with such a

frightened air? I can see no reason why I should not go."

'No, I suppose there is no reason," he said, frowning.

"That is precisely what I said myself," she replied, tranquilly, drawing on her long, perfumed glove.

"Anna, in Heaven's name, what has come over you?" he exclaimed, seeking, as her own husband had often done, to awaken her from some trance or dream.

"I do not understand what you wish."

"You know very well that you can not go there."

"Why not? I shall not be alone. The princess has gone to change her costume, and will accompany me."

Again he raised his shoulders, discouraged.

"Do you not know—?" he began.

"I know nothing," she cried; "and I wish to know nothing. I do not repent of anything that I have done. I would do it all over again. There is only one thing of importance between you and myself, and that is to know if we love each other. The rest is nothing. Why do we live here cut off from all the world? Why can I not go where I wish? I love *you*, and if you have not changed toward me, nothing else matters to me. Why do you look at me like that?"

He was looking at her wonderful beauty, and this very beauty and elegance was precisely what irritated him.

"You know very well that my feelings can never change; but I beg you not to go."

Though his face was stern and cold, there was entreaty in his voice.

She merely noticed his looks, and answered in a tone of annoyance:

"And I—I beg you to explain to me why I should not go."

"Because it will subject you—" he paused, troubled.

"I do not understand you. Toushkewitch can not compromise me; and, as for the princess, she is no worse than any one else. Ah! here she is!"

CHAPTER XVI

ANNA AT THE THEATRE

FOR perhaps the first time in his life, Wronsky was fairly angry. What troubled him was his inability to explain to Anna that, in appearing at the opera with a person like the princess, she was throwing down the glove to public opinion, which would vote her a lost woman, and effectually dissipate any chance of her re-entrance into society.

"Why does she not understand?" he asked himself. "What is passing within her?"

He found Yashvine still smoking and consuming vast quantities of brandy and soda. For a time they resumed their talk of horses, racing, and other kindred matters; but Wronsky could not drive from his mind the thought of Anna and her strange behavior, and Yashvine soon saw that his companion was ill at ease and paying little heed to his own remarks.

"Well, let us go," he said at last. "It is getting late."

"No, I shall not go," said Wronsky, gloomily.

"Very well," replied the other; "I must, for I promised. *Au revoir*. If you change your mind, you had better take Krasinski's stall—you will find it vacant."

"A wife is sometimes tiresome," thought the prince as he left the hotel, "but a mistress is still worse."

Wronsky sat alone, thinking over all that had happened, and picturing Anna exposed to the gaze and criticisms of the whole of St. Petersburg society.

"And I? Why am I afraid?" he suddenly said to himself. "Why have I left it to Toushkewitch to protect her? It is absurd. Why has she placed me in such a foolish position?"

He rose from his chair, rang for his valet, and dressed himself for the opera. When he reached the theater, the brilliant and crowded audience was listening breathlessly to the liquid notes of the great prima-donna. When her song was ended and the house rang with applause, he made his way to the vacant seat and examined the rows of boxes through his lorgnette.

His eyes soon discovered Anna sitting in front of a box above him, tapping one hand gently with her fan and looking straight before her with the evident intention of disregarding something which was passing beside her. Yashvine was by her side, and from the way in which he was biting his huge mustache, a heavy frown upon his face, it was plain that he, too, was ill at ease.

In the box next to them were the Kartasofs, people with whom Anna had formerly been intimate. Madame Kartasof, a small, thin woman, was standing up, her back turned upon Anna, and arranging on her shoulders the cloak which her husband held for her; her face was pale, as if with anger, and she was speaking hurriedly and with agitation.

The husband, a stout, bald-headed man, while glancing at Anna, was using all his efforts to calm his wife. In a few moments their box was empty.

Though Wronsky understood nothing of the scene, he felt sure that something had happened to humiliate Anna. He quickly left his seat, for the *entr'acte* was now in progress, and went upstairs to his brother's box. His mother was sitting there, while Maria and a friend were standing, talking by the open door. Maria at once took Wronsky's arm and led him to one side.

"It was vile and mean!" she exclaimed, excitedly. "Madame Kartasof had no right to do it!"

"What was it? I know nothing at all," he said.

"Have you not heard?"

"You know very well that there are some things which I am the last to hear. What has Madame Kartasof done?"

"It was my husband who told me. She has insulted Madame Karénine. Her husband spoke to Madame Karénine, in the next box to theirs, and she made a scene—she used some offensive term in a loud tone and then left the box."

At this moment his mother sent for Wronsky to come and speak to her.

"I am always expecting you," she said as he entered the box; "but nowadays I never see you. How is it that you are not paying court to Madame Karénine? She has made the sensation of the evening. Even Patti is forgotten."

"I have begged you not to talk to me like that," said Wronsky, gravely.

"I only say what all the world says."

Wronsky said no more on the subject, and presently left the box. He felt that he had some duty to perform—but what? He was full of anger, furious at the false position in which Anna had placed herself and him, and yet he felt a great pity for her.

He entered her box.

"It seems to me," said Anna, addressing him, "that you have come very late; you have certainly missed the best piece," and her tone was bitter and mocking.

"I am a poor judge," he answered, looking at her with a serious look.

"Like Prince Yashvine," she said, with a smile, "who thinks that Patti sings too loud."

As she finished speaking, a tremor passed her lips. She rose from her seat and retired to the back of the box.

The last act had hardly commenced, when Wronsky, looking up from his seat, saw that Anna's box was empty. He left the theater and returned to the hotel.

Anna had just arrived. When he entered the room, she was sitting on the nearest sofa, looking straight before her, just as she had been when he first saw her at the opera. She threw a glance at him, but did not move.

"Anna—" he began.

"It is you—you who are the cause of everything!" she cried, rising from her seat, tears of rage and despair in her voice.

"I prayed you, I begged you not to go. I knew that you were drawing something disagreeable on yourself."

"Disagreeable!" she interrupted. "It was horrible! If I were to live for a hundred years, I could never forget it. She said that she was disgraced by sitting near me!"

"The speech of a fool! But why have you risked it? Why expose yourself to—"

"I hate your quietness. You should not have driven me to this. If you had any love for me—"

"Anna, why talk like that now?"

"Yes, I say again, if you loved me as I love you; if you suffered as I am suffering—" and there was a look of absolute terror on her face.

He was filled with pity for her, and began to protest his love, which he saw was the only means of calming her; but, at the bottom of his heart, he felt angry and bitter toward her.

She, on the contrary, greedily drank in his words of love, and, by degrees, recovered her composure.

Two days later they left St. Petersburg for the country, completely reconciled.

PART V

CHAPTER I

SUMMER

The invitation which Levine and his wife extended to Dolly and the Princess Cherbatzky to pass the summer on their estate was readily accepted. Stépane, so far as his wife was concerned, was delighted with the arrangement. His own country house was in sad need of repairs, and as his occupations compelled his frequent presence in Moscow,

he was only able to join the party from time to time. Like most mothers, the Princess Cherbatzky considered her presence indispensable for the well-being of Kitty in her present state of health, and watched the young wife's every movement with maternal solicitude and care.

It was not long before Dolly discovered that Wronsky and Anna were spending the summer at a small estate of the former's, distant some seventy versts from the Levine mansion. She at once made up her mind to visit Anna, of whom, in former times, she had always been extremely fond, and who, in any case, was her own husband's sister.

With some hesitation she announced her intention to Levine, asking him where she could best hire horses and a conveyance for the journey.

"Why should you imagine that I could feel at all annoyed at the idea of your meeting Wronsky?" he said; "and, moreover, you will really offend me if you talk about using any other horses than mine, even if I would allow you to hire them. Those you would get could never make a trip of seventy versts."

So Dolly was forced to submit, and on the appointed day she set out, entirely alone, in a roomy, old-fashioned carriage of Levine's.

The drive was long and uninteresting, and the afternoon was well advanced when the carriage, containing its tired and dusty occupant, entered the grounds of Wronsky's house.

Anna and Wronsky met her on the steps in front of the house.

"Dolly! What an unlooked-for pleasure!" cried Anna, embracing her. "You can not tell how glad I am to see you! Alexis"—turning to Wronsky—"is it not nice?"

He raised his hat and greeted Dolly cordially. "Your visit makes us both very happy," he said; and then, addressing Anna: "What room shall we give the princess?"

"The corner room, facing the balcony —it is nearest to my own. I hope you

are going to stay some time with us, Dolly. What? Only one day? Impossible!"

"I have promised to return to-morrow on account of the children," said Dolly.

"Oh, but it can not be! However, we will talk about that later on. Let me take you to your room now;" and with the gladness of a young girl, she led Dolly upstairs to the beautifully furnished chamber near her own.

"You are looking at me," she said, with a sigh, "and wondering how, in my position, I can be so happy. I will own that it is very wrong of me. But I am like one enchanted. My past unhappiness seems like a nightmare—especially since we came here."

"I am glad to hear you speak like that," said Dolly. "But why have you never written to me?"

"I had not the courage."

"Courage? To write to *me?* If you knew—"

"Tell me," said Anna, interrupting her, "what do you really think of me?"

"I think nothing," answered Dolly. "I love you, and have always loved you. When one loves a person, one loves her for what she is, not for what one, perhaps, would wish her to be."

"If I had not feared that you would misunderstand me, I would have asked you all to come and see us. Stiva is an old friend of Alexis'," said Anna, blushing.

Dolly was confused, and hardly knew what to say.

"The joy of seeing you makes me unreasonable," said Anna, again embracing her. "But you must promise to be quite frank with me, and to keep nothing back from me, now that you are going to see what my present life is. My one aim is to live so as to bring evil on no one but myself. But we will talk of all this later on."

"And your little daughter, how is she?" asked Dolly.

"Anny? Oh, she is very well. Would you like to see her? Come with me, and I will show her to you. We have had much trouble with the wet nurse—an Italian woman—but as the baby is very fond of her, we have been obliged to keep her."

"But what have you done—" began Dolly, wishing to ask what name the child bore. She stopped short, seeing a cloud gather on Anna's face. "Have you not weaned her yourself?" she added, quickly.

"That was not what you were going to say," replied Anna, reading her sister-in-law's silence. "You were thinking of the child's name, were you not? It is Alexis' one trouble that she has none but Karénine."

The nursery was a spacious, well-furnished room, equipped with every new and costly luxury for enhancing infantine comfort. An English nurse, a woman of vulgar, and—in Dolly's eyes—unpleasant appearance, was with the child. The little girl, with her black hair, healthy looks, and amusing ways went straight to Dolly's heart; but there was something displeasing to her in the general aspect of the nursery. How could Anna keep a woman such as the nurse was, whose appearance suggested how little she had been used to "respectable" households? Anna herself seemed like a stranger in her own child's nursery. She knew nothing of its toys and such trifles, and could not answer the dozen little questions which one

mother puts to another when she sees her child.

"I feel that I am useless here," she said, as they left the room. "How different it was with the elder one!"

"On the contrary," began Dolly, timidly, "I should have thought—"

"Oh, no! You know I looked after Serge entirely myself," said Anna, with that fixed look as if she were seeking something far off. "But I am like some creature dying of hunger, and who, finding itself in the presence of plenty to eat, does not know what to commence with. It is you who have brought me this plenty, and to whom, if not to you, can I open and lay bare my heart? But now we must go down-stairs and join Alexis."

CHAPTER II

HE WILL DESPISE ME!

DURING the afternoon Dolly found herself alone with Wronsky. Anna had been called away on some domestic matter.

"I think I am right," he said, gravely, "in looking upon you as one of Anna's truest friends."

Dolly felt uneasy. What was he going to say or ask of her? To beg her to receive Anna in her own circle when they should come to Moscow; or, perhaps, to make some inquiry as to Kitty's welfare and condition?

"Anna loves you very dearly," he continued, after a moment's silence. "Will you use your influence over her in my behalf? Of all her former friends, you are the only one—I speak of friends—who has come to see her. I know that it is not from any approval of our relations, but simply that you are sufficiently attached to her to be anxious to make her situation more supportable. Am I not right?"

"Yes; but—"

"No one could feel more bitterly than myself"—he went on, interrupting her —"the difficulties of our life. Unless you consider me utterly heartless, you will give me credit for so much."

"Most assuredly," said Dolly, touched by the sincerity with which he spoke. "But do you not exaggerate these difficulties? The world, perhaps, condemns you—"

"It is simply purgatory! You can not picture the agony which Anna suffered at St. Petersburg."

"But not here. And neither you nor she, I suppose, have any wish to return to your old world?"

"How could I wish it?" exclaimed Wronsky, impetuously.

"You are spending a pleasant life here, and can continue to do so. As for Anna, from what she has had time to tell me, she is perfectly happy."

"Yes," he replied; "but will that happiness last? I am frightened of the future. Have we acted for the best or the worst? The die is cast; we are joined together for life. We have a child, and may have others; but," he added, "my daughter is Karénine's. If I were to have a son to-morrow, he would be a Karénine, unable to inherit my name or my property. Can you not understand what a frightful thought this is? Picture to yourself the feelings of a man who knows that his children—the children of the woman he adores—do not belong to him; that for a father they have a man who must necessarily hate them, and who will never recognize them. Is it not horrible?"

He stopped, overcome by his emotion. "But what can Anna do?"

"Now," said Wronsky, controlling himself, "you have touched upon the real subject of our talk. Anna can obtain a divorce. Your husband obtained Monsieur Karénine's consent to it, and all that was required was that Anna should have written to him. And that is why I am repeating to you, princess, as the one friend who can assist us: help me to convince Anna of the necessity for demanding a divorce."

"Willingly, very willingly," said Dolly, recalling her interview with Karénine; but her first thought was: "Why has not Anna reasoned with herself like this?"

"Yes," she added, aloud, "I will certainly speak to her;" and their conversation ended as dinner was announced.

It was not until they had retired for the night that Dolly and Anna found opportunity for their talk. As Dolly was undressing, the door of her room opened, and Anna, clothed in a white dressing-gown, came in.

"And how is Kitty?" asked Anna, seated near the window and looking at Dolly with a curious air of humility. "Tell me the truth: does she not bear me a grudge, and dislike me?"

"No, no," said Dolly, smiling; "but you know there are some things a woman never forgives another."

"That is very true," said Anna, quietly, gazing out through the open window. "Kitty is happy, is she not? I am told her husband is an excellent man."

"There is none better. Kitty is very happy. But now tell me about yourself. I have had a talk with—" She paused.

not knowing by what name to speak of Wronsky.

"With Alexis," interposed Anna, "and I can guess what your conversation was about; but still I would like you to tell me."

"We spoke on a subject which I should have avoided with you had he himself not mentioned it—of the possibility of rendering your present position right and formal in the eyes of the world."

"You mean through a divorce? Betsy Tverskoï has urged the same thing; not that I wish to compare you two for a moment—she is the most depraved woman in existence. Well, what did he say?"

"That he is suffering on your account and on his own. If that implies selfishness, it springs from a sense of honor. He would legitimize your daughter, become your husband, and assume a husband's rights."

"Could a wife belong to her husband more completely than I do to him? I am his slave."

"But he can not bear to see you suffer And, then it would legitimize your children—give them a name to bear."

"What children?"

"Anny, and those you still may have."

"Oh, you can be easy on that point. I shall not have any more."

"Anna! How can you speak like that?"

"Because I do not wish to have any. You think I am wicked and immoral, but you must remember that such children would be unfortunate creatures, compelled to blush for their parents and their own birth."

"That is precisely why you should obtain a divorce."

"Perhaps, if it were possible," said Anna, quietly.

"I am told your husband would consent."

"He would *not* consent. He is under the influence of the Countess Lydia."

"But why not try?" urged Dolly, gently, her heart full of sympathy for Anna.

"Supposing I were to try—even supposing I were to succeed, after humbling myself in the dust before him—would he let me have my son? No He will grow up in his father's house—the father whom I have deserted—and learn to despise me. Picture it! The two people whom I love most, whom I love equally—Serge and Alexis—can never come together!"

She passed up and down the room, her hands pressed against her breast, her face full of grief.

"They are all I have to love in the world," she continued, "and I can not unite them. Nothing else matters to me. You do not know what I suffer." She sat down beside Dolly and took her hand. "Do not despise me—I don't deserve it; but rather pity me, for what woman was ever more wretched?" And she broke down and wept.

* * * * * * *

In spite of the persuasions of her hosts, Dolly was firm in her resolve to return home the next morning. She breathed more freely when at last she found herself some distance from the house and the horses' heads turned toward their own stable. Her leave-taking of Anna had been very sad, for Anna felt that perhaps the last attempt had been made to restore her to her former and her better self, and Dolly, on her part, could see no light ahead in the life of her unhappy friend.

She found her children well and anxiously awaiting their mother's return. To the others she described the elegance of Wronsky's house and the cordiality of her reception, but would not allow herself to make any critical remarks.

"To understand just how they are," she said, "one must see them at their own home."

CHAPTER III

ANNA'S LETTER

WRONSKY and Anna spent the whole summer and a great part of the autumn in the country without any thought or plan for their future movements.

During October the elections for the government of Kachine—the province in which Wronsky's estate was situated —took place, and, in fulfillment of a promise given some time before, he decided to assist in person.

It was not until the eve of his departure that he told Anna of his coming absence for several days, and even then he spoke coldly and curtly, dreading an outbreak of unreasonable jealousy on her part.

To his surprise, she received the news quite calmly, merely asking him the exact date of his return.

"I hope you will not be lonely while I am away," he said, trying to read her real feelings from the expression of her face.

"Oh, no," she answered quietly; "I have just received a parcel of books from Moscow. They will occupy my time."

He went away without any further explanation, but with a vague sense of uneasiness in his mind. The little scene, though so few words had been spoken, left a painful impression in the minds of both.

Anna, though she made heroic efforts to accept his absence stoically, was hurt by the cold and imperious manner in which he announced his departure. "Of course," she said to herself, "he has the right to go and come as he pleases—he has all the rights, while I have none. Still, it was not very generous of him to make me feel it. And his looks? Surely he is wearying of me."

During the day she occupied her mind and endeavored to banish all such thoughts with her household cares and duties; to gain rest at night she had recourse to morphine. In the state of mind at which she had now arrived, a divorce seemed to her the only means by which she could prevent Wronsky from abandoning her. Divorce implied marriage, and she resolved that so soon as he should again broach the subject, she would no longer resist.

So five days passed, and on the sixth her little daughter was attacked by some childish and trifling indisposition. Anna sent a message by special dispatch, telling Wronsky of the child's severe illness, and no sooner had it gone than she regretted having sent it. What would he say and think on finding that the child's illness had been a mere passing trifle? Yet his return would mean happiness for her. Doubtless he would regret his liberty and find his domestic ties irksome: but he would be there;

she would see him, and would not lose sight of him again.

She sat by the table, endeavoring to read by the light of a shaded lamp the latest work of Taive and listening to the wind and storm outside. Her nervousness increased each movement. She begrudged the child its recovery to health, for now the emptiness of her excuse for recalling him was apparent.

When she heard at last, however, the wheels of his carriage, every other thought vanished but that she was about to see *him,* her lover. She ran downstairs and met him in the hall as he was removing his traveling cloak and wraps.

"How is Anny?" he asked at once, before she reached him.

"Much better. And you?" She seized both his hands and drew him toward her.

"I am very well," he said, coldly examining the dress which he knew she had put on to please him. Though such attentions pleased him, they had done so now for a long time, and the fixed look of sternness did not leave his face. "How have you been yourself?" he asked, kissing her hand, and they passed upstairs.

The evening passed cheerfully enough. Wronsky related the different episodes of the election in which his party had been victorious, and Anna told him of all the little trifles which had occurred during his absence and which she thought would please him.

Before retiring for the night, Anna determined to discover what effect her message had had.

"Own that my letter displeased you," she said, "and that you do not believe what I said was true."

"Yes," he answered—and in spite of the tenderness of his manner she could see that he had not forgiven her—"it was certainly very strange. You wrote me that you were exceedingly uneasy about her, and yet you expressed a wish to come to me."

"Both were true."

"I do not doubt it."

"Yes, you do doubt it; I can see that you are annoyed."

"Not at all. The only fault I have to find is that you will not admit the possibility of my ever having business of importance to attend to. However, we will say no more about it."

"And why not?"

"I have only this to say—speaking of business—it is absolutely necessary for me to go to Moscow."

"So," said Anna, with a sudden change in her tone, "you return one day, only to leave again the next. If you are tired of this life—"

"Anna, do not be unkind. You know that I am ready to sacrifice everything for you."

But she went on, without appearing to hear him:

"When you go to Moscow I shall go with you. I will not remain here alone. Let us live together or separate forever."

"My only wish is to live with you; but, for that, it will be necessary—"

"A divorce? I will write at once. I see now that I can not continue to live like this. I will follow you to Moscow."

"You say it in a very threatening tone," said Wronsky, smiling; "but it is all that I myself wish for."

His look, as he said this, was that of a man exasperated by continual persecution, and Anna saw it and understood it. The impression she gained in that moment never afterward left her mind.

She wrote to Karénine, demanding a divorce, and toward the end of November arrived with Wronsky in Moscow.

CHAPTER IV

THE CALL

THE Levines had been in Moscow for two months, in order that Kitty might avail herself of the best medical attendance during her confinement, which was now close at hand.

While her husband looked forward to the event with fear and trembling, she herself was quite calm and confident. For her, the little one already existed, the proof of which was best shown by her frequent sufferings. She felt a new love springing up in her heart. Never had her happiness been so complete; never had she been so caressed and petted by all around her. The only shadow to her joy was her husband's condition; he was restless, gloomy, and excited by turns; his quiet dignity and composure, to which she had become accustomed, were gone, and she felt a genuine pity for him. Moscow could furnish no fitting occupation for him; the life of such friends as Oblowsky had no charm for him, and for this Kitty was devoutly thankful. Nor did he care for the society of women, even of those who now belonged to his own family.

The most important event of Kitty's life at this time was her meeting with Wronsky—a meeting which took place one day at the house of her godmother, the Princess Marie Borissowna. She was calling there with her father, and when Wronsky was announced, she felt her heart begin to beat tumultuously, and as if every drop of blood in her veins had rushed to her face.

The old princess hastened to draw Wronsky into a political discussion, and Kitty soon felt that she had regained entire control over herself. She exchanged some words with Wronsky, joked with him about his prominent part in the recent Kachine elections, and then, devoting her conversation to her godmother, did not turn her head toward Wronsky until he rose to take his leave; then she bid him a simple and courteous adieu.

When Wronsky had gone, her father made no remark whatever concerning the unexpected meeting; but Kitty could see that he was well pleased with her and the manner in which she had borne herself.

When she next saw her husband, she told him of the meeting.

"I was sorry you were not present," she said, "or, rather, I would have liked you to be looking at and listening to us through the keyhole; for, had you been there, I should probably have lost my self-command. See how I am blushing even now."

Levine himself was blushing even more than she. Her words and sincere look dissipated any annoyance he might have felt at his wife's meeting with Wronsky. Hitherto he had avoided all chance of meeting the count, but now he said to himself that the idea of flying from any man, however much he might formerly have been mixed up in his life, was childish and absurd. In future he would rather court than avoid such meeting. The opportunity to prove his words came even sooner than he expected. Dining one evening with Sté-

pane Oblowsky at his club, they met
Count Wronsky in the smoking-room.

"I think you have both met before,"
said Stépane, full of the good humor
consequent upon an excellent dinner and
still more excellent wine. "Levine," he
added, addressing Wronsky, "is one of
my two dearest friends, and as you are
the other, I want to see you both as
friendly to each other as I am."

"Then all we have to do is to embrace
immediately," said Wronsky, laughing,
as he held out his hand to Levine. The
latter pressed the hand which was offered him, and said, cordially: "I shall
be very pleased to carry out Stépane's
wishes."

"And I also," rejoined Wronsky; but
in spite of their mutual satisfaction in
meeting, they were both at a loss what
next to say.

"Levine has not yet met Anna, you
know," said Stépane, "and I want to
introduce him."

"She will be changed," answered
Wronsky. "I would ask you to come
with me at once; but I must stay here
and look after Yashvine, who has been
dining too well, and is now in the card-
room. He is quite capable of losing
everything he possesses, and I am the
only one who seems to have any influence over him;" and he left the room
to rejoin his friend.

"Why should we not call on Anna
without him?" said Stépane, taking the
other's arm. "I have promised for a
long time to take you. What are you
doing this evening?"

"Nothing at all. I will go with you
with pleasure."

"Agreed!" said Stépane; and having
ordered his carriage, the two men left
the club and drove to Anna's house.

CHAPTER V

A REMARKABLE WOMAN

As they entered the house, Levine
felt decidedly nervous. He followed
Stépane up the stairs, glancing in the
mirrors which lined the stair-way, to
see if his confusion was apparent in his
face. Madame, the servant told them,
was in the library with a visitor—Monsieur Varkouef.

They passed into an anteroom in
which hung the portrait of Anna,
painted by Mikhaïlof, in Italy. Levine
stood before it fascinated. To his mind,
a more beautiful woman could not exist.

"I am very glad to see you," said a
voice, evidently addressed to him; and,
in the half obscurity of the room, Levine recognized the original of the picture, dressed in a simple, tasteful
fashion, but bearing the same charm
which the artist had been quick to note.

She welcomed him most warmly, and
led the two men into the library, where
she introduced them to her other visitor
—Varkouef.

"I am glad to meet you," she said to
Levine, "for—thanks to Stiva and your
wife—I seem to have known you for a
long time. I shall never forget the impression the Princess Kitty made upon
me—she is like some beautiful flower.
I hear she is soon to become a mother."

She spoke so naturally that Levine at
once felt at his ease, and as if they
were old acquaintances.

"May we smoke?" asked Oblowsky.

"It is for that purpose we have taken
refuge in Alexis' library," she answered,
offering a cigarette-case to Levine and
taking one herself.

"And how are you to-day?" asked
Stiva.

"Oh, very well; rather nervous, as usual," she answered, carelessly. "If you will take some tea with me, I will ring," rising from her seat and removing a book which lay upon the table.

"Will you let me see that?" said Varkouef, pointing to the book, which had been written by herself.

"No, no; it is stupid and amateurish. I am sure Monsieur Levine would—"

"I have already told him about it," interrupted Stépane.

"You were wrong. My little scribblings are like the works written by prisoners, which their friends outside the prison sell for them—they are works of patience."

In Levine's eyes the *abandon* with which this woman spoke was an additional charm; she seemed to have no wish to avoid the thorns and difficulties of her situation, and her serious expression heightened the beauty of her face. A feeling of tenderness and pity for her overpowered him. Anna allowed her two visitors to pass into the salon, and herself remained behind to talk with Stiva. Of what was she speaking? Of the divorce? of Wronsky? Levine was so moved by his own thoughts that he did not hear a single word of the rhapsodies Varkouef poured forth on the book which she had written. As they drank their tea, the conversation became general; but through it all Levine was listening only to Anna, admiring her intelligence and culture, her wonderful, yet natural tact, and seeking to analyze her inner thoughts and sentiments. He who had formerly been so prompt and severe in his judgment of her, now thought only how to make excuses for her, and the idea that she was suffering and that Wronsky was unconscious of it grieved him to the heart.

It was quite late when they rose to take their leave; but to Levine it seemed as if their visit had lasted but a few minutes.

"Good-bye," said Anna, holding his hand, and with a look in her eyes which troubled him. "I am glad the ice is broken. Tell your wife that I think as much of her as formerly, and if she can not condone the position I am in, tell her how fervently I hope she may never come to understand it; for, before one can forgive, one must have suffered."

"I will tell her," answered Levine, simply.

"Was I not right?" asked Stépane, when they had left the house. "Is she not a remarkable woman?"

"Yes," answered his friend, "she *is* a remarkable woman. One can see that her attraction is not merely outward. She has a good heart; but she is suffering."

"Yes, her situation is sadder than ever it was. We have been arranging for the divorce—her husband has given his consent, but difficulties have arisen on account of her child, and for three months matters have not advanced at all. However, I hope everything will soon be arranged. When the divorce has been granted, she will marry Wronsky and her position will then be acknowledged and secure."

Their ways lying different, they bid each other good-night and parted.

CHAPTER VI

THE BARRIER

WHEN her visitors had gone, Anna commenced to pace up and down the room, deep in thought. She did not conceal from herself that for some time past she had found it possible to indulge in a certain amount of coquetry or worse toward different men, and, in this case, she owned that she had done her best to turn Levine's head. But although he had pleased her, and although, like Kitty, she found some secret likeness between him and Wronsky, it was not of Levine she was now thinking. One idea, and one idea only, possessed her.

"Why, if I can exercise an attraction over a married man, and one who is in love with his wife, can I no longer attract *him?* Why has he become so cold? He loves me still, but there is something dividing us. He has kept away all evening, with the excuse of taking care of Yashvine—as if Yashvine were a child! Can he not understand the horror of the life I am leading?" and tears of pity for her own lot started to her eyes.

The bell sounded, and Anna hastily recovered herself, and taking up a book, made a pretense of reading.

Wronsky entered the room, and coming to her, asked in a cheerful and animated tone, if she had not grown tired of waiting for him.

"Oh, no," she answered; "I have ceased to do that, and, besides, Stiva and Levine called upon me."

"Yes, I know. And were you pleased with Levine?" he asked, seating himself by her.

"Very much; they have only just left. What did you do with Yashvine?"

"What a terrible gambler he is! He won seventeen thousand roubles, and I succeeded in getting him away from the game. Then he gave me the slip, went back, and at this moment has probably lost everything."

"Then why look after him?" said Anna, curtly, raising her head and meeting Wronsky's cold glance. "After telling Stiva that you would stay with him and keep him from playing, you end up by deserting him."

"In the first place, I gave Stiva no authority to say anything of the sort," answered Wronsky in a cold and decisive tone. "In the next, I am not given to lying; and, lastly, I have acted exactly as it suited me to act." Then after a moment's silence, he added: "Anna, Anna, why this fault-finding?" He held out his hand to her, hoping that she would place her own in it. Her ill-temper held her back.

"There can be no doubt," she said, as Wronsky sharply drew back his hand, "of your having done exactly as you pleased. But why make a point of that? It is a question of stubbornness and obstinacy, and resolves itself into this— which of us shall prevail? If you only knew how, seeing your attitude against me, I feel as if I were on the brink of a precipice, how frightened I am of myself!" And she turned away her head to hide her sobs.

"But what is it all about?" cried Wronsky, frightened at this despair, and taking her hand to raise it to his lips. "Do you reproach me for seeking distraction outside? Do I not shun the society of every woman?"

"There is no necessity for that."

"Come, now," he said, "tell me what I can do to make you happy? I would do anything to save you a single grief!"

It touched him to see her so unhappy.

"It is nothing," she answered; "only being alone, perhaps—and my nerves;

let us speak no more of it. Tell me what you were doing all afternoon. Did you go to the races?" She strove to conceal the pride she felt in having forced this strong and resolute nature to bend before her.

Wronsky, while they sat at supper, told her of all his doings during the day; but his voice and his look became colder each moment, and Anna quickly understood that she must pay for the victory she had gained, and that he would not forgive her words, "I am afraid of myself; I feel as if I were on the brink of a precipice." It was a dangerous weapon to have used, and one which could no longer serve her. She felt that it had raised a barrier between them, which, strive as they might, neither she nor Wronsky could break down.

CHAPTER VII

REFUSAL

ABOUT this time Stépane Oblowsky's private affairs necessitated his presence in St. Petersburg. Before leaving Moscow for the capital, he promised Anna that he would see Karénine again on the subject of the divorce. On the pretense of submitting a scheme he had formulated in regard to the public finances, Stépane called upon Karénine, and was at once admitted. They discussed the *pros* and *cons* of Oblowsky's scheme, and the latter, indeed, was only too glad to postpone the inevitable moment when he must enter into the more delicate and family matter. At last, however, he was forced to speak.

"There is another matter I wish to speak to you about," he said, feeling uncomfortable and ill at ease. "You can guess what it is. Anna—"

Karénine's face at once assumed an expression of severity. "What is it now, that you wish of me?" he asked, taking his seat again.

"Some definite decision, Alexis Alexandrovitch. I am speaking to you now, not as"—he was about to say, "a deceived husband," but stopped himself in time—"not as a statesman and a public character, but as an ordinary Christian, a man possessed of a heart. Have pity on her."

"In what way?" asked Karénine, quietly.

"It would give you infinite pain if you could see her. Her position is a cruel one."

"I was under the impression," said Karénine, dryly, "that Anna Arcadievna had obtained all she desired."

"Do not let us bandy words, Alexis Alexandrovitch; we are not dealing with the past; what she now wishes for is a divorce."

"I understood that, in case I insisted on keeping my son, Anna Arcadievna refused a divorce. My silence, therefore, was equivalent to an answer, for I look upon that point as definitely settled," said Karénine, quite hotly.

"Let us review the whole matter calmly," replied Stépane. "At the time you separated, with unheard-of generosity you consented to let her have possession of the boy, and consented to a divorce. Then she felt too guilty toward you and too humiliated to accept the offer; but the intervening time has proved to her that, by so doing, she brought an unbearable condition of affairs upon herself."

"Anna Arcadievna's condition is of no

interest to me whatever," said Karénine, raising his eyebrows.

"You must allow me to doubt the truth of that," replied Oblowsky, quietly. "Admitting that she herself deserves all that she suffers, the fact still remains that we are all made unhappy thereby, and beg you to have compassion. Who can profit by her misery?"

"Really, one would imagine that I am to blame for it."

"No, no; I simply wish to persuade you that you can lose nothing by lightening her load of suffering. Besides, you have already promised; let me arrange the whole thing—you yourself shall not be troubled at all."

"My consent certainly was given," said Karénine, his lips trembling visibly; "but on conditions which I should have thought Anna Arcadievna would at least have had the grace to understand—"

"She no longer asks for the child. She merely wishes the means of escaping from her present position. To her it is a matter of life or death. For the last six months she has been living in a fever of doubt and expectation. Her position is like that of a criminal condemned to death, but who has no inkling as to when the fatal moment is to arrive. Again I ask you to have pity on her; and as to any scruples—"

"No need to speak of those," interrupted Karénine in a tone of disgust. "But it is possible that I promised more than I had the right to."

"Then you refuse?"

"I do not refuse as yet; but I demand time to reflect. You, I am aware, are a free thinker—I am not; and in a question so grave as this there is more than man's law to be considered."

"Does not our church sanction divorce, then?" asked Oblowsky, springing from his seat.

"Not in this sense."

"I can not understand you. It was you yourself who formerly said—"

"I shall be obliged if you will cut this conversation short," interrupted Karénine, rising suddenly and trembling in every limb.

"Forgive me for having pained you," said Oblowsky, confused, and holding out his hand; "but I was obliged to carry out the mission I was charged with."

Karénine placed his hand in Stépane's, and, after a moment's reflection, said:

"You shall have my positive answer within two days. I have much to think over, and must consult others."

Within the appointed time Stépane received from Karénine his definite refusal on the subject of divorce. He had little difficulty in ascribing the result as largely due to the Countess Lydia's influence.

CHAPTER VIII

TORMENT

NOTHING so complicates the ordinary details of life as a want of accord between the man and woman. Often one sees a family suffering for years from the effects of trifling differences which, at the start, a little mutual reasoning would have easily dissipated.

Wronsky and Anna had arrived at this condition. Spring came and turned to summer, and summer, in its turn, to autumn, and they still remained in Moscow, though their sojourn there was equally hateful to both. And yet there was no serious cause for misunderstanding between them save Anna's nervous irritability and Wronsky's cold reserve. Day by day the breach widened. For Anna there was no other object in life but love and her lover, nor could she bring herself to look upon things from any other point of view. If the count did not devote himself entirely to her, she suspected him of infidelity, and her blind jealousy caused her to suspect every woman whom she knew. Sometimes she suspected him of the gross material loves open to him as a bachelor; at others, certain women of society aroused her jealousy, and especially the young girl whom, in case of any rupture with herself, she felt sure he would marry. This particular distrust had been planted in her mind by an imprudent confidence of Wronsky's, who one day alluded to his mother's want of tact in imagining that he could and would propose to the young Princess Sarokine. Jealousy led her to such lengths that she came to look upon him, the man whom she adored, as responsible for their long stay in Moscow, the uncertainty of the life she was now living, and, worst of all, for the grievous separation from her son. Wronsky, on his side, rebelled against the false position in which Anna's obstinacy had placed him, and held her responsible for the increase of difficulties in their lives. If, in some rare moments, he lapsed into tenderness, Anna made no sign of appreciation, but seemed to look upon it as simply her right.

One evening Anna was waiting in Wronsky's library for his return from a bachelor dinner he had been forced to attend. Their last interview had been marked by a disagreement on some trivial subject which had resulted in some unjust and bitter words from her as she made her escape from the room.

In solitude during the whole afternoon she had had time to reflect, and, deeply wounded as she was by her lover's coldness, she determined to take all blame upon herself and effect a reconciliation at any cost.

"It is my foolish jealousy," she argued with herself, "which makes me so irritable. When I have obtained his forgiveness, we will go to the country, and there I shall grow calm." Her thoughts again veered round to her own sense of injury. "If he seeks to offend and hurt me, it is because he loves me no longer, because he loves another—" But with an effort she broke away from this constant and fatal thought, and, to distract her mind, gave some orders to the servants in regard to the preparations for leaving town.

Wronsky returned home about ten o'clock.

"Well, and how did the dinner pass off?" asked Anna, going toward him with a conciliating air.

"Just as such affairs always do," he answered, noticing the change in her manner. "But what is this?" he added, noticing the half-filled trunks. "Packing up? That is good!"

"Yes; we may as well leave town. The walk I took to-day made me long for the country, and there is nothing to keep us here."

"All I ask is to get away. Will you order tea while I change my coat?"

His approval of the preparations for departure was given—so it seemed to Anna—in a tone of patronizing superiority; he spoke as one might to a spoiled child whose caprices must be indulged. Anna felt an inclination to resist come over her. Why should she humble herself before this arrogance? Yet, when he returned to the room, she controlled herself and spoke quietly of the plans she had formed for leaving Moscow.

"It came upon me like an inspiration," she said; "it will at least cut short this state of ceaseless expectation. I wish to forget all about the divorce. Am I not right?"

"Certainly," he answered, noticing, with uneasiness, the emotion she displayed. "When shall we leave?"

"The sooner the better. I am afraid I can not be ready by to-morrow; but the day after—"

"That will be Sunday, and I am obliged to go to see my mother."

He noticed a look of suspicion come into her face at once. The fact that the Princess Sarokine was staying with his mother, the countess, flashed across her mind.

"Could you not go there to-morrow?" she asked.

"Impossible. The procuration to which I have to get her signature will not be ready, and without that I can not get the money I want."

"Then we will not go at all."

"And why not?"

"Sunday, or not at all."

"There is no sense in that!" cried Wronsky, astonished.

"Not in your eyes, perhaps, for you think only of yourself, and have no wish to understand what I suffer here."

"It is you who willfully and purposely misunderstand *me*," replied Wronsky. "I am always thinking of you and for you."

"That is not true; and for one who boasts of his rights—"

"I am neither accustomed to boast nor to lie," said Wronsky, with difficulty repressing his anger, "and I very much regret that you do not respect—"

"Respect," she interrupted, "was invented to conceal the absence of love. If you no longer love me, it would be more honorable in you to acknowledge it."

"This is intolerable!" exclaimed the count, approaching her almost threateningly. "There are limits to my patience —why prove them?"

"What do you mean by that?" she asked, frightened at the rancorous look he turned upon her.

"It is I who, rather, have the right to ask what you claim from me?"

"What can I claim except that you do not abandon me, as you have every intention of doing. Everything else is of small importance. I wish to keep your love, and if you no longer love me all is over."

She walked toward the door.

"Stay," said Wronsky, holding her by the arm, "what is this difference between us? I express a wish not to leave here for three days, and you reply by telling me that I lie, and that I am not an honorable man."

"Yes, and I repeat it. A man who can throw in my face the sacrifices he has made for me is worse than dishonorable—he is heartless!"

"My patience is exhausted!" exclaimed Wronsky, allowing her to go.

Anna went into her room and threw herself upon a sofa.

"He hates me!" she sobbed. "I am sure of it now, and surer still that he loves another. All is over! I must go away; but how, and where?"

All sorts of contradictory thoughts passed through her mind. Should she go to her aunt who had brought her up as a girl, to Dolly, or simply among strangers? Would this rupture be definite? What would her husband and all St. Petersburg say? A vague, half-formed idea troubled her. She recalled some words she had said to Karénine during her convalescence: "Why am I not dead?" and again the same feeling came over her. "Yes, to die is the only means of escape. My own shame, the dishonor I have brought upon my husband and my son, will all be wiped out by my death. Then *he* will regret me, and will love me."

"Anna," said a voice near her, "I am willing to do anything. We will leave the day after to-morrow."

Wronsky had quietly entered the room and was speaking in an affectionate tone. She heard his words, but did not raise her head.

"Well?" he asked.

"Do as you wish," she answered, and the sobs broke out again. "Leave me, leave me!" she murmured. "I will go away—I will do more! What am I? A lost, dishonored woman, a stone around your neck. I will trouble you no more. You love some one else; I will relieve you of myself."

Wronsky implored her to be calm, swore to her that she had no cause at all for jealousy, and strongly protested his own love for her.

"Why torment yourself like this?" he asked.

Anna imagined that she could notice the tears in his eyes and in his voice. Passing suddenly from jealousy to the most passionate tenderness, she covered her lover's face and hands with kisses.

CHAPTER IX

OUTWARD RECONCILIATION

OUTWARDLY the reconciliation was complete. As soon as morning came, Anna, without fixing the time of their departure, busied herself with packing and the various preparations. To her surprise, for the hour was still early, Wronsky entered the room dressed and ready to go out.

"I am going at once to see my mother," he said. "Perhaps she will be able to send me the money, and then we can leave to-morrow."

The idea of this visit disturbed Anna's good humor.

"No," she said; "there is no occasion to trouble yourself. I shall not be ready myself by then; but do exactly as you wish. Now, if you will go to breakfast, I will join you in a few minutes."

As she entered the dining-room, his valet brought Wronsky a telegram.

"From whom is it?" she asked.

"From Stiva," he answered, carelessly.

"Then why do you not show it to me? What secret can there be between my brother and myself?"

"Stiva has a mania for telegraphing. What need had he to send me a dispatch simply to say that nothing had been decided."

"As regards the divorce?"

"Yes. He claims that he can not get a definite answer; but read it for yourself."

Anna took the telegram with trembling fingers. Its closing words were:

"Small hope; but, possible or impossible, I will do everything in my power."

"Did I not tell you last night," she said, "that it was a matter of indifference to me. There was no necessity for your trying to conceal it from me. I was in hopes that you were as little interested as myself."

"I am interested because I like to have things clearly defined."

"Why, what need have you of a divorce, if love exists?"

"Always 'love'!" said Wronsky to himself, with a slight grimace. "You know very well," he said, aloud, "that if I wish it it is on your account and your children's."

"There will be no more children."

"So much the worse. I am sorry."

"You think only of the children, and not of me," she said, forgetting that he had included her in his wish.

"On the contrary, I do think of you, for I am convinced that your irritability is mainly owing to the falseness of your position," he replied in a cold, abrupt manner.

"I can not see how my position can affect my irritability," said Anna. "The situation seems perfectly clear to me. Am I not absolutely in your power?"

"Yes; but you distrust me and grudge me the slightest liberty."

"Oh, as to that, you can reassure yourself," she said in a provoking tone. "Your mother's plans for your marriage trouble me very little."

"We will not talk of her."

"Certainly; for I assure you a heartless woman, young or old, has no interest at all for me."

"Anna, I must beg you to have some respect for my mother."

"A woman who can not see where her son's honor lies can have no heart."

"I ask you again not to speak so of her," repeated Wronsky, raising his voice. "Whatever my mother may be, I must—"

"You must take her part," interrupted Anna; "and as for myself, I know what there is left for me to do," and she rose to leave the room.

At that moment, the door opened and Yashvine was announced. Anna, striving to conceal her agitation, wished him good-morning, then, "Have they paid you your money?" she asked—for she knew that, the previous day, Yashvine had won an immense sum.

"I shall probably receive it this morning," answered the giant, perfectly conscious that his arrival had been at an inopportune moment. "When do you leave?"

"The day after to-morrow, I think," said Wronsky.

"Do you never pity the unfortunate men who lose to you?" continued Anna, still addressing Yashvine.

"It is a question I have never considered, Anna Arcadievna. My whole fortune is here," he said, touching his pocket; "rich at this moment, I may be penniless when I leave the club to-night. I would lose my very boots to the man I am playing with, and not grumble; it is the struggle and excitement which give me pleasure."

As he spoke, another caller was announced—a man with whom Wronsky had some business—and Anna left the dining-room.

Before leaving the house, Wronsky came to the room in which she was, and searched for something among the papers on his writing-desk. Anna at first pretended not to notice him, but ashamed of such deceit, asked:

"What are you looking for?"

"The certificate of a horse I am just going to sell," he answered, indifferently.

As he left the room, having found the paper, he thought that Anna called him.

"What is it, Anna?" he asked, standing by the door.

"Nothing," she answered, coldly.

"So much the worse," he said.

In a mirror on the wall he caught sight of a face so full of sadness that the idea came to him to go back and comfort her. But it was too late; the door was already closing behind him. He spent the whole day away from the house, and when he returned home, the maid informed him that Anna Arcadievna was unwell and had begged not to be disturbed.

CHAPTER X

THE VIAL OF OPIUM

NEVER before had a whole day passed without a reconciliation, and to Anna it seemed as if this last quarrel meant indeed a rupture.

She pictured to herself the manner and the very words with which he would break off from her. "I will not hold you back," he would say; "you can go. As you will not accept a divorce, it must be that you count upon returning to your husband. If you should require any money, you have only to let me know the amount." And then, the next moment, she said to herself: "But only yesterday he swore that he loved me, and me only. He is an honest and truthful man. Have I not causelessly distressed myself before now?"

When evening came, she retired to her own room, and gave to her maid the message that she was ill. "If, in spite of that," she thought, "he comes to me, I shall know that he still loves me; if not, all is finished, and I shall know what to do."

She heard his carriage roll up to the door, his steps as he mounted the stairs, and his colloquy with the maid, Annouchka. Then his footsteps passed away, he entered his library, and Anna knew that the die was cast. Death appeared to her the only means by which she could punish Wronsky, triumph over him, and regain his love. Their departure for the country, the decision as to a divorce, were matters of no importance whatever; the one thing was— his punishment!

She took the vial of opium, and thought how easily its contents could effect all that she now desired. Then, all at once, her feelings changed, and a great fear of death came over her. "No, no," she said; "anything rather than death! I love him; he loves me also. These evil days will pass away." To shake off her fears, she took a candle and went to Wronsky's library. He was sleeping quietly. She stood gazing at him, crying softly, but careful not to awake him and doubtless meet that stern and freezing look. She returned to her room, poured out and drank a double dose of opium, and had soon forgotten everything in a heavy, dreamless sleep. When she awoke, the events of the previous day came slowly back to her.

"Why should I have given way to such despair?" she asked herself. "On account of a quarrel? It was not the first. Then I pretended to be ill, and he was unwilling to disturb me. To-morrow we must go away. I must see him, speak to him, and hasten our departure."

When she had risen, she went toward Wronsky's room; but as she passed through the salon, the noise of wheels attracted her attention and she looked out through the window. A coupé had just stopped at the door. Its occupant was a young, and, so far as she could see, a remarkably pretty girl. She heard Wronsky descend, saw him go down the outside steps and approach the carriage bareheaded. The girl handed him a package, smiling as she spoke to him; then, after a short conversation, the carriage drove away, and Wronsky again mounted the stairs.

This little scene dissipated the numbness which had come over Anna's mind, and the impression of the past evening returned more vividly than ever. How could she so abase herself as to pass another day under his roof?

She entered the library to make her intentions known to Wronsky.

"The Princess Sarokine," said Wronsky at once in a perfectly easy tone, "has just brought me the papers and the money from my mother. How are you this morning?" he added, not noticing the somber and tragic look upon her face.

She stood in the middle of the room, watching him as he glanced over the papers in his hand, and said not a word. Then she turned slowly away, and was passing from the room.

"By the way," he exclaimed, "is it settled that we leave to-morrow?"

"You, but not I," she answered.

"Anna, it is impossible for us to continue living like this!"

"You, but not I," she repeated.

"This is intolerable!"

"You—will be sorry for this," she said, and went out.

Frightened at her words and manner, his first impulse was to follow her; but he reflected for a moment, and muttering between his teeth: "I have tried every means I could think of. I must see what indifference will do," he left the room, and, presently, the house.

Anna heard him pass through the dining-room, stop in the ante-chamber and give some orders about the horse he was about to sell. She heard the carriage drive up to the door, and, running to the window, was in time to see him give some order to the coachman, and then, sitting in his usual position, with one leg crossed above the other, he was driven away.

As the carriage turned the corner of the street, he disappeared from Anna's sight.

CHAPTER XI

IN THE COUNTRY

"HE has gone!" said Anna to herself, standing by the window, and the old feeling of horror came over her. She was afraid to remain alone. She rang, and walked to the door to meet the servant.

"Find out where the count has gone," she said.

"To the stables, madame; and he left word that you should be informed that the carriage would come back and be at your disposal."

"Very well; I am going to write a note which you will take to the stables at once."

She sat down and wrote:

"I am to blame, but, in God's name,

come back. All shall be explained. I am afraid."

She sealed the note and gave it to the servant, and then, dreading to be alone, she went to her little daughter's nursery.

The little one was sitting at a table, playing with some toys in front of her. She looked up when her mother entered the room, and the movement of her eyes, the sound of her laugh, reminded Anna so vividly of Wronsky that she could not bear it. She hurried from the room. "Is is possible that the end has come?" she thought. "He will come back; but how can he explain his animation and his smile when he was talking to *her?* I will accept any excuse from him. If the worst comes, I have a remedy, and shall not begrudge it."

Ten, fifteen, twenty minutes passed, and Wronsky did not return. She looked at her watch. "Ten minutes to go, ten minutes to return; he should be here by now;" and she began to count each minute as it passed on the face of the little dial.

A carriage drove up to the door, but she did not hear his step upon the stairs. The valet brought to her the note she had given him. "The count had already gone to the Nijni railway-station," he said.

"Well, take the note to him immediately, at his mother's country house, and bring me back the answer."

What should she do while away the time of waiting? She would call on Dolly. A sudden thought came to her—she could telegraph to him.

She wrote out and sent a message: "I must speak with you. Come back quickly."

A few minutes later she was dressed in out-door costume, and on her way to Oblowsky's house.

The weather was clear and fine. During the morning a light rain had fallen, and the roofs of the houses still glittered in the bright May sunlight. It was three o'clock, and the streets were crowded and full of life and bustle.

"Are there any visitors?" she asked, as she entered the ante-chamber in Dolly's house.

"Catherine Alexandrovna Levine," the servant answered.

"Kitty—the Kitty that *he* was in love with, and whom he regrets not having married, while he curses the day when he met me."

The two sisters at that moment were deep in consultation over the nourishment of the little child that had been born to Kitty. When Anna was announced, Dolly alone came to the saloon to receive her.

"Not gone yet?" she said. "I was thinking whether I should find you if I called. I have had a letter from Stiva."

"We received a dispatch from him," said Anna, turning to see if Kitty, too, were coming.

"He writes that he can hardly understand exactly what Alexis Alexandrovitch wishes; but he will not leave without obtaining a definite answer."

"You have visitors?"

"Yes—Kitty," answered Dolly, somewhat confused. "She is in the nursery. She has been quite ill since her child's birth, you know."

"So I heard. Can you show me Stiva's letter?"

"Certainly; I will go and get it. Alexis Alexandrovitch has not refused;

on the contrary, Stiva has great hopes," she said, pausing by the open door.

"I myself hope and wish for nothing." "Will Kitty think it beneath her dignity to meet me?" thought Anna, when she was alone. "Perhaps she has a right to, though it is not for her, who was once in love with him, to try and teach *me* a lesson. I have sacrificed everything for him, and this is my reward! Ah! how I hate him! Why did I come here? If I wish to see Kitty, it is only to show her that I am insensible to everything, that I have no faith in anything."

Dolly came back with the letter. Anna glanced over it and handed it back to her.

"I knew that already," said Anna. "I do not care at all."

"Why not?" asked Dolly. "I myself have every hope." She had never seen Anna in such a mood before. "When do you leave?"

Anna half closed her eyes and looked straight before her without answering. "Is Kitty afraid of me?" she asked, glancing toward the door.

"What an idea! She is nursing the child, and can hardly leave it just yet. On the contrary, she will be delighted to see you. Ah! here she is!" for during her absence from the room, Dolly had, with much difficulty, persuaded her sister to see Anna.

Kitty came in, blushing, and held out her hand to Anna.

"I am very glad to see you," she said in an unsteady voice. All her prejudice against this "wicked" woman vanished at the sight of Anna's face.

"I should not have blamed you for refusing to see me," said Anna. "You have been ill, they tell me. You are very much changed since I saw you."

Kitty attributed Anna's hard, dry tone to embarrassment caused by her false position. The girl's heart went out to her in compassion.

They talked of Kitty's illness, of her child, of Stiva; but Anna's preoccupation was evident.

"I came to make my adieus," she said to Dolly, as she rose.

"When do you go?"

Again Anna did not answer. She turned to Kitty with a smile. "I am very glad to have seen you again. I have heard so much about you, even from your husband. You know he came to see me. I like him very much," she added, with an ill-natured intention. "Where is he at present?"

"In the country," answered Kitty, blushing.

"Please give him my warmest regards. Don't forget."

"I will be sure and do so," said Kitty, with a look of pity.

"Good-bye, Dolly," said Anna, embracing her.

When Dolly had escorted her to the door, the two sisters talked together of Anna. Even Kitty could see that she was unusually unhappy.

"She is not herself to-day," said Dolly. "I thought she would have burst into tears just now in the antechamber."

CHAPTER XII

THE TRAIN

SEATED again in her carriage, Anna felt more unhappy than ever. Her meeting with Kitty had awakened, to a painful extent, the sense of her own moral degradation, and a new suffering weighed upon her. Almost without knowing it, she ordered the coachman to drive home.

"They both looked upon me," she thought, "as some strange, incomprehensible being. And I had thought of confiding everything to Dolly! I was right to keep silent; my misfortune would have given her pleasure, although she would have tried to hide it. And Kitty? She would have been still more pleased—I could read it in her face. She hates me because I took the man away from her whom she would have married. Ah! if I was what she thinks I am, how easily I could have turned her husband's head! The thought of doing so did strike me, I will admit."

So lost in her thoughts had she been, she was surprised when the carriage stopped at her door.

"Has any answer come?" she asked the footman.

He handed her a telegram.

"I can not return before ten o'clock.
"WRONSKY."

"And the messenger?" she asked.

"He has not returned yet, madame," said the man.

As Anna mounted the staircase, a longing for revenge arose within her. "I will go and find him myself," she thought; "before leaving him forever, I will tell him what he has done. Never have I hated any one as I now hate this man!" The sight of one of Wronsky's hats in the ante-chamber caused her to shudder as if with disgust. She had not considered that the telegram was merely an answer to her own, and not to the message which could not yet have reached him. "He is at his mother's house, laughing and talking, careless of the suffering he has caused. I must go at once," she said to herself, without knowing whither she should go; "take the train, and follow him, humiliate him!" She consulted a guide, and saw that the evening train would leave at a few minutes past eight. "I shall get there in time." Ordering fresh horses to be put to the carriage, she hastily filled a small hand-bag with such things as were necessary for an absence of some days. She had decided not to return to the house. After her interview with him at his mother's house or at the railway-station was over, she would go on by the Nijni line and stop at the first town she came to.

Dinner was served, but she could eat nothing. She went to the carriage as soon as it came to the door, and was driven to the Nijni terminus.

Her mind was still in a turmoil and almost devoid of sense and reasoning power. She endeavored to pick up the thread of the thoughts which had flitted through her brain as she drove home from Dolly's house, but without much success. She could not fix her attention on any one point. For the first time, by the aid of some mysterious enlightenment, her true relations with Wronsky, and the life she had been leading, were revealed to her. "What did he seek for in me? The satisfaction of his vanity rather than that of love?" Wronsky's words and his expression of dog-like submission after the first moment of their *liaison* returned to her memory and confirmed this thought: "What he strove for, above everything, was the triumph of success. He loved me, but chiefly out of vanity. Now that he is no longer proud of me, everything is over. Having taken all that he could take from me, and finding nothing more worth boasting of, he feels that I am a burden to him. Perhaps he still has some love for me—but of what sort? At the bottom of his heart he will be glad to be relieved of me. While my love has from day to day become more passionate, his has gradually faded away. I have sought to draw him to me; he has tried to escape from me. He accuses me of being ridiculously jealous. I acknowledge it, but, in truth, it is because my love has not been satisfied. If I could, I would be a reasonable and reasoning friend to him, not a passionate mistress; but I can not change. What can happen that could bring me happiness? Supposing Alexis Alexandrovitch consents to a divorce; that he gives up Serge to me; that I marry Wronsky! Will Kitty respect me any the more? Will not Serge still ask me why I have *two* husbands? Will not Wronsky change toward me? Can the relations between him and myself ever bring me—I will not say happiness—but freedom from torture?"

The footman's voice at the carriage window broke through her thoughts: "Shall I take a ticket for Obiralowka?"

It was some moments before she could realize where she was and the meaning of his words.

"Yes," she answered, giving him her purse, and stepping from the carriage with the little bag in her hand.

She took her place in the railway carriage which the footman had secured for her; she heard the conductor close the doors, the third bell rang, the locomotive gave a shrill whistle, and she saw the walls of the station glide slowly past the windows, as if the train were yet standing still.

For a time the motion and the fresh air revived her; but she soon sunk back into the same train of thought. When she arrived at her destination and left the carriage, she walked behind the crowd, seeking to avoid any contact with the outside world, and waited on the platform, asking herself what she was going to do next. The carrying out of her original plan, half formed as it had been at first, seemed now almost impossible. Her one thought was: Where should she take refuge from every one? At last she forced herself to ask a station hand if Count Wronsky's coachman had not arrived at the station with a message.

"Count Wronsky? Why, he is visiting the Princess Sarokine and her daughter. Is not this the coachman?"

At that moment Anna saw the coachman, Michel, approaching her, carrying a note with an air of proud importance at having executed his mission. She tore it open, and, with a breaking heart, read:

"I am sorry your note did not reach me in Moscow. I will return at ten o'clock.   WRONSKY."

"It is all right. This is what I was waiting for," she said, with a queer, sardonic smile. "You can return home now." She spoke gently and quietly, though the beating of her heart almost suffocated her. "No," she thought, "I will not permit you to make me suffer again like this;" and she began to walk up and down the platform. "My God! where shall I fly to?" she asked herself, noticing the passers-by examining her face and rich costume.

When she reached the end of the platform, she stopped. Some women and children were standing talking to an elderly man wearing spectacles, whom probably they had come to meet. They also ceased their conversation and turned to look at Anna as she passed. She quickened her steps. A freight train was approaching the station, its heavy cars causing the platform to shake. She could imagine she was again in a moving train. Suddenly she remembered the man who had been crushed to death on the day she first met Wronsky at Moscow, and at last she understood what was left for her to do. With a quick and light step she descended the steps which ran down from the end of the platform to the track, and walked in front of the train. She calmly looked at the large driving-wheel of the locomotive, its thick spokes and axles, and tried to measure with her eyes the distance between the front and hind wheels of the first car.

"There," she said to herself, looking at the shadow cast by the car upon the gravel mixed with small pieces of coal which covered the ties, "there, in the middle. He will be punished, and I shall be freed from every one and from myself."

The slight difficulty she had in removing the little traveling-bag from her arm caused her to miss the proper moment for throwing herself underneath the first car; she waited for the second. A feeling such as in by-gone days she had experienced before plunging into the water, came over her, and she made the sign of the cross. The familiar gesture awoke in her mind a crowd of memories of her youth and infancy; life, with its fugitive joys, shone for one moment before her; but she kept her eyes fixed upon the car, and when the space between its two sets of wheels appeared, she threw aside her bag, bent her head between her shoulders, and with her hands joined together in front of her, threw herself upon her knees under the car. For the space of an instant she had time in which to feel afraid. "Where am I? Why?" she thought to herself, making an effort to throw herself back again; but an enormous, unyielding mass struck her upon the head and seemed to clutch her by the back. "Lord, pardon me," she murmured, conscious of the utter uselessness of struggling. And the light which for this poor unfortunate had illumined the book of life with its troubles, its treacheries, and its griefs, rent the darkness, shone with the brightest rays, then flickered, and went out forever.

CHAPTER XIII

ETERNAL POISON

Two months had passed away.

The neighborhood of the terminus of the Koursk railway was crowded with carriages bringing volunteers and their friends to the train which was to bear them on their way to the seat of war.

Among the bustling, hurrying crowd which filled the station was Serge Ivanitch, who was about to visit his brother, Constantin Levine, at the latter's home.

As he walked along the platform, he was stopped by one of the numerous ladies who were present, carrying large bouquets with which to do honor to the departing heroes.

"I am going into the country, to my brother's, princess," he said in answer to her questioning. "I need a change. You, however, I see," he added, with a smile, "are not going to leave your post."

"No, indeed. Tell me, is it true that we have already equipped eight hundred men?"

"Nearly a thousand, counting those who do not go direct from Moscow."

"Splendid! Have you seen the latest dispatches? We have beaten the Turks again. By the way, do you know who is leaving to-day? Count Wronsky."

"I heard that he was going, but did not know he left to-day."

"I have just seen him. He is here with his mother. As a matter of fact, 't is the best thing he could do."

"Certainly; without a doubt," said Serge Ivanitch.

"Whatever they may say," the princess went on, "I am sorry for poor Wronsky. I never liked him myself; but what he is now doing should wipe out a great many faults. You are aware that he has equipped a company at his own expense? There he is!"

Wronsky at that moment passed along the platform. He wore a long military cloak, and his face was almost hidden by a soft, wide hat. His mother leaned upon his arm. As he passed the princess and Serge Ivanitch he raised his hat and showed his features aged and worn by grief. The next moment he had disappeared among the crowd.

Having taken leave of the princess, Serge Ivanitch walked toward his own carriage. On the way he passed that in which the Wronskys were. The old countess was seated near the window. She called him to her.

"I am going as far as Koursk with Alexis," she said.

"So I have heard," replied Serge, noticing that Wronsky was absent from the carriage. "He is doing a sensible and wise thing."

"What else would you have, after his misfortune?"

"It was a terrible affair!"

"Terrible! that is no word to describe it. But come in and sit with me until Alexis returns," said the countess, making room for him. "You can form no idea of what I suffered. For six weeks he never opened his mouth, and it was all I could do to induce him to take food. We were really frightened about him. You know that he nearly killed himself once before on her account. Yes"—and the countess's face darkened—"that woman died as she had lived, shamefully and miserably."

"It is not for us to judge her, countess," said Serge, gravely; "but I can understand how you yourself suffered."

"Don't speak of it. My son was at my house, where I spend the summer, when a note was brought to him which he immediately answered. No one suspected that she was at the station. During the evening, my maid told me that a woman had thrown herself beneath a train. I immediately suspected, and said at once: 'Don't let the count hear of it!' but he had been already told—his coachman was at the station and saw it all. I hastened to my son. He was like a madman. Without a word he left the house. When he came back, he was so changed I could hardly recognize him. Soon after he lost his reason and was delirious. Ah! that woman was thoroughly bad. Can you understand a passion of that sort? What did she expect to prove by her death? She ruined the lives of two men, both of exceptional merit—her husband and my son—and went to perdition herself."

"What has the husband done?"

"He has adopted the little girl. At first Alexis consented to everything; now he is sorry that he has given his daughter to a stranger. But can he be blamed? Karénine was present at the funeral. We contrived to prevent a meeting between him and Alexis. For the husband, her death was a deliverance; but my poor son, who had sacrificed everything for this woman—his own mother, his position in society, his career—and to end like this! No; say what you will, her end was that of a creature utterly without religion. May God pardon me, but when I think of the evil she has done my son, I can only curse her memory!"

"How is he now?"

"This war has saved him. It has brought him back to life. His friend Yashvine, who has ruined himself at play, goes with him to Servia. The preparations distracted his attention. Have a talk with him, I beg of you. He is so sad; but I know he will be glad to see you. There he is, across the platform."

Serge Ivanitch left the carriage and made his way toward Wronsky. At first it seemed to him that the latter wished to avoid a meeting; but thinking of the promise to the mother, Serge went up to him, and a cordial greeting passed between the two men.

"Perhaps you would have preferred my leaving you to yourself," said Serge. "You must excuse my insistence; I want to offer you my services."

"There is no one I would avoid less than yourself," answered Wronsky. "Pardon me for any apparent rudeness; life offers me few enough agreeables."

"I can understand that. I have thought that a letter to Ristich or to Milan might be of use to you," said Serge, struck by the look of deep suffering in the count's face.

"Oh, no," he answered, as if hardly comprehending the other's words. "Shall we walk a little? The carriages are so close and stuffy. A letter? No, thank you. Does one need a letter in order to be killed? In that case, one to the Turks, perhaps—" he added, with a poor attempt at a smile.

"Well, as you wish. I want to tell you, though, how glad I was to hear of your determination. You have done infinite good to the volunteer cause which so many people have been attacking."

"My only merit," answered Wronsky, "is that I am willing to give up my life. As to energy, I know that I shall not be found wanting, and it is a consolation to me to put the existence with which I am burdened to a useful end."

"Allow me to predict," said Serge Ivanitch, touched by his words, "that you are going to enter into a new life. May God give you all success, and send you the peace of mind you are so sorely in need of."

"I am little more than a wreck," said Wronsky in a low tone, pressing the hand which Serge held out to him. His eyes fell upon the tender of the locomotive as it came sliding smoothly and quietly along the rails, to be attached to the train. The sight brought back his grief in its cruelest form to him. He saw *her* again, or, rather, what was left of her, lying in a wooden shed close by the railway track, where they had carried her. He saw the body covered with blood, stretched out before the prying eyes of every one; the head untouched, with its thick braids of hair and light curls about the temples, was thrown back, the eyes half closed; the lips, slightly open, seemed about to utter over again their terrible threat, and to predict, as at his last interview with her, "You will be sorry for this!" It was always thus. Though he strove to recall her image as he first met her at this very station—her poetical and charming beauty, her life and gayety, the happiness she seemed to enjoy and to shed on all around her—it was not so that he saw her; but always a face full of anger and an implacable desire for revenge came before his eyes, and the joys of the past were poisoned for all time.

His whole body was shaken by a sob.

The signal was given for the train to start; the two men again pressed each other by the hand, and parted.

The Kreutzer Sonata

CHAPTER I

PASSENGERS

It was early spring. We had passed two weary days and a night in the train. Passengers riding for short distances were continually coming in and getting out, but there were three others besides myself who had come the whole way from the terminus at which the train had started: a lady, no longer young or attractive, addicted to smoking, attired in a man's great-coat, and wearing a little soft hat on her head, and whose face spoke of long and profound suffering; an acquaintance of hers, a talkative gentleman of forty, faultlessly attired in brand-new clothes; and another gentleman, short of stature, and of fitful, nervous movements, not yet old, although his curly hair was prematurely gray. His eyes wandered rapidly from object to object as he sat aloof from all the other passengers.

He wore an old great-coat made evidently by an expensive tailor, with Astrakhan collar and Astrakhan cap to match. Underneath his great-coat, when unbuttoned, a jacket could be seen and an embroidered shirt, of the kind known as "Russian" shirts. It was characteristic of this person that he uttered from time to time peculiar sounds resembling short coughs or laughter just begun and suddenly broken off. During the journey he sedulously avoided making the acquaintance of, or communicating with, his fellow-passengers: to all their attempts at conversation he gave curt and churlish replies, and would either take to reading or to smoking, looking out through the window in the latter case, or else would draw forth his provisions from an old bag and make tea for himself, or eat a little. It seemed to me that his loneliness oppressed him, and I made more than one effort to enter into conversation with him, but each time our eyes met—and it happened pretty frequently, for he sat on the further end of the seat opposite to me—he always turned away, burying himself in his book or looking out through the window.

During the stop we made at a large station on the evening of the second day, this nervous passenger went out to fetch boiling water to make himself some tea. The gentleman with the brand-new clothes—a lawyer, as I afterward gathered—went to the refreshment-room to have tea with the lady smoker in the man's great-coat. While they were away several new passengers entered the carriage, among them a tall, clean-shaven old man—evidently a merchant—his face full of the wrinkles of age, wearing an ample fur coat, made from the skins of American skunks, and a cloth cap with a huge peak. He sat down on the seat opposite to that occupied by the lady and the lawyer, and without more ado entered into a conversation with a young man, apparently a merchant's clerk, who had got in at this same station.

I was sitting on the further end of the

seat opposite, and, as the train was standing still, I could distinguish snatches of their conversation, whenever there was no one walking along the passage. The merchant began by volunteering the information that he was bound for his estate, situated close by the next station. Then they spoke, as is always done in such cases, about prices, about trade, discussed the state of business in Moscow at that moment, and then went on to talk of the Fair of Nischny Novgorod. The clerk began to describe the drinking bouts and other wild pranks of a well-known rich merchant at the fair, but the old man did not allow him to tell his story to the end, but interrupted him with tales of revelries of by-gone times at the Fair of Kunavin, in which he himself took part. He took evident pride in his participation in these saturnalia, and with visible delight went on to relate how he and that same rich merchant had once in Kunavin, under the influence of liquor, played such a trick that it could not even be described otherwise than in a whisper; it made the clerk, when he heard it, roar with laughter till his voice resounded from one end of the carriage to the other, the old man also laughing the while and displaying two yellow teeth. Not expecting to hear anything interesting, I arose and moved toward the door with the intention of walking to and fro on the platform till the departure of the train. On the threshold I met the lawyer and the lady engaged in a lively conversation on their way back to their places. "You'll not have time," exclaimed the communicative lawyer, addressing me; "the second bell is about to be rung this moment."

And he was right. Scarcely had I reached the end of the train, when the second bell was rung. I returned and found the lawyer and the lady continuing their lively discussion. The old merchant seated opposite them was looking straight before him, occasionally pursing his lips disapprovingly. "Then she told her husband right out," the lawyer said, with a smile, as I was moving past him to my seat, "that she could not and would not live with him any longer, inasmuch as . . ." The rest of the story I could not catch, for no sooner had I taken my place than other passengers came in; then the guard entered; soon afterward a luggage porter rushed in, and for a considerable time such a noise was kept up, that I could not hear the conversation.

When the din had subsided, and the lawyer's voice again became audible, I noticed that the conversation had taken a new turn, and, from being private, had drifted into general topics. The lawyer was remarking that the question of divorce was now claiming and receiving the serious attention of the public in all Europe, and that even in Russia the cases in which it was granted were growing more and more frequent. Becoming suddenly aware that his was the only voice heard in the carriage, he ceased speaking, and turning to the old man: "In old times there was nothing like that, I am sure, was there?" he said, blandly, smiling. The merchant was about to make some reply, but at this moment the train started, and, taking off his cap, he began to make the sign of the cross, and to mutter his prayers in a low whisper. The lawyer, turning away his eyes, courteously waited till he had done. Having finished his prayer and crossed himself three times, the old man put his cap on, pressed it well on his head, made himself comfortable in his seat, and then began to speak.

"It used to happen in old times, too, sir," he observed, "only not so often as it does now. But at present it could not be otherwise than it is. People have become so surprisingly enlightened."

The train, moving faster and faster groaned and clanked, and made it very difficult for me to hear what was being said, and, as the conversation interested me, I moved nearer to the speakers. My neighbor, the nervous passenger with the glowing eyes, was also, I could see, interested; and he, too, made a visible effort to catch what was being said, but without rising or leaving his place.

"In what respect is education an evil?" asked the lady, with a scarcely perceptible smile on her lips. "Surely it can not be contended that it is better to marry as they did in old times, the bride and bridegroom not having as much as seen each other before the wedding?" she continued, after the manner of many ladies, replying not to the words of her interlocutor but to the remarks which she supposed he would make. "They did not know whether they liked each other, whether they could possibly like each other, and yet they married they knew not whom, making themselves miserable for all their lives. And yet that is a better state of things, in your opinion?" she went on, unmistakably addressing her remarks to the lawyer and myself, and scarcely, if at all, to the old man with whom she was ostensibly talking.

"Nowadays people have become surprisingly enlightened," repeated the merchant, contemptuously eyeing the lady and leaving her query unanswered.

"It would give me pleasure to hear how you explain the connection between education and discord in married life," exclaimed the lawyer, smiling almost imperceptibly.

The merchant was about to say something, when the lady interrupted him, saying: "No, those times are gone for good."

The lawyer, however, checked her, and exclaimed: "Pray allow him to explain his meaning!"

"Folly comes from education," cried the merchant in a dogmatic manner.

"They join in marriage people who do not love each other, and then they are astonished that such couples do not live happily," hurriedly exclaimed the lady turning round to look at the lawyer, at me, and even at the clerk, who, having risen from his place, was leaning on the back of the seat, smiling and listening to the discussion. "It is only animals that you can treat in that way," she continued, with the evident intention of stinging the merchant, "pairing and coupling them as their owner thinks fit; but men and women have their own inclinations and attachments."

"You ought not to talk in that way, ma'am," observed the merchant; "an animal is a beast, but a law has been given to man."

"Yes, but how are you to live with a man if you have no love for him?" cried the lady, apparently in haste to give utterance to thoughts which she probably believed to be very original.

"In former times no heed was given to such things," said the merchant in a solemn, peremptory manner; "it is only in our days that they have come into vogue. The moment the slightest hitch occurs, the wife bristles up with her 'I'll not live with you.' The very peasants have adopted the new fashion, and are conducting themselves accordingly. 'Here,' cries a countryman's mate, 'here, take your blouses and your drawers, I'll go off with Jack. He has a finer curly head than you have.' Talk about wonders happening after this! The first and chief thing that should be looked for in a woman is fear."

The clerk looked at the lawyer, the lady, and at me, keeping back his smile in reserve, and ready either to ridicule or to approve the merchant's discourse, according to the reception it met with.

"What kind of fear?" asked the lady.

"The kind meant by the words: 'And she shall fear her husband.' That's the kind of fear."

"Those days are long since past and gone, my good man," exclaimed the lady, with a certain touch of bitterness.

"No, ma'am, those days can not pass away. As Eve, the woman, once was created from the man's rib, so she will remain till the end of time." These words the old man uttered solemnly, shaking his head so triumphantly the while that the clerk at once decided that the victory would be on his side, and consequently he burst out laughing.

"Yes, that's the way you men reason out the question," exclaimed the lady, reluctant to surrender, and looking away from us. "You give yourselves liberty, while you want to keep us women behind bolts and bars. You take very good care, I am sure, to allow yourselves every liberty."

"Nobody accords us permission; a man, you know, brings no increase into the house by misconduct outside it. But a woman, a wife, you see, is a frail vessel."

The emphasis and gravity with which the merchant delivered himself of these

judgments had evidently a powerfully persuasive effect on his hearers. Even the lady was conscious of defeat: still, however, she refused to give in.

"Yes, but I think for all that you will admit that a woman is a human being, endowed with feeling, just as a man is. Now what is she to do if she does not love her husband?"

"If she does not love her husband?" angrily repeated the merchant, moving his brows and his lips simultaneously. "Don't you fear, she'll learn to love him!"

This unlooked-for argument especially tickled the clerk's fancy, and he uttered an inarticulate sound significative of approval.

"Oh, but she will not learn to love him," declared the lady; "and if love is lacking, it is not force that can engender it."

"Well, but suppose a woman has proved unfaithful to her husband; how then?" asked the lawyer.

"That has not to be taken into account at all," replied the old man. "One should always take effective measures to prevent it."

"Yes, but suppose it should occur in spite of your measures; it's a fact that it does take place; what then?"

"Wherever else it happens, it is unknown in our circles," was the merchant's reply.

All became silent. The clerk shifted his position, moved a little nearer, and apparently not wishing to be behind the others, began with a smile as follows:

"Yes, here now is a scandalous affair that took place among our people, and a hard one to disentangle, too! She was a queer woman, a loose sort, you know. And she did go in for games, I tell you!

Her husband was a well enough sort of man in his way, and had all his wits about him. She began tricks with the shop-boy. Her husband tried to bring her round, and get her to keep straight by soft talk and advice. But she wouldn't knuckle down. She did no end of queer things, that woman. She got to such a pitch that she made no bones of stealing his money. He beat her then. Well, and what do you think came of it? Why, she got worse and worse, and at last she went off with an unbaptized fellow—a Jew! Now, what was her husband to do, I ask you? He shook her off altogether; and now he's living like a bachelor, and she's going from bad to worse."

"Because he's a fool!" exclaimed the old man. "If he had put a spoke in her wheel from the very outset; if he had given her a thorough good taming, I'll go bail she'd be living with him to-day. Never let them have their way from the very beginning. 'Don't trust your horse in the field nor your wife in your home,' as the saying is."

At this point in the conversation the guard came in to collect the tickets for the next station. The old man gave up his. "Yes, sir, women must be tamed in time, or else all's lost." .

"Well, but how do you reconcile that with what you yourself related a short time ago about what the men did at the Fair of Kunavin?" I asked, unable to keep silent any longer.

"Oh, that's a different thing alto-gether," he answered, and relapsed im-mediately into silence.

Shortly afterward the shrill whistle of the engine was heard, and he rose, drag-ged out a bag from under the seat, pulled his fur coat closer about him, and, slightly raising his cap, left the carriage to take his place on the little platform near the break.

CHAPTER II

LOVE DEFINED

SCARCELY had he left the carriage when the conversation began again, several voices being heard simultaneously.

"There goes a patriarchal old grand-father!" exclaimed the clerk.

"The incarnation of tyrannical home government," ejaculated the lady. "What a barbarous conception of women and of marriage he has!"

"Yes, we are still far off from Euro-pean views on marriage," observed the lawyer.

"The strangest thing of all about such people," resumed the lady, "is that they do not understand that marriage without love is not marriage at all; that the only thing that can hallow marriage is love, and that the only genuine marriage is that which is hallowed by love."

The clerk listened and smiled, desirous of impressing on his memory for future use as many enlightened remarks as pos-sible. In the middle of the lady's talk a noise was heard as of suppressed laugh-ter or a smothered sob, and, turning round, we beheld my neighbor, the gray-haired, lonely man with the lustrous eyes, who during the course of the conversa-tion, which evidently interested him, had moved quite close to us, without being observed. He was standing with his arms resting on the back of the seat, and he appeared very excited, his face being quite red, and the nervous twitching of the facial muscles being painfully visible.

"What kind of love do you mean— the love that hallows marriage?" he asked, stammering.

Noticing the state of agitation in which her interlocutor addressed her, the lady put as much gentleness and thoroughness into her reply as was possible.

"Real, genuine love," she explained; "if such love exists between the man and the woman, marriage is possible."

"Yes; but what are we to understand by real, genuine love?" insisted the man with the glowing eyes, smiling awkwardly, and displaying great timidity as he put the question.

"Surely, every one knows what is meant by love!" exclaimed the lady.

"I do not," objected her questioner; "you should define what you mean by—"

"What? Why, it's very simple," replied the lady, who, nevertheless, became thoughtful and silent for a few moments. Then resuming, "What is love?" she repeated, "love is the preference of one person for another, to the exclusion of every one else."

"Preference for what period of time? For a month? For two days? Or for half an hour?" queried the passenger, with a laugh.

"No: it is clear you have something else in mind," said the lady.

"No; I am speaking of the same thing as you are."

"The lady maintains," said the advocate, interposing, "that marriage should be the outcome in the first place of an attachment (or call it love, if you will), and that if such a sentiment exists, then, and not otherwise, is marriage hallowed, so to say. In the next place, that every marriage not based upon this natural predilection (or love, if you prefer the term), is devoid of the element that makes it morally binding. Have I interpreted you aright?" he asked, turning to the lady.

The lady by a nod of her head signified her approval of the lawyer's exposition.

"In the next place—" the lawyer went on; but the nervous gentleman, with the glowing eyes, which now resembled two coals of fire, was evidently unable any longer to control himself, for breaking in on the lawyer's speech, he began:

"No, I am speaking of exactly the same thing, the predilection of one person for another, only I ask how long is this predilection to last?"

"How long? A long time, sometimes a whole life-time," answered the lady, shrugging her shoulders.

"Yes, but that is only in novels. In life it is never so. In life this predilection of one person for another lasts in very rare instances for years; generally for months, and sometimes for weeks, for days, for hours," he exclaimed, obviously conscious that he was startling us all by this expression of opinion, and satisfied that it should be so.

"Oh, how can you! No, but— Pardon me, but—" all three of us began simultaneously. Even the clerk uttered some sound of disapproval.

"Yes, I know," he exclaimed, in a high voice, "you are talking of that which is supposed to be, whereas I was speaking of that which is. Every man feels what you call love toward every pretty woman."

"Oh, that's horrible—to say such things. It is certain that there is such a sentiment as love—love that is given us not for months or years, but for our life-time. Is not that so?" asked the lady.

"Certainly not. Even if we admit that a man may conceive a predilection for a certain woman, and that it lasts all his life, it is most highly probable that the woman's predilection will be for some one else. So it has ever been, and so it will ever continue to be in this world of ours." Having delivered himself of this opinion, he took out his cigarette-case and began to smoke.

"It may be reciprocal," urged the lawyer.

"No, it can not be," he answered; "just as in a cartload of peas no two peas will lie exactly side by side. Besides, we are not dealing in this case with mere improbabilities; one of the certain elements of the question is satiation. To say that you can love one person all your life is just like saying that one candle will continue burning as long as you live." As he said this, he greedily drew in the smoke of his cigarette.

"You are speaking of another sort of love," objected the lady: "don't you admit the existence of love founded on identity of ideals, on spiritual kinship?"

"Identity of ideals!" he repeated, uttering his strange noise; "but in that case there is no reason why they should sleep together—pardon me this coarseness. The idea of people sleeping together because their ideals are identical!" and he laughed nervously.

"Allow me to point out," interposed the lawyer, "that the facts are dead against you. We see that marriages exist; that all mankind, or at least the great majority, contract matrimonial unions, and that many live honorably during a long married life."

The gray-haired passenger again laughed.

"You maintain," he said, "that marriages are based on love. But when I express my doubts as to the existence of any but physical love, you set about proving the existence of love by pointing to the existence of marriages. Marriage in our days is nothing but deceit."

"I beg your pardon," exclaimed the lawyer, "all I affirm is that marriages have existed, and do still exist."

"Marriages exist! Yes, but why do they exist? They existed and still exist among those peoples who discern something mysterious, sacramental in marriage; a sacrament which has a binding power in the sight of God. Among such people marriages do indeed subsist, but not among us. In our country people contract matrimonial unions who in marriage see nothing of the sort, and the result is deceit or violence. If deceit, it is more easily borne; the husband and wife merely deceive others, leading them to believe that they are living in real marriage, whereas they are living in polygamy and polyandry. This is bad; it is tolerable, however; but when, as is more frequently the case, husband and wife have taken upon themselves the outward obligation of living together as long as life is given them, and yet from the second month of married life already hate each other, and although eagerly desirous to separate, yet continue to live together—life at last becomes a terrible hell, from which they endeavor to escape by drinking themselves to death, blowing out their brains, poisoning and killing themselves and each other." He spoke rapidly, allowing no one to interpose a word, and grew more and more excited as he spoke.

We all remained silent, feeling ill at ease.

"Yes, undoubtedly critical episodes do occur in married life," said the lawyer, at last breaking the awkward silence with the object of putting an end to the discussion, which was becoming unduly heated.

"I see you know who I am?" said the gray-haired passenger quietly, and, as it seemed, calmly.

"No, I have not the pleasure."

"Well, the pleasure is not much. I am Pozdnischeff, the person to whom occurred that 'critical episode' to which you allude, the episode that consisted in his killing his wife," he exclaimed, looking hurriedly at each of us in turn. As none of us hit upon any remark appropriate to such an occasion, we remained silent. "Well, it's all the same," he continued, making that strange noise to which he was addicted. "Anyhow, I ask your pardon. Ah! I will not embarrass you any longer with my presence!"

"But not at all; don't mention such a thing; not at all!" exclaimed the lawyer, not exactly knowing what he meant by "not at all." Pozdnischeff, however, paid no attention to what he said, and turning round, went back to his place. The gentleman began to converse with the lady in whispers.

CHAPTER III

THE TALE OF POZDNISCHEFF

I was seated opposite Pozdnischeff, but as I could not think of anything appropriate to say to him, and as it was too dark to read, I closed my eyes and simulated a desire to sleep. We remained thus till we reached the next station, where the gentleman and lady got into another carriage, after having previously arranged the matter with the guard. The clerk, having made himself comfortable on the seat,

had gone to sleep. Pozdnischeff was all the time smoking and drinking tea— the tea he had made at the previous station. No sooner did I open my eyes and look about me than he addressed me with determination in his manner and irritation in his voice:

"Perhaps it is disagreeable to you to sit near me, now that you know who I am. If so, I will go away."

"Not at all. Please don't think such a thing."

"Well, then, can I offer you some? It is somewhat strong, I fear." With this he poured me out some tea.

"They talk . . . but what they say is all lies—"

"To what are you referring?" I inquired.

"To the same subject, of course; to that love of theirs, and to its nature. You are not sleepy?"

"No; not in the least."

"Well, if you like, I'll tell you how it was that I was led by this very love to do what I did?"

"Certainly, if the effort is not too painful for you—"

"Not at all. To keep silence is painful. Have some more tea? Or is it too strong for you?"

The tea was in truth very strong; it was almost like beer; however, I drank a tumbler of it. Just then the conductor passed through the carriage; Pozdnischeff scowled at him, and did not begin till he had left.

"Well, then, I'll tell you the story. But are you really sure you care to hear it?"

I assured him that I desired it very much. He remained silent a moment, then rubbed his face with his hands and began:

"Before marriage I lived as all other men live in our social stratum. I am a land-owner, a candidate of the university, and at one time was marshal of the nobility. Until I married I lived like everybody else—that is to say, not morally—and, like men in my own walk of life, fancied that by living in this way I was performing my duty. I considered myself a model, and believed that I was a thoroughly moral man. Not being a seducer, nor possessed of depraved tastes, I did not make pleasure the main object of my life, as did many men of my own age and station. I yielded moderately, decently, for the sake of health. I avoided women who by conceiving a strong affection for me might fetter me in any way. For the rest, for aught I know, there may have been attachments, but I acted as if they did not exist. And not merely did I hold this to be moral conduct, but I was actually proud of it."

Here he stopped short and uttered that peculiar sound which he apparently always made whenever a new thought occurred to him.

"It was this," he continued, "that constituted the hideousness of my conduct. It is not anything physical that imports; what is wrong is the exemption of one's self from all moral relations when terms of intimacy exist. And it was precisely this exemption of myself from all such moral ties that I regarded as my peculiar merit. I remember how terribly I suffered once when I had failed to acknowledge, by means of a present of money, a woman who had most probably fallen in love with me. Nor did I recover my wonted tranquillity until I had forwarded her money, and thereby made it clear to her that I considered myself perfectly untrammeled by any kind of moral ties.

"You need not shake your head as if you agreed with me," he suddenly exclaimed. "I know this trick well. Every man, and you among the rest, unless you are a rare exception, shares these very views in accordance with which I acted. It's all the same, however; forgive me," he continued, "but the truth is that all this is very terrible."

"What is terrible?" I asked.

"The abyss of delusions in which we live concerning women and our relations toward them. Yes; I am unable to speak calmly of it, not because of the 'episode,' as he termed it, which occurred to me in connection therewith, but because ever since it took place my eyes have been opened, and I see things in quite a different light. Everything is turned inside out; yes, inside out."

He lighted a cigarette, and, resting his elbows on his knees, resumed. In the darkness I could not distinguish his face; I could only hear, high above the creaking and noise of the train, the sound of his impressive and agreeable voice.

CHAPTER IV

HIGH PRIESTS OF SCIENCE

"YES, it was only after I had been tortured and agonized, and, thanks to this torture and agony, that I understood wherein lay the root of the evil; it is only since I learned what ought to be, that I realize so fully the hideousness of that which is.

"Let me now tell you when and how

those circumstances originated which led up to that terrible episode of my life. I was not quite sixteen years old when I took the first step on that fatal journey. It happened when I was still a pupil in the gymnasium, and my elder brother a freshmen at the university. I had never known a woman before, but at the same time I possessed no more claim to be called an innocent boy than did any of the unfortunate children of our social stratum. For nearly two years previously my soul had been defiled by my comrades, and already the bare thought of woman, not of any particular woman, but of a woman in general, tormented me.

"My thoughts, when alone, were therefore, no longer pure. I tortured myself as ninety-nine one hundredths of our boys torture themselves. I was horrified, I was agonized, I prayed, and I fell. I had already, therefore, been corrupted in imagination. I was perishing alone, and had not as yet laid violent hands upon other human beings, in order to involve them in my ruin.

"It was at this conjuncture that one day a friend of my brother's, also a student, a gay youth, and what is commonly called a right good fellow—that is, a worthless villain—who had taught us to drink and to gamble, persuaded us one night, after a drinking bout, to go *there*. And we went. My brother was also innocent up to then, and fell on the same night And I, a mere stripling of sixteen, fell also, not realizing what I did.

"I had never heard from any one of my elders that what I was doing was wrong. And, what is more, even now, boys of the present generation never hear it. True, it is to be found in the Decalogue, but then the Decalogue exists only to be repeated by heart at examinations in schools and universities, and even in that capacity it is not very necessary; certainly not by any means as indispensable as is the grammatical commandment that the Latin particle *ut* is to be employed in the conditional clauses of a sentence. At all events, I never heard from any of my elders, whose opinion I respected, that what I was doing was wrong. On the contrary, I heard from people whom I esteemed that I was doing quite right. I was told that, once done, all my struggles and my sufferings would disappear. This I had both heard and read. I had not been told by my elders that I was doing wrong; the men I knew regarded their conduct as a sort of heroism, as it were. So that, altogether, it was clear that it could have none but good effects. Had I any fear of evil consequences? Even that had been foreseen, and a provident government had taken thought of it. Salaried doctors are employed to look after these matters. This is as it ought to be. It is the doctors who affirm what is indispensable to good health, and it is they who sanction a system of conduct. I am personally acquainted with mothers who take measures precisely as the doctors direct in these matters. It is science that is responsible."

"Why science?" I asked.

"Who are the doctors," he answered, "if not the high priests of science? Who demoralizes our youth by affirming what is indispensable to good health? And then, with airs of unutterable self-importance, they set about curing complaints."

"And why should they not cure complaints?" I asked.

"Because if the one hundredth part of the efforts made to cure had been directed to the extirpation of indulgence, these complaints would have long ago disappeared. But no; all those efforts are put forth, not for the purpose of rooting out evil, but with the express object of encouraging it, of guaranteeing those who practice it from risks of evil accompanying it. But that is not the point I was driving at. What I wanted to emphasize is the circumstance that what happened to me is exactly what befalls nine tenths, if not more, of the members, not only of our social sphere, but of all classes and conditions of our society, not excepting even the peasants: I fell without even the excuse that I was yielding to natural love. No; it was not love that caused me to fall; I fell, simply because those persons in whose midst I lived looked upon that which constituted my fall, some as a lawful and useful action, others as a most natural, and not only excusable, but perfectly innocent amusement for a young man to engage in. As for me, I had not a suspicion that I had done anything that could be appropriately described as a fall. I simply began to give myself up to what was partly a pleasure and partly, as I was assured, a necessity, just as I had taken to drink and to smoke. And yet in this first fall there was something peculiar, something pathetic. I remember that the very instant I had fallen I was overwhelmed with sadness, and I felt that I should like to sit down and weep. Yes, I could have wept over the loss of my innocence, over the wrong I had committed, which no ages could ever wash away.

"Yes, I could never again hope to look upon woman in the simple, natural way characteristic of the pure and the innocent. Just as the opium-eater, the drunkard, and the immoderate smoker are not normal men, so is he who has fallen as I did; he is a tainted, corrupted man. As an opium-eater, or a drunkard, is readily recognizable by his face his gait, his manner, so also is such a man as I became. He may succeed in exercising a certain self-mastery, in repressing tell-tale movements and looks that have become spontaneous—in a word, he may still struggle with himself and his proclivities, but he can never again recover those simple, clear, pure relations with womankind, relations as of a brother toward his sister.

"And I became a voluptuary, and remained one. And this it was that worked my ruin."

CHAPTER V

HER STUPEFACTION

"AFTER this I sank deeper and deeper into the slough. And yet what I recall is what *I* did—I who was a continual butt for the scornful gibes of my comrades, owing to my relative 'innocence.' What if you were to hear of the doings of the gilded youth, of army officers, of 'Parisians'! And yet all these persons, myself included, when we were profligates of thirty years of age, our souls laden with hundreds of multiform crimes, how often have we entered the salon or the ballroom, spruce and neat, washed, shaved, perfumed in spotless linen and irreproachable evening dress or faultless uniform—as emblems of purity! How charming!

"Just reflect for a moment upon what ought to be, and confront it with what really is. What ought to be is this: when a person of this description in society approaches my sister or my daughter, I, knowing his life, should walk up to him, draw him aside, and, addressing him in a whisper, say: 'Friend, I know the kind of life you lead, how you spend your nights and with whom. This is no fit place for you. Here there are spotless innocent girls. Withdraw!' This is what ought to take place. What really does occur is this: when such a person makes his appearance and dances with my sister or my daughter, encircling her waist with his arm, we laugh at it if he is rich and has powerful friends. Oh, abomination! How long shall we have to wait for the time when this execrable state of things, this tissue of damnable lies, will be finally shown up and exploded?"

He again made those peculiar sounds of his several times in succession, and again took tea. The tea, I must say, was extremely strong, and there was no water at hand with which to weaken it. I felt extremely stimulated by the two glasses of it that I had drunk. It doubtlessly affected him, too, in a similar way, for the more tea he drank the more excited he grew. His voice became more and more sonorous and expressive; he was continually changing his position, and now putting on his cap, now taking it off; and his face seemed to undergo strange transfigurations in the gathering darkness.

"In this way I lived," he resumed, "till I was thirty years of age, never for a single moment giving up my intention to marry, settle down, and lead the purest and most ideal family life conceivable. With this object in view, I carefully sought for a suitable young girl. I looked around with critical gaze in search of a girl whose purity would qualify her to aspire to the dignity of becoming my wife. I slighted and rejected several because, forsooth, they were not immaculate enough for me. At last, however, my search was successful: I discovered a person whom I regarded as worthy of myself.

"She was one of two daughters of a land-owner of Penza, once a wealthy man, but at that time ruined and in straitened circumstances. One evening she and I had been out boating together, and when night came on, and we were returning home, lighted by the soft rays of the moon, and I sat side by side with her, admiring her bewitching curls and her well-shaped figure, becomingly set off in a well-fitting jersey, I suddenly decided that she was the person. I fancied that night that she comprehended everything that I felt and thought, and that what I felt and thought was sublime to a degree. In truth, at the root of this fancy lay her curls and her jersey, which became her remarkably well, and the desire for greater proximity.

"What a strange illusion it is to suppose that beauty is goodness! A beautiful woman utters absurdities; we listen and we hear not the absurdities, but wise thoughts. She speaks, she does odious things, and yet we are only conscious of something agreeable. If she refrains from absurd or hateful words and acts, and if she is beautiful to boot, we are straightway convinced that she is a paragon of wisdom and morality. As for me, I returned home in ecstasies, deciding that she was the pink of moral perfection, and for this reason worthy to be my wife. The next day I proposed for her.

"What an absurd entanglement of ideas! Out of a thousand men who marry, not only in our social sphere, but also unfortunately in the rank of the people, there is scarcely one who has not, like Don Juan, been married before innumerable times. (True, there are now, I hear, and I have personal experience of what I say, pure young men who feel and know that purity is no laughing matter, but a most important affair. May God succor them! But in my time there was not one such in ten thousand.) Everybody is perfectly well aware that this is the normal state of things, and yet everybody feigns to believe that it is entirely different.

"All novels are full of detailed descriptions of the feelings of their heroes, and the appearance of the lakes and trees round which they ramble. But when their love for a young girl is touched upon, no mention whatever is made about the previous experiences of the interesting hero. Or if such novels exist, they are never put in the hands of the persons most concerned to know these things—namely, young girls. At first a pretense is made to girls that the wickedness which fills up half the life of a man in our cities and villages does not exist at all. In time we grow so accustomed to this hypocrisy that we honestly begin to believe that we are all moral people and live in a moral world. Girls, poor things,

believe this quite seriously. It was also the conviction of my unfortunate wife. Once before our marriage I showed her my diary containing entries from which she could gain a glimpse of certain episodes of my former life, especially of my last *liaison*, which I felt it advisable to bring to her knowledge, lest it should be communicated to her by others. I well recollect the horror, the despair, the stupefaction which she felt when she knew and understood what had taken place. I saw that she wanted to break off all relations with me then and there."

"And what prevented her from breaking off?" I queried.

He uttered again that peculiar sound of his, remained silent, and drank a little tea.

"Anyhow, it is better so, yes, it is better so," he exclaimed. "It serves me right."

CHAPTER VI

DECEIVED DAUGHTERS

"But that is not the point. What I wanted to say is that the only persons who are really deceived in all this are the unfortunate girls. The mothers, initiated by their husbands, see through it all, and, while simulating belief in the purity of men, act in a manner wholly incompatible with such a belief. They know with what bait to catch men for themselves and for their daughters.

"It is only we men who do not know this, and we are ignorant of it simply because we do not wish to know. Women are well aware that what is commonly called sublime and poetical love depends not upon moral qualities, but on frequent meetings, and on the style in which the hair is done up, and on the color and cut of the dress. Ask an experienced coquette eagerly bent upon captivating a man, which of the two risks she would rather incur: that of being convicted of deceit, cruelty, or even of immoral conduct in presence of the man whom she is endeavoring to attract, or of appearing before him in a badly made and ugly dress. She will unhesitatingly prefer the first. For she well knows that men are continually lying about lofty sentiments; that what they really want is only the woman herself and that they consequently freely condone every species of bad conduct, while they will never forgive a dress that is badly cut, tastelessly trimmed, or suggestive of *mauvais ton*. Every coquette is keenly conscious of this; every innocent girl is unconsciously aware of this: Hence these odious jerseys and projections behind, these exposed shoulders, arms, and almost open breasts. Women, particularly those who have passed through the masculine school, are alive to the fact that conversations on lofty themes are mere hollow phrases; that the object of a man's desire is the person, and whatever sets that out in its most seductive light; and they act in strict accordance with this knowledge.

"If we could only throw aside that familiarity with shocking conventions which has become second nature to us, and look at life among the higher classes as it really is, we should find it absolutely shameful. You don't agree with me? I will prove it to you," he said, interrupting me. "You maintain that women of our social sphere live for interests other than those which play a part in the life of lost women, but I tell you that it is not so, and I will make good my contention.

"If people wholly differ in their aims of life, in the significance they ascribe to human existence, this divergence will be assuredly reflected in their outward conduct; and their external appearance will be as different as are their views. Look now upon the unfortunate and despised sisterhood of fallen woman and compare them with the ladies of the highest society. What do you observe? The same toilets, the same costumes, the same perfumes, the same exposure of the arms and shoulders, the same projections behind, the same passion for jewelry, for costly glittering ornaments, the same amusements, dances, music, and song. And as the former class of women employ all of these things for the purposes of seduction, so also do the latter. There is absolutely no difference between them."

CHAPTER VII

CONTRIVED PASSION

"IT was thus, then, that I was caught by these jerseys, curls, and projections. It was easy to catch me, seeing that I had been brought up under conditions calculated to breed young lovers, somewhat as cucumbers are forced in hot-houses. Consider our stimulating, superfluous food, combined as it is with complete physical inactivity.

"You may wonder or not wonder, just as you like, but so it is. I myself did not discover this till very lately.

And it causes me profound suffering to reflect that nobody is aware of it now, and that people utter in consequence such absurdities as those to which that lady here gave expression a short time ago.

"Last spring a number of peasants were working in our neighborhood on a railway embankment. The usual food of a strong peasant when engaged in light field labor consists of bread (kvass), onions, and this keeps him alive, active, and healthy. When he enters into the service of a railway company his food is porridge, and a pound of meat daily. This meat he gives out again in the form of sixteen hours' labor, driving a wheelbarrow of thirty poods, which is just as much as he is able to perform. We, on the other hand, eat game, meat, and fish, besides sundry other kinds of heat-giving food and drink. Now where, may I ask, does all this go? To produce excesses, abnormal excitement, which, passing through the prism of our artificial life, assumes the form of falling in love.

"Thus I fell in love, as all men do, and none of the characteristic traits of that state were wanting. Ecstasies, tenderness, and poetry were all there, in appearance at least, but in reality my love was the result of the contrivances of the mamma and the dress-maker on the one hand, and good dinners and inactivity on the other. If, on the one hand, there had been no boating excursions, no dress-makers to arrange wasp-like waists, and so on; had my wife been dressed in a plain gown and stayed at home; and if, on the other hand, I had been leading a normal life. I should not have fallen

in love, and all that took place subsequently and in consequence of that, would never have occurred."

CHAPTER VIII

TAKE MY LILY!

"As it was, however, my frame of mind, the becoming dress, and the rowing in the boat, contributed to make the thing a success. Twenty times over it had failed before; this time it succeeded, and I fell into what may be described as a kind of trap.

"I am not joking when I say that marriages in our days are arranged like traps. What is there natural about them? A girl grows up and must be married. It seems a very simple problem on the face of it, especially if she is not a scarecrow, and there is a sufficiency of men desirous of marrying. In old times it was very plain sailing. The girl became of age, and the parents arranged the match. It is still so with the Chinese, Indians, Mohammedans, the lower orders of Russians; in a word, with ninety-nine hundredths of all mankind. It remained for the one hundredth part or even less of debased humanity to make the discovery that this was not the proper way of solving the problem and to devise a new method. Now, what are the essential cha_acteristics of this new system? The girls sit at home and the young men go, as it were, to the market, and choose them, the girls anxiously waiting and thinking, but not daring to say plainly. 'Pray take me, dear! No, take me. Not her, but me, please. Look what shoulders I have got!' And we men, meanwhile, walk up and down, scrutinizing them and feeling perfectly satisfied, each one saying to himself, 'I know, forsooth, that I shall not be taken in.' And so we stroll backward and forward, delighted that everything is so nicely arranged for us, when suddenly one of us trips up, falls, and is caught in the trap."

"Well, but what would you have?" I asked. "Surely you would not wish the girls to propose to the men?"

"I really do not know what I would have, I only feel that if there is to be equality, let there be real equality.

"If match-making by professional match-makers is found to be debasing, our system is a thousand times more degrading, for in the former case the rights and chances are equal on both sides, whereas in the latter the woman is either a slave in the market or a mere decoy.

"Tell a mother or her daughter the plain truth, namely, that all her efforts are directed to the one end of catching a husband. Heavens! what an insult that would be! And yet they all do this, and there is nothing else for them to do; it is peculiarly harrowing to see sometimes very young, poor, innocent girls occupied in this way. Lamentable as all this is, if it were, at least, done openly, above board, it would be different, but as a matter of fact it is all deceit.

"'Ah! "The Origin of Species"— how interesting!' a mamma would exclaim. 'Oh, Lily is very much interested in painting!' 'And you, do you propose going to the exhibition?' 'How instructive!' 'Driving in a drosky!' 'The play!' 'The concert!' 'Ah! how wonderful!' 'Lily is simply wild about music!' 'And you, how is it that you

do not share these convictions?' 'Boating parties!—ah! boating parties!'

"The thought underlying all these ejaculations is one and the same. Put into words it is this: 'Take me; do, please, take me!' 'Take my Lily!' 'No, take me, dear!' Oh, abomination! damnable lie!" And having swallowed the remainder of his tea, he set about removing the cups and vessels.

CHAPTER IX

MERETRICIOUS COSTUMES

"YES," he resumed, putting away his tea and sugar in a bag, "this is the origin of the ascendency of women, from which the entire world is suffering."

"How the ascendency of women?" I asked. "All rights and privileges are on the side of the men."

"Yes, yes; precisely what I was about to say," he interrupted me. "This gives us the clew to the strange circumstance that while, on the one hand, women are reduced to the lowest degree of humiliation, they are all-powerful on the other. Their position in that respect is perfectly analogous to that of the Jews. As these make up for their oppression by acquiring influence and power in other ways, so do women. 'Ah! you ordain,' the Jews seem to say, 'that we should be more tradesmen? Very well; then we, as tradesmen, shall acquire ascendancy over you.' 'Ah! you ordain that we should be merely instruments of pleasure?' exclaim the women. 'Very well; we shall enslave you.'

"The denial of woman's rights does not consist in her disqualification to vote, to occupy a place upon the bench, to take a part in the conduct of these or those affairs, but in her inferiority to man in all those social acts and functions which are based on the relations of the sexes. Thus it is not in her power to choose her husband, but she must wait to be chosen by him.

"You say that it would be monstrous to confer upon her these rights? Very well; then let the men be deprived of them. At present they constitute a monopoly for men, and so in order to compensate for the loss of these rights, woman acts upon the senses of the man, and through his senses so completely enslaves him that his right of choice dwindles away to a mere formality. In reality it is she who chooses, and when once she has mastered these means of conquest she abuses them, and acquires thereby a terrible power over men."

"Yes, but in what does this peculiar power manifest itself?" I asked.

"In everything and everywhere," he answered. "Pass by the shops, for instance, in any large city; it is impossible to estimate the untold wealth exhibited in the windows, or to gauge the amount of man's labor which produced it. Observe them well, and in nine tenths of these shops you will find nothing destined for the use of the male members of the community: all the trade in the luxuries of life is called into existence and sustained by the requirements of women. Count up all the factories: by far the greatest number of them turn out useless ornaments, equipages, furniture, toys—for women. Millions of people, generations of slaves, perish in this penal servitude of the factories merely in order to satisfy the whim of woman. Women, like empresses, condemn to imprisonment and hard labor nine tenths of mankind.

"Such is the form assumed by their vengeance on us men for having degraded them and deprived them of equal rights. All these contrivances and stratagems are calculated to act upon the immoral part of our nature and thus to entice us into the nets they have spread for us. Yes, this is the root of the abnormal state of things I have described. Woman has transformed herself into an object of pleasure of such terrible effect that a man can not calmly approach her. No sooner does a man draw near a woman than he falls under the power of her spell, and his senses are forthwith paralyzed. Even in former times I always felt ill at ease in presence of a lady arrayed in all the splendor of ball-dress: at present I positively shudder at the sight, for I recognize therein a palpable danger to people in general, a danger that has no legal right to exist; and I feel prompted to call in a policeman, to appeal for protection against this danger that threatens me, and to insist on its removal or suppression.

"This makes you laugh!" he exclaimed all at once, addressing me; "does it? But this is no joking matter, I can assure you. A time will come, and it may come very soon, when people will realize this, and will ask themselves in wonderment, how it was possible for a society to hold together in which acts like those just described, fraught as they were with danger to the public peace, were tolerated. Can it for a moment be pretended that that bedecking of the human body which our society connives at in women, and which is calculated directly to provoke passion, is devoid of social danger? Positively it is just the same as if you were to set traps and spread nets on the streets and public walks, on the highways and by-ways. Nay, it is still worse. Why is it, let me ask you, that games of hazard are prohibited, while women attired in meretricious costumes are not prohibited? And yet the latter are a thousand times more dangerous than the former!"

CHAPTER X

ONLY A CONDITION

"It was thus that I, too, was caught. I was what is termed 'in love.' Not only did I represent her to myself as the pink of perfection, but all the time that I was paying my addresses to her I fancied myself also a model of what a man should be. As a matter of fact, the world does not contain a scoundrel of however deep a dye who, if he only made a thorough search, would not discover another scoundrel in some respects worse than himself, and a reason therefore for feeling proud of, and satisfied with, himself.

"That was my case. I did not marry money. Love of lucre played no part in my choice, as it did in that of most of my acquaintances, who married for the sake of their wife's dowry or influential friends. I was wealthy, she was poor. This was one consideration. Another circumstance in which I took equal pride was that others married with the deliberate intention of continuing the irregular lives which they had led before marriage. I, on the contrary, had taken the firm resolution to remain faithful to my wife, after marriage, and there were no bounds to the high opinion I had of myself in consequence. Yes, for this I flattered myself that I was an angel.

"I was only engaged for a short time, and yet I can not recall that period of life without shame. What an abomination! The love that united us was supposed to be of a spiritual character. But if our love and communings had been of a spiritual nature, all the words, phrases, and conversations that passed between us should have expressed this. As a matter of fact, nothing of the kind took place. We found it extremely difficult to converse when left alone; it was a labor of Sisyphus. I would think of something to say, say it, relapse into silence, and then rack my brain for something else—there was absolutely nothing to converse about. All the topics referring to the new life which awaited us, to our future plans, had already been discussed, and what was there further to say? If we had been animals, we should at least have known that we were not expected to converse, but not being mere animals we were forced to speak, notwithstanding that there was absolutely nothing to speak about. Add to all this that disgraceful custom of eating sweets and dinners, and all those abominable preparations for marriage, usual under the circumstances, such as discussions about lodgings, morning robes for my wife, morning coats for myself, linen, toilet, and so on.

"Of course if people contracted marriage in accordance with the rules and counsels of the fathers of the early Russian Church, as the old merchant insisted here this afternoon that they should, down mattresses, the dowry, the bed and bedstead and such-like things would sink to the level of mere details that go along with the sacrament. But in our country, where out of ten who enter into matrimony there is scarcely one who believes, I do not say in the reality of the Sacrament, but in the attribute of the union to create something in the nature of an obligation; where out of one hundred men there is scarcely one who has not been practically married before, or one in fifty who does not propose to commit infidelities whenever a favorable opportunity presents itself; in our country, I say, where the majority look upon the church ceremonies as neither more nor less than a condition, the fulfillment of which entitles them to take possession of a certain woman."

CHAPTER XI

TO BE COMBATED

"THUS it is that all people marry; thus it was that I married. Then began the much-lauded period called the honeymoon. What bathos is contained in the very name!

"Strolling about Paris one day," he said, "looking at all the shows and spectacles, I espied a sign-board with the effigy of a woman with a beard and a walrus. I went in to look, and found that the bearded woman was merely a man in a low-bodied woman's dress, and the sea-monster a common dog covered with a walrus's skin swimming about in a bath filled with water. The whole thing was extremely uninteresting. When leaving, the showman deferentially accompanied me, and addressing the public standing outside the door, he pointed at me and said, 'You can ask this gentleman whether the show is worth looking at. Walk in, walk in! One franc a head.' I was ashamed to declare that it was not worth looking at, and the showman undoubtedly relied upon that feeling. It is probably the same with those who have experienced all the fatuities of

the honey-moon, and refuse to disabuse others. Nor did I disabuse any one, but I do not see why I should not now tell the truth. Indeed, I feel it incumbent upon me to proclaim the truth about it.

"The fact is it was irksome, miserable, and above all things wearisome, inconceivably wearisome! It reminded me to some extent of the feelings I experienced when I was learning to smoke, years ago, when the nausea in my stomach foreboded sickness, and my mouth was filling with saliva, which I made haste to swallow, endeavoring to look as if the whole thing were pleasant."

"You are speaking curiously of the affairs of a honey-moon," I said. "How are you going to continue the human race if you proceed on the assumption that the fact of two persons living together produces this nausea?"

"Ah! yes; what's to be done, lest the human race perish?" he repeated, maliciously, as if he had been waiting for this conscientious and familiar objection. "Preach abstention from child-bearing, in order that English lords may be always supplied with the wherewithal to wax fat, and no one will find fault with you. But merely hint the advisability of abstaining from child-bearing in the name of morality, and, great heavens! what a cry will be raised!

"But I trust you'll pardon me. That light up there is disagreeable to me," he said, pointing to the lantern; "have you any objection to my drawing the shade round it?" On my replying that it was a matter of indifference to me, he rose—as he did everything—precipitately, got up on the seat, and drew the woolen shade over the lantern.

"Still," I urged, "if every one were to accept this doctrine as a law of practica...

conduct, the human race would soon cease to exist."

He did not immediately reply.

"You want to know how the human race is to perpetuate itself?" he said, re-seating himself opposite to me, stretching out his feet widely apart, and resting his elbows on his knees. "Why should the human race be perpetuated?" he asked.

"Why?" I exclaimed; "because otherwise we should not exist."

"But why should we exist?"

"Why should we? In order to live, of course."

"Well, but why should we live? If there be no purpose, no aim; if life be given to us for life's sake only, then there is no object in living. And if that be so, Schopenhauer and the Buddhists are perfectly right. On the other hand, if there be an end and object in human existence, it is clear that humanity must cease to exist when that object is attained. This is perfectly evident," he repeated with visible emotion, clearly setting a high value upon his thought.

"Yes, this is perfectly evident. Now, mark my words well: if the object for which humanity exists is bliss, goodness, love, or by whatever other name you like to call it, if it is what the ancient prophets have proclaimed it to be, namely, that all men be united in love, that their swords be turned into plow-shares, and so on, what hinders the accomplishment of this object? The passions do. Now, of all the passions, the strongest, the most wicked, the most stubborn, is the passion of the senses. Consequently, if we succeed in rooting up the passions, and with them this last and most powerful, the prophecies will come to pass; men will be united by the

bond of love, the aim and mission of humanity will have been fulfilled, and there will be no longer any reason for the further existence of the human race.

"As long as humanity subsists, it tends toward an ideal; and its ideal is assuredly not that of rabbits who increase and multiply as much as possible; it is an ideal of goodness attainable by continence, abstemiousness, purity. Toward this ideal people have always been and still are tending.

"Look now at the upshot of all this: love, passion, appears in the role of a safety-valve. The present generation of men has not accomplished the mission for which it is here in the world; and why? Because of its passions, the strongest of which is the passion of sense. On the other hand, such passion not being extirpated, a new generation arises, and humanity has the renewed possibility of arriving at the goal by the efforts of the new men. If they are unsuccessful, it is for the same reason, and failure brings with it the possibility of success later on, and so on ad infinitum, till such times as the object is accomplished, the prophecy comes to pass, and all men are joined together in union.

"What would happen were things otherwise? If God had created men, for instance, for the purpose of accomplishing a certain mission, and had made them mortal and devoid of passions or immortal? In the former case they would live without having attained the end and object of their existence, and would then die; and God would have to resort to another creative act, in order that the purpose in question should be fulfilled. In the latter case, that is, if men had been created immortal, let us suppose that after many thousand years they at tained their end—a most unlikely thing to postulate, seeing that it is much easier for new generations to correct the errors of the old and tend toward perfection, than for the same creatures to turn from their mistakes and change their lines of conduct. What would be the aim and purpose of their further existence? What should be done with them then? Evidently things are better as they are.

"But perhaps you dislike the form in which I have expressed all this? Perhaps you are an evolutionist? But even so, you can not fail to see the truth of this contention. The highest race of animals is the human race. In order to hold its own in the struggle with other races it must keep closely together, unite like a swarm of bees, and not go on endlessly multiplying and increasing; and like the bees it should bring up the sexless; that is to say, it ought to aim at restraint, and not by any means contribute to inflame the passions as our social life seems deliberately instituted to do."

He was silent for a time. Then he resumed: "The human race will cease? Yes; but is it possible that any one, no matter from what point of view he contemplated the world, could have ever entertained a doubt about that? Why, it is as inevitable as death. All ecclesiastical doctrines are based on the theory that this world of ours will sooner or later come to an end; modern science propagates the same teaching. Why should we be surprised that ethics inculcates the same lesson?"

Having ceased speaking, he remained a considerable time silent, drinking and smoking the while. Having smoked his cigarette to the end, he took several more

out of his bag and began to put them into his old, soiled cigarette-case.

"I understand your position," I said; "something similar to that is taught by the Shakers."

"Yes, yes; and they are right," he exclaimed. "Passion, no matter with what forms it may be hedged round, is an evil, a terrible evil, to be combated, not fostered, as it is in our society. The words of the Gospel that 'whosoever looketh on a woman to lust after her, hath committed adultery with her already in his heart,' apply not only to other men's wives, but also and mainly to one's own. In our world as at present constituted, the prevalent views are exactly contrary to this, and consequently to what they ought to be. What are these wedding tours and excursions, and that isolation of the young married couple authorized by their elders, but a license to unlimited pleasure?"

CHAPTER XII

PUNISHMENT

"But sooner or later the moral law visits us with condign punishment for every violation of it. Thus all my efforts to make the honey-moon a success were doomed to failure. It was a period of shame, tediousness, and it soon became an unbearable torture.

"Things took this turn very early indeed. Finding my wife bored one day—I think it was the third or fourth day after marriage—I inquired the cause of her gloom, and began to embrace her, this being, to my thinking, all that she could possibly expect or desire from me; but she put my arms off, and began to shed tears. 'What is the matter?' She was unable to say what, but she was evidently very sad and depressed. Probably her nerves revealed to her the nature of our relations; but she could not formulate what she instinctively felt. I continued to question her, and she muttered something about being lonely without her mother. I felt that this was not true, and I set about consoling her without making any reference to her mother. I did not realize that she was simply depressed in spirits, and that her mother was merely a pretext; and yet she at once took offense at my not mentioning her mother, as if I disbelieved what she had told me. She could now see, she said, that I did not love her. On this, I rebuked her for being capricious, and all at once a change came over her face; the sadness that had settled upon it gave way to an expression of irritation, and she began to reproach me in the most spiteful words with being egoistic and cruel. I looked intently upon her; all her features combined to express perfect coldness and hostility—I might almost say hatred—toward me.

"I remember the horror that seized me then; what did it mean? How could it be? Love, the blending of souls in one! And instead of that, this is what it had come to! 'Can it be?' I asked myself. 'Surely this is not she!'

"I endeavored to soothe and calm her, but soon found myself face to face with such an impregnable wall of cold, venomous hostility, that before I knew where I was I was lashed into a state of extreme irritation, with the result that we addressed a number of unpleasant remarks to each other.

"The impression left by that first quarrel of ours was indescribably horrible. I have called it a quarrel, but in truth it was nothing of the kind; it was merely the discovery of the abyss that yawned between us. What we called love had been exhausted, and there we stood face to face in our true mutual relations; two egoists, perfect strangers to each other.

"I have given the name of 'quarrel' to what passed between us. But it was not a quarrel; it was simply a glimpse of our real relation to each other. I did not then perceive that this coldness and hostility constituted our normal relation to each other, because during that first period of our married life those sentiments were soon again hidden from our observation by the vapors raised by 'love,' and I took it that we had merely quarreled and become reconciled, and that no such misunderstandings should ever occur again.

"But it was not long before, during the first month of the honey-moon, another period set in, during which we again ceased for a time to be necessary to each other, and in consequence of which another quarrel broke out. This second misunderstanding impressed me more profoundly than the first. 'The first was not, therefore, a mere accident,' I said to myself; 'it was the result of a necessity, and will again occur in virtue of the same necessity.' Another reason why I was struck more profoundly by this second quarrel, was its absurdly insufficient pretext. It was something about money, which I never grudged and could not dream of grudging my wife; I only remember that she put such an interpretation upon the matter as to make a remark of mine seem the expression of a wish on my part to acquire an undue ascendency over her by means of money to which she pretended that claimed an exclusive right. The accu sation was groundless, silly, vile, unnatural.

"I lost my temper and upbraided her with lack of delicacy; she accused me in turn, and in the expression of her face and eyes I read the same cruel, deliberate enmity that had struck coldness to my heart before.

"With my father, with my brother, I had quarreled, I remember, occasionally; but there never had subsisted between us that peculiarly bitter hatred that had sprung up between my wife and me. It was not long, however, before this mutual hatred was disguised once more by so-called love, and I was once more engaged in consoling myself that these two quarrels were mistakes, mere misunderstandings which might be easily cleared up. The occurrence of the third and fourth quarrels, however, dispelled this delusion; I recognized clearly that this was no accident, no misunderstanding, but the outcome of necessity; that it could not be otherwise, that it would recur again and again.

"And my heart froze within me at the perspective before me. My suffering was still further intensified by the thought that I alone was living with my wife in such perpetual discord, so different from the way I used to flatter myself we would live; that other people were more fortunate than we were. I was ignorant then that this is the common lot, that other people believe their misery to be—as I believed mine—exceptional; that they not only hide it from others, but endeavor to disguise it to themselves.

"In our case it began immediately after the wedding, and went on gaining gradually in intensity and savageness. From the very first weeks of our married life I knew in the bottom of my heart that I was caught in a trap, that what I had realized was not what I had had in view and confidently expected, that my marriage, far from being a source of happiness, was a burden very hard to bear; but, like every one else, I refused to admit this, not only to others—I should not own to it now if it were not ended forever—but even to myself.

"Whenever I think of it now, it is a mystery to me how I could have remained blind to my real condition. One sure sign by which we might have easily recognized it was the circumstance that all our quarrels turned upon mere bagatelles; indeed, their origin was so absurdly trivial that, once over, we could not recollect how they had come about. The reasoning faculty was not quick enough to conjure up specious pretexts fast enough for the outburst of cordial hostility which continued to subsist between us without break or change. Still more striking, however, was the insufficiency of the pretexts for reconciliation. Occasionally they assumed the form of words, explanations, even tears, but at times—and even now the recollection of it fills me with disgust—while launching the most bitter and venomous reproaches at each other, a period of silence would begin, filled up with smiles, kisses, embraces."

CHAPTER XIII

TWO WAYS OUT

At this point two passengers entered the carriage and began to install themselves on the far-off seat. Pozdnischeff ceased speaking till they had finally taken their places. As soon as they were settled down, and the noise caused by their movements had subsided, he began again where he had left off, obviously never for a moment losing the thread of his thoughts.

"What is peculiarly revolting about all this," he resumed, "is that whereas in theory love is described as an ideal state, a sublime sentiment, in practice it is a thing which can not be mentioned or called to mind without a feeling of disgust. It was not without cause that nature made it so. But if it be revolting, let it be proclaimed so without any disguise. Instead of that, however, people go about preaching and teaching that it is something splendid and sublime.

" 'What,' I asked myself in astonishment, 'could give rise to the deadly malignity which we entertained toward each other?' And yet the source of it was perfectly obvious. This malignity was neither more nor less than the protest of human nature against the other nature that was crushing it in both of us. I was amazed at our reciprocal hatred. And yet it was impossible that we should feel anything but hatred for each other. This sentiment was, in kind, identical with the hatred which accomplices in a crime feel for each other, both for instigating and for actually taking part in the crime.

"Perhaps you think that I am wandering from the point? Not in the least. I am unfolding to you the story of how I killed my wife. They asked me on my trial with what and how I killed her. Fools that they are, to suppose that I murdered her with the knife on the 5th of October. It was not then that I killed her; it was very long before, just as they are all killing their wives at this moment—all, ay, all of them."

"How so?" I asked.

"It is the most extraordinary thing conceivable that no one wants to see what is so clear and evident, what physicians should know and inculcate, but about which they are obstinately silent.

"The thing is so extremely simple. Now the number of women in the world is about equal to that of men. The inference is clear: it is drawn and acted upon by the lower animals, and it requires no rare wisdom on the part of men to discover it; it is that restraint is indispensable. But simple as is the discovery, it has not yet been made. Science has discovered some new kind of animalculæ that swim about in the blood, and a hundred other superfluous absurdities, but it has not advanced to the point necessary to apprehend this truth yet. At least one does not hear of any such doctrines being put forward by men of science.

"And so a woman has but two ways out of the difficulty. The first is by annihilating once for all or destroying, whenever the circumstances seem to require it, her faculty of becoming a mother. The second is not, properly speaking, a way out of the difficulty at all; it is simply a direct violation of the laws of nature: the woman is obliged to nurse her child and be the mistress of her husband at one and the same time. This is the origin in our social sphere of hysterics and nerves, and in the peasant class of 'possession.' So it is in Russia. Nor is it otherwise in Europe. And both women suffering from 'possession' and the female patients of Professor Charcot are in the true sense of the word cripples; and of such the world is full.

"It needs but little reflection to realize how important, how sublime, is that which is taking place when a woman bears within her, or is tending and feeding, the being that will prove a continuation of, a substitute for, ourselves. And these holy functions are interrupted, and for what? . . . And in the face of this they prate about freedom, about woman's rights. Why, the cannibals might just as well boast that they were solicitous for the rights and liberty of the prisoners of war whom they feed and fatten for food."

All this was new to me, and deeply impressed me.

"What would you do?" I asked. "If you are right you will annihilate the relation of husband and wife; and men, as you are aware—"

"Yes, I know," he interrupted. "This is another of the favorite doctrines of physicians, those precious priests of science. I would, if I could, condemn these magicians to discharge the functions of these very women whom they affirm to be so indispensable to men, in order to hear what they then would say upon the question. Impress a man with the idea that alcohol is indispensable to him, that he can not get on without tobacco, that opium is a necessity of life, and all these things will straightway become indispensable. Is it to be supposed that God did not know what was needful to man, and that not having taken counsel of the physicians He scamped His work?

"It was a question, as you perceive, of reconciling two conditions diametrically opposed to each other. How was the difficulty to be overcome? Put your trust in the doctors; they will make things smooth. And they did. They found as issue out of the difficulty. Oh, that those villains were divorced from their frauds! It is indeed high time! You see what it has come to already. People go mad and blow their brains out, and all owing to this. And how could it be otherwise?

"Brute beasts seem to be instinctively aware that their progeny serves to perpetuate the race, and they observe a certain law in this connection. Man alone does not know this, and does not want to know it. He wrecks and ruins one half of the human race; he transforms all women, who should be active coadjutors aiding humanity to move onward toward truth and happiness, into enemies of progress and development. Look around you and say what or who it is that impedes the advance of humanity. Womankind. And why do they act so? For the reason just explained.

"Yes, yes," he repeated several times, beginning to stir himself a little, and he took out a cigarette and began to smoke it, obviously striving to calm himself.

CHAPTER XIV

THE DEVIL'S CUNNING

"I LIVED this life like everybody else, and, what was still worse, I flattered myself that because I did not commit adultery I was leading a pure family life, was a truly moral man, perfectly blameless, and that if quarrels did disturb the quiet of our lives my wife was in fault, it was her character that was to blame. Needless to say the blame did not really rest with her. She was like other women, like the majority of women. She had been brought up in such a way as to qualify her to play the part assigned to women in our society, which is equivalent to saying that her training was in nowise different from that of other women of the well-to-do classes.

"It is the fashion nowadays to talk about some new system of female education, but all that is arrant nonsense. Women are actually trained and educated in perfect harmony with the views really and truly held in modern society respecting the mission of their sex, and female education will always be regulated in strict accordance with man's conception of woman. Now no one ignores what men's views of women are. Wine, women, and song—so say the poets in verse. Read the poetry of all ages and countries, examine all the productions of painting and sculpture, commencing with erotic poems and Venuses and Phyrnes, and you can not fail to perceive that in the highest society, as well as in the lowest, woman is merely an instrument of pleasure.

"And mark the devil's cunning; it is not enough that she should be so degraded, but the fact must be deftly disguised. Thus in by-gone times we read of the gallant knights who went about protesting that they idolized woman, apotheosized her; in our days men profess that they honor and respect woman; they yield up their places to her, pick up her pocket-handkerchief, and some even go so far as to admit her right to occupy all civil positions of trust, to have a share in the government, and so on. And in the face of all these professions and protestations the world's view of woman's mission and position is un-

modified; she is still what she was—an object of pleasure; and she is well aware that it is so.

"We notice exactly the same state of things, the same contradiction between professions and acts in the matter of slavery. Slavery is the enjoyment by a few of the involuntary labor of the many, and before slavery can become a thing of the past, people must cease to desire the enjoyment of the forced labor of others, must hold it to be sinful or shameful. But no, they simply set to work to abolish the outward form of slavery, to render it impossible legally to purchase or sell a slave, and execute a deed of sale; and this done, they delude themselves into the belief that slavery no longer exists, overlooking the circumstance that it continues to be just as rife as before, because people still consider it good and just to profit by the labor of others. And as long as they hold it to be good and just there will never be any lack of persons stronger or more cunning than their fellows who can transform this opinion into an act.

"It is just the same with the thralldom of woman. Woman's serfdom consists in the circumstance that she is looked upon and sought after as an instrument of pleasure, and that this view is considered the right one. And then woman is solemnly enfranchised, is invested with extensive rights, equal to those exercised by men, but people continue to regard her as an instrument of pleasure, continue to educate her accordingly, instilling those views into her mind first in her childhood, and later on by means of public opinion. And so she remains what she was, a degraded, demoralized serf, as the man remains what he was, a demoralized slave-owner. We enfranchise woman in high schools and hospital wards, and yet continue to look upon her as before. Train her, as she is trained in Russia, to regard herself in that light, and she will remain forever a being of a lower order. Gymnasiums and high schools are powerless to change this; it can only be altered by a change in men's views of women and women's views of themselves. It can only be supplanted by a better state of things when woman considers that the highest condition to which she, as woman, can attain is that of maidenhood—a state which she now regards as one of shame and disgrace. Until this change of ideas takes place, the ideal of every girl, whatever her education may be, will necessarily remain what it now is—to attract as many men as possible, in order to secure for herself the possibility of choosing; and the circumstance that one girl knows more mathematics, or another can play the harp, does not change one iota. A woman is happy, and attains all that she desires, when she captivates a man; hence the great object of her life is to master the art of captivating men. So it has ever been, and so it will be. In the life of a young girl in our sphere this tendency is clearly observable, and she carries it with her into the married state. To the maiden it is indispensable in order that she may have an extensive choice; to the married woman that she may strengthen her ascendency over her husband. The only event that puts an end to this tendency, or at least represses it for awhile, is the birth of children, and even that has no effect if the mother is a monster—that is, does not nurse her own children. But here again the doctors interfere.

"My wife, who suckled her five other children, fell ill soon after the birth of the first. The precious doctors who cynically touched and examined her, for which I had to thank and pay them, decreed that she should not suckle her child, and, in consequence of this sentence, she was deprived of the sole means whereby she would have been effectually delivered from coquettishness. We hired a wet-nurse—that is to say, we took advantage of the poverty, the misery, and the ignorance of another woman, enticed her away from her own child to ours, and in return decked her out with a head-dress and tawdry laces. But this by the way. The point is that my wife's exemption from the cares and duties of a mother manifested itself in the awakening of that female coquettishness which had previously lain dormant in her, while I began to be tortured with the agonies of jealousy, which had never given me a moment's rest during my married life, but now grew unbearably excruciating. This feeling of jealousy is no peculiar characteristic of mine; it is the common lot of all husbands who live with their wives as I lived with mine."

CHAPTER XV

PANGS OF JEALOUSY

"DURING the whole course of my married life I never once enjoyed a moment's relief from the maddening pangs of jealousy. There were times, however, when my torments were unusually acute; and one of these periods began after the birth of my first child when the doctors forbid my wife to nurse it.

"There was a twofold reason for this intensity of jealousy during the period in question. In the first place, the circumstance that my wife experienced that uneasiness peculiar to mothers which provokes a general disturbance in the natural course of life; and secondly, because, having seen with what a light heart she set at naught the moral obligations of a mother, I naturally, if unconsciously, concluded that she might with equal facility trample upon the duties of wife, especially as she was in the enjoyment of perfect health, and, in spite of the prohibition of the precious physicians, nursed the children who were born subsequently without the slightest inconvenience to herself."

"You do not seem enamored of doctors?" I said, noticing an especially bitter tone of voice whenever he alluded to them or their profession.

"It's not a matter of like or dislike," he answered. "My life has been utterly wrecked by doctors, and they have ruined and are still ruining the lives of thousands, nay, of hundreds of thousands, and I can not well help putting cause and effect together. Of course it is natural enough that, like lawyers and members of other professions, they should be somewhat keen about earning money, and I must say that I would most willingly cede them half my yearly income, and I am sure every one else would gladly follow my example, if their influence for evil were made clear, on condition that they would refrain from meddling in other people's family affairs, that they would keep to themselves and leave others in peace. Although I never collected statistics on the subject, I am acquainted with scores of cases—and there are countless similar ones—in which they killed now the unborn child, now the mother, on the pretext of performing an operation. Yet nobody ever regards these murders, as no one ever added up the murders committed by the Inquisition, because, forsooth, they are all done for the good of mankind. It would be impossible to count the number of crimes committed by the medical profession. And yet they are all as dust in the balance, compared with that moral depravation, the pollution of materialism, which they introduce into the world through the medium of women. If you hearken to their counsels—so numerous and dangerous are the germs of disease that lurk in wait for you at every step you take—whatever you do will tend not to draw you closer to your fellow-men, but to separate you from them more than ever. If the doctors' behests were faithfully carried out, every one of us should sit apart, completely isolated from every one else, and would never think of putting the syringe with the carbolic acid out of his hand. (Of late, I am told, they have discovered that carbolic acid is ineffectual.) This, however, is merely by the way. The real poison of their influence lies in the demoralization of the people, especially of the women, which marks their track. Nowadays it would be a solecism to say: 'You, friend, are leading a bad, irregular life; live better.' No one would ever think of addressing such words to himself or to others. If you are leading a bad life, the cause is to be sought for in the nervous centers, in one of which something must have gone wrong; and you can not do better than put yourself in the hands of a physician who will prescribe a shilling's worth of medicine for you, which you will duly take as ordered. You will then grow worse, on which you must have more doctors and more medicines. A precious system!

"But all this by the way. I wanted to say that my wife nursed the children herself with excellent results, and that this child-bearing and child-nursing were the only things that contributed to ease the sufferings I endured from jealousy. Indeed, had it not been for them, the catastrophe would have occurred much sooner. It was the children who saved both her and me. In the course of eight years she gave birth to five children and nursed them all herself."

"Where are they now—your children, I mean?" I asked.

"The children?" he repeated, with a frightened look.

"I beg your pardon; perhaps I have unwittingly awakened very painful memories."

"No, it's nothing. My sister-in-law and her brother took charge of the children. I gave them my fortune, but they refused to give me the custody of my children. You see I am a sort of insane person. I am now journeying away from them. I saw them, but they would not give them up to me. If I had charge of them, I should educate them so that they would not resemble their parents; and this is precisely what is not wanted. It is required that they should be exactly such as we were. Well, there is no

help for it, I dare say. It is natural enough for them to keep the children from me and to disbelieve me. Besides, I am not at all sure that I have the energy needed to educate them; indeed, I am inclined to think not: I am but a ruin now, a cripple. One thing, however, I have; I know—yes, *this* is true, I do know what most other people will not soon learn. Yes, the children are all living, and growing up just such savages as all those around them. I saw them. Three times I saw them. I can do nothing for them. Nothing. I am now on my way to my place in the south, where I have a little house and garden. Yes, it will take some time before people will know what I know. It is easy to learn whether there is much iron in the sun, and what other metals there are in the sun and the stars; but it is hard, yes, frightfully hard, to discover that which convicts us of immorality. You are listening, and even for that I am grateful."

CHAPTER XVI

A BLESSING AND JOY

"You just mentioned the children. There again, just consider what lying goes on concerning children. Children are a blessing from God, children are a joy. Now all this is a lie. It was true once, but has long since ceased to contain a grain of truth. Children are a torment, and nothing more. The majority of mothers distinctly feel this, and at times, when off their guard, say so very plainly. Question the general run of mothers in our social circles, people who live in affluence, and they will tell you that from fear lest their children should sicken and die, they don't wish to have any children at all; and if any are born, they refuse to nurse them, lest they should become too much attached to them and be made unhappy in consequence. The pleasure they receive from the contemplation of the child, the charms of its tiny hands, its pretty little feet, and its diminutive little body, are less than the sufferings they undergo in consequence of—I do not say the illness or loss of the child, but of—the mere apprehension of the possibility of illness or death. Having weighed the advantages and the drawbacks, it turns out that the balance is not in favor of the former, and they therefore decide that it is not desirable to have children. These sentiments they express artlessly, fearlessly, thinking that they spring from affection for children—an excellent, praiseworthy feeling in which they take pride. They do not perceive that by reasoning in this way, they are disavowing love, and merely proclaiming their own selfishness. Their pleasure is lessened by fear for the child, and consequently they do not wish to have a child whom they would be fond of. They sacrifice, not themselves for a beloved creature, but the beloved creature who is on the point of coming into existence for themselves. It is pretty clear that this is not love but egoism.

"On the other hand, one has not the heart to condemn these mothers of well-to-do families for their egoism, when one bears in mind all that they have to suffer for the sake of their children's health, owing once more to those doctors who play such an important part in our lives. Even now

the bare recollection of what my wife went through, and the continual state of anxiety she was in during the first years of our married life, when we had three and four children who engrossed all her attention, makes me shudder. We led a dog's life. It does not deserve the name of life; it was one never-ending danger hanging over us, followed by momentary escapes from it, after which it would again loom threatening until we once more escaped for a time, and so on without end—our condition being for all the world like that of the crew of a sinking vessel. There were times when I imagined that all this was feigned, and that she was merely pretending to be anxious about the children in order to get the whip hand of me, so effectually did it contribute to settle all questions between us in her favor. It seemed as if everything she said and did was said and done as the result of a preconcerted plan. This, however, was not really so. She was continually worrying and tormenting herself to death with the children, with their health and their illnesses, and it was a martyrdom for her as well as for me. She felt that strong attachment to children, that animal need of nursing, fondling, and nestling them which is common to most mothers. But she did not enjoy, as animals do, immunity from imagination and reasoning. The hen, for instance, has no fear of what may be in store for her chick, has not the faintest notion what the diseases are to which it may fall a prey; knows nothing of the means by which people fondly imagine that they can save themselves from sickness and death; and consequently her young are not a torment to her. She does for her chicks what it is in her nature to do for them, and what is therefore a pleasure for her to do, and it is only natural that her young should be a joy to her. And the instant one of her chicks falls ill, her duties become very clearly determined: she has only to warm and feed it, and having done this feels that she has performed all that is needful. If it comes to pass, in spite of her care, that it dies, she does not ask why and whither it has gone; she clucks for awhile, ceases, and lives on as before.

"With our unhappy women, and with my wife in particular, the case is very different. Independently of the question of children's diseases and the way to treat them, there were numbers of other topics always cropping up, such, for instance, as how to educate them, how to discipline their minds, about which she had heard and read an infinite number of ever-varying rules and prescriptions. They should be fed thus, and only with that and that; no, not so, not with that, but thus and with such and such a food. On the subjects of clothing them, bathing them, putting them to sleep, sending them to walk, regulating the quality of the air they breathe, both of us were discovering, but especially she was discovering, new rules every week. It was just as if children had only begun to be born into the world yesterday. It was all because the poor child was not fed properly, or did not get its bath in due time, that it fell ill; consequently she felt that it was she who should bear the blame, for not having taken the needful precautions, for not

having done what should have been done.

"Thus under the most favorable circumstances, that is, when in thriving health, children are a torment; but when they fall ill, life is positively not worth living, it is simply a hell on earth. We start with the postulate that diseases can be cured, that there is a science which has their treatment for its object, and that there are people called physicians who know how to cure them. Not, of course, that every doctor is capable of treating them successfully, but the best among the profession. And now, the child being ill, the problem to be solved is how to get at the very best doctor, the man who saves; this done, the infant is saved. If you can not consult him, if you are living in a different part of the city from where he resides, and can not summon him in time, the child is lost. And observe, it is not the belief of my wife only to which I am now giving expression, it is the faith of all the women of her social sphere. On all sides scraps of conversation like the following fell frequently on her ears: 'Mrs. A——'s three children, poor dear things, died because Doctor Z—— was not sent for in time. He saved Mrs. D——'s eldest little girl, you know. The Petroffs, by advice of the doctor, isolated themselves in time and went to live at different hotels, and saved their lives by doing so. The others who did not isolate themselves lost their children. Mrs. So-and-So's little girl was very weak until, by advice of the doctor, they went to live in the south, and saved the child's life.' How could she do otherwise than fret, and chafe, and tremble, from year's end to year's end, at the thought that the life of her children, to whom she was attached by the bonds of strong animal affection, depended wholly on her learning in good time what Doctor Ivan Zakharievitch had to say on the subject. And yet nobody knew what Ivan Zakharievitch would say, he himself least of all, because he was and is well aware that he knows nothing and has no help to give, and so all he does is to shuffle and trim as best he can, so that people should not cease to believe that he knows what he is talking about.

"If she had been in all respects an animal, she would not have tortured herself as she did. If she had been in all respects a human being, she would have been animated by faith in God, and would have spoken, and thought like the peasant women, who exclaim: 'God gave and God has taken away; you can not escape from God.' She would have felt that the life and death of all mankind, and of her children among the rest, are beyond the power of man, in the hands of God alone, and she would not therefore have racked her mind with the thought that it was in her power to hinder the sickness and death of her children, and that yet she failed to do so. As a matter of fact, her position was extremely complicated: she had charge of the most frail creatures conceivable, weak little things exposed to countless mishaps. She was drawn toward them by vehement animal affection. Moreover, these beings were confided to her care, and yet the means of preserving them unharmed were hidden from her and revealed to men who were perfect strangers to her, whose services and counsels she could not obtain otherwise than by paying considerable sums of money, and not always even then. How could she do otherwise than torture herself?

"And this she did without respite. Just when our angry passions would be slowly subsiding after some scene of jealousy or a common quarrel, and were making ready to regulate our lives anew, to begin a course of reading or to take some enterprise in hand, word would be suddenly brought that Vasa was taken sick; that Mary had a bowel complaint; that a rash had broken out on Andy's face or body, and from that moment began our martyrdom anew. To what part of the city should we rush off, which doctor should we send for, in what room should we isolate the sick child? And then began the endless series of injections, measurings of temperature, mixtures, potions, and doctors. And before this came to an end, something else would crop up unexpectedly, and so on without end; a regular, family life being wholly out of the question. As I said before, it was one continual escape from fancied and from real dangers. And the same thing goes on still in the majority of families. In our family it was painfully palpable. My wife loved her children dearly, and was credulous; so that the presence of children, far from contributing to better our life, only poisoned it.

"Moreover, the children were for us a new pretext for quarreling. Each of us specially favored one child, which was our pet instrument in the quarrel. Thus, I generally employed Vasa (the eldest); she made use of Liza. Later on, when they grew up and their characters unfolded themselves, they gradually became our allies, whom we sought to enlist on our side by every means at our disposal. The results told terribly on their bringing up, poor things; but we had no time or desire during our endless warfare to give this a thought. The girl was usually my partisan; the eldest boy, who resembled his mother, and frequently espoused her cause, was often hateful to me."

CHAPTER XVII

HOSTILE

"And in this manner we continued to live, our relations growing gradually more and more hostile, until at last it was no longer difference of views that produced enmity, but settled enmity that engendered difference of views. No matter what opinion she might advance, no matter what wish she might express, I always dissented in advance, and she treated me in the same way. In the fourth year of our marriage we tacitly came to the conclusion that there was no hope of our ever being able to understand each other, to agree with each other, and so we ceased to make any further attempts to come to an agreement. Each of us held his or her own opinion about the most matter-of-fact subjects—about everything connected with the children, for instance. The views that I advocated were not by any means so dear to me that I could not sacrifice them; but she was of the opposite way of thinking; and to give up my opinion would mean to yield to her; and, whatever else I might agree to, this I could not think of doing. It was the same with her. She looked upon herself as having acted rightly and justly by me,

and I, in my own eyes, was invariably immaculate. When together, we were reduced to something like silence, to such conversations as the very brutes, I am convinced, can carry on among themselves. 'What o'clock is it?' 'Is it time to go to bed?' 'What shall we have for dinner to-day?' 'Where shall we drive?' 'What's in the newspapers?' 'Shall I send for the doctor? Mary has a sore throat.'

"A single step beyond the bounds of this circumscribed circle of conversational topics was enough to provoke the renewal of hostilities. Skirmishes and expressions of hatred were called forth by the coffee, the table-cloth, the carriage, the card played at whist—in a word, by things and incidents that could not possibly be of the slightest importance to us. Speaking for myself, I can say that I was boiling with hatred toward her. I would watch her pouring out the tea, waving her foot to and fro, lifting up the spoon to her mouth, smacking her lips and drawing in the liquid; and I hated her for all that as if she had committed a really bad action. I did not remark at the time that these periods of hatred recurred regularly, uniformly, and invariably corresponded with the periods of what we termed love.

"The periods and the degrees corresponded: after a period of love came a period of hatred; a period of vehement love was followed by a long period of hatred; a shorter period of hatred succeeded a weaker manifestation of love. We were not then aware that this love and hatred were the two opposite poles of one and the same feeling.

"It would have been terrible to live

thus, had we realized and understood our position; but we did not understand it. And herein lies the salvation, as well as the punishment, of men who lead irregular lives; that they can always raise a cloud before their eyes which hides from them the misery of their situation. It was thus that we acted. She sought to forget the dreadful reality by giving her attention to absorbing and always urgent occupations: household cares, the furniture, her own dresses and those of the children, their schooling, and their health. As for me, I had my own ways of intoxicating myself. There was the intoxication of my daily work, the intoxication of the chase, the intoxication of cards. Thus we were both of us always occupied; and both of us felt that the more assiduously we were occupied, the more spiteful and malicious we could be to each other.

" 'It's all right for you to go on making your grimaces,' I would say of her to myself; 'but you worried me to death all last night with those scenes you made; and here now I've got to go to the meeting of the committee.' 'You have no reason to feel uneasy,' she on her side would not only think, but say aloud to me, 'but I have not slept a wink all night with the child.'

"All these new-fangled theories about hypnotism, psychical disorders, hysterics, and the rest, are an absurdity, not a simple absurdity, however, but a wicked, baneful absurdity. There is not the slightest doubt that Charcot would have pronounced my wife to be hysterical and myself abnormal, and it is likely enough that he would set about treating us. And yet there was absolutely nothing to cure us of.

"And thus we lived in a perpetual fog, unable to see and realize the position in which we were. And if the episode which occurred later on had not taken place at all, I might live to be an old man without once ceasing to cherish the belief that I had led a good life; not a remarkably good one, but not a bad life. I might never have got a glimpse of that abyss of misery and odious lying in which I was floundering hopelessly. We were two prisoners hating each other and chained together. We poisoned each other's lives, and tried to shut our eyes to what we were doing. I did not know at that time that ninety-nine per cent of all married people are plunged in just such a hell as mine. I was not aware then that I was in such a hell, and consequently never imagined that others were.

"It is wonderful what striking coincidences may be found in the course of a regular humdrum life, and even in quite an irregular life. Thus, just when the parents have rendered each other's life unbearable, it becomes necessary, in the interests of their children's education, to come to live in a city where the conditions for education are favorable." He was silent for awhile. Then he uttered those peculiar sounds, which now resembled suppressed sobs. We were nearing a station. "What o'clock is it?" he asked me. I looked at my watch—it was two o'clock, A. M. "Are you not tired?" he exclaimed. "No, I am not, but you are fatigued," I replied. "I am choking," he said; "excuse me, I will get out for awhile at the station and take a drink of water;" and reeling down the passage in the middle of the carriage, he left the train. I remained seated alone in the compartment, turning over in my mind all that he had been telling me, and so absorbed was I by my reflections that I did not remark his return by the opposite door.

CHAPTER XVIII

NO CURB

"I KNOW I am continually wandering away from the subject, but the fact is I have pondered long and carefully over it all, and I have come to look upon many things from a new angle of vision, and I would rather explain all this to you in detail.

"As I was saying, we left the country and came to settle in the city. In a city unhappy people breathe much more freely than in the country. A man may live a hundred years in a city without the fact ever once dawning upon him that he has been dead and rotten for ever so long. He has no leisure to take stock of himself; he is always occupied; there are social rounds and duties, the arts, his own and his children's health to look after, their education to superintend; he must receive the visits of these people and of those, must in turn visit these acquaintances and those friends, must see this person and hear that one. A city, no matter when you consider it, is never without one or more celebrities, of whose presence it is absolutely incumbent upon you to avail yourself; now you must have yourself treated for this or that complaint, or have your children prescribed for; then again you have to see the teacher, the tutor,

the governess—and your life is a hollow sham.

"It was thus that we lived, growing less susceptible to the sufferings caused by our daily intercourse. Moreover, at first we had the pleasing pastime of settling down in the city, establishing ourselves in our new lodgings, and the consequent journeying to and fro between the city and the country.

"The second winter after our arrival an incident occurred without which none of the subsequent episodes of my life would ever have taken place. She was delicate in health, and the scoundrelly doctors forbid her ever again to become a mother. And they taught her the means of executing their commands. To me this was an abomination, and I set my face against it; but she insisted on obeying the doctors, stubbornly refusing to yield to my representations. To the peasant workman children are necessary, although he finds it hard enough to support them; but they are necessary, and this is the justification of his conjugal relations. To us who possess children already, they are not a necessity; on the contrary, they are a source of new anxiety, of expense—they are a burden, in a word. Consequently we are without any justification of the life we lead. Either we escape from having children by artificial means, or else—what is still worse—we regard them as a misfortune, the result of carelessness on our part. But justification we have already absolutely none. So low are we fallen, however, from a moral point of view, that we do not feel the need of any justification. The overwhelming majority of the present educated classes give themselves up to this species of life without the least remorse of conscience. Nor would it be easy to expect remorse, seeing that there is no such thing as conscience in our life, unless we consent to give that name to the conscience of public opinion, of the criminal law. And in the present case neither of the two is shocked or in any way called into play. There is no reason why one should be ashamed to look society in the face, for all its members do likewise, Mrs. P——, and Ivan Zakharievitch, and the rest. Neither need one be in awe of the criminal law. It is only ugly country girls and soldiers' wives who throw their children into wells and ponds: and it is of course only just that such depraved characters as they are should be put in jail. We arranged all these things in good time, decently, respectably.

"Two years more rolled by, and it became evident that the means supplied by the doctors were beginning to act. My wife's appearance improved; she grew more attractive than ever with the last mellow beauty, as it were, of summer. She felt this, and thought much about herself. Her beauty was of a provoking, perturbing kind, such as would naturally characterize a pretty woman of thirty, well-fed, irritable, and no longer fatigued by the cares and responsibilities of motherhood. Whenever she passed she was sure to attract the looks of men, to magnetize them, as it were. She resembled a well-fed, wanton, harnessed horse that has long stood inactive in the stables, and from whom the bridle has been suddenly removed. There was no curb of any kind, as there is no curb of any

kind to hold in ninety-nine per cent of our women. I felt this, and I was seized with horror."

CHAPTER XIX

THE VIOLINIST

HE suddenly rose and moved nearer to the window. "I ask your pardon," he said, and silently fixing his eyes on the window, remained thus three or four minutes. Then, heaving a deep sigh, he again rose and reseated himself opposite me.

His face underwent a total change; there was a piteous expression in his eyes, and a strange kind of smile played about his lips. "I am a little tired. But I will go on with my story. There's still plenty of time, the day has not dawned yet."

"Yes," he began, after having lighted a cigarette, "she throve and grew stouter from the time when she ceased to bear children, and her malady—the endless worry and anxiety about the children—began to disappear. It seemed as if she were recovering.

"Yes, she seemed to have recovered her senses as after a drunken fit, to have awakened to the fact that there was a whole God's world full of joys and happiness which she had somehow forgotten, in which she had not known how to live. 'I must endeavor not to let this slip away from my grasp; time will fly by very quickly, and it will be too late.' This at least is what I fancied she thought, or, rather, felt; and I do not see how she could have thought or felt otherwise, seeing that all her education had had but the one object of persuading her that there is only one thing worthy of attention in the world, that thing being so-called 'love.' She had married, and had experienced something of that 'love,' but not by any means as much as she had expected, not that which she had promised herself, and which she longed for. Moreover, she had met with many disappointments, disillusions, sufferings in marriage, among them the torture of which she had never even dreamed—children. This species of suffering had wearied and harassed her until the obliging doctors came along and informed her how to shirk the duties of motherhood. So she rejoiced, tried the doctors' method, and revived; living and breathing for one sole purpose—'love.'

"But love with a husband whom jealousy and hate rendered odious was not what she yearned for, and she began to dream of another love, pure and new—at least, I thought so—looking about her in vague expectation, as it were, of something. I saw this, and could not but feel uneasy in consequence, especially as about this time she would lose no opportunity of expressing such thoughts in conversation with others, intending them, of course, for my ear; and this notwithstanding the fact that only an hour previously she might have said just the opposite. Thus she would often maintain, half seriously, half in jest, that maternal solicitude is a delusion; that it is a pity to sacrifice one's youth for one's children instead of taking one's share of the joys of living. She cared less for her children then, and more for herself, attending to her personal appearance—though she tried to conceal this—to her pleasures, and even seek-

ing to perfect herself in certain accomplishments. Thus she set herself again to practice music—she had formerly played the piano with a certain technical skill and delicacy—and this was the visible beginning of the catastrophe." He again turned toward the window, and looked out with wearied eyes; but making a visible effort to control himself, he continued. "Yes, it was then that that individual appeared on the scene." He faltered, and twice made the peculiar noise that characterized him. I could see that it was extremely painful to him to name that man, to mention or in any way allude to him. But he made an effort, and having, as it were, broken through the barrier that held him back, he went on with determination—"A vile fellow he was in my eyes. This I say, not because of the important part he played in my life, but because it is really so. But the fact that he was a sorry character only shows what an irresponsible being she was. Had it not been this man it would have been another. It was necessary that this thing should come to pass." He was again silent for a moment. "He was a musician, a violinist, partly a professional, partly a fashionable amateur. His father, a land-owner, had been my father's neighbor, and had ruined himself financially years ago. He had three children, all boys, who were provided for in one way or another; the youngest being sent to his god-mother in Paris, where he had studied in the Academy of Music, as he had a gift for music, and he came out a violinist and took part in public concerts. He was a man who—"

Wishing to say something bitter,

Pozdnischeff made an evident effort to restrain himself, and, speaking very rapidly, continued:

"I don't know how he lived then, I only know that he came back to Russia that year and called upon me. He had almond-shaped humid eyes, rosy smiling lips, waxed mustaches, his hair was cut and dressed in the latest fashion, his face was of the insipidly agreeable kind which women term 'not bad-looking,' he was of weak build, but not misshapen. He was inclined to strike up a tone of familiarity to the full extent which the circumstances seemed to justify, but he was at the same time peculiarly sensitive, and always prepared to stop short if he met with the slightest check or discouragement—not, however, without a due regard for his own outward dignity. His boots, of the approved Parisian shade, were with buttons, his necktie always of some crying color—in a word, he had adopted all those little peculiarities which take the attention of all foreigners in Paris, and by their originality and novelty catch the eye of a woman and prepossess her in favor of the wearer. Outwardly he was always good-humored. He had a way of speaking about everything by means of allusions and fragmentary expressions, just as if you knew all about it and remembered it vividly, and could finish his phrases for him. This was the man who with his music was the cause of all that followed.

"On my trial all the facts of the case were dove-tailed together in such a manner as to make it appear as if I had killed my wife from jealousy. This was not so; at least, I mean it requires to be considerably modified before it can be said to be true. No doubt was entertained in court that my wife had sinned against me, and that I had killed her to avenge my outraged honor—that is what they call it—and I was acquitted in consequence. I endeavored on my trial to put the facts in their true light, but my efforts were interpreted as the result of a desire on my part to rehabilitate my wife's good name. But in truth her relations to that musician, whatever they may have been, mattered really very little to me or to her either. What did matter very much is what I have already related to you. It was all caused by the fact that there was that yawning bottomless abyss between her and me because of the terrible strain of mutual hatred whereby the slightest touch, the least impulsion, was quite sufficient to precipitate the crisis. Quarrels, too, had grown very frequent between us at that time, and were unusually savage; alternating, as of old, with outbursts of headstrong animal appetites. If he had not come upon the scene some one else would have played his part as effectually. If one pretext of jealousy had not been forthcoming another would have been unearthed. What I mean to affirm is that all husbands who live as I live must sooner or later give themselves up to indulgence or separate from their wives, or else must kill themselves or their wives as I killed mine. If there are people to whom none of these alternatives has proved a necessity, they are very rare exceptions. Before I ended as I did I was several times on the point of committing suicide, and more than once my wife had attempted to poison herself."

CHAPTER XX

LIAR! LIAR!

"SOMETHING of the kind had taken place a short time before the catastrophe. We had been living for a little while, during a cessation of hostilities, a kind of informal truce, and in the absence of grounds for violating it we began to talk about a certain dog at the exhibition which had, I said, obtained a medal. 'Not a medal,' she replied, 'but an honorable mention.' And then the dispute began, during which we jumped from one topic to another, reproaching each other at every step: 'Ah! yes, I knew that long ago; it's always so with you.' 'You said so yourself.' 'No, I said nothing of the kind.' 'I am a liar, then I suppose,' and so on; and you feel that a minute more and a terrible struggle will begin, in which you would like to kill yourself or your antagonist. You know that it will begin presently, and you are in terror of it, and would like to restrain yourself, but hatred takes possession of your whole being. Her state was, if possible, still worse than mine; she deliberately put a wrong construction upon everything I said; and every word that she uttered herself was saturated with venom, and she was careful to prick my tender spots and reopen old sores, with every one of which she was perfectly familiar. As the dispute advanced matters grew worse. 'Silence!' I thundered at last, or some such exclamation to this effect. She rushes out of the room in the direction of the nursery, I following and striving to stop her in order that she should hear me out. As I seize her by the sleeve she pretends that I have hurt her, and screams out, 'Children, here's your father beating me!' On which I roar out, 'Don't tell lies!' To which she replies in the same high key, 'This is not the first time you've done it.' The children run up to her, and she calms them, while I continue, 'Don't make believe.' 'It's all make believe in your eyes. You are quite capable of killing a person and then saying that she only pretends to be dead. Oh, I've found you out by this time. This is what you are longing for.'

"'I wish you were dead like a dog!' I shout out in reply. I remember how surprised and horrified I was when I uttered these terribly coarse words, and I can not explain how they could have passed my lips. As soon as I had pronounced them I ran out of the room into my study, sat down and began to smoke. From there I could hear her in the antechamber making ready to go out. I called out, 'Where are you going?' But she made no reply. 'The devil speed her!' I say to myself, as, going back to my study, I lie down again and smoke. A thousand different plans of revenge crowded into my brain, and ingenious combinations by means of which I was to make everything good again and repair what had been said and done. I ponder upon all this, smoking the while with all my might. It occurs to me to run away from her, to conceal myself, to emigrate to America; I actually go so far as to consider how I can best rid myself of her altogether, and please my fancy with the thought that after that consummation everything will again be as it should be, I shall then link myself to another lovely woman, fresh and pure; and the way of getting rid of her will be her natural death, or else I shall sue for a divorce; and then I mentally discuss with myself the best means of bringing this about. Then I become aware of the fact that I am wandering from the point at issue, that my thoughts are not what they should be, and in order to cloud my clear consciousness of this I smoke.

"Meanwhile, things at home were taking their usual course. The governess arrives and inquires, 'Where is madame? When will she return?' The lackey asks, 'Shall I serve the tea?' I repair to the dining-room; the children are there, and they look at me interrogatively, reproachfully, especially Liza, who is already beginning to understand the meaning of these things. We drink our tea in silence; *she* is not come yet. The whole evening passes away, and still she has not returned. Meanwhile, two different feelings alternately take possession of my soul: anger that she is torturing the children and me by her absence, the upshot of which will be that she will come back in the end; and fear that she will never return, that she will lay violent hands upon herself. I would go and fetch her, but where is she? At her sister's? But it would look so ridiculous for me to go there and make inquiries; and besides, I don't care; if she wants to pain me, then let her torment herself too. If I were to worry myself and run hither and thither to look for her, I should be merely playing into her hands, for that is just the end she had in view when she left the house, and she would thus be encouraged to do worse next time. But what if she be

not at her sister's; what if she has in some way made away with herself? Eleven o'clock has struck. Twelve o'clock. I do not go into the bedroom; it would be stupid of me to lie down by myself there and wait. But even here in my study I do not lie down; I wish to undertake some kind of work that will occupy me—to write letters or to read, for instance; but I find that I am incapable of doing anything, and so I watch and wait by myself in my study, tormenting myself, boiling with rage, listening to every sound, real and imaginary. It is already three o'clock. It has struck four, and she is not yet come. Toward morning I fell asleep. When I awoke she had not returned. Meanwhile, everything in the household went on as before, only every one had a puzzled, dissatisfied air, and they all looked at me interrogatively and reproachfully, as if they felt that all this had been caused by me. And all this while my soul was the arena in which the same struggle for the mastery went on as before, between anger at her having left me, and fear lest something had happened to her. At eleven o'clock her sister drove up as her envoy, and the old procedure was gone over again as if it were new. 'She is in a terrible state; what's it all about?' 'Nothing has happened.' I emphasize her impossible character, and affirm that I did nothing to her. 'Yes, but things can not remain as they now are, at all events,' her sister exclaims. 'That's her affair, not mine,' I answer. 'I will not make the first advances. If we are to separate, then let us separate.' And so her sister returned without having accomplished anything. I had said boldly that I would not move first in the matter, but as soon as she had gone, and I went out and saw the sad and frightened faces of the children, I was perfectly willing to take the first step. I began to walk to and fro as before, and to smoke. I drank vodka and wine at lunch, and attained thereby the object I had in view, which was to hide from myself the stupidity of my own position.

"About three o'clock she drove up herself. As she made no remark when she saw me, I inferred that she had resolved to make peace, and I told her that it was she who had provoked me with her reproaches, and thus originated the quarrel. She turned to me with a harsh, uncompromising look in her face, which bore traces of profound suffering, and intimated that she had come not to ask for terms, but to take away the children, as it was impossible for us to live any longer together. On this I began to explain that I was not to blame, that it was she who had lashed me into fury with her stinging reproaches. She again fixed her harsh, triumphant gaze upon me, and exclaimed, 'Say no more, you have repented.' To which I answered that I hated comedies. She then screamed out something which I did not catch, and rushed off to her room and turned the key in the door. I pushed the door several times, but elicited no reply. I then went off infuriated. Half an hour later Liza ran up to me in tears: 'What has happened? I can not hear mamma.' We go together to her room. I push the door, and the bolt being badly drawn, both of the folding-doors open at once, and I walk up to the bed. She is lying in an uncomfortable position

on the bed, dressed in her petticoats and high boots; on the table by the bedside there is an empty bottle that has had opium in it. We bring her to herself, and tears follow closely on the first signs of returning consciousness, and everything winds up with a reconciliation. In our hearts, however, we foster the same hatred for each other, to which is superadded the feeling of exasperation caused by the pain and suffering that accompanied this quarrel, which each puts down to the account of the other. But it was indispensable to end this in one way or another, and life moves forward again in its old groove.

"And such quarrels as these, and still worse ones, were continually occurring; now once a week, now once a month, now every day. And always the same old story, without variations or modifications. Once things went so far that I applied for a foreign passport. That quarrel lasted two days; but it, too, finished with a half-hearted explanation and reconciliation, and I did not go abroad."

CHAPTER XXI

A STRANGE FATAL FORCE

"THIS is the sort of life we led, these were the relations in which we stood to each other when that man—Trookhatschevsky was his name—made his appearance. He came to Moscow and called upon me one morning. I bid the servant show him in. In former times he and I had been on terms of familiarity: now he felt his way carefully before venturing to treat me on the old footing, and employed expressions and spoke in a tone equally far removed from distant formality and the familiarity of comrades. I quickly solved his doubts by treating him as a mere acquaintance, and he took his cue readily, without a moment's hesitation or awkwardness.

"I disliked him exceedingly from the first moment I looked upon him. But some strange fatal force moved me not only to refrain from repelling him, but to draw him nearer to me. What could be simpler than to exchange a few words with him, to bid him good-bye chillingly, and not to introduce him to my wife? But no; I must talk about his playing, and tell him that I had heard he had given up music. He said it was not so; that he had never practiced more assiduously all his life than at that moment; and passing from himself to me, reminded me that I, too, had played in times gone by. To this I replied that I did not play now, but that my wife was a good musician. It is very curious! From the very first day, from the very first hour I saw him, my relations toward him were such as they could only have been subsequently to everything that occurred later on. There was something very strained in my intercourse with him; I took note of every word, every expression uttered by him or by myself, and invested them with a significance justified by nothing that I then knew. I introduced him to my wife, and the conversation at once turned upon music, and he proffered his services to accompany her on the violin. That morning, as during all that later period, my wife looked extremely elegant, seductive, and provokingly beautiful. It was evident that he pleased her from the very first; moreover, she was also delighted at the prospect of being accompanied on the violin by him—a pleasure which she relished so highly that she had hired a musician of one of the theaters to accompany her. This satisfaction was reflected in her looks; but as soon as her eyes met mine, she guessed my feelings, and instantaneously changed the expression of her face; and then began the game of mutual deception all round. I smiled graciously, and looked as if I were delighted.

"He, eyeing my wife as all immoral men look upon pretty women, pretended to be interested exclusively in the topic under discussion—that is to say, in the very thing that was utterly devoid of interest in his eyes. She endeavored to seem indifferent, but was disconcerted somewhat by that false smile on my face which denoted the jealous man and was quite familiar to her, and by his gaze. I saw that her eyes gleamed with a peculiar brightness from the moment she first saw him, and that owing, perhaps, to my jealousy an electric current seemed to connect them and establish uniformity in their looks and smiles; so that when she would blush he would blush, and as soon as she smiled he smiled also. We chatted a little about music, Paris, and various trivial commonplaces, and then he rose to leave, and smiling, with his hat pressed against his quivering thigh, stood looking now at her, then at me, as if waiting to see what we should do.

"I distinctly remember that moment, because during those short-lived seconds it lay in my power not to invite him to our house, and then that episode would never have occurred. But I glanced at him and at her: 'Do not for a moment delude yourself with the idea that I am jealous of you,' I mentally said to her, 'or that I have any fear of you,' I mentally said to him; and I thereupon asked him to come and see us in the evening, and to bring his violin with him, to accompany my wife. She looked at me in astonishment, blushed, and was fluttered and frightened, as it were, began to decline the offer, saying that she could not play well enough for that. This refusal of hers only irritated me, and I insisted the more strongly. I well recollect the strange feeling with which I looked at the back of his head and his white neck, set off by the black hair which was carefully combed back on both sides of his head, as with a frisky, saltatory motion, suggestive of the hopping of a bird, he walked out. I could not disguise from myself the fact that this man's presence was a torture to me; it is in my power, I said to myself, to act in such a way that we shall never be troubled by his visits any more. But to act thus is to admit that I go in fear of him. And I have not the slightest fear of him; that would be too degrading, I said to myself. And in the antechamber, as he was preparing to go, I insisted, knowing that my wife would hear everything I was saying, on his coming again in the evening, bringing his violin with him. This he promised to do, and left.

"In the evening he came, and they played together; but for a long time their play was inharmonious; they had not the music that my wife wanted, and she was unable to play without preparation the music they had. I was very fond of music myself, and I rather liked the idea of their playing together; and I arranged the music-stand and turned over the leaves for him. They managed at last to execute a few pieces: some songs without words and a sonata of Mozart. He played magnificently; for he possessed in the highest degree what is termed *ton*, over and above which he was endowed with a delicate, refined taste which seemed wholly out of harmony with his character. He played much better than my wife, of course, and assisted her, at the same time respectfully praising her play. She seemed interested only in the music, and behaved simply and naturally. As for me, although I pretended to be interested in the music, I was suffering indescribable torture from jealousy all the evening.

"What considerably augmented the pain I experienced was the knowledge that the only feeling she entertained for me was one of chronic irritation, only interrupted occasionally for a short while, as before; while, on the other hand, he was qualified by his elegant appearance, the fact that he was a new-comer, and, above all, by reason of his undoubted musical talent, to produce a profound impression on her. In virtue of all this, and also of the fact that they must necessarily be frequently thrown in each other's society by playing together, and, thanks to the influence of music, especially that of the violin, on impressionable natures, this man must not merely take her fancy, but conquer her completely. I could not help noticing all this, and I suffered horribly in consequence. And yet, in spite of this, or, rather, perhaps, by reason of it, an invisible power compelled me against my will to be not only extremely courteous, but affectionate toward him. I am unable to specify the motive which prompted me to act thus; whether it was to prove to my wife and to him that I was not actuated by fear, or to deceive myself, I can not say; I only know that from the very first my relations with him were not natural and unaffected.

"In order not to give myself up to the desire to kill him on the spot, I felt compelled to treat him cordially. I entertained him at supper with expensive wines, went into ecstasies over his musical talents, spoke to him with a peculiarly affectionate smile, and invited him to dinner on the following Sunday, and to accompany my wife in the evening. I said that I would ask some musical friends of mine to come and hear him. And so that day came to an end."

Here Pozdnischeff was overcome with emotion, and, changing his position, again made that peculiar noise.

"It is surprising how I was affected by the presence of that man," he resumed, manifestly putting forth a strong effort to compose himself. "I was returning from the Exhibition three or four days after this, and, on entering the house, I suddenly felt oppressed at heart, as if a heavy stone were weighing me down; and at first I saw nothing to account for the feeling. Then I remembered that it originated in my having descried something, as I was passing through the antechamber, which reminded me of *him*. It was only when I was in my study that I was conscious of what that something was, and I immediately returned to verify the discovery. Yes, I was not mistaken; it was his overcoat. You know, a fashionable great-coat. I was extremely sensitive to everything relating in any

way to him, noticing it at once, even though I was not always distinctly conscious of it. I then asked the servant. Yes, he was there. I then went to my room, not through the parlor, but through the children's class-room. My daughter Liza was reading a book, and the nurse at the table with the youngest child was spinning the cover of some vessel. The door leading into the drawing-room was open, and I could hear the measured *arpeggio* and the sound of her voice and his. I listened, but could not distinguish any words. It was evident that the notes of the piano were evoked merely for the purpose of drowning their conversation— their kisses, perhaps. Good God! what a wild beast was roused up within me! What horrible imaginings thronged my mind! Even now I am filled with horror at the mere recollection of the fury that then took possession of my soul.

"My heart contracted, stopped, and then suddenly thumped against my breast like a sledge-hammer. The predominating feeling in this, as in all rage and hatred, was pity for myself. 'Before the children, before the nurse,' I said to myself. There must have been something terrible in my face, for Liza looked at me with terror reflected in her eyes. 'What am I to do?' I asked myself. 'To go in? I can not. God only knows what I shall do if I go in. And yet I can not go away!' The nurse looked at me as if she understood my position.

"'I can not but go in,' I said to myself, and quickly threw open the door. He was seated at the piano practicing the *arpeggio* with his large white fingers turned upward; she stood at a corner of the piano, some open music spread

out before her. She was the first to
see or hear me, and she turned her eyes
upon me. Was she frightened, and her
external composure only simulated, or
was she really composed? I can not
say; but certain it is that she did not
start or move in any way when I entered; she merely blushed; and even
that was not till afterward.

" 'I am so glad you have come; we
have not yet decided what to play next
Sunday,' she said in a tone of voice
that she would never have employed
had we been alone. This and the 'we,'
referring to him and herself, incensed
me. I saluted him in silence; he shook
me by the hand, and immediately went
on to explain to me, with a smile that
I considered derisive, that he had
brought some music in order to prepare
for Sunday, but that they were not
agreed what to play; whether it was
to be something difficult and classical—
namely, one of Beethoven's sonatas,
with the violin—or light, trivial pieces?
All this was so simple and natural that
I could not find anything to cavil at,
and, at the same time, I saw and was
convinced that it was wholly untrue,
and that they had been concerting
measures to play me false.

"There can be nothing more agoniz-
ing for jealous people—and in our
social life all men are jealous—than
certain of the conditions of fashionable
life which render the closest and most
dangerous contact between man and
woman permissible. It is impossible,
without making one's self the laughing-
stock of the world, to hinder this proximity between men and women dancing
at balls, between doctors and their
women patients, between artists, painters, and musicians working together.

"Two persons are cultivating the
noblest art—music—together; this requires a certain proximity, in which
there is nothing unseemly, and no one
but a stupid, jealous husband, forsooth.
could find anything reprehensible therein. And yet every one knows full well
that it is, thanks to these very occupations, especially musical studies,
prosecuted together, that by far the
greatest proportion of wickedness takes
place in our society.

"It was clear that I disconcerted the
pair by my own embarrassment: for a
long time I could say nothing; I resembled a bottle turned up side down, from
which the liquid can not escape, owing
to the bottle being too full. I wanted
to load them with reproaches, to expel
him from the house, but I felt, on the
other hand, that I ought to appear
amiable and affectionate toward him.
And I appeared so: I pretended to approve of everything—in obedience to
the impulse that made me increase my
outward civility and cordiality toward
him in proportion as the mental sufferings caused by his presence grew more
acute. I said that I felt perfect confidence in his taste, and I advised her to
follow my example. He remained just
as long as was absolutely necessary to
remove the disagreeable impression
which I had caused by suddenly walking into the room with a terrified face,
and continuing to preserve an awkward
silence after I had entered. Then he
left, pretending that now they had determined what pieces they would execute on the morrow. I was persuaded
that the question of the musical pro-
gramme was utterly indifferent to them.
I accompanied him with marked obsequiousness to the antechamber—how

could I treat less courteously the man who had come to disturb the peace and ruin the happiness of my family?—and I pressed with unwonted warmth his soft white hand."

CHAPTER XXII

INSANE RAGE

"ALL that day I did not speak to my wife. I could not. Proximity to her produced such an upheaval of hatred within me that I was frightened of myself. At dinner she asked me in presence of the children when I intended to go to the country—I was obliged to go to the country the following week, to attend the district sittings of the Zemstvo. I mentioned the date. She asked me whether I needed anything for the journey. I said not, and sat on in silence till the end of the dinner, and in silence rose up from the table and went to my study. Of late she never used to come to my room, especially at that time of day. I had lain down in my study, and was giving myself up to angry thoughts, when suddenly the horrid, absurd idea entered my head that she was coming to hide her sin—like Uriah's wife—and that that was why she was about to call upon me at that unusual hour. 'Can it be that she is really coming to me?' I asked myself, as I heard her footsteps approaching nearer and nearer. 'If so, it is evident that I was right, then; she—' And I felt an inexpressible hatred for her. Nearer and still nearer; is it possible that she will not pass by and go into the drawing-room? No; the door suddenly creaked on its hinges, and there on the threshold stood her tall, well-proportioned, handsome figure, her face and eyes expressive of timidity, of a desire to ingratiate herself with me, a desire which she endeavored to conceal, but which did not escape my notice, and the meaning of which I well knew. I held my breath so long that I was nearly suffocated, and continuing to regard her, I caught hold of the cigarette-case and began to smoke.

"'How can you, now? A person comes to sit down and have a quiet chat with you, and here you take out your cigarettes and smoke!' and she seated herself on the sofa beside me, leaning gently up against me. I moved a little further off, so as not to be in contact with her. 'I see that you are annoyed that I am going to play on Sunday?' she said. 'I'm not annoyed in the least,' I answered. 'Do you think I don't see it?' 'I can only congratulate you if you do. The only thing that I can see is, that you conduct yourself like a *cocotte*—' 'Oh, if you want to abuse me in such language, I will go.' 'Go; but mark this, if the honor of the family is not dear to you, it is not you who are dear to me—the devil take you!—but the honor of the family is.' 'What—what do you mean?' 'Leave the room; leave the room, for God's sake!' I do not know whether she only made believe that she did not understand me, or she really did not understand me, but she took offense. She rose, but did not go, and continued standing in the middle of the room: 'You are making yourself positively unbearable. You have a character that makes it impossible even for an angel to live with you;' and bent as usual upon stinging me in the most sensitive place, she reminded me of how I had once treated my sister. (I had once lost my temper and spoken very coarsely to my sister, and the recollection of this was always extremely painful to me. Hence she chose this sore place to prick me.) 'If you treat your own sister in that way, nothing that you could do would surprise me,' she concluded. 'Yes, she is not content with offending me, humiliating me, disgracing me, but she must make it appear that I am to blame for it all,' I said to myself; and I conceived such a consuming hatred for her as I had never in my whole life felt before. For the first time I longed to give my hatred physical expression. I started to my feet and moved toward her, but just as I was doing so I remember I became conscious that I was moved by angry passion, and I asked myself whether I was doing right to abandon myself to its power, and instantaneously came the answer that it was right, because that would terrify her, and so instead of withstanding, combating my rage, I began to fan it into a still more powerful flame, taking a peculiar delight in the contemplation of its rapid spread and growing intensity.

" 'Leave me, or I'll kill you!' I screamed, and going up to her I caught her by the arm. When pronouncing these words I deliberately pitched my voice in a higher key to express my anger; and no doubt I did look terrible, for she was so terror-stricken that she had not the force to leave the room. She only said: 'Vasa, what's the matter with you?' 'Leave me,' I vociferated still louder; 'only you can drive me mad; I can't answer for what may happen!'

"Having let loose my angry passion, I drank it in with inebriating delight, and I felt a desire to do something extraordinary, something which would mark the culminating point of my insane rage.

"I conceived an almost insuperable desire to beat her, to kill her, but I was aware that this could not be; therefore, in order to give loose reins to my rage, I seized the *presse-papier* that lay on the table, and screaming out once more, 'Leave me!' I dashed it to the ground close to where she stood. I had carefully aimed so as to miss her. Thereupon she left the room, but remained standing on the threshold; and while she was still looking at me—I did it expressly that she should look—I snatched up various articles that were on the table—the candle-stick, the ink-bottle—and flung them to the ground, continuing to cry out, 'Leave me! take yourself off! I can not answer for what I may do!' She left, and I instantaneously ceased. An hour later the nurse came and said that my wife was in hysterics. I went to her room; she was sobbing and laughing by turns; she could not speak a word, and her whole body trembled violently. She was not making believe, but was really ill.

"Toward morning she grew calm, and we made up the quarrel under the influence of that feeling which we call 'love.' In the morning, when, after the reconciliation, I confessed to her that I was jealous of Trookhatschevsky, she was not at all confused, but laughed in the most natural way conceivable—so queer did it seem to her, she said, that an attachment on her part for such a man should be deemed a possibility.

" 'Can such a man as he cause any other feelings in a respectable woman than pleasure at his musical performances? If you like, I am willing to refuse to see him any more, even on Sunday—although all the guests have been invited—write to say I am unwell, and there's an end to the matter. There is only one thing irritating about it—that is, that any one, especially that he himself, should for a moment suppose that he is dangerous. And I have too much pride to let anything of the kind be imagined.' And this was not a lie. She honestly believed what she was saying; indeed, she hoped by these words to evoke within herself a feeling of contempt for him, and by means of it to defend herself from his attacks. But she failed. Everything was against her, especially that accursed music.

"In this way the incident was wound up, and on Sunday the guests gathered together, and the two performed again."

CHAPTER XXIII

THE SONATA

"I DEEM it superfluous to say that I was extremely vain. Life without vanity is become almost an impossibility. On Sunday I endeavored to the best of my power to give a *recherché* dinner, and to arrange the *soirée musicale* with taste and success. I even went out myself to purchase certain things for the dinner, and personally called on the guests. By six o'clock the guests had come, and he also was there in evening dress with diamond shirt studs of questionable taste. He seemed perfectly at his ease, replied to all questions hurriedly, with a smile of assent and approval, and with that peculiar expression which is meant to suggest that everything you say or do is precisely what he had been expecting.

All his unfavorable traits and characteristics were noted by me with unusual satisfaction that evening, because they were calculated to tranquillize me and prove to me that the level on which he stood was too low for my wife, who could not degrade herself to stoop down to it. I did not permit myself to be jealous now. In the first place, I had suffered from the pangs of jealousy till the furthest limits of endurance were reached, and I now needed repose; and in the second place I desired to put faith in my wife's assurances, and I did put faith in them. But, although I was not at all jealous, yet, do what I would, I could not be natural in my intercourse with him and with her during the dinner, and all the first half of the evening until the music began. I was continually watching and scanning their movements and their looks. The dinner was, as dinners generally are, tedious, conventional. The music began at an early hour.

"Ah! how I remember all the circumstances, even the most trivial incidents, of that *soirée;* how he brought in his violin, opened the box, removed the covering, which had been worked for him by a lady, took out the instrument, and began to tune it; how my wife took her place at the piano with a look of indifference beneath which I could see that she concealed considerable diffidence, chiefly diffidence in her own powers; how, as soon as she was seated, the usual preparatory notes were extracted from the piano and the violin, the usual rustling sound of the music was heard as it was spread out on the stands; then how they looked at each other, glanced rapidly at the guests who were seating themselves, and began. He took the first accords, his face instantaneously becoming serious, severe, sympathetic, and, as he listened to the notes he was producing, he drew his fingers cautiously along the chords. The piano answered him, and the concert began."

Here Pozdnischeff stopped and uttered that peculiar sound of his several times in succession. He was about to resume his story, but merely snuffled, and lapsed again into silence. After a pause he went on.

"They played the 'Kreutzer Sonata' of Beethoven; do you know the first *presto?* Eh? Ah! . . ." he exclaimed, "it is a strange piece of music, that sonata, especially the first part of it. And music generally is a strange thing. I can not comprehend it. What is music? What effect does it produce? And in virtue of what does it produce the effect that we see it produce?

"Music, they say, acts on one by elevating the soul. That is absurd. It acts upon us, it is true, acts with terrible effect—at least I am speaking for myself—but is far from elevating the soul. It neither elevates nor depresses the soul, but irritates it. How shall I make my meaning clear? Music forces me to forget myself and my true state; it transports me to some other state which is not mine. Under its influence I fancy I experience what I really do not feel, that I understand what I do not comprehend, that I am able to do what is completely beyond my power. I explain this by the supposition that music acts like yawning or laughing; thus, although not sleepy, I yawn if I see others yawning; although I see nothing to laugh at I burst out laughing simply if I hear others laughing.

Music instantaneously throws me into that state of feeling in which the composer of it found himself when he wrote it. My soul blends with his, and together with him I am transported from one frame of mind to another. But why I am so ravished out of myself I know not. He who composed the piece —Beethoven, for instance, in the case of the 'Kreutzer Sonata'—knew perfectly well why he was in that mood; it was that mood that determined him to do certain things, and therefore for him that state of mind has a meaning; for me it has absolutely none. This is why it is that music only causes irritation, never ends anything. It is a different thing if a military march is played; then the soldiers move forward, keeping time to the music, and the end is attained; if dance music is played, people dance to it, and the object is also accomplished; if a mass is sung, I receive Holy Communion, and here, too, the music is not in vain; but in other cases there is nothing but irritation, and no light how to act during this irritation. Hence the terrible effects that music occasionally produces. In China music is a state concern, and this is as it ought to be. Could it be tolerated in any country that any one who takes the fancy may hypnotize any one else and then do with him whatever he has a mind to, especially if this magnetizer is—Heaven knows who!— an immoral character, for instance?

"It is indeed a terrible weapon in the hands of those who know how to employ it. Take the 'Kreutzer Sonata,' for example: is it right to play that first *presto* in a drawing-room to ladies in low dresses? to play that *presto*, then to applaud it, and immediately afterward to eat ice creams and discuss the latest scandal? Such pieces as this are only to be executed in rare and solemn circumstances of life, and even then only if certain important deeds that harmonize with this music are to be performed. It is meant to be played and then to be followed by the feats for which it nerves you; but to call into life the energy of a sentiment which is not destined to manifest itself by any deed, how can that be otherwise than baneful?

"Upon me, at least, this piece produced a terrible effect; it seemed as if new feelings were revealed to me, new possibilities unfolded to my gaze, of which I had never even dreamed before. 'It is thus that I should live and think, and not as I have hitherto lived and thought,' a voice seemed to whisper in my soul. What that new object of knowledge was, I could not satisfactorily explain to myself; but the consciousness of its existence was most delightful. All the people whom I knew, my wife and he among the number, appeared to me in an entirely new light. After this *presto* they executed the splendid but traditional *andante,* which has nothing new in it, with the commonplace variations and very weak *finale.* Then, at the request of the guests, they performed an elegy of Ernst and several other light pieces, all of them excellent in their way, but which did not make even the one hundredth part of the impression on me which the first piece produced. I was cheerful and good-humored for the rest of the evening. I had never before seen my wife as she appeared to me that evening: those gleaming eyes, that severity and gravity of mien while she

played, that dissolving languor, and that soft, melting, blissful smile that played over her features when they had finished. I saw all that, but put no other construction upon it than that she was undergoing the same experience as myself; that feelings new and never before experienced were revealed to her— brought dimly within the range of her consciousness. The *soirée,* which was a complete success, came to an end at last, and the guests took their leave.

"Knowing that I should have to leave for the interior in two days' time, Trookhatschevsky said, as he was bidding me good-night, that the next time he came he hoped to renew the pleasure he had experienced that evening. I inferred from this that he did not deem it possible to visit my house in my absence, and this gave me satisfaction. It was clear that as I should not return before his departure from Moscow, we should not see each other any more. For the first time I shook his hand with unfeigned pleasure, and thanked him for the treat. He also took a final leave of my wife, and their leave-taking appeared to me in the highest degree natural and correct. My wife and myself were both quite delighted with the *soirée.*"

CHAPTER XXIV

CONSUMMATION

"Two days afterward I departed for the country in the calmest and happiest frame of mind, after having taken leave of my wife. In the country I had always found plenty of work awaiting me, and a new life, an original little world, different from the one in which I usually lived. I worked for ten hours a day, two days in succession, in the department. The day after my arrival in the country I was sitting in the department, engaged in my work, when a letter from my wife was delivered to me. I opened and read it there and then. She wrote about the children, about her uncle, the nurse, about various purchases which she had made, and added at the fag end, and as if it were a most trivial circumstance, 'Trookhatschevsky has called and brought the music that he promised me, and offered to play again, but I declined.' Now, I had no recollection of his having promised to bring any music, and I certainly had the impression that he had taken leave forever, and this piece of news was consequently extremely disagreeable to me. But I had so much to attend to just then that I had no spare time to think the matter over, and it was only in the evening, when I had got back to my lodging, that I read the letter over again. Besides, the circumstance that Trookhatschevsky had called in my absence, the whole tone of the letter appeared to me enigmatical. The furious wild beast of jealousy within me roared in his den and endeavored to escape thence; but, fearing he might succeed, I made haste to shut the door.

"'What an odious feeling this jealousy is!' I said to myself, 'and what could be more natural than what she writes?' And I went to bed and commenced to think about the affairs that I should have to take in hand the next day. During these sittings of the Zemstvo I never could go asleep very soon, owing partly, no doubt, to the unfamiliar place; this night, however, I very quickly fell asleep.

"And as often happens in such cases, I felt something in the nature of an electric shock and suddenly awoke. I awoke thinking of her, of my love for her, and of Trookhatschevsky. Horror and rage crushed my heart between them; but I strove to listen to the promptings of reason. 'What absurd suspicions!' I said to myself; 'there's not the shadow of a foundation for them. And how can I thus degrade my wife? Here on the one hand is a fellow who might almost be described as a hired fiddler, known to be disreputable, and on the other an estimable, respected mother of a family—*my* wife. How preposterous!' This was one current of ideas. There was also another; and the thoughts that composed it were very different: 'Why should it not happen? What incongruity is there in supposing that such a natural and intelligible thing may have occurred? He is not married, well-fed, sleek, and not only devoid of principle, but guided by the rule that one should enjoy whatever pleasures one finds in one's way. And between these two beings there is the connecting bond of music—the most refined lust of the senses. What considerations are likely to keep him in bounds? None. On the contrary, everything conspires to attract him. And she? What is she? She is the mystery that she ever was. I do not know her. I know her only as a creature of instinct. And nothing is capable of restraining a creature of instinct.

"It was only at that moment that I called to mind their faces as I saw them that memorable Sunday evening when, after they had executed the 'Kreutzer Sonata,' they played some little piece, I forget by whom, I only remember that it was passionate to excess. 'How could I have been foolish enough to leave the city?' I asked myself as I called their faces to mind. 'Was it not as clear as daylight that everything was consummated between them on that evening; was it not manifest that on that evening not only was there no barrier subsisting between them, but that they both, especially she, felt some little shame at the recollection of what had taken place between them? I recollect how she smiled feebly, tenderly, and blissfully, wiping the perspiration from her flushed face, as I approached the piano. Already then they avoided looking at each other, and it was only at supper, when he was pouring her out some water, that they glanced at each other and smiled almost imperceptibly. I now shuddered when the look that I caught on their faces came back to my mind, accompanied as it was by that feeble smile. 'Yes, everything is now consummated,' one voice whispered into my ear. 'You are half demented; don't you know that that can not be?' exclaimed the other voice. There was something very weird and ghastly, it seemed to me, in my lying there in the darkness, a prey to these thoughts; so I struck a match, and all at once a feeling of indescribable dread came over me, as I looked around me in that little room with the yellow wallpapers. I lighted a cigarette, and as it always occurs to you to smoke when you are moving round and round, as I was, in the same circle of insoluble contradictions, I smoked cigarette after cigarette for the purpose of clouding my reason and avoiding the sight of the contradictions. I did not fall asleep any more that night, and at five o'clock,

having come to the conclusion that I would no longer remain in that state of mental tension, I got out of bed, called the door-keeper who usually waited upon me, and sent him for the horses. I scribbled a note to the department, to say that I had been summoned to Moscow on very urgent business, and to request that, in the meanwhile, my place be temporarily taken by another member. At eight o'clock I took my seat in the tarantass and drove off. . . ."

CHAPTER XXV

ABSORPTION

THE conductor entered the carriage, and perceiving that our candle had burned down to the socket, blew it out, without lighting another. Day was already breaking. Pozdnischeff was silent, sighing heavily from time to time, until the conductor again went out, leaving us in obscurity. Nothing was audible but the clinking of the glass windows, the rumbling and creaking of the rolling carriages, and the regular, monotonous snore of the clerk. In the uncertain gray of the dawn, I could not distinguish the figure of Pozdnischeff; but his voice grew louder as it became more piteous and excited.

"I had to drive thirty miles in the tarantass and then travel eight hours by rail. The drive was magnificent. It was a frosty autumn morning with bright, cheerful sunshine; the roads were smooth, the rays of the sun brilliant, and the air bracing. The riding in the tarantass was pleasant. As soon as day broke and I set out, I felt eased at heart. Looking at the horses, the fields, the people on foot we met, made me forget whither I was bound. At times it seemed as if I were only out for a drive, and that none of the circumstances that had combined to make me undertake the journey had ever had any existence in reality. And I felt a peculiar pleasure in thus forgetting myself. Whenever I did recollect on what errand I was bound, I said to myself, 'Don't think about that now; we'll see afterward what's to be done.' When we got half-way to the station, an incident occurred which stopped my progress and distracted me still more from my thoughts—the tarantass broke down and had to be mended. This accident was of still greater importance than was at first apparent, inasmuch as it occasioned the delay on the road which prevented my catching the express, and so I had to wait some hours and go on with the passenger train, thus getting into Moscow not, as I had intended, at five o'clock, but at midnight, thus reaching my own house toward one o'clock. The drive over, the search of a country wagon, the work of repairing, the payment, tea at the inn, and my conversation with the doorkeeper— all these things diverted my thoughts from what might otherwise seem their natural channel. By dusk, everything was ready, and I resumed my journey, which was still more pleasant after dark than during the day. There was a young moon, a slight frost, a splendid road, a jovial driver; and I drove forward, scarcely once reverting in thought to what was awaiting me; or was it that I enjoyed myself so thoroughly precisely because I knew what I had to expect, and was taking leave of all the joys of life? At all events this calm state of mind and the power of controlling my feelings came to an end with the drive in the tarantass.

"The moment I entered the train the conditions changed completely. This eight hours' journey in a railway carriage was a terrible experience for me, something I shall never forget to my dying day. Whether it was that having once taken my seat in the train I realized in a more lively manner than before that I was nearing the goal of my journey, or that railway traveling in general produces feverishness and unrest, I can not decide; I only know that from the moment I entered the compartment I lost all control over my imagination, which went on without cease, painting in the most vivid colors an endless series of pictures one after the other, one more cynical than the other, and all of a nature to inflame my jealousy, all treating the one theme— the doings that were going on at home in my absence, and how she was proving false to me. I was consumed with indignation, hatred, and a strange feeling of inebriation produced by my very dishonor, as I contemplated these pictures; powerless to tear myself away from them, unable to avoid looking at them, impotent to rub them out, too passive to hinder them from rising up before me. Nay, more, the longer I looked at them the more firmly did I believe in their reality. The life-like vividness with which these pictures presented themselves to my mind seemed to stamp with the impress of truth the scenes they delineated, and thus the phantoms of my brain succeeded in assuming all the appearance of reality. It seemed as if against my will some devil were employed in fabricating and suggesting to me the most horrible fancies and conjectures. A conversation that I had had many years before with Trookhatschevsky's brother recurred to me now, and applying it to Trookhatschevsky himself and my wife, I employed it to lacerate my heart. Trookhatschevsky's brother—although it had happened many years previously, it all came back to me now with great distinctness—in answer to the question whether he went to irregular places, replied that he did not, seeing that one could always establish relations in good society. And here now this man's brother had established relations with my wife. 'No, this thing is impossible!' I would then say to myself, terrified: 'It can not, can not be! Nay, there are not the slenderest grounds for supposing anything of the kind. Did she not herself assure me that she regarded the very possibility of my being jealous of him as dishonoring? She certainly did; but then she lies; yes, she is always lying,' I exclaimed, and thereupon everything began again *da capo*. There were only two passengers in the compartment —an old woman and her husband, both of them very silent, and even they got out at one of the intermediate stations, and I remained alone. I was exactly like a wild beast in a cage; now I would suddenly jump up and run to the window; then, reeling to the middle of the compartment, I would begin to pace rapidly forward as if trying to overtake the railway carriage; and the carriage with all its seats and windows went on shivering and shaking, just as ours is doing at this moment."

And here Pozdnischeff started to his feet, paced up and down for a few seconds, and then sat down again.

"Oh, how I fear, how I fear these railway carriages! They fill me with dread.

"Yes, it was a terrible time," he resumed. "I would say to myself, 'Come, I must think of something else. Let it be the proprietor of the road-side inn where I drank tea to-day.' And then before the eyes of my imagination I would see the door-keeper rising up, with his long beard, and his grandson, a little boy of the same age as my Vasa. My Vasa! My Vasa will see how a musician kisses his mother.' What will take place in his poor soul at the sight? But what does she care? She is in love, forsooth. . . . And the whole thing began again. 'No, no! Let me think of the inspection of the hospital; yes, yesterday, I recollect, a patient complained of the doctor—the doctor with the mustaches like Trookhatschevsky's. How shamelessly, how impudently he deceived me—they both deceived me— when he said that he was going to leave Moscow!' And then the same racking thoughts began again. There was no subject that I could think of that was not in some way connected with them. I suffered terribly. What tormented me most was the uncertainty, the doubt, the vacillation, the ignorance I was in, whether I ought to love or hate her. My anguish was so excruciating that I remember it occurred to me to go on to the line, lie down on the rails, let the train pass over me, and end my pains. And the idea pleased me, for then, at least, I reflected, I should be troubled no more with torturing doubts. The only consideration that prevented me from acting on this impulse was pity for myself, which, in turn, instantaneously called forth hatred toward her. Toward him I had a very strange feeling of hatred, mingled with the consciousness of my humiliation and his triumph; but for her my hatred was terrible. 'I can not make away with myself, and leave her behind me,' I said to myself; 'it is only right that she should suffer somewhat, that she should at least feel that I have suffered.'

"I got out at all the stations on the way to seek for distractions. At one station I saw people drinking in the refreshment-room, and I at once went up and poured myself out some vodka. A Jew stood beside me at the counter, and entered into conversation with me; and in order not to be quite alone in my carriage, I followed him to his third-class compartment, filthy though it was, reeking with stale tobacco smoke, and littered over with the husks of sunflower seeds; and I sat down on the wooden bench beside him. He was relating a number of anecdotes to me, which I did not understand nor even hear, because I continued to think of what was absorbing my own mind. He noticed this, and began to demand my attention to what he was saying, and then I got up and went back again to my own carriage. 'I must think it all over again,' I said to myself, 'I must sift and compare all the *pros* and *cons,* and see whether there is really any ground for the anguish I am causing myself. And I sat down with the intention of weighing the matter calmly in my mind, but that very instant, instead of a calm analysis, the old train of thoughts was started afresh, and in lieu of arguments I saw the old pictures and imaginings.

" 'How often have I tortured myself,' I then thought, 'exactly in the same way before'—I here called to mind my former paroxysms of jealousy—'and all utterly groundless, as it afterward proved! It may be that my present suspicions are equally groundless—indeed, I am sure they are; when I get home I shall find her asleep, and by her words and looks I shall feel that nothing wrong has taken place, and that it was all a phantom of my brain. Oh, how delightful that would be!' 'But no, it has been so too often; this time it will assuredly be otherwise,' an interior voice seemed to say, . . . and the flood of bitter, corroding thoughts rushed in upon me again. Yes, that was in truth a torture! It is not, I thought, into a hospital that I would take a young man to show him the results of evil-doing, but into my own soul, to let him glance at the devils that are tearing it to pieces! A very revolting feature in all this was, that I was convinced I possessed an indefeasible right to my wife, just as if she were myself, and at the same time I felt that I could not possess her, that she was not mine, and that she could dispose of herself as she liked, and that she was minded to dispose of herself in a manner that I did not approve. And I could do nothing to him, and still less to her. If she has not deceived me, but is bent upon deceiving me—and I know perfectly well that she is so bent—the situation is still worse; it would be much better if she did deceive me, so that I should know for certain what to think, and get rid of all these horrid doubts and fears.' I could not formulate what I wanted or desired. It was madness pure and simple."

CHAPTER XXVI

SHE IS—

"AT the last station but one, when the guard came in to collect the tickets, I got all my things together, and went out on the platform where the brake is worked; and standing there, the consciousness that the consummation was near only intensified my feverishness. I felt a sensation of extreme cold, which was soon followed by the chattering of my teeth. We reached our destination at last, and I left the station mechanically with the crowd, called a drosky, took my place, and drove home. During the ride home I gazed at the rare passers-by, the door-keepers of the houses, and the shadows projected by the vehicle now before, now behind, thinking of nothing the while. When we had gone about half a mile from the station, my feet became extremely cold, and I remembered that I had taken off my woolen stockings in the train, and put them in my traveling-bag. Where was my traveling-bag? Was it there in the drosky? It was. And where was the trunk? Then I became aware that I had forgotten all about my luggage; but having searched for and found the receipt for it, I decided that it was not worth my while to go back for it now; so I drove on. I have never been able since then to recall the state of mind in which I was during that drive home from the station. What were my thoughts? What were my wishes? All that is now an utter blank.

"I only remember that I was conscious that something terrible was brewing, an event of extreme importance in my life impending. Whether that important thing was taking place because I thought thus, or because I foreboded it, I can not say. It may be that after that which subsequently happened, all the moments that immediately preceded it were tinged with dismal hues in my memory.

"I drove up to the door. It was near one o'clock. A few cabmen were stationed before the street door waiting for fares—a reasonable expectation enough, to judge by the light in the windows—in our lodgings the windows of the drawing-room and parlor were brilliantly lighted up. Without attempting to explain to myself why the light was burning in our rooms at such a late hour, I walked up the doorsteps in that same state of expectancy—foreboding something terrible—and rang the bell. George, the lackey, a good, zealous, but extremely stupid man, opened the door. The first thing that struck me in the antechamber was the great-coat hanging from the clothes-rack along with other hats and coats. I ought to have been astonished at this, but I did not feel the least surprise, because I expected it. 'Just what I thought,' was the mental commentary I made when, in reply to my question, 'Who is here?' George mentioned the name of Trookhatschevsky. 'Any one else?' I asked. 'No, no one else.' I remember the tone of voice in which he said this, as if he were desirous of giving me pleasure and dispelling my apprehensions that there might be somebody else there. 'Exactly,' I muttered, as if aloud to myself; 'and the children?' 'The children, thank God, are well. They have been asleep ever so long, sir.' I could not breathe out freely, nor could I stop the chattering of my teeth. 'So,' I said to myself, 'it is not then as I thought it might be.'

Hitherto I had been wont to imagine misfortunes, only to find that I had been mistaken, and that all was well. This time it is not as of yore: I am now face to face in grim reality with all that existed in my imagination, and, as I believed, only in my imagination. Here I find it all perfectly life-like and real.

"I was on the point of sobbing aloud, but at that moment the devil whispered: Whine and pule, give yourself up to sickly sentimentality, and give them time to separate, and then pass your life in heart-corroding doubts and torments. And all at once tenderness for myself disappeared, and was succeeded by a strange feeling: you will scarcely believe it—a feeling of joy that my torture was about to come to an end, that I could punish her now, rid myself of her, give loose reins to my hatred. And I did let loose my hatred, and it metamorphosed me into a wild beast, a malignant, cunning, savage beast. 'Stop! stop!' I cried to George, who was about to go into the parlor; 'look here; take a drosky and drive over to the station as quickly as ever you can and get my luggage. Here's the receipt. Lose no time.' He went along the corridor to get his overcoat. Apprehensive lest he should disturb the pair, I accompanied him to his little room and stood by while he was putting his great-coat on. Through the parlor, from which I was separated by another room, came the sound of voices and the noise of knives and plates. They were evidently eating, and had not heard the bell. 'I pray Heaven they may not leave the room yet!' I mentally ejaculated. George at last put on his coat and departed. I let him out and shut the door behind

him, and I was seized with a weird, shuddering feeling when I saw myself quite alone and bound to act quickly. To act how? I did not know yet; I only knew that it was all over then, that there could be no longer any doubts about her guilt, that I would punish her presently, and break off all relations with her forever. Heretofore I had had hesitations; I had said to myself, 'Perhaps it is not true, perhaps I am mistaken.' I did not say or think so now; everything was decided once for all, irrevocably. 'Alone with him, without my knowledge, and at night! This argues complete forgetfulness of everything.' Or still worse: 'This audacity was adopted as the result of cool calculation; this assurance in committing crime was relied upon as a proof of innocence.' It is all perfectly clear. There can be no manner of doubt about it. The only thing I felt any uneasiness about was that they might escape, might hit upon some new way to baffle and deceive me, and might thus deprive me of the evidence of my senses, the possibility of proving their crime.

"And in order to lose no time in coming upon them and catching them, I went to the drawing-room where they were sitting, not through the parlor, but along the corridor and through the nursery, walking on the tips of my toes. In the first of the two rooms of which the nursery was composed the boys were sound asleep. In the second the nurse stirred and moved as if she were about to awake, and I had a very vivid presentiment of what she would think if she knew what was going on. I was thereupon filled with such profound pity for myself that I could not hold back my tears, and in order not to wake the child, I ran back along the corridor on the tips of my toes to my study, where I flung myself on the sofa and sobbed aloud.

"I, an honest man, the son of such respectable parents; I, who all my life cherished the dream of domestic happiness in the bosom of my family; I, her husband, who was never unfaithful to her—I have lived to see this thing! She, the mother of five children, and to throw herself into the arms of a musician because he has rosy lips! No, she is not a human being, she is . . . And all this in the room next the nursery where the children are, the children whom she has all her life been pretending to love. And then again to send me such a letter as she sent me! Nay, how do I know?—possibly this has been going on for ever so long. Had I come to-morrow, instead of to-night, she would have met me, her hair tastefully done up, her slender waist becomingly set off, with her languid, graceful movements, and the wild beast of jealousy imprisoned forever within me would have torn my heart to pieces. What will the nurse think? and George? and poor little Liza? (She was already of an age to understand something of what was going on.) 'And this shamelessness! this hypocrisy!' I exclaimed to myself.

"I wanted to rise, but I could not. My heart beat so violently that I could not stand on my feet. 'I shall have a fit and drop down dead,' I thought. 'She will indeed be the death of me. That's what she wants; killing would be nothing to her. But no, my death would be too much of a godsend to her; I must not give her this pleasure. Why, here am I sitting in my room while this very moment they are eating and laughing. . . . Oh, why did I not strangle her then?' I asked myself, as I called to mind the moment, a week ago, when I thrust her out of my study and smashed the things on the table. I had a most lively recollection of the state of mind I was in at that time; and not merely a recollection, but I experienced the very same desire to beat, to destroy, that animated me then. I remember how I burned to do something, to act, and how all considerations, except those that were indispensable for action, vanished from my mind in a twinkling, and I was left in a mood identical with that of a wild beast or of a human being under the influence of physical excitement in time of danger when a man naturally acts with precision, not hurriedly, yet without losing a single moment, and all with a single, definite object in view."

CHAPTER XXVII

HER LOOKS BETRAY

"The first thing I did was to take off my boots, and then in my stockings I went to the wall where my guns and daggers were suspended above the sofa, and took down a crooked Damascus blade that had never been used, and was exceedingly sharp. I unsheathed it. The scabbard slipped from my hands and fell down behind the sofa, and I remember saying to myself, 'I must look for it afterward, or it may get lost.' Then I divested myself of my great-coat, which I had worn all the time, and, stepping out softly in my stockings, I went *there;* and, stealing up inaudibly, I suddenly threw open the door.

"I remember the expression of their faces. I remember it because at the time it afforded me an excruciating pleasure. It was an expression of terror, and that was precisely what I desired. To my dying day I shall not forget the regard of mingled despair and terror that was visible on their faces the first moment they beheld me. He was seated, I think, at the table, and as soon as he saw me he started to his feet and stationed himself with his back leaning against the cupboard. His features were expressive of unmistakable abject terror. Her face wore the same expression; but there was something else there besides; and had it not been for that something else, had I discovered no trace of anything but terror, perhaps that which happened a little later would have never taken place at all. For an instant, and only for an instant, her looks betrayed her—to my thinking, at least—the disappointment, the vexation she felt at being disturbed, at having the happiness which his society gave her broken in upon. She seemed to have but one thought, but one wish—namely, to be left alone to enjoy her happiness unmolested. Both of those expressions lingered but a second on their faces; his was instantaneously replaced by an interrogative glance at her which plainly said, 'Is it possible to right things by lying? If so, then it is time to begin. If not, something else will take place; but what?' Her look of vexation and disappointment was succeeded, I fancied, the moment her eyes met his, by solicitude for him. For an instant I stood on the threshold, holding the dagger behind my back, and that instant he smiled and began to speak in a tone of voice so studiously

unconcerned that it seemed positively comical. 'And we were at our music—' he began.

"'Well, this is a surprise!' she exclaimed the same moment, following up the cue he had given her.

"But neither he nor she finished what they were going to say. The insane frenzy that I had felt a week previously had again taken possession of me; once more I experienced the same mania for destroying, for using violence, for assuring the triumph of madness; and I yielded myself up to it body and soul.

"They never finished the sentences they had begun. That other alternative happened which he was so greatly afraid of, and it swept away in a trice all that they were going to say. I threw myself upon her, hiding all the time the dagger, lest he should hinder me from plunging it into her side, under her breast. (I chose this spot from the very first.) Just as I was flinging myself upon her, he saw what I was about, and—what surprised me very much from him—caught me by the arm, and shouted out at the top of his voice, 'Think of what you are doing! Help!'

"I freed my arm and rushed upon him without uttering a word. His eyes encountering mine, he all at once turned as pale as a sheet, his very lips became bloodless and white, his eyes glistened with an unwonted luster, and—what likewise surprised me very much—he dived under the piano and fled from the room.

"I rushed after him, but felt a heavy weight suspended from my left arm. It was she. I struggled, and tried to tear myself from her; but she weighed me down still more heavily, and effectually prevented me from moving. This unlooked-for hindrance, the dragging weight, and her touch, from which I shrunk as from a loathsome thing, served only to inflame me still more. I felt that I was perfectly raging, and that I could not but appall her, and I exulted in the thought.

"Striking backward with my left arm with all the force I could gather, I hit her with my elbow in the face. She screamed and let go my arm.

"I was on the point of running out in pursuit of him, when it occurred to me that it would be ridiculous to rush off in my stockings after the lover of my wife, and I did not wish to be ridiculous, but to be terrible. Notwithstanding the irrepressible fury that was driving me, I was conscious all the time of the impression I produced on others. At times, indeed, that impression served to guide me.

"I turned round to her. She had fallen on the couch, and, holding her hands up to her bruised eyes, was looking at me. Her face was expressive of terror and of hatred for me, her enemy; it was just such a look as a rat might give when the trap in which he has been caught is being raised up to the light. At least I saw nothing but fear and hatred in her features, just such fear and hatred for me which love for another would inevitably call forth in her. Still, I might perhaps have restrained myself yet, and might not have done what I did, if she had only remained silent.

"But she all at once began to speak and to clutch at my hand, the hand that held the dagger.

"'Think of what you are doing. Nothing has passed between him and me, nothing. I swear to you! Noth-

ing.' I might still have wavered had it not been for those concluding words, from which I inferred that the opposite was true, that everything had taken place. These words required a reply. And the reply would have to correspond to the state of frenzy up to which I had lashed myself, and which went on *crescendo,* and would still go on gaining in intensity. Fury has its laws as well as other mental states.

"'Do not lie, hell-hag!' I screamed, seizing her arm with my left hand. But she wrenched herself away from my grasp. Then, without relinquishing my hold of the dagger. I caught her with my left hand by the throat, threw her over on her back, and began to strangle her. How tough her neck seemed! She seized my arms with both her hands, tearing them away from her throat; and, as if I had only been waiting for this, I struck the dagger with all the strength I could muster, into her left side, under the ribs. . . .

"Whenever people assert that in a paroxysm of madness they do not remember what they are doing, they are either talking nonsense—or lying. I knew very well what I was doing, and did not for a single second cease to be conscious of it. The more I fanned the flame of my fury, the brighter burned within me the light of consciousness, lighting up every nook and corner of my soul, so that I could not help seeing everything I was doing. I can not affirm that I knew in advance what I was going to do, but the very moment I was doing anything, and I fancy some seconds beforehand, I was conscious of what I was doing, in order, as it were, that I might repent of it in time, that I might afterward have it to say that I could have stayed my hand. Thus, I was aware that I was striking her below the ribs, and that the blade would penetrate. The moment I was doing this, I knew that I was doing something terrible, a thing I had never done before, an action that would be fraught with frightful consequences. But that consciousness was instantaneous, like a flash of lightning, and the deed followed so close upon it as to be almost simultaneous with it. My consciousness of the deed and of its nature was painfully distinct. I felt and still remember the momentary resistance of the corset, and of something else, and then the passage of the knife cutting its way through the soft parts of the body. She seized the dagger with both her hands, wounding them, but without staying its progress.

"Afterward, in prison, when a moral revolution had already worked radical changes in my being, I would ponder for hours at a time on the thoughts and sensations that had filled my mind during that fatal instant, recalling all possible details. I remember that a second, but barely a second, before the act was accomplished, I was terribly conscious that I was killing, that I had killed, a woman, a defenseless woman, my own wife. I recollect the indescribable horror of this state of mind, and I infer from it, and in fact I may add that I have a dim remembrance, that having plunged the dagger into her body, I instantaneously drew it out again, anxious thereby to remedy what I had done, to stay my hand. I then stood motionless for an instant, waiting to see what would happen, and whether it was possible to undo it.

"She suddenly sprung to her feet and screamed out: 'Nurse, he has murdered me!' The nurse, having heard the noise, was already on the threshold. I was still standing motionless, expectant, incredulous. Suddenly the blood welled forth from under her corset.

"Then I saw that what I had done was past remedying, and the same instant I decided that it was not desirable that it should be remedied, that this very thing was what I wanted to do, and what ought to have been done. I lingered on still, till she fell, and the nurse exclaiming 'Good God!' ran to her assistance; it was only then that I flung away the dagger and quitted the room. 'I must not get excited; I must think of what I am doing,' I said to myself, not looking at her or the nurse.

"The nurse began to scream and call the maid.

"I walked along the corridor, sent the maid to her mistress, and went to my room. 'What must I do now?' I asked myself—and the answer at once suggested itself. Going into my study, I went up to the wall, took down the revolver, examined it—it was loaded—and placed it on the table. I next picked up the scabbard from behind the sofa, and then seated myself on the sofa. I remained thus seated for a long time, thinking of nothing, recollecting nothing. I was conscious, however, of a considerable stir in the other rooms. I heard a vehicle driving up to the door with some one, then another. Then I heard and saw George coming into my study with my luggage—as if any one wanted it! 'Did you hear what has happened?' I asked him. 'Tell the house-porter to go and inform the police.'

"He went out without making any reply. I rose from the sofa, took out my cigarettes and the matches, and began to smoke. Before I had finished one cigarette I was overcome by drowsiness and fell asleep.

"I slept for about two hours. I dreamed that she and I were living on terms of affection; that we had quarreled, but were making it up, and that there was some little obstacle in the way, but that at bottom we were friends.

"I was awakened by a knocking at the door.

"'That is the police,' I thought; 'I fancy I murdered her. But perhaps it is she herself who is knocking, and that nothing at all has happened.' The knocking at the door went on. I did not answer it, but strove to decide the question, Had all that really taken place or not? Yes, it had. I remembered the resistance of the corset, and the passage of the blade through the body, and the recollection sent an icy cold chill along my back, and made my flesh creep. . . .

"Yes, it had taken place. There was no mistake about that. Now it's my turn, I thought, to lay hands upon myself; but while I was still saying that to myself, I knew that I would not kill myself. And yet I rose and took up the revolver again. It seemed strange; I remember how many times before that I had been on the point of committing suicide—the night before, in the train, for instance—and it had always seemed to me such an easy thing to do; it had seemed easy, because I considered that to be the most effectual means of striking terror into her. But now not only could I not take my own life, but I could not even harbor the thought. 'Why should I kill myself?' I asked.

And no answer was forthcoming. The knocking at the door continued. 'Ah, yes, I must first see who is at the door. There will be always time enough for this,' I thought, as I laid the revolver down on the table and covered it over with a newspaper. I then went to the door, and drew back the bolt. It was my wife's sister, a well-meaning, silly widow.

"'Vasa, what's all this?' she exclaimed, and the tears—always ready with her—flowed abundantly.

"'What do you want?' I asked, gruffly. I knew that I ought not to be rude to her, that I had no reason to be rude, but I could not hit upon any other tone.

"'Vasa, she's dying; Ivan Zakharievitch said so.'

Ivan Zakharievitch was the doctor—her doctor and adviser. 'Is he here?' I inquired, and all my hatred for her revived.

"'Well, and what if she is?' I continued.

"'Vasa, go to her. Ah! this is dreadful!' she sighed.

"'Shall I go to her?' I asked myself. And I at once decided that it was my duty to go to her, that it was the correct thing to do in such cases; that when a husband kills his wife, as I had done, he is bound to go to her. If it is always done, I reasoned, then I suppose I must go. Yes, if it should prove needful—I said to myself, thinking of my intention to commit suicide—I shall have plenty of time to do it afterward; and I followed my wife's sister. 'Now I shall have to prepare for grimaces and phrases,' I said to myself; 'but I must not let them affect me.' 'Wait a moment,' I exclaimed to my sister-in-law;

'it is so stupid to go without boots; let me just draw on my slippers.'"

CHAPTER XXVIII

GOOD-BYE!

"STRANGE as it may seem, as I left my study and passed through the familiar rooms, I once more conceived a hope that all this had not really taken place; but the pungent smell of the abominable drugs, of iodoform, of carbolic acid, overpowered me, and I knew that it was a dread reality.

"Passing along the corridor by the nursery, I saw Liza. She gazed at me with a terrified look in her eyes. I fancied all my five children were there, and were steadfastly looking at me. I went up to the door of *her* room, and the maid opened it and went out.

"The first thing that struck me was her light gray dress lying on the chair, all black with blood. She was in bed, in my bed, which was easier of access than her own, lying on pillows in a very sloping position, her knees upraised, her camisole unbuttoned. Something had been laid on the place where the wound was. A nauseous smell of iodoform pervaded the room. What impressed me in the first place, and more profoundly than anything else, was her swollen, bruised face, the eyes and part of the nose being of a bluish-black color—the effect of the blow I had struck her with my elbow when she was trying to hold me back. No trace of beauty was left, but instead of it I noticed something repulsive in her. I stopped at the threshold.

"'Go up to her—go up to her!' exclaimed her sister.

"'Yes, she probably wants to repent,' I thought. 'Shall I forgive her? Yes, as she is dying I suppose I may forgive her,' I decided within myself, striving to be magnanimous.

"I then went up close to her bedside. With difficulty she raised up her eyes to me, one of which was greatly bruised, and said, falteringly, stammering over the words, 'You have your way now; you have killed me;' and I observed on her face the expression which was struggling with physical pain for the mastery; in spite of the nearness of death it was that of the old, familiar, cold, animal hatred. 'The children—you—shall not—have; I will—not give—them —to you! She' (her sister)—'will take them.'

"As to that which was the most important point of all, for me—her guilt, her faithlessness—she did not consider it deserving of even a passing allusion.

"'Yes, admire what you have done!' she exclaimed, slowly turning her eyes in the direction of the door and sobbing. On the threshold stood her sister with the children. 'Yes, see what you have done!'

"I looked at the children and then at her bruised, blue face, and for the first time I forgot myself, my rights, my pride; for the first time I saw in her a human being, and so frivolous and mean did everything appear that had wounded me, even my jealousy, and so grave, so fateful the thing that I had done, that I was ready to fall at her feet, take her hand in mine, and exclaim, 'Forgive me!' But I did not dare. She closed her eyes and remained silent, evidently too weak to speak. All at once her distorted face quivered, a frown passed over it, and she pushed me feebly away from her. 'Why has all this happened? Oh, why?'

'Forgive me!' I exclaimed. 'Forgiveness; all that is rubbish. Oh, if I could only keep from dying!" she ejaculated, raising herself up a little and fixing on me her eyes that gleamed with a feverish luster. 'You have worked your will. I hate you! Oh, ah!' she exclaimed, evidently frightened of something, as her mind began to wander. 'Kill me now, kill me; I'm not afraid. Only kill them all—kill him too. He's gone—he's gone!' The delirium continued to the end. She recognized no one. The same day at noon she passed away.

"Before this, at eight o'clock in the morning, I was taken to the police station and transferred from there to the prison, where I remained eleven months, awaiting my trial. It was there that I meditated upon myself and my past life, and succeeded in getting a true insight into its meaning. Three days afterward they took me over to the house—" He was going to say something more, but he could not muster strength enough to repress his sobs, and was obliged to stop. Making an effort, he continued:

"I only began to see things in their true light after I had looked upon her in her coffin." He sobbed again, but went on hurriedly: "It was only when I had gazed upon her dead face that I realized what I had done. I then felt and realized that it was I, I who killed her, that through my instrumentality it had come to pass that she who a little while before was living, moving, warm, was now still, wax-like, cold, and that this could be righted nowhere, never, by no one. He who has not experienced this is not capable of understanding. . . . Oh, oh, oh!" he ejaculated several times, and lapsed into silence.

We remained seated in silence for a long while, he sobbing and shivering opposite me. "Good-bye," he called out at last, and, turning his back to me, lay down on the seat, covering himself up with his plaid.

When we came to the station where I had to get out—it was eight o'clock in the morning—I went up to where he lay, to take leave of him. Whether he was asleep, or only pretended to be asleep, I could not tell, but he did not move. I touched him with my hand. He uncovered himself, and then I saw that he was not sleeping. "Good-bye," I exclaimed, holding out my hand to him. He stretched out his hand and smiled, almost imperceptibly, but so piteously that I was moved almost to tears.

"Yes, good-bye," he said, employing as his last adieu to me the same words with which he had finished the story of his life.

The Cossacks

CHAPTER I

MOSCOW

Moscow has become quiet. Only very rarely does one hear the sound of wheels in the wintry streets. There are no longer any lights in the windows, and the street lamps have been extinguished. From the church towers come the sound of bells which, borne over the sleepy city, remind one of morning. The streets are empty. Every now and then a sledge plows its way through the mixture of snow and sand and, crossing over to another street corner, the driver stops to wait for another fare. An old woman passes by on her way to the church, where a few irregularly placed wax candles are already burning with a red light which is reflected from the gilt mountings of the icons. Workmen are already getting up after their long winter night, and are going to their work. But for the gentlefolk it is still evening!

Through chinks beneath the shutters of Chevalier's Restaurant, lights—unlawful at this hour—are still visible. At the entrance stand, closely crowded, a carriage and a number of sledges. Also a three-horsed post sledge is there. The yard porter, muffled up and pinched with cold, seems to be hiding behind the corner of the house.

"And what's the good of all this jawing?" thinks the attendant who, with a haggard look on his face, is sitting in the hall. "This is what always happens when I am on duty!"

From the adjoining brightly illuminated little room are heard the voices of three young men. On the table in the room are the remnants of supper and wine. One, a plain clean thin little man, sits looking with kindly, tired eyes at the friend about to depart. Another, a tall man, playing with his watch key, is lying on a sofa near the table on which stand the empty bottles. The third, in a new sheepskin coat, is pacing up and down. Every now and then he stops to crack an almond between his fingers, which are strong and thick, with carefully cleaned nails. He is constantly smiling at something, and his eyes and face are all aglow. He speaks with warmth, and gesticulates; but evidently he cannot find the words he wants, and those that come to his lips seem inadequate to express all that fills his heart.

"Now I can speak out," says the traveler. "I am not defending myself, but I want you, at least, to understand me as I understand myself, and not to look at the matter superficially. You say I've treated her badly?" he continues, addressing the man who was looking at him with kindly eyes.

"Yes, you are to blame," says the latter, and his look seems to express still more kindness and weariness.

"I know why you say that," continues the traveler. "You think that to be loved is as great a happiness as to love, and should suffice for a whole lifetime, once you have attained it."

"Yes, my dear fellow, it is quite sufficient, more than sufficient," insists the plain little man, opening and closing his eyes.

"But why should not a man also love?" says the traveler, thoughtfully, looking at his friend as if with pity. "Why shouldn't one love? Love doesn't come. . . . No, to be beloved is a misfortune! It is a misfortune when it makes you feel guilty because you do not, and cannot, give back what you receive. Ah, my God!" and he waves his arm. "If only these things happened logically! But it's all topsy-turvy, and doesn't depend on us—it comes as it will. Why, it's as if I had stolen that love! You think so too. Don't deny it, you must think so! But, will you believe it? Of all the stupid and horrid things I have found time to do in my life, this is one I do not and cannot repent of. Neither when it began, nor afterwards, did I consciously deceive myself or her. It seemed to me that I had at last fallen in love; but later on I discovered that I had been unconsciously deceiving myself— that it is impossible to love like that— and I could not go on, and then she went and. . . . Is it my fault that I couldn't? What was I to do?"

"Well, anyhow, it's all over now!" says his friend, lighting a cigar to keep awake. "Only you have never yet loved and do not know what love is!"

The man in the sheepskin was going to speak again, and put his hands to his head, but could not express what he wanted to say.

"Never loved! . . . Yes, quite true, I never have! But after all, I have within me a desire to love, and nothing could be stronger than that desire! But then, again, does such love exist? There always remains something incomplete. Ah well! What's the use of talking? I've made an awful mess of life! But anyhow, it's all over now; you are quite right. And I feel that I am beginning a new life."

"Which you will again make a mess of," said the man who lay on the sofa playing with his watch key. But the traveler did not listen to him.

"I am sad, and yet glad to go," he continued. "Why I am sad, I don't know."

And the traveler went on talking about himself, without noticing that this did not interest the others as much as it did him. A man is never such an egotist as at moments of spiritual ecstasy. At such times it seems to him that there is nothing on earth more splendid and interesting than himself.

"Dmitry Andreich! The coachman won't wait any longer!" said a young serf, entering the room in a sheepskin coat with a scarf tied round his head. "The horses have been standing since twelve, and it's now four o'clock!"

Dmitry Andreich looked at his serf, Vanyusha. The scarf round Vanyusha's head, his felt boots, and sleepy face, seemed to be calling his master to a new life of labor, hardship, and activity.

"True enough! Good-by!" said he, feeling for the unfastened hook and eye on his coat.

In spite of advice to mollify the

coachman by another tip, he put on his cap, and stood in the middle of the room. The friends kissed once, then again, and after a pause, a third time. The man in the sheepskin coat approached the table and emptied a champagne glass, then took the plain little man's hand and blushed.

"Ah well, I will speak out all the same. . . . I must, and will be frank with you, because I am fond of you. . . . Of course you love her—I always thought so—don't you?"

"Yes," answered his friend, smiling still more gently.

"And perhaps . . ."

"Please, sir, I have orders to put out the candles," said the sleepy attendant, who had been listening to the last part of the conversation and wondering why gentlefolk always talk about one and the same thing. "To whom shall I make out the bill? To you, sir?" he added, knowing whom to address, and turning to the tall man.

"To me," replied the tall man. "How much?"

"Twenty-six rubles."

The tall man considered for a moment, but said nothing, and put the bill in his pocket.

The other two continued their talk.

"Good-by, you are a capital fellow!" said the short plain man with the mild eyes.

Tears filled the eyes of both. They stepped into the porch.

"Oh, by the bye," said the traveler, turning with a blush to the tall man, "will you settle Chevalier's bill, and write and let me know?"

"All right, all right!" said the tall man, pulling on his gloves. "How I envy you!" he added quite unexpectedly when they were out in the porch.

The traveler got into his sledge, wrapped his sheepskin about him, and said: "Well then, come along!" He even moved a little to make room in the sledge for the man who said he envied him; his voice trembled.

"Good-by, Mitya! I hope that with God's help you . . ." said the tall one. But his wish was that the other would go away quickly, and so he could not finish the sentence.

They were silent a moment. Then some one again said, "Good-by," and a voice cried, "Ready," and the coachman touched up the horses.

"Hy, Elisar!" one of the friends called out, and the other coachman and the sledge drivers began moving, clicking their tongues and pulling at the reins. Then the stiffened carriage wheels rolled squeaking over the frozen snow.

"A fine fellow, that Olenin!" said one of the friends. "But what an idea, to go to the Caucasus—as a cadet, too! I wouldn't do it for a bob. . . . Are you dining at the club to-morrow?"

"Yes."

They separated.

The traveler felt warm, his sheepskin seemed too hot. He sat on the bottom of the sledge and unfastened his coat, and the three shaggy post horses dragged themselves out of one dark street into another, past houses he had never before seen. It seemed to Olenin that only travelers starting on a long journey went through those streets. All was dark and silent and dull around him, but his soul was full of memories, love, regrets, and a pleasant tearful feeling.

CHAPTER II

OLENIN

"I'm fond of them, very fond! . . . First-rate fellows! . . . Fine!" he kept repeating, and felt ready to cry. But why he wanted to cry; who were the first-rate fellows; whom he was so fond of—was more than he quite knew. Now and then he looked round at some house and wondered why it was so curiously built; sometimes he began wondering why the postboy and Vanyusha, who were so different from him, sat so near, and together with him were being jerked about and swayed by the tugs the side horses gave at the frozen traces: and again he repeated: "First rate . . . very fond!" and once more he even said: "And it seizes one . . . excellent!" and wondered what made him say it. "Dear me, am I drunk?" he asked himself. He had had a couple of bottles of wine, but it was not the wine alone that was having this effect on Olenin. He remembered all the words of friendship heartily, bashfully, spontaneously (as he believed) addressed to him on his departure. He remembered the clasp of hands, glances, the moments of silence, and the sound of a voice saying, "Good-by, Mitya!" when he was already in the sledge. He remembered his own deliberate frankness. And all this had a touching significance for him. Not only friends and relatives, not only people who had been indifferent to him, but even those who did not like him, seemed to have agreed to become fonder of him, or to forgive him, before his departure, as people do before confession or death.

"Perhaps I shall not return from the Caucasus," he thought. And he felt that he loved his friends and some one besides. He was sorry for himself. But it was not love for his friends that so stirred and uplifted his heart that he could not repress the meaningless words that seemed to rise of themselves to his lips; nor was it love for a woman (he had never yet been in love) that had brought on this mood. Love for himself, love full of hope—warm young love for all that was good in his own soul (and at that moment it seemed to him that there was nothing but good in it)—compelled him to weep and to mutter incoherent words.

Olenin was a youth who had never completed his university course, never served anywhere (having only a nominal post in some government office or other), who had squandered half his fortune, and had reached the age of twenty-four without having done anything or even chosen a career. He was what in Moscow society is termed un jeune homme.

At the age of eighteen he was free—as only rich young Russians in the 'forties, who had lost their parents at an early age, could be. Neither physical nor moral fetters of any kind existed for him; he could do as he liked, lacking nothing and bound by nothing. Neither relatives, nor fatherland, nor religion, nor wants, existed for him. He believed in nothing and admitted nothing. But although he believed in nothing he was not a morose or blasé young man, nor argumentative, but on the contrary continually let himself be carried away. He had come to the conclusion that there is no such thing as love, yet his heart always overflowed in the presence of any young and attractive woman. He had long been aware that honors and position were nonsense, yet involuntarily he felt pleased when, at a ball, Prince Sergius came up and spoke to him affably. But he yielded to his impulses only in so far as they did not limit his freedom.

As soon as he had yielded to any influence and became conscious of its leading on to labor and struggle, he instinctively hastened to free himself from the feeling or activity into which he was being drawn, and to regain his freedom. In this way he experimented with society life, the civil service, farming, music—to which at one time he intended to devote his life—and even with the love of women, in which he did not believe. He meditated on the use to which he should devote that power of youth which is granted to man only once in a lifetime: that force which gives a man the power of making himself, or even—as it seemed to him—of making the universe, into anything he wishes: should it be to art, to science, to love of woman, or to practical activities? It is true that some people are devoid of this impulse, and on entering life at once place their necks under the first yoke that offers itself, and honestly labor under it for the rest of their lives. But Olenin was too strongly conscious of the presence of that all-powerful God of Youth—of that capacity to be entirely transformed into an aspiration or idea —the capacity to wish and to do—to throw oneself headlong into a bottomless abyss without knowing why or wherefore. He bore this consciousness within himself, was proud of it, and, without knowing it, was happy in that

consciousness. Up to that time he had loved only himself, and could not help loving himself, for he expected nothing but good of himself, and had not yet had time to be disillusioned. On leaving Moscow he was in that happy state of mind in which a young man, conscious of past mistakes, suddenly says to himself, "That was not the real thing." All that had gone before was accidental and unimportant. Till then he had not really tried to live, but now, with his departure from Moscow, a new life was beginning—a life in which there would be no mistakes, no remorse, and certainly nothing but happiness.

It is always the case on a long journey that, till the first two or three stages have been passed, imagination continues to dwell on the place left behind, but with the first morning on the road it leaps to the end of the journey, and there begins building castles in the air. So it happened to Olenin.

After leaving the town behind, he gazed at the snowy fields, and felt glad to be alone in their midst. Wrapping himself in his fur coat, he lay at the bottom of the sledge, became tranquil, and fell into a doze. The parting with his friends had touched him deeply, and memories of that last winter spent in Moscow and images of the past, mingled with vague thoughts and regrets, rose unbidden in his imagination.

He remembered the friend who had seen him off, and his relations with the girl they had talked about. The girl was rich. "How could he love her, knowing that she loved me?" thought he, and evil suspicions crossed his mind. "There is much dishonesty in men, when one comes to reflect." Then he was confronted by the question: "But really, how is it I have never been in love? Every one tells me that I never have. Can it be that I am a moral monstrosity?" And he began to recall all his infatuations. He recalled his entry into society, and a friend's sister with whom he spent several evenings at a table with a lamp on it which lit up her slender fingers busy with needlework, and the lower part of her pretty delicate face. He recalled their conversations, that dragged on like the game in which one passes on a stick which one keeps alight as long as possible, and the general awkwardness and restraint, and his continual feeling of rebellion at all that conventionality. Some voice had always whispered: "That's not it, that's not it," and so it had proved. Then he remembered a ball, and the mazurka he danced with the beautiful D——. "How much in love I was that night, and how happy! And how hurt and vexed I was next morning, when I woke and felt myself still free! Why does not love come and bind me hand and foot?" thought he. "No, there is no such thing as love! That neighbor who used to tell me, as she told Dubrovin and the Marshal, that she loved the stars, was not *it* either."

And now his farming and work in the country recurred to his mind, and in those recollections also there was nothing to dwell on with pleasure. "Will they long talk of my departure?" came into his head; but who "they" were, he did not quite know. Next came a thought that made him wince and mutter incoherently. It was the recollection of M. Cappel, the tailor,

and the 678 rubles he still owed him, and he recalled the words in which he had begged him to wait another year, and the look of perplexity and resignation which had appeared on the tailor's face. "Oh, my God, my God!" he repeated, wincing and trying to drive away the intolerable thought. "All the same, and in spite of everything, she loved me," thought he of the girl they had talked about at the farewell supper. "Yes, had I married her I should not now be owing anything, and as it is I am in debt to Vasilyev." Then he remembered that last night he had played with Vasilyev at the club (just after leaving her), and he recalled his humiliating requests for another game, and the other's cold refusal. "A year's economizing, and they will all be paid, and the Devil take them!" . . . But despite this assurance he again began calculating his outstanding debts, their dates, and when he could hope to pay them off. "And I owe something to Morell as well as to Chevalier," thought he, recalling the night when he had run up so large a debt. It was at a drinking bout with the gypsies, arranged by some fellows from Petersburg: Sashka B——, an aid-de-camp to the Tsar, Prince D——, and that pompous old ——. "How is it those gentlemen are so self-satisfied?" thought he, "and by what right do they form a clique, to which they think others must be highly flattered to be admitted? Can it be because they are aids-de-camp? Why, it's awful what fools and scoundrels they consider other people to be! But I showed them that I, on the contrary, at any rate, do not at all want their intimacy. All the same, I fancy Andrew, the steward, would be amazed to know that I am on familiar terms with a man like Sashka B——, a colonel and an aid-de-camp to the Tsar! Yes, and no one drank more than I did that evening, and I taught the gypsies a new song, and every one listened to it. Though I have done many foolish things, all the same I am a very good fellow," thought he.

Morning found him at the third post stage. He drank tea, and himself helped Vanyusha to move his bundles and trunks, and sat down among them, sensible, erect, and precise, knowing where all his belongings were, how much money he had and where it was, where he had put his passport and the post-horse requisition and toll gate papers; and it all seemed to him so well arranged that he grew quite cheerful and the long journey before him seemed an extended pleasure trip.

All that morning and noon he was deep in calculations of how many versts he had traveled, how many remained to the next stage, how many to the next town, to the place where he would dine, to the place where he would drink tea, and to Stavropol, and what fraction of the whole journey was already accomplished. He also calculated how much money he had with him, how much would be left over, how much would pay off all his debts, and what proportion of his income he would spend each month. Toward evening, after tea, he calculated that to Stavropol there still remained seven-elevenths of the whole journey; that his debts would require seven months' economy and one-eighth of his whole fortune; and then, tranquilized, he wrapped himself up, lay down in the sledge, and again dozed off. His imagination was now turned to the future: to the Caucasus. All his dreams of the future were mingled with pictures of Amalat-Beks, Circassian women, mountains, precipices, terrible torrents, and dangers. All these things were vague and dim, but the love of fame and the danger of death furnished the interest of that future. Now, with unprecedented courage and a strength that amazed everyone, he slew and subdued an innumerable host of hillsmen; now he was himself a hillsman, and with them was maintaining their independence against the Russians. As soon as he pictured anything definite, familiar Moscow figures always appeared on the scene. Sashka B—— fights with the Russians or the hillsmen against him. Even the tailor, Cappel, in some strange way, takes part in the conqueror's triumph. Amid all this he remembered his former humiliations, weaknesses, and mistakes, and the recollection was not disagreeable. It was clear that there among the mountains, waterfalls, fair Circassians, and dangers, such mistakes could not recur. Having once made full confession to himself, there was an end of it all. One other vision, the sweetest of them all, mingled with the young man's every thought of the future—the vision of a woman. And there, among the mountains, she appeared to his imagination as a Circassian slave, a fine figure with a long plait of hair and deep submissive eyes. He pictured a lonely hut in the mountains, and on the threshold *she* stands awaiting him, when, tired and covered with dust, blood, and fame, he returns to her. He is conscious of her kisses, her shoulders, her sweet voice.

and her submissiveness. She is enchanting, but uneducated, wild, and rough. In the long winter evenings he begins her education. She is clever and gifted, and quickly acquires all the knowledge essential. Why not? She can quite easily learn foreign languages, read the French masterpieces and understand them: *Notre Dame de Paris,* for instance, is sure to please her. She can also speak French. In a drawing-room she can show more innate dignity than a lady of the highest society. She can sing, simply, powerfully, and passionately. . . . "Oh, what nonsense!" said he to himself. But here they reached a post station, and he had to change into another sledge and give some tips. But his fancy again began searching for the "nonsense" he had relinquished, and again fair Circassians, glory, and his return to Russia with an appointment as aid-de-camp and a lovely wife, rose before his imagination. "But there's no such thing as love," said he to himself. "Fame is all rubbish. But the 678 rubles? . . . And the conquered land, that will bring me more wealth than I need for a lifetime? It will not be right, though, to keep all that wealth for myself. I shall have to distribute it. But to whom? Well, 678 rubles to Cappel, and then we'll see." . . . Quite vague visions now cloud his mind, and only Vanyusha's voice and the interrupted motion of the sledge break his healthy youthful slumber. Scarcely conscious, he changes into another sledge at the next stage and continues his journey.

Next morning everything goes on just the same: the same kind of post stations and tea drinking, the same moving horses' cruppers, the same short talks with Vanyusha, the same vague dreams and drowsiness, and the same tired, healthy, youthful sleep at night.

CHAPTER III

SPRING

THE farther Olenin traveled from Central Russia, the farther he left his memories behind and the nearer he drew to the Caucasus, the lighter his heart became. "I'll stay away for good, and never return to show myself in society," was a thought that sometimes occurred to him. "These people whom I see here are *not* people. None of them know me, and none of them can ever enter the Moscow society I was in, or find out about my past. And no one in that society will ever know what I am doing, living among these people." And quite a new feeling of freedom from his whole past came over him among the rough beings he met on the road, whom he did not consider to be *people* in the sense that his Moscow acquaintances were.

The rougher the people and the fewer the signs of civilization, the freer he felt. Stavropol, through which he had to pass, irked him. The signboards, some of them even in French, ladies in carriages, cabs in the market place, and a gentleman wearing a fur cloak and tall hat who was walking along the boulevard and staring at the passers-by, quite upset him. "Perhaps these people know some of my acquaintances," he thought; and the club, his tailor, cards, society . . . came back to his mind. But, after Stavropol, everything was satisfactory—wild and also beautiful and warlike, and Olenin felt happier and happier. All the Cossacks, post boys and post-station masters seemed to him simple folk, with whom he could jest and converse simply, without having to consider to what class they belonged. They all belonged to the human race, which, without his thinking about it, all appeared dear to Olenin; and they all treated him in a friendly way.

Already, in the province of the Don Cossacks, his sledge had been exchanged for a cart; and beyond Stavropol it became so warm that Olenin traveled without wearing his sheepskin. It was already Spring—an unexpected joyous Spring for Olenin. At night he was no longer allowed to leave the Cossack villages, and they said it was dangerous to travel in the evening. Vanyusha began to be uneasy, and they carried a loaded gun in the cart. Olenin became still more joyful. At one of the post stations the postmaster told of a terrible murder that had been committed recently on the highroad. They began to meet armed men. "So this is where it begins!" thought Olenin, and kept expecting to see the snowy mountains, of which mention was so often made. Once, toward evening, the Nogay driver pointed with his whip to the mountains shrouded in clouds. Olenin looked eagerly, but it was dull, and the mountains were almost hidden by the clouds. Olenin made out something gray and white and fleecy, but, try as he would, he could find nothing beautiful in the mountains of which he had so often read and heard. The mountains and the clouds appeared to him quite alike, and he thought the special beauty of the snow peaks, of which he had so often been told, was as much an invention as Bach's music

and the love for women, which he did not believe in. So he gave up looking forward to see the mountains.

But early next morning, being awakened in his cart by the freshness of the air, he glanced carelessly to the right. The morning was perfectly clear. Suddenly he saw, about twenty paces away as it seemed to him at first glance, pure white gigantic masses with delicate contours, the distinct fantastic outlines of their summits showing sharply against the far-off sky. When he had realized the distance between himself and them and the sky, and the whole immensity of the mountains, and felt the infinitude of all that beauty, he became afraid that it was but a phantasm or a dream. He gave himself a shake to rouse himself, but the mountains were still the same.

"What's that? What is it?" he said to the driver.

"Why, the mountains," answered the Nogay driver with indifference.

"And I too have been looking at them for a long while," said Vanyusha. "Aren't they fine? They won't believe it at home."

The quick progress of the three-horsed cart along the smooth road caused the mountains to appear to be running along the horizon, while their rosy crests glittered in the light of the rising sun. At first Olenin was only astonished at the sight, then gladdened by it; but later on, gazing more and more intently at that snow-peaked chain, that seemed to rise not from behind other, black, mountains, but straight out of the plain, and to glide away into the distance, he began by slow degrees to be penetrated by their beauty, and at length to *feel* the mountains. From that moment all he saw, all he thought, and all he felt, acquired for him a new character, sternly majestic, like the mountains! All his Moscow reminiscences, shame and repentance, and his trivial dreams about the Caucasus, vanished and did not return. "Now it has begun," a solemn voice seemed to say to him. The road, and the Terek, just becoming visible in the distance, and the Cossack villages and the people, all no longer appeared to him as a joke. He looked at himself or Vanyusha, and again thought of the mountains. . . . Two Cossacks ride by, their guns in their cases swinging rhythmically behind their backs, the white and bay legs of their horses mingling confusedly . . . and the mountains! Beyond the Terek rises the smoke from a Tartar village . . . and the mountains! The sun has risen and glitters on the Terek now visible beyond the reeds . . . and the mountains! From the village comes a Tartar wagon, and women, beautiful young women, pass by . . . and the mountains! "Abreks canter about the plain, and here am I driving along and do not fear them! I have a gun, and strength, and youth . . . and the mountains!"

CHAPTER IV

DOCTRINES

THAT whole part of the Terek line (about fifty miles) along which lie the villages of the Grebensk Cossacks, is uniform in character, both as to the country and the inhabitants. The Terek, which separates the Cossacks from the hill tribes, still flows turbid and rapid though already broad and smooth, always depositing grayish sand on its low reedy right bank, and washing away the steep, though not high, left bank, with its roots of century-old oaks, its rotting plane trees and young brushwood. On the right bank lie the villages of pro-Russian, though still somewhat restless, Tartars. Along the left bank, back half a mile from the river and standing five or six miles apart from one another, are Cossack villages. In olden times most of these villages were situated on the banks of the river; but the Terek, shifting northward from the mountains year by year, washed away these banks, and now there remain only the ruins of the old villages, and of the gardens of pear and plum trees and poplars, all overgrown with blackberry bushes and wild vines. No one lives there now, and one only sees the tracks of the deer, the wolves, the hares, and the pheasants, who have learned to love these places. From village to village runs a road cut through the forest as a cannon shot might fly. Along the roads are cordons of Cossacks, and watch towers with sentinels in them. Only a narrow strip of about seven hundred yards of fertile wooded soil belongs to the Cossacks. To the north of it begin the sand drifts of the Nogay or Mozdok Steppes, which stretch far to the north and run, Heaven knows where, into the Trukhmen, Astrakhan and Kirghiz-Kaisatsk Steppes. To the south, beyond the Terek, are the great Chechnya river, the Kochkalov range, the Black Mountains, yet another range, and at last the snow mountains, which can just be seen but have never yet been scaled. In this fertile wooded strip, rich in vegetation, has dwelt, as far back as memory runs, the fine war-like and prosperous Russian tribe belonging to the sect of Old Believers, and called the Grebensk Cossacks.

Long long ago their Old Believer ancestors fled from Russia, and settled beyond the Terek among the Chechens on the Greben, the first range of wooded mountains of Chechnya. Living among the Chechens, the Cossacks intermarried with them, and adopted the manners and customs of the hill tribes, though they still retained the Russian language in all its purity, as well as their Old Faith. A tradition, still fresh among them, declares that Tsar John the Terrible came to the Terek, sent for their Elders, and gave them the land on this side of the river, exhorting them to remain friendly to Russia, and promising not to enforce his rule upon them nor oblige them to change their faith. Even now the Cossack families claim relationship with the Chechens, and the love of freedom, of leisure, of plunder and of war, still form their chief characteristics. Only the harmful side of Russian influence is apparent—by interference at elections, by confiscation of church bells, and by the troops who are quartered in the country, or march through it.

A Cossack is inclined to hate less the dzhigit hillsman, who maybe has killed his brother, than the soldier quartered on him to defend his village, but who has defiled his hut with tobacco smoke. He respects his enemy the hillsman, and despises the soldier; who is in his eyes an alien and an oppressor. In reality, from a Cossack's point of view, a Russian peasant is a foreign, savage, despicable creature, of whom he sees a sample in the hawkers who come to the country, and in the Little-Russian immigrants whom the Cossack contemptuously calls "woolbeaters." For him, to be smartly dressed, means to be dressed like a Circassian. The best weapons are obtained from the hillsmen, and the best horses are bought, or stolen, from them. A dashing young Cossack likes to show off his knowledge of Tartar, and when carousing talks Tartar even to his fellow Cossack.

In spite of all these things this small Christian clan, stranded in a tiny corner of the earth, surrounded by half-savage Mohammedan tribes and by soldiers, considers itself highly advanced, acknowledges none but Cossacks as human beings, and despises everybody else. The Cossack spends most of his time in the cordon, in action, or in hunting and fishing. He hardly ever works at home. When he stays in the village, it is an exception to the general rule, and then he is holiday making. All Cossacks make their own wine, and drunkenness is not so much a general tendency as a rite, the nonfulfillment of which would be considered apostasy. The Cossack looks upon a woman as an instrument for his welfare; only the unmarried girls are allowed to amuse themselves. A married woman has to work for her husband from youth to very old age: his demands on her are the Oriental ones of submission and labor. In consequence of this outlook, women are strongly developed, both physically and mentally; and though they are—as everywhere in the East— nominally in subjection, they possess far greater influence and importance in family life than Western women. The exclusion from public life and inurement to heavy male labor give the women all the more power and importance in the household. A Cossack, who before strangers considers it improper to speak affectionately or needlessly to his wife, when alone with her is voluntarily conscious of her superiority. His house and all his property, in fact the entire homestead, has been acquired and is kept together solely by her labor and care. Though firmly convinced that labor is degrading to a Cossack, and is only proper for a Nogay laborer or a woman, he is vaguely aware of the fact that all he makes use of and calls his own is the result of that toil, and that it is in the power of the woman (his mother or his wife) whom he considers his slave, to deprive him of all he possesses. Besides, the continuous performance of man's heavy work and the responsibilities intrusted to her, have endowed the Grebensk women with a peculiarly independent, masculine character, and have remarkably developed their physical powers, common sense, resolution, and stability. The women are in most cases stronger, more intelligent, more developed, and handsomer, than the men. A striking feature of a Grebensk woman's beauty is the combination of the purest Circassian type of face with the broad and powerful build of Northern women. Cossack women wear the Circassian dress: a Tartar smock, beshmet, and soft slippers; but they tie their kerchiefs round their heads in the Russian fashion. Smartness, cleanliness and elegance in dress and in the arrangement of their huts, are with them a custom and a necessity. In their relations with men the women, and especially the unmarried girls, enjoy perfect freedom.

Novomlinsk village was considered the very heart of Grebensk Cossackdom. In it more than elsewhere the customs of the old Grebensk population have been preserved; and its women have from time immemorial been renowned all over the Caucasus for their beauty. A Cossack's livelihood is derived from vineyards, fruit gardens, watermelon and pumpkin plantations, from fishing, hunting, maize and millet growing, and from war plunder. Novomlinsk village lies about two and a half miles away from the Terek, from which it is separated by a dense forest. On one side of the road, which runs through the village, is the river; on the other, green vineyards and orchards, beyond which are seen the drift sands of the Nogay Steppe. The village is surrounded by earth banks and prickly bramble hedges, and is entered by tall gates hung on posts, and covered with little reed-thatched roofs. Beside them stands, on a wooden gun carriage, an unwieldy cannon, captured by the Cossacks at some time or other, and which has not been fired for a hundred years. A uniformed Cossack sentinel, with dagger and gun, sometimes stands, and sometimes does not stand, on guard beside the gate, and sometimes presents arms to a passing officer, and sometimes does not.

Below the roof of the gateway is written in black letters on a white board: "Houses 266: male inhabitants 897: female 1012." The Cossacks' houses are all raised on pillars two-and-a-half feet from the ground. They are carefully thatched with reeds, and have large carved gables. If not new, they are at least all straight and clean, with high porches of different shapes; and they are not built close together but have ample space around them, and are all picturesquely placed along broad streets and lanes. In front of the large clear windows of many of the houses, beyond the kitchen gardens, dark green poplars and acacias with their delicate pale verdure and scented white blossoms overtop the houses, and beside them grow bold-faced yellow sunflowers, creepers, and grapevines. In the broad open square are three shops, where drapery, sunflower and pumpkin seeds, locust beans and gingerbreads are sold; and surrounded by a tall fence, loftier and larger than the other houses, stands, behind a row of tall poplars, the Regimental Commander's dwelling with its casement windows. Few people are to be seen in the streets of the village on weekdays, especially in summer. The young men are on duty in the cordons, or on military expeditions; the old ones are fishing or helping the women in the orchards and gardens. Only the very old, the sick, and the children remain at home.

CHAPTER V

MARYANKA

IT was one of those rare evenings that occur only in the Caucasus. The sun had sunk behind the mountains, but it was yet light. The evening glow had spread over a third of the sky, and against its light the dull white immensity of the mountains was sharply defined. The air was rarefied, motionless, and full of sound. The shadow of the mountains reached for several miles over the steppe. The steppe, the opposite side of the river, and the roads, were all deserted. If, very occasionally, mounted men appeared, the Cossacks in the cordon and the Chechens in their aouls (villages) watched them with surprised curiosity, and tried to guess who those questionable men could be.

At nightfall people from fear of one another flock to their dwellings, and only birds and beasts fearless of man prowl in those deserted spaces. Talking merrily, the women, who have been tying up the vines, hurry away from the gardens before sunset. The vineyards, like all the surrounding district, are deserted, but the villages become very animated at that time of the evening. From all sides, walking, riding, or driving in their creaking carts, people move toward the village. Girls with their smocks tucked up and twigs in their hands, run chatting merrily to the village gates to meet the cattle that are crowding together in a cloud of dust and mosquitoes which they bring with them from the steppe. The well-fed cows and buffaloes disperse at a run all over the streets, and Cossack women in colored beshmets go to and fro among them. You can hear their merry laughter and shrieks mingling with the lowing of the cattle. There an armed and mounted Cossack, on leave from the cordon, rides up to a hut and, leaning toward the window, knocks. In answer to the knock the handsome head of a young woman appears at the window, and you can hear caressing, laughing voices. There a tattered Nogay laborer with prominent cheek-bones, brings a load of reeds from the steppes, turns his creaking cart into the Cossack captain's broad and clean courtyard, and lifts the yoke off the oxen, that stand tossing their heads, while he and his master shout to one another in Tartar. Past a puddle that reaches nearly across the street, a barefooted Cossack woman, with a bundle of firewood on her back, makes her laborious way by clinging to the fences, holding her smock high and exposing her white legs. A Cossack returning from shooting calls out in jest: "Lift it higher, shameless thing!" and points his gun at her. The woman lets down her smock and drops the wood. An old Cossack, returning home from fishing with his trousers tucked up and his hairy gray chest uncovered, has a net across his shoulder containing silvery fish that are still struggling; and, to take a short cut, climbs over his neighbor's broken fence and gives a tug to his coat which has caught on the fence. There a woman is dragging a dry branch along, and from round the corner comes the sound of an ax. Cossack children, spinning their tops wherever there is a smooth place in the street, are shrieking; women are climbing over fences to avoid going round. From every chimney rises the scented kisyak smoke. From every homestead comes the sound of increased bustle, precursor to the stillness of night.

Granny Ulitka, the wife of the Cossack Cornet who is also Teacher in the regimental school, goes out to the gates of her yard, like the other women, and waits for the cattle which her daughter Maryanka is driving along the street. Before she has had time fully to open the wattle gate in the fence, an enormous buffalo cow, surrounded by mosquitoes, rushes up bellowing, and squeezes in. Several well-fed cows slowly follow her, their large eyes gazing with recognition at their mistress as they swish their sides with their tails.

The beautiful and shapely Maryanka enters at the gate and, throwing away her switch, quickly slams the gate to, and rushes with all the speed of her nimble feet to separate and drive the cattle into their sheds. "Take off your slippers, you devil's wench!" shouts her mother, "you'll wear them into holes!" Maryanka is not at all offended at being called a "devil's wench," but, accepting it as a term of endearment, cheerfully goes on with her task. Her face is covered with a kerchief tied round her head. She is wearing a pink smock and a green beshmet. She disappears inside the lean-to shed in the yard, following the big fat cattle; and from the shed comes her voice as she speaks gently and persuasively to the buffalo: "Won't she stand still? What a creature! Come now, come, old dear!" Soon the girl and the old woman pass from the shed to the outhouse, carrying two large pots of milk, the day's yield. From the chimney of the outhouse rises a thin cloud of kisyak smoke: the milk is being used to make into clotted cream. The girl makes up the fire, while her mother goes to the gate. Twilight has fallen on the village. The air is full of the smell of vegetables, cattle, and scented kisyak smoke. From the gates and along the streets Cossack women come running, carrying burning rags. From the yards, one hears the snorting and quiet chewing of the cattle, eased of their milk; while in the street only the voices of women and children sound, as they call to one another. It is rare on a week day to hear the drunken voice of a man.

One of the Cossack wives, a tall, masculine old woman, approaches Granny Ulitka from the homestead opposite, and asks her for a light. In her hand she holds a rag.

"Have you cleared up, Granny?"

"The girl is lighting the fire. Is it fire you want?" says Granny Ulitka, proud of being able to oblige her neighbor.

Both women enter the hut, and coarse hands, unused to dealing with small articles, tremblingly remove the lid of a match box, which is rare in the Caucasus. The masculine-looking newcomer sits down on the doorstep, with the evident intention of having a chat.

"And is your man at the school, Mother?" she asked.

"He's always teaching the youngsters, Mother. But he writes that he'll come home for the holidays," said the Teacher's wife.

"Yes, he's a clever man, one sees; it all comes useful."

"Of course it does."

"And my Lukashka is at the cordon; they won't let him come home," said the visitor, though the Teacher's wife had known all this long ago. She wanted to talk about her Lukashka, whom she had lately fitted out for service in the Cossack regiment, and whom she wished to marry to the Teacher's daughter, Maryanka.

"So he's at the cordon?"

"He is, Mother. He's not been home since last holidays. The other day I sent him some shirts by Fomushkin. He says he's all right, and that his superiors are satisfied. He says they

are looking out for abreks again. Lukashka is quite happy, he says."

"Ah well, thank God," said the Teacher's wife. "'Snatcher' is certainly the only word for him." Lukashka was surnamed "the Snatcher" because of his bravery in snatching a boy from a watery grave, and the Teacher's wife alluded to this, wishing in her turn to say something agreeable to Lukashka's mother.

"I thank God, Mother, that he's a good son! He's a fine fellow, everyone praises him," says Lukashka's mother. "All I wish is, to get him married; then I could die in peace."

"Well, aren't there plenty of young women in the village?" answered the Teacher's sly wife, as she carefully replaced the lid of the match box with her horny hands.

"Plenty, Mother, plenty," remarked Lukashka's mother, shaking her head. "There's your girl now, your Maryanka —that's the sort of girl! You'd have to search through the whole place to find such another!"

The Teacher's wife knows what Lukashka's mother is after; but though she believes him to be a good Cossack, she hangs back: first because she is a Teacher's wife and rich, while Lukashka is the son of a simple Cossack and fatherless; secondly because she does not want to part with her daughter yet; but chiefly, because propriety demands it.

"Well, when Maryanka grows up she'll be marriageable too," she answers soberly and modestly.

"I'll send the matchmakers to you— I'll send them! Only let me get the vineyard done, and then we'll come and make our bows to you," says Lukashka's mother. "And we'll make our bows to Elias Vasilich too."

"Elias, indeed!" says the Teacher's wife, proudly. "It's to me you must speak! All in its own good time."

Lukashka's mother sees by the stern face of the Teacher's wife that it is not the time to say anything more just now, so she lights her rag with the match, and says, rising: "Don't refuse us, think of my words. I'll go; it is time to light the fire."

As she crosses the road, swinging the burning rag, she meets Maryanka, who bows.

"Ah, she's a regular queen, a splendid worker, that girl!" she thinks, looking at the beautiful maiden. "What need for her to grow any more? It's time she was married, and into a good home; married to Lukashka!"

But Granny Ulitka had her own cares, and she remained sitting on the threshold, thinking hard about something, till the girl called her.

CHAPTER VI

UNCLE EROSHKA

THE male population of the village spend their time on military expeditions and in the cordon—or "at their posts," as the Cossacks say. Toward evening, the same Lukashka the Snatcher, about whom the old women had been talking, was standing on a watchtower of the Nizhne-Prototsk post, situated on the very banks of the Terek. Leaning on the railing of the tower and screwing up his eyes, he looked, now far into the distance beyond the Terek, now down at his fellow Cossacks, and occasionally he addressed the latter. The sun was already approaching the snowy

range that gleamed white above the fleecy clouds. The clouds undulating at the base of the mountains grew darker and darker. The clearness of evening was noticeable in the air. A sense of freshness came from the woods, though round the post it was still hot. The voices of the talking Cossacks vibrated more sonorously than before. The moving mass of the Terek's rapid brown waters contrasted more vividly with its motionless banks. The waters were beginning to subside, and here and there the wet sands gleamed drab on the banks and in the shallows. The other side of the river, just opposite the cordon, was deserted; only an immense waste of low-growing reeds stretched far away to the very foot of the mountains. On the low bank, a little to one side, could be seen the flat-roofed clay houses and the funnel-shaped chimneys of a Chechen village. The sharp eyes of the Cossack who stood on the watchtower followed, through the evening smoke of the pro-Russian village, the tiny moving figures of the Chechen women, visible in the distance in their red and blue garments.

Although the Cossacks expected abreks to cross over and attack them from the Tartar side at any moment, especially as it was May, when the woods by the Terek are so dense that it is difficult to pass through them on foot and the river is shallow enough in places for a horseman to ford it, and despite the fact that a couple of days before a Cossack had arrived with a circular from the Commander of the regiment, announcing that spies had reported the intention of a party of some eight men to cross the Terek, and ordering special vigilance—no special vigilance was being observed in the cordon. The Cossacks, unarmed and with their horses unsaddled, just as if they were at home, spent their time some in fishing, some in drinking, and some in hunting. Only the horse of the man on duty was saddled and, with its feet hobbled, was moving about by the brambles near the wood; and only the sentinel had his Circassian coat on and carried a gun and sword. The Corporal, a tall thin Cossack with an exceptionally long back and small hands and feet, was sitting on the earth bank of a hut, with his beshmet unbuttoned. On his face was the lazy, bored expression of a superior, and, having shut his eyes, had dropped his head upon the palm first of one hand and then of the other. An elderly Cossack, with a broad grayish black beard, was lying in his shirt, girdled with a black strap, close to the river and gazing lazily at the waves of the Terek as they monotonously foamed and swirled. Others, also overcome by the heat and half naked, were rinsing clothes in the Terek, plaiting a fishing line, or humming tunes as they lay on the hot sand of the river bank. One Cossack, with a thin face burnt black by the sun, lay near the hut, evidently dead drunk, by a wall which, though it had been in shadow some two hours previously, was now exposed to the sun's fierce slanting rays.

Lukashka, who stood on the watchtower, was a tall, handsome lad about twenty years old, and very like his mother. His face and whole build, in spite of the angularity of youth, indicated great strength, both physical and moral. Though he had only lately joined the Cossacks at the front, it was

evident from the expression of his face and the calm assurance of his attitude that he had already acquired the somewhat proud and warlike bearing peculiar to Cossacks and to men generally who continually carry arms; and that he felt he was a Cossack and fully knew his own value. His ample Circassian coat was torn in some places; his cap was on the back of his head, Chechen fashion, and his leggings had slipped below his knees. His clothing was not rich, but he wore it with that peculiar Cossack foppishness which consists in imitating the Chechen brave. Everything on a real brave is ample, ragged, and neglected; only his weapons are costly. But these ragged clothes and these weapons are belted and worn with a certain air and matched in a certain manner, neither of which can be acquired by everybody, and which at once strike the eye of a Cossack or a hillsman. Lukashka had this resemblance to a brave. With his hands folded behind his cap, and his eyes nearly closed, he kept looking at the distant Tartar village. Taken separately, his features were not beautiful, but anyone who saw his stately carriage, and his dark-browed intelligent face, would involuntarily say "What a fine fellow!"

"Look at the women, what a lot of them are walking about in the village," said he in a sharp voice, languidly showing his brilliant white teeth, and not addressing anyone in particular. But Nazarka, who was lying below, immediately lifted his head, and remarked:

"They must be going for water."

"Supposing one scared them with

a gun?" said Lukashka, laughing. "Wouldn't they be frightened?"

"It wouldn't reach."

"What! Mine would carry beyond. Just wait a bit, and when their feast comes round I'll go and visit Girey Khan and drink buza there," said Lukashka, angrily swishing away the mosquitoes which clung about him.

A rustling in the thicket drew the Cossack's attention. A pied mongrel half-setter, searching for a scent and violently wagging its scantily furred tail, came running to the cordon. Lukashka recognized the dog as one belonging to his neighbor, Uncle Eroshka, a hunter, and saw, following it through the thicket, the approaching figure of the hunter himself.

Uncle Eroshka was a gigantic Cossack with a broad, snow-white beard, and such broad shoulders and chest that in the wood where there was no one to compare him with, he did not look particularly tall, so well proportioned were his powerful limbs. He wore a tattered coat and, over the bands with which his legs were swathed, sandals made of undressed deer's hide, tied on with strings; while on his head he had a rough little white cap. He carried over one shoulder a screen to hide behind when shooting pheasants, and a bag containing a hen for luring hawks, and a small falcon; over the other shoulder, attached by a strap, was a wildcat he had killed; and stuck in his belt behind were some little bags containing bullets, gunpowder and bread; a horse's tail to swish away the mosquitoes, a large dagger in a torn scabbard smeared with old bloodstains, and two dead pheasants. Having glanced at the cordon, he halted.

"Hi, Lyam!" he called to the dog, in such a ringing bass that it awoke an echo far away in the wood; and throwing over his shoulder his big gun, of the kind the Cossacks call a "flint," he raised his cap.

"Had a good day, good people, eh?" he said, addressing the Cossacks in the same strong and cheerful voice, quite without effort but as loudly as if he were shouting to some one on the other bank of the river.

"Yes, yes, Uncle!" answered from all sides the voices of the young Cossacks.

"What have you seen? Tell us!" shouted Uncle Eroshka, wiping the sweat from his broad red face with the sleeve of his coat.

"Ah, there's a vulture living in the plane tree here, Uncle. As soon as night comes he begins hovering round," said Nazarka, winking, and jerking his shoulder and leg.

"Come, come!" said the old man incredulously.

"Really, Uncle! You just watch," replied Nazarka, with a laugh.

The other Cossacks began laughing.

The wag had not seen any vulture at all, but it had long been the custom of the young Cossacks in the cordon to tease and mislead Uncle Eroshka every time he came to them.

"Eh, you fool, always lying!" exclaimed Lukashka from the tower to Nazarka.

Nazarka was immediately silenced.

"It must be watched. I'll watch," answered the old man, to the great delight of all the Cossacks. "But have you seen any boars?"

"Watching for boars, are you?" said the Corporal, bending forward and scratching his back with both hands.

very pleased at the chance of some distraction. "It's abreks one has to hunt here, and not boars! You've not heard anything, Uncle, have you?" he added, needlessly screwing up his eyes, and showing his close-set white teeth.

"Abreks?" said the old man. "No, I've not. I say, have you any chikhir? Let me have a drink, there's a good man. I'm really quite done up. When the time comes, I'll bring you some fresh meat, I really will. Give me a drink!" he added.

"Well, and are you going to watch?" inquired the Corporal, as though he had not heard what the other said.

"I did mean to watch to-night," replied Uncle Eroshka. "Maybe, with God's help, I shall kill something for the holiday. Then you shall have a share, you shall indeed!"

"Uncle! Hallo, Uncle!" called out Lukashka sharply from above, attracting everybody's attention. All the Cossacks looked up at him. "Just go to the upper watercourse, there's a fine herd of boars there. I'm not inventing, really! The other day one of our Cossacks shot one there. I'm telling you the truth," added he, readjusting the musket at his back, and in a tone that showed he was not joking.

"Ah! Lukashka the Snatcher is here!" said the old man, looking up. "Where has he been shooting?"

"Haven't you seen? I suppose you're too young!" said Lukashka. "Close by the ditch," he went on seriously, with a shake of the head. "We were just going along the ditch when all at once we heard something crackling, but my gun was in its case. Elias fired suddenly. . . . But I'll show you the place. it's not far. You just

wait a bit. I know every one of their footpaths. . . . Daddy Mosey," said he, turning resolutely and almost commandingly to the Corporal, "it's time to relieve guard!" and, holding aloft his gun, he began to descend from the watchtower, without waiting for the order.

"Come down!" said the Corporal, after Lukashka had started, and glanced round. "Is it your turn, Gurka? Then go. . . . True enough, your Lukashka has become very skillful," he went on, addressing the old man. "He keeps going about just like you, he doesn't stay at home. The other day he killed a boar."

CHAPTER VII

BOARS!

THE sun had already set, and the shades of night were rapidly spreading from the edge of the wood. The Cossacks finished their task round the cordon, and gathered in the hut for supper. Only the old man still stayed under the plane tree, watching for the vulture and pulling the string tied to the falcon's leg, but though a vulture was really perching on the plane tree it declined to swoop down on the lure. Lukashka, singing one song after another, was leisurely placing nets among the very thickest brambles to trap pheasants. In spite of his tall stature and big hands, every kind of work, both rough and delicate, prospered under Lukashka's fingers.

"Hallo, Luke!" came Nazarka's shrill, sharp voice calling him from the thicket close by. "The Cossacks have gone in to supper." And Nazarka, carrying a live pheasant under his arm, forced his way through the brambles, and emerged into full sight on the footpath.

"Oh!" said Lukashka, breaking off in his song, "where did you get that cock pheasant? I suppose it was in my trap?"

Nazarka was of the same age as Lukashka, and had also only been at the front since the previous spring. He was plain, thin and puny, with a shrill voice that rang in one's ears. They were neighbors and comrades. Lukashka was sitting on the grass, cross-legged like a Tartar, adjusting his nets.

"I don't know whose it was—yours, I expect."

"Was it beyond the pit, by the plane tree? Then it is mine! I set the nets last night."

Lukashka rose and examined the captured pheasant. After stroking the dark burnished head of the bird, which rolled its eyes and stretched out its neck in terror, Lukashka took the pheasant in his hands.

"We'll have it in a pilav to-night. You go and kill and pluck it."

"And shall we eat it ourselves, or give it to the Corporal?"

"He has plenty!"

"I don't like killing them," said Nazarka.

"Give it here!"

Lukashka drew a little knife from under his dagger and gave it a swift jerk. The bird fluttered, but before it could spread its wings the bleeding head bent and quivered. "That's how one should do it!" said Lukashka, throwing down the pheasant. "It will make a fat pilav."

Nazarka shuddered as he looked at the bird.

"I say, Lukashka, that fiend will be sending us to lie in ambush again to-night," he said, taking up the bird. (He was alluding to the Corporal.) "He has sent Fomushkin to get wine, and it ought to be his turn. He always puts it on us."

Lukashka went whistling along the cordon. "Take the string with you," he shouted; and Nazarka obeyed.

"I'll give him a bit of my mind, to-day, I really will," continued Nazarka. "Let's say we won't go; we're tired out, and there's an end of it! No, really, you tell them; they'll listen to you. It's too bad!"

"Get along with you! What a thing to make a fuss about!" said Lukashka, evidently thinking of something else. "What bosh! If he made us turn out of the village at night now, that would be annoying: there one can have some fun, but here, what is there? It's all one whether we're in the cordon or in ambush. What a chap you are!"

"And are you going to the village?"

"I'll go for the holidays."

"Gurka says your Dunayka is carrying on with Fomushkin," said Nazarka suddenly.

"Well, let her go to the devil," said Lukashka, showing his regular white teeth, though he did not laugh. "As if I couldn't find another!"

"Gurka says he went to her house. Her husband was out, and there was Fomushkin sitting and eating pie. Gurka stopped awhile and then went away, and passing by the window he heard her say, 'He's gone, the fiend. . . . Why don't you eat your pie, my own? You needn't go home for the night,' she says. And Gurka under the window, says to himself, 'Fine, that!' "

"You're making it up."

"No, quite true, by Heaven!"

"Well, if she's found another, let her go to the devil," said Lukashka, after a pause. "There's no lack of girls, and I was sick of her anyway."

"Well, see what a devil you are!" said Nazarka. "You should make up to the Teacher's girl, Maryanka. Why doesn't she walk out with anyone?"

Lukashka frowned. "What of Maryanka? They're all alike," said he.

"Well, you just try . . ."

"What do you think? Are girls so scarce in the village?"

And Lukashka recommenced whistling, and went along the cordon, pulling leaves and branches from the bushes as he went. Suddenly, catching sight of a smooth sapling, he drew the knife from the handle of his dagger, and cut it down. "What a ramrod it will make," he said, swinging the sapling till it whistled through the air.

. . . . . .

The Cossacks were sitting round a low Tartar table on the earthen floor of the clay-plastered outer room of the hut, when the question of whose turn it was to lie in ambush was raised.

"Who is to go-tonight?" shouted one of the Cossacks, through the open door, to the Corporal in the next room.

"Who is to go?" the Corporal shouted back. "Uncle Burlak has been, and Fomushkin too," said he, not quite confidently. "You two had better go, you and Nazarka," he went on, addressing Lukashka. "And Ergushov must go too; surely he has slept it off?"

"You don't sleep it off yourself, so why should he?" said Nazarka in a subdued voice.

The Cossacks laughed.

Ergushov was the Cossack who had been lying drunk and asleep near the hut. He had only that moment staggered into the room, rubbing his eyes.

Lukashka had already risen, and was getting his gun ready.

"Be quick and go! Finish your supper and go!" said the Sergeant; and without waiting for an expression of consent he shut the door, evidently not expecting the Cossack to obey. "Of course," thought he, "if I hadn't been ordered to, I wouldn't send anyone; but an officer might turn up at any moment. As it is, they say eight abreks have crossed over."

"Well, I suppose I must go," remarked Ergushov, "it's the regulation. Can't be helped! The times are such. I say, we must go."

Meanwhile Lukashka, holding a big piece of pheasant to his mouth with both hands, and glancing now at Nazarka, now at Ergushov, seemed quite indifferent to what passed, and only laughed at them both. Before the Cossacks were ready to go into ambush, Uncle Eroshka, who had been vainly waiting under the plane tree till night fell, entered the dark outer room.

"Well, lads," his loud bass resounded through the low-roofed room, drowning all the other voices, "I'm going with you. You'll watch for Chechens, and I for boars!"

CHAPTER VIII

THE LOOK-OUT

It was quite dark when Uncle Eroshka and the three Cossacks, in their cloaks and shouldering their guns, left the cordon and went toward the place on the Terek where they were to lie in ambush.

Nazarka did not want to go at all, but Lukashka shouted at him, and they soon started. After they had gone a few steps in silence, the Cossacks turned aside from the ditch and went along a path almost hidden by reeds, till they reached the river. On its bank lay a thick black log cast up by the water. The reeds around it had been recently beaten down.

"Shall we lie here?" asked Nazarka.

"Why not?" answered Lukashka. "Sit down here, and I'll be back in a minute. I'll only show Daddy where to go."

"This is the best place; here we can see and not be seen," said Ergushov, "so it's here we'll lie. It's a first-rate place!"

Nazarka and Ergushov spread out their cloaks and settled down behind the log, while Lukashka went on with Uncle Eroshka.

"It's not far from here, Daddy," said Lukashka, stepping softly in front of the old man; "I'll show you where they've been—I'm the only one that knows, Daddy."

"Show me! You're a fine fellow, a regular Snatcher!" replied the old man, also whispering.

Having gone a few steps, Lukashka stopped, stooped down over a puddle, and whistled. "That's where they come to drink, d'you see?" He spoke in a scarcely audible voice, pointing to fresh hoof-prints.

"Christ bless you," answered the old man. "The boar will be in the hollow beyond the ditch," he added. "I'll watch, and you can go."

Lukashka pulled his cloak up higher and walked back alone, throwing swift glances, now to the left at the wall of reeds, now to the Terek rushing by below the bank. "I daresay he's watching or creeping along somewhere," thought he of a possible Chechen hillsman. Suddenly a loud rustling and a splash in the water made him start and seize his musket. From under the bank a boar leapt out—his dark outline showing for a moment against the glassy surface of the water and then disappearing among the reeds. Lukashka pulled out his gun and aimed; but, before he could fire, the boar had disappeared in the thicket. Lukashka spat with vexation, and went on. On approaching the ambuscade he halted again, and whistled softly. His whistle was answered and he stepped up to his comrades.

Nazarka, all curled up, was already asleep. Ergushov sat with his legs crossed, and moved slightly to make room for Lukashka.

"How jolly it is to sit here! It's really a good place," said he. "Did you take him there?"

"Showed him where," answered Lukashka, spreading out his cloak. "But what a big boar I roused just now, close to the water! I expect it was the very one! You must have heard the crash?"

"I did hear a beast crashing through. I knew at once it was a beast. I thought to myself: 'Lukashka has roused a beast,'" Ergushov said, wrapping himself up in his cloak. "Now I'll go to sleep," he added. "Wake me when the cocks crow. We must have discipline. I'll lie down and have a nap; and then you will have a nap and I'll watch—that's the way."

"Luckily, I don't want to sleep," answered Lukashka.

The night was dark, warm, and still. Only on one side of the sky the stars were shining; the other and greater part was overcast by one huge cloud, stretching from the mountain tops. The black cloud, blending, in the absence of any wind, with the mountains, moved slowly onwards, its curved edges sharply defined against the deep starry sky. Only in front of him could the Cossack discern the Terek and the distance beyond. Behind, and on both sides, he was surrounded by a wall of reeds. Occasionally the reeds would sway and rustle against one another, apparently without cause. Seen from down below, against the clear part of the sky, their waving tufts looked like the feathery branches of trees. Close in front, at his very feet, was the bank, and at its base the rushing torrent. A little farther on was the moving mass of glassy brown water, which eddied rhythmically along the bank and round the shallows. Farther still, water, banks and cloud all merged together in impenetrable gloom. Along the surface of the water floated black shadows, in which the experienced eyes of the Cossack detected trees carried down by the current. Only very rarely sheet lightning, mirrored in the water as in a black glass, disclosed the sloping bank opposite. The rhythmic sounds of night—the rustling of the reeds, the snoring of the Cossacks, the hum of mosquitoes, and the rushing water, were every now and then broken by a shot fired in the distance, or by the gurgling of water when a piece of bank slipped down, the splash of a big fish, or the crashing of an animal breaking through the thick undergrowth in the wood. Once an owl flew past along the Terek, flapping one wing against the other rhythmically at every second beat. Just above the Cossack's head it turned toward the wood, and then, striking its wings, no longer after every other flap, but at every flap, it flew to an old plane tree, where it rustled about for a long time before settling down among the branches. At every one of these unexpected sounds the watching Cossack listened intently, straining his hearing, and his eyes screwed up while he deliberately felt for his musket.

The greater part of the night was past. The black cloud that had moved westward revealed, from under its torn edge, the clear starry sky, and the golden upturned crescent of the moon shone above the mountains with a reddish light. The cold began to be penetrating. Nazarka awoke, spoke a little, and fell asleep again. Lukashka, feeling bored, got up, drew the knife from his dagger handle, and began to fashion his stick into a ramrod. His head was full of the Chechens who lived over there in the mountains, and of how their brave lads came across and were not afraid of the Cossacks, and might even now be crossing the river at some other spot. He thrust himself out of his hiding place and looked along the river, but could see nothing. And as he continued looking out at intervals upon the river and at the opposite bank, now faintly distinguishable from the water in the faint moonlight, he no longer thought about the Chechens, but only of when it would be time to wake his comrades, and of going home to the village. In the village, he imagined Dunka, his "little soul," as the Cossacks call a man's mistress, and thought of her with vexation. Silvery mists, a sign of coming morning, glittered white above the water, and not far from him young eagles were whistling and flapping their wings. At last the crowing of a cock reached him from the distant village, followed by the long-sustained note of another, which was again answered by yet other voices.

"Time to wake them," thought Lukashka, who had finished his ramrod and felt his eyes growing heavy. Turning to his comrades he managed to make out which pair of legs belonged to whom, when it suddenly seemed to him that he heard something splash on the other side of the Terek. He turned again toward the horizon beyond the hills, where day was breaking under the upturned crescent, glanced at the outline of the opposite bank, at the Terek, and at the now distinctly visible driftwood upon it. For one instant it seemed to him that he was moving and that the Terek with the drifting wood remained stationary. Again he peered out. One large black log with a branch particularly attracted his attention. The tree was floating in a strange way right down the middle of the stream, neither rocking nor whirling. It even appeared not to be floating altogether with the current, but to be crossing it in the direction of the shallows. Lukashka, stretching out his neck, watched it intently. The tree floated to the shallows, stopped, and shifted in a peculiar

manner. Lukashka thought he saw an arm stretched out from beneath the tree.

"Supposing I killed an abrek all by myself!" he thought, and seized his gun with a swift, unhurried movement, putting up his gun rest, placing the gun upon it, and holding it noiselessly in position. Cocking the trigger, with bated breath he took aim, still peering out intently.

"I won't wake them," he thought. But his heart began beating so fast that he remained motionless, listening. Suddenly the trunk gave a plunge and began again to float across the stream toward our bank.

"Suppose I miss? . . ." thought he, and now by the faint light of the moon he caught a glimpse of a Tartar's head in front of the floating wood. He aimed straight at the head, which appeared to be quite near—just at the end of his musket's barrel. He glanced across. "Right enough, it is an abrek!" he thought joyfully, and suddenly, rising to his knees, he again took aim. Having found the mark, just visible in a line with the end of his gun, he said: "In the name of the Father and of the Son," in the Cossack way learned in his childhood, and pulled the trigger. A flash of lightning lit up for an instant the reeds and the water; and the sharp, abrupt report of the shot was carried across the river, changing into a prolonged roll somewhere in the far distance. The piece of driftwood now floated not across, but with, the current, rocking and whirling.

"Hold, I say!" exclaimed Ergushov, seizing his musket, and raising himself behind the log near which he was lying. "Shut up, you devil," whispered Lukashka, grinding his teeth. "Abreks!"

"Whom have you shot?" asked Nazarka. "Who was it, Lukashka?"

Lukashka did not answer. He was reloading his gun and watching the floating wood. A little way off, it stopped on a sand bank, and from behind it something large, that rocked in the water, came into view.

"What did you shoot? Why don't you speak?" insisted the Cossacks.

"Abreks, I tell you!" said Lukashka.

"Don't humbug! Did the gun go off? . . ."

"I've killed an abrek, that's what I fired at," muttered Lukaska in a voice choked by emotion, as he jumped to his feet. "A man was swimming . . ." he said, pointing to the sand bank. "I killed him. Just look there."

"Have done with your humbugging!" said Ergushov again, rubbing his eyes.

"Have done with what? Look there," said Lukashka, seizing him by the shoulders, and pulling him with such force that Ergushov groaned.

He looked in the direction in which Lukashka pointed, and discerning a body, immediately changed his tone.

"Oh my! But I say, more will come! I tell you the truth," said he softly, and began examining his musket. "That was a scout swimming across: either the others are here already, or are not far off on the other side—I tell you true!"

Lukashka was unfastening his belt and taking off his Circassian coat.

"What are you up to, you idiot?" exclaimed Ergushov. "Only show yourself, and you're lost, all for nothing, I tell you true! If you've killed him, he won't escape. Let me have a little powder for my musket pan—you have

some? Nazar, you go back to the cordon, and look alive; but don't go along the bank, or you'll be killed,—I tell you true."

"Catch me going alone! Go yourself!" said Nazarka angrily.

Having taken off his coat, Lukashka went down to the bank.

"Don't go in, I tell you!" said Ergushov, putting some powder on the pan. "Look, he is not moving. I can see. It's nearly morning; wait till they come from the cordon. You go, Nazarka. You're afraid! Don't be afraid, I tell you."

"Luke, I say, Lukashka! Tell us how you did it!" said Nazarka.

Lukashka changed his mind about going into the water just then. "Go quick to the cordon, and I will watch. Tell the Cossacks to send out the patrol. If the abreks are on this side, they must be caught," said he.

"That's what I say. They'll get off," said Ergushov, rising. "True, they must be caught!"

Ergushov and Nazarka rose, and, crossing themselves, started off for the cordon—not along the river bank, but breaking their way through the brambles to reach a path in the wood.

"Now mind, Lukashka—they may cut you down here, so you'd best keep a sharp lookout, I tell you!"

"Go along; I know," muttered Lukashka; and having examined his gun again, he sat down behind the log.

Lukashka remained alone, and sat gazing at the shallows and listening for the Cossacks; but it was some distance to the cordon, and he was tormented by impatience. He kept thinking that the other abreks who were with the one he had killed would escape. He was vexed with the abreks who were going to escape, just as he had been with the boar that had escaped the evening before. He glanced round and at the opposite bank, expecting every moment to see a man; and having arranged his gun rest, he was ready to fire. The idea that he might himself be killed never entered his head.

CHAPTER IX

THE BODY

It was growing light. The Chechen's body, which was gently rocking in the shallow water, was now clearly visible. Suddenly the reeds rustled not far from Luke, and he heard steps and saw the feathery tops of the reeds moving. He set his gun at full cock and muttered: "In the name of the Father and of the Son," but when the cock clicked. the sound of steps ceased.

"Hullo, Cossacks! Don't kill your Daddy!" calmly said a deep bass voice; and, moving the reeds apart, Daddy Eroshka came up close to Luke.

"I very nearly killed you, by God I did!" said Lukashka.

"What have you shot?" asked the old man. His sonorous voice sounded through the wood and downward along the river, suddenly dispelling the mysterious quiet of night around the Cossack. It was as if everything had suddenly become lighter and more distinct.

"There now, Uncle, you have not seen anything, but I've killed a beast," said Lukashka, uncocking his gun, and getting up with unnatural calmness.

The old man was staring very intently at the white back, now clearly visible, against which rippled the Terek.

"He was swimming with a log on his back. I spied him out! . . . Look there. There! He's got blue trousers, and a gun, I think. . . . Do you see?" inquired Luke.

"How can one help seeing?" said the old man angrily, and a serious and stern expression appeared on his face. "You've killed a brave," he said, apparently with regret.

"Well, I sat here, and suddenly I saw something dark on the other side. I spied him when he was still over there. It was as if a man had come there and fallen in. Strange! And a piece of driftwood, a good-sized piece, comes floating, not with the stream, but across it; and what do I see but a head appearing from under it! Strange! I stretched out of the reeds, but could see nothing; then I rose, and he must have heard, the beast, and crept out into the shallow and looked about. 'No, you don't!' I said, as soon as he landed and looked around, 'you'll not get away!' Oh, there was something choking me! I got my gun ready, but did not stir, and looked out. He waited a little and then swam out again; and when he came into the moonlight I could see his whole back. 'In the name of the Father and of the Son and of the Holy Ghost' . . . and through the smoke I see him struggling. He moaned, or so it seemed to me. 'Ah,' I thought, 'the Lord be thanked, I've killed him!' And when he drifted on to the sand bank I could see him distinctly: he tried to get up, but couldn't. He struggled a bit, and then lay down. Everything could be seen. Look, he does not move—he must be dead! The Cossacks have gone back to the cordon in case there should be any more of them."

"And so you had him!" said the old man. "He is far away now, my lad! . . ." And again he shook his head sadly.

Just then the sound reached them of breaking bushes, and the loud voices of Cossacks approaching along the bank on horseback and on foot. "Are you bringing the skiff?" shouted Lukashka.

"You're a trump, Luke! Lug it to the bank!" shouted one of the Cossacks.

Without waiting for the skiff, Lukashka began to undress, keeping an eye all the while on his prey.

"Wait a bit, Nazarka is bringing the skiff," shouted the Corporal.

"You fool! Maybe he is alive and only pretending! Take your dagger with you!" shouted another Cossack.

"Get along," cried Luke, pulling off his trousers. He quickly undressed and, crossing himself, jumped, plunging with a splash into the river. Then with long strokes of his white arms, lifting his back high out of the water and breathing deeply, he swam across the current of the Terek toward the shallows. A crowd of Cossacks stood on the bank, talking loudly. Three horsemen rode off to patrol. The skiff appeared round a bend. Lukashka stood up on the sand bank, leaned over the body, and gave it a couple of shakes. "Quite dead!" he shouted in a shrill voice.

The Chechen had been shot in the head. He had on a pair of blue trousers, a shirt, and a Circassian coat, and a gun and dagger were tied to his back. Above all these a large branch was tied, and that it was which at first had misled Lukashka.

"What a carp you've landed!" cried one of the Cossacks who had assembled in a circle, as the body, lifted out of the skiff, was laid on the bank, pressing down the grass.

"How yellow he is!" said another.

"Where have our fellows gone to search? I expect the rest of them are on the other bank. If this one had not been a scout he would not have swum that way. Why else should he swim alone?" said a third.

"Must have been a smart one, to offer himself before the others; a regular brave!" said Lukashka mockingly, as he stood shivering at the bottom of the bank, wringing out his wet clothes.

"His beard is dyed, and cropped."

"And he has tied a bag with a coat in it to his back."

"That would make it easier for him to swim," said some one.

"I say, Lukashka," said the Corporal, who was holding the dagger and gun taken from the dead man. "Keep that dagger for yourself and the coat too; but I'll give you three rubles for the gun. You see it has a hole in it," said he, blowing into the muzzle. "I want it just for a souvenir."

Lukashka did not answer. Evidently this sort of begging vexed him, but he knew it could not be avoided.

"See, what a devil!" said he, frowning and throwing down the Chechen's coat. "If at least it were a good coat, but it's a mere rag."

"It'll do to fetch firewood in," said one of the Cossacks.

"Mosev, I'll go home," said Lukashka, evidently forgetting his vexation and wishing to get some advantage out of having to give a present to his superior.

"All right, you may go!"

"Take the body beyond the cordon, lads," said the Corporal, still examining the gun, "and put a shelter over him from the sun. Perhaps they'll send from the mountains to ransom it."

"It isn't hot yet," said some one.

"And supposing a jackal tears him? Would that be well?" remarked another Cossack.

"We'll set a watch; for should they come to ransom him, it won't do for him to have been torn."

"Well, Lukashka, whatever you do, you must stand a pail of vodka for the lads," said the Corporal gayly.

"Of course! That's the custom," chimed in the Cossacks. "See what luck God has sent you! Without ever having seen anything of the kind before, you've killed a brave!"

"Buy the dagger and coat, and don't be stingy, and I'll let you have the trousers too," said Lukashka. "They're too tight for me; he was a thin devil."

One Cossack bought the coat for a ruble, and another gave the price of two pails of vodka, for the dagger.

"Drink, lads! I'll stand you a pail!" said Luke. "I'll bring it myself from the village."

"And cut up the trousers into kerchiefs for the girls!" said Nazarka.

The Cossacks burst out laughing.

"Have done laughing!" said the Corporal. "And take the body away. Why have you put the nasty thing by the hut?"

"What are you standing there for? Haul him along, lads!" shouted Lukashka in a commanding voice to the Cossacks, who reluctantly took hold of the body, obeying him as though he were their chief. After dragging the body along for a few steps, the Cossacks let fall the legs, which dropped with a lifeless jerk; and stepping apart they then stood silent for a few moments. Nazarka came up and straightened the head, which was turned to one side, so that the round wound above the temple and the whole of the dead man's face were visible.

"See what a mark he has made, right in the brain," he said. "He'll not get lost. His owners will always know him!"

No one answered, and again the Angel of Silence flew over the Cossacks.

The sun had risen high and its diverging beams were lighting up the dewy grass. Near by, the Terek murmured in the awakened wood, and, greeting the morning, the pheasants called to one another. The Cossacks stood still and silent around the dead man, gazing at him. The brown body, with nothing on but the wet blue trousers held by a girdle over the sunken stomach, was well-shaped and handsome. The muscular arms lay stretched straight out by his sides; the blue, freshly shaven, round head with the clotted wound on one side of it, was thrown back. The smooth tanned forehead contrasted sharply with the shaven part of the head. The open glassy eyes with lowered pupils, stared upwards, seeming to gaze past everything. Under the red, trimmed mustache, the fine lips, drawn at the corners, seemed stiffened into a smile of good-natured subtle raillery. The fingers of the small hands, covered with red hairs, were bent inward, and the nails were dyed red.

Lukashka had not yet dressed. He was wet. His neck was redder and his eyes brighter than usual; his broad jaws twitched, and from his healthy body a hardly perceptible steam rose in the fresh morning air.

"He too was a man!" he muttered, evidently admiring the corpse.

"Yes, if you had fallen into his hands, you would have had short shrift," said one of the Cossacks.

The Angel of Silence had taken wing. The Cossacks began bustling about and talking. Two of them went to cut down bushes for a shelter, others strolled toward the cordon. Luke and Nazarka ran to get ready to go to the village.

Half an hour later Lukashka and Nazarka were on their way homewards, talking incessantly, and almost running through the dense woods which separated the Terek from the village.

"Mind, don't tell her I sent you, but just go and find out if her husband is at home," Luke was saying in his shrill voice.

"And I'll go round to Yamka too," said the devoted Nazarka. "We'll have a spree, shall we?"

"When should we have one, if not to-day?" replied Luke.

When they reached the village the two Cossacks drank, and lay down to sleep till evening.

CHAPTER X

HER UNTAMED LOOK

On the third day after the events above described, two companies of a Caucasian infantry regiment arrived at the Cossack village of Novomlinsk. The horses had been unharnessed, and the companies' wagons were standing in the square. The cooks had dug a pit and with logs gathered from various yards (where they had not been sufficiently securely stored) were now cooking the food; the pay sergeants were settling accounts with the soldiers. The Service Corps men were driving piles in the ground to which to tie the horses; and the quartermasters were going about the streets just as if they were at home, showing officers and men to their quarters. Here were green ammunition boxes in a line, artillery wagons, horses, and caldrons in which buckwheat porridge was being cooked.

Here were the Captain and the Lieutenant and the Sergeant Major, Onisim Mikhaylovich; and all this was in the Cossack village where it was reported that the companies were ordered to take up their quarters: therefore they were at home here.

But why they were stationed there; who the Cossacks were; and whether they wanted the troops to be there; and whether they were Old Believers or not —was all quite immaterial. Having received their pay and been dismissed tired out and covered with dust, the soldiers noisily and in disorder, like a swarm of bees about to settle, spread over the squares and streets.

Quite regardless of the Cossacks' ill will, chattering merrily, and with their muskets clinking, by twos and threes they entered the huts and hung up their accouterments, unpacked their bags, and joked with the women. At their favorite spot, round the porridge caldrons, a large group of soldiers assembled, and with little pipes between their teeth they gazed, now at the smoke which rose into the hot sky, becoming visible when it thickened into white clouds as it rose, and now at the camp fires which were quivering in the pure air, like molten glass; and bantered and made fun of the Cossack men and women, because they do not live at all like Russians. In all the yards one could see soldiers and hear their laughter, and the exasperated and shrill cries of Cossack women defending their houses and refusing to give the soldiers water or cooking utensils. Little boys and girls clinging to their mothers and to each other, followed all the movements of the troopers (never before seen by them) with frightened curiosity or ran after them at a respectful distance.

The old Cossacks came out silently and dismally and sat on the earthen embankments of their huts and watched the soldiers' activity with an air of leaving it all to the will of God, without understanding what would come of it.

Olenin, who had joined the Caucasian Army as a cadet three months before, was quartered in one of the best houses in the village, the house of the Teacher, Elias Vasilich—that is to say in Granny Ulitka's.

"Goodness knows what it will be like, Dmitry Andreich," said the panting Vanyusha to Olenin, who, dressed in a Circassian coat and mounted on a Kabarda horse which he had bought in Groznoe, was, after a five hours' march, gayly entering the yard of the quarters assigned to him.

"Why, what's the matter?" he asked, caressing his horse, and looking merrily at the perspiring, disheveled, and worried Vanyusha, who had arrived with the baggage wagons and was unpacking.

Olenin looked quite a different man. In place of his clean-shaven lips and chin, he had a youthful mustache and a small beard. In place of his sallow complexion, the result of nights turned into day, his cheeks, his forehead, and the skin behind his ears were now red with healthy sunburn. In place of a clean new black suit, he wore a dirty white Circassian coat with a deeply pleated skirt, and he bore arms. Instead of a freshly starched collar, his neck was tightly clasped by the red band of his silk beshmet. He wore the Circassian dress, but did not wear it well, and any one would have known him for a Russian and not a Tartar brave. It was the thing—but not the real thing. But for all that, his whole person breathed health, joy, and satisfaction.

"Yes, it seems funny to you," said Vanyusha; "but just try to talk to these people yourself: they set themselves against one and there's an end of it. You can't get as much as a word out of them." Vanyusha angrily threw down a pail on the threshold. "Somehow they don't seem like Russians."

"You should speak to the Chief of the Village!"

"But I don't know where he lives," said Vanyusha, in an offended tone.

"Who has upset you so much?" asked Olenin, looking round.

"The devil only knows. Faugh! There is no real master here. They say he has gone to some kind of kriga, and the old woman is a real devil. God preserve us!" answered Vanyusha putting his hands to his head. "How we shall live here, I don't know. They are worse than Tartars, I do declare— though they consider themselves Christians! A Tartar is bad enough, but all the same he is more noble. Gone to the kriga indeed! What this kriga they have invented is I don't know!" concluded Vanyusha, and turned aside.

"It's not as it is in the serfs' quarters at home, eh?" chaffed Olenin without dismounting.

"Please, sir, may I have your horse?" said Vanyusha, evidently perplexed by this new order of things, but resigning himself to his fate.

"So a Tartar is more noble, eh, Vanyusha?" repeated Olenin, dismounting and slapping the saddle.

"Yes, you're laughing! You think it funny," muttered Vanyusha angrily.

"Come, don't be angry, Vanyusha," replied Olenin, still smiling. "Wait a minute, I'll go and speak to the people of the house; you'll see I shall arrange everything. You don't know what a jolly life we shall have here. Only don't get upset."

Vanyusha did not answer. Screwing up his eyes, he looked contemptuously after his master, and shook his head. Vanyusha regarded Olenin as only his master, and Olenin regarded Vanyusha as only his servant; and they would both have been much surprised if anyone had told them that they were friends, as they really were without knowing it themselves. Vanyusha had been taken into his proprietor's house when he was only eleven, and when Olenin was the same age. When Olenin was fifteen he gave Vanyusha lessons for a time, and taught him to read French, of which the latter was inordinately proud; and when in specially good spirits he still let off French words, always laughing stupidly when he did so.

Olenin ran up the steps of the porch; and pushed open the door of the hut. Maryanka, wearing nothing but a pink smock, as all Cossack women do in the house, jumped, frightened, away from the door and pressing herself against the wall covered the lower part of her face with the broad sleeve of her Tartar smock. Having opened the door wider, Olenin, in the semidarkness of the passage, saw the whole tall, shapely figure of the young Cossack girl. With the quick eager curiosity of youth, he involuntarily noticed the firm maidenly form revealed by the fine print smock, and the beautiful black eyes fixed on him with child-like terror and wild curiosity.

"This is *she*," thought Olenin. "But there will be many others like her," came at once into his head, and he opened the inner door.

Old Granny Ulitka, also dressed only in a smock, was stooping, with her back turned to him, sweeping the floor.

"Good day to you, Mother! I've come about my lodgings," he began.

The Cossack woman, without unbending, turned her severe but still handsome face toward him.

"What have you come here for? Want to mock at us, eh? I'll teach you to mock; may the black plague seize you!" she shouted, looking askance from under her frowning brow at the newcomer.

Olenin had at first imagined that the wayworn, gallant Caucasian Army (of which he was a member) would be everywhere received joyfully, and especially by the Cossacks, our comrades in the war; and he therefore felt perplexed by this reception. Without losing presence of mind, however, he tried to explain that he meant to pay for his lodgings, but the old woman would not give him a hearing.

"What have you come for? Who wants a pest like you, with your scraped face? You just wait a bit; when the master returns he'll show you your place.

I don't want your dirty money! A likely thing—just as if we had never seen any! You'll stink the house out with your beastly tobacco, and want to put it right with money! Think we've never seen a pest! May you be shot in your bowels and your heart!" shrieked the old woman in a piercing voice, interrupting Olenin.

"It seems Vanyusha was right!" thought Olenin. "'A Tartar would be nobler,'" and, followed by Granny Ulitka's abuse, he went out of the hut. As he was leaving, Maryanka, still wearing only her pink smock, but with her face now hidden right up to her eyes in a white kerchief, suddenly slipped out from the passage past him. Pattering rapidly down the steps with her bare feet, she ran down from the porch, stopped, and, looking round hastily with laughing eyes at the young man, vanished round the corner of the hut.

Her firm youthful step, the untamed look of the eyes glistening from under the white kerchief, and the firm stately build of the young beauty, struck Olenin even more powerfully than before.

"Yes, it must be *she*," he thought, and troubling his head still less about the lodgings, he kept looking round at Maryanka as he approached Vanyusha.

"There, you see, the girl too is quite a savage, just like a wild filly!" said Vanyusha, who, though still busy with the luggage wagon, had now cheered up a bit. *"La fame!"* he added in a loud triumphant voice, and burst out laughing.

CHAPTER XI

LODGINGS

Toward evening the master of the house returned from his fishing, and having learnt that the cadet would pay for the lodging, pacified the old woman and satisfied Vanyusha's demands.

Everything was settled in the new quarters. Their hosts moved into the winter hut, and let their summer hut to the cadet for three rubles a month. Olenin had something to eat and went to sleep. Toward evening he woke up, washed, and made himself tidy; dined and, having lit a cigarette, sat down by the window that looked on to the street. It was cooler. The slanting shadow of the hut with its ornamental gables fell across the dusty road, and even bent upwards at the base of the wall of the house opposite. The steep reed-thatched roof of that house shone in the rays of the setting sun. The air grew fresher. Everything was peaceful in the village. The soldiers had settled down and become quiet. The herds had not yet been driven home, and the people had not returned from their work.

Olenin's lodging was situated almost at the end of the village. At rare intervals, from somewhere far beyond the Terek in those parts whence Olenin had just come (the Chechen or the Kumytsk plain), came muffled sounds of firing. Olenin was feeling very well contented after three months of bivouac life. His newly washed face was fresh and his powerful body clean (an unaccustomed sensation after the campaign) and in all his rested limbs he was conscious of a feeling of tranquillity and strength. His mind, too, felt fresh and clear. He thought of the campaign and of past dangers. He remembered that he had faced them no worse than other men, and that he was accepted as a comrade among the valiant Caucasians. His Moscow recollections were left behind,

Heaven knows how far! The old life was wiped out, and a quite new life had begun in which there were, as yet, no mistakes. Here, as a new man among new men, he could gain a new and good reputation. He was conscious of a youthful and unreasoning joy of life. Looking now out of the window at the boys spinning their tops in the shadow of the house, now round his new little lodging, he thought how pleasantly he would settle down to this new Cossack village life. Now and then he glanced at the mountains and the blue sky, and an appreciation of the solemn grandeur of nature mingled with his reminiscences and dreams. His new life had begun, not as he imagined it would when he left Moscow, but unexpectedly well. "The mountains, the mountains, the mountains!" they permeated all his thoughts and feelings.

"He's drunk his bitch, and licked the jug! . . . Daddy Eroshka has drunk his bitch!" suddenly the little Cossacks, who had been spinning their tops under the window, shouted, looking toward the side street.

"He's drunk his bitch, and his dagger!" shouted the boys, crowding together and stepping backwards.

Those shouts were addressed to Daddy Eroshka who, with his gun on his shoulder and some pheasants hanging at his girdle, was returning from his shooting expedition.

"I have done wrong, lads, I have!" he said, vigorously swinging his arms and looking up at the windows on both sides of the street. "I have drunk the bitch; it was wrong," he repeated, evidently vexed, but pretending not to care.

Olenin was surprised by the boys' behavior toward the old hunter, but was still more struck by the expressive, intelligent face and the powerful build of the man whom they called Daddy Eroshka.

"Here, Daddy, here, Cossack!" he called. "Come here!"

The old man looked into the window and stopped.

"Good evening, good man," he said, lifting his little cap off his cropped head.

"Good evening, good man," replied Olenin. "What is it the youngsters are shouting at you?"

Daddy Eroshka came up to the windows. "Why, they're teasing the old man. No matter, I like it. Let them joke about their old daddy," he said with those firm musical intonations with which old and venerable people speak. "Are you an army commander?" he added.

"No, I am a cadet. But where did you kill those pheasants?" asked Olenin.

"I dispatched these three hens in the forest," answered the old man, turning his broad back toward the window, to show the hen pheasants, which were hanging with their heads tucked into his belt and staining his coat with blood.

"Haven't you seen any?" he asked. "If you like, take a brace! Here you are," and he handed two of the pheasants in at the window. "Are you a sportsman yourself?" he asked.

"I am. During the campaign I killed four, myself."

"Four? What a lot!" said the old man sarcastically. "And are you a drinker? Do you drink chikhir?"

"Why not? I like a drink."

"Ah, I see you are a trump! We shall be kunaks, you and I," said Daddy Eroshka.

"Step in," said Olenin. "We'll have a drop of chikhir."

"I might as well," said the old man, "but take the pheasants." The old man's face showed that he liked the cadet. He had seen at once that he could get free drinks from him, and that therefore it would be all right to give him a brace of pheasants.

Soon Daddy Eroshka's figure appeared in the doorway of the hut; and it was only then that Olenin became fully conscious of the enormous size and sturdy build of this man, whose red-brown face, with its perfectly white broad beard, was all furrowed by deep lines produced by age and toil. For an old man, the muscles of his legs, arms, and shoulders were quite exceptionally large and prominent. There were deep scars on his head, under the short-cropped hair. His thick sinewy neck was covered with deep intersecting folds like a bull's. His horny hands were bruised and scratched. He stepped lightly and easily over the threshold, unslung his gun and placed it in a corner, and casting a rapid glance round the room noted the value of the goods and chattels deposited in the hut, and with outturned toes stepped softly, in his sandals of rawhide, into the middle of the room. He brought with him a penetrating but not unpleasant smell of chikhir wine, vodka, gunpowder and congealed blood.

Daddy Eroshka bowed down before the icons, smoothed his beard, and approaching Olenin, held out his thick brown hand. "Koshkildy," said he. "That is Tartar for 'Good day'—'Peace be unto you,' it means in their tongue."

"Koshkildy, I know," answered Olenin, shaking hands.

"Eh, but you don't, you won't know the right order! Fool!" said Daddy Eroshka, shaking his head reproachfully. "If anyone says Koshkildy to you, you must say 'Allah rasi bo sun,' that is, 'God save you.' That's the way, my dear fellow, and not 'Koshkildy.' But I'll teach you all about it. We had a fellow, Elias Mosevich here, one of your Russians, he and I were kunaks. He was a trump, a drunkard, a thief, a sportsman,—and what a sportsman! I taught him everything."

"And what will you teach me?" asked Olenin, who was becoming more and more interested in the old man.

"I'll take you hunting, and teach you to fish. I'll show you the Chechens, and find a girl for you, if you like—even that! That's the sort I am! I'm a wag!"—and the old man laughed. "I'll sit down. I'm tired. Karga?" he added, inquiringly.

"And what does 'Karga' mean?" asked Olenin.

"Why, that means 'All right' in Georgian. But I say it just so. It's a way I have, it's my favorite word. Karga, Karga. I say it just so; in fun I mean. Well, lad, won't you order the chikhir? You've got an orderly, haven't you?"

"Yes."

"Hey, Ivan!" shouted the old man. "All your soldiers are Ivans. Is yours Ivan?"

"True enough, his name is Ivan—Vanyusha. Here, Vanyusha! Please get some chikhir from our landlady, and bring it here."

"Ivan or Vanyusha, that's all one. Why are all your soldiers Ivans? Ivan, old fellow," said the old man, "you tell them to give you some from the barrel that they have begun. They have the best chikhir in the village. But don't give more than thirty kopeks for the pint, mind, because that witch would be only too glad. . . . Our people are anathema people; stupid people," Daddy Eroshka continued in a confidential tone after Vanyusha had gone out. "They do not look upon you as on men; you are worse than a Tartar in their eyes. 'Worldly Russians,' they say. But as for me, though you are a soldier, you are still a man, and have a soul in you. Isn't that right? Elias Mosevich was a soldier, and yet what a treasure of a man he was! Isn't that so, my dear fellow? That's why our people don't like me; but I don't care! I'm a merry fellow, and I like everybody. I'm Eroshka; yes, my dear fellow."

And the old Cossack patted the young man affectionately on the shoulder.

CHAPTER XII

WHERE'S THE SIN?

VANYUSHA, who meanwhile had finished his housekeeping arrangements and had even got shaved by the company's barber and had pulled his trousers out of his high boots as a sign that the company was stationed in comfortable quarters, was in excellent spirits. He looked attentively, but not benevolently, at Eroshka, as at a wild beast he had never seen before, shook his head at the floor which the old man had dirtied, and, having taken two bottles from under a bench, went to the landlady.

"Good evening, kind people," he said, having made up his mind to be very gentle. "My master has sent me to get some chikhir; will you draw some for me, good folk?"

The old woman gave no answer. The girl, who was arranging the kerchief on her head before a little Tartar mirror, looked round at Vanyusha in silence.

"I'll pay money for it, honored people," said Vanyusha, jingling the coppers in his pocket. "Be kind to us and we too will be kind to you," he added.

"How much?" asked the old woman abruptly.

"A pint."

"Go, my own, draw some for them," said Granny Ulitka to her daughter. "Take it from the cask that's begun, my precious."

The girl took the keys and a decanter, and went out of the hut with Vanyusha.

"Tell me, who is that young woman?" asked Olenin, pointing to Maryanka who was passing the window. The old man winked, and nudged the young man with his elbow.

"Wait a bit," said he, and reached out of the window. "Khm," he coughed, and bellowed, "Maryanka dear. Hallo, Maryanka, my girlie, won't you love me, darling? I'm a wag," he added in a whisper to Olenin. The girl, not turning her head and swinging her arms regularly and vigorously, passed the window with the peculiarly elegant and bold gait of a Cossack woman, and only turned her dark shaded eyes slowly toward the old man.

"Love me, and you'll be happy," shouted Eroshka, and, winking, he looked questioningly at the cadet. "I'm a fine fellow, I'm a wag!" he added. "She's a regular queen, that girl. Eh?"

"She is lovely," said Olenin. "Call her here!"

"No, no," said the old man. "For

that one, a match is being arranged with Lukashka, Luke, a fine Cossack, a brave, who killed an abrek the other day. I'll find you a better one. I'l find you one that will go about clothed in silk and silver. Once I've said it, I'll do it. I'll get you a regular beauty!"

"You, an old man—and say such things," replied Olenin. "Why, it's a sin!"

"A sin? Where's the sin?" said the old man emphatically. "A sin to look at a nice girl? A sin to have some fun with her? Or is it a sin to love her? Is that so in your parts? . . . No, my dear fellow, it's not a sin, it's salvation! God made you, and God made the girl, too. He made it all; so it is no sin to look at a nice girl. That's what she was made for; to be loved and to give joy. That's how I judge it, my good fellow."

Having crossed the yard and entered a cool dark storeroom filled with barrels, Maryanka went up to one of them and repeating the usual prayer, plunged a dipper into it. Vanyusha, standing in the doorway, smiled as he looked at her. He thought it awfully funny that she only had a smock on, close-fitting behind and tucked up in front, and still funnier that she wore a necklace of silver coins. He thought this quite un-Russian, and that they would all laugh in the serfs' quarters at home, if they saw a girl like that. *La fille comme c'est très bien,* for a change," he thought. "I'll tell that to my master."

"What are you standing in the light for, you devil!" the girl suddenly shouted. "Why don't you hand me the decanter!"

Having filled the decanter with cool red wine, Maryanka handed it to Vanyusha.

"Give the money to Mammy," she said, pushing away the hand in which he held the money.

Vanyusha laughed. "Why are you so cross, little dear?" he said good-naturedly, irresolutely shuffling with his feet while the girl was covering the barrel.

She began to laugh.

"And you! Are you kind?"

"We, my master and I, are very kind," Vanyusha answered decidedly. "We are so kind, that wherever we have stayed our hosts were always very grateful. It's because he's a nobleman."

The girl stood listening.

"And is your master married?" she asked.

"No. The master is young and unmarried, because noble gentlemen can never marry young," said Vanyusha didactically.

"A likely thing! See what a fed-up buffalo he is, and too young to marry! Is he the chief of you all?" she asked.

"My master is a cadet; that means he's not yet an officer, but he's more important than a general—he's an important man! Because not only our colonel, but the Tsar himself, knows him," proudly explained Vanyusha. "We are not like those other beggars of the line regiment, and our papa himself was a Senator. He had more than a thousand serfs, all his own, and they send us a thousand rubles at a time. That's why everyone likes us. Another may be a captain, but have no money. What's the use of that?"

"Go, I'll lock up," said the girl, interrupting him.

Vanyusha brought Olenin the wine,

and announced that *"La fille c'est très jolie,"* and, laughing stupidly, at once went out.

CHAPTER XIII

NIGHT LOVE

MEANWHILE the tattoo had sounded in the village square. The people had returned from their work. The herd lowed, as in clouds of golden dust it crowded at the village gate. The girls and women hurried through the streets and yards, turning in their cattle. The sun had quite hidden itself behind the distant snowy peaks. One pale bluish shadow spread over land and sky. Above the darkened gardens, stars just discernible were kindling, and the sounds were gradually hushed in the village. The cattle having been attended to and left for the night, the women came out and gathered at the corners of the streets and, cracking sunflower seeds with their teeth, settled down on the earthen embankments of the houses. Later on, Maryanka, having finished milking a buffalo and the two cows, also joined one of these groups. The group consisted of several women and girls and one old Cossack man. They were talking about the abrek who had been killed. The Cossack was narrating and the women questioning him.

"I expect he'll get a handsome reward," said one of the women.

"Of course. It's said that they'll send him a cross."

"Mosev did try to wrong him. Took the gun away from him; but the authorities at Kizlyar heard of it."

"A mean creature that Mosev is!"

"They say Lukashka has come home," remarked one of the girls.

"He and Nazarka are merrymaking at Yamka's." (Yamka was an unmarried, disreputable Cossack woman who kept an illicit pothouse.) "I heard say they had drunk half a pailful."

"What luck that snatcher has," somebody remarked. "A real snatcher. But there's no denying he's a fine lad, smart enough for anything, a right-minded lad! His father was just such another, Daddy Kiryak was: he takes after his father. When he was killed the whole village howled. Look, there they are," added the speaker, pointing to the Cossacks who were coming down the street toward them. "And Ergushov has also managed to come along with them! The drunkard!"

Lukashka, Nazarka, and Ergushov, having emptied half a pail of vodka, were coming toward the girls. The faces of all three, but especially that of the old Cossack, were redder than usual. Ergushov was reeling, and kept laughing and nudging Nazarka in the ribs.

"Why are you not singing?" he shouted to the girls. "Sing to our merrymaking, I tell you!"

They were welcomed with the words, "Had a good day? Had a good day?"

"Why sing? It's not a holiday," said one of the women. "You're tight, so you go and sing."

Ergushov roared with laughter, and nudged Nazarka. "You'd better sing. And I'll begin too. I'm clever, I tell you."

"Are you asleep, fair ones?" said Nazarka. "We've come from the cordon to drink your health. We've already drunk Lukashka's health."

Lukashka, when he reached the group, slowly raised his cap and stopped in front of the girls. His broad cheek-bones and neck were red. He stood and spoke softly and sedately, but in his tranquillity and sedateness there was more of animation and strength than in all Nazarka's loquacity and bustle. He reminded one of a playful colt, that with a snort and a flourish of its tail suddenly stops short and stands as though nailed to the ground with all four feet. Lukashka stood quietly in front of the girls; his eyes laughed, and he spoke but little as he glanced now at his drunken companions and now at the girls.

When Maryanka joined the group he raised his cap with a firm deliberate movement, moved out of her way, and then stepped in front of her with one foot a little forward and with his thumbs in his belt, fingering his dagger. Maryanka answered his greeting with a leisurely bow of her head, settled down on the earthbank, and took some seeds out of the bosom of her smock. Lukashka, keeping his eyes fixed on Maryanka, slowly cracked seeds and spat out the shells. All were quiet when Maryanka joined the group.

"Have you come for long?" asked a woman, breaking the silence.

"Till to-morrow morning," quietly replied Lukashka.

"Well, God willing, you've got a good chance," said the Cossack; "I'm glad of it, as I've just been saying."

"And I say so too," put in the tipsy Ergushov, laughing. "What a lot of visitors have come," he added, pointing to a soldier who was passing by. "The soldiers' vodka is good—I like it."

"They've sent three of the devils to us," said one of the women. "Grandad went to the village Elders, but they say nothing can be done."

"Ah, ha! Have you met with trouble?" said Ergushov.

"I expect they have smoked you out with their tobacco?" asked another woman. "Smoke as much as you like in the yard, I say, but we won't allow it inside the hut. Not if the Elder himself comes; I won't allow it. Besides, they may rob you. He's not quartered any of them himself, no fear, that devil's son of an Elder."

"You don't like it?" Ergushov began again.

"And I've also heard say that the girls will have to make the soldiers' beds and offer them chikhir and honey," said Nazarka, putting one foot forward and tilting his cap like Lukashka.

Ergushov burst into a roar of laughter, and seizing the girl nearest him, he embraced her. "I tell you true."

"Now then, you black pitch!" squealed the girl, "I'll tell your old woman."

"Tell her," shouted he, "that's quite right what Nazarka says; a circular has been sent round. He can read, you know. Quite true!" And he began embracing the next girl.

"Where are you getting to, you beast?" squealed the rosy, round-faced Ustenka, laughing and lifting her arm to hit him.

The Cossack stepped aside, and nearly fell. "There, they say girls have no strength, and you nearly killed me."

"Get away, you black pitch, what devil has brought you from the cordon?" said Ustenka, and turning away from him she again burst out laughing. "You were asleep and missed the abrek, didn't you? Suppose he had done for you; it would have been all the better"

"You'd have howled, I expect," said Nazarka, laughing.

"Howled! A likely thing."

"Just look, she doesn't care. She'd howl, Nazarka, eh? Would she?" said Ergushov.

Lukashka all this time had stood silently looking at Maryanka. His gaze evidently confused the girl. "Well, Maryanka! I hear they've quartered one of the chiefs on you?" he said, drawing nearer.

Maryanka, as was her wont, waited before she replied, and, slowly raising her eyes, looked at the Cossack. Lukashka's eyes were laughing, as if something special, apart from what was said, was taking place between himself and the girl.

"Yes, it's all right for them, as they have two huts," replied an old woman on Maryanka's behalf, "but at Formushkin's now, they also have one of the chiefs quartered on them, and they say one whole corner is packed full with his things, and the family have nowhere to go. Was such a thing ever heard of, as that they should turn a whole horde loose in the village?" she said. "And what the plague are they going to do here?"

"I've heard say they'll build a bridge across the Terek," said one of the girls.

"And I've been told that they will dig a pit to put the girls in, because they don't love the lads," said Nazarka, approaching Ustenka; and he again made a whimsical gesture which set everybody laughing, and Ergushov, passing by Maryanka, who was next in turn, began to embrace an old woman.

"Why don't you hug Maryanka? You should do it to each in turn," said Nazarka.

"No, my old one is sweeter," shouted the Cossack, kissing the struggling old woman.

"You'll throttle me," she screamed, laughing.

The tramp of regular footsteps at the other end of the street interrupted their laughter. Three soldiers in their cloaks, with their muskets on their shoulders, were marching in step to relieve guard by the ammunition wagon.

The Corporal, an old cavalryman, looked angrily at the Cossacks and led his men straight along the road where Lukashka and Nazarka were standing, so that they should have to get out of the way. Nazarka moved, but Lukashka only screwed up his eyes and turned his broad back, without moving from his place. "People are standing here, so you go round," he muttered, only half turning his head and tossing it contemptuously in the direction of the soldiers. The soldiers passed by in silence, keeping step regularly along the dusty road. Maryanka began laughing, and all the other girls chimed in.

"What swells!" said Nazarka. "Just like long-skirted choristers," and he walked a few steps down the road, imitating the soldiers. Again everyone broke into peals of laughter.

Lukashka slowly came up to Maryanka. "And where have you put up the chief?" he asked.

Maryanka thought for a moment. "We've let him have the new hut," she said.

"And is he old or young?" asked Lukashka, sitting down beside her.

"Do you think I've asked?" answered

the girl. "I went to get him some chikhir, and saw him sitting by the window with Daddy Eroshka. Red-headed he seemed. They've brought a whole cartload of things;" and she dropped her eyes.

"Oh, how glad I am that I got leave from the cordon!" said Lukashka, moving closer to the girl, and looking straight in her eyes all the time he was speaking.

"And have you come for long?" asked Maryanka, smiling slightly.

"Till the morning. Give me some seeds," he said, holding out his hand.

Maryanka now smiled outright, and unfastening the neckband of her smock, said, "Don't take them all."

"Really, I felt so dull all the time without you, I swear I did," he said in a restrained, calm whisper, helping himself to some seeds out of the bosom of the girl's smock; and stooping still closer over her, he continued with laughing eyes to talk to her in low tones.

"I won't come. I tell you," Maryanka suddenly said aloud, leaning away from him.

"No really . . . what I wanted to say to you," . . . whispered Lukashka. "By the Heavens! Do come!"

Maryanka shook her head, but did so with a smile.

"Nursey Maryanka! Hallo, Nursey! Mammy is calling! Supper time!" shouted Maryanka's little brother, running toward the group.

"I'm coming," replied the girl. "Go, my dear, go alone—I'll come in a minute."

Lukashka rose and raised his cap. "I expect I had better go home too; that will be best," he said, trying to appear unconcerned but hardly able to repress a smile, and he disappeared behind the corner of the house.

Meanwhile, night had entirely enveloped the village. Bright stars were scattered over the dark sky. The streets became dark and empty. Nazarka remained with the woman on the earth bank, and their laughter was still heard, but Lukashka, having slowly moved away from the girls, crouched down like a cat and then suddenly started running lightly, holding his dagger to steady it: not homeward, however, but toward the Teacher's house. Having passed two streets he turned into a lane, and lifting the skirt of his coat he sat down on the ground in the shadow of a fence. "A regular Teacher's daughter!" he thought about Maryanka. "Won't even have a lark—the devil! But just wait a bit."

The approaching footsteps of a woman attracted his attention. He began listening, and laughed all by himself.

Maryanka with bowed head, striking the pales of the fences with a switch, was walking with rapid regular strides straight toward him. Lukashka rose. Maryanka started and stopped.

"What an accursed devil! You frightened me! So you have not gone home?" she said, and laughed aloud.

Lukashka put one arm around her and with the other hand raised her face. "What I wanted to tell you, by Heaven!" his voice trembled and broke.

"What are you talking of, at night-time!" answered Maryanka. "Mammy is waiting for me, and you'd better go to your sweetheart." And, freeing herself from his arms, she ran away a few steps. When she had reached the wattle fence of her home, she stopped and turned to the Cossack, who was running beside her and still trying to persuade her to stay a while with him.

"Well, what do you want to say, midnight gad-about?" and she again began laughing.

"Don't laugh at me, Maryanka! By the Heaven! Well, what if I have a sweetheart? May the devil take her! Only say the word and now I'll love you—I'll do anything you wish. Here they are!" and he jingled the money in his pocket. "Now we can live splendidly. Others have pleasures, and I? I get no pleasure from you, Maryanka, dear!"

The girl did not answer. She stood before him, breaking her switch into little bits with a rapid movement of her fingers.

Lukashka suddenly clenched his teeth and fists.

"And why keep waiting and waiting! Don't I love you, darling! You can do what you like with me," said he suddenly, frowning angrily and seizing both her hands.

The calm expression of Maryanka's face and voice did not change.

"Don't bluster, Lukashka, but listen to me," she answered, not pulling away her hands, but holding the Cossack at arm's length. "It's true I am a girl, but you listen to me! It does not depend on me, but if you love me I'll tell you this. Let go my hands, I'll tell you without—I'll marry you, but you'll never get any nonsense from me," said Maryanka without turning her face.

"What, you'll marry me? Marriage does not depend on us. Love me yourself, Maryanka, dear," said Lukashka, from sullen and furious becoming again gentle, submissive, and tender, and smiling as he looked closely into her eyes. Maryanka clung to him and kissed him firmly on the lips. "Brother dear!" she whispered, pressing him convulsively to her. Then, suddenly tearing herself away, she ran into the gate of her house without looking round.

In spite of the Cossack's entreaties to wait another minute to hear what he had to say, Maryanka did not stop.

"Go," she cried, "you'll be seen! I do believe that devil, our lodger, is walking about the yard."

"Teacher's daughter," thought Lukashka, "she will marry me. Marriage is all very well, but you just love me!"

He found Nazarka at Yamka's house, and after having a spree with him, went to Dunayka's house, where, in spite of her not being faithful to him, he spent the night.

CHAPTER XIV

THE ANIMAL'S EXAMPLE

IT was quite true that Olenin had been walking about the yard when Maryanka entered the gate, and had heard her say, "That devil, our lodger, is walking about." He had spent that evening with Daddy Eroshka in the porch of his new lodging. He had had a table, a samovar, wine and a lighted candle, brought out, and over a cup of tea he listened to the tales the old man told seated on the threshold at his feet. Though the air was still, the candle dripped and flickered: now lighting up the post of the porch, now the table and crockery, now the cropped white head of the old man. Moths circled round the flame and, shedding the dust of their wings, fluttered on the table and in the glasses, flew into the candle flame, and disappeared in the black space beyond. Olenin and Eroshka had emptied five bottles of chikhir. Eroshka filled the glasses every time, offering one to Olenin, drinking his health, and talking untiringly. He told of the Cossack life in the old days; of his father, "The Blood," who alone had carried on his back a boar's carcass weighing three hundredweight, and drank two pails of chikhir at one sitting. He told of his own days and his chum Girchik, with whom, during the plague, he used to smuggle felt cloaks across the Terek. He told how one morning he had killed two deer, and about his "little soul" who used to run to him at the cordon at night. He told all this so eloquently and picturesquely that Olenin did not notice how time passed. "Ah, yes, my dear fellow, you did not know me in my golden days; then I'd have shown you things. To-day it's 'Eroshka licks the jug,' but then Eroshka was famous in the whole regiment. Whose was the finest horse? Who had a Gurda sword? To whom should one go to get a drink? With whom go on the spree? Who should be sent to the mountains to kill Ahmet Khan? Why, always Eroshka! Whom did the girls love? Always Eroshka had to answer for it. Because I was a real brave; a drinker; a thief (I used to seize herds of horses in the mountains); a singer; I was a master of every art! There are no Cossacks like that nowadays. It's disgusting to look at them. When they're that

high (Eroshka held his hand three feet from the ground) they put on idiotic boots and keep looking at them—that's all the pleasure they know. Or they'll drink themselves foolish, not like men, but all wrong. And who was I? I was Eroshka, the thief; they knew me not only in this village, but up in the mountains. Tartar princes, my kunaks, used to come to see me! I used to be everybody's kunak. If he was a Tartar—with a Tartar; an Armenian—with an Armenian; a soldier—with a soldier; an officer—with an officer! I didn't care, as long as he was a drinker. He says you should cleanse yourself from intercourse with the world: not drink with soldiers, not eat with a Tartar."

"Who says all that?" asked Olenin.

"Why, our teacher! But listen to a Mullah or a Tartar Cadi. He says, 'You unbelieving Giaours, why do you eat pig?' That shows that everyone has his own law. But I think it's all one. God has made everything for the joy of man. There is no sin in any of it.

"Take example from an animal. It lives in the Tartar's reeds, or in ours. Wherever it happens to go, there is its home! Whatever God gives it, that it eats! But our people say we have to lick red-hot plates in hell, for that. And I think it is all a fraud," he added after a pause.

"What is a fraud?" asked Olenin.

"Why, what the preachers say. We had an army captain in Chervlena who was my kunak: a fine fellow, just like me. He was killed in Chechnya. Well, he used to say that the preachers invent all that out of their own heads. 'When you die the grass will grow on your grave, and that's all!'" The old man laughed. "He was a desperate fellow."

"And how old are you?" asked Olenin.

"The Lord only knows! I must be about seventy. When a Tsaritsa reigned in Russia I was no longer little. So you can reckon it out. I must be seventy."

"Yes, you must, but you are still a fine fellow."

"Well, thank Heaven, I am healthy, quite healthy, except that a woman, a witch, has harmed me. . . ."

"How?"

"Oh, just harmed me."

"And so when you die, the grass will grow?" repeated Olenin.

Eroshka evidently did not wish to express his thought clearly. He was silent for a while. "And what did you think? Drink!" he shouted suddenly, smiling and handing Olenin some wine.

CHAPTER XV

FOOLS AND MOTHS

"WELL, what was I saying?" he continued, trying to remember. "Yes, that's the sort of man I am. I am a hunter. There is no hunter to equal me in the regiment. I will find and show you any animal, and any bird, and what, and where. I know it all! I have dogs, and two guns and nets, and a screen and a hawk. I have everything, thank the Lord! If you are not bragging but are a real sportsman, I'll show you everything. Do you know what a man I am! When I have found a track—I know the animal. I know where he will lie down, and where he'll drink or roll about. I

make myself a perch and sit there all night, watching. What's the good of staying at home! One only gets into mischief, gets drunk. And here women come and chatter, and boys shout at me: enough to drive one mad.

"It's a different matter when you go out at nightfall, choose yourself a place, press down the reeds and sit there and sit, waiting, like a jolly fellow. One knows everything that goes on in the woods. One looks up at the sky: the stars move, you look at them and find out from them how the time goes. One looks round—the wood is rustling; one goes on waiting, now, there comes a crackling—a boar comes to rub himself; one listens to hear the young eaglets screech, and then the cocks give voice in the village, or the geese. When you hear the geese, you know it is not yet midnight. And I know all about it! Or when a gun is fired, somewhere far away, thoughts come to one. One thinks, who is that firing? Is it another Cossack like myself, who has been watching for some animal? And has he killed it? Or only wounded it, so that now the poor dear goes through the reeds smearing them with its blood all for nothing? I don't like that! Oh, how I dislike it! Why injure a beast? You fool, you fool! Or one thinks, 'Maybe an abrek has killed some silly little Cossack.' All this passes through one's mind. And once as I sat watching by the river, I saw a cradle floating down. It was sound, except for one corner which was broken off. Thoughts did come that time! I thought, some of your soldiers, the devils, must have got into a Tartar village and seized the Chechen women; and one of the devils has killed the little one: taken it by its legs, and hit its head against a wall. Don't they do such things? Sh! Men have no souls! And thoughts came to me that filled me with pity. I thought: they've thrown away the cradle and driven the wife out, and her brave has taken his gun and come across to our side to rob us. One watches and thinks. And when one hears a litter breaking through the thicket, something begins to knock inside one. Dear one, come this way! 'They'll scent me,' one thinks; and one sits and does not stir, while one's heart goes dun! dun! dun! and simply lifts you. Once this spring a fine litter came near me. I saw something black. 'In the name of the Father and the Son,' and I was just about to fire when she grunts to her pigs: 'Danger, children,' she says, 'there's a man here,' and off they all ran, breaking through the bushes. I felt I should like to get my teeth into her."

"How could a sow tell her brood that a man was there?" asked Olenin.

"What do you think? You think, the beast's a fool? No, he is wiser than a man, though you do call him a pig! He knows everything.

"Take this, for instance. A man will pass along your track, and not notice it; but a pig as soon as it gets on to your track, turns and runs at once: that shows there is wisdom in him, since he scents your smell, and you don't. And there is this to be said too: you wish to kill it, and it wishes to go about the woods alive. You have one law, and it has another. It is a pig, but it is no worse than you— it too is God's creature. Ah, dear! Man is foolish, foolish, foolish!" The old man repeated this several times, and then letting his head drop, he sat thinking.

Olenin also became thoughtful, and descending from the porch, with his hands behind his back begun pacing up and down the yard.

Eroshka, rousing himself, raised his head and began gazing intently at the moths circling round the flickering flame of the candle and burning themselves in it.

"Fool, fool!" he said. "Where are you flying to? Fool, fool!" He rose and with his thick fingers began to drive away the moths.

"You'll burn, little fool! Fly this way, there's plenty of room." He spoke tenderly, trying to catch them with his thick fingers delicately by their wings, and then letting them fly again. "You are killing yourself, and I am sorry for you!"

He sat a long time, chattering, and sipping out of the bottle. Olenin paced up and down the yard. Suddenly he was struck by the sound of whispering outside the gate. Involuntarily holding his breath, he heard a woman's laughter, a man's voice, and the sound of a kiss. Intentionally rustling the grass under his feet, he crossed to the opposite side of the yard; but after a while the wattle fence creaked. A Cossack in a dark Circassian coat and a white sheepskin cap passed along the other side of the fence (it was Luke), and a tall woman with a white kerchief on her head went past Olenin. "I and you have nothing to do with one another," was what Maryanka's firm step gave him to understand. He followed her with his eyes to the porch of the hut, and he even saw her, through the window, take off her kerchief and sit down. And suddenly a feeling of lonely depression, and some vague longings and hopes, and envy of some one or other, overcame the young man's soul.

The last lights had been put out in the

huts. The last sounds had died away in the village. The wattle fences and the cattle gleaming white in the yards, the roofs of the houses and the stately poplars, all seemed to be sleeping the laborers' healthy peaceful sleep. Only the incessant ringing voices of frogs from the damp distance reached the young man. In the east the stars were growing fewer and seemed to be melting in the increasing light; but overhead they were denser and deeper than before. The old man was dozing with his head on his hand. A cock crowed in the yard opposite, but Olenin still paced the yard, thinking of something. The sound of a song sung by several voices reached him, and he stepped up to the fence and listened. The voices of several young Cossacks caroled a merry song, and one voice was distinguishable among them all by its firm strength.

"Do you know who is singing there?" said the old man, rousing himself. "It is the brave Lukashka. He has killed a Chechen, and now he rejoices. And what is there to rejoice at? . . . The fool, the fool!"

"And have you ever killed people?" asked Olenin.

"You devil!" shouted the old man. "What are you asking? One must not talk so. It is a serious thing to destroy a human being. . . . Ah, a very serious thing! Good-by, my dear fellow. I've eaten my fill and am drunk," he said, rising. "Shall I come tomorrow, to go shooting?"

"Yes, come!"

"Mind, get up early; if you oversleep you will be fined!"

"Never fear, I'll be up before you," answered Olenin.

The old man left. The song ceased, but one could hear footsteps and merry talk. A little later the singing broke out again, but farther away, and Eroshka's loud voice chimed in with the other.

"What people, what a life!" thought Olenin with a sigh, as he returned alone to his hut.

CHAPTER XVI

TORTOISE

DADDY EROSHKA was a superannuated and solitary Cossack: twenty years ago his wife went over to the Orthodox Church, and ran away from him and married a Russian sergeant major, and he had no children. He was not bragging when he spoke of himself as having been the boldest daredevil in the village when he was young. Everybody in the regiment knew of his old-time prowess. The death of more than one Russian, as well as Chechen, lay on his conscience. He used to go plundering in the mountains, and robbed the Russians too; and he had twice been in prison. The greater part of his life was spent in the forests, hunting. There he lived for days on a crust of bread and drank nothing but water. But, on the other hand, when he was in the village he made merry from morning to night. After leaving Olenin he slept for a couple of hours and awoke before it was light. He lay on his bed thinking of the man he had become acquainted with the evening before. Olenin's "simplicity" (simplicity in the sense of not grudging him a drink) pleased him very much, and so did Olenin himself. He wondered why the Russians were all "simple" and so rich, and why they knew nothing and yet were educated. He pondered on these questions, and also considered what he might get out of Olenin.

Daddy Eroshka's hut was of a good size and not old, but the absence of a woman was very noticeable in it. Contrary to the usual cleanliness of the Cossacks, the whole of this hut was filthy and exceedingly untidy. A blood-stained coat had been thrown onto the table; half a dough cake lay beside a plucked and mangled crow with which to feed the hawk. Sandals of rawhide, a gun, a dagger, a little bag, wet clothes and sundry rags lay scattered on the benches. In a corner stood a tub of stinking water, in which another pair of sandals were being steeped; and near by was a gun and a hunting screen. On the floor a net had been thrown down and several dead pheasants lay there, while a hen tied by its leg was walking about near the table pecking among the dirt. In the unheated oven stood a broken pot with some kind of milky liquid. On the top of the oven a falcon was screeching and trying to break the cord by which it was tied, and a molting hawk sat quietly on the edge of the oven, looking askance at the hen and occasionally bowing its head to right and left.

Daddy Eroshka, in his shirt, was lying prone on a short bed rigged up between the wall and the oven, with his strong legs raised and his feet on the oven. He was picking with his thick fingers at the scratches left on his hands by the hawk, which he was accustomed to carry without wearing gloves. The whole room, especially near the old man, was filled with that strong but not unpleasant mixture of smells that he always carried about with him.

"Uyde-ma, Daddy?" (Is Daddy in?) through the window came a sharp voice, which he at once recognized as Lukashka's. "Uyde, Uyde, Uyde."

"I am in!" shouted the old man. "Come in, neighbor Mark, Luke Mark. Come to see Daddy? On your way to the cordon?"

The hawk, at the sound of his master's shout, flapped his wings and pulled at his cord.

The old man was fond of Lukashka, who was the only man he excepted from his general contempt for the younger generation of Cossacks. Besides which, Lukashka and his mother, as near neighbors, often gave the old man wine, clotted cream, and other home produce which Eroshka did not possess. Daddy Eroshka, who all his life had allowed himself to get carried away, always explained his infatuations from a practical point of view. "Well, why not?" he used to say to himself. "I'll give them some fresh meat, or a bird, and they won't forget Daddy: they'll sometimes bring a cake or a piece of pie."

"Good morning, Mark! I am glad to see you," shouted the old man cheerfully, and, quickly putting down his bare feet, he jumped off his bed and walked a step or two along the creaking floor, looked down at his outturned toes, and suddenly, amused by the appearance of his feet, he smiled, stamped with his bare heel on the ground, stamped again, and then performed a funny dance step.

"That was clever, eh?" he asked, his small eyes glistening.

Lukashka smiled faintly.

"Going back to the cordon?" asked the old man.

"I have brought the chikhir I promised you when we were at the cordon."

"May Christ save you!" said the old man, who took up the extremely wide trousers that were lying on the floor and his beshmet, put them on, fastened a strap round his waist, poured some water over his hands from an earthenware pot, wiped them on the old trousers, smoothed his beard with a bit of comb, and stopped in front of Lukashka.

"Ready," he said.

Lukashka fetched a cup, wiped it, and filled it with wine, and then handed it to the old man.

"Your health! To the Father and the Son!" said the old man, accepting the wine with solemnity. "May you have what you desire, may you always be a hero, and receive the cross."

Lukashka also drank a little, after repeating a prayer, and then put the wine on the table.

The old man rose and brought out some dried fish which he laid on the threshold, where he beat it with a stick to make it tender; then, having put it with his horny hands on a blue plate (his only one), he placed it on the table.

"I have all I want. I have victuals, thank God!" he said proudly. "Well, and what of Mosev?" he added.

Lukashka, evidently wishing to know the old man's opinion, told him how the officer had taken the gun from him. "Never mind the gun," said the old man. "If you don't give away the gun, you will get no reward."

"But they say, Daddy, it's little reward a fellow gets when he is not yet a mounted Cossack; and the gun is a fine one, worth eighty rubles."

"Eh, let it go! I had a dispute like that with an officer: he wanted my horse. 'Give it me and you'll be made a Teacher,' says he. I wouldn't and I got nothing!"

"Yes, Daddy, but you see I have to buy a horse; and they say you can't get one the other side of the river under fifty rubles, and mother has not yet sold our wine."

"Eh, we didn't bother,' said the old man; "when Daddy Eroshka was your age, he already stole herds of horses from the Nogay folk, and drove them across the Terek. Sometimes we'd give a fine horse for a quart of vodka or a cloak."

"Why so cheap?" asked Lukashka.

"You're a fool, a fool, Mark," said the old man contemptuously. "Why, that's what one steals for; so as not to be stingy! As for you, I suppose you have not so much as seen how one drives off a herd of horses? Why don't you speak?"

"What's one to say, Daddy?" replied Lukashka. "It seems we are not the same sort of men as you were."

"You're a fool! Mark, a fool! not the same sort of men!" retorted the old man, mimicking the Cossack lad. "I was not that sort of Cossack at your age."

"How's that?" asked Lukashka.

The old man shook his head contemptuously. "Daddy Eroshka was *simple;* he did not grudge anything! That's why I was kunak with all Chechnya. A kunak would come to visit me, and I'd make him drunk with vodka and make him happy, and put him to sleep with me; and when I went to see him I'd take him a present—a dagger! That's the way it is done, and not as you do nowadays: the only amusement lads have now is to crack seeds and spit out the shells!" The old man finished contemptuously, imitating the present-day Cossacks cracking seeds and spitting out the shells.

"Yes, I know," said Lukashka; "that's so!"

"If you wish to be a fellow of the right sort, be a brave, and not a peasant! Because even a peasant can buy a horse,—pay the money and take the horse."

They were silent for a while.

"Well, of course it is dull both in the village and the cordon, Daddy: but there's nowhere one can go for a bit of sport. All our fellows are so timid. Take Nazarka. The other day when we went to the Tartar village, Girey Khan asked us to come to Nogay to take some horses, but no one went; and how was I to go alone?"

"And what of Daddy? Do you think I am quite dried up? . . . No, I'm not dried up. Let me have a horse, and I'll be off to Nogay at once."

"What's the good of talking nonsense!" said Luke. "You'd better tell me what to do about Girey Khan. He says, 'Only bring horses to the Terek, and then even if you bring a whole stud, I'll find a place for them.' You see, he's also a shaven-headed Tartar—how's one to believe him?"

"You may trust Girey Khan, all his kin were good people. His father too was a faithful kunak. But listen to Daddy and I won't teach you wrong; make him take an oath, then it will be all right. And if you go with him, have your pistol ready all the same; especially when it comes to dividing up the horses. I was nearly killed that way once by a Chechen. I wanted ten rubles from him for a horse. Trusting is all right, but don't go to sleep without a gun."

Lukashka listened attentively to the old man.

"I say, Daddy, have you any stone-break grass?" he asked after a pause.

"I have none, but I'll teach you how to get it. You're a good lad, and won't forget the old man. . . . Shall I tell you?"

"Tell me, Daddy."

"You know a tortoise? She's a devil, the tortoise is!"

"Of course I know!"

"Find her nest and fence it round, so that she can't get in. Well, she'll come, go round it, and will then go off to find the stone-break grass, and will bring some along and destroy the fence. Anyhow, next morning come in good time, and where the fence is broken, there you'll find the stone-break grass lying. Take it wherever you like. No lock and no bar will be able to stop you."

"Have you tried it yourself, Daddy?"

"As for trying, I have not tried it, but I was told of it by good people. I used only one charm: that was to repeat the 'Hail Rhyme' when mounting my horse; and no one ever killed me!"

"What is the 'Hail Rhyme,' Daddy?"

"What, don't you know it? Oh, what people! You're right to ask Daddy. Well, listen, and repeat after me:

> "Hail! Ye, living in Sion,
> This is your King,
> Our steeds we shall sit on,
> Sophonia is weeping.
> Zacharias is speaking,
> Father Mandrych,
> Mankind ever loving."

"Kind ever loving," the old man repeated. "Do you know it now? Try it."

Lukashka laughed.

"Come, Daddy, was it that that hindered their killing you? Maybe it just happened so!"

"You've grown too clever! You learn it all, and say it. It will do you no harm. Well, suppose you have sung 'Mandrych,' it's all right," and the old man himself began laughing.

"But just one thing! Luke, don't you go to Nogay!"

"Why?"

"Times have changed. You are not the same men. You've become rubbishy Cossacks! And see how many Russians have come down on us! You'd get to prison. Really, give it up! Just as if you could! Now Girchik and I, we used . . ." And the old man was about to begin one of his unending tales, but Lukashka glanced at the window and interrupted him.

"It is quite light, Daddy. It's time to be off. Look us up, some day."

"May Christ save you! I'll go to the army man; I promised to take him out shooting. He seems a good fellow."

CHAPTER XVII

LUKASHKA'S DUMB SISTER

FROM Eroshka's hut Lukashka went home. As he returned, the dewy mists were rising from the ground and enveloped the village. Though the cattle were out of sight, you could hear them on all sides beginning to stir. The cocks called to one another with increasing frequency and insistence. The air was becoming more transparent, and the villagers were getting up. Not till he was close to it, could Lukashka discern the fence of his yard, all wet with dew, the porch of the hut and the open shed. From the misty yard he heard the sound of an ax chop-

ping wood. Lukashka entered the hut. His mother was up, and stood at the oven, throwing wood into it. His little sister was still lying in bed asleep.

"Well, Lukashka, had enough holiday making?" softly asked his mother. "Where did you spend the night?"

"I was in the village," reluctantly replied her son, reaching for his musket, which he drew from its cover and examined carefully.

His mother shook her head.

Lukashka poured a little gunpowder onto the pan, took out a little bag from which he drew some empty cartridge cases which he began filling, carefully plugging each one with a ball wrapped in a rag. Then, having tested the loaded cartridges with his teeth and examined them, he put down the bag.

"I say, Mother, I told you my socks wanted mending; have they been done?" he asked.

"Oh, yes, our dumb girl was mending something last night. Why, is it time for you to be going back to the cordon? I haven't seen anything of you!"

"Yes, as soon as I have got ready I shall have to go," answered Lukashka, tying up the gunpowder. "And where is our dumb one? Outside?"

"Chopping wood, I expect. She kept fretting for you. 'I shall not see him at all!' she said. She puts her hand to her face like this and clicks her tongue, and presses her hands to her heart, as much as to say—'sorry.' Shall I call her in? She understood all about the abrek."

"Call her," said Lukashka. "And I had some tallow there; bring it: I must grease my sword."

The old woman went out, and a few minutes later Lukashka's dumb sister came up the creaking steps and entered the hut. She was six years older than her brother, and would have been extremely like him, had it not been for the dull and coarsely changeable expression (common to all deaf and dumb people) of her face.

She wore a coarse smock all patched; her feet were bare and muddy, and on her head she had an old blue kerchief. Her neck, arms, and face were sinewy like a peasant's. Her clothing and her whole appearance indicated that she always did the hard work of a man.

She brought in a heap of logs, which she threw down by the oven. Then she went up to her brother, and with a joyful smile which made her whole face pucker up, touched him on the shoulder and began making rapid signs to him with her hands, her face, and whole body.

"That's right, that's right, Stepka is a trump!" answered the brother, nodding. "She's fetched everything, and mended everything, she's a trump! Here, take this for it!" He brought out two pieces of gingerbread from his pocket and gave them to her.

The dumb woman's face flushed with pleasure, and she began making a weird noise for joy. Having seized the gingerbread, she began to gesticulate still more rapidly, frequently pointing in one direction, and passing her thick finger over her eyebrows and her face. Lukashka understood her, and kept nodding, while he smiled slightly. She was telling him to give the girls dainties, and that the girls liked him, and that one girl, Maryanka—the best of them all—loved him. She indicated Maryanka by rapidly pointing in the direction of Maryanka's home and to her own eyebrows and face, and by smacking her lips and shaking her head. "Love" she expressed by pressing her hands to her breast, kissing her hand, and pretending to embrace some one. Their mother returned to the hut, and seeing what her dumb daughter was saying, smiled and shook her head. Her daughter showed her the gingerbread, and again made the noise which expressed joy.

"I told Ulitka the other day that I'd send a match-maker to them," said the mother. "She took my word well."

Lukashka looked silently at his mother. "But how about selling the wine, mother? I need a horse."

"I'll cart it when I have time. I must get the barrels ready," said the mother, evidently not wishing her son to meddle in domestic matters. "When you go out, you'll find a bag in the passage. I borrowed it from the neighbors, and got something for you to take back to the cordon; or shall I put it in your sack?"

"All right," answered Lukashka. "And if Girey Khan should come across the river, send him to me at the cordon, for I shall not get leave again for a long time now! I have some business with him."

He began to get ready to start.

"I will send him on," said the old woman. "It seems you have been spreeing at Yamka's all the time. I went out in the night to see to the cattle, and I think it was your voice I heard singing songs."

Lukashka did not reply, but went out into the passage, threw his bags over his shoulder, tucked up the skirts of his coat, took his musket, and then stopped for a moment on the threshold.

"Good-by, Mother!" he said as he closed the gate behind him. "Send me a small barrel with Nazarka. I promised it to the lads, and he'll call for it."

"May Christ keep you, Lukashka. God be with you! I'll send you some, some from the new barrel," said the old woman, going to the fence: "But listen," she added, leaning over the fence.

The Cossack stopped.

"You've been making merry here; well, that's all right. Why should not a young man amuse himself? God has sent you luck, and that's good. But now look out and mind, my son. Don't you go and get into mischief. Above all, honor your superiors: one has to! And I will sell the wine and find money for a horse, and will arrange a match with the girl for you."

"All right, all right!" answered her son, frowning.

His deaf sister shouted to attract his attention. She pointed to her head and the palm of her hand, to indicate the shaved head of a Chechen. Then she frowned and pretended to aim a gun, she shrieked and began rapidly humming and shaking her head. This meant that Lukashka should kill another Chechen.

Lukashka understood. He smiled, and shifting the gun at his back under his cloak, stepped lightly and rapidly, and soon disappeared in the thick mist.

Silently the old woman, having stood a little while at the gate, returned to the hut and immediately began working.

CHAPTER XVIII

TEACHER ELIAS

LUKASHKA returned to the cordon, and at the same time Daddy Eroshka whistled to his dogs and, climbing over his wattle fence, went to Olenin's lodging, passing by the back of the houses (he disliked meeting women before going out hunting or shooting).

He found Olenin still asleep, and even Vanyusha, though awake, was still in bed and was looking round the room, considering whether it was not time to get up, when Daddy Eroshka, gun on shoulder and in full hunter's trappings, opened the door. "A cudgel!" he shouted in his deep voice, "An alarm! The Chechens are upon us! Ivan! Get the samovar ready for your master; and get up yourself—quick!" cried the old man. "That's our way, my good man! Why, even the girls are already up! Look out of the window. See, she's going for water, and you're still sleeping!"

Olenin awoke and jumped up, feeling fresh and light-hearted at the sight of the old man and at the sound of his voice. "Quick, Vanyusha, quick!" he cried.

"Is that the way you go hunting?" said the old man. "Others are having their breakfast, and you are asleep! Lyam! Here!" he called to his dog.

"Is your gun ready?" he shouted, as loud as if a whole crowd were in the hut.

"Well, it's true I'm guilty, but it can't be helped! The powder, Vanyusha, and the wads!" said Olenin.

"A fine!" shouted the old man.

"*Du tay voulay vou?*" asked Vanyusha, grinning.

"You're not one of us, your gabble is not like our speech, you devil!" the old man shouted at Vanyusha, showing the stumps of his teeth.

"A first offense must be forgiven," said Olenin playfully, drawing on his high boots.

"The first offense shall be forgiven,"

answered Eroshka, "but if you oversleep another time you'll be fined a pail of chikhir. When it gets warmer you'll not find the deer."

"And even if we do find him, he is wiser than we are," said Olenin, repeating the words spoken by the old man the evening before, "and you can't deceive him!"

"Yes, laugh away! You kill one first, and then you may talk. Now then, hurry up! Look, there's the master himself coming to see you," added Eroshka, looking out of the window. "Just see how he's got himself up. He's put on a new coat so that you should see that he is an officer. Ah, these people, these people!" and, right enough, Vanyusha came in and announced that the master of the house wished to see Olenin.

"L'arjan!" he remarked profoundly, to forewarn his master of the meaning of this visitation. Following him, the master of the house, in a new Circassian coat with an officer's stripes on the shoulders and with polished boots (quite exceptional among Cossacks) entered the room, swaying from side to side and congratulating his lodger on its being a holiday.

The Teacher, Elias Vasilich, was an *educated* Cossack. He had been to Russia proper, was a regimental schoolteacher, and above all, he was noble. He wished to appear noble, but one could not help feeling that beneath his grotesque pretense of polish, his affectation, his self-confidence, and his absurd way of speaking, he was just the same as Daddy Eroshka. This could also clearly be seen by his sunburnt face and his hands and his red nose. Olenin asked him to sit down.

"Good morning, Father Elias Vasilich," said Eroshka, rising with (or so it seemed to Olenin) an ironically low bow.

"Good morning, Daddy. So you're here already," said the Teacher, with a careless nod.

The Teacher was a man of about forty, with a gray pointed beard, skinny and lean, but handsome and very fresh-looking for his age. Having come to see Olenin, he was evidently afraid of being taken for an ordinary Cossack, and wanted to let Olenin feel his importance from the first.

"That's our Egyptian Nimrod," he remarked, addressing Olenin, and pointing to the old man with a self-satisfied smile. "A mighty hunter before the Lord! He's our foremost man on every hand. You've already been pleased to get acquainted with him."

Daddy Eroshka gazed at his feet, in their shoes of wet rawhide, and shook his head thoughtfully at the Teacher's ability and learning, and muttered to himself: "Gyptian Nimvrod! What things he invents!"

"Yes, you see, we mean to go hunting," answered Olenin.

"Yes, sir, exactly," said the Teacher, "but I have a small business with you."

"What do you want?"

"Seeing that you are a gentleman," began the Teacher, "and as I may understand myself to be in the rank of an officer too, and therefore we may always progressively negotiate, as gentlemen do . . ." (He stopped and looked with a smile at Olenin and at the old man.) "But if you have the desire with my consent, then, as my wife is a foolish woman of our class, she could not quite comprehend your words of yesterday's date. Therefore my quarters might be let for six rubles to the Regimental Adjutant, without the stables; but I can always avert it from myself free of charge. But, as you desire, therefore I, being myself of an officer's rank, can come to an agreement with you in everything, personally, as an inhabitant of this district, not according to our customs, but can maintain the conditions in every way. . . ."

"Speaks clearly!" muttered the old man.

The Teacher continued in the same strain for a long time. At last, not without difficulty, Olenin gathered that the Teacher wished to let his rooms to him, Olenin, for six rubles a month. The latter gladly agreed to this, and offered his visitor a glass of tea. The Teacher declined it.

"According to our silly custom we consider it a sort of sin to drink out of a 'worldly' tumbler," he said. "Though, of course, with my education I may understand, but my wife from her human weakness . . ."

"Well, then, will you have some tea?"

"If you will permit me, I will bring my own particular glass," answered the Teacher, and stepped out into the porch. "Bring me my glass!" he cried.

In a few minutes the door opened, and a young sunburnt arm in a print sleeve thrust itself in, holding a tumbler in the hand. The Teacher went up, took it, and whispered something to his daughter. Olenin poured tea for the Teacher into the latter's own "particular" glass, and for Eroshka into a "worldly" glass.

"However, I do not desire to detain you," said the Teacher, scalding his lips and emptying his tumbler. "I too have a great liking for fishing, and I am here, so to say, only on leave of absence for recreation from my duties. I too have the desire to tempt fortune and see whether some *Gifts of the Terek* may not fall to my share. I hope you too will come and see us and have a drink of our wine, according to the custom of our village," he added. The Teacher bowed, shook hands with Olenin, and went out. While Olenin was getting ready, he heard the Teacher giving orders to his family in an authoritative and sensible tone, and a few minutes later he saw him pass by the window in a tattered coat, with his trousers rolled up to his knees, and a fishing net over his shoulder.

"A rascal!" said Daddy Eroshka, emptying his "worldly" tumbler. "And will you really pay him six rubles? Was such a thing ever heard of? They would let you the best hut in the village for two rubles. What a beast! Why, I'd let you have mine for three!"

"No, I'll remain here," said Olenin.

"Six rubles! . . . Clearly it's a fool's money. Eh, eh, eh!" answered the old man. "Let's have some chikhir, Ivan!"

Having had a snack and a drink of vodka to prepare themselves for the road, Olenin and the old man went out together before eight o'clock. At the gate they came up against a wagon, to which a pair of oxen were harnessed. With a white kerchief tied round her head nearly to her eyes, a coat over her smock, and wearing high boots. Maryanka, with a long switch in her hand, was dragging the oxen by a cord tied to their horns.

"Mammy," said the old man, pretending that he was going to seize her.

Maryanka flourished her switch at him, and glanced merrily at them both with her beautiful eyes.

Olenin felt still more light-hearted.

"Now then, come on, come on," he said, throwing his gun on his shoulder and conscious of the girl's eyes upon him.

"Gee, gee!" sounded Maryanka's voice behind them, followed by the creak of the moving wagon.

As long as their road lay through the pastures at the back of the village, Eroshka went on talking. He could not forget the Teacher, and kept on abusing him.

"Why are you so angry with him?" asked Olenin.

"He's stingy. I don't like it," answered the old man. "He'll leave it all behind when he dies! Then who's he saving up for? He's built two houses, and he's got a second garden from his brother by a lawsuit. And in the matter of papers what a dog he is! They come to him from other villages to fill up documents. As he writes it out, exactly so it happens. He gets it quite exact. But who is he saving for? He's only got one boy and the girl; when she is married who'll be left?"

"Well then, he's saving up for her dowry," said Olenin.

"What dowry? The girl is sought after, she's a fine girl. But he's such a devil that he must yet marry her to a rich fellow. He wants to get a big price for her. There's Luke, a Cossack, a neighbor and a nephew of mine, a fine lad. It's he who killed the Chechen—he has been wooing her for a long time, but he hasn't let him have her. He's given one excuse and another, and a third. 'The girl is too young,' he says. But I know what he is thinking. He wants to keep them bowing to him. What a lot of scandal there has been about her lately. Still they will get her for Lukashka, because he is the best Cossack in the village, a brave, who has killed an abrek, and will be rewarded with a cross."

"But how about this? When I was walking up and down the yard last night, I saw my landlord's daughter and some Cossack kissing," said Olenin.

"You're pretending!" cried the old man, stopping.

"On my word," said Olenin.

"Women are the devil," said Eroshka, pondering. "But what Cossack was it?"

"I couldn't see."

"Well, what sort of a cap had he, a white one?"

"Yes."

"And a red coat? About your height?"

"Not a bit taller."

"It's he!" and Eroshka burst out laughing. "It's himself, it's Mark. He is Luke, but I call him Mark for a joke. His very self! I love him. I was just such a one myself. What's the good of minding them? My sweetheart used to sleep with her mother and sister-in-law, but I managed to get in. She used to sleep upstairs; that witch her mother was a regular demon; it's awful how she hated me. Well, I used to come with a chum, Girchik his name was. We'd come under her window, and I'd climb on his shoulders, push up the window and begin groping about. She used to sleep just there on a bench. Once I woke her up and she nearly called out. She had not recognized me. 'Who is there?' she said, and I could not answer. Her mother was even beginning to stir, but I took off my cap and shoved it over her mouth; and she at once knew it, by a seam in it, and ran out to me. I used not to want anything then. She'd bring along clotted cream and grapes and everything," added Eroshka (who always explained things practically), "and she was not the only one. It was a life!"

"And what now?"

"Now we'll follow the dog, get a pheasant to settle on a tree, and then you may fire."

"Would you have made up to Maryanka?"

"Attend to the dogs. I'll tell you tonight," said the old man, pointing to his favorite dog, Lyamka.

After a pause they continued talking while they went about a hundred paces. Then the old man stopped again and pointed to a twig that lay across the path.

"What do you think of that?" he said. "You think it's nothing? It's bad that this stick is lying so."

"Why is it bad?"

He smiled.

"Ah, you don't know anything. Just listen to me. When a stick lies like that, don't you step across it, but go round it, or throw it off the path, this way, and say 'Father and Son and Holy Ghost,' and then go on with God's blessing. Nothing will happen to you. That's what the old men used to teach me."

"Come, what rubbish!" said Olenin. "You'd better tell me more about Maryanka. Does she carry on with Lukashka?"

"Hush, . . . be quiet now!" the old man again interrupted in a whisper: "just listen, we'll go round by the wood."

And the old man, stepping quietly in his soft shoes, led the way by a narrow path into the dense, wild, overgrown forest. Now and again with a frown he turned to look at Olenin, who rustled and clattered with his heavy boots and, carrying his gun carelessly, several times caught the twigs of the trees that grew across the path.

"Don't make a noise. Step softly, soldier!" the old man whispered angrily.

There was a feeling in the air that the sun had risen. The mist was dissolving, but it still enveloped the tops of the trees. The forest looked terribly high. At every step the aspect changed: what had appeared like a tree proved to be a bush, and a reed looked like a tree.

CHAPTER XIX

THE FOREST CRASH

IT was calm. The sounds from the village, audible at first, now no longer reached the sportsmen. Only the branches cracked as the dogs ran under them, and now and then birds called to one another. Olenin knew that danger lurked in the forest, that abreks always hid in such places. But he knew too that in the forest, for a man on foot, a gun is a great protection. Not that he was afraid, but he felt that another in his place might be; and looking into the damp misty forest and listening to the rare and faint sounds with strained attention, he changed his hold on his gun and experienced a pleasant feeling that was new to him. Daddy Eroshka went in front, stopping and carefully scanning every puddle where an animal had left a double track, and pointing it out to Olenin. He hardly spoke at all, and only occasionally made remarks in a whisper. The track they were following had once been made by wagons, but the grass had long overgrown it. The elm and plane-tree forest, on both sides of them, was so dense and overgrown with creepers that it was impossible to see anything through it. Nearly every tree was enveloped from top to bottom with wild grapevines, and dark bramble bushes thickly covered the ground. Every little glade was overgrown with blackberry bushes and gray feathery reeds. In places large hoofprints and small funnel-shaped pheasant trails led from the path into the thicket. The vigor of the growth of this forest untrampled by cattle struck Olenin at every turn, for he had never seen anything like it. This forest, the danger, the old man and his mysterious whispering, Maryanka with her virile upright bearing, and the mountains—all this seemed to him like a dream.

"A pheasant has settled," whispered the old man, looking round and pulling his cap over his face—"Cover your mug! A pheasant!" he moved his arm angrily at Olenin, and pushed forward almost on all fours. "He don't like a man's mug."

Olenin was still behind him when the old man stopped and began examining a tree. A cock pheasant on the tree clucked at the dog that was barking at it, and Olenin saw the pheasant; but at that moment a report, as of a cannon, came from Eroshka's enormous gun; the bird fluttered up and, losing some feathers, fell to the ground. Coming up to the old man, Olenin disturbed another, and raising his gun aimed and fired. The pheasant flew swiftly up, and then, catching at the branches as he fell, dropped like a stone to the ground.

"Good man!" the old man (who could not hit a flying bird) shouted, laughing.

Having picked up the pheasants, they went on. Olenin, excited by the exercise and the praise, kept addressing remarks to the old man.

"Stop! Come this way," the old man interrupted. "I noticed the track of deer here, yesterday."

After they had turned into the thicket and gone some three hundred paces, they scrambled through into a glade overgrown with reeds and partly under water. Olenin failed to keep up with the old huntsman, and presently Daddy Eroshka, some twenty paces in front, stooped down, nodding and beckoning with his arm. On coming up with him, Olenin saw a man's footprint to which the old man was pointing.

"D'you see?"

"Yes, well?" said Olenin, trying to speak as calmly as he could. "A man's footstep!"

Involuntarily a thought of Cooper's *Pathfinder* and of abreks flashed through Olenin's mind, but noticing the mysterious manner with which the old man moved on, he hesitated to question him, and remained in doubt whether this mysteriousness was caused by fear of danger, or by the sport.

"No, it's my own footprint," the old man said quietly, and pointed to some grass, under which the track of an animal was just perceptible.

The old man went on, and Olenin kept up with him. Descending to lower ground some twenty paces farther on, they came upon a spreading pear tree, under which, on the black earth, lay the fresh dung of some animal. The spot, all covered over with wild vines, was like a cozy arbor, dark and cool.

"He's been here this morning," said the old man with a sigh; "the lair is still damp; quite fresh."

Suddenly they heard a terrible crash in the forest some ten paces from where they stood. They both started and seized their guns, but they could see nothing and only heard the branches breaking. The rhythmical rapid thud of galloping was heard for a moment and then changed into a hollow rumble which resounded farther and farther off, reëchoing in wider and wider circles through the forest. Olenin felt as though something had snapped in his heart. He peered carefully, but vainly, into the green thicket, and then turned to the old man. Daddy Eroshka, with his gun pressed to his breast, stood motionless; his cap was thrust backwards, his eyes gleamed with an unwonted glow, and his mouth open, with its worn yellow teeth, seemed to have stiffened in that position.

"A horned stag!" he muttered, and throwing down his gun in despair he began pulling at his gray beard. "Here it stood. We should have come round by the path. . . . Fool! fool!" and he gave his beard an angry tug. "Fool! Pig!" he repeated, pulling painfully at his own beard.

Through the forest something seemed to fly away in the mist, and ever farther and farther off was heard the sound of the flight of the stag.

It was already dusk when, hungry, tired, but full of vigor, Olenin returned with the old man. Dinner was ready. He ate and drank with the old man till he felt warm and merry. Olenin then

went out into the porch. Again westwards before his eyes rose the mountains. Again the old man told his endless stories of hunting, of abreks, of sweethearts, and of all that free and reckless life. Again the fair Maryanka went in and out and across the yard, and her smock outlined the powerful form of the beautiful maiden.

CHAPTER XX

OLENIN'S FRIGHT

THE next day, Olenin went alone to the spot where he and the old man had startled the stag. Instead of passing round through the gate, he climbed over the prickly hedge, as everybody else did, and before he had had time to pull out the thorns that had caught in his coat, his dog, which had run on in front, started two pheasants. He had hardly stepped among the briers, when the pheasants began to rise at every step (the old man had not shown him that place the day before, as he meant to keep it for shooting from behind the screen). Olenin fired twelve times, and killed five pheasants, but clambering after them through the briers he got so fatigued that he was drenched with perspiration. He called off his dog, uncocked his gun, put in a bullet above the small shot, and, brushing away the mosquitoes with the wide sleeve of his Circassian coat, he went slowly to the spot where they had been the day before. It was, however, impossible to keep back the dog, who found trails on the very path, and Olenin killed two more pheasants, so that, after being detained by this, it was getting toward noon before he began to find the place he was looking for.

The day was perfectly clear, calm, and hot. The morning moisture had dried up even in the forest, and myriads of mosquitoes literally covered his face, his back, and his arms. His dog had turned from black to gray, its back being covered with mosquitoes, and so had Olenin's coat, through which the insects thrust their stings. Olenin was ready to run away from them, and it seemed to him that it was impossible to live in this country in the summer. He was about to go home, but remembering that other people managed to endure such pain, he resolved to bear it, and gave himself up to be devoured. And, strange to say, by noontime the feeling became actually pleasant. He even felt that without this mosquito-filled atmosphere around him, and that mosquito-paste mingled with perspiration which his hand smeared over his face, and that unceasing irritation all over his body, the forest would lose for him some of its character and charm. These myriads of insects were so well suited to that monstrously lavish wild vegetation, these multitudes of birds and beasts which filled the forest, this dark foliage, this hot scented air, these runlets filled with turbid water which everywhere soaked through from the Terek and gurgled here and there under the overhanging leaves, that the very thing which had at first seemed to him dreadful and intolerable, now seemed pleasant. After going round the place where yesterday they had found the animal, and not finding anything, he felt inclined to rest. The sun stood right above the forest and poured its perpendicular rays down on his back and head whenever he came out into a glade, or on to the road. The seven heavy pheasants dragged painfully at his waist. Having found the traces of yesterday's stag, he crept under a bush into the thicket just where the stag had lain, and lay down in its lair. He examined the dark foliage around him, the place marked by the stag's perspiration, and yesterday's dung, the imprint of the stag's knees, the bit of black earth it had kicked up, and his own footprints of the day before. He felt cool and comfortable and did not think of or wish for anything. And suddenly he was overcome by such a strange feeling of causeless joy, and of love for everything, that, from an old habit of his childhood, he began crossing himself and thanking some one. Suddenly, with extraordinary clearness, he thought: "Here am I, Dmitry Olenin, a being quite distinct from every other being, now lying all alone, Heaven only knows where,—where a stag used to live—an old stag, a beautiful stag, who perhaps had never seen a man, and in a place where no human being has ever sat, or thought these thoughts. Here I sit, and around me stand old and young trees, one of them festooned with wild grape-vines, and pheasants are fluttering, driving one another about and perhaps scenting their murdered brothers." He felt his pheasants, examined them, and wiped the warm blood off his hand on to his coat. "Perhaps the jackals scent them, and with dissatisfied faces go off in another direction: above me, flying in among the leaves, which to them seem enormous islands, mosquitoes hang in the air and buzz: one, two, three, four, a hundred, a thousand, a million mosquitoes, and all of them buzz something or other, and each one of them is separate from all else, and is just such a separate Dmitry Olenin as I am myself." He imagined vividly what the mosquitoes buzzed: "This way, this way, lads! Here's some one we can eat!" They buzzed, and stuck to him. And it was clear to him that he was not a Russian nobleman, a member of Moscow society, the friend and relation of so-and-so and so-and-so, but just such a mosquito, or pheasant, or deer, as those that were now living all round him. "Just as they, just as Daddy Eroshka, I shall live awhile and die, and as he says truly: grass will grow and nothing more.

"But what though the grass does grow?" he continued thinking, "still I must live, and be happy, because happiness is all I desire. Never mind what I am—an animal like all the rest, above whom the grass will grow, and nothing more; or a frame in which a bit of the one God has been set,—still I must live in the very best way. How then must I live to be happy, and why was I not happy before?" And he began to recall his former life, and he felt disgusted with himself. He appeared to himself to have been terribly exacting and selfish, though he now saw that all the while he really needed nothing for himself. And he looked round at the foliage with the light shining through it, at the setting sun and the clear sky, and he felt just as happy as before.

"Why am I happy, and what used I to live for?" thought he. "How much I exacted for myself; how I schemed and did not manage to gain anything but shame and sorrow; and, there now, I require nothing to be happy"; and suddenly a new light seemed to reveal itself to him. "Happiness is this!" he said to himself. "Happiness lies in living for others. That is evident. The desire for happiness is innate in every man; therefore it is legitimate. When trying to satisfy it selfishly—that is, by seeking for oneself riches, fame, comforts, or love—it may happen that circumstances arise which make it impossible to satisfy these desires. It follows that it is these desires that are illegitimate, but not the need for happiness. But what desires can always be satisfied, despite external circumstances? What are they? Love, self-sacrifice." He was so glad and excited when he had discovered this, as it seemed to him, new truth, that he jumped up and began impatiently seeking some one to sacrifice himself for, to do good to, and to love. "Since one wants nothing for oneself," he kept thinking, "why not live for others?"

He took up his gun with the intention of returning home quickly to think this out and to find an opportunity of doing good. He made his way out of the thicket.

When he had come out into the glade he looked around him; the sun was no longer visible above the tree tops. It had grown cooler, and the place seemed to him quite strange, and not like the country round the village. Everything seemed changed—the weather and the character of the forest; the sky was wrapped in clouds, the wind was rustling in the tree tops, and all around nothing was visible but reeds and dying broken-down trees. He called to his dog, who had run away to follow some animal, and his voice came back as in a desert. And suddenly he was seized with a terrible sense of weirdness. He grew frightened. He remembered the abreks, and the murders he had been told about.

and he expected every moment that an abrek would spring from behind every bush, and he would have to defend his life and die, or be a coward. He thought of God and of the future life as for long he had not thought about them. And all around was that same gloomy stern wild nature. "And is it worth while living for oneself," thought he, "when at any moment you may die, and die without having done any good; and so that no one will know of it?" He went in the direction where he fancied the village lay. Of his shooting he had no further thought; but he felt tired to death, and peered round at every bush and tree with particular attention and almost with terror, every moment expecting to be called to account for his life. After having wandered about for a considerable time, he came upon a ditch down which was flowing cold sandy water from the Terek, and, not to go astray any longer, he decided to follow it. He went on, without knowing whither the ditch would lead him. Suddenly the reeds behind him crackled. He shuddered and seized his gun. He felt ashamed of himself: the overexcited dog, panting hard, had thrown itself into the cold water of the ditch, and was lapping it!

He too had a drink, and then followed the dog in the direction it wished to go, thinking it would lead him to the village. But despite the dog's company, everything around him seemed still more dreary. The forest grew darker, and the wind grew stronger and stronger in the tops of the broken old trees. Some large birds circled, screeching, round their nests in those trees. The vegetation grew poorer, and he came oftener and oftener upon rustling reeds

and bare sandy spaces, covered with animal footprints. To the howling of the wind was added another kind of cheerless monotonous roar. Altogether his spirits became gloomy. Putting his hand behind him he felt his pheasants, and found one missing. It had broken off and was lost, and only the bleeding head and beak remained sticking in his belt. He felt more frightened than he had ever been before. He began to pray to God, and feared above all that he might die without having done anything good or kind; and he so wanted to live, and to live so as to perform a feat of self-sacrifice.

CHAPTER XXI

COSSACK LAUGHTER

SUDDENLY it was as though the sun had shone into his soul. He heard Russian being spoken, and also heard the rapid smooth flow of the Terek, and a few steps farther in front of him saw the brown moving surface of the river with the dim-colored wet sand of its banks and shallows, the distant steppe, the cordon watchtower outlined above the water, a saddled, hobbled horse among the brambles, and then the mountains opening out before him. The red sun appeared for an instant from under a cloud, and its last rays glittered brightly along the river over the reeds, on the watchtower and on a group of Cossacks, among whom Lukashka's vigorous figure attracted Olenin's involuntary attention.

Olenin felt that he was again, without any apparent cause, perfectly happy. He had come upon the Nizhne-Prototsk post on the Terek, opposite a pro-Russian Tartar village on the other bank of the river. He accosted the Cossacks, but not finding as yet any excuse for doing anyone a kindness he entered the hut; nor in the hut did he find any such opportunity. The Cossacks received him coldly. On entering the mud hut he lit a cigarette. The Cossacks paid little attention to him, first because he was smoking a cigarette, and secondly because they had something else to divert them that evening. Some hostile Chechens, relatives of the abrek who had been killed, had come from the hills with a scout to ransom the body; and the Cossacks were waiting for their Commanding Officer's arrival from the village. The dead man's brother, tall and well-shaped, with a short cropped beard which was dyed red, despite his very tattered coat and cap was calm and majestic as a king. His face was very like that of the dead abrek. He did not deign to look at anyone and never once glanced at the dead body, but, sitting on his heels in the shade, he spat as he smoked his short pipe, and occasionally uttered some few guttural sounds of command, which were respectfully listened to by his companion. He was evidently a brave who had met Russians more than once before in quite other circumstances, and nothing about them could astonish or even interest him. Olenin was about to approach the dead body and had begun to look at it, when the brother, looking up at him from under his brows with calm contempt, said something sharply and angrily. The scout hastened to cover the dead man's face with his coat. Olenin was struck by the dignified and stern expression of the brave's face. He began to speak to him, asking from what village he came, but the Chechen, scarcely giving him a glance, spat contemptuously and turned away. Olenin was so surprised at the Chechen not being interested in him, that he could only put it down to the man's stupidity or ignorance of Russian; so he turned to the scout who also acted as interpreter. The scout was as ragged as the other, but instead of being red-haired he was black-haired, fidgety, with extremely white gleaming teeth and sparkling black eyes. The scout willingly entered into conversation, and asked for a cigarette.

"There were five brothers," began the scout in his broken Russian. "This is the third brother the Russians have killed; only two are left. He is a brave, a great brave!" he said, pointing to the Chechen. "When they killed Ahmet Khan (the dead brave) this one was sitting on the opposite bank among the reeds. He saw it all. Saw him laid in the skiff and brought to the bank. He sat there till the night and wished to kill the old man, but the others would not let him."

Lukashka went up to the speaker, and sat down.

"Of what village?" asked he.

"From here in the hills," replied the scout, pointing to the misty bluish gorge beyond the Terek. "Do you know Suzuk-su? It is about eight miles beyond that."

"Do you know Girey Khan in Suzuk-su?" asked Lukashka, evidently proud of the acquaintance. "He is my kunak."

"He is my neighbor," answered the scout.

"He's a trump!" and Lukashka, evidently much interested, began talking in Tartar to the scout.

Presently a Cossack captain and the head of the village arrived on horseback, with a suite of two Cossacks. The captain—one of the new type of Cossack officers—wished the Cossacks "Good health," but none shouted in reply, "Hail! Good health to your honor," as is customary in the Russian Army, and only a few replied with a bow. Some, and among them, Lukashka, rose and stood erect. The corporal replied that all was well at the outposts. All this seemed ridiculous: it was as if these Cossacks were playing at being soldiers. But these formalities soon gave place to ordinary ways of behavior, and the captain, who was a smart Cossack, just like the others, began speaking fluently in Tartar to the interpreter. They filled in some document, gave it to the scout, and received from him some money. Then they approached the body.

"Which of you is Luke Gavrilov?" asked the captain.

Lukashka took off his cap and came forward.

"I have reported your exploit to the commander. I don't know what will come of it. I have recommended you for a cross; you're too young to be made a sergeant. Can you read?"

"I can't."

"But what a fine fellow to look at!" said the captain, again playing the commander. "Put on your cap. Which of the Gavrilovs does he come of? . . . the Broad, eh?"

"His nephew," replied the corporal.

"I know, I know. Well, lend a hand, help them," he said, turning to the Cossacks.

Lukashka's face shone with joy and seemed handsomer than usual. He moved away from the corporal, and having put on his cap, sat down beside Olenin.

When the body had been carried to the skiff, the brother Chechen descended to the bank. The Cossacks involuntarily stepped aside to let him pass. He jumped into the boat, and pushed off from the bank with his powerful leg, and now, as Olenin noticed, for the first time threw a rapid glance at all the Cossacks, and then abruptly asked his companion a question. The latter answered something, and pointed to Lukashka. The Chechen looked at him and, turning slowly away, gazed at the opposite bank. That look expressed not hatred, but cold contempt. He again made some remark.

"What is he saying?" Olenin asked of the fidgety scout.

"Yours kill ours, ours slay yours. It's always the game," replied the scout, evidently inventing, and he smiled, showing his white teeth, as he jumped into the skiff.

The dead man's brother sat motionless, gazing at the opposite bank. He was so full of hatred and contempt that there was nothing on this side of the river that moved his curiosity. The scout, standing up at one end of the skiff and dipping his paddle now on one and then on the other, steered skillfully, while talking incessantly. The skiff became smaller and smaller as it moved obliquely across the stream; the voices became scarcely audible, and at last, still within sight, they landed on the opposite bank, where their horses stood waiting. There they lifted out the corpse, and (though the horse shied) laid it across one of the saddles, mounted, and rode at a foot pace along the road past a Tartar village, from which a crowd came out to look at them.

The Cossacks on the Russian side of the river were highly satisfied and jolly. Laughter and jokes were heard on all sides. The captain and the head of the village entered the mud hut to regale themselves. Lukashka, vainly striving to impart a sedate expression to his merry face, sat down with his elbows on his knees beside Olenin, and whittled away at a stick.

"Why do you smoke?" he said with assumed curiosity. "Is it good?"

He evidently spoke because he noticed Olenin felt ill at ease and isolated among the Cossacks.

"It's just a habit," answered Olenin. "Why?"

"H'm, if one of us were to smoke there would be a row! Look there now, the mountains are not far off," continued Lukashka, "yet you can't get there! How will you get back alone? It's getting dark. I'll take you, if you like. You ask the corporal to give me leave."

"What a fine fellow!" thought Olenin, looking at the Cossack's bright face. He remembered Maryanka and the kiss he had heard by the gate, and he was sorry for Lukashka, and his want of culture. "What confusion it is," he thought. "A man kills another, and is happy and satisfied with himself as if he had done something excellent. Can it be that nothing tells him that it is not a reason for any rejoicing, and that happiness lies not in killing, but in sacrificing oneself?"

"Well, you had better not meet him again now, mate!" said one of the Cossacks who had seen the skiff off, addressing Lukashka. "Did you hear him asking about you?"

Lukashka raised his head. "My godson?" said Lukashka, meaning by that word the dead Chechen.

"Your godson won't rise, but the red one is the godson's brother!"

"Let him thank God that he got off whole himself," replied Lukashka.

"What are you glad about?" asked Olenin. "Supposing your brother had been killed, would you be glad?"

The Cossack looked at Olenin with laughing eyes. He seemed to have understood all that Olenin wished to say to him, but to be above such considerations.

"Well, that happens too! Don't our fellows get killed, sometimes?"

CHAPTER XXII

THE PRESENT

THE captain and the head of the village rode away; and Olenin, to please Lukashka as well as to avoid going back alone through the dark forest, asked the corporal to give Lukashka leave, and the corporal did so. Olenin thought that Lukashka wanted to see Maryanka, and he was also glad of the companionship of such a pleasant-looking and sociable Cossack. Lukashka and Maryanka he involuntarily united in his mind, and he found pleasure in thinking about them. "He loves Maryanka," thought Olenin, "and I could love her," and a powerful novel emotion of tenderness overcame him as they walked homewards together through the dark forest. Lukashka too felt happy; something akin to love made itself felt between these two very different young men. Every time they glanced at one another they wanted to laugh.

"By which gates do you enter?" asked Olenin.

"By the middle ones. But I'll see you as far as the marsh. After that you have nothing to fear."

Olenin laughed.

"Do you think I am afraid? Go back, and thank you. I can get on alone."

"It's all right! What have I to do? And how can you help being afraid? Even we are afraid," said Lukashka to set Olenin's self-esteem at rest, and laughed too.

"Then come in with me. We'll have a talk and a drink, and in the morning you can go back."

"Couldn't I find a place to spend the night!" laughed Lukashka. "But the corporal asked me to go back."

"I heard you singing last night, and also saw you."

"Every one . . ." and Luke moved his head.

"Is it true you are getting married?" asked Olenin.

"Mother wants me to marry. But I have not got a house yet."

"Aren't you in the regular service?"

"Oh, dear no! I've only just joined, and have not got a horse yet, and don't know how to get one. That's why the marriage does not come off."

"And what would a horse cost?"

"We were bargaining for one beyond the river the other day, and they would not take sixty rubles for it, though it is a Nogay horse."

"Will you come and be my drabant?" (A drabant was a kind of orderly attached to an officer when campaigning.) "I'll get it arranged and will give you a horse," said Olenin suddenly. "Really now, I have two and I don't want it."

"How—don't want it?" Lukashka said, laughing. "Why should you make us a present? We'll get on by ourselves, by God's help."

"No, really! Or don't you want to be a drabant?" said Olenin, glad that it had entered his head to give a horse to Lukashka, though, without his knowing why, he felt uncomfortable and confused and did not know what to say when he tried to speak.

Lukashka was the first to break the silence.

"Have you a house of your own in Russia?" he asked.

Olenin could not refrain from replying that he had not only one, but several houses.

"A good house? Bigger than ours?" asked Lukashka, good-naturedly.

"Much bigger; ten times as big, and three stories high," replied Olenin.

"And have you steeds such as ours?"

"I have a hundred horses, worth three or four hundred rubles each, but they are not like yours. They are trotters, you know! But still, I like the horses here best."

"Well, and did you come here of your own free will, or were you sent?" said Lukashka, laughing at him. "Look! that's where you lost your way," he added, "you should have turned to the right."

"I came by my own wish," replied Olenin. "I wanted to see your parts and to join some expeditions."

"I would go on an expedition any day," said Lukashka. "D'you hear the jackals howling?" he added, listening.

"I say, don't you feel any horror at having killed a man?" asked Olenin.

"What's there to be frightened about? But I should like to join an expedition," Lukashka repeated. "How I want to! How I want to!"

"Perhaps we may be going together. Our company is going before the holidays, and your hundred too."

"And what did you want to come here for? You've a house, and horses, and serfs. In your place I'd do nothing but make merry! And what is your rank?"

"I am a cadet, but have been presented for a commission."

"Well, if you're not bragging about your home, if I were you I'd never have left it! Yes, I'd never have gone away anywhere. Do you find it pleasant living among us?"

"Yes, very pleasant," answered Olenin.

It had grown quite dark before, talking in this way, they approached the village. They were still surrounded by the deep gloom of the forest. The wind howled through the tree tops. The jackals suddenly seemed to be crying close beside them: howling, chuckling, and sobbing, but ahead of them in the village the sounds of women's voices and the barking of dogs could already be heard; the outlines of the huts were clearly to be seen; lights gleamed, and the air was filled with the peculiar smell of kizyak smoke. Olenin felt keenly, that night, especially, that here in this village was his home, his family, all his happiness, and that he had never and would never live so happily anywhere as he did in this Cossack village. He was so fond of everybody and especially of Lu-

kashka that night. On reaching home, to Lukashka's great surprise, Olenin led out of the shed with his own hands a horse he had bought in Groznoe—it was not the one he usually rode but another—not a bad horse though no longer young, and gave it to Lukashka.

"Why should you give me a present?" said Lukashka, "I have not yet done anything for you."

"Really it is nothing," answered Olenin. "Take it, and you will give me a present, and we'll go an expedition against the enemy together."

Lukashka became confused.

"But what d'you mean by it? As if a horse were of small value," he said without looking at the horse.

"Take it, take it! If you don't, you will offend me. Vanyusha! Take the gray horse to his house."

Lukashka took hold of the halter.

"Well, then, thank you! This is something unexpected, undreamt of."

Olenin was as happy as a boy of twelve.

"Tie it up here. It's a good horse. I bought it in Groznoe; it gallops splendidly! Vanyusha, bring us some chikhir. Come into the hut."

The wine was brought. Lukashka sat down and took the wine bowl.

"God willing, I'll find a way to repay you," he said, finishing his wine. "How are you called?"

"Dmitry Andreich."

"Well, 'Mitry Andreich, God bless you. We will be kunaks. Now you must come to see us. Though we are not rich people, still we can treat a kunak, and I will tell mother that if you need anything—clotted cream, or grapes—and if you come to the cordon I'm your servant to go hunting, or to go across the river, anywhere you like! There now, only the other day, what a boar I killed, and I divided it among the Cossacks; but if I had only known, I'd have given it to you."

"That's all right, thank you! But don't harness the horse, it has never been in harness."

"Why harness the horse? And there is something else I'll tell you, if you like," said Lukashka; bending his head. "I have a kunak, Girey Khan. He asked me to lie in ambush by the road where they come down from the mountains. Shall we go together? I'll not betray you. I'll be your murid."

"Yes, we'll go; we'll go some day."

Lukashka seemed quite to have quieted down and to have understood Olenin's attitude toward him. His calmness, and the ease of his behavior, surprised Olenin, and he even did not quite like it. They talked long, and it was late when Lukashka, not tipsy (he never was tipsy) but having drunk a good deal, left Olenin after shaking hands. Olenin looked out of the window to see what he would do. Lukashka went out hanging his head. Then, having led the horse out of the gate, he suddenly shook his head, sprang on to its back like a cat, gathered up the reins of the halter, gave a shout and galloped down the street.

Olenin expected that Lukashka would go to share his joy with Maryanka, but, though he did not do so, Olenin still felt his soul more at ease than ever before in his life. He was as delighted as a boy, and could not refrain from telling Vanyusha, not only that he had given Lukashka the horse, but also why he had done it,

as well as his new theory of happiness.

Vanyusha did not approve of this theory, and announced that *"l'argent il n'y a pas!"* and that therefore it was all nonsense.

Lukashka rode home, jumped off the horse, and handed it over to his mother, telling her to let it out with the communal Cossack herd. He himself had to return to the cordon that same night. His deaf sister undertook to take the horse, and explained by signs that when she saw the man who had given the horse, she would bow down at his feet. The old woman only shook her head at her son's story, and decided in her own mind that he had stolen it. She therefore told the deaf girl to take it to the herd before daybreak.

Lukashka went back alone to the cordon pondering over Olenin's action. Though he did not consider the horse a good one, yet it was worth at least forty rubles and Lukashka was very glad to have the present. But why it had been given him he could not at all understand, and therefore he did not experience the least feeling of gratitude. On the contrary, vague suspicions that the cadet had some evil intentions filled his mind. What those intentions were he could not decide, but neither could he admit the idea that a stranger would give him a horse worth forty rubles, for nothing, just out of kindness; it seemed impossible. Had he been drunk, one might understand it! He might have wished to show off. But the cadet had been sober, and therefore must have wished to bribe him to do something wrong.

"Eh, humbug!" thought Lukashka. "Haven't I got the horse, and we'll see later on. I'm not a fool myself, and we shall see who'll get the better of the other," he thought, feeling the necessity of being on his guard and therefore arousing in himself unfriendly feelings toward Olenin. He told no one how he had got the horse. To some he said he had bought it, to others he replied evasively. However, the truth soon got about in the village, and Lukashka's mother, and Maryanka, as well as Elias Vasilich and other Cossacks, when they heard of Olenin's unnecessary gift, were perplexed, and began to be on their guard against the cadet. But despite their fears, his action aroused in them a great respect for his simplicity and wealth.

"Have you heard," said one, "that the cadet quartered on Elias Vasilich has thrown a forty-ruble horse at Lukashka?"

"He's rich! . . ."

"Yes, I heard of it," replied another profoundly, "he must have done him some great service. We shall see what will come of this cadet. Eh! what luck that snatcher has!"

"Those cadets are crafty, awfully crafty," said a third. "See if he don't go setting fire to a building, or doing something!"

CHAPTER XXIII

PRINCE BELETSKY

OLENIN's life went on with monotonous regularity. He had little intercourse with the commanding officers or with his equals. The position of a rich cadet in the Caucasus was peculiarly advantageous in this respect. He was not sent out to work, or for training. As a reward for going on an expedition, he was recommended for a commission, and meanwhile he was left in peace. The officers regarded him as an aristocrat, and behaved toward him with dignity. Card playing and the officers' carousals accompanied by the soldier singers, of which he had had experience when he was with the detachment, did not seem to him attractive, and he also avoided the society and the life of the officers in the village. The life of officers stationed in a Cossack village has long had its own definite form. Just as every cadet or officer when in a fort regularly drinks porter, plays cards and discusses the rewards given for taking part in the expeditions, so in the Cossack villages he regularly drinks chikhir with his hosts, treats the girls to sweet-meats and honey, dangles after the Cossack women, and falls in love, and occasionally marries there. Olenin always took his own path and had an unconscious objection to the beaten tracks. And here, too, he did not follow the ruts of a Caucasian officer's life.

It came quite naturally to him to wake up at daybreak. After drinking tea and admiring from his porch the mountains, the morning, and Maryanka, he would put on a tattered ox-hide coat, sandals of soaked rawhide, buckle on a dagger, take a gun, with cigarettes and some lunch in a little bag, call his dog, and soon after five o'clock he would start for the forest beyond the village. Toward seven in the evening he returned tired and hungry, with five or six pheasants hanging from his belt (sometimes with some other animal) and with his bag of food and cigarettes untouched. If the thoughts in his head had lain like the lunch and cigarettes in the bag, one might have seen that during all those fourteen hours not a single thought had moved in it.

He returned morally fresh, strong, and perfectly happy, and he could not tell what he had been thinking about all the time. Were they ideas, memories, or dreams, that had been flitting through his mind? They were frequently all three. He would rouse himself and ask what he had been thinking about; and would see himself as a Cossack, working in a vineyard with his Cossack wife, or an abrek in the mountains, or a boar running away from himself. And all the time he kept peering and watching for a pheasant, a boar, or a deer.

In the evening, Daddy Eroshka would be sure to be sitting with him. Vanyusha would bring a jug of chikhir, and they would converse quietly, drink, and separate to go quite contentedly to bed. The next day he would again go shooting, again be healthily weary, again they would sit conversing and drink their fill, and again be happy. Sometimes, on a holiday or a day of rest, Olenin spent the whole day at home. Then his chief occupation was watching Maryanka, whose every movement, without realizing it himself, he followed greedily from his window or his porch. He regarded Maryanka and loved her (so he thought) just as he loved the beauty of the mountains and the sky, and he had no thought of entering into any relations with her. It seemed to him that between him and her such relations as there were between her and

the Cossack Lukashka, could not exist, and still less, such as often existed between rich officers and other Cossack girls. It seemed to him that if he tried to do as his fellow officers did, he would exchange his complete enjoyment of contemplation for an abyss of suffering, disillusionment and remorse. Besides, he had already achieved a triumph of self-sacrifice in connection with her, which had given him great pleasure; but above all he was in a way afraid of Maryanka, and would not for anything have ventured to utter a word of love to her lightly.

Once during the summer when Olenin had not gone out shooting but was sitting at home, quite unexpectedly a Moscow acquaintance, a very young man whom he had met in society, came in.

"Ah, *mon cher,* my dear fellow, how glad I was when I heard that you were here!" he began in his Moscow French, and he went on intermingling French words in his remarks. "They said, 'Olenin.' What Olenin? and I was so pleased. . . . Fancy fate bringing us together here! Well, and how are you? How? Why?" and Prince Beletsky told his whole story: how he had temporarily entered the regiment, how the Commander in Chief had offered to take him as an aid-de-camp, and how he would take up the post after this campaign, although personally he felt quite indifferent about it.

"Living here, in this hole, one must at least make a career—get a cross— or a rank—be transferred to the Guards. That is quite indispensable, not for myself, but for the sake of my relations and friends. The prince received me very well; he is a very decent fellow," said Beletsky, and went on unceasingly. "I have been recommended for the St. Ann's Cross, for the expedition. Now I shall stay here a bit until we start on the campaign. It's capital here. What women! Well, and how are you getting on? I was told by our captain, Startsev, you know, a kind-hearted, stupid creature. . . . Well, he said you were living like an awful savage, seeing no one! I quite understand you don't want to be mixed up with the set of officers we have here. I am so glad now, you and I will be able to see something of one another. I have put up at the police officer's house. There is such a girl there, Ustenka! I tell you, she is just charming."

And more and more French and Russian words came pouring forth from that world which Olenin thought he had left forever.

The general opinion about Beletsky was that he was a nice good-natured fellow. Perhaps he really was; but in spite of his pretty, good-natured face, Olenin thought him extremely unpleasant. He seemed just to exhale that filthiness which Olenin had forsworn. What vexed him most, was that he could not—had not the strength—abruptly to repulse this man, who came from that world: as if that old world he used to belong to had an irresistible claim on him. Olenin felt angry with Beletsky and with himself, yet, against his wish, he introduced French phrases into his own conversation, was interested in the Commander in Chief and in their Moscow acquaintances, and because he and Beletsky in this Cossack village both spoke French, he spoke contemptuously of their fellow officers, and of the Cossacks, and was friendly with Beletsky, promising to visit him and inviting him to drop in to see him. Olenin, however, did not himself go to see Beletsky.

Vanyusha for his part approved of Beletsky; remarking that he was a real gentleman.

Beletsky at once adopted the customary life of a rich officer in a Cossack village.

Before Olenin's eyes, in one month he came to be like an old resident of the village; he made the old men drunk, arranged evening parties, and himself went to parties arranged by the girls,—bragged of his conquests, and even got so far that, for some unknown reason, the women and girls began calling him grandad, and the Cossacks, to whom a man who loved wine and women was clearly understandable, got used to him and even liked him better than they did Olenin, who was a puzzle to them.

CHAPTER XXIV

DUSK

It was five in the morning. Vanyusha was in the porch heating the samovar, and using the leg of a long boot instead of bellows. Olenin had already ridden off to bathe in the Terek. (He had recently invented a new amusement: to swim his horse in the river.) His landlady was in her outhouse and the dense smoke of the kindling fire rose from the chimney. The girl was milking the buffalo cow in the shed. "Can't keep quiet, the damned thing!" came her impatient voice, followed by the rhythmical sound of milking.

From the street in front of the house.

horses' hoofs were heard clattering briskly, and Olenin, riding bareback on a handsome dark gray horse which was still wet and shining, rode up to the gate. Maryanka's handsome head, tied round with a red kerchief, appeared from the shed, and again disappeared. Olenin was wearing a red silk shirt, a white Circassian coat girdled with a strap which carried a dagger, and a tall cap. He sat his wet, well-fed horse with a slightly conscious elegance and, holding his gun at his back, stooped to open the gate. His hair was still wet, and his face shone with youth and health. He thought himself handsome, agile, and like a brave; but he was mistaken. To any experienced Caucasian, he was still only a soldier.

When he noticed that the girl had put out her head, he stooped with particular smartness, threw open the gate and, tightening the reins, swished his whip and entered the yard. "Is tea ready, Vanyusha?" he cried gayly, not looking at the door of the shed. He felt with pleasure how his fine horse, pressing down its flanks, pulling at the bridle and with every muscle quivering, and with each foot ready to leap over the fence, pranced on the hard clay of the yard. *"C'est prêt,"* answered Vanyusha. Olenin felt as if Maryanka's beautiful head was still looking out of the shed, but he did not turn to look at her. As he jumped down from his horse he made an awkward movement, and caught his gun against the porch and turned a frightened look toward the shed, where there was no one to be seen and whence the sound of milking could still be heard.

Soon after he had entered the hut he came out again and sat down with his pipe and a book on the side of the porch which was not yet exposed to the rays of the sun. He meant not to go anywhere before dinner that day, and to write some long-postponed letters; but somehow he felt disinclined to leave his place in the porch, and he was as reluctant to go back into the hut as if it had been a prison. The housewife had heated her oven, and the girl, having driven the cattle, had come back and was collecting kisyak and heaping it up along the fence. Olenin went on reading but did not understand a word of what was written in the book that lay open before him. He kept lifting his eyes from it and looking at the powerful young woman who was moving about. Whether she stepped into the moist morning shadow thrown by the house, or went out into the middle of the yard lit up by the joyous young light so that the whole of her stately figure in its bright-colored garment gleamed in the sunshine and cast a black shadow—always he feared to lose any one of her movements. It delighted him to see how freely and gracefully her figure bent: into what folds her only garment, a pink smock, draped itself on her bosom and down her shapely legs; how she drew herself up and her tight-drawn smock showed the outline of her breathing bosom; how the soles of her narrow feet in her worn red slippers stood on the ground without altering their shape; how her strong arms with the sleeves rolled up, exerting the muscles, used the spade almost as if in anger, and how her deep dark eyes sometimes glanced at him. Though the delicate brows frowned, yet her eyes expressed pleasure, and a knowledge of her own beauty.

"I say, Olenin, have you been up long?" said Beletsky, as he entered the yard, dressed in the coat of a Caucasian officer.

"Ah, Beletsky," replied Olenin, holding out his hand. "How is it you are out so early?"

"I had to. I was driven out; we are having a ball to-night. Maryanka,—of course you'll come to Ustenka's?" he added, turning to the girl. Olenin felt surprised that Beletsky could address this woman so easily. But Maryanka, as though she had not heard him, bent her head, and throwing the spade across her shoulder, went with her firm masculine tread toward the outhouse.

"She's shy, the wench is shy," Beletsky called after her. "Shy of you," he added as, smiling gayly, he ran up the steps of the porch.

"How is it you are having a ball, and have been driven out?"

"It is at Ustenka's, at my landlady's, that the ball is, and you two are invited. A ball consists of a pie and a gathering of girls."

"What should we do there?"

Beletsky smiled knowingly and winked, jerking his head in the direction of the outhouse into which Maryanka had disappeared.

Olenin shrugged his shoulders and blushed.

"Well, really, you are a strange fellow!" said he.

"Come now, don't pretend!"

Olenin frowned, and Beletsky noticing this, smiled insinuatingly.

"Oh, come, what do you mean?" he said, "living in the same house—and such a fine girl, a splendid girl, a perfect beauty——"

"Wonderfully beautiful! I never saw such a woman before," replied Olenin.

"Well, then?" said Beletsky, quite unable to understand the situation.

"It may be strange," replied Olenin, "but why should I not say what is true? Since I have lived here, women don't seem to exist for me. And it is so good, really! Now what can there be in common between us and women like these? Eroshka—that's a different matter! He and I have a passion in common—sport."

"There now! In common! And what have I in common with Amalia Ivanovna? It's the same thing! You may say they're not very clean; that's another matter . . . *A la guerre, comme à la guerre!* . . ."

"But I have never known any Amalia Ivanovnas, and have never known how to behave with women of that sort," replied Olenin. "One cannot respect them; but these I do respect."

"Well, go on respecting them! Who wants to prevent you?"

Olenin did not reply. He evidently wanted to complete what he had begun to say. It was very near to his heart.

"I know I'm an exception. . . ." He was visibly confused. "But my life has so shaped itself that I not only see no necessity to renounce my rules, but that I could not live here, let alone live as happily as I am doing, were I to live as you do. Therefore I look for something quite different from what you look for."

Beletsky raised his eyebrows incredulously. "Anyhow, come to me this evening; Maryanka will be there and I will make you acquainted. Do come, please! If you feel dull you can go away. Will you come?"

"I would come, but to speak frankly, I am afraid of being seriously carried away."

"Oh, oh, oh!" shouted Beletsky. "Only come, and I will comfort you. Will you? On your word?"

"I would come, but really I don't understand what we shall do; what part we shall play!"

"Please, I beg of you. You will come?"

"Yes, perhaps I'll come," said Olenin.

"Really now! Charming women such as one sees nowhere else, and to live like a monk! What an idea! Why spoil your life and not make use of what is at hand? Have you heard that our company is ordered to Vozdvizhensk?"

"Hardly. I was told the 8th Company would be sent there," said Olenin.

"No. I have had a letter from the aid-de-camp. He writes that the Prince himself will take part in the campaign. I am very glad I shall see something of him. I'm beginning to get tired of this place."

"I hear we shall start on a raid soon."

"I have not heard of it; but I have heard that Krinovitsin has received the Order of St. Ann, for a raid. He expected a lieutenancy," said Beletsky, laughing. "He was let in! He has set off for headquarters."

It was growing dusk and Olenin began thinking about the party. The invitation he had received worried him. He felt inclined to go, but what might take place there seemed strange, absurd and even rather alarming. He knew that neither Cossack men nor older women, nor anyone besides the girls, were to be there. What was going to happen? How was he to behave? What would they talk about? What connection was there between him and those wild Cossack girls? Beletsky had told him of such curious cynical, and yet rigid relations. It seemed strange to think that he would be there in the same hut with Maryanka and perhaps might have to talk to her. It seemed to him impossible when he remembered her majestic bearing. But Beletsky spoke of it as if it were all perfectly simple. "Is it possible that Beletsky will treat Maryanka in the same way? That is interesting," thought he. "No, better not go. It's all so horrid, so vulgar, and above all—it leads to nothing!" But again he was worried by the question of what would take place; and besides, he felt as if bound by a promise. He went out without having made up his mind one way or the other; but he walked as far as Beletsky's, and went in there.

The hut in which Beletsky lived was like Olenin's. It was raised nearly five feet from the ground on wooden piles, and had two rooms. In the first (which Olenin entered by the steep flight of steps) feather beds, rugs, blankets and cushions were tastefully and handsomely arranged, Cossack fashion, along the main wall. On the side wall hung brass basins and weapons, while on the floor, under a bench, lay watermelons and pumpkins. In the second room there was a big brick oven, a table, and sectarian icons. It was here that Beletsky was quartered, with his camp bed and his pack and trunks. His weapons hung on the wall with a little rug behind them, and on the table were his toilet appliances and some portraits. A silk dressing gown had been thrown on to the bench. Beletsky himself, clean and good looking, lay on the bed in his underclothing, reading Les Trois Mousquetaires.

He jumped up.

"There you see how I have arranged things. Fine! Well, that's right, that you have come. They are working furiously. Do you know what the pie is made of? Dough, with a stuffing of pork and grapes. But that's not the point. You just look at the commotion out there!"

And really, on looking out of the window they saw an unusual bustle going on in the hut. Girls ran in and out, now for one thing and now for another. "Will it soon be ready?" cried Beletsky.

"Very soon! Why? Is Grandad hungry?" and from the hut came the sounds of ringing laughter.

Ustenka, plump, small, rosy, and pretty, with her sleeves turned up, ran into Beletsky's hut to fetch some plates.

"Get away, or I shall smash the plates!" she squeaked, escaping from Beletsky. "You'd better come and help," she shouted, laughing, to Olenin. "And don't forget to get some refreshments for the girls." ("Refreshments" meaning spice-bread and sweets.)

"And has Maryanka come?"

"Of course! She brought some dough."

"Do you know," said Beletsky, "if one were to dress Ustenka up and clean and polish her up a bit, she'd be better than all our beauties. Have you ever seen that Cossack woman who married a colonel; she was charming! Borsheva? What dignity! Where do they get it. . . ."

"I have not seen Borsheva, but I think nothing could be better than the costume they wear here."

"Ah, I'm first rate at fitting into any kind of life," said Beletsky with a sigh of pleasure. "I'll go and see what they are up to." He threw his dressing gown over his shoulders and ran out, shouting, "And you look after the 'refreshments.' "

Olenin sent Beletsky's orderly to buy spice-bread and honey; but it suddenly seemed to him so disgusting to give money (as if he were bribing some one) that he gave no definite reply to the orderly's question: "How much spice-bread with peppermint, and how much with honey?"

"Just as you please."

"Shall I spend all the money?" asked the old soldier, impressively. "The peppermint is dearer. It's sixteen kopeks."

"Yes, yes, spend it all," answered Olenin, and sat down by the window, surprised that his heart was thumping as if he were preparing himself for something serious and wicked. He heard screaming and shrieking in the girls' hut when Beletsky went there, and a few moments later saw how, accompanied by shrieks, bustle, and laughter, he jumped out and ran down the steps. "Turned out," he said.

A little later Ustenka entered, and solemnly invited her visitors to come in: announcing that all was ready.

When they came into the room they saw that everything was really ready. Ustenka was rearranging the cushions along the wall. On the table, which was covered by a disproportionately small cloth, was a decanter of shikhir and some dried fish. The room smelt of dough and grapes. Some half dozen girls in smart tunics, with their heads not covered, as usual, with kerchiefs, were huddled together in a corner behind the oven, whispering, giggling, and spluttering with laughter.

"I humbly beg you to do honor to my

patron saint," said Ustenka, inviting her guests to the table.

Olenin noticed Maryanka among the group of girls, who without exception were all handsome, and he felt vexed and hurt that he met her in such vulgar and awkward circumstances. He felt stupid and awkward, and made up his mind to do what Beletsky did. Beletsky stepped to the table somewhat solemnly, yet with confidence and ease, drank a glass of wine to Ustenka's health, and invited the others to do the same. Ustenka announced that girls don't drink.

"We might, with a little honey," exclaimed a voice from among the group of girls.

The orderly, who had just returned with the honey and spice-cakes, was called in. He looked askance (whether with envy or with contempt) at the gentlemen, who in his opinion were on the spree; and carefully and conscientiously handed over to them a piece of honeycomb and the cakes, wrapped up in a piece of grayish paper, and began explaining circumstantially all about the prices and the change, but Beletsky sent him away. Having mixed honey with wine in the glasses, and having lavishly scattered the three pounds of spice-cakes on the table, Beletsky dragged the girls from their corners by force, made them sit down at the table, and began distributing the cakes among them. Olenin involuntarily noticed how Maryanka's sunburnt but small hand closed on two round peppermint nuts and one brown one, and that she did not know what to do with them. The conversation was halting and ungenial, in spite of Ustenka's and Beletsky's free and easy manner and their wish to enliven the company. Olenin faltered and tried to think of something to say, feeling that he was exciting curiosity and perhaps provoking ridicule and infecting the others with his shyness. He blushed, and it seemed to him that Maryanka in particular was feeling uncomfortable. "Most likely they are expecting us to give them some money," thought he. "How are we to do it? And how can we manage quickest to give it and get away?"

CHAPTER XXV

USTENKA

"How is it you don't know your own lodger?" said Beletsky, addressing Maryanka.

"How is one to know him if he never comes to see us?" answered Maryanka with a look at Olenin.

Olenin felt frightened, he did not know of what. He flushed, and, hardly knowing what he was saying, remarked:

"I'm afraid of your mother. She gave me such a scolding the first time I went in."

Maryanka burst out laughing.

"And so you were frightened?" she said; and glanced at him and turned away.

It was the first time Olenin had seen the whole of her beautiful face. Till then he had seen her with her kerchief covering her to the eyes. It was not for nothing that she was reckoned the beauty of the village.

Ustenka was a pretty girl, small, plump, rosy, with merry brown eyes and red lips which were perpetually smiling and chattering. Maryanka, on the contrary, was certainly not pretty, but beautiful. Her features might have been considered too masculine and almost harsh, had it not been for her tall stately figure, her powerful chest and shoulders, and especially the severe yet tender expression of her long dark eyes, which were darkly shadowed beneath their black brows, and for the gentle expression of her mouth and smile. She rarely smiled, but her smile was always striking. She seemed to radiate virginal strength and health. All the girls were good-looking, but they themselves, and Beletsky, and the orderly when he brought in the spice-cakes, all involuntarily gazed at Maryanka, and anyone addressing the girls was sure to address her. She seemed a proud and happy queen among them.

Beletsky, trying to keep up the spirit of the party, chattered incessantly, made the girls hand round chikhir, fooled about with them, and kept making improper remarks in French about Maryanka's beauty to Olenin, calling her "yours" (*la vôtre*), and advising him to behave as he did himself. Olenin felt more and more uncomfortable. He was devising an excuse to get out and run away, when Beletsky announced that Ustenka, whose saint's day it was, must offer chikhir to everybody with a kiss. She consented, on condition that they should put money on her plate, as is the custom at weddings.

"What fiend brought me to this disgusting feast!" thought Olenin, rising to go away.

"Where are you off to?"

"I'll fetch some tobacco," he said, meaning to escape; but Beletsky seized his hand, saying in French, "I have some money, one can't go away."

"One has to pay here," thought Olenin bitterly, vexed at his own awkwardness. "Can't I really behave like Bel-

etsky? I ought not to have come, but once I am here I must not spoil their fun. I must drink like a Cossack," and taking the wooden bowl (holding about eight tumblers) he almost filled it with chikhir and drank it up. The girls looked at him, surprised and almost frightened, while he drank. It seemed to them strange and not right. Ustenka brought them another glass each, and kissed them both.

"There, girls, now we'll have some fun," she said, clinking on the plate the four rubles the men had put there. Olenin no longer felt awkward, but became talkative.

"Now, Maryanka, it's your turn to offer us wine and a kiss," said Beletsky, seizing her hand.

"Yes, I'll give you such a kiss!" she said, playfully, preparing to strike at him.

"One can kiss Grandad without payment," said another girl.

"There's a wise girl," said Beletsky, kissing the struggling girl. "No, you must offer it," he insisted, addressing Maryanka. "Offer a glass to your lodger."

And taking her by the hand he led her to the bench and sat her down beside Olenin.

"What a beauty," he said, turning her head to see it in profile.

Maryanka did not resist, but, proudly smiling, turned her long eyes toward Olenin.

"A beautiful girl," repeated Beletsky, and Maryanka's look seemed to affirm, "Yes, see what a beauty I am."

Without considering what he was doing, Olenin embraced Maryanka and was going to kiss her, but she suddenly extricated herself, upsetting Beletsky and pushing the top off the table, and sprang away toward the oven. There was much shouting and laughter. Then Beletsky whispered something to the girls, and suddenly they all ran out into the passage and locked the door behind them.

"Why did you kiss Beletsky and won't kiss me?" asked Olenin.

"Oh, just so. I don't want to; that's all!" she answered, pouting and frowning. "He's Grandad," she added with a smile. She went to the door and began to bang at it. "Why have you locked the door, you devils?"

"Well, let them be there, and us be here," said Olenin, drawing closer to her.

She frowned, and sternly pushed him away with her hand. And again she appeared so majestically handsome to Olenin, that he came to his senses and felt ashamed of what he was doing. He went to the door, and began pulling at it himself. "Beletsky! Open the door! What a stupid joke!"

Maryanka again gave a bright, happy laugh. "Ah, you're afraid of me?" she said.

"Yes, you know you're as cross as your mother."

"You spent more of your time with Eroshka; that will make the girls love you!" And she smiled, looking straight and close into his eyes. He did not know what to reply.

"And if I were to come to see you—" he let fall.

"That would be a different matter," she replied, tossing her head.

At that moment Beletsky pushed the door open, and Maryanka sprang away from Olenin, and in doing so her thigh struck his leg. "It's all nonsense what I have been thinking about, love and

self-sacrifice and Lukashka. Happiness is the one thing. He who is happy is right," flashed through Olenin's mind, and with a strength unexpected to himself, he seized and kissed the beautiful Maryanka on her temple and her cheek. Maryanka was not angry, but only burst into a loud laugh and ran out to the other girls.

That was the end of the party. Ustenka's mother, returned from her work, gave all the girls a scolding, and turned them all out.

CHAPTER XXVI

RADIANCE

"YES," thought Olenin, as he walked home. "I need only slacken the reins a bit and I might fall desperately in love with this Cossack girl." He went to bed with these thoughts, but expected it all to blow over, and that he would continue to live as before. But the old life did not return. His relations to Maryanka were changed. The wall that had separated them was broken down. Olenin now greeted her every time they met.

The master of the house having returned to collect the rent, on hearing of Olenin's wealth and generosity, invited him to his hut. The old woman received him kindly and, from the day of the party onwards, Olenin often went in of an evening and sat with them till late at night. He seemed to be living in the village just as he used to, but within him everything had changed. He spent his days in the forest, and toward eight o'clock, when it began to grow dusk, he would go to see his hosts, alone or with Daddy Eroshka. They grew so used to him that they were surprised when he stayed away. He paid well for his wine, and was a quiet fellow. Vanyusha would bring him his tea, and he would sit down in a corner near the oven. The old woman did not mind him, but went on with her work, and they talked over their tea or their chikhir about Cossack affairs, about the neighbors, or about Russia: Olenin relating and the others inquiring. Sometimes he brought a book and read to himself. Maryanka crouched like a wild goat with her feet drawn up under her, sometimes on the top of the oven, sometimes in a dark corner. She did not take part in the conversations, but Olenin saw her eyes and face and heard her moving, or cracking sunflower seeds, and he felt that she listened with her whole being when he spoke, and was aware of his presence while he silently read to himself. Sometimes he thought her eyes were fixed on him and, meeting their radiance, he involuntarily became silent and gazed at her. Then she would instantly hide her face, and he would pretend to be deep in conversation with the old woman, while he listened all the time to her breathing and to her every movement, and waited for her to look at him again. In the presence of others she was generally bright and friendly with him, but when they were alone together she was shy and rough. Sometimes he came in before Maryanka had returned home. Suddenly he would hear her firm footsteps and catch a glimmer of her blue cotton smock at the open door. Then she would step into the middle of the hut, catch sight of him, and her eyes would give a scarcely perceptible kindly smile, and he would feel happy and frightened.

He neither sought for nor wished for anything from her, but every day her presence became more and more necessary to him.

Olenin had so fully entered into the life of the Cossack village that his past seemed quite foreign to him. As to the future, especially a future outside the world in which he was now living, it did not interest him at all. When he received letters from home, from relatives and friends, he was offended by the evident distress with which they regarded him as a lost man, while he, in his village, considered those as lost who did not live as he was living. He felt sure he would never repent of having broken away from his former surroundings and of having settled down in this village to such a solitary and original life. When out on expeditions and when quartered at one of the forts, he felt happy too; but it was here, from under Daddy Eroshka's wing, from the forest and from his hut at the end of the village, and especially when he thought of Maryanka and Lukashka, that he seemed to see the falseness of his former life. That falseness used to rouse his indignation even before, but now it seemed inexpressibly vile and ridiculous. Here he felt freer and freer every day, and more and more of a man. The Caucasus now appeared entirely different to what his imaginations had painted it. He had found nothing at all like his dreams, nor like the descriptions of the Caucasus he had heard and read. "There are none of all those chestnut trees, precipices, Amalet Beks, heroes or villains," thought he. "The people live as nature lives: they die, are born, unite, and more are born—they fight, eat and drink, rejoice and die, without any restrictions but those that nature imposes on sun and grass, on animal and

tree. They have no other laws." Therefore, these people, compared to himself,
appeared to him beautiful, strong, and
free, and the sight of them made him
feel ashamed and sorry for himself.
Often it seriously occurred to him to
throw up everything, to get registered
as a Cossack, to buy a hut and cattle,
and marry a Cossack woman (only not
Maryanka, whom he conceded to Lukashka), and to live with Daddy
Eroshka, and go shooting and fishing
with him, and go with the Cossacks on
their expeditions. "Why ever don't I
do it? What am I waiting for?" he
asked himself, and he egged himself on,
and shamed himself. "Am I afraid of
doing what I hold to be reasonable and
right? Is the wish to be a simple Cossack, to live close to nature, not to injure anyone, but even to do good to
others, more stupid than my former
dreams, such as those of becoming a
minister of state, or a colonel?" but a
voice seemed to say that he should wait
and not take any decision. He was held
back by a dim consciousness that he
could not live altogether like Eroshka
and Lukashka, because he had a different idea of happiness—he was held
back by the thought that happiness lies
in self-sacrifice. What he had done for
Lukashka continued to give him joy. He
kept looking for occasions to sacrifice
himself for others, but did not meet
with them. Sometimes he forgot this
newly discovered recipe for happiness,
and considered himself capable of iden-
tifying his life with Daddy Eroshka's,
but he then quickly bethought himself,
and promptly clutched at the idea of
conscious self-sacrifice, and from that
basis looked calmly and proudly at all
men and at their happiness.

CHAPTER XXVII

HIS BRAGGING

JUST before the vintage, Lukashka
came on horseback to see Olenin. He
looked more dashing than ever.

"Well? Are you getting married?"
asked Olenin, greeting him merrily.

Lukashka gave no direct reply.
"There, I've exchanged your horse across
the river. There *is* a horse! A Kabarda
horse from the Lov stud. I know
horses."

They examined the new horse and
made him caracole about the yard. The
horse really was an exceptionally fine
one, a broad and long bay gelding, with
glossy coat, thick silky tail and the soft
fine mane and crest of a thoroughbred.
He was so well fed that "you might go
to sleep on his back" as Lukashka expressed it. His hoofs, eyes, teeth, were
exquisitely shaped and sharply outlined,
as one only finds them in very pure-bred
horses. Olenin could not help admiring
the horse; he had not yet met with such
a beauty in the Caucasus.

"And how it goes!" said Lukashka,
patting its neck. "What a step! And
so clever—he simply runs after his master."

"Did you have to add much to make
the exchange?" asked Olenin.

"I did not count it," answered Lukashka with a smile. "I got him from a
kunak."

"A wonderfully beautiful horse! What
would you take for it?" asked Olenin.

"I have been offered a hundred and
fifty rubles for it, but I'll give it you
for nothing," said Lukashka, merrily.
"Only say the word, and it's yours. I'll
unsaddle it, and you may take it. Only

give me some sort of a horse for my duties."

"No, on no account."

"Well, then, here is a dagger I've brought you," said Lukashka, unfastening his girdle and taking out one of the two daggers which hung from it. "I got it from across the river."

"Oh, thank you!"

"And mother has promised to bring you some grapes herself."

"That's quite unnecessary. We'll balance up some day. You see I don't offer you any money for the dagger!"

"How could you, we are kunaks. It's just the same as when Girey Khan, across the river, took me into his home, and said, 'Choose what you like!' So I took this sword. It's our custom."

They went into the hut and had a drink.

"Are you staying here awhile?" asked Olenin.

"No, I have come to say good-by. They are sending me from the cordon to a company beyond the Terek. I am going to-night with my comrade, Nazarka."

"And when is the wedding to be?"

"I shall be coming back for the betrothal, and then I shall return to the company again," Lukashka replied, reluctantly.

"What, and see nothing of your betrothed?"

"Just so—what is the good of looking at her? When you go on campaign, ask in our company for Lukashka the Broad. But what a lot of boars there are in our parts! I've killed two. I'll take you. Well, good-by! Christ save you." Lukashka mounted his horse, and without calling on Maryanka, rode caracol-

ing down the street, where Nazarka was already awaiting him.

"I say, shan't we call round?" asked Nazarka, winking in the direction of Yamka's house.

"That's a good one!" said Lukashka. "Here, take my horse to her, and, if I don't come soon, give him some hay. I shall reach the company by the morning."

"Hasn't the cadet given you anything more?"

"I am thankful to have paid him back with a dagger—he was going to ask for the horse," said Lukashka, dismounting and handing over the horse to Nazarka.

He darted into the yard, past Olenin's very window, and came up to the window of the teacher's hut. It was already quite dark. Maryanka, wearing only her smock, was combing her hair, preparing for bed. "It's I—" whispered the Cossack.

Maryanka's look was severely indifferent; but her face suddenly brightened up when she heard her name. She opened the window and leaned out, frightened and joyous.

"What—what do you want?" she said.

"Open!" uttered Lukashka. "Let me in for a minute. I am so sick of waiting! It's awful!"

He took hold of her head through the window and kissed her.

"Really, do open!"

"Why do you talk nonsense? I've told you I won't. Have you come for long?"

He did not answer, but went on kissing her, and she did not ask again.

"There, through the window, one

can't even hug you properly," said Lukashka.

"Maryanka dear!" came the voice of her mother, "who is that with you?"

Lukashka took off his cap, which might have been seen, and crouched down by the window.

"Go, be quick!" whispered Maryanka. "Lukashka has called round," she answered; "he is asking for Daddy."

"Well, then send him here!"

"He's gone; says he's in a hurry."

In fact, Lukashka, stooping as with big strides he passed under the windows, ran out through the yard and toward Yamka's house, unseen by anyone but Olenin. After drinking two bowls of chikhir he and Nazarka rode away to the outpost. The night was warm, dark, and calm. They rode in silence; only the footfall of their horses was heard. Lukashka started a song about the Cossack, Mingal, but stopped before he had finished the first verse, and, after a pause, turning to Nazarka, said:

"I say, she wouldn't let me in!"

"Oh?" rejoined Nazarka. "I knew she wouldn't. D'you know what Yamka told me? The cadet has begun going to their house. Daddy Eroshka brags that he got a gun from the cadet for getting him Maryanka."

"He lies, the old devil!" said Lukashka, angrily. "She's not such a girl. If he does not look out, I'll whallop the devil's sides," and he began his favorite song:

"From the village of Izmaylov,
From the master's favorite garden,
A bright-eyed falcon from his cage once
  flew there,
And soon after him a huntsman young
  came riding.

With his hand he beckoned to the
  bright-eyed falcon.
The bright-eyed falcon then made
  answer:
'In a golden cage you knew not how
  to keep me,
On your right hand you knew not how
  to hold me.
So now I'll fly to the blue sea, far, far
  away,
And there I will kill a white swan for
  myself,
And I will get my fill of the sweet
  swan-flesh.'"

CHAPTER XXVIII

BETROTHAL

The betrothal was taking place in the teacher's hut. Lukashka had returned to the village, but had not been to see Olenin; and Olenin had not gone to the betrothal though he had been invited. He was sad, as he had never been since he settled in this Cossack village. He had seen Lukashka earlier in the evening, and he was worried by the question why Lukashka was so cold toward him. Olenin shut himself up in his hut and began writing in his diary as follows:

"Many things have I pondered over lately, and much have I changed," wrote he, "and I have come back to the copybook maxim: The one way to be happy is to love, to love self-denyingly, to love everybody and everything; to spread a web of love on all sides and to take all who come into it. In this way I caught Vanyusha, Daddy Eroshka, Lukashka, and Maryanka."

As Olenin was finishing this sentence, Daddy Eroshka entered the room.

Eroshka was in the happiest frame of mind. A few evenings before this, Olenin had gone to see him, and had found him with a proud and happy face deftly skinning the carcass of a boar with a small knife in the yard. The dogs (Lyamka his pet among them) were lying close by, watching what he was doing, and gently wagging their tails. The little boys were respectfully looking at him through the fence, and not even teasing him as was their wont. His women neighbors, who were as a rule not too gracious toward him, greeted him and brought him, one a jug of chikhir, another some clotted cream, and a third a little flour. The next day Eroshka sat in his store-room, all covered with blood, and distributed pounds of boar flesh, taking in payment money from some and wine from others. His face clearly expressed, "God has sent me luck. I have killed a boar; so now I am wanted." Consequently, he naturally began to drink, and had gone on for four days, never leaving the village. Besides which he had had something to drink at the betrothal.

He came to Olenin quite drunk: his face red, his beard tangled, but wearing a new beshmet trimmed with gold braid; and he brought with him a balalayka which he had obtained beyond the river. He had long promised Olenin this treat, and felt in the mood for it, so that he was sorry to find Olenin writing.

"Write on, write on, my lad," he whispered, as if he thought that a spirit sat between him and the paper and must not be frightened away, and he softly and silently sat down on the floor. When Daddy Eroshka was drunk, his favorite position was on the floor.

Olenin looked round, ordered some wine to be brought, and continued to write. Eroshka found it dull to drink by himself, and he wished to talk.

"I've been to the betrothal at the Teacher's. But there! They're shwine! —Don't want them!—Have come to you."

"And where did you get your balalayka?" asked Olenin, still writing.

"I've been beyond the river and got it there, brother mine," he answered, also very quietly. "I'm a master at it. Tartar or Cossack, squire or peasant songs, any kind you please."

Olenin looked at him again, smiled, and went on writing.

That smile emboldened the old man.

"Come, leave off, my lad, leave off!" he said with sudden firmness.

"Well, perhaps I will."

"Come, people have injured you, but leave them alone, spit at them! Come, what's the use of writing and writing, what's the good?"

And he tried to mimic Olenin by tapping the floor with his thick fingers, and then twisted his big face to express contempt.

"What's the good of writing quibbles! Better have a spree and show you're a man!"

No other conception of writing found place in his head, except that of legal chicanery. Olenin burst out laughing and so did Eroshka. Then, jumping up from the floor, the latter began to show off his skill on the balalayka, and to sing Tartar songs.

"Why write, my good fellow! You'd better listen to what I'll sing to you. When you're dead you'll not hear any more songs. Make merry now!"

First he sang a song of his own composing, accompanied by a dance:

"Ah, dee, dee, dee, dee, dee, dim,
Say, where did they last see him?
In a booth, at the fair,
He was selling pins, there."

Then he sang a song he had learned from his former sergeant major:

"Deep I fell in love on Monday,
Tuesday nothing did but sigh,
Wednesday I popped the question,
Thursday waited her reply.
Friday, late, it came at last,
Then all hope for me was past!
Saturday my life to take
I determined like a man,
But for my salvation's sake
Sunday morning changed my plan!"

Then he sang again:

"Oh, dee, dee, dee, dee, dee, dim,
Say, where did they last see him."

And after that, winking, shrugging his shoulders and footing it to the tune he sang:

"I will kiss you and embrace,
Ribbons red twine round you;
And I'll call you little Grace.
Oh! you little Grace, now do
Tell me, do you love me true?"

And he became so excited that with a sudden daring movement he started dancing all alone around the room.

Songs like "Dee, dee, dee"—"gentlemen's songs"—he sang for Olenin's benefit, but after drinking three more tumblers of chikhir he remembered old times and began singing real Cossack and Tartar songs. In the midst of one of his favorite songs his voice suddenly trembled, and he ceased singing, and only continued strumming on the balalayka.

"Oh, my dear friend!" he said.

The peculiar sound of his voice made Olenin look round. The old man was weeping. Tears stood in his eyes, and one tear was running down his cheek. "You are gone, my young days, and will never come back!" he said, blubbering and halting. "Drink, why don't you drink!" he suddenly shouted with a deafening roar, without wiping away his tears.

There was one Tartar song that specially moved him. It had few words, but its charm lay in the sad refrain. "Ay day, dalalay!" Eroshka translated the words of the song: "A youth drove his sheep from the aoul to the mountains: the Russians came and burnt the aoul, they killed all the men, and took all the women into bondage. The youth returned from the mountains. Where the aoul had stood was an empty space; his mother not there, nor his brothers, nor his house; one tree alone was left standing. The youth sat beneath the tree and wept. 'Alone like thee, alone am I left,'" and Eroshka began singing: "Ay day, dalalay!" and the old man repeated several times this wailing, heart-rending refrain.

When he had finished the refrain, Eroshka suddenly seized a gun that hung on the wall, rushed out into the yard, and fired off both barrels into the air. Then again he began, more dolefully, his "Ay day, dalalay—ah, ah," and ceased.

Olenin followed him into the porch

and looked up into the starry sky in the direction where the shots had flashed. In the Teacher's house there were lights, and the sounds of voices. In the yard girls were crowding round the porch and the windows, and running backwards and forwards between the hut and the outhouse. Some Cossacks rushed out of the hut, and could not refrain from shouting, reëchoing the refrain of Daddy Eroshka's song and his shots.

"Why are you not at the betrothal?" asked Olenin.

"Never mind them! Never mind them!" muttered the old man, who had evidently been offended by something there. "Don't like them, I don't. Oh, those people! Come back into the hut! Let them make merry by themselves and we'll make merry by ourselves."

Olenin went in.

"And Lukashka, is he happy? Won't he come to see me?" he asked.

"What, Lukashka? They've lied to him and said I am getting his girl for you," whispered the old man. "But what's the girl? She will be ours if we want her. Give enough money—and she's ours. I'll fix it up for you. Really!"

"No, Daddy, money can do nothing if she does not love me. You'd better not talk like that!"

"We are not loved, you and I. We are forlorn," suddenly said Daddy Eroshka, and again he began to cry.

Listening to the old man's talk, Olenin had drunk more than usual. "So now my Lukashka is happy," thought he; yet he felt sad. The old man had drunk so much that evening that he fell down on the floor, and Vanyusha had to call soldiers in to help,

and spat as they dragged the old man out. He was so angry with the old man for his bad behavior that he did not even say a single French word.

CHAPTER XXIX

AUGUST

It was August. For days the sky had been cloudless; the sun scorched unbearably, and from early morning the warm wind raised a whirl of hot sand from the sand drifts and from the road, and bore it in the air through the reeds, the trees, and the village.

The grass and the leaves on the trees were covered with dust; the roads and dried-up salt marshes were baked so hard that they rang when trodden on. The water had long since subsided in the Terek, and rapidly vanished and dried up in the ditches. The slimy banks of the pond near the village were trodden bare by the cattle, and all day long you could hear the splashing of water, and the shouting of bathing girls and boys. The sand drifts and the reeds were already drying up in the steppes, and the cattle, lowing, ran into the fields in the daytime. The boars migrated into the distant reed beds and to the hills beyond the Terek. Mosquitoes and gnats swarmed in thick clouds over the lowlands and villages. The snow peaks were hidden in gray mist. The air was rarefied and smoky. It was said that abreks had crossed the now shallow river, and were prowling on this side of it. Every night the sun set in a glowing red blaze. It was the busiest time of the year. The villagers all swarmed in the plantations and the vineyards. The vineyards thickly overgrown with twining verdure lay in cool, deep shade. Everywhere between the broad translucent leaves, ripe, heavy, black clusters peeped out. Along the dusty road from the vineyards, slowly moved the creaking carts heaped with black grapes. Clusters of them, crushed by the wheels, lay in the dirt. Boys and girls in smocks stained with grape juice, with grapes in their hands and mouths, ran after their mothers. On the road you continually came across tattered laborers with baskets of grapes on their powerful shoulders; Cossack maidens, wrapped in kerchiefs to their eyes, drove bullocks harnessed to carts laden high with grapes. Soldiers who happened to meet these carts, asked for grapes, and these maidens, clambering up without stopping their carts, would take an armful of grapes and drop them into the skirts of the soldiers' coats. In some homesteads they had already begun pressing the grapes; and the smell of the emptied skins filled the air. One saw the blood-red troughs in the penthouses in the yards, and Nogay laborers with their trousers rolled up and their legs stained with the juice. Grunting pigs gorged themselves with the empty skins, and rolled about in them. The flat roofs of the outhouses were all spread over with black clusters that were drying in the sun. Daws and magpies crowded round the roofs, picking the seeds from the grapes and fluttering from one place to another.

The fruits of the year's labor were being merrily gathered in; and this year the fruit was unusually fine and plentiful.

In the shady green vineyards, amid a sea of vines, on all sides laughter, songs, merriment, and the voices of women were to be heard and glimpses of their bright-colored garments could be seen.

Just at noon, Maryanka was sitting in their vineyard in the shade of a peach tree, getting out the family dinner from under an unharnessed cart. Opposite her, on a spread-out horse cloth, sat the Teacher (who had returned from the school) washing his hands by pouring water on them from a little jug. Her little brother, who had just come straight out of the pond, stood wiping his face with his wide sleeves, gazed anxiously at his sister and his mother and breathed deeply, awaiting his dinner. The old mother, with her sleeves rolled up over her strong sunburnt arms, was arranging grapes, dried fish, and clotted cream on a little low circular Tartar table. The Teacher wiped his hands, took off his cap, crossed himself, and moved nearer to the table. The boy seized the jug and eagerly began to drink. The mother and daughter crossed their legs under them and sat down by the table. Even in the shade it was intolerably hot. The air above the vineyard smelt unpleasant: the strong warm wind passing amid the branches brought no coolness, but only monotonously bent the tops of the pear, peach, and mulberry trees with which the vineyard was sprinkled. The Teacher, having crossed himself once more, took a little jug of chikhir that stood behind him covered with a vine leaf, and having had a drink from the mouth of the jug passed it to the old woman. He had nothing on over his shirt, which was unfastened at the neck, and showing his shaggy muscular chest. His fine-featured cunning face looked cheerful; neither in his attitude nor in his words was his usual wiliness to be seen; he was cheerful and natural.

"Shall we finish the bit beyond the shed to-night?" he asked, wiping his wet beard.

"We'll manage it," replied his wife, "if only the weather does not hinder us. The Demkins have not half finished yet," she added. "Only Ustenka is at work there, wearing herself out."

"What can you expect of them?" said the old man proudly.

"Here, have a drink, Maryanka dear!" said the old woman, passing the jug to the girl. "God willing, we'll have enough to pay for the wedding feast," added the old woman.

"That's not yet awhile," said the Teacher with a slight frown.

The girl hung her head.

"Why shouldn't we mention it?" said the old woman, "the affair is settled, and the time is drawing near too."

"Don't make plans beforehand," said the Teacher. "Now we have the harvest to get in."

"Have you seen Lukashka's new horse?" asked the old woman. "That which Dmitry Andreich Olenin gave him is gone—he's exchanged it."

"No, I have not; but I spoke with the servant to-day," said the Teacher, "and he said his master has again received a thousand rubles."

"Rolling in riches, in short," said the old woman, briefly.

The whole family felt cheerful and contented. The work was progressing successfully. The grapes were more abundant and finer than they had expected. After dinner Maryanka threw some grass to the oxen, folded her beshmet for a pillow, and lay down under the wagon on the juicy down-trodden grass. She had on only a red kerchief over her head, and a faded blue print smock; yet she felt unbearably hot. Her face was burning and she did not know where to put her feet; her eyes were moist with sleepiness and weariness; her lips parted involuntarily, and her chest heaved heavily and deeply.

The busy time of the year had begun a fortnight ago, and the continuous heavy labor had filled the girl's life. At dawn she jumped up, washed her face with cold water, wrapped herself in a shawl, and ran out barefoot to see to the cattle. Then she hurriedly put on her shoes and her beshmet and, taking a small bundle of bread, she harnessed the bullocks and drove away to the vineyards for the whole day. There she cut the grapes and carried the baskets, with only one hour's interval for rest, and in the evening she returned to the village, bright and not tired, dragging the bullocks by a rope or driving them with a long stick. After attending to the cattle, she took some sunflower seeds in the wide sleeve of her smock and went to the corner of the street to crack them and have some fun with the other girls. But as soon as it was dusk, she returned home, and after having supper with her parents and her brother in the dark outhouse, she went into the hut, healthy, and free from care, and climbed on to the oven, where, half drowsing, she listened to their lodger's conversation. As soon as he went away, she would throw herself down on her bed and sleep soundly and quietly till morning. And so it went on day after day. She had not seen Lukashka since the day of their betrothal, but calmly awaited the wedding.

She had got used to their lodger and felt his intent looks with pleasure.

CHAPTER XXX

AND THE SIN!

ALTHOUGH there was no escape from the heat, and the mosquitoes swarmed in the cool shadow of the wagons, and her little brother tossing about beside her kept pushing her, Maryanka, having drawn her kerchief over her head, was just falling asleep, when suddenly their neighbor Ustenka came running toward her, and, diving under the wagon, lay down beside her.

"Sleep, girls, sleep!" said Ustenka, making herself comfortable under the wagon. "Wait a bit," she exclaimed, "that won't do!" She jumped up, plucked some green branches, and stuck them through the wheels on both sides of the wagon, and hung her beshmet over them. "Let me in," she shouted to the little boy, as she again crept under the wagon. "Is this the place for a Cossack; with the girls? Go away!" When alone under the wagon with her friend, Ustenka suddenly put both her arms round her and clinging to her, began kissing her cheeks and neck.

"Darling, brotherkin," she kept repeating, between bursts of shrill, clear laughter.

"Why, you've learned it from grandad," said Maryanka, struggling. "Stop it!"

And they both broke into such peals of laughter that Maryanka's mother shouted to them to be quiet.

"Are you envious?" asked Ustenka in a whisper.

"What humbug! Let us sleep. What have you come for?"

But Ustenka kept on, "I say! But 1 wanted to tell you such a thing."

Maryanka raised herself on her elbow and arranged the kerchief which had slipped off.

"Well, what is it?"

"I know something about your lodger!"

"There's nothing to know," said Maryanka.

"Oh, you rogue of a girl!" said Ustenka, nudging her with her elbow and laughing. "Won't tell anything. Does he come to you?"

"He does. What of that?" said Maryanka, with a sudden blush.

"Now I'm a simple lass. I tell everybody. Why should I pretend?" said Ustenka; and her bright rosy face suddenly became pensive. "Whom do I hurt? I love him, that's all about it."

"Grandad, do you mean?"

"Well, yes!"

"And the sin?"

"Ah, Maryanka! When is one to have a good time if not while one's still free? When I marry a Cossack, I shall bear children and shall have cares. There now, when you get married to Lukashka not even a thought of joy will enter your head: children will come, and work!"

"Well? Some who are married live happily. It makes no difference!" Maryanka replied quietly.

"Do tell me just this once, what has passed between you and Lukashka?"

"What has passed? A match was proposed. Father put it off for a year; but now it's been settled, and they'll marry us in the autumn."

"But what did he say to you?"

Maryanka smiled.

"What should he say? He said he

loved me. He kept asking me to come to the vineyards with him."

"Just see what pitch! But you did not go, did you? And what a daredevil he has become: the first among the braves. He makes merry out there in the army too! The other day our Kirka came home; he says: What a horse Lukashka's got in exchange! But all the same I expect he frets after you. And what else did he say?"

"Must you know everything?" said Maryanka laughing. "One night he came to my window, tipsy, and asked me to let him in."

"And you didn't let him?"

"Let him, indeed! Once I have said a thing, I keep to it, firm as a rock," answered Maryanka seriously.

"A fine fellow! If he wanted her, no girl would refuse him."

"Well, let him go to the others," proudly replied Maryanka.

"You don't pity him?"

"I do pity him, but will have no nonsense. It is wrong."

Ustenka suddenly dropped her head on her friend's breast, seized hold of her and shook with smothered laughter. "You silly fool!" she exclaimed, quite out of breath. "You don't want to be happy," and she began tickling Maryanka.

"Ay, leave off!" said Maryanka, screaming and laughing. "You've crushed Lazutka."

"Hark at those young devils! Quite frisky! Not tired yet!" came the old woman's sleepy voice from the wagon.

"Don't want happiness," repeated Ustenka in a whisper, insistently. "But you are lucky, that you are! How they love you! You are so haughty, and yet they love you. Ah, were I in

your place I'd soon turn the lodger's head! I noticed him when you were at our house. He was ready to eat you with his eyes. What things grandad has given me! And yours, they say, is the richest of the Russians. His orderly says they have serfs of their own."

Maryanka raised herself, and after thinking a moment, smiled.

"Do you know what he once told me: the lodger, I mean?" she said, biting a bit of grass. "He said, 'I'd like to be Lukashka the Cossack, or your brother Lazutka—.' What do you think he meant?"

"Oh, just chattering what came into his head," answered Ustenka. "What does mine not say! Just as if he was possessed!"

Maryanka dropped her head on her folded beshmet, threw her arm over Ustenka's shoulder, and shut her eyes. "He wanted to come and work in the vineyard to-day: father asked him," she said, and after a short silence she fell asleep.

CHAPTER XXXI

I AM ALONE!

THE sun had come out from behind the pear tree that had shaded the wagon, and, even through the branches that Ustenka had fixed up, it scorched the faces of the sleeping girls. Maryanka woke up and began arranging the kerchief on her head. Looking about her, beyond the pear tree, she noticed their lodger, who, with his gun on his shoulder, stood talking to her father. She nudged Ustenka and smilingly pointed him out to her.

"I went yesterday, and didn't find a

single one," Olenin was saying as he looked about uneasily, not seeing Maryanka through the branches.

"Ah, you should go out there, to that direction, go right round as by compasses, there, in a disused vineyard, denominated as the Waste, hares are always to be found," said the Teacher, having at once changed his manner of speech.

"A fine thing to go looking for hares in these busy times! You had better come and help us, and do some work with the girls," the old woman said merrily. "Now then, girls, up with you!" she cried.

Maryanka and Ustenka under the cart were whispering, and could hardly restrain their laughter.

Since it had become known that Olenin had given a horse worth fifty rubles to Lukashka, his hosts had become more amiable, and the Teacher in particular saw with pleasure his daughter's growing intimacy with Olenin.

"But I don't know how to do the work," replied Olenin, trying not to look through the green branches under the wagon, where he had now noticed Maryanka's blue smock and red kerchief.

"Come, I'll give you some peaches," said the old woman.

"It's only according to the ancient Cossack hospitality. It's her old woman's silliness," said the Teacher, explaining, and apparently correcting, his wife's words. "In Russia, I expect it's not so much peaches as pineapple jam and preserves you have been accustomed to eat at your pleasure."

"So you say hares are to be found in the disused vineyard?" asked Olenin. "I will go there," and throwing a hasty glance through the green branches, he raised his cap and disappeared between the regular rows of green vines.

The sun had already sunk behind the fence of the vineyards, and its broken rays glittered through the translucent leaves, when Olenin returned to his host's vineyard. The wind was falling, and a cool freshness was beginning to spread around. By some instinct Olenin recognized from afar Maryanka's blue smock among the rows of vines, and, picking grapes on his way, he approached her. His highly excited dog also now and then seized a low-hanging cluster of grapes in his slobbering mouth.

Maryanka, her face flushed, her sleeves rolled up, and her kerchief down below her chin, was rapidly cutting the heavy clusters and laying them in a basket. Without letting go of the vine she had hold of, she stopped to smile pleasantly at him, and resumed her work. Olenin drew near, and threw his gun behind his back to have his hands free. "Where are your people? May God aid you! Are you alone?" he meant to say, but did not say, and only raised his cap in silence.

"You'll be shooting the women with your gun like that," said Maryanka.

"No, I shan't shoot them." They were both silent, and then, after a pause, she said: "You should help me." He took out his knife and began silently to cut off the clusters. He reached from under the leaves, low down, a thick bunch, weighing about three pounds, the grapes of which grew so close that they flattened each other for want of space. He showed it to Maryanka.

"Must they all be cut? Isn't this one too green?"

"Give it here."

Their hands touched. Olenin took her hand, and she looked at him smiling.

"Are you going to be married soon?" he asked.

She did not answer, but turned away with a stern look.

"Do you love Lukashka?"

"What's that to you?"

"I envy him!"

"Very likely!"

"No, really. You are so beautiful!"

And he suddenly felt terribly ashamed of having said it, so commonplace did the words seem to him. He flushed, lost control of himself, and seized both her hands. "Whatever I am, I'm not for you. Why do you make fun of me?" replied Maryanka, but her look showed how certainly she knew he was not making fun.

"Making fun? If you only knew how I——"

The words sounded still more commonplace, they accorded still less with what he felt; but yet he continued, "I don't know what I would not do for you——"

"Leave me alone, you pitch!"

But her face, her shining eyes, her swelling bosom, her shapely legs, said something quite different. It seemed to him that she understood how petty were all the things he had said, but that she was superior to such considerations. It seemed to him she had long known all he wished, and was not able, to tell her, but wanted to hear how he would say it.

"And how can she help knowing," he thought, "since I only want to tell her all that she herself is? But she does not wish to understand, does not wish to reply."

"Hullo!" suddenly came from behind the vine at no great distance Ustenka's high voice, followed by her shrill laugh. "Come and help me, Dmitry Andreich. I am all alone," she cried, thrusting her round, naïve little face through the vines.

Olenin did not answer, nor move from his place.

Maryanka went on cutting and continually looked up at Olenin. He was about to say something, but stopped, shrugged his shoulders and, having jerked up his gun, with rapid strides walked out of the vineyard.

CHAPTER XXXII

ALL NIGHT

He stopped once or twice, listening to the ringing laughter of Maryanka and Ustenka who, having come together, were shouting something. Olenin spent the whole evening hunting in the forest. Without having killed anything, he returned home at dusk. When crossing the road, he noticed her open the door of the outhouse, and her blue smock showed through it. He called to Vanyusha very loud, so as to let her know that he was back, and then sat down in the porch in his usual place. His hosts now returned from the vineyard; they came out of the outhouse and into their hut, but did not ask him in. Maryanka went twice out of the gate. Once in the twilight it seemed to him that she was looking at him. He eagerly followed her every movement, but could not make up his mind to approach her. When she disappeared into the hut he left the porch and began pacing up and down the yard; but Maryanka did not again come out. Olenin spent the whole sleepless night out in the yard, listening to every sound in his hosts' hut. He heard them talking early in the evening, heard them having, their supper, and pulling out their cushions, and going to bed; he heard Maryanka laughing at something, and then heard everything growing gradually quiet.

The Teacher and his wife talked a while in whispers, and some one was breathing. Olenin reëntered his hut. Vanyusha lay asleep in his clothes. Olenin envied him, and again went out to pace the yard, always expecting something, but no one came, no one moved, and he only heard the regular breathing of three people. He knew Maryanka's breathing and listened to it and to the beating of his own heart. In the village everything was quiet. The waning moon rose late and the deep-breathing cattle in the yard became more visible as they lay down and slowly rose. Olenin angrily asked himself, "What is it I want?" but could not tear himself away from the enchantment of the night. Suddenly he thought he distinctly heard the floor creak and the sound of footsteps in his hosts' hut. He rushed to the door, but all was silent again, except for the sound of regular breathing, and in the yard the buffalo cow, after a deep sigh, again moved, rose on her front knees and then on her feet, swished her tail, and something splashed steadily on the dry clay ground, and then she lay down again in the dim moonlight. He asked himself: "What am I to do?" and definitely decided to go to bed, but again he heard a sound, and in his imagination there rose the image of Maryanka coming out into this moonlit misty night, and again he rushed to her window, and again heard the sound of footsteps. Not

till just before dawn did he go up to her window and push at the shutter and then run to the door, and this time he really heard Maryanka's deep breathing and her footsteps. He took hold of the latch and knocked. The floor hardly creaked under the bare cautious footsteps which approached the door. The latch clicked, the door creaked, and he noticed a faint smell of marjoram and pumpkin, and Maryanka's whole figure appeared in the doorway. He saw her only for an instant in the moonlight. She slammed the door and, muttering something, ran lightly back again. Olenin began rapping softly, but nothing responded. He ran to the window and listened. Suddenly he was startled by a shrill squeaky man's voice.

"Fine!" exclaimed a rather small young Cossack, in a white cap, coming across the yard close to Olenin. "I saw . . . fine!"

Olenin recognized Nazarka, and was silent, not knowing what to do or say.

"Fine! I'll go and tell them at the office, and I'll tell her father! That's a fine Teacher's daughter! One's not enough for her."

"What do you want of me, what are you after?" uttered Olenin.

"Nothing; only I'll tell them at the office."

Nazarka spoke very loud, and evidently did so intentionally, adding: "Just see what a clever cadet!"

Olenin trembled and grew pale. "Come here, here!"

He seized the Cossack firmly by the arm, and drew him toward his hut: "Nothing happened, she did not let me in and I, too, mean no harm. She is an honest girl——"

"Eh, discuss——"

"Yes; but all the same I'll give you something now. Wait a bit!"

Nazarka said nothing. Olenin ran into his hut and brought out ten rubles, which he gave to the Cossack.

"Nothing happened, but still I was to blame, so I give this!— Only for God's sake don't let anyone know, for nothing happened——"

"I wish you joy," said Nazarka, laughing, and went away.

Nazarka had come to the village that night, at Lukashka's bidding, to find a place to hide a stolen horse, and now, passing by on his way home, had heard the sound of footsteps. When he returned next morning to his company, he bragged to his chum, and told him how cleverly he had got ten rubles.

Next morning Olenin met his hosts, and they knew nothing about the events of the night. He did not speak to Maryanka, and she only laughed a little when she looked at him. Next night he also passed without sleep, vainly wandering about the yard. The day after, he purposely spent shooting, and in the evening he went to see Beletsky, to escape from his own thoughts. He was afraid of himself, and promised himself not to go to his host's hut any more.

That night he was roused by the Sergeant Major. His company was ordered to start at once on a raid.

Olenin was glad this had happened, and thought he would not again return to the village.

The raid lasted four days. The Commander, who was a relative of Olenin's, wished to see him, and offered to let him remain with the staff, but this Olenin declined. He found that he could not live away from the village, and asked to be allowed to return to it. For having taken part in the raid, he received a soldier's cross, which he had formerly so much desired. Now he was quite indifferent about it, and even more indifferent about his promotion, the order for which had still not arrived.

Accompanied by Vanyusha, he rode back to the cordon without any accident, several hours in advance of the rest of the company. He spent the whole evening in his porch, watching Maryanka, and he again walked about the yard, without aim or thought, all night.

CHAPTER XXXIII

HIS WRITING

IT was late when he awoke the next day. His hosts were no longer in. He did not go shooting, but now took up a book, and now went out into the porch, and now again reëntered the hut and lay down on the bed. Vanyusha thought he was ill.

Toward evening Olenin got up, resolutely began writing, and wrote on till late at night. He wrote a letter, but did not post it, because he felt that no one would have understood what he wanted to say; and, besides, it was not necessary that anyone but himself should understand it.

This is what he wrote:

"I receive letters of condolence from Russia. They are afraid that I shall perish, buried in these wilds. They say about me: 'He will become coarse; he will be behind the times in everything; he will take to drink, and who knows but that he may marry a Cossack girl.' It was not for nothing, they say, that Ermolov declared: 'Anyone serving in the Caucasus for ten years either becomes a confirmed drunkard, or marries a loose woman.' How terrible! Indeed, it won't do for me to ruin myself when I might have the great happiness of even becoming the Countess B——'s husband or a Court chamberlain, or a *Maréchal de noblesse* of my district. Oh, how repulsive and pitiable you all seem to me! You do not know what happiness is, and what life is! One must once taste life in all its natural beauty! Must see and understand what I see every day before me; those eternally unapproachable snowy peaks, and a majestic woman in that primitive beauty in which the first woman must have come from her Creator's hands— and then it becomes clear who is ruining himself, and who is living truly or falsely: you or I. If you only knew how despicable and pitiable you, in your delusions, seem to me! When I picture to myself, in place of my hut, my forests, and my love, those drawingrooms, those women with their pomatum-greased hair eked out with false curls, these unnaturally grimacing lips, these hidden, feeble, distorted limbs, and that chatter of obligatory drawingroom conversation, which has no right to the name—I feel unendurably revolted. I then see before me those obtuse faces, those rich eligible girls, whose looks seem to say: 'It's all right, you may come near, though I am rich and eligible,'—and that arranging and rearranging of seats, that shameless matchmaking, and that eternal tittletattle and pretense; those rules—with whom to shake hands, to whom only

to nod, with whom to converse (and all this done deliberately with a conviction of its inevitability), that continual ennui in the blood passing on from generation to generation. Try to understand or believe just this one thing: you need only see and comprehend what truth and beauty are, and all that you now say and think, and all your wishes for me and for yourselves will fly to atoms!

"Happiness is being with nature, seeing her, and conversing with her. 'He may even (God forbid) marry a common Cossack girl, and be quite lost socially,' I can imagine them saying of me with sincere pity! Yet the one thing I desire is to be quite 'lost,' in your sense of the word. I wish to marry a common Cossack girl, and dare not, because it would be a height of happiness of which I am unworthy.

"Three months have passed since I first saw the Cossack girl, Maryanka. The views and prejudices of the world I had left were still fresh in me. I did not then believe that I could love that woman. I delighted in her beauty just as I delighted in the beauty of the mountains and the sky, nor could I help delighting in her, for she is as beautiful as they. I found that the sight of her beauty had become a necessity of my life, and I began asking myself whether I did not love her. But I could find nothing within myself at all like love, as I had imagined it to be. Mine was not the restlessness of loneliness and desire for marriage, nor was it platonic, still less a carnal love, such as I have experienced. I needed only to see her, to hear her, to know that she was near; and if I was not happy, I was at peace.

"After an evening gathering at which

I met her and touched her, I felt that between that woman and myself there existed an indissoluble though unacknowledged bond against which I could not struggle, yet I did struggle. I asked myself: 'Is it possible to love a woman who will never understand the profoundest interests of my life? Is it possible to love a woman simply for her beauty, to love the statue of a woman?' But I was already in love with her; though I did not yet trust to my feelings.

"After that evening, when I first spoke to her, our relations changed. Before that, she had been to me an extraneous but majestic object of external nature: but since that, she has become a human being. I began to meet her, to talk to her, and sometimes to go to work for her father and to spend whole evenings with them, and in this intimate intercourse she remained still in my eyes just as pure, inaccessible, and majestic. She always responded with equal calm, pride, and cheerful equanimity. Sometimes she was friendly, but generally her every look, every word, and her every movement expressed equanimity—not contemptuous, but crushing and bewitching. Every day, with a feigned smile on my lips, I tried to play a part, and with torments of passion and desire in my heart I spoke banteringly to her. She saw that I was dissembling, but looked straight at me, cheerfully and simply. This position became unbearable. I wished not to deceive her, but to tell her all I felt and thought. I was extremely agitated. We were in the vineyard when I began to tell her of my love, in words I am now ashamed to remember. I am ashamed because I ought not to have dared to speak so to her, because she stood far above such words, and above the feeling they were meant to express. I said no more, but from that day my position has been intolerable. I did not wish to demean myself by continuing our former flippant relations, and at the same time I felt that I had not yet reached the level of straight and simple relations with her. I asked myself despairingly, 'What am I to do?' In foolish dreams I imagined her, now as my mistress and now as my wife, but rejected both ideas with disgust. To make her a wanton woman would be dreadful. It would be murder. To turn her into a fine lady, the wife of Dmitry Andreich Olenin, like a Cossack woman here who is married to one of our officers, would be still worse. Now could I turn Cossack, like Lukashka, and steal horses, get drunk on chikhir, sing rollicking songs, kill people, and when drunk climb up at her window for the night without a thought of who and what I am, it would be different: then we might understand one another, and I might be happy.

"I tried to throw myself into that kind of life, but was still more conscious of my own weakness and artificiality. I cannot forget myself and my complex, distorted past; and my future appears to me still more hopeless. Every day I have before me the distant snowy mountains, and this majestic, happy woman. But not for me is the only happiness possible in the world; I cannot have this woman! What is most terrible and yet sweetest in my condition is that I feel that I understand her, but that she will never understand me; not because she is inferior:

on the contrary she ought not to understand me. She is happy, she is like nature: consistent, calm, and self-contained; and I, a weak distorted being, want her to understand my deformity and my torments! I have not slept at night, but have aimlessly passed under her windows, not rendering account to myself of what was happening to me.

"On the 18th our company started on a raid, and I spent three days away from the village. I was sad and apathetic, the usual songs, cards, drinking bouts, and talk of rewards in the regiment, were more repulsive than usual to me. Yesterday I returned home, and saw her, my hut, Daddy Eroshka, and the snowy mountains from my porch, and was seized by such a strong, new feeling of joy that I understood it all. I love this woman; I feel real love for the first and only time in my life. I know what has befallen me. I do not fear to be degraded by this feeling; I am not ashamed of my love, I am proud of it. It is not my fault that I love. It has come about against my will. I tried to escape from my love by self-renunciation, and tried to devise a joy in the Cossack Lukashka's and Maryanka's love, but thereby only stirred up my own love and jealousy.

"This is not the ideal, the so-called exalted love, which I have known before; not that sort of attachment in which you admire your own love, and feel that the source of your emotion is within yourself, and do everything yourself. I have felt that too. It is still less a desire for enjoyment: it is something different. Perhaps in her I love nature: the personification of all that is beautiful in nature; but yet I am not acting by my own will, but some elemental force loves through me; the whole of God's world, all nature, presses this love into my soul, and says, 'Love her.' I love her not with my mind, or my imagination, but with my whole being. Loving her, I feel myself to be an integral part of all God's joyous world.

"I wrote before about the new convictions to which my solitary life had brought me; but no one knows with what labor they shaped themselves within me, and with what joy I realized them, and saw a new way of life opening out before me; nothing was dearer to me than those convictions. . . . Well! . . . love has come, and neither they, nor any regrets for them, remain!

"It is even difficult for me to believe that I could prize such a one-sided, cold, and abstract state of mind. Beauty came and scattered to the winds all that laborious inward toil; and no regret remains for what has vanished! Self-renunciation is all nonsense and absurdity! That is pride, a refuge from well-merited unhappiness, and salvation from the envy of other's happiness: 'Live for others, and do good!'—Why? when in my soul there is only love for myself, and the desire to love her, and to live her life with her. Not for others, not for Lukashka, I now desire happiness. I do not now love those others. Formerly I should have told myself that this is wrong. I should have tormented myself with the questions: What will become of her, of me, and of Lukashka? Now I don't care. I do not live my own life, there is something stronger than me which directs me. I suffer; but formerly I was dead, and only now do I live. To-day I will go to their house, and will tell her everything."

CHAPTER XXXIV

COSSACK GIRLS

LATE that evening, after writing this letter, Olenin went to his hosts' hut. The old woman was sitting on a bench behind the oven, unwinding cocoons. Maryanka, with her head uncovered, sat sewing by the light of a candle. On seeing Olenin she jumped up, took her kerchief and stepped to the oven.

"Maryanka, dear," said her mother, "won't you sit here with me a bit?"

"No, I'm bareheaded," she replied, and sprang up on the oven.

Olenin could only see a knee and one of her shapely legs hanging down from the oven. He treated the old woman to tea. She treated her guest to clotted cream, which she sent Maryanka to fetch. But, having put a plateful on the table, Maryanka again sprang on the oven, from whence Olenin felt her eyes upon him. They talked about household matters. Granny Ulitka became animated, and went into raptures of hospitality. She brought Olenin preserved grapes and a grape tart, and some of her best wine, and pressed him to eat and drink with the rough yet proud hospitality of country folk, only found among those who produce their bread by the labor of their own hands.

The old woman, who had at first struck Olenin so much by her rudeness, now often touched him by her simple tenderness toward her daughter.

"Yes, we need not offend the Lord by grumbling! We have enough of everything, thank God. We have pressed sufficient chikhir, and have pre-

served, and shall sell, three or four barrels of grapes, and have enough left to drink. Don't be in a hurry to leave us. We will make merry together at the wedding."

"And when is the wedding to be?" asked Olenin, feeling his blood suddenly rush to his face, while his heart beat irregularly and painfully. He heard a movement on the oven, and the sound of seeds being cracked.

"Well, you know, it ought to be next week. We are quite ready," replied the old woman, as simply and quietly as though Olenin did not exist. "I have prepared, and have procured everything for Maryanka. We will give her away properly. Only there's one thing not quite right. Our Lukashka has been running rather wild. He has been too much on the spree! He's up to tricks! The other day a Cossack came here from his company and said he had been to Nogay."

"He must mind he does not get caught," said Olenin.

"Yes, that's what I tell him. 'Mind, Lukashka, don't you get into mischief. Well, of course a young fellow naturally wants to cut a dash. But there's a time for everything. Well, you've captured or stolen something, and killed an abrek! Well, you're a fine fellow! But now you should live quietly for a bit, or else there'll be trouble.'"

"Yes, I saw him a time or two in the division; he was always merrymaking. He has sold another horse," said Olenin, and glanced toward the oven.

A pair of large, dark, and hostile eyes glittered as they gazed severely at him.

He became ashamed of what he had said. "What of it? He does no one any harm," suddenly remarked Maryanka. "He makes merry with his own money," and lowering her legs she jumped down from the oven and went out, banging the door. Olenin followed her with his eyes as long as she was in the hut; and then looked at the door and waited, understanding nothing of what Granny Ulitka was telling him.

A few minutes later some visitors arrived: an old man, Granny Ulitka's brother, with Daddy Eroshka, and following them came Maryanka and Ustenka.

"Good evening," squeaked Ustenka. "Still on holiday?" she added, turning to Olenin. "Yes, still on holiday," he replied, and felt, he did not know why, ashamed and ill at ease.

He wished to go away, but could not. It also seemed to him impossible to keep silent. The old man helped him by asking for a drink, and they had a drink. Olenin drank with Eroshka, with the other Cossack, and again with Eroshka, and the more he drank the heavier was his heart. But the two old men grew merry. The girls climbed to the oven, where they sat whispering and looking at the men, who drank till it was late. Olenin did not talk, but drank more than the others. The Cossacks were shouting. The old woman would not let them have any more chikhir, and at last turned them out. The girls laughed at Daddy Eroshka, and it was past ten when they all went out into the porch. The old men invited themselves to finish their merrymaking at Olenin's. Ustenka ran off home, and Eroshka led the old Cossack to Vanyusha. The old woman went out to tidy up the shed. Maryanka remained alone in the hut. Olenin felt fresh and joyous, as if he had only just waked

up. He noticed everything, and having let the old men pass ahead, he turned back to the hut where Maryanka was preparing for bed. He went up to her and wished to say something, but his voice broke. She moved away from him, sat down crosslegged on her bed in the corner, and silently looked at him with wild and frightened eyes. She was evidently afraid of him. Olenin felt this. He felt sorry and ashamed of himself, and at the same time felt proud and pleased that he aroused even that feeling in her.

"Maryanka!" he said, "will you never take pity on me? I can't tell you how I love you."

She moved still farther away and said: "Just hear how the wine is speaking! . . . You'll get nothing from me!"

"No, it is not the wine. Do not marry Lukashka. I will marry you. What am I saying?" he thought as he uttered these words. "Shall I be able to say the same to-morrow?" "Yes, I shall, I am sure I shall, and I will repeat them now," replied an inner voice.

"Will you marry me?"

She looked at him seriously, and her fear seemed to have passed.

"Maryanka, I shall go out of my mind! I am not myself. I will do whatever you command," and madly tender words came from his lips of their own accord.

"Now then, what are you driveling about?" she interrupted, suddenly seizing the arm he was stretching toward her. She did not push his arm away, but pressed it firmly with her strong hard fingers.

"Do gentlemen marry Cossack girls? Go away!"

"But will you? Everything . . ."

"And what shall we do with Lukashka?" said she, laughing.

He snatched away the arm she was holding, and firmly embraced her young body, but she sprang away like a fawn and ran barefooted into the porch: Olenin came to his senses and was terrified at himself. He again felt himself inexpressibly vile compared to her, yet not repenting for an instant of what he had said, he went home and, without even glancing at the old men who were drinking in his room, he lay down and fell asleep more soundly than he had done for a long time.

CHAPTER XXXV

BELETSKY'S HUT

THE next day was a holiday. In the evening all the villagers, their holiday clothes shining in the sunset, were out in the street. That season more wine than usual had been produced, and the people were now free from their labors. In a month the Cossacks were to start on a campaign, and in many families preparations were being made for weddings.

Most of the people were standing in the square, in front of the Cossack Government Office and near the two shops, in one of which cakes and pumpkin seeds were sold, in the other kerchiefs and cotton prints. On the earth embankment of the office building sat or stood the old men in sober gray or black coats, without gold trimmings or any kind of ornament. They conversed among themselves quietly, in measured tones, about the harvest, about the young folk, about village affairs, and about old times, looking

with dignified equanimity at the younger generation. Passing by them, the women and girls stopped and bent their heads. The young Cossacks respectfully slackened their pace and raised their caps, holding them for a while over their heads. The old men then stopped speaking. Some of them watched the passers-by severely, others kindly, and in their turn slowly took off their caps and put them on again.

The Cossack girls had not yet started dancing their horovods, but having gathered in groups, they in their bright-colored beshmets, with white kerchiefs on their heads pulled down to their eyes, sat, either on the ground or on the earth banks about the huts, sheltered from the oblique rays of the sun, and laughed and chattered in their ringing voices. Little boys and girls, playing in the square, sent their balls high up into the clear sky, and ran about squealing and shouting. The rather older girls had started dancing their horovods; and were timidly singing in their thin shrill voices. Clerks, lads not in the service, or home for the holiday, bright-faced, and wearing smart white or new red Circassian gold-trimmed coats, went about arm in arm, in twos or threes, from one group of women or girls to another, and stopped, joking and chatting with the Cossack girls. The Armenian shopkeeper, in a gold-trimmed coat of fine blue cloth, stood at the open door, through which piles of folded bright-colored kerchiefs were visible, and conscious of his own importance and with the pride of an oriental tradesman, waited for customers. Two red-bearded, barefooted Chechens, who had come from beyond the Terek to see the fête, sat on their heels outside the house of a friend, negligently smoking their little pipes and occasionally spitting, watching the villagers and exchanging remarks with one another in their rapid guttural speech. Occasionally a workaday-looking soldier in an old overcoat passed among the bright-clad girls. Here and there the songs of tipsy Cossacks who were merrymaking, could already be heard. All the huts were locked up; the porches had been scrubbed clean the day before. Even the old women were out in the street, which was everywhere sprinkled with pumpkin and melon seed shells. The air was warm and still, the sky deep and clear. Beyond the roofs the dead-white mountain range, which seemed very near, was turning rosy in the glow of the evening sun. Now and then, from the other side of the river, came the distant roar of a cannon, but above the village, mingling with one another, floated all sorts of merry holiday sounds.

Olenin had been pacing the yard all that morning, hoping to see Maryanka. But she went to Mass at the chapel, and afterwards sat with the other girls on an earth embankment, cracking seeds; sometimes, again, together with her companions, she ran home, and each time gave the lodger a bright and kindly look. Olenin felt afraid to address her playfully, or in the presence of others. He wished to finish telling her what he had begun to say the night before, and to get her to give him a definite answer. He waited for another moment like that of yesterday evening; but the moment did not come, and he felt that he could not remain any longer in this uncertainty. She

went out into the street again, and after waiting a while he too went out, and without knowing where he was going he followed her. He passed by the corner where she was sitting in her shining blue satin beshmet, and with an aching heart he heard behind him the girls laughing.

Beletsky's hut looked out on to the square. As Olenin was passing it he heard Beletsky's voice calling to him, "Come in," and in he went.

After a short talk they both sat down by the window, and were soon joined by Eroshka, who entered, dressed in a new beshmet, and sat down on the floor beside them.

"There, that's the aristocratic party," said Beletsky, pointing with his cigarette to a brightly colored group at the corner. "Mine is there too. Do you see her? in red. That's a new beshmet. Why don't you start the horovod?" he shouted, leaning out of the window. "Wait a bit, and then, when it grows dark, let us go too. Then we will invite them to Ustenka's. We must arrange a ball for them!"

"And I will come to Ustenka's," said Olenin in a decided tone. "Will Maryanka be there?"

"Yes, she'll be there. Do come!" said Beletsky, without the least surprise. "But isn't it a pretty picture?" he added, pointing to the motley crowds.

"Yes, very!" Olenin assented, trying to appear indifferent. "Holidays of this kind," he added, "always make me wonder why all these people should suddenly be contented and jolly. Today, for instance, just because it happens to be the fifteenth of the month, everything is festive. Eyes and faces, and voices and movements and garments, and the air and the sun, are all in a holiday mood. And we have no longer any holidays!"

"Yes," said Beletsky, who did not like such reflections. "And why are you not drinking, old fellow?" he said, turning to Eroshka.

Eroshka winked at Olenin, pointing to Beletsky. "Eh, he's a proud one, that kunak of yours," he said.

Beletsky raised his glass.

"Allah birdy!" he said, emptying his glass. (Allah birdy, "God gave," is the usual greeting of Caucasians, when drinking together.)

"Sau bul" ("Your health"), answered Eroshka smiling, and emptied his glass.

"Talking about holidays!" he said, turning to Olenin as he rose and looked out of the window. "What sort of holiday is that? You should have seen them make merry in the old days! The women used to come out in their gold-trimmed sarafans. Two rows of gold coins hanging round their necks, and gold-cloth diadems on their heads, and when they passed they made a noise, 'flu, flu,' with their dresses.

"Every woman looked like a princess. Sometimes they'd come out, a whole herd of them, and begin singing songs so that the air seemed to rumble, and they went on making merry all night. And the Cossacks would roll out a barrel into the yards, and sit down and drink till break of day, or they would go hand-in-hand sweeping the village. Whoever they met they seized and took along with them, and went from house to house. Sometimes they used to make merry for three days on end. Father used to come home—I still remember it—quite red

and swollen, without a cap, having lost everything: he'd come and lie down. Mother knew what to do: she would bring him some fresh caviar, and a little chikhir to sober him up, and would herself run about in the village looking for his cap. Then he'd sleep for two days! That's the kind of fellows they were then! But now what are they?"

"Well, and the girls in the sarafans, did they make merry all by themselves?" asked Beletsky.

"Yes, they did! Sometimes Cossacks would come on foot or on horse and say, 'Let's break up the beyond,' and they'd go, but the girls would take up cudgels. Carnival week, some young fellow would come galloping up, and they'd cudgel his horse and cudgel him too. But he'd break through, seize the one he loved, and carry her off. 'Mammy, darling! . . .' Oh! how he would love her! Yes, the girls in those days, they were regular queens!"

CHAPTER XXXVI

THE DUMB GIRL

Just then tow men rode out of the side street into the square. One of them was Nazarka. The other, Lukashka, sat slightly sideways on his well-fed bay Kabarda horse, which stepped lightly over the hard road, jerking its beautiful head with the fine glossy crest. The well-adjusted gun in its cover, the pistol at his back, and the cloak rolled up behind the saddle, showed that Lukashka had not come from a peaceful place, or from one near by. The smart way in which he sat a little sideways on his horse, the careless motion with which he touched the horse under its belly with his whip, and especially his half-closed black eyes, glistening as he looked proudly around him, all expressed the conscious strength and self-confidence of youth. "Ever seen as fine a lad?" his eyes, looking from side to side, seemed to say. The elegant horse with its silver ornaments and trappings, the weapons, and the handsome Cossack himself, attracted the attention of everyone in the square. Nazarka, lean and short, was much less well dressed. As he rode past the old men, Lukashka paused and raised his curly, white, sheepskin cap above his closely cropped black head.

"Well, have you carried off many Nogay horses?" asked a lean old man, with a frowning, lowering look.

"Have you counted them, grandad, that you ask?" replied Lukashka, turning away.

"That's all very well, but you need not take my lad along with you," the old man muttered, with a still darker frown.

"Just see the old devil, he knows everything," muttered Lukashka to himself, and a worried expression came over his face; but then, noticing a corner where a number of Cossack girls were standing, he turned his horse toward them.

"Good evening, girls!" he shouted in his powerful, resonant voice, suddenly checking his horse. "You've grown old, without me, you witches!" and he laughed.

"Good evening, Lukashka! Good evening, laddie!" the merry voices answered.

"Have you brought much money? Buy some sweets for the girls! . . ."

Have you come for long? True enough, it's long since we saw you. . . ."

"Nazarka and I have just flown across to make a night of it," replied Lukashka, raising his whip and riding straight at the girls.

"Why, Maryanka has quite forgotten you," said Ustenka, nudging Maryanka with her elbow and breaking into a shrill laugh.

Maryanka moved away from the horse and, throwing back her head, calmly looked at the Cossack with her large sparkling eyes.

"True enough, you have not been for a long time! Why are you trampling us under your horse?" she remarked dryly, and turned away.

Lukashka had appeared particularly merry. His face shone with audacity and joy. Obviously staggered by Maryanka's cold reply, he suddenly knitted his brow.

"Step up on my stirrup and I'll carry you away to the mountains, Mammy!" he suddenly exclaimed, and, as if to disperse his dark thoughts, he caracoled among the girls. Stooping down toward Maryanka, he said. "I'll kiss, oh, how I'll kiss you! . . ."

Maryanka's eyes met his, and she suddenly blushed and stepped back.

"Oh, bother you! you'll crush my feet," she said, and bending her head looked at her well-shaped feet in their tightly fitting light blue stockings with clocks, and her new red slippers trimmed with narrow silver braid.

Lukashka turned toward Ustenka, and Maryanka sat down next to a woman with a baby in her arms. The baby stretched his plump little arms toward the girl, and seized the string of coins that hung down on to her blue beshmet. Maryanka bent toward the child and glanced at Lukashka from the corner of her eyes. Lukashka just then was getting out from under his coat, out of the pocket of his black beshmet, a bundle of sweetmeats and seeds.

"There, I give them to all of you," he said, handing the bundle to Ustenka and smiling at Maryanka.

A confused expression again appeared on the girl's face. It was as though a mist gathered over her beautiful eyes. She drew her kerchief down from her lips, and leaning her head over the fair-skinned face of the baby that still held her by her coin necklace, she suddenly began to kiss it greedily. The baby pressed his little hands against the girl's high breasts, and opening his toothless mouth, screamed loudly.

"You're smothering the boy!" said the little one's mother, taking him away; and she unfastened her beshmet to give him the breast. "You'd better go and welcome the lad."

"I'll only go and put up my horse, and then Nazarka and I will come back; we'll make merry all night," said Lukashka, touching his horse with his whip and riding away from the girls. Turning into a side street, he and Nazarka rode up to two huts that stood side by side.

"Here we are, all right, old fellow! Be quick and come soon!" called Lukashka to his comrade, dismounting in front of one of the huts; then he carefully led his horse in at the gate of the wattle fence of his own home.

"How d'you do, Stepka?" he said to his dumb sister, who, smartly dressed like the others, came in from the street to take his horse, and he made signs to her to take the horse to the hay, but not to unsaddle it.

The dumb girl made her usual humming noise, smacked her lips as she pointed to the horse, and kissed it on the nose, as much as to say that she loved it and that it was a fine horse.

"How d'you do, mother? How is it that you have not gone out yet?" shouted Lukashka, holding his gun in place, as he mounted the steps of the porch.

His old mother opened the door. "Dear me! I never expected, never thought, you'd come," said the old woman. "Why, Kirka said you'd not be here."

"Go and bring some chikhir, mother. Nazarka is coming here and we will celebrate the feast day."

"Directly, Lukashka, directly!" answered the old woman. "Our women are making merry. I expect our dumb one has gone too."

She took her keys, and hurriedly went to the outhouse.

Nazarka, after putting up his horse and taking the gun off his shoulder, returned to Lukashka's house and went in.

CHAPTER XXXVII

THE HORSE COMPASS

"Your health!" said Lukashka, taking from his mother's hands a cup filled to the brim with chikhir, and carefully raising it to his bowed head.

"A bad business!" said Nazarka. "You heard how Daddy Burlak said, 'Have you stolen many horses?' He seems to know!"

"A regular wizard!" Lukashka replied shortly. "But what of that!" he added, tossing his head. "They are across the river by now. Go and find them."

"Still, it's a bad lookout."

"What's a bad lookout? Go and take some chikhir to him to-morrow, and nothing will come of it. Now let's make merry. Drink!" shouted Lukashka, just in the tone in which old Eroshka uttered the word. "We'll go out into the street and make merry with the girls. You go and get some honey; or no, I'll send our dumb wench. We'll make merry till morning."

Nazarka smiled. "Are we stopping here long?" he asked.

"Till we've had a bit of fun. Run and get some vodka. Here's the money."

Nazarka ran off obediently to get the vodka from Yamka's.

Daddy Eroshka and Ergushov, like birds of prey, scenting where the merry-making was going on, tumbled into the hut one after the other, both tipsy.

"Bring us another half-pail," shouted Lukashka to his mother, by way of reply to their greeting.

"Now then, tell us, where did you steal them, you devil?" shouted Eroshka. "Fine fellow, I'm fond of you!"

"Fond indeed . . ." answered Lukashka, laughing, "carrying sweets from cadets to lasses! Eh, you old . . ."

"That's not true, not true! . . . Oh, Mark," and the old man burst out laughing. "And how that devil begged me. 'Go,' he said, 'and arrange it.' He offered me a gun! But, no. I'd have managed it, but I feel for you. Now tell us, where have you been?" And the old man began speaking in Tartar.

Lukashka answered him promptly.

Ergushov, who did not know much Tartar, only occasionally put in a word in Russian:

"What I say is, he's driven away the horses. I know it for a fact," he chimed in.

"Girey and I went together." (His speaking of Girey Khan as "Girey" was, to the Cossack mind, evidence of his boldness.) "Just beyond the river he kept bragging that he knew the whole of the steppe, and would lead the way straight, but we rode on and the night was dark, and my Girey lost his way, and began wandering in a circle without getting anywhere: couldn't find the village, and there we were. We must have gone too much to the right. I believe we wandered about wellnigh till midnight. Then, thank goodness, we heard dogs howling."

"Fools!" said Daddy Eroshka. "There now, we too used to lose our way in the steppe. (Who the devil can follow it?) But I used to ride up a hillock and start howling like the wolves, like this!" He placed his hands before his mouth, and howled like a pack of wolves, all on one note. "The dogs would answer at once. . . . Well, go on,—so you found them?"

"We soon led them away! Nazarka was nearly caught by some Nogay women, he was!"

"Caught, indeed," Nazarka, who had just come back, said in an injured tone.

"We rode off again, and again Girey lost his way, and almost landed us among the sand drifts. We thought we were just getting to the Terek, but we were riding away from it all the time!"

"You should have steered by the stars," said Daddy Eroshka.

"That's what I say," interjected Ergushov.

"Yes, steer when all is black; I tried and tried all about . . . and at last I put the bridle on one of the mares, and let my own horse go free—thinking he'll lead us out; and what do you think! he just gave a snort or two with his nose to the ground, galloped ahead, and led us straight to our village. Thank goodness!"

"It was getting quite light. We barely had time to hide them in the forest. Nagim came across the river, and took them away."

Ergushov shook his head. "It's just what I said. Smart. Did you get much for them?"

"It's all here," said Lukashka, slapping his pocket.

Just then his mother came into the room, and Lukashka did not finish what he was saying.

"Drink!" he shouted.

"We too, Girich and I, rode out late one night . . ." began Eroshka.

"Oh, bother, we'll never hear the end of you!" said Lukashka. "I am going." And having emptied his cup and tightened the strap of his belt, he went out.

CHAPTER XXXVIII

KISSES FIVE

It was already dark when Lukashka went out into the street. The autumn night was fresh and calm. The full golden moon floated up behind the tall dark poplars that grew on one side of the square. From the chimneys of the outhouses smoke rose and spread above the village, mingling with the mist. Here and there lights shone through the windows, and the air was laden with the smell of kisyak, grape pulp, and mist. The sounds of voices, laughter, songs, and the cracking of seeds mingled just as they had done in the daytime, but were now more distinct. Clusters of white kerchiefs and caps gleamed through the darkness near the houses and by the fences.

In the square, before the shop door, which was lit up and open, the black and white figures of Cossack men and maids showed through the darkness, and one heard from the afar their loud songs and laughter and talk. The girls, hand in hand, went round and round in a circle, stepping lightly in the dusty square. A skinny girl, plainest of them all, set the tune:

"From beyond the wood, from the forest dark,
From the garden green, and the shady park,
There came out, there came two young fellows gay.
They were brave and smart, bach'lors both were they!
And they walked and walked, then stood still, each man,
So they stood and soon to dispute began!
Then a maid came out; as she came along,
Said, 'To one of you, I shall soon belong!'
'Twas the fair-faced lad got the maiden fair,
Yes, the fair-faced lad with the golden hair!
Her right hand so white, in his own took he,

And he led her round, for his mates
    to see!
And he said, 'Have you, mates, in all
    your life,
Met a lass as fair as my little wife?' "

The old women stood round, listening
to the songs. The little boys and girls
ran about chasing one another in the
dark. The men stood by, catching at
the girls as the latter moved round,
and sometimes breaking the ring and
entering it. On the dark side of the
doorway stood Beletsky and Olenin,
in their Circassian coats and sheepskin
caps, and in a style of speech unlike
that of the Cossacks talked together in
low but distinct tones, conscious that
they were attracting attention.

Next to one another, in the horovod
circle, moved plump little Ustenka in
her red beshmet and the stately Maryanka in her new smock and beshmet.
Olenin and Beletsky were discussing
how to snatch Ustenka and Maryanka
out of the ring. Beletsky thought
that Olenin wished only to amuse himself, while Olenin was expecting his
fate to be decided. He wanted, at
any cost, to see Maryanka alone that
very day, and to tell her everything,
and ask her whether she could and
would be his wife. Although that
question had long been answered in the
negative in his own mind, he hoped he
would be able to tell her all he felt,
and that she would understand him.

"Why did you not tell me sooner?"
said Beletsky. "I would have got
Ustenka to arrange it for you. You
are such a queer fellow! . . ."

"What's to be done! . . . Some
day, very soon, I'll tell you all about it.
Only now, for Heaven's sake arrange

so that she should come to Ustenka's."

"All right, that's easily done! Well,
Maryanka, will you belong to the 'fair-
faced lad,' and not to Lukashka?" said
Beletsky, speaking to Maryanka first
for propriety's sake, but, having received
no reply, he went up to Ustenka and
begged her to bring Maryanka home
with her. He had hardly time to finish
what he was saying before the leader
began another song, and the girls
started pulling each other round in the
ring by the hand. They sang:

"Past the garden, the garden,
A young lad came strolling down,
Up the street and through the town;
And the first time, as he passed,
He did wave his strong right hand.
As the second time he passed
Waved his hat with silken band.
And the third time as he passed
He stood still: did not depart.
He this time did not depart, but he
    made himself look smart.

" 'I have wished to come to thee
Just to have a bit of talk.
Why is it that thou, my dear,
In the park don't come to walk?

" 'Come now, answer me, my dear,
Dost thou hold me in contempt?
Later on, thou knowest, dear,
Thou'lt get sober and repent.
Soon to woo thee, I will come,
And when we shall married be,
Thou shalt weep because of me!'

"Though I knew what to reply,
Yet I dared not him deny,
No I dared not him deny!
In the park to walk went I,
In the park my lad to meet.

There my dear one I did greet.
As I bowed, so it befell,
To the ground my kerchief fell.

"Up he picked it, where it lay,
'In thy white hand take it, pray.
Please accept it, dear, from me,
Say I am beloved by thee,
I don't know at all, I fear,
What I am to give thee, dear!
To my dear I think I will
Of a shawl a present make—
Kisses five for it I'll take.' "

Lukashka and Nazarka broke into the ring and started walking about among the girls. Lukashka joined in the singing, taking seconds in his clear voice as he walked in the middle of the ring swinging his arms.

"Well, come in, one of you!" he said. The other girls pushed Maryanka, but she would not enter the ring. The sound of shrill laughter, slaps, kisses, and whispers, mingled with the singing. As he went past Olenin, Lukashka gave a friendly nod.

"Dmitry Andreich! Have you, too, come to have a look?" he said.

"Yes," answered Olenin, dryly.

Beletsky stooped and whispered something into Ustenka's ear. She had not time to reply till she came round again, when she said, "All right, we'll come."

"And Maryanka too?"

Olenin stooped toward Maryanka. "You'll come? Please do, if only for a minute. I must speak to you."

"If the other girls come, I will."

"Will you answer my question?" said he, bending toward her. "You are in good spirits to-day."

She had already moved past him. He went after her. "Will you?"

"What question?"

"The one I asked you the other day," said Olenin, stooping to her ear. "Will you marry me?"

Maryanka thought for a moment. "I'll tell you," said she, "I'll tell you to-night," and through the darkness her eyes gleamed brightly and kindly at the young man.

He still followed her. He enjoyed stooping closer to her.

But Lukashka, without ceasing to sing, suddenly seized her firmly by the hand and pulled her from her place in the ring of girls, into the middle. Olenin had only time to say, "Come to Ustenka's," and stepped back to his companion. The song came to an end. Lukashka wiped his lips. Maryanka did the same, and they kissed.

"No, no, kisses five!" said Lukashka. Chatter, laughter, and running about, succeeded to the rhythmic movements and sound. Lukashka, who seemed to have drunk a great deal, began to distribute sweetmeats to the girls. "I offer them to everyone!" he said, with proud, comically pathetic self-admiration. "But anyone who goes after soldiers, get out of the ring!" he suddenly added with an angry glance of Olenin.

The girls grabbed his sweetmeats from him, and laughing, struggled for them among themselves. Beletsky and Olenin stepped aside.

Lukashka, as if ashamed of his generosity, took off his cap and wiping his forehead with his sleeve, came up to Maryanka and Ustenka. "Answer me, my dear, dost thou hold me in contempt?" he said, in the words of the song they had just been singing, and turning to Maryanka, he angrily repeated the words: "Dost thou hold me in contempt? When we shall married be, thou shalt weep because of me!" he added, embracing Ustenka and Maryanka both together. Ustenka tore herself away, and swinging her arm gave him such a blow on the back that she hurt her hand.

"Well, are you going to have another turn?" he asked.

"The other girls may if they like," answered Ustenka, "but I am going home, and Maryanka was coming to our house too."

With his arm still round her, Lukashka led Maryanka away from the crowd to the darker corner of a house.

"Don't go, Maryanka," he said, "let's have some fun for the last time. Go home and I will come to you!"

"What am I to do at home? Holidays are meant for merrymaking. I am going to Ustenka's," replied Maryanka."

"I'll marry you, all the same, you know!"

"All right," said Maryanka, "we shall see when the time comes."

"So you are going," said Lukashka sternly, and, pressing her close, he kissed her on the cheek.

"There, leave off! Don't bother," and Maryanka, wrenching herself from his arms, moved away.

"Ah, my girl, it will turn out badly," said Lukashka reproachfully, and stood still shaking his head. "Thou shalt weep because of me . . ." and turning away from her, he shouted to the other girls.

"Now then! Play away!"

What he had said seemed to have frightened and vexed Maryanka. She stopped, "What will turn out badly?"

"Why, that!"

"That what?"

"Why, that you keep company with a soldier-lodger and no longer care for me!"

"I'll care just as long as I choose. You're not my father, nor my mother. What do you want? I'll care for whom I like!"

"Well, all right . . ." said Lukashka, "but remember!" He moved toward the shop. "Girls!" he shouted, "why have you stopped? Go on dancing. Nazarka, fetch some more chikhir."

"Well, will they come?" asked Olenin, addressing Beletsky.

"They'll come directly," replied Beletsky. "Come along, we must prepare the ball."

CHAPTER XXXIX

JOY AND PAIN

IT was already late in the night when Olenin came out of Beletsky's hut, following Maryanka and Ustenka. He saw in the dark street before him the gleam of the girl's white kerchief. The golden moon was descending toward the steppe. A silvery mist hung over the village. All was still; there were no lights anywhere, and one heard only the retreating footsteps of the young women. Olenin's heart beat fast. The fresh moist atmosphere cooled his burning face. He glanced at the sky and turned to look at the hut he had just come out of: the candle was already out. Then he again peered through the darkness at the girls' retreating shadows. The white kerchief disappeared in the mist. He was afraid to remain alone, he was so happy. He jumped down from the porch and ran after the girls.

"Bother you, some one may see . . ." said Ustenka.

"Never mind!"

Olenin ran up to Maryanka, and embraced her. Maryanka did not resist.

"Haven't you kissed enough yet?" said Ustenka. "Marry and then kiss, but now you'd better wait."

"Good night, Maryanka, to-morrow I will come to see your father, and tell him. Don't you say anything."

"Why should I!" answered Maryanka.

Both the girls started running. Olenin went on by himself, thinking over all that had happened. He had spent the whole evening alone with her in a corner by the oven. Ustenka had not left the hut for a single moment, but had romped about with the other girls and with Beletsky all the time. Olenin had talked in whispers to Maryanka.

"Will you marry me?" he had asked.

"You'll deceive me and not have me," she replied cheerfully and calmly.

"But do you love me? Tell me for God's sake!"

"Why shouldn't I love you? You don't squint," answered Maryanka, laughing, and with her hard hands squeezing his . . .

"What whi-ite, whi-i-te, soft hands you've got—so like clotted cream," she said.

"I am in earnest. Tell me, will you marry me?"

"Why not, if father gives me to you?"

"Well then, remember, I shall go mad if you deceive me. To-morrow I will tell your mother and father. I shall come and propose."

Maryanka suddenly burst out laughing.

"What's the matter?"

"It seems so funny!"

"It's true! I will buy a vineyard and a house, and will enroll myself as a Cossack."

"Mind you don't go after other women, then. I am severe about that."

Olenin joyfully repeated all these words to himself. The memory of them now gave him pain, and now such joy that it took away his breath. The pain was because she had remained as calm as usual while talking to him. She did not seem at all agitated by these new conditions. It was as if she did not trust him, and did not think of the future. It seemed to him that she only loved him for the present moment, and that in her mind there was no future with him. He was happy, because her words sounded to him true, and she had consented to be his.

"Yes," thought he to himself, "we shall only understand one another when she is quite mine. For such love, there are no words. It needs life—the whole of life. To-morrow everything will be cleared up. I cannot live like this any longer; to-morrow I will tell everything to her father, to Beletsky, and to the whole village."

Lukashka, after two sleepless nights, had drunk so much at the fête, that for the first time in his life, his feet would not carry him, and he slept in Yamka's house.

CHAPTER XL

COSSACK SCOUTS

THE next day Olenin awoke earlier than usual and immediately remembered what lay before him, and he joyfully recalled her kisses, the pressure of her hard hands, and her words, "What white hands you have!"

He jumped up and wished to go at once to his hosts' hut to ask for their consent to his marriage with Maryanka. The sun had not yet risen, but it seemed that there was an unusual bustle in the street and side street: people were moving about on foot and on horseback, and talking. He threw on his Circassian coat and hastened out into the porch. His hosts were not yet up. Five Cossacks were riding past and talking loudly together. In front rode Lukashka, on his broad-backed Kabarda horse. The Cossacks were all speaking and shouting so that it was impossible to make out exactly what they were saying.

"Ride to the Upper Post," shouted one.

"Saddle, and catch us up, be quick," said another.

"It's nearer through the other gate!"

"What are you talking about!" cried Lukashka. "We must go through the middle gates, of course."

"So we must, it's nearer that way," said one of the Cossacks, who was covered with dust and rode a perspiring horse.

Lukashka's face was red and swollen after the drinking of the previous night, and his cap was pushed to the back of his head. He was calling out with authority, as though he were an officer.

"What is the matter? Where are you going?" asked Olenin, with difficulty attracting the Cossacks' attention.

"We are off to catch abreks. They're hiding among the sand drifts. We are just off, but there are not enough of us yet." And the Cossacks continued to shout, more and more of them joining as they rode down the street. It occurred to Olenin that it would not look well for him to stay behind; besides he thought he could soon come back. He dressed, loaded his gun with bullets, jumped on to his horse, which Vanyusha had saddled more or less well, and overtook the Cossacks at the village gates. The Cossacks had dismounted, and filling a wooden bowl with chikhir from a little cask which they had brought with them, they passed the bowl round to one another, and drank to the success of their expedition. Among them was a smartly-dressed young teacher, who happened to be in the village and who took command of the group of nine Cossacks who had joined for the expedition. All these Cossacks were privates, and although the Teacher assumed the airs of a commanding officer they only obeyed Lukashka.

Of Olenin they took no notice at all and when they had all mounted and started, and Olenin rode up to the Teacher, and began asking him what was taking place, the Teacher, who was usually quite friendly, treated him with marked condescension. It was with great difficulty that Olenin managed to find out from him what was happening. Scouts, who had been sent out to search for abreks, had come upon several hillsmen some six miles from the village. These abreks had taken shelter in pits and had fired at the scouts, declaring they would not surrender. A corporal, who had been scouting with two Cossacks, had remained to watch the abreks and had sent one Cossack back to get help.

The sun was just rising. Three miles beyond the village the steppe spread out and nothing was visible except the dry, monotonous, sandy, dismal plain covered with the footmarks of cattle, and here and there with tufts of withered grass, with low reeds in the flats, and rare, little-trodden footpaths, and the camps of the nomad Nogay tribe just visible far away. The absence of shade and the austere aspect of the place were striking. The sun always rises and sets red in the steppe. When it is windy whole hills of sand are carried by the wind from place to place. When it is calm, as it was that morning, the silence, uninterrupted by any movement or sound, is peculiarly striking. That morning in the steppe it was quiet and dull, though the sun had already risen. It all seemed specially soft and desolate. The air was hushed; the footfalls and the snorting of the horses were the only sounds to be heard, and even they quickly died away. The men rode almost silently. A Cossack always carries his weapons so that they neither jingle nor rattle. Jingling weapons are a terrible disgrace to a Cossack. Two other Cossacks from the village caught the party up and exchanged a few words. Lukashka's horse either stumbled or caught its foot in some grass, and became restive—which is a sign of bad luck among the Cossacks, and at such a time was of special importance. The others exchanged glances, and turned away, trying not to notice what had happened. Lukashka, pulled at the reins, frowned sternly, set his teeth, and flourished his whip above his head. His good Kabarda horse, prancing from one foot to another, not knowing with which to start, seemed to wish to fly upwards on wings. But Lukashka hit its well-fed sides with his whip once, then again, and a third time, and the horse, showing its teeth and spreading out its tail, snorted and reared and stepped on its hind legs a few paces away from the others. "Ah, a good steed that!" said the Teacher. That he said *steed* instead of *horse*, indicated special praise.

"A lion of a horse," assented one of the others, an old Cossack.

The Cossacks rode silently forward, now at a foot-pace, then at a trot, and these changes were the only incidents that for a moment interrupted the stillness and solemnity of their movements.

Riding through the steppe for about six miles, they passed nothing but one Nogay tent, placed on a cart and moving slowly along at a distance of about a mile from them. A Nogay family was moving from one part of the steppe to another. Afterwards they met two tattered Nogay women with high cheekbones, who with baskets on their backs were gathering dung left by the cattle that wandered over the steppe. The Teacher, who did not know their language well, tried to question them, but they did not understand him, and, obviously frightened, looked at one another.

Lukashka rode up to them both, stopped his horse and promptly uttered the usual greeting. The Nogay women were evidently relieved, and began speaking to him quite freely as to a brother.

"Ay-ay, kop abrek!" they said plaintively, pointing in the direction the Cossacks were going. Olenin understood that they were saying, "Many abreks."

Never having seen an engagement of that kind, and having formed an idea of them only from Daddy Eroshka's tales, Olenin wished not to be left behind by the Cossacks, but wanted to see it all. He admired the Cossacks, and was on the watch, looking and listening and making his own observations. Though he had brought his sword and a loaded gun with him, when he noticed that the Cossacks avoided him he decided to take no part in the action, as in his opinion his courage had already been sufficiently proved when he was with his detachment, and also because he was very happy. Suddenly a shot was heard in the distance. The Teacher became excited, and began giving orders to the Cossacks as to how they should divide and from which side they should approach. But the Cossacks did not appear to pay any attention to these orders, listening only to what Lukashka said, and looking to him alone. Lukashka's face and figure were expressive of a calm solemnity. He put his horse to a trot with which the others were unable to keep pace, and screwing up his eyes, he kept looking ahead.

"There's a man on horseback," he said, reining in his horse and keeping in line with the others.

Olenin looked intently, but could not see anything.

The Cossacks soon distinguished two riders, and quietly rode straight toward them.

"Are those the abreks?" asked Olenin.

The Cossacks did not answer his question, which appeared meaningless to them. The abreks would have been fools to venture across the river on horseback.

"That's friend Rodka waving to us I do believe," said Lukashka, pointing to the two mounted men, who were now clearly visible. "Look, he's coming to us."

A few minutes later it became plain that the two horsemen were the Cossack scouts. The corporal rode up to Lukashka.

CHAPTER XLI

THE DEAD

"ARE they far?" was all Lukashka said.

Just then they heard a sharp shot some thirty paces off. The corporal smiled slightly.

"Our Gurka is having shots at them," he said, nodding in the direction of the shot.

Having gone a few paces farther they saw Gurka sitting behind a sand hillock and loading his gun. To while away the time, he was exchanging shots with the abreks, who were behind another sand heap. A bullet came whistling from their side. The Teacher was pale and grew confused. Lukashka dismounted from his horse, threw the reins to one of the other Cossacks, and went up to Gurka. Olenin also dismounted, and bending down, followed Lukashka. They had hardly reached Gurka when two bullets whistled above them. Lukashka looked around laughing at Olenin, and stooped a little.

"Look out, or they will kill you, Dmitry Andreich," he said. "You'd better go away—you have no business here."

But Olenin wanted absolutely to see the abreks. From behind the mound he saw caps and muskets some two hundred paces off. Suddenly a little cloud of smoke appeared from thence, and again a bullet whistled past. The abreks were hiding in a marsh at the foot of the hill. Olenin was much impressed by the place in which they sat. In reality it was very much like the rest of the steppe, but because the abreks sat there, it seemed to detach itself from all the rest and to have become distinguished. Indeed it appeared to Olenin that it was the very spot for abreks to occupy. Lukashka went back to his horse, and Olenin followed him.

"We must get a hay cart," said Lukashka, "or they will be killing some of us. There, behind that mound, is a Nogay cart with a load of hay." The Teacher listened to him and the Corporal agreed. The cart of hay was fetched, and the Cossacks, hiding behind it, pushed it forward. Olenin rode up a hillock from whence he could see everything. The hay cart moved on, and the Cossacks crowded together behind it. The Cossacks advanced, but the Chechens, of whom there were nine, sat with their knees in a row and did not fire.

All was quiet. Suddenly from the Chechens arose the sound of a mournful song, something like Daddy Eroshka's "Ay day, dalalay." The Chechens knew that they could not escape, and to prevent themselves from being tempted to take to flight they had strapped themselves together, knee to knee, had got their guns ready, and were singing their death song.

The Cossacks with their hay cart drew closer and closer, and Olenin expected the firing to begin any moment, but the silence was only broken by the abreks' mournful song. Suddenly the song ceased; there was a sharp report, a bullet struck the front of the cart, and Chechen curses and yells broke the silence, and shot followed on shot, and one bullet after another struck the cart. The Cossacks did not fire, and were now only five paces distant.

Another moment passed, and the Cossacks with a whoop rushed out on both sides, from behind the cart— Lukashka in front of them. Olenin heard only a few shots, then shouting and moans. He thought he saw smoke and blood, and abandoning his horse and quite beside himself, he ran toward the Cossacks. Horror seemed to blind him. He could not make out anything, but understood that all was over. Lukashka, pale as death, was holding a wounded Chechen by the arms, and shouting, "Don't kill him. I'll take him alive!" The Chechen was the red-haired man who had fetched his brother's body away after Lukashka had killed him. Lukashka was twisting his arms. Suddenly the Chechen wrenched himself free and fired his revolver. Lukashka fell, and blood began to flow from his stomach. He jumped up, but fell again, swearing in Russian and in Tartar. More and more blood appeared on his clothes and under him. Some Cossacks approached him and began loosening his girdle.

One of them, Nazarka, before beginning to help, fumbled for some time, unable to put his sword in its sheath; it would not go the right way. The blade of the sword was bloodstained.

The Chechens, with their red hair and clipped mustaches, lay dead and hacked about. Only the one we know of, who had fired at Lukashka, though wounded in many places, was still alive. Like a wounded hawk, all covered with blood (blood was flowing from a wound under his right eye), pale and gloomy, he looked about him with wide-open excited eyes and clenched teeth, as he crouched, dagger in hand, still prepared to defend himself. The Teacher went up to him as if intending to pass by, and with a quick movement shot him in the ear. The Chechen started up, but it was too late, and he fell.

The Cossacks, quite out of breath, dragged the bodies aside and took the weapons from them. Each of the redhaired Chechens had been a man, and each one had his own individual expression. Lukashka was carried to the cart. He continued to swear in Russian and in Tartar.

"No fear, I'll strangle him with my hands. Anna seni!" he cried, struggling. But he soon became quiet from weakness.

Olenin rode home. In the evening he was told that Lukashka was at death's door, but that a Tartar from beyond the river had undertaken to cure him with herbs.

The bodies were brought to the village office. The women and the little boys all hastened to look at them.

It was growing dark when Olenin returned, and he could not collect himself after what he had seen. But toward night memories of the evening before came rushing to his mind. He looked out of the window, Maryanka was passing to and fro, from the house to the cow shed, putting things straight. Her mother had gone to the vineyard and her father to the office. Olenin could not wait till she had quite finished her work, but went out to meet her. She was in the hut, standing with her back toward him. Olenin thought she felt shy.

"Maryanka," said he, "I say Maryanka! May I come in?"

She suddenly turned. There was a scarcely perceptible trace of tears in her eyes, and her face was beautiful in its sadness. She looked at him in silent dignity.

Olenin again said: "Maryanka, I have come——"

"Leave me alone!" she said. Her face did not change, but the tears ran down her cheeks.

"What are you crying for? What is it?"

"What?" she repeated in a rough voice. "Cossacks have been killed, that's all."

"Lukashka?" said Olenin.

"Go away! What do you want?"

"Maryanka!" said Olenin approaching her.

"You will never get anything from me!"

"Maryanka, don't speak like that," Olenin entreated.

"Get away. I'm sick of you!" shouted the girl, stamping her foot, and moved threateningly toward him. And her face expressed such abhorrence, such contempt, and such anger, that Olenin suddenly understood that there was no hope for him, and that his

rst impression of this woman's inac-
essibility had been perfectly correct.

Olenin said nothing more, but ran
ut of the hut.

CHAPTER XLII

THE BULLET

FOR two hours after returning home
e lay on his bed motionless. Then
e went to his company commander
nd obtained leave to join the staff.
Without taking leave of anyone, and
ending Vanyusha to settle his accounts
ith his landlord, he prepared to leave
or the fort where his regiment was
tationed. Daddy Eroshka was the
nly one to see him off. They had a
rink, and then a second, and then yet
nother. Again, as on the night of his
eparture from Moscow, a three-
orsed post chaise stood waiting at the
oor. But Olenin did not confer with
imself as he had done then, and did
ot say to himself that all he had
hought and done here was "not it."
e did not promise himself a new life.
e loved Maryanka more than ever,
nd knew that he could never be loved
y her.

"Well, good-by, my lad!" said Daddy
roshka. "When you go on an expedi-
ion, be wise, and listen to my words—
he words of an old man. When you
re out on a raid, or the like (you
now I'm an old wolf and have seen
hings), and when they begin firing,
on't get into a crowd, where there
re many men. When you fellows get
rightened, you always try to get close
ogether with a lot of others. You
hink it is merrier to be with others,
ut that's where it is worst of all!

They always aim at a crowd. Now I
used to keep farther away from the
others, and went alone, and I've never
been wounded. Yet what things
haven't I seen in my day?"

"But you've got a bullet in your
back," remarked Vanyusha, who was
clearing up the room.

"That was the Cossacks fooling
about," answered Eroshka.

"Cossacks? How was that?" asked
Olenin.

"Oh, just so. We were drinking.
Vanka Sitkin, one of the Cossacks, got
merry, and puff! he gave me one from
his pistol, just here."

"Yes, and did it hurt?" asked Olenin. "Vanyusha, will you soon be
ready?" he added.

"Ah, where's the hurry! Let me tell
you. When he banged into me, the
bullet did not break the bone, but remained here. And I say: 'You've
killed me, brother. Eh? What have
you done to me? I won't let you off!
You'll have to stand me a pailful!'"

"Well, but did it hurt?" Olenin asked
again, scarcely listening to the tale.

"Let me finish. He stood a pailful;
and we drank it, but the blood went on
flowing. The whole room was drenched
and covered with blood. Grandad
Burlak, he says, 'The lad will give up
the ghost. Stand a bottle of the sweet
sort, or we shall have you taken up!'
They brought more drink, and boozed
and boozed——"

"Yes, but did it hurt you much?"
Olenin asked once more.

"Hurt, indeed! Don't interrupt: I
don't like it. Let me finish. We
boozed and boozed till morning, and I
fell asleep on the top of the oven.

drunk. When I woke in the morning I could not unbend myself anyhow——"

"Was it very painful?" repeated Olenin, thinking that now he would at last get an answer to his question.

"Did I tell you it was painful? I did not say it was painful, but I could not bend and I could not walk."

"And then it healed up?" said Olenin, not even laughing, so heavy was his heart.

"It healed up, but the bullet is still there. Just feel it!" And lifting his shirt he showed his powerful back, where just near the bone a bullet could be felt and rolled about.

"Feel how it rolls," he said, evidently amusing himself with the bullet as with a toy. "There now, it has rolled to the back."

"And Lukashka, will he recover?" asked Olenin.

"Heaven only knows! There's no doctor. They've gone for one."

"Where will they get one? From Groznoe?" asked Olenin.

"No, my lad. Were I the Tzar, I'd have hung all your Russian doctors long ago. Cutting is all they know! There's our Cossack Baklashka, no longer a real man now that they've cut off his leg! That shows they're fools! What's Baklashka good for now? No, my lad, in the mountains there are real doctors. There was my chum, Vorchik, he was on an expedition and was wounded just here in the chest. Well, your doctors gave him up, but one of theirs came from the mountains and cured him! They understand herbs, my lad!"

"Come, stop talking rubbish," said Olenin. "I'd better send a doctor from headquarters."

"Rubbish!" the old man said, mockingly. "Fool, fool! Rubbish. You'll send a doctor!— If yours cured people, Cossacks and Chechens would go to you for treatment, but, as it is, your officers and colonels send to the mountains for doctors. Yours are all humbugs, all humbugs."

Olenin did not answer. He agreed only too fully, that all was humbug in the world in which he had lived and to which he was now returning.

"How is Lukashka? You've been to see him?" he asked.

"He just lies as if he were dead. He does not eat nor drink. Vodka is the only thing his soul accepts. But as long as he drinks vodka, it's well. I'd be sorry to lose the lad. A fine lad—a brave, like me. I too lay dying like that once. The old women were already wailing. My head was burning. They had already laid me out under the holy icons. So I lay there and above me, on the oven—little drummers, no bigger than this, beat the tattoo. I shout at them and they drum all the harder." (The old man laughed.) "The women brought our church elder. They were getting ready to bury me. They said, 'he defiled himself with worldly unbelievers; he made merry with women; he ruined people; he did not fast, and he played the balalayka. Confess,' they said. So I began to confess. 'I've sinned!' I said. Whatever the priest said, I always answered 'I've sinned.' He began to ask me about the balalayka. 'Where is the accursed thing,' he says. 'Show it me and smash it.' But say, I've not got it.' I'd hidden it myself in a net in the out-house. I knew they could not find it. So they left me. Yet after all I recovered. When I went for my balalayka— What was I saying?" he continued. "Listen to me, and keep farther away from the other men, or you'll get killed foolishly. I feel for you, truly: you are a drinker—I love you! And fellows like you like riding up the mounds. There was one who lived here, who had come from Russia, he always would ride up the mounds (he called the mounds so funnily, 'hillocks'). Whenever he saw a mound, off he'd gallop. Once he galloped off that way and rode to the top, quite pleased, but a Chechen fired at him, and killed him! Ah, how well they shoot from their gun rests, those Chechens! Some of them shoot even better than I do. I don't like it when a fellow gets killed so foolishly! Sometimes I used to look at your soldiers and wonder at them. There's foolishness for you! They go, the poor fellows, all in a clump, and even sew red collars to their coats! How can they help being hit! One gets killed, they drag him away, and another takes his place! What foolishness!" the old man repeated, shaking his head. "Why not scatter and go one by one? So you just go like that, and they'll not notice you. That's what you must do."

"Well, thank you! Good-by, Daddy. God willing, we may meet again," said Olenin, getting up and moving toward the passage. The old man, who was sitting on the floor, did not rise.

"Is that the way one says 'Good-by'? Fool, fool!" he began. "Oh, dear, what has come to people! We've kept company, kept company for wellnigh a year, and now 'Good-by!' and off he goes! Why, I love you, and how I pity you! You are so forlorn, always alone, always alone. You're somehow so unsociable. At times I can't sleep for thinking about you. I am so sorry for you. As the song has it:

"'It is very hard, dear brother,
   In a foreign land to live.'

So it is with you."

"Well, good-by," said Olenin again. The old man rose and held out his hand. Olenin pressed it and turned to go.

"Give us your mug, your mug!" And the old man took Olenin by the head with both hands and kissed him three times with wet mustaches and lips, and began to cry.

"I love you, good-by!"

Olenin got into the post chaise.

"Well, is that how you're going? You might give me something for a remembrance. Give me a gun! What do you want two for?" said the old man, sobbing quite sincerely.

Olenin got out a musket and gave it to him.

"What a lot you've given the old fellow," murmured Vanyusha, "he'll never have enough! A regular old beggar. They are all such irregular people," he remarked, as he wrapped himself in his overcoat and took his seat on the box.

"Hold your tongue, swine!" exclaimed the old man, laughing. "What a stingy fellow!"

Maryanka came out of the cow shed, glanced indifferently at the post chaise, bowed and went toward the hut.

"*La fille!*" said Vanyusha, with a wink, and burst out into a silly laugh.

"Go on!" shouted Olenin, angrily.

"Good-by, my lad! Good-by. I won't forget you!" shouted Eroshka.

Olenin turned round. Daddy Eroshka was talking to Maryanka, evidently about his own affairs, and neither the old man nor the girl looked at Olenin.

Master and Man

CHAPTER I

THE SEXTON

IT was in the seventies, the day after the feast of Saint Nicholas in the winter. There had been a festival in the parish, and the church sexton, Vassili Andreitch Brekhunoff, (who was also a merchant of the second guild), had been forced to remain at home, since not only was his presence necessary at the church, but he had been receiving and entertaining some of his friends and relations. Now, however, the last of his guests had departed, and he was able to get himself ready to visit a neighbouring landowner, for the purpose of buying some timber for which he had long been in treaty. He was in a hurry to be off, lest rival buyers from the town should deprive him of this eligible bargain. The only reason why the young landowner had asked ten thousand roubles for the timber was that Vassili Andreitch had offered him seven—and seven represented about a third of its value. Perhaps Vassili might have gone on haggling still further (for the wood was in his own district, and there was a recognized agreement between the local merchants and himself that one merchant should not bid against another in the same district), were it not that he had heard that the Government forest contractors were also thinking of coming to treat for the Goviatchkinsky timber, and therefore he had better make up his mind to go at once and clinch the

matter. So, as soon as ever the festival was over, he took seven hundred roubles of his own out of the strong-box, added to them two thousand three hundred more out of the church funds which he had by him (making three thousand in all), and counted them carefully. Then he placed them in his pocket-book and got ready to go.

Nikita—the only one of Vassili's workmen who was not drunk that day— ran to put the horse in. Nikita was not drunk that day for the reason that he had formerly been a toper, but, after pawning his jacket and leather boots for drink during the flesh-eating days, had suddenly foresworn liquor altogether, and drunk nothing during the second month. Even on the present occasion he had kept his vow, in spite of the temptation of the liquor which had flowed in all directions during the first two days of the festival.

He was a muzhik of about fifty, and hailed from a neighbouring village— where, however, it was said that he was not a householder, but had lived most of his life among strangers. Everywhere he was valued for his handiness, industry and strength, as well as, still more, for his kindly, cheerful disposition. Yet he had never remained long in any one place, since twice a year, or more, he had been accustomed to get drunk, and at those times would not only pawn everything he possessed, but

575

grow uproarious and quarrelsome as well. Vassili himself had dismissed him more than once, yet had always taken him on again because of the store which he set by his honesty, care for animals, and (most important of all) cheapness. In fact, Vassili allowed Nikita a wage, not of eighty roubles a year—the true market value of such a workman—but of forty only. Moreover, this wage was doled out irregularly and in driblets, as well as, for the most part, not in cash at all, but in the form of goods purchased at a high price from Vassili's own store.

Nikita's wife, Martha—a rugged dame who had once been good-looking—lived at home with their little lad and two girls, but never invited her husband to come and see her; since, in the first place, she had lived for the last twenty years with a cooper (originally a muzhik from a distant village who had come to lodge in the hut), and, in the second, because, although she could do what she liked with her husband when he was sober, she dreaded him like fire when he was drunk. Once, for instance, when drunk at home he had seized the occasion to avenge himself upon his wife for all his submissiveness to her when sober by breaking into her private box, possessing himself of her best clothes, laying all the gowns and other gewgaws upon the wood-block, and chopping them into shreds with an axe. Yet all his earnings were handed over to Martha. Never once had he disputed this arrangement. In fact, only a couple of days before the festival she had driven over to Vassili's store, and been supplied by him with white meal, tea, sugar, and a pint of vodka, to the value of three roubles, as well as with five roubles in

cash—for all of which she had thanked Vassili as for a particular favour, although, as a matter of fact, Vassili was in Nikita's debt to the extent of at least twenty roubles.

"What agreement need you and I make together?" Vassili had said to Nikita. "Take what you need as you earn it. I don't do business as other folks do—keep my creditors waiting, and go in for detailed accounts and deductions and so on. You and I can trust one another. Only serve me well, and I shall never fail you."

In saying this, Vassili really had believed that he was being good to Nikita, for he could speak so persuasively and had always been so entirely supported in his decisions by his dependents, from Nikita upwards, that even he himself had come to feel comfortably persuaded that he was not cheating them, but actually benefiting them.

"Yes, yes, I understand you, Vassili Andreitch," Nikita had replied. "I understand you perfectly well, and will serve and work for you as for my own father."

Nevertheless Nikita had not been ignorant that Vassili was cheating him. He had only felt that it would be no use his trying to get a detailed account out of his master, and that, in default of another place to go to, he had better grin and bear it and take what he could get.

So, when ordered to harness the horse, Nikita proceeded to the stable in his usual cheerful, good-natured manner, and with the usual easy stride of his rather waddling legs. There he took down from a peg the heavy headstall, with its straps and tassels, and, rattling the bit against the side-pieces, proceeded to the stall where the horse was standing which he was to get ready.

"Oh ho, so you find time long, do you, my little beauty?" he said in reply to the low whinny of welcome which greeted him from the shapely, middle-sized, low-rumped, dark-brown stallion cob which was the sole occupant of the loose-box.

"Nay, nay," he went on. "You are in a hurry to be off, I daresay, but I must water you first," (he always spoke to the animal as one might speak to a being capable of understanding human speech). Then, having wiped the sleek, though dusty and harness-galled, back of the cob with a cloth, he adjusted the headstall to the handsome young head, pulled the ears and forehead-tuft through, let down the halter, and led the animal out to drink. As soon as Brownie had picked his way gingerly out of the dung-heaped stall he grew lively and threw up his heels, pretending that he wanted to kick Nikita as the latter trotted beside him to the water-trough.

"Quiet then, quiet then, you little rascal!" exclaimed Nikita, though well aware that Brownie was taking good care to throw out his hind leg in such a manner as only to graze Nikita's greasy fur coat, not strike it direct—a trick which Nikita always admired. Having drunk his fill of cold water, the animal snorted as he stood twitching his strong, wet lips, from the hairs of which the bright, transparent drops kept dripping back into the trough. Then he stood motionless for an instant or two, as though engaged in thought, and then suddenly gave a loud neigh.

"You don't want any more. You wouldn't get it even if you did, so you needn't ask for it," said Nikita, explaining his conduct to Brownie with abso-lute gravity and precision. Then he set off running back to the stable, holding the spirited young cob by the halter as the animal kicked and snorted all across the yard. None of the other workmen were about—only the cook's husband, who had come over for the festival from another village.

"Go in, will you, my boy," said Nikita to this man, "and ask which sledge I am to get ready—the big one or the little one?"

The man disappeared into the house (which was iron-roofed and stood upon a raised foundation), and returned in a moment with a message that it was the little sledge which was to be used. Meanwhile Nikita had slipped the collar over the cob's head and adjusted the brass-studded saddle-piece, and was now walking, with the light-painted douga in one hand and the end of the cob's halter in the other, towards the two sledges standing beneath the shed.

"If the little sledge, then the little sledge," he remarked, and proceeded to back the clever little animal into the shafts (it pretending meanwhile to bite him) and, with the other man's assistance, to harness it to the vehicle. When all was ready and there remained only the reins to be put on, Nikita sent his assistant to the stable for some straw, and then to the store-house for a sack.

"There now, that will do," said Nikita as he stuffed into the sledge the freshly-cut oaten straw which the man had brought. "But nay, nay" (to Brownie). "You need not prick your ears like that! —Well, suppose we put the straw so, and the sack on the top of it. Then it will be comfortable to sit upon,"—and he suited the action to the words by tucking the edges of the sack under the straw disposed around the seat.

"Thank you, my boy," he added to the cook's husband. "Two pairs of hands work quicker than one." After that he buckled the loose ends of the reins together, mounted the splashboard, and drove the good little steed, all impatient to be off, across the frozen dung of the yard to the entrance-gates.

"Uncle Mikit, Uncle Mikit!" came the shrill little voice of a seven-year-old boy from behind him, as the youngster ran hastily out of the porch into the yard— a youngster who was dressed in a short jacket of black fur, new white bast shoes, and a cosy cap. "Let *me* get up too," he implored, fastening his jacket as he ran.

"Well, well! Come here then, my dear," said Nikita, pulling up. Then, seating his master's pale, thin little son behind him, he drove the boy, beaming with pleasure, out into the street.

It was now three o'clock in the afternoon and freezing hard, the thermometer registering only ten degrees; yet the weather was dull and gusty, and fully half the sky was covered by a low, dark bank of cloud. In the courtyard the air was still, but directly one stepped into the street outside the wind became more noticeable and the snow could be seen twirling itself about in wreaths as it was swept from the roof of a neighbouring outbuilding into the corner near the bathhouse. Hardly had Nikita returned through the gates and turned the cob's head towards the steps when Vassili Andreitch—a cigarette between his lips, and a sheepskin coat upon his shoulders, fastened tightly and low down with a belt—came out of the house-door upon the high, snow-trampled flight of steps,

making them creak loudly under his felt boots as he did so.

Drawing the last whiff from his cigarette, he threw down the fag end and stamped it out. Then, puffing the smoke out of his moustache, he glanced at the cob as it re-entered the gates, and began to turn out the corners of his coat-collar in such a way that the fur should be next his face on either side (his face was clean-shaven, except for a moustache), and yet not liable to be fouled with his breath.

"So you have managed it, you little monkey?" he exclaimed as he caught sight of his little boy seated in the sledge. Vassili was a little animated with the wine which he had been drinking with his guests, and therefore the more ready to approve of all that belonged to him and all that he had done in life. The aspect of his little son at that moment—of the little boy whom he intended to be his heir—afforded him the greatest satisfaction as he stood blinking at him and grinning with his long teeth. In the porch behind Vassili stood his pale, thin wife, Vassilia Andreitcha. She was enceinte, and had her head and shoulders muffled up in a woolen shawl, so that only her eyes were visible.

"Had not you better take Nikita with you?" she said, stepping timidly forward from the porch. Vassili returned her no answer, but merely frowned angrily as though somehow displeased at her words, and spat upon the ground.

"You see, you will be travelling with money on you," she continued in the same anxious tone. "Besides, the weather might grow worse."

"Don't I know the road, then, that I must needs have a guide with me?" burst out Vassili with that unnatural stiffening of his lips which marked his intercourse with buyers and sellers when he was particularly desirous of enunciating each syllable distinctly.

"Yes, do take him, for heaven's sake, I implore you," repeated his wife as she shifted her shawl to protect the other side of her face.

"Goodness! Why, you stick to me like a bathing-towel!" cried Vassili. "Where can I find room for him on the sledge?"

"I am quite ready to go," put in Nikita, cheerfully. "Only, someone else must feed the other horses while I am away," (this last to his mistress).

"Yes, yes, I will see to that, Nikita," she replied. "I will tell Simon to do it."

"Then I am to go with you, Vassili Andreitch?" said Nikita, expectantly.

"Well, I suppose I must humour the good lady," answered Vassili. "Only, if you go, you had better put on a rather better, not to say warmer, diplomatist's uniform than that,"—and he smiled and winked one eye at Nikita's fur jacket, which, truth to tell, had holes under its two arms, down the back, and round the sides, besides being greasy, matted, shorn of hooks, and torn into strips round the edges.

"Here, my good fellow! Come and hold the cob, will you?" shouted Nikita across the yard to the cook's husband.

"No, no, let *me* do it," cried the little boy, drawing his small, red, frozen hands out of his pockets and catching hold of the chilly reins.

"Don't be too long over your new uniform, please," said Vassili to Nikita with a grin.

"No, no, Vassili Andreitch—I shan't be a moment," protested Nikita as he went shuffling hurriedly off in his old

felt boots towards the servants' quarters across the yard.

"Now, then, my good Arininshka, give me my khalat from the stove! I am going with master!" shouted Nikita as he burst into the hut and seized his belt from a peg. The cook, who had been enjoying a good sleep after dinner and was now getting tea ready for her husband, greeted Nikita cheerfully, and, catching the infection of his haste, began to bustle about as briskly as he himself. First she took from near the stove a shabby, but well-aired, cloth khalat, and set about shaking and smoothing it out with all possible speed.

"*You* are far more fit to go with the master than I am," he said to the cook, in accordance with his usual habit of saying something civil to everyone with whom he came in contact. Then, twisting about him the shabby, well-worn belt, he succeeded first in compressing his not over-prominent stomach, and then in drawing the belt with a great effort over his fur coat.

"There you are!" he said (not to the cook but to the belt) as he tucked its ends in. "You can't very well burst apart like that." Then, with a hoist and much heaving of the shoulders, he drew the cloth khalat over all (stretching its back well, to give looseness in the arms), and patted it into place under the armpits. Finally he took his mittens from a shelf.

"Now," said he, "I am all right."

"But you have forgotten about your feet," cried the cook. "Those boots are awful."

Nikita stopped as if struck by this.

"Yes, perhaps I ought to ch—" he began, but changed his mind, and exclaiming. "No, he might go without me if

I did—I have not far to walk," bolted off into the yard.

"But won't you be cold in that khalat only, Nikita?" said his mistress when he reached the sledge.

"No indeed! How should I? It is *very* warm," answered Nikita as he disposed the straw over the forepart of the sledge in such a manner as would conceal his feet after he had mounted, and thrust the whip (not needed for so willing a steed) under the straw.

Vassili had already taken his seat, his broad back, with its double covering of furs, filling almost the entire rear part of the sledge. Then, taking up the reins, he flicked the cob with them, while Nikita jumped into the forepart of the sledge just as it started, and sat leaning forward to the left and sticking out one leg.

CHAPTER II

LOST

THE good little cob moved the sledge rapidly along with a light creaking of the runners as he trotted at a round pace over the well-beaten, frozen piece of road leading to the village.

"Hullo! What have *you* jumped up for?" cried Vassili, suddenly, clearly enjoying the fact that an unauthorized passenger was trying to perch himself upon the runners behind. ("Give me the whip, Nikita!" he interjected). "*I'll* thrash you, you young rascal! Run along home to your mother!"

The boy jumped off. Brownie broke into a gallop, but soon changed to a trot again.

Kresti, where Vassili lived, was a hamlet of six houses only, and when they had got beyond the blacksmith's hut at the end they at once perceived that the wind was much stronger than they had thought it to be, and that the road ahead was almost invisible. The track of the sledge became snowed over almost as fast as made, and only the fact that the road was a little higher than the ground on either side of it rendered it at all distinguishable. The snow was whirling over the whole country-side and blotting out the horizon, while the Teliatinsky forest—generally clearly visible—now showed only as a dark mass looming at intervals through the snow-dust. The wind was blowing from the left, and kept turning Brownie's mane over his thick, fat neck and blowing his feathery tail,—bound at the top in a plain knot,—across his flank. Owing to the wind, too, Nikita's tall coat-collar, where he sat on the weather side of the sledge, kept pressing itself tightly against his cheeks and nose.

"The cob can't get up much of a pace to-day; there's too much snow on the ground," said Vassili, who prided himself on the excellence of his steed. "Once I drove him to Pashutino in half an hour."

"What did you say?" asked Nikita, whose tall coat-collar had prevented him from hearing what was said.

"I said that I have driven to Pashutino in half an hour," bawled Vassili.

"That's something to boast of indeed! He's a good animal if ever there was one!" commented Nikita, after which they kept silence for a while. Vassili, however, was inclined to be talkative.

"What do you think? I told your wife the other day not to let her cooper drink all the tea," he bawled once more, in the firm conviction that Nikita must be feeling flattered at being talked to by such an important and highly-educated man as himself, as well as so greatly taken with his own joke about the cooper that it never entered into his head that the topic might be distasteful to Nikita. However, the latter had once more failed to catch his master's words for the violence of the wind, so Vassili repeated his pleasantry at the very top of his "educated" voice.

"God be with her, Vassili Andreitch!" returned Nikita when he understood. "I never interfere with their affairs. She has given me little cause for blame, and, so long as she treats the lad well, I merely say, 'God be with her!'"

"Well, well," said Vassili, and changed the subject. "Are you going to buy a horse in the spring?" he continued.

"I only wish I could," replied Nikita as he turned his coat-collar back a little and leant over towards his master. The new topic interested him, and he wanted to catch every word. "My little lad is fast growing up and ought to learn to plough, but I have squandered all my money."

"Well, if you'll take the low-rumped nag off my hands I won't ask you much for it," said Vassili, whose spirits were rising, and who therefore recurred instinctively to his ruling passion—the passion which absorbed his whole faculties —namely, the pursuit of bargains.

"I would rather you lent me fifteen roubles and let me go and buy one in the horse-market," answered Nikita, knowing full well that the low-rumped nag which Vassili was asking him to buy was worth no more than seven roubles at the outside, but that as soon as ever Vassili had handed him over the animal he would swear that it was worth at least twenty-

five, and therefore retain about half a year's wages to cover the amount.

"The horse is a splendid one," went on Vassili in his precise, business-like tones. "I want to do you a service as well as myself. Honestly, now. Brekhunoff would never do *any* man a bad turn. I would rather be out of pocket myself than see others so. Yes, on my honour. The horse is a magnificent one."

"I am sure of it," said Nikita with a sigh. Then, finding it useless to try and listen further, he turned up his coat-collar again, and his face and ear became covered in a twinkling. For about half an hour they drove in silence. The wind kept getting down Nikita's legs and through a hole in his mitten, but he hunched his shoulders and breathed into the coat-collar muffled over his mouth, so that he did not feel the cold very much after all.

"What do you think? Shall we go round by Karamishevo or straight on?" asked Vassili presently. The road by way of Karamishevo was the longer and the rougher one, yet, on the other hand, it was clearly defined by posts on either side. The road straight on was a good deal nearer, but used by few travellers, as well as either altogether devoid of posts or marked only by small ones which would now be almost drifted over. Nikita debated matters for a moment.

"The road by Karamishevo is longer than the other one, but a good deal the easier to drive over," he decided at length.

"Yet, if we go straight on," pursued Vassili, who was inclined towards the route he named, "we have only to get into the hollow, and then we can't possibly lose our way. It will be splendid going through the forest."

"As you wish," said Nikita, and turned up his coat-collar again.

Accordingly Vassili had his way, and after driving about half a verst further on, turned to the left where a tall young oak tree stood. Its branches and the few dead leaves which still clung to them were being madly dashed about by the wind, which, after the turning, met the travellers almost full in the face. Light snow began to fall, and Vassili tightened the reins, puffed out his cheeks, and let the breath escape slowly from under his moustache, while Nikita dozed. They had driven like this in silence for about ten minutes when Vassili gave an exclamation.

"What is it?" asked Nikita, opening his eyes.

Vassili returned no answer, but twisted himself round to look back. Then he gazed ahead. The cob was still trotting along, his flanks steaming with sweat.

"What is it?" asked Nikita again.

"What is it, do you say?" cried Vassili in angry mimicry of the question. "Why, only that I can't see any posts now. We must be off the road."

"Wait a minute, then, while I go and look for it," said Nikita as he leapt lightly from the sledge and, taking the whip from beneath the straw, went ahead and towards the left—the side on which he had been sitting. The snow had not been very deep that year, so that, as yet, the road had been easily passable the whole way along; but here there were patches where it reached knee-high and smothered Nikita's boot-tops. He kept on trying the ground, both with his feet and the whip, as he walked along; yet the road had vanished.

"Well?" said Vassili when Nikita returned to the sledge.

"No road on this side," answered Nikita. "I must try the other."

"There seems to be something dark showing ahead," remarked Vassili. "Go and see what it is."

Nikita did so, and found it to be only a spot where the naked sprouts of some winter corn sown on a piece of black earth were making a dark patch on the snow as they waved before the wind. Nikita circled round to the right, and then returned to the sledge again, beat the snow from his khalat and boots, and remounted.

"We must go to the right," he said with decision. "The wind was on our left a moment ago, but now it is straight in our faces. Yes, to the right," he concluded with an air of conviction.

Vassili just managed to catch what he said, and turned the cob in the direction indicated; yet no road revealed itself there, although they went on for a considerable time. Meanwhile the wind showed no signs of dropping, and the snow continued.

"Well, we are altogether lost now, Vassili Andreitch," observed Nikita, suddenly, and half as though he were pleased at the fact. "What is this, though?" he went on, pointing to a blackened potato-top which was projecting above the snow. Vassili at once stopped the cob, which was now sweating heavily and moving its stout flanks with difficulty.

"Yes, what is it?" he echoed.

"It means that we are on the Zakharo-vek estate. That is where we have got to."

"Surely not?" exclaimed Vassili.

"Yes, it is as I say," insisted Nikita, "You can tell, too, by the sound of the sledge-runners that we are driving over a potato-field. Look at the bits of potato-tops which they have dragged off. Yes, these are the Zakharovek market-gardens."

"A fine place to get landed in!" said Vassili. "Well, what is to be done now?"

"We must keep on going to the right, and we shall be sure to come out somewhere or other," answered Nikita. "If we don't actually strike Zakharovek we shall at all events come across some tenant's farm."

Vassili assented, and drove the cob forward in the direction Nikita had advised. They proceeded thus for a considerable time, now coming upon bare grass, now upon rough patches of frozen ground, over which the sledge went grating loudly. Then, again, they would find themselves passing over stubble of winter or spring corn, with the dead straw or sticks of weeds projecting above the snow and waving madly before the wind. More than once they found themselves labouring through deep, level, pure-white drifts, with nothing whatever showing above the top. All the while the snowfall continued and the snow-dust whirled about the ground. The cob was evidently failing now, for his flanks were white and steaming with sweat, and he proceeded only at a foot's pace. Suddenly he stumbled, and then plunged forward into some ditch or gully. Vassili was for pulling up, but Nikita shouted to him:

"Why stop? Go on, go on! We must get him out of this. Now then, my beauty! Now then, my pet!" he went on to the cob encouragingly as he leapt from the sledge—only to stick fast in the ditch himself. However, the cob extricated himself presently, and scrambled back onto the frozen ridge which

lined the bank. Evidently it was a ditch dug out by hand.

"Where are we now?" queried Vassili.

"We must find that out," answered Nikita. "Let us push on a bit, and we shall arrive somewhere."

"Isn't that the Goviatchkinsky forest, surely?" said his master presently, pointing to something black looming through the snow ahead.

"It may be. We had better push on and find out," rejoined Nikita. As a matter of fact, he had already distinguished the oblong patches of some withered vine-leaves showing against the blackness of the object in question, and knew, therefore, that it was more likely to be a habitation of some kind than a forest; yet he hesitated to speak before he knew for certain. Sure enough, they had not proceeded more than twenty yards beyond the ditch when trees showed up clearly before them and some melancholy sound became audible. Nikita had guessed rightly. It was not a forest they had come to, but a row of tall vines, with a few withered leaves still quivering upon them. Evidently they marked the trench of a threshing-floor. Just as the travellers had almost reached these vines and could tell that the melancholy sound arose from the wind sweeping through their rustling leaves, the cob took a sudden plunge upwards with his fore hoofs, pulled up his hind-quarters after them, turned to the left, and went on with the snow no longer reaching to his knees. It was the road again!

"Now we have reached it!" exclaimed Nikita, "but the Lord only knows where!"

The cob, however, never faltered, but went straight ahead along the snow-swept road; until, just as they had covered about a hundred yards, there uprose before them the rectangular outlines of a wattled barn, with its roof piled with snow and the snow-dust blowing from it in clouds. Passing the barn, the road wound back into the wind a little, and they found themselves in a snowdrift. A short way further on could be seen an opening between two buildings, so that it was clear that the road lay through the snowdrift, and that the latter must be surmounted. Sure enough, they had no sooner accomplished this than they found themselves in a village street, in the nearest courtyard of which some frozen linen was hanging from a line and rustling distractedly in the wind. It comprised two shirts (one of them white and the other one red), a pair of drawers, some leggings, and a petticoat, of which the white shirt was particularly abandoned in its antics as it waved its sleeves before the wind.

"Ugh, the lazy woman—though I am sorry to have to say it of her!" said Nikita with a glance at the waving shirts. "To think of not getting one's linen ready for the festival!"

CHAPTER III

WHOSE MEN

THE wind was as strong at the entrance to the street as it had been in the open country, and the roadway piled with snow, but in the middle of the hamlet everything seemed warm and quiet and cheerful. A dog came barking out of a yard, while in another yard an old woman came running from somewhere, with her head swathed in a handkerchief, but stopped as she was making for the door of the hut and stood for a moment on the threshold to gaze at the new arrivals. From the middle of the village came the sound of girls singing, and altogether there seemed to be less wind and cold and snow here than outside.

"Why, this must be Grishkino," said Vassili.

"It is," replied Nikita; and Grishkino it was.

It turned out afterwards that they had left the road upon their right, and travelled some eight versts at a tangent to their former direction—though still more or less in the direction of their proper goal. Yet Goviatchkina was fully five versts from Grishkino.

Halfway up the street they encountered a tall man walking in the centre of the roadway.

"Who are you?" he cried as he stopped. Then, recognizing Vassili, he caught hold of one of the shafts, rested his hands upon it, and climbed to the seat of the sledge. It was a friend of Vassili's named Isai, known as the worst horse-thief in the district.

"Well, and whither is God taking you now?" said Isai, suffusing Nikita with the smell of the vodka which he had been drinking.

"We have been trying to get to Goviatchkina."

"What a way to take, then! You should have gone by Malakhovo."

"It's no good saying what we *should* have done when we didn't do it," retorted Vassili as he pulled up the cob.

"That is a good animal," remarked Isai, looking the cob over, and passing his hand under the now drooping stump of its stout, knotted tail in his usual horsey manner. "Are you going to stay the night here?"

"No, my friend. We have further to go yet."

"You had much better stay. But who is this? Why, if it isn't Nikita Stepanitch!"

"Yes, no one else," replied Nikita. "But pray tell us, brother, how to avoid losing our way again."

"How to avoid losing your way again? Why, turn back, go right along the street, and the road is straight in front of you. Don't turn to the left, but keep on until you come nearly to a large village, and then—to the right."

"But whereabouts is the turning near that village?" asked Nikita again. "Is it on the summer or the winter road?"

"The winter. You will come to a copse there, and exactly opposite the copse there stands a tall, ragged oaken post. That is where you are to turn off."

Accordingly Vassili turned the cob's head round, and drove off down the street again.

"You had better have stayed the night here," shouted Isai after them, but Vassili shook up the cob and returned no answer. To cover five versts of level road, of which two would run through forest, seemed an easy enough prospect, especially in view of the fact that the snow now seemed to them to have ccased and the wind to have dropped.

Passing from the street again, with its roadway trampled hard and showing black here and there with patches of fresh dung, they drove past the yard where the linen was hanging out to dry (the white shirt had now partly torn away from the line and was dangling by one frozen sleeve only), and went on until they came to the vine-stocks with their quaintly murmuring leaves. Here they were in the open country again— only to discover that the blizzard had in no way abated, but rather, on the con-

trary, increased. The road was drifted over ahead, and nothing but the posts alongside could keep them from leaving it. These posts, too, were difficult to distinguish, since the wind was head on.

Vassili knit his brows as he bent forward to watch for the posts, but gave the cob more rein than before, and trusted to its sagacity. Sure enough, the cob never faltered, but went on turning to the left or right, according to the windings of the road, and feeling for it with his hoofs; so that, despite the fact that the wind kept rising and the snow falling ever thicker and thicker, the posts remained plainly visible on either side.

They had been driving like this for about ten minutes when there suddenly loomed up something black in front of the cob—something which was moving along in a tangled whirl of wind-driven snow. It was a party of fellow-travellers whom Brownie had outpaced, and the back of whose sledge he had actually struck into with his fore-hoofs.

"Pull out! Hi! Look out in front of you!" came in a chorus of shouts from this vehicle, and Vassili pulled out accordingly. In the sledge were seated three muzhiks and an old woman. Evidently they were guests returning from the village festival. One of the men was lashing the snow-covered flanks of their pony with a dry branch, his two comrades were shouting and gesticulating at one another in the forepart of the sledge, and the old woman—muffled up and white over with snow—was seated motionless at the back.

"Whose men are you?" shouted Vassili.

"A-a-a-skie!" was all that could be heard in answer.

"Eh?"

"A-a-a-skie!" repeated one of the muzhiks at the top of his voice, but it was impossible to distinguish precisely what he said.

"Lay on! Don't give way to them!" shouted another to the one belabouring the pony with the branch.

"You are returning from the festival, I suppose?"

"They are gaining, they are gaining! Lay on, Semka! Pull out, you! Lay on!"

The sledges kept bumping against each other, almost interlocking, and then parting again, until finally the muzhik's sledge began to be overhauled. Their shaggy, fat-bellied, snow-covered pony, blowing heavily under its low douga, and evidently frantic (though in vain) to escape from the flagellation of the dry branch, kept shuffling along on its stumpy legs through the deep snow, although at times they almost gave way beneath it. Its muzzle—that, apparently, of a young animal, with its lower lip projecting like a fish's, the nostrils distended, and the ears laid back in terror—kept level with Nikita's shoulder for a few seconds, and then began to drop behind.

"That's what drink will make them do," observed Nikita. "The pony will be ruined by treatment like that. What Asiatic brutes the fellows are!"

For several minutes the sobbing of the distressed pony's nostrils could be heard behind them, as well as the drunken shouts of the muzhiks. Then the first sound died away, and presently the second also. Nothing whatever was to be heard now except the whistling of the wind in the travellers' ears and an occasional faint scrape of the runners over patches which the wind had swept bare.

This contest with the rival sledge had cheered and enlivened Vassili, so that he drove the cob with greater assurance than ever, and without watching for the posts at all—leaving matters, in fact, to the cob entirely. Nikita also had nothing to do, so that, as usual with him when thus situated, he fell into a doze, in order to make up for arrears of sleep at other times. Suddenly the cob stopped short, almost pitching Nikita forward out of the sledge.

"We have gone wrong again," said Vassili.

"How do you know?"

"Because there are no posts to be seen. We must have left the road."

"Well, if we have, I must look for it again," remarked Nikita abruptly as he got out and began to trudge about the snow, stepping as lightly as possible on the balls of his splayed-out feet. He kept this up for a long time—now disappearing from view, now reappearing, now vanishing again—and then returned.

"No road there," he remarked as he mounted the sledge. "It must be somewhere ahead."

The dusk was now coming on, and although the blizzard had not increased it also had not lessened.

"If only we could hear those muzhiks!" sighed Vassili.

"They won't overtake us now," replied Nikita, "for we must have left the road a long way back. Perhaps they have done the same," he added, as an afterthought.

"Well, which way now?" inquired Vassili.

"Give the cob his head," advised Nikita, "and perhaps he will take us right. Here, give me the reins."

Vassili relinquished them none the less readily because his hands were half frozen in their warm mittens. Nikita took the reins, but let them lie quite passively in his fingers, endeavoring not to give them the slightest twitch. In fact, he took keen pleasure in thus trying the intelligence of his favourite. Sure enough, after pricking his ears first to the one side and then to the other, the clever animal started to turn round.

"He can almost speak!" cried Nikita. "My word, how well he knows what to do! On you go, then! On with you! Tchk, tchk!"

The wind was now at their backs again, and it seemed warmer.

"Ah, what a knowing fellow he is!" went on Nikita, delighted with his pet. "Kirghizenok is strong enough, of course, but an absolute fool; whereas this fellow—well, see what he found out with his ears alone! No need of telegraphs for him, when he can smell out a road a verst away!"

And, indeed, less than half an hour later a black object—either a wood or a village—began to loom ahead, while the posts reappeared on their right, placing it beyond doubt that the travelers had hit the road once more.

"If this isn't Grishkino again!" exclaimed Nikita suddenly.

And Grishkino it was. On their left showed the barn with the snow-dust blowing from its roof, while further on could be seen the clothes-line, with its burden of shirts and drawers still fluttering in the wind. Once again they drove up the street and found everything grow suddenly quiet and warm and cheerful. Once again the miry roadway appeared, voices and singing became audible, and the dog barked as before. The dusk, however, was now so far advanced that lights could be seen gleaming in some of the windows.

Half-way up the street Vassili turned the cob's head towards a large hut with a double coping of bricks, and pulled up at the steps. Nikita approached the gleaming, snow-encrusted window, in the light of which the dancing snowflakes glittered brightly, and knocked at a pane with the butt-end of his whip.

"Who is there?" cried a voice in answer to Nikita's summons.

"The Brekhunoffs from Kresti, brother," replied Nikita. "Please let us in."

Someone could be heard moving away from the window, and in another two minutes the sound of the inner door opening with a wrench. Then the latch of the outer door rattled, and there came out a tall old white-bearded muzhik, holding the door half-closed behind him to keep the wind from blowing into the hut. He was clad in a fur coat, hastily thrown over a white holiday shirt, while behind him stood a young fellow in a red shirt and tall boots.

"How is it with you, Andreitch?" inquired the old man.

"We have lost our way, my friend," replied Vassili. "We tried to get to Goviatchkina, but landed here. Then we set off again, and have just missed the road for the second time."

"But how came you to go wrong?" asked the old man. "Here, Petrushka"— and he turned to the young fellow in the red shirt— "go and open the yard-gates."

"Certainly," responded the youngster cheerfully, and ran forward out of the porch.

"No, no. We must not stop the night," interposed Vassili.

"But where can you be going now? It is nearly dark. You had much better stay here."

"I should have been only too glad to do so, but I simply cannot. Business, you see, my friend—and business won't wait."

"Then at least come in and warm yourselves with some tea," said the old man.

"Yes, we might do that," replied Vassili. "The night won't grow any darker than it is now, for the moon will soon be rising. Shall we go in and warm ourselves, Nikita?"

"Yes, I could do with something to warm me," replied Nikita, who was desperately cold, and only too eager to thaw his frozen limbs before a stove.

Vassili thereupon entered the hut with the old man, while Nikita drove the sledge through the yard-gates, duly opened for him by Petrushka. Under the latter's guidance he then led the cob under the roof of a shed. The shed was heaped high with dung, so that the cob's lofty douga caught upon a beam; whereupon the cock and hens which were roosting there were moved to uneasy flutterings and scratchings of their claws, some sheep darted away in terror, with much pattering of their hoofs over the frozen dung, and a dog whined loudly, then growled in angry alarm, and finally barked at the intruder in puppy fashion.

Nikita had a word for them all. He begged the hens' pardon, and quieted them by saying that he would not disturb them further; chided the sheep for their unreasoning nervousness; and never ceased to make overtures to the dog as he tied up his steed.

"We shall be all right now," he said as he beat the snow from his clothes.

"Hush, then, how he growls!" he added to the dog. "It is all right now. Quiet, then, stupid! Be quiet! You are only disturbing yourself for nothing. We are not thieves."

"They are what we might call our three domestic councillors," remarked Petrushka as he drew the sledge under the shed with his powerful hands.

"Why 'councillors'?" asked Nikita.

"Because," said Petrushka, with a smile, "you will find it written in Paulson's book: 'When a thief is sneaking up to a house the dog barks out in his own language—Wake up! the cock sings out—Get up! and the cat starts washing herself—meaning thereby to say: A guest is at hand, so let us be ready to receive him!'"

Petrushka, it seemed, was of a literary turn, and knew by heart the only book which he possessed—some book or other by Paulson. He was particularly fond of it when he had had a little to drink—as now—and would quote such extracts from it as might seem to him to fit the occasion.

"That is just right," observed Nikita.

"Yes, isn't it?" answered Petrushka. "But you are simply frozen. Shall I take you in to tea now, my boy?"

"Yes, by all means," replied Nikita. and they crossed the yard to the hut door.

CHAPTER IV

NIKITA

THE homestead where Vassili had pulled up was one of the richest in the village, for the family held no less than five lots of land, as well as rented some, while in the stables stood six horses, three cows, two draught-bullocks, and a flock of twenty sheep. In all, there lived around the courtyard of the homestead twenty-two souls—namely, four married sons, six grandchildren (of whom one—Petrushka—was married), two great-grandchildren, three orphans, and four daughters-in-law, with their children. In addition to these there were two sons employed as water-carriers in Moscow, while a third was in the army. At the present moment there were at home only the old man, his wife, the second of the married sons, the elder of the two sons who worked at Moscow (come over for the festival), the various wives and children, and a neighbouring gossip.

It was one of those rare households which are still to be found undivided, yet one in which there were already at work those deep-rooted internal dissensions which generally originate among the women of a family, and which would break up this family also in time.

Over the table in the hut there hung a shaded lamp, throwing a clear light upon the crockery below, upon a bottle of vodka, and upon sundry viands, as well as over the clay walls of the room. In one corner—the "corner beautiful"—there hung some ikons, with pictures on either side of them. In the place of honour at the table sat Vassili, stripped now to his black under-jacket, and chewing his frozen moustache as he gazed round the hut and at those about him with his prominent, hawklike eyes. Next to him sat the bald, white-bearded head of the family (dressed in a white shirt of home manufacture), while, further on, were the son who had come over from Moscow for the festival (straight-backed, square-shouldered, and wearing a similar shirt to his father's, but of finer material), a second square-shouldered son (the eldest of those living at home), and,

lastly, the neighbour—a red-haired, lanky muzhik.

These muzhiks had had their supper and vodka, and were just about to drink tea when the travellers arrived. Consequently, the samovar on the floor by the stove was already boiling. Near the stove, also, and in shelf-bunks could be seen various children, while the old woman—her face covered in every direction with fine wrinkles, furrowing even her lips—bustled about behind Vassili. As Nikita entered the hut she was just taking her guest some vodka, which she had poured out into a tumbler of thick glass.

"You must not refuse it, Vassili Andreitch," she said. "No, you really must not. You need something to refresh you. Drink it down, my dear sir."

Nikita found himself greatly excited by the smell of the vodka—especially now that he was so cold and hungry. He knit his brows and, shaking the snow from his hat and khalat, halted for a moment before the ikons, with his eyes turned away from the company. He crossed himself three times and made a genuflexion, after which he turned first to his host and saluted him, then to those present at the table, and then to the women standing by the stove. Finally, with a general greeting of "A merry festival to you all!" he started to take off his khalat—though still without looking at the table.

"But you are frozen all over, my brother!" cried the eldest brother as he stared at Nikita's snow-caked eyes, beard and face. For answer, Nikita divested himself of his khalat, shook it out, and hung it over the stove; after which he at length approached the table. Offered vodka, he had almost taken the glass and tilted the fragrant, shining liquor into his mouth, when he glanced at Vassili and remembered the pawned boots, as well as the cooper and the young son for whom he had promised to buy a horse in the spring. So he ended by declining the vodka with a sigh.

"I would rather not drink it, I thank you humbly," he said with knitted brows, and seated himself on a bench by the window.

"But why?" asked the eldest brother.

"Because I would rather not. I would rather not," Nikita replied without raising his eyes as he squinted down at his short beard and moustache and thawed the icicles out of them.

"It does not suit him," put in Vassili, smacking his lips over a cracknel washed down with vodka.

"Well, give me the tea-pot, then," said the kindly old woman. "I will get you some tea, for you must be frozen. Why are you so long with the samovar, my good women?"

"It is quite ready," retorted one of the younger ones as she wiped the covered samovar with a napkin. Then, raising it with some difficulty, she came and plumped it down on the table.

Meanwhile, Vassili had been relating how he and his companion had missed their way, wandered about, fallen in with the drunken muzhiks, and twice returned to the village. His hosts marvelled at the story, and then went on to explain how and where they had gone wrong, who the drunken muzhiks had been, and the route which Vassili and Nikita must take when they set off again.

"Why, even a child could find the way as far as Moltchanovka," said the neighbour; "and, once there, you only have to hit the turning near the village.

You will see a copse there. To think that you never got so far!"

"But hadn't you better stay the night here?" put in the old woman, persuasively. "The women shall get you a bed ready."

"Yes, do so, for if you were to get lost again it might be a terrible business," added her husband.

"No, no, I really cannot, my good friend," replied Vassili. "Business is business. Delay an hour, and you lose a year," he added, remembering the timber and the rival buyers who might forestall him. "Shall we go now?" (this last to Nikita).

Nikita returned no answer for a moment, and seemed absorbed in the task of thawing out his beard and moustache. At length he muttered gruffly:

"It would hardly do to get lost again, would it?"

As a matter of fact, he was gruff because he wanted the vodka so badly, and the only thing which would assuage that yearning of his was tea—which he had not yet been offered.

"But we need only to reach that turning," protested Vassili, "and we simply *can't* lose our way afterwards. From there onwards it will be all forest road."

"Well, it is for you to say, Vassili Andreitch," said Nikita as he took the tumbler of tea now proffered him. "If we must go, we must, that's all."

"Drink up the tea, then, and quick march."

Nikita said no more (although he shook his head disapprovingly), but poured the tea out carefully into the saucer and began to warm his work-swollen fingers in the steam. Then, having bitten off a crumb from his lump of sugar, he bowed to his hosts, said "A good health to you all!" and poured the grateful liquid down his throat.

"If only we had someone to guide us to the turning!" sighed Vassili.

"That could be managed," said the eldest brother. "Petrushka could harness a horse and go with you as far as that."

"Harness up, then, brother, and my best thanks to you," exclaimed Vassili.

"And to you also, good sir," said the hospitable old woman. "We have been only too pleased to see you."

"Petrushka, off you go and harness the mare," ordered the eldest brother.

"Very well," replied Petrushka smilingly as he seized his cap from a peg and departed.

Whilst the horses were being got ready the conversation passed to the subject which had been interrupted when Vassili drove up to the window. It seemed that the old man had been complaining to the neighbour (who was also the local starosta) about his third son, who had sent him no gift for the festival, but had given his wife a French shawl.

"The young people are getting out of hand nowadays," said the old man.

"Indeed they are!" agreed the neighbour. "There is no living with them. They are growing much too clever. Look at Demotchkin, who broke his father's arm the other day—all through his being too clever, of course!"

Nikita kept listening and looking from one to the other of the speakers' faces with an evident desire to join in the conversation, but he was too full of tea to do so, and therefore merely nodded his head approvingly at intervals. He had drunk tumbler after tumbler of tea, until he had grown warmer and warmer and more and more good-humoured.

The conversation lasted for quite a long time on this subject—on the evil of dividing up families—and proved too absorbing to be successfully diverted, so that in time it passed to the dissensions in this particular household—to the separation which the second son (who had been sitting by meanwhile and maintaining a sullen silence) was demanding. Evidently it was a moot point, and the question above all others which was exercising the household, yet politeness had hitherto prevented the family from discussing such a private affair before strangers. At length, however, the old man could not forbear, and with tears in his voice went on to say that, so long as he lived, he would never permit the separation; that he maintained his household to the glory of God; and that, once it were divided, it would become scattered all over the world.

"Yes, that is what happened to the Matvieffs," observed the neighbour. "They were a comfortable household once, but separated—and now not a single one of them has anything left."

"That is what you desire for *us*, I suppose?" said the old man, turning to his son.

The son returned no answer, and an awkward silence ensued until interrupted by Petrushka, who had duly harnessed his horse and been back in the hut for some minutes past, smiling the whole time.

"It reminds me of a fable in Paulson," he said. "A father gave his son a broom to tear across. None of them could tear it: but, twig by twig—well, that was easy enough. So also it will be in our case," he added with a broad smile. "But I am quite ready to start now."

"Then, if you are ready, let us be off," said Vassili. "About that separation, good grandfather—do not give in. It is *you* who have made the household, and therefore it should be *you* who are master of it. If necessary, refer the matter to the mirovoi. He would settle it for you."

"But to behave like this, to behave like this!" cried the old man, with unrestrained grief. "There is no living with them. It is the Devil's doing entirely."

Meanwhile Nikita, his fifth tumbler of tea swallowed, had placed the empty glass by his side instead of returning it, in the hope that he would be given a sixth. But there was no more water left in the samovar, and so the hostess brewed no more tea, while Vassili was already putting his fur coat on. Accordingly, there being nothing else for it, Nikita rose, replaced his lump of sugar (which he had nibbled on every side) in the sugar-basin, wiped his perspiring face with the lappet of his jacket, and went to put on his khalat. This done, he sighed heavily. Then he thanked and took leave of his hosts, and left the warm, bright living-room for the cold, dark porch, which was rattling with the wind which hurtled through it and which had drifted the snow through the chinks of the quaking outer door until it lay in heaps upon the floor. Thence he passed into the dark courtyard.

Petrushka, clad in a sheepskin jacket, was standing by his horse in the middle of the yard and smilingly quoting some verses from Paulson:

"The lowering tempest hides the sky.
The whirlwind brings the driving snow;

Now like a wild beast it doth cry,
Now like a child it whimpers low."

Nikita nodded his head approvingly and unhooked the reins, while the old man brought a lantern into the porch to guide Vassili to the sledge. He tried to light him with it, but it was blown out in a twinkling. Even in the yard it was easy to tell that the storm was worse than ever.

"What fearful weather!" thought Vassili to himself. "Perhaps we shall never get there. However, there is business to be thought of. Besides, I have got myself ready now, and my host's horse has been put in. God send we get there, though!"

The old man likewise was thinking that it would be better for them not to set out, but he had already tried to dissuade them, and they had not listened to him. It would be no use asking them again.

"Perhaps, too, it is only old age which makes me so nervous, and they will arrive safely," he thought. "Let us ourselves at least go to bed in the meanwhile. Enough of talking for to-night."

Petrushka, at all events, had no thought of danger. He knew the road and the whole neighbourhood too well for that. Moreover, he had been greatly put upon his mettle by the couplet about the whirlwind and the snow, which seemed to him to describe with extraordinary exactness what was to be seen in the yard. As for Nikita, he had no wish to go at all, but he had been too long accustomed not to have his own way and to serve others; so that in the end there was no one to prevent them from setting out.

CHAPTER V

HALTED

VASSILI walked through the porch, peered about in the darkness till he discerned where the sledge was, took the reins, and climbed in.

"All right in front!" he cried. Petrushka, kneeling in his own sledge, started his horse, and Brownie, with a loud neigh as he scented the mare in front of him, dashed away after her. They issued thus into the village street, passed the outskirts, and took the same road as before—the road which ran past the yard with the frozen linen (although the linen was quite invisible now), past the barn heaped with snow, and from the gables of which a cloud of snow-dust kept blowing, and past the bending vines with their mysterious murmurings and pipings. Then once more the travellers were launched upon a sea of snow, which raged both above and below them. The wind was so strong that when it was upon their flank and their wrappings filled before it, it actually careened the sledge to one side and threw the cob out of his stride. Petrushka kept shouting encouragement as he drove his stout mare ahead of them, while the cob followed her closely.

After about ten minutes' driving, Petrushka turned aside and shouted something, but neither Vassili nor Nikita could tell what he said for the sound of the wind. They guessed, however, that they had reached the turning. Sure enough, Petrushka had wheeled to the right, and the wind, which had hitherto been chiefly on their flank, now met them full in the face, whilst something could be seen showing black through the snow on their right hand. It was the copse which marked the turning.

"God go with you!" cried Petrushka.

"Thank you, thank you, Petrushka!"

"The lowering tempest hides the sky," shouted the lad once more, and vanished.

"Goodness, what a poetry-spouter!" remarked Vassili as he started the cob again.

"Yes, he is a fine young fellow, a real honest muzhik," returned Nikita, and they went on. In order not to squander the warmth engendered by the tea which he had drunk in the hut, Nikita wrapped himself up well, hunched his shoulders until his short beard covered his throat, and sat perfectly silent. In front of him he could see the two dark lines of the shafts forever cheating his eye, and looking to him like the ruts of a beaten road; the cob's tossing flank and knotted, wind-blown tail; and, further ahead, the animal's lofty douga, nodding head and neck, and dishevelled mane. At intervals posts would leap into sight, and he would know that the sledge was still keeping the road and that there was nothing for him to do. Vassili held the reins loosely, leaving it to the cob to guide himself. Nevertheless, although Brownie had had a long rest in the village, he went unwillingly, and as though he would like to turn aside at any moment, so that Vassili frequently had to straighten him again.

"There goes a post on the right—two —three," counted Vassili. "And there is the forest in front," he went on to himself as he gazed at something showing dark ahead of them. However, what had seemed to him a forest proved to be only a bush. This they passed, and had covered another fifty yards or so—when, behold! there was neither forest nor a fourth post to be seen!

"Never mind; we shall be at the forest in a moment," thought Vassili as, excited by the vodka and tea, he jerked the reins again instead of pulling up. The willing, docile animal obeyed and, now at an amble and now at a moderate trot, went whither he was driven, although he knew that it was in the wrong direction. Another ten minutes passed, and still there was no forest.

"We have missed the road again!" exclaimed Vassili, at last pulling up. Without speaking, Nikita descended from the sledge, and, after tucking up his khalat, which sometimes clung to him and sometimes flapped up and down, according to the strength of the gusts of wind, began to flounder about over the snow. First he tried the one side, and then the other, and thrice vanished altogether. At last, however, he returned, and took the reins from Vassili's hands.

"We must go towards the right," he said brusquely and decisively as he turned the cob in that direction.

"Very well; if to the right, to the right," agreed Vassili as he surrendered the reins and thrust his numbed hands up his sleeves. Nikita said nothing more beyond crying, "Now do your best, my pet!" to the cob. Nevertheless, the animal moved forward only at a foot's pace, in spite of all Nikita's shaking of the reins. The snow was knee-deep in places, and the sledge moved through it in jerks with each stride of the animal. Presently Nikita took up the whip, which had been hanging over the splash-board, and used it once; whereupon the good cob, unused to its lash, plunged forward and broke into a trot—only, however, to subside again into an alternative amble

and walk. They proceeded thus for about five minutes. It was so dark, and there was such a swirl of snow both around them and on the ground, that it was scarcely possible for them even to see the cob's douga. Sometimes, indeed, it was almost as though the sledge were standing still and the ground gliding backwards from it.

Suddenly the cob stopped short, as though he had scented something in front of him. Nikita threw down the reins and leapt lightly out, in order to go to the cob's head and see what he was jibbing at; but hardly had he taken a single stride ahead of the animal when his legs shot up and he rolled down some steep declivity.

"Phew, phew, phew!" he kept exclaiming all the time he was descending and trying in vain to stop himself, but his course was only arrested when his legs ploughed their way into a deep snowdrift at the bottom, while, shaken by his struggles, the drift overhanging the bank above him descended upon his head and crammed a large portion of its mass down the back of his neck.

"What a one you are, then!" said Nikita, reproachfully, both to the snowdrift and to the ravine, as he attempted to shake the snow out of his coat-collar.

"Nikita, Nikita!" came in a shout from Vassili above, but Nikita sent no answering call. He was too busy for that, for he was employing all his energies in shaking himself and searching for the whip, which had rolled away somewhere while he was shooting down the declivity. Having found it at last, he tried to reascend at the spot where he had come down, but found it impossible to do so, since he merely slid back with each successive attempt; so that finally he was forced to proceed along the bottom to find a way out. Nevertheless, only a few yards from the point where he had descended he found a place where he managed to creep up on all fours, after which he began to walk along the edge towards the spot where he judged the cob to be. Both cob and sledge were wholly invisible, but inasmuch as he was walking against the wind, he could hear Vassili's shouts and Brownie's welcoming neigh some moments before he actually caught sight of them.

"I am coming, I am coming," he exclaimed. "Why make such a fuss about it?"

It was not until he was almost upon the sledge that he was able to distinguish the cob, with Vassili standing beside it— the latter looming very large in the obscurity.

"How the devil did you manage to lose yourself?" began his master, angrily. "We must turn back and at least try to return to Grishkino."

"I should be only too glad," retorted Nikita. "But which way are we to go? If we fall into this ravine we might never get out of it again. I myself have just found it pretty hard to do so."

"Yet we cannot stay here, can we? We *must* go *some*where," retorted Vassili.

Nikita said nothing, but sat down on the rim of the sledge, pulled off his boots, and shook out the snow which had collected in them. That done, he gathered up a handful of straw and carefully plugged a hole in the left one.

Vassili also said nothing, as though he meant now to leave everything to Nikita. When the latter had finished pulling on his boots again, he tucked his legs onto the sledge, put on his mittens, took up the reins, and turned the cob parallel to the ravine. They had not gone more than a hundred yards, however, before the animal pulled up short. In front of them lay the ravine again!

Once more Nikita got out and went probing about over the snow. He was absent for some time, but at length reappeared on the opposite side of the sledge to that which he had started from.

"Are you there, Andreitch?" he shouted.

"Yes," replied Vassili. "Well, what now?"

"There is no getting out this way; it is too dark, and there are too many ravines about. We must try driving back against the wind."

After doing so for a little while they stopped, and Nikita once more alighted and went creeping about over the snow. Then he remounted, but only to alight again almost immediately; until at length he came to a halt by the sledge in a perfectly breathless condition.

"Well, what?" inquired Vassili.

"Only that I am fairly done, and the cob nearly so too."

"What are we to do, then?"

"Wait a minute." Nikita departed again, but returned in a moment or two.

"Keep close behind me," he cried as he walked on before the cob. Vassili had now ceased to give orders, but humbly obeyed Nikita's directions.

"This way—after me," cried the latter again as he turned sharply to the right and, taking Brownie by the head, led him downwards towards a snowdrift. The cob held back at first, and then made a plunge forward as though to leap the snowdrift. Failing in the attempt, he sank in up to the collar.

"Get out of the sledge," cried Nikita to Vassili, who had retained his seat meanwhile. Then, grasping one of the shafts, he exerted all his strength to help the cob to drag the sledge out of the drift.

"Pull, my pet!" he cried to Brownie. "One good pull and the thing is done. Now, now! Just one good pull!"

The cob made a brave effort, and yet another, but, failing to extricate himself, settled down as though to reflect upon the situation.

"Come, come, my pet; this won't do," Nikita adjured Brownie. "Now then, once again!" and he tugged at the shaft on his side, while Vassili tugged at the other. The cob shook his head for a moment, and then plunged forward suddenly in another attempt.

"That's it! You're not going to be buried this time, eh?" cried Nikita, encouragingly.

Another plunge—a second—a third—and the cob had cleared the drift and stopped short, shaking himself all over and breathing heavily. Nikita was for dragging the sledge a little further yet, but Vassili was so exhausted with the weight of his two heavy coats that he gave up and climbed in again.

"Let me rest a minute," he said, as he loosened the handkerchief which he had wound round his coat-collar before leaving the village.

"Very well; there is no great hurry," returned Nikita. "Sit still, and I will lead the cob."

Accordingly Vassili remained in the sledge, while Nikita led the animal forward for about ten yards, down a slope, then up again a little way, and finally came to a halt.

The spot where he had done so was not actually in the ravine itself, where the snow blowing off the hillocks and accumulating might have buried them entirely, but in a spot partly sheltered by the lee side of the ravine. Occasionally the wind seemed to drop a little, but it was not for long; whilst, as if to make up for such lulls, the blizzard would increase ten-fold after they were over, and tear and swirl around the travellers more cruelly than ever. One of these violent gusts struck the sledge just as Vassili was descending from it to go and take counsel with Nikita as to what they should do next, with the result that they could only cower down without speaking until the fury of the squall was spent. As for Brownie, he flattened his ears and shook his head in disgust. When the squall had abated a little, Nikita took off his mittens, tucked them into his belt, blew upon his hands, and set to work to unfasten the bow-rein from the douga.

"Why are you doing that?" asked Vassili.

"Because there is nothing else to be done," replied Nikita, though half-apologetically. "I am absolutely tired out now."

"Then aren't we going to try and get any further?"

"No, for we are only exhausting the cob for nothing," said Nikita, pointing to the animal where it stood patiently waiting for what might be required of it, yet scarcely able to hold itself upright on its stout, sweat-belathered flanks. "Brownie is willing enough, but he can hardly stand on his legs. There is nothing for it but to spend the night here."

Nikita said this as if he were proposing to put up in an inn-yard, and went on unfastening the collar-thong until the two clasps of the collar fell apart.

"But we shall freeze to death here!" cried Vassili.

"Well? What if we do? It cannot be helped," was all that Nikita vouchsafed to reply.

CHAPTER VI

WOLVES CRYING

VASSILI was warm enough in his two heavy coats, especially after his exertions in the snowdrift. Yet, for all that, the frost seemed to breathe down his back when he understood that they had to spend the night there. To calm his apprehensions, he sat down in the sledge and pulled out his matches and cigarettes.

Meanwhile Nikita unharnessed the cob. He undid the belly-band and saddle-piece, ran the reins out, unfastened the traces, and took off the douga, talking cheerily to the animal the while.

"Out you come, out you come," he said as he led it out of the shafts. "Let me take off your bit and tie you up here, and then you shall have some straw." He suited the action to the word. "Eat away, and you will feel all the better for it."

Nevertheless, Brownie did not seem to grow easier under Nikita's touch, but kept fidgeting about as he stood tail onwards to the wind. Every moment he would shift his legs, press up to the sledge, and rub his head against Nikita's sleeve. However, as if unwilling to seem churlish about the meal of straw which Nikita had strewn before his nose, he took an occasional straw from the sledge, but appeared at once to come to the conclusion that straw did not meet the case, and threw it down again; whereupon

the wind caught it in a twinkling, whirled it away, and buried it in the snow.

"Suppose we make a signal of distress," said Nikita, presently. He turned the sledge a little towards the wind, tied the shafts together with the belly-band, turned them up, and rested them against the splashboard.

"Now, if anyone passes this way they will be able to see us by the shafts, and come and dig us out. I learnt that trick from the old people," and he clapped his mittens together and put them on.

Meanwhile Vassili had unhooked his fur coat and made a shelter of its skirts. Then he struck match after match against the steel match-box, but his hands were shaking so violently with the cold that each successive match either failed to light at all or was blown out by the wind as he was in the act of lifting it to his cigarette. At length a match did flare up properly, illuminating for a brief second the pelt of his fur coat, his hand with the gold ring on its curved index finger, and the snow-covered straw which projected from under the sacking. The cigarette lighted, he drew a couple of greedy whiffs, swallowed the smoke, and puffed it out again through his moustache. Then he was about to take a third whiff, when the wind caught the lighted end of the cigarette and carried it away to join the wisps of straw!

Nevertheless, even these meagre mouthfuls of smoke had exercised a cheering effect upon him. "If we *must* spend the night here, well, we must, that's all," he said undauntedly. "Wait a moment and I will rig up a flag."

Picking up the handkerchief which he had unwound from his neck and thrown down upon the floor of the sledge, he took off his mittens, climbed onto the splashboard, stretched himself on tip-toe to reach the belly-band, and tied the handkerchief round one end of it and of the shaft in a stout knot. The handkerchief at once began to wave wildly—now clinging to the shaft, now suddenly filling out again and straining at the knot as its folds cracked in the wind.

"Is not that clever of me?" said Vassili as he stepped down again, much pleased with his handiwork. "Now, if we could lie together, that would be the warmest way, but I'm afraid that there isn't room for both of us."

"Never mind; I will find a place for myself," answered Nikita. "Only, I must cover the cob over first, for he has been sweating a lot and is tired out. Wait a minute"—and, diving into the sledge, he dragged the sacking from under Vassili. Possessed of this, he folded it double, and, removing the saddle-piece and crupper from Brownie's back, covered him over.

"You will be warmer like this, little fool," he said as he replaced the saddle-piece and crupper. "And now," he added to Vassili, "I will take the apron if you don't want it to-night. Give me some straw, too," and, thus taking one thing and another from beneath Vassili, he went to the back of the sledge, dug a hole in the snow there, and lined it with straw. Then he pulled his cap over his eyes, wrapped his khalat about him, with the apron over all, and squatted down upon the straw with his back resting against the bark tail-board of the sledge, that it might protect him from the wind and snow.

Vassili shook his head in disapproval of Nikita's proceedings (it was contrary to his habit to encourage the peasantry in their rude, uncouth ways), and then set about making his own preparations for the night. First of all, he smoothed out what straw was left in the sledge, padding it a little thicker where his thigh-bone was to rest. Then he pulled on his mittens and lay down with his head in one of the corners near the splashboard, that the latter might protect him from the wind.

Somehow he did not feel sleepy, but lay thinking. He thought chiefly of the one thing which constituted his whole pride, ideal, aim and joy in life—namely, the making of money, and yet more money. He thought of the means by which certain acquaintances of his had made their money, how they were using it, and the means by which he, like they, might make a great deal more than he already possessed. The purchase of the Goviatchkinsky forest seemed to him a matter of vast importance, since out of this forest he hoped to make, at one stroke, a sum, possibly, of ten thousand roubles. He mentally reckoned up the value of the timber which he had viewed in the autumn, and on the basis of the two dessiatins he had then inspected went on to calculate the whole.

"The oak-wood will do for sledge-runners if cut up, and for beams as they stand," he said to himself. "And after they are felled there should be left about 30 sazhens of firewood to the dessiatin." Thus calculating, he could see that the total value of the forest worked out at about 12,000 roubles, but could not reckon to an exact figure in the absence of tables. "All the same," he went on, "I am not going to give even so much as 10,000 for it—only 8000—and that subject to deductions for open spaces. I will grease the surveyor's palm with a hundred roubles, or perhaps a hundred and fifty, and he will measure me off the clearings at at least five dessiatins. Yes, the owner will be glad to let the forest go at 8000 roubles. I have 3000 ready for him here," thought Vassili as he felt for his pocket-book with the inside of his fore-arm; "and that should melt him. How on earth we came to miss that turning God only knows. There must be a forest and a forest-keeper somewhere about there. His dog ought to have heard us. The cursed brutes never bark when they're wanted to."

He turned back his coat-collar from his ear and listened. Nothing was to be heard but the whistling of the wind, the rustling and cracking of the handkerchief on the shafts, and the swish of the snow as it lashed the bark sides of the sledge. He covered his ear over again.

"If only I had known that we should have to spend the night here!" he thought. "Well, we shall get there to-morrow, all the same. It will only mean one day lost. Besides, those other fellows wouldn't come either—not in such weather."

Suddenly he remembered that on the 9th of the month he was to be paid some money for wethers by the butcher.

"I ought to be back by then to receive it. He couldn't take me in over the price, whereas my wife doesn't in the least know how to bargain. In fact, she doesn't understand how to talk to *anyone*," he went on as he remembered her failure to make conversation to the stanovoi, who had been one of their guests of yesterday for the festival. "She is a *woman*—that is the long and short of it. Moreover, what had she ever seen before I married her? Her father was only a well-to-do muzhik. A shabby little farm—that was all his property. But what have I not acquired in fifteen years? A store, two taverns, a mill, a granary, two rented holdings, and an iron-roofed villa and warehouse combined." He swelled with pride. "Rather different to her father, I think! In fact, who is the chief man in the district to-day? Why, Vassili Brekhunoff, of course!"

"And why so?" he continued presently. "Because I devote my whole attention to business and work hard—not like some people who lie abed and play the fool. *I* don't sleep whole nights away. No. Blizzard or no blizzard, out I go if necessary, and my business gets done. They think me a fool, and laugh at my money-making: but never mind, Vassili—go on working hard, even if it makes your head ache. If necessary, spend a night in the open like this rather than lose time. Never mind if you cannot sleep, either. To be able to think such thoughts is a pillow in itself," he concluded proudly.

"Some people seem to think that riches come to one by chance. Pooh! There is only one Mironoff in a million. No. Work hard, and God will give you the rest. If only He give you health and strength, that alone should be sufficient."

And the mere thought that he might one day become such a millionaire as Mironoff, who had risen from nothing, so fired Vassili with ecstasy that he yearned to have someone to speak to. Yet there was no one. Oh, but, once he could win to Goviatchkina, he would have a landowner to speak to—and to bamboozle as well!

"Good heavens, how it blows!" he continued as he listened to a squall of wind which was beating against the splashboard and bending it inwards as

It lashed the bark planking with snow. 'It is drifting the snow so much that perhaps we shall never get out in the morning."

Nothing could be seen in the white swirl of obscurity but Brownie's dark head and tail and the sack covering his back. At intervals the wind would toss the corners of the sack aloft, while in front and behind and on either side of the sledge whirled the same uniform mass of whiteness—now lightening a little, now suddenly becoming denser.

"I was a fool ever to have listened to Nikita," he thought. "We ought to have gone on again, and we should have landed somewhere. We might have reached Grishkino again, and been able to put up at Tarass's place after all. Yet here we have to stick all night! What is the good of that? God gives to those who help themselves, but not to loafers, sluggards and fools. I must try smoking again."

He sat up, got out a cigarette, and then rolled over on his stomach to shield the flame of the match from the wind with the flap of his coat. Yet the wind found an entry somehow, and blew out the matches, one by one. At length he contrived to keep one alight, and started smoking. He felt greatly pleased with his success, and although the wind got more of the smoke than he did, he managed to draw three whiffs, and was much cheered by them. He rolled himself back into a sitting posture, wrapped himself up again, and started once more to think over and consider matters; until suddenly, and without warning, he lost consciousness and went off into a doze.

All at once something seemed to jostle him, and he awoke. It might have been Brownie pulling away straw from beneath him, or it might have been the result of some internal disturbance, but at all events he awoke—and with his heart beating so fast and so furiously that the very sledge seemed to be shaking under him. He opened his eyes. The scene around him appeared exactly the same, except that it seemed lighter.

"It must be the dawn," he thought to himself. "It will soon be morning now."

Then all at once he remembered that the fact of its getting lighter could only mean that the moon was rising. He raised himself again, and looked at the cob. Brownie was standing with his hindquarters to the wind, and shaking all over. The snow-heaped sacking was turned up over his back on the windward side, and the crupper was slipping down over his flank, while his snow-powdered head and wind-tossed mane and forehead-tuft were more clearly visible than before. As for Nikita, he was still squatting in the same position as when he had first sat down, with his feet and the apron with which he had covered his head all piled with snow.

"A muzhik never freezes," thought Vassili as he bent over the back of the sledge and looked at him. "No, not for all his poor clothes. He can be trusted for that. Yet the muzhiks are a stupid lot—a mere welter of ignorance."

For a moment he thought of taking the sacking off the cob's back and covering Nikita over with it, but it was too cold to get up and make the effort. Moreover, he was afraid of the cob starving if he did.

"What on earth did I take Nikita for?" he reflected. "I have *her* stupidity to thank for it all," (he was thinking of his wife). Then he rolled back into his former position by the splashboard. "My uncle spent a night in the snow like this," he went on, "yet he took no harm. Sebastian, too, once had to be dug out," he continued as another instance occurred to him. "Sebastian died, though, for he was frozen stiff as a carcase. If only we had stayed at Grishkino!"

Wrapping his coat more carefully about him, so that the protection of the fur should not be wasted at any point, but keep him warm from head to heels, he closed his eyes and tried to sleep again. Yet for all his efforts, he could not succeed, but, on the contrary, continued absolutely alert and wakeful. Once more he began to make business calculations and to run over his outstanding debts. Once more, too, he began to appraise himself and to congratulate himself on his position in the world.

None the less, his every thought seemed to be broken in upon by a sort of haunting fear, as well as by a feeling of vexation that they had not stayed at Grishkino.

"To think of it!" he murmured. "Why, at this moment I might have been lying in a warm bed!"

More than once he turned himself over and resettled himself, in a vain endeavour to find an easier position and one more protected from the wind, but each new posture proved more uncomfortable than the last. At length he raised himself again, changed his position altogether, wrapped his legs up carefully, closed his eyes, and tried to lie perfectly still. Yet, either his feet, squeezed into their stiff top-boots, had begun to ache, or the wind was catching him somewhere, but at all events he had not been lying long in this position before he found himself angrily

remembering that at this very moment he might have been lying in a warm hut at Grishkino. Again he raised himself, again he wrapped his coat about him, and resettled himself. Once he thought he heard the far-off sound of cocks crowing, whereupon he turned down the collar of his coat in a tremor of joy and listened attentively; yet, for all his straining of his ears, he could hear nothing but the whistling of the wind through the shafts, the flapping of the handkerchief, and the lashing of the snow against the bark sides of the sledge.

As for Nikita, he remained squatting as he had done since the previous evening. Never once had he stirred, nor returned any answer to Vassili's shouts, although the latter had called to him more than once.

"*He* seems to have no difficulty in sleeping," thought Vassili with irritation as he leant over the back of the sledge and looked at the snow-covered Nikita.

In all, Vassili must have got up and lain down again at least twenty times. It seemed to him as if the night would never end.

"Surely it must be nearly morning now?" he thought once as he raised himself and glanced about him. "How would it be to look at my watch? But no; I might get frozen if I unhooked my coat. Yet, once I knew that it was drawing towards morning, things would seem better, and we would set about harnessing the cob."

In the depths of his soul, however, Vassili knew quite well that it could not be near morning yet. The truth was that his nervous panic was increasing to such an extent that he wished both to verify his supposition and to deceive himself. In the end he finished by carefully unhooking his fur coat, thrusting his hand in, and groping about till he dug down to his waistcoat. A further series of efforts enabled him to draw out his silver watch, with its enamelled chasing of flowers. Then he tried to look at it, but nothing could be seen without a light. Once more he lay down upon his elbows and stomach (as he had done when getting ready to smoke), pulled out his matches, and set about striking one. By this time he had grown more expert at the business, and, feeling for the match with the largest head of sulphur, he contrived to light it at the first attempt. Then, thrusting the dial of the watch under the light, he looked at it, and could hardly believe his eyes! It was only ten minutes past one! The whole night lay before him!

"Oh, the long, long night!" he groaned, feeling as though the frost were striking down his back already. Then, hooking his coat up again and wrapping it about him, he sat back in the corner of the sledge, and prepared to wait with what patience he might.

Suddenly, above the monotonous wail of the wind he heard a new sound—a sound made by some living creature. It grew steadily louder, attained its maximum, and began as steadily to die away again. There could be no doubt what it was. It was a wolf. Nor was the beast so far off that the wind could drown the gradations of tone in its howl as it moved its jaws from side to side. Vassili put back his coat-collar from his ear and listened strainedly. Brownie was doing the same, his ears sharply pricked, and when the howl ceased he changed his legs and snorted uneasily. After this Vassili found it

more than ever impossible to sleep—found it impossible to steady his nerves for a moment. The more he tried to think of his business affairs and accounts, his reputation, dignity and wealth, the more did terror begin to master him; while, above all other thoughts, and yet mixed up with them, floated the persistent question—"Why did we not stop the night at Grishkino?"

"God be with that landowner and his forest," he thought to himself, "yet I wish I had never come across either of them. To have to spend the night here! They say that men who have been drinking always freeze readily, and I have been drinking to-night."

Listening thus to his own suggestions, he could feel himself beginning to tremble, though he hardly knew why—whether from cold, that is to say, or from fear. He tried to cover himself up and lie down as before, but found this impossible. He could not remain still, even for a second, but felt as if he must be up and doing something to stifle the terror which was rising in him, and against which he felt himself powerless. He got out his matches and cigarettes once more, but of the former there remained but three, and they of the sorriest kind. Indeed, all of them fizzled out without lighting when struck.

"The devil take you, you cursed bit of rubbish! Go and be hanged to you!" he burst out (though hardly knowing what it was he was swearing at) as he hurled the battered cigarette away. The match-box was about to follow it, when he stayed his hand, and thrust the box into his pocket. Such a fit of restlessness now seized upon him that he could stay no longer where he was. Leaping from the sledge, and standing with his back to the wind, he began lowering and tightening up his belt again.

"Why should we lie here, waiting for death to come?" he exclaimed as a new idea suddenly struck him. "Why not mount the cob and ride away? With only a man on his back he would never stick fast." Then he thought of Nikita. "Oh, but it would be nothing to him to die," he went on. "What can his life matter to him? He has nothing much to lose with it, whereas I have much to gain with mine."

So he untied the cob, threw the halter over its neck, and tried to mount, but his fur coat and boots weighed him down, and he slipped back every time. Then he climbed onto the sledge and tried to mount from there, but the sledge kept rocking under his weight, and he failed again. At length, and for the third time, he drew the cob close to the sledge, balanced himself cautiously on the rim, and succeeded so far as to find himself stretched face downwards athwart the animal's back. Lying thus, he wriggled himself forward once or twice until he had got his leg over and seated himself, his toes resting in the trace-loops of the saddle-piece. But the jolting of the sledge as it shook under Vassili's weight had awakened Nikita, who now raised himself and seemed to Vassili to be saying something.

"Look here, you fool," shouted Vassili. "It's all through you that we have got into this plight—got into it for nothing, too," and, tucking the flapping skirts of his greatcoat beneath his knees, he turned the cob round, and rode away from the sledge in the direction where he thought the forest and the forest-keeper's lodge must be.

CHAPTER VII

LOST CONSCIOUSNESS

Up to this moment Nikita had never once stirred since he first squatted down behind the sledge and covered himself over with the apron. Like all people who live in close contact with nature and are familiar with hardship, he was patient, and could sit waiting for hours, or even for days, without growing restless or losing his temper. He had heard his master call out to him twice, yet had returned no answer, for the sole reason that he did not feel inclined to stir or to go to the trouble of raising his voice. Although he was warm enough at the time he had sat down, both with the tea which he had drunk and with the exertion of plunging through snowdrifts, he knew that that would not last long, and that he would be powerless to restore the warmth by exercising himself, since he felt as utterly worn out as a horse feels when he stops and can go no further, despite the severest whipping, and his master sees that no further work can be got out of him until he has been rested and fed. Moreover, one of his feet had got frost-bitten through its ragged boot, so that the big toe had lost all sensation and his whole body was becoming steadily colder and colder. Consequently, in time, the thought began to enter his head that he might have to die that night. Yet the thought was neither particularly unwelcome nor particularly awe-inspiring. It was not particularly unwelcome, for the reason that his life had not been exactly an uninterrupted holiday, but, on the contrary, a life of ceaseless servitude, of which he was beginning to grow weary.

Nor did the thought seem to him particularly awe-inspiring, for the reason that, over and above the masters whom he had served on earth—masters such as Vassili Andreitch—he had always felt himself dependent upon the Great Master who had sent him into this life, and knew that, in dying, he would still remain that Master's servant, and that that Master would be good to him.

"Should I be sorry to leave the life in which I am settled and which I am accustomed to?" he thought. "Well, even if I have to go, I cannot help myself, and it were best to prepare for the new one."

"My sins?" he went on presently as he remembered his drunken orgies, the money squandered on drink, his insults to his wife, his frequent oaths, his neglect of church-going, his non-observance of fast-days, and all the many things for which the priest had reproved him at confession time. "Well, of course they were sins—I have never denied that; but it was God who made me what I am. Yet, what terrible sins they have been! What will become of me for such sins?"

Then, from thinking of what might be in store for him that night he passed, without recurring to that thought, to memories which came into his head at random. He thought of Martha's arrival, of the workmen's carouse, of his refusal to share their liquor, of the present expedition, of Tarass's hut, of the talk about family separations, of his little lad, of Brownie (now, doubtless, growing warm under his sacking), and of the master who was making the sledge creak above him as he tossed and turned.

"Well, I had plenty of tea to drink there and was tired," he thought. "*I* had no wish to start out again. *I* had no wish to leave such good living to come and die in this hole. Yet *he* wished otherwise."

Then all these memories swam together and jumbled themselves up in his head, and he went off into a doze.

From this doze he was awakened by Vassili shaking the sledge as he mounted the cob—shaking it so violently that it slewed right round and struck Nikita in the back with one of its runners, forcing him, willy-nilly, to shift his position. Stretching out his legs with some difficulty and sweeping the snow off them, he raised himself a little, and at once felt a pang shoot through his body. Understanding at the first glance what Vassili intended to do, he begged him to leave the sacking behind, since the cob no longer needed it and it would make an additional covering for himself. He shouted to Vassili to that effect, but the latter disappeared in the snow-dust without heeding him. Left alone, Nikita considered what he had better do. He felt that he had not sufficient strength also to go off in search of a human habitation, while it was impossible for him to resume his old seat, since the snow had filled up the hole already. Even if he got into the sledge, things would not mend, for he had no extra covering, and his khalat and fur jacket no longer kept him warm. He could not have felt colder if he had been clad only in a shirt.

The situation was becoming one of positive agony.

"Little Father—our Little Father in Heaven!" he cried aloud; and the knowledge that he was not alone, but that there was One who could hear him and would never abandon him, brought him comfort. He drew a deep sigh and, with the apron still covering his head, crept into the sledge and lay down where his master had been. Even there, however, he could not grow warm. At first he kept shivering all over. Then the shivering fit passed away, and he began to lose consciousness. He might have been dead or asleep, for all he could tell, yet felt prepared for either eventuality.

CHAPTER VIII

BROWNIE!

MEANWHILE Vassili was using his heels and the spare end of the halter to urge the cob in the direction where, for some reason or another, he supposed the forest and the forest-keeper to be. The snow blinded his eyes and the wind seemed as if it were struggling to stop him, but, bending forward at times to double the skirts of his coat and tuck them between his knees and the icy saddle-piece which made his seat such an uncomfortable one, he pressed the cob onwards unceasingly. The animal moved with difficulty, yet proceeded whither it was directed in its usual docile manner.

For what seemed to him some five minutes Vassili rode straight ahead, seeing nothing in front of him but the cob's head and ears and a sea of whiteness, and hearing nothing but the whistling of the wind over the cob's ears and round the collar of his fur coat. Suddenly, however, something black showed up before him. His heart began to beat hopefully, and he rode towards the object, imagining that he already discerned in its outlines the

walls of the houses forming a village. The object did not keep still, however, but was forever waving from side to side. In fact, it turned out to be, not a village, but a tall piece of wormwood, which, growing out of a boundary ridge and projecting above the snow, bent violently over to one side each time that the wind struck it and went whistling through its stems. Somehow the sight of this wormwood thus tortured by the cruel wind caused Vassili to shudder, and he re-started the cob in haste, without noticing that, in turning aside to the wormwood, he had deviated from his former direction, and was now riding at a tangent to it. None the less, he imagined himself still to be bearing in the fancied direction of the forest-keeper's hut, and, although the cob kept trying to swerve to the right, he as often straightened it again to the left.

For the second time a dark object loomed up before him, filling his heart with joy, since he felt certain this time that here was a village at last: yet it proved to be only another boundary ridge topped with wormwood. As in the case of the first one, the sound of the wind wailing through the dried stems seemed to fill Vassili with fear. This piece of wormwood was exactly similar to the other piece in all respects save one—namely, that beside this second piece ran the track of a horse's hoofs, slightly powdered over with snow. Vassili pulled up, leaned forward, and looked at the track carefully. It was the track of a small-sized hoof, and the covering of snow upon it was, as yet, a mere sprinkling. In short, it was the track of his own cob! He had described a complete circle, and that not a large one.

"So this is how I am to perish!" he thought. Then, lest he should yield to his terror, he started forward again, and urged on the cob even more strenuously than before. At every moment, as he strained his eyes into the swirl of whiteness before him, he seemed to see dark points stand out for a second and then vanish as soon as he looked at them. Once he thought he heard what might have been either the barking of a dog or the howl of a wolf, but the sound was so faint and uncertain that he could not be sure whether he had really heard anything or whether it had been only his fancy. He stopped and listened attentively.

Suddenly a weird, startling cry sounded in his very ears, and everything beneath him seemed to heave and tremble. He clutched the cob's mane, yet found that that too was quivering, while the cry grew ever more and more piercing. For some seconds Vassili could not frame a thought or understand in the least what was happening. Yet all that had happened was that the cob had been seized with the idea either of inspiriting himself or of calling for help, and had neighed loudly in his raucous, guttural tones.

"How the beast frightened me, be hanged to it!" gasped Vassili to himself. Yet, although he understood now the cause of his terror, he could not shake himself free from it.

"I must consider things a moment and steady myself," he thought. Yet it was all to no purpose, for he could not master himself—could not keep from urging the cob on; taking no heed the while that he was now riding before the wind instead of against it. His body was chilled and aching all over, but especially in the lower part, next the saddle-piece, where his coat was unhooked, whilst his hands and feet were shaking violently and his breath came in gasps. He felt sure now that he was to perish in the midst of this fearful waste of snow, and that nothing could save him.

Suddenly the cob gave a groan as it stuck fast in a snowdrift, and, struggling violently, began to sink sideways onto its flank. Vassili leapt off, displacing as he did so the trace-loops in which his feet had been resting, and so also the saddle-piece on which he had been seated. Yet he had no sooner dismounted than the cob righted himself, lurched forward, took a couple of plunges, and disappeared with a loud neigh, trailing behind him the sacking and harness, and leaving Vassili stranded in the snowdrift. Vassili made a rush to catch him, but the snow was so deep, and his fur coat so heavy, that he sank knee-deep at every step, and had taken no more than twenty strides when his breath failed him, and he had to stop.

"The timber, the wethers for the butcher, the rent-hold land, the store, the taverns, the iron-roofed villa and warehouse, my little heir—am I to leave them all?" he thought. "Is it to end like this? No, no, it cannot be!"

For some reason or another there came into his mind at that moment a picture of the wormwood waving in the wind, and of himself twice riding up to it. Such terror seized upon him that he could hardly believe in the reality of what was happening. "I must be dreaming it all," he thought, and tried, as it were, to awake from his dream: yet there was no awakening for him. It was real snow that was lashing his face, heaping his form over, and chilling his right hand, which had lost its mitten. It was a real desert, too, in which he was now left lonely—as lonely as the wormwood—and in which he must await an imminent, a swift, and an unthinkable death.

"O Queen of Heaven! O Holy Father Saint Nicholas who teachest us abstinence!" he began, with a dim recollection of the thanksgiving service of yesterday, of the ikon with its blackened face and golden vestment, and of the candles for that ikon which he had sold, and which, returned to him straightway, he had replaced in his locker after lighting them for a brief moment. Again and again he besought the wonder-working Saint Nicholas to save him from his fate, promising in return a thanksgiving and many candles. Yet all the time he knew beyond the possibility of doubt that, although that blackened face and golden vestment, as well as the candles, the priest, and the thanksgivings, were all of them very important and necessary there in the church, they could do nothing for him here, and that between those candles and thanksgivings on the one hand, and his present forlorn plight on the other, there could be no real connection whatever.

"Still, I must not despair," he thought. "I have only to follow the cob's track before it gets snowed over, and it will bring me out somewhere. Only, I must not hurry too much, or I might plunge into another snowdrift and be worse off than ever."

Nevertheless, for all his determina-tion to go quietly, he could not help quickening his pace, breaking into a run, tumbling down continually, picking himself up again, and once more falling. Moreover, the cob's track was almost invisible where the snow was not deep.

"I am done for!" he said at last. "I am not following the cob's track at all, but only losing myself."

Just as he said this, however, he happened to glance ahead, and caught sight of something dark there. It was Brownie! And not Brownie alone, but also the shafts and the handkerchief! The cob was standing beside the sledge, with the harness and sacking still dangling down his flank—but standing in a different position to before, since he was just under the shafts, and had his head (which he kept shaking at intervals) drawn close to the ground by the halter, which had caught round his pastern. It seemed that Vassili had stuck fast in the same ravine as that into which Nikita and he had previously blundered—that, as a matter of fact, the cob had been carrying him straight back to the sledge, and that, at the moment when he jumped off, he had only been fifty paces from it!

CHAPTER IX

I KNOW!

STAGGERING up to the sledge, Vassili grasped hold of it and stood for a long time without moving as he endeavoured to steady himself and regain his breath. There was nothing to be seen of Nikita in his old position, but in the sledge there lay something heaped with snow, which Vassili guessed to be his servant. Vassili's terrors had now vanished—or, if any were left, it was merely lest he should have a return of the horrible panic which he had experienced on the cob's back, and, still more, when he found himself left in the snowdrift. At all costs he must not give way to that panic again; and if he would avoid that, he must be up and doing something—must be occupying his thoughts with something. First of all he planted himself with his back to the wind, and unfastened his fur coat to cool himself. Then, when he had regained his breath a little, he shook the snow off his boots and left-hand mitten (the other one was hopelessly lost, and probably lying somewhere a couple of inches below the snow), and refastened his belt tightly—much as he was accustomed to do when he was about to step out of his store to buy cartloads of grain which the muzhiks had brought. This done, he set about exerting himself. The first thing which it occurred to him to do was to disentangle the cob's leg, and, the halter thus freed, he tied Brownie up to the rim of the splashboard where he had been tied before. Next, he had just gone behind the cob to straighten the crupper, sacking and saddle-piece on his back, when he saw something stir in the sledge, and then the head of Nikita emerge from beneath the snow which covered it. The frozen man raised himself a little—though evidently with a great effort—and made a strange gesture with his hand in front of his face, as though he were brushing away a fly. As he did this he seemed to Vassili to be saying something— probably Vassili's name—so the latter left the sacking unstraightened and stepped up to the sledge.

"How is it with you now?" he asked, "and what are you trying to say?"

"Only that I—I am dying," answered Nikita with difficulty and in gasps. "Give my wages to the little lad or to the wife—it does not matter which."

"Are you frozen, then?" said Vassili.

"Yes—and dying; I know it quite well," replied Nikita in a choking voice, and still fluttering his hand before his face as though to brush away a fly. "Pardon me, for Christ's sake."

For about half a minute Vassili stood without moving and in silence. Then all at once, and with the same air of decision as marked him when he had struck hands over a good bargain, he took a step backwards, tucked up the sleeves of his coat, and began with both hands to rake the snow off Nikita and out of the sledge. This done, he un-hooked his belt, opened his fur coat, pushed Nikita hastily into a straight posture, and lay down upon him in such a way that the latter should be covered, not only with the coat, but with Vassili's own warm, overheated body. With one skirt of the coat tucked between Nikita's form and the side of the sledge, and the tail of it grasped between his ankles, Vassili remained lying prone, with his head resting upon the splashboard and his ears deaf either to the movements of the cob or to the howling of the wind, but intent only on listening to Nikita's breathing. For a long time Nikita lay without moving. Then he gave a deep sigh, and stirred faintly.

"There you are, you see, and yet you talk of dying!" began Vassili. "Just you lie still and grow warm, and we—"

To his great surprise Vassili found that he could say no more, for tears were welling from his eyes and his lower jaw was working. He broke off short, and swallowed a lump in his throat.

"How absurdly weak and nervous I have made myself," he thought. Yet not only did he find this weakness far from unpleasant, but it actually gave him a sensation of joy such as he had never yet experienced.

"Yes, we shall manage it all right like this," he said to himself, conscious of a rapturous feeling of emotion. After this he lay for a long time in silence, merely wiping his eyes against the fur of the coat, and tucking back its right-hand skirt as the wind blew it up at intervals; but at length he felt as though he must communicate his joy to a fellow-creature.

"Nikita," he said.

"That is better. I am getting warm now," came from underneath him.

"Nikita, my old friend, I thought we were done for. You would have been frozen, and I—"

Once more Vassili's cheeks started quivering and his eyes filled with tears, so that he could say no more.

"No, it is no good," he said to himself. "Yet I know what I know," and he remained silent. Still he lay there. Warmth seemed to be passing into his body from Nikita below and from the fur coat above. Only the hands with which he held the skirts of the coat against Nikita's sides, and his feet, from between which the wind kept blowing the skirts away, were beginning to feel frozen. His mittenless right hand in particular felt numbed. Yet he never thought of his hands or feet—only of how he could best warm the peasant who was lying beneath him.

More than once he glanced at the cob and saw that its back was uncov-

ered, since the sacking had now slipped off altogether and was lying on the snow. He felt as if he ought to go and cover the animal over again; yet could not make up his mind to leave Nikita, even for a moment, and thus break the spell of that rapturous joy which now possessed him. As for his terrors, they had long since fled away.

"By heavens, I am not going to be beaten!" he said to himself with reference to his efforts to warm Nikita—speaking, indeed, in just the same boastful tone in which he had been accustomed to speak of his sales or purchases.

He lay for an hour—for two—for three, but took no heed of the passing of time. At first there danced before his vision dim pictures of the storm, of the shafts, and of the cob under its high douga. Then these pictures became exchanged for jumbled memories of the festival, of his wife, of the stanovoi, and of the candle-locker—but beneath the picture of the candle-locker lay Nikita. Then again he saw the muzhiks trading with him, and the white, iron-roofed walls of his house—but beneath the picture of those walls again lay Nikita. Then everything became confused. One thing ran into another, until at last these various scattered impressions came together as the colours of a rainbow merge into a beam of white light, and he fell asleep. For long he slept without dreaming, but just before the dawn came, there came also some sleep-visions. He seemed to be standing by the candle-locker, while old mother Tikhonova was asking him for a five-copeck candle for the festival. He tried to take the candle out and give it to her, but his hands remained glued in his pockets. Then he tried to walk round the locker, but his legs refused to move, and his new, clean shoes stuck fast to the stone floor, so that he could not even raise his feet to take the shoes off.

Then suddenly the locker was not a locker at all, but a bed, and on that bed Vassili could see himself lying, face downwards—lying on his own bed at home. He was lying on the bed, and could not rise, although it was necessary for him to do so, seeing that Ivan Matveitch, the stanovoi, was coming to see him presently, and he must go with Ivan either to buy some timber or to put the crupper straight on the cob's back—he could not be sure which. He kept asking his wife, "Has he not come yet, Mikolovna?" and she kept answering him, "No, not yet." Then he could hear someone driving up to the steps outside. Surely it must be he? But no—the vehicle had driven past. "Is he not come yet, Mikolovna?" he asked his wife once more, and once more she replied, "No, not yet." Thus he lay and lay upon the bed, unable to rise, and ever waiting—waiting: and the waiting was at once painful and joyous. Suddenly the joy of it was filled to the full! He for whose coming he had been waiting, was now at hand and it was not Ivan Matveitch nor anyone else. Yet still it was the Man for whom he had been waiting. He entered—did that Man—and called him: and this Man who had called him cried out to him again and bade him go and lie down upon Nikita. And Vassili was glad that this Someone had come. "Yes, I will go!" he cried in his joy, and with that cry Vassili awoke.

Yes, he awoke—but awoke a very different man to what he had been when he fell asleep. He tried to rise, and could not. He tried to move his hand, and could not. He tried to move his leg, and could not. Then he tried to turn his head, but that also he could not do. This surprised him, yet in no way troubled him. Then he remembered that Nikita was lying beneath him, and that Nikita was growing warm and was coming back to life. It seemed to him that he was Nikita, and Nikita he, and that his life was no longer within himself, but within Nikita. He strained his ears till he caught the sound of breathing—yes, the faint, deep breathing of Nikita. "Nikita is alive!" he cried to himself in triumph, "and therefore so also am I!"

Then he began to think about his money, his store, his house, his sales and purchases, and Mironoff's millions. He could not understand how that man whom men called Vassili Brekhunoff could bear to interest himself in such things as he did. "That man can never have known what is the greatest thing of all," he thought of this Vassili Brekhunoff. "He can never have known what I know. Yes, I know it for certain now. At last—I KNOW!"

Once again he heard the Man calling him who had called to him before, and his whole being seemed to respond in joy and loving-kindness as he replied: "I am coming, I am coming!" For he felt that he was free at last, and that nothing could hold him further.

And, indeed, nothing further than that did Vassili Andreitch see or hear or feel in this world.

Around him the tempest still kept on. The same swirls of snow kept circling in eddies and covering the coats of the dead Vassili Andreitch and the trembling Brownie, the sledge (now almost invisible) and, stretched out upon its floor, the now reviving Nikita as he lay prone beneath the body of his dead master.

CHAPTER X

NEXT MORNING

JUST before morning Nikita awoke. It was the frost making its way down his back which aroused him. He had just been dreaming that he was driving from the mill with a load of his master's flour, and that, instead of taking the bridge over the stream, he went by the ford, and stuck fast. He could see himself getting under the load and trying to lift it as he straightened his back. Yet, strange to say, the load would not move, but clung always to his back, so that he could neither move the cart nor withdraw himself from beneath it. It seemed to be breaking his very loins. And how cold it felt! At all costs he must get away from beneath it. "Hold on," he found himself saying to the someone who was causing the load to break his back. "Take off some of the sacks." Yet the load kept growing colder and colder, and pressing more and more heavily upon him. Then suddenly something gave a loud bang, and he became fully awake and remembered all that had happened. That chilly load—it was his dead frozen master. That loud bang—it had been caused by Brownie striking his hoofs against the sledge.

"Andreitch, Andreitch!" he cried cautiously to his master (though he half guessed the truth already) as he raised his back stiffly. But Andreitch returned no answer, while his body and

legs were cold and stiff and heavy as weights.

"There is no doubt that he is dead," thought Nikita. He turned his head round, pushed the snow away from in front of his face, and opened his eyes. It was quite light now. The wind was still humming through the shafts and the snow streaming down—but with this difference, that the snow was no longer dashing itself against the sides of the sledge, but piling itself up in silence over sledge and cob—from the latter of which not even the sound of breathing was now to be heard.

"Brownie too must be frozen," thought Nikita. And, indeed, those two loud hoof-strokes upon the sledge which had awakened him had been the last efforts of the now dead and frozen animal to keep upon his legs.

"O God, Little Father of ours, surely thou wilt call me also?" said Nikita. "If so, Thy will be done. It would be hard that two of us should be taken and the other left. Let death come when it will," and he drew his hand in again, closed his eyes and fell asleep, firmly convinced that this time he was really and truly dead.

It was about the time of the midday meal next day when some muzhiks dug out Vassili and Nikita—seventy yards only from the road, and half a verst from the village.

The snow had drifted completely over the sledge, but the shafts, with the handkerchief on them, were still visible. Brownie, belly-deep in the snow, stood a white frozen mass, his dead muzzle pressed tightly inwards against his rigid neck, his nostrils fringed with icicles, and his eyes coated over and glazed with ice as with frozen tears. Moreover, he had so wasted away in that one night that there remained of him but skin and bones. As for Vassili, he too was as stiff as a frozen carcase, and when his legs were pulled aside the corpse rolled off Nikita in a solid lump. His prominent, hawk-like eyes were frozen hard, and his mouth (open a little under his cropped moustache) filled with snow. Nikita only was alive, though frost-bitten all over. Yet, when brought to himself, he could not be persuaded that he was not dead, and that all that was now happening to him was not taking place in the next world instead of in this. Indeed, his first feeling when he heard the muzhiks shouting above him as they dug out the sledge and then rolled the stiffened Vassili off him was one of surprise that muzhiks shouted in the next world even as they had shouted in this, and had similar bodies! When at length he understood that he was really here—here in this present world—he felt vexed rather than pleased, especially as he could feel that the fingers of both his hands were frostbitten.

For about two months he lay in hospital. Three of his fingers had to be amputated, but the others healed, so that he was able to go to work again and to live twenty years longer—first as a labourer, and then, in his old age, as a watchman. Indeed, he died only this year—at home and under the ikons, with a lighted wax candle in his hands, just as he had always wished. Before his death he took leave of his old wife, and pardoned her for the cooper. He took leave also of his son and grand-children, and died thoroughly happy to think that his death left his son and daughter-in-law freed from the burden of having a supernumerary mouth to feed, and that this time he himself would really pass from a life which had grown wearisome to him to that other life which had been growing more and more familiar and alluring to him each year and hour. Is he better or worse off now where he has awakened after his death—the death which really came that time? Is he disillusioned, or has he really found what he expected? Soon we shall all know.

The Snow-Storm

CHAPTER I

THE START

It was past six o'clock in the evening, after drinking tea, that I set out from a posting-station, the name of which I have forgotten, though I remember that it was somewhere in the Don Cossack district, near Novotcherkask. It was quite dark as I wrapped myself in my fur cloak and fur rug and settled myself beside Alyoshka in the sledge. Under the lee of the station-house it seemed warm and still. Though there was no snow falling, there was not a star to be seen overhead, and the sky seemed extraordinarily low and black in contrast with the pure, snowy plain stretched out before us.

As soon as we had driven out of the village, passing the dark figures of some windmills, one of which was clumsily waving its great sails, I noticed that the road was heavier and thicker with snow, and the wind began to blow more keenly on my left, tossed the horses' tails and manes on one side, and persistently lifted and blew away the snow as it was stirred up by the sledge-runners and the horses' hoofs. The tinkle of the bell died away, a draught of cold air made its way through some aperture in my sleeve and blew down my back, and I recalled the advice of the overseer of the station that I should do better not to start that night, or I might be out all night and get frozen on the way.

"Don't you think we might get lost?" I said to the driver. But receiving no reply, I put the question more definitely, "What do you say, shall we reach the next station? Sha'n't we lose the way?"

"God knows," he answered, without turning his head. "How it drives along the ground! Can't see the road a bit. Lord 'a' mercy!"

"Well, but you tell me, do you expect to get to the next station or not?" I persisted in inquiring. "Shall we manage to get there?"

"We've got to get there," said the driver, and he said something more which I could not catch in the wind.

I did not want to turn back; but to spend the night driving in the frost and the snow-storm about the absolutely desolate steppe of that part of the Don Cossack district was a very cheerless prospect. And although in the dark I could not see my driver distinctly, I somehow did not take to him, and felt no confidence in him. He was sitting with his legs hanging down before him exactly in the middle of his seat instead of on one side. His voice sounded listless; he wore a big hat with a wavering brim, not a coachman's cap, and besides he did not drive in correct style, but held the reins in both hands, like a footman who has taken the coachman's place on the box. And what prejudiced me most of all was that he had tied a kerchief over his ears. In short, the serious, bent back before my eyes impressed me unfavourably and seemed to promise no good.

"Well, I think it would be better to turn back," said Alyoshka; "it's poor fun being lost."

"Lord, 'a' mercy! how the snow is flying; no chance of seeing the road; one's eyes choked up entirely. . . . Lord, 'a' mercy!" grumbled the driver.

We had not driven on another quarter of an hour, when the driver, pulling up the horses, handed the reins to Alyoshka, clumsily extricated his legs from the box, and walked off to look for the road, his big boots crunching in the snow.

"Where are you going? Are we off the road, eh?" I inquired, but the driver did not answer. Turning his head to avoid the wind, which was cutting straight in his face, he walked away from the sledge.

"Well, found it?" I questioned him again, when he had come back.

"No, nothing," he said with sudden impatience and annoyance, as though I were to blame for his having got off the road, and deliberately tucking his big feet back again under the box, he picked up the reins with his frozen gloves.

"What are we going to do?" I asked, as we started again.

"What are we to do? Go whither God leads us."

And we drove on at the same slow trot, unmistakably on no sort of road; at one moment in snow that was soft and deep, and the next over brittle, bare ice.

Although it was so cold, the snow on my fur collar melted very quickly; the drifting snow blew more and more thickly near the ground, and a few flakes of frozen snow began falling overhead.

It was evident that we were going astray, because after driving another quarter of an hour, we had not seen a single verst post.

"Come, what do you think," I asked the driver again, "can we manage to get to the station?"

"To which station? . . . We shall get back all right if we let the horses go as they please, they'll take us there; but I doubt our getting to the other station; only lose our lives, may be."

"Well, then let us go back," said I. "And really . . ."

"Turn back then?" repeated the driver.

"Yes, yes, turn back!"

The driver let the reins go. The horses went at a better pace, and though I did not notice that we turned round, the wind changed and soon the mills could be seen through the snow. The driver plucked up his spirits and began talking. "The other day they were driving back from the next station like this in a snow-storm," said he, "and

they spent the night in some stacks and only arrived next morning. And a good job they did get into the stacks, or they'd have all been clean frozen to death—it was a frost. As it was, one had his feet frost-bitten; and he died of it three weeks after."

"But now it's not so cold and the wind seems dropping," said I; "couldn't we manage it?"

"Warmer it may be, but the snow's drifting just the same. Now it's behind us, so it seems a bit quieter, but it's blowing hard. We might have to go if we'd the mail or anything; but it's a different matter going of our own accord; it's no joke to let one's fare freeze. What if I've to answer for your honour afterwards?"

CHAPTER II

THE OTHER SLEDGE

At that moment we heard the bells of several sledges behind us, overtaking us at a smart pace.

"It's the mail express bell," said my driver; "there's only one like that at the station."

And certainly the bells of the foremost sledge were particularly fine; their clear, rich, mellow and somewhat jangled notes reached us distinctly on the wind. As I learned afterwards, it was a set of bells such as sportsmen have on their sledges—three bells, a big one in the middle, with a "raspberry note," as it is called, and two little bells pitched at the interval of a third up and down the scale. The cadence of these thirds and the jangling fifth ringing in the air was uncommonly striking and strangely sweet in the desolate dumb steppe.

"It's the post," said my driver, when the foremost of the three sledges was level with us. "How's the road, can one get along?" he shouted to the hindmost of the drivers; but the latter only shouted to his horses without answering him.

The music of the bells quickly died away in the wind as soon as the post had passed us. I suppose my driver felt ashamed.

"Suppose we go on, sir!" he said to me; "folks have driven along the road, and now their tracks will be fresh."

I assented and we turned, facing the wind again, and pushing on through the deep snow. I watched the road at the side, that we might not go off the tracks made by the sledges. For two versts their track was distinctly visible; then only a slight unevenness could be detected below the runners, and soon I was utterly unable to say whether there was a track or simply a crease blown by the wind in the snow. My eyes were dazed by watching the snow flying monotonously by under our runners, and I began looking straight before me. The third verst post we saw, but the fourth we could not find; just as before we drove against the wind and with the wind, to the right and to the left, and at last things came to such a pass that the driver said we were too much to the right; I said too much to the left; and Alyoshka maintained that we were going straight back. Again we pulled up several times, and the driver extricated his long legs and clambered out to seek the road, but always in vain. I, too, got out once to see whether something I fancied I descried might not be the road. But scarcely had I struggled six steps against the wind and satisfied myself that there was nothing but regular, uniform white drifts of snow everywhere, and that I had seen the road only in imagination, when I lost sight of the sledge. I shouted "Driver! Alyoshka!" but my voice I felt was caught up by the wind out of my very mouth and in one second carried far away from me. I went in the direction where the sledge had been—there was no sledge there. I went to the right, it was not there. I am ashamed when I remember the loud, shrill, almost despairing, voice in which I shouted once more, "Driver!" when he was only a couple of paces from me. His black figure, with his whip and his huge hat flapping down on one side, suddenly started up before me. He led me to the sledge.

"We must be thankful, too, that it's warm," said he; "if the frost gets sharp, it's a bad look-out. . . . Lord, 'a' mercy!"

"Let the horses go, let them take us back," I said, settling myself in the sledge. "They'll take us back, driver, eh?"

"They ought to."

He put down the reins, gave the shaft horse three strokes about the pad with his whip, and we started off again. We drove for another half-hour. All at once we heard ahead of us bells, which I recognised as the sportsmen's set of bells and two others. But this time the bells were coming to meet us. The same three sledges, having delivered the post, were returning to their station with their change of horses tied on behind. The three stalwart horses of the express sledge with the sporting bells galloped swiftly in front. There was only one driver in it. He was sitting on the box-seat, shouting briskly and frequently to his horses. Behind, in the inside of the emptied sledge, there were a couple of drivers; we could hear their loud, cheerful talk. One of them was smoking a pipe, and its spark, glowing in the wind, lighted up part of his face. Looking at them I felt ashamed of having been afraid to go on, and my driver must have had the same feeling, for with one voice we said, "Let us follow them."

CHAPTER III

FOLLOW THEM!

WITHOUT waiting for the hindmost sledge to get by, my driver began turning awkwardly and ran his shafts into the horses tied on at the back of it. One team of three started aside, broke their rein, and galloped away.

"Ah, the cross-eyed devil doesn't see where he's turning to—right into people! . . . The devil!" scolded a short driver in a husky, cracked voice—an old man, as I inferred from his voice and figure. He jumped nimbly out of the hindmost sledge and ran after the horses, still keeping up his coarse and cruel abuse of my driver.

But the horses would not let themselves be caught. The old man ran after them, and in one moment horses and man vanished in the white darkness of the snow-storm.

"Vassily—y! give us the bay here; there's no catching them like this," we heard his voice again.

One of the drivers, a very tall man, got out of the sledge, unyoked his three horses, pulled himself up by the head on to one of them, and crunching

over the snow at a shuffling gallop vanished in the same direction.

In company with the two other sledges we pushed on without a road, following the express sledge which ran ahead at full gallop with its ringing bells.

"What! he catch them!" said my driver, referring to the man who had run to catch the horses. "If it won't join the other horses of itself—it's a vicious beast—it'll lead him a fine dance, and he won't catch it."

From the time that he turned back, my driver seemed in better spirits and was more conversational, and as I was not sleepy I did not fail of course to take advantage of it. I began asking him where he came from, how he came here, and what he was; and soon learned that he was from my province, a Tula man, a serf from the village of Kirpitchny, that they had too little land, and that the corn had given up yielding any crop at all ever since the cholera year. There were two brothers at home, a third had gone for a soldier; they hadn't bread enough to last till Christmas, and lived on what they could earn. His younger brother, he told me, was the head of the house because he was married, while he himself was a widower. Every year gangs of men from his village came here as drivers, though he hadn't himself ever been a driver before; but now he had gone into the posting service so as to be a help to his brother. That he earned, thank God, one hundred and twenty roubles a year here, and sent a hundred of them home, and that it would be a pleasant life, too, "but the mail men were a brutal lot, very, and, indeed, all the people in these parts were a rough lot.

"Now, why did that driver abuse me? Lord, 'a' mercy on us! Did I set the horses loose on purpose? Am I a man to do any one a mischief? And what did he gallop after them for? They'd have got home by themselves. He's only wearing out his horses, and he'll be lost himself too," repeated the God-fearing peasant.

"And what's that blackness?" I asked, noticing several black objects ahead of us.

"Why, a train of waggons. That's a pleasant way of travelling!" he went on, as we overtook the huge waggons on wheels, covered with hemp sacking, following one another. "Look, not a man to be seen—they're all asleep. The clever mare knows the way herself, there's no making her stray off the road. . . . I've driven with a train of waggons too," he added, "so I know."

Truly it was strange to look at those huge waggons, covered with snow from their sacking top down to the wheels, moving along quite alone. But in the corner of the foremost the snow-covered sacking was lifted a little on two fingers, and a cap emerged from it for an instant when our bells were ringing close to the waggons. The big, piebald horse, stretching its neck and dragging with its back, stepped evenly along the completely buried road, and rhythmically shook its shaggy head under the whitened yoke. It pricked up one snowy ear as we came up to it.

After we had driven on another half-hour, my driver addressed me again.

"Well, what do you think, sir, are we going right?"

"I don't know," I answered.

"The wind was this way, sir, before, but now we're going with our backs to the weather. No, we're not going the right way, we're astray again," he concluded with complete serenity.

It was clear that though he was very timorous, even death, as they say, is pleasant in company; he had become perfectly composed since we were a large party, and he had not to be the guide and responsible person. With great coolness he made observations on the mistakes of the driver of the foremost sledge, as though he had not the slightest interest in the matter. I did notice, indeed, that the foremost sledge was sometimes visible in profile on my left, sometimes on the right; it positively seemed to me as though we were going round in a very small space. This might, however, have been an illusion of the senses, just as sometimes it looked to me as though the first sledge were driving up-hill, or along a slope, or down-hill, though the steppe was everywhere level.

We had driven on a good while longer, when I discerned—far away, it seemed to me, on the very horizon—a long black moving streak. But a minute later it was evident to me that this was the same train of waggons we had overtaken before. Just as before, the snow lay on the creaking wheels, some of which did not turn at all, indeed. As before, all the men were asleep under the sacking covers, and as before, the piebald horse in front, with inflated nostrils, sniffed out the road and pricked up its ears.

"There, we've gone round and round, and we've come back to the same waggons again!" said my driver in a tone of dissatisfaction. "The mail horses are good ones, and so he can drive them in this mad way; but ours will come to a dead stop if we go on like this all night."

He cleared his throat.

"Let us turn back, sir, before we come to harm."

"What for? Why, we shall get somewhere."

"Get somewhere! Why, we shall spend the night on the steppe. How the snow does blow! . . . Lord, 'a' mercy on us!"

Though I was surprised that the foremost driver, who had obviously lost both the road and the direction, did not attempt to look for the road, but calling merrily to his horses drove on still at full trot, I did not feel inclined now to drop behind the other sledges.

"Follow them!" I said.

My driver went on, but he drove the horses now with less eagerness than before, and he did not address another syllable to me.

CHAPTER IV

THE STORM

THE storm became more and more violent, and fine frozen snow was falling from the sky. It seemed as though it were beginning to freeze; my nose and cheeks felt the cold more keenly; more often a draught of cold air crept in under my fur cloak, and I had to wrap myself up more closely. From time to time the sledge jolted over a bare, broken crust of ice where the snow had blown away. Though I was much interested in seeing how our wanderings would end, yet, as I had been travelling six hundred versts without stopping for a night, I could not help shutting my eyes and I dropped into a doze. Once when I opened my eyes, I was struck by what seemed to me for the first minute the bright light shed over the white plain. The horizon had grown noticeably wider; the black, lowering sky had suddenly vanished; on all sides one could see the white, slanting lines of falling snow; the outlines of the horses of the front sledge were more distinctly visible, and when I looked upwards it seemed to me for the first minute that the storm-clouds had parted and that only the falling snow hid the sky. While I had been dozing, the moon had risen and cast its cold, bright light through the thin clouds and falling snow. All that I could see distinctly was my own sledge with the horse and driver and the three sledges with their horses ahead of us. In the first, the mail sledge, the one driver still sat on the box driving his horses at a smart trot. In the second there were two men, who, letting go their reins and making themselves a shelter out of a cloak, were all the time smoking a pipe, as we could see from the gleaming sparks. In the third sledge no one was to be seen; the driver was presumably asleep in the middle of it. The driver in front had, when I waked, begun stopping his horses and looking for the road. Then, as soon as we stopped, the howling of the wind became more audible, and the astoundingly immense mass of snow driving in the air was more evident to me. I could see in the moonlight, veiled by the drifting snow, the short figure of the driver holding a big whip with which he was trying the snow in front of him. He moved backwards and forwards in the white darkness, came back to the sledge again, jumped sideways on the front seat, and again through the monotonous whistling of the wind we could hear his jaunty, musical calling to his horses and the ringing of the bells. Every time that the front driver got out to search for signs of the road or of stacks, a brisk self-confident voice from the second sledge shouted to him—

"I say, Ignashka, we've gone right off to the left! Keep more to the right, away from the storm." Or, "Why do you go round and round like a fool? Go the way of the snow, you'll get there all right." Or, "To the right, go on to the right, my lad! See, there's something black—a verst post may be." Or, "What are you pottering about for? Unyoke the piebald and let him go first; he'll bring you on the road in a trice. That'll be the best plan."

The man who gave this advice did not himself unyoke the trace-horse, nor get out into the snow to look for the road; he did not so much as poke his nose out beyond the shelter of the cloak, and when Ignashka in reply to one of his counsels, shouted to him that he'd better ride on in front himself as he knew which way to go, the giver of good advice answered that, if he were driving the mail horses, he would ride on and would soon bring them on to the road. "But our horses won't lead the way in a storm!" he shouted; "they're not that sort!"

"Don't meddle then!" answered Ignashka, whistling merrily to his horses.

The other driver, sitting in the same sledge as the counsellor, said nothing to Ignashka, and refrained altogether from taking part in the proceedings,

though he was not yet asleep, as I concluded from his still glowing pipe, and from the fact that when we stopped I heard his regular, continuous talk. He was telling a tale. Only once, when Ignashka stopped for the sixth or seventh time, apparently vexed at the interruption in his enjoyment of the drive, he shouted to him—

"Why, what are you stopping for? . . . Trying to find the road, indeed! Don't you see, there's a snow-storm! The land-surveyor himself couldn't find the road now; you should drive on as long as the horses will go. We sha'n't freeze to death, I don't suppose. . . . Do go on!"

"I dare say! A postillion was frozen to death last year, sure enough!" my driver retorted.

The man in the third sledge did not wake up all the time. Only once, while we were halting, the counsellor shouted—

"Filip, aye . . . Filip!" And receiving no reply, he remarked, "I say, he's not frozen, is he? . . . You'd better look, Ignashka."

Ignashka, who did everything, went up to the sledge and began to poke the sleeper.

"I say, one drink has done for him. If you're frozen, just say so!" he said, shaking him.

The sleeping man muttered some words of abuse.

"Alive, lads!" said Ignashka, and he ran ahead again, and again we drove on, and so fast indeed that the little sorrel trace-horse of my sledge, who was constantly being lashed about its tail, more than once broke into a clumsy gallop.

CHAPTER V

A WHITE UNIVERSE

It was, I think, about midnight when the old man and Vassily, who had gone in pursuit of the strayed horses, rode up to us. They had caught the horses, and found and overtook us. But how they managed to do this in the dark, blinding blizzard, across the bare steppe, has always remained a mystery to me. The old man with his elbows and legs jogging, trotted up on the shaft-horse (the other two horses were fastened to the yoke; horses cannot be left loose in a blizzard). On overtaking us, he began railing at my driver again.

"You see, you cross-eyed devil, what a . . ."

"Hey, Uncle Mitritch," shouted the story-teller from the second sledge, "alive are you? . . . Come in to us."

But the old man, making no answer, went on scolding. When he judged he had said enough, he rode up to the second sledge.

"Caught them all?" was asked him from the sledge.

"I should think so!"

And his little figure bent forward with his breast on the horse's back while it was at full trot; then he slipped off into the snow, and without stopping an instant ran after the sledge, and tumbled into it, pulling his legs up over the side. The tall Vassily seated himself as before, in silence, in the front sledge with Ignashka, and began looking for the road with him.

"You see what an abusive fellow . . . Lord 'a' mercy on us!" muttered my driver.

For a long while after this we drove on without a halt over the white wilderness, in the cold, luminous, and flickering twilight of the snow-storm.

I open my eyes. The same clumsy cap and back, covered with snow, are standing up in front of me; the same low-arched yoke, under which, between the tight, leather reins, the head of the shaft-horse shakes up and down always at the same distance away, with its black mane blown rhythmically by the wind in one direction. Over its back on the right there is a glimpse of the bay trace-horse with its tail tied up short and the swinging bar behind it knocking now and then against the framework of the sledge. If I look down—the same crunching snow torn up by the sledge runners, and the wind persistently lifting it and carrying it off, always in the same direction. In front the foremost sledge is running on, always at the same distance; on the right and left everything is white and wavering. In vain the eye seeks some new object; not a post, not a stack, not a hedge—nothing to be seen. Everywhere all is white, white and moving. At one moment the horizon seems inconceivably remote, at the next closed in, two paces away on all sides. Suddenly a high, white wall shoots up on the right, and runs alongside the sledge, then all at once it vanishes and springs up ahead, to flee further and further away, and vanish again. One looks upwards; it seems light for the first minute—one seems to see stars shining through a mist; but the stars fly further and further away from the sight, and one can see nothing but the snow, which falls past the eyes into the face and the collar of one's cloak. Everywhere the sky is equally light, equally white, colourless, alike and ever moving. The wind seems to shift; at one time it blows in our faces and glues our eyes up with snow, then teasingly it flings one's fur collar on one's head and flaps it mockingly in one's face, then it drones behind in some chink of the sledge. One hears the faint, never-ceasing crunch of hoofs and runners over the snow, and the jingle of the bells, dying down as we drive over deep snow. Only at times when we are going against the wind and over some bare, frozen headland, Ignashka's vigorous whistling and the melodious tinkle of the bells with the jangling fifth float clearly to one's hearing, and these sounds make a comforting break in the desolateness of the snowy waste, and then again the bells fall back into the same monotonous jingle, with intolerable correctness ringing ever the same phrase, which I cannot help picturing to myself in musical notes.

One of my legs began to get chilled, and when I turned over to wrap myself up closer, the snow on my collar and cap slipped down my neck and made me shiver; but on the whole, in my fur cloak, warmed through by the heat of my body, I still kept warm and was beginning to feel drowsy.

CHAPTER VI

DROWNING

MEMORIES and fancies followed one another with increased rapidity in my imagination.

"The counsellor, that keeps on calling out advice from the second sledge, what sort of peasant is he likely to be? Sure to be a red-haired, thick-set fellow with short legs," I thought, "somewhat like Fyodor Filippitch, our old butler."

And then I see the staircase of our great house and five house-serfs, who are stepping heavily, dragging along on strips of coarse linen a piano from the lodge. I see Fyodor Filippitch, with the sleeves of his nankin coat turned up, carrying nothing but one pedal, running on ahead, pulling open bolts, tugging at a strip of linen here, shoving there, creeping between people's legs, getting in every one's way, and in a voice of anxiety shouting assiduously.

"You now, in front, in front! That's it, the tail end upwards, upwards, upwards, through the doorway! That's it."

"You only let us be, Fyodor Filippitch, we'll do it by ourselves," timidly ventured the gardener, squeezed against the banisters, and red with exertion, as, putting out all his strength, he held up one corner of the piano.

But Fyodor Filippitch would not desist.

"And what is it?" I reflected. "Does he suppose he's necessary to the business in hand, or is he simply pleased God has given him that conceited, convincing flow of words and enjoys the exercise of it? That's what it must be."

And for some reason I recall the pond, and the tired house-serfs, knee-deep in the water, dragging the draw-net, and again Fyodor Filippitch running along the bank with the watering-pot, shouting to all of them, and only approaching the water at intervals to take hold of the golden carp, to let out the muddy water, and to pour over them fresh.

And again it is midday in July. I am wandering over the freshly mown grass of the garden, under the burning sun straight above my head. I am still very young; there is an emptiness, a yearning for something in my heart. I walk to my favourite spot near the pond, between a thicket of wild rose and the birch-tree avenue, and lie down to go to sleep. I remember the sensation with which, as I lay there, I looked through the red, thorny stems of the rose at the black earth, dried into little clods, and at the shining, bright blue mirror of the pond. It was with a feeling of naïve self-satisfaction and melancholy. Everything around me was so beautiful; its beauty had such an intense effect on me that it seemed to me I was beautiful myself, and my only vexation was that there was no one to admire me.

It is hot. I try to console myself by going to sleep. But the flies, the intolerable flies, will not even here give me any peace; they begin to gather together about me and persistently, stolidly, as it were like pellets, they shoot from forehead to hand. A bee buzzes not far from me, right in the hottest spot; yellow butterflies flutter languidly, it seems, from stalk to stalk. I look upwards, it makes my eyes ache; the sun is too dazzling through the bright foliage of the leafy birch-tree, that gently swings its branches high above me, and I feel hotter than ever. I cover my face with my handkerchief; it becomes stifling, and the flies simply stick to my moist hands. Sparrows are twittering in the thickest of the clump of roses. One of them hops on the ground a yard from me; twice he makes a feint of pecking vigorously at the earth, and with a snapping of twigs and a merry chirrup flies out of the bush. Another, too, hops on the ground, perks up his tail, looks round, and with a chirrup he too flies out like an arrow after the first. From the pond comes the sounds of wet linen being beaten with washing-bats in the water, and the blows seem to echo and be carried over the surface of the pond. There is the sound of laughter, chatter, and the splashing of bathers. A gust of wind rustles in the tree-tops at a distance; it comes closer, and I hear it ruffling up the grass, and now the leaves of the wild rose tremble and beat upon the stems; and now it lifts the corner of the handkerchief and a fresh breath of air passes over me, tickling my moist face. A fly flies in under the lifted kerchief and buzzes in a frightened way about my damp mouth. A dead twig sticks into me under my spine. No, it's no good lying down; I'll go and have a bath. But suddenly close to my nook, I hear hurried footsteps and the frightened voices of women.

"Oh, mercy on us! What can we do! and not a man here!"

"What is it, what is it?" I ask, running out into the sunshine and addressing a serf-woman, who runs past me, groaning. She simply looks round, wrings her hands and runs on. But here come Matrona, an old woman of seventy, holding on her kerchief as it falls back off her head, limping and dragging one leg in a worsted stocking, as she runs towards the pond. Two little girls run along, hand in hand, and a boy of ten, wearing his father's coat, hurries behind, clinging to the hempen skirt of one of them.

"What has happened?" I inquire of them.

"A peasant is drowning."

"Where?"

"In our pond."

"Who? one of ours?"

"No; a stranger."

The coachman Ivan, struggling over the newly mown grass in his big boots, and the stout bailiff, Yakov, breathing hard, run towards the pond, and I run after them.

I recall the feeling that said to me, "Come, jump in, and pull out the man, save him, and they will all admire you," which was just what I was desiring.

"Where? where is he?" I ask of the crowd of house-serfs gathered together on the bank.

"Over yonder, near the deepest pool, towards that bank, almost at the bath-house," says a washerwoman, getting in her wet linen in a yoke. "I saw him plunge in; and he comes up so and goes down again, and comes up again and screams, 'I'm drowning, mercy!' and again he went down to the bottom, and only bubbles came up. Then I saw the man was drowning. And I yelled, 'Mercy on us, the peasant's drowning!'"

And the washerwoman hoists the yoke on to her shoulder, and, bending one one side, walks along the path away from the pond.

"My word, what a shame!" says Yakov Ivanov, the bailiff, in a voice of despair: "what a to-do we shall have now with the district court—we shall never hear the last of it!"

A peasant with a scythe makes his way through the throng of women, children, and old people crowding about the bank, and hanging his scythe in the branches of a willow, begins deliberately pulling off his boots.

"Where, where did he sink?" I keep on asking, longing to throw myself in, and do something extraordinary.

But they point to the smooth surface of the pond, broken into ripples here and there by the rushing wind. It is inconceivable to me that he is drowned while the water stands just as smooth and beautiful and untroubled over him, shining with glints of gold in the mid-day sun, and it seems to me that I can do nothing, can astonish no one, especially as I am a very poor swimmer. And the peasant is already pulling his shirt over his head, and in an instant will plunge in. Every one watches him with hope and a sinking heart: but when he has waded in up to his shoulders, the peasant slowly turns back and puts on his shirt again—he cannot swim.

People still run up; the crowd gets bigger and bigger: the women cling to each other; but no one does anything to help. Those who have only just reached the pond give advice, and groan, and their faces express horror and despair. Of those who had arrived on the scene earlier some, tired of standing, sit down on the grass; others go back. Old Matrona asks her daughter whether she has shut the door of the oven; the boy in his father's coat flings stones with careful aim into the pond.

But now Trezorka, Fyodor Filippitch's dog, comes running down-hill from the house, barking and looking round in perplexity; and the figure of Fyodor himself, running down the hill and shouting something, comes into sight behind the thicket of wild rose.

"Why are you standing still?" he shouts, taking off his coat as he runs. "A man's drowning, and they do nothing. . . . Give us a cord!"

All gaze in hope and dread at Fyodor

Filippitch, while leaning on the shoulder of an obliging house-serf he kicks off his right boot with the tip of his left one.

"Over there, where the crowd is; over there, a little to the right of the willow, Fyodor Filippitch, over there," says some one.

"I know," he answers, and knitting his brows, probably in acknowledgment of symptoms of outraged delicacy in the crowd of women, he takes off his shirt and his cross, handing the latter to the gardener's boy, who stands obsequiously before him. Then stepping vigorously over the mown grass, he goes to the pond.

Trezorka, who had stood still near the crowd, eating some blades of grass from the water's edge, and smacking his lips, looks inquiringly at his master, wondering at the rapidity of his movements. All at once, with a whine of delight, he plunges with his master into the water. For the first minute there is nothing to be seen but frothing bubbles, which float right up to us. But soon Fyodor Filippitch is seen swimming smartly towards the further bank, his arms making a graceful sweep, and his back rising and sinking regularly at every fathom's length. Trezorka, after swallowing a mouthful of water, hurriedly turns back, shakes himself in the crowd, and rolls on his back on the bank. While Fyodor Filippitch is swimming towards the further bank, the two coachmen run round to the willow with a net rolled round a pole. Fyodor Filippitch, for some reason or other, raises his hands above his head, and dives, once, twice, thrice; every time a stream of water runs out of his mouth, he tosses his hair with a

fine gesture, and makes no reply to the questions which are showered upon him from all sides. At last he comes out on the bank, and, as far as I can see, simply gives orders for the casting of the net. The net is drawn up, but in it there is nothing except weed and a few carp struggling in it. While the net is being cast a second time, I walk round to that side.

Nothing is to be heard but the voice of Fyodor Filippitch giving directions, the splashing of the water through the wet cords, and sighs of horror. The wet cordage fastened to the right beam is more and more thickly covered with weed, as it comes further and further out of the water.

"Now pull together, all at once!" shouts the voice of Fyodor Filippitch. The butt-ends of the beams come into view covered with water.

"There is something; it pulls heavy, lads," says some one.

And now the beams of the net in which two or three carp struggle, splashing and crushing the weed, are dragged on to the bank. And through the shallow, shifting layer of muddy water something white comes into sight in the tightly strained net. A sigh of horror passes over the crowd, subdued but distinctly audible in the deathlike stillness.

"Pull all together, pull it on to dry land!" cries Fyodor Filippitch's resolute voice. And with the iron hook they drag the drowned man over the chopped stalks of dock and agrimony towards the willow.

And here I see my kind old aunt in her silk gown; I see her fringed, lilac parasol, which seems somehow oddly incongruous with this scene of death, so awful in its simplicity. I see her face on the point of shedding tears. I recall her look of disappointment that in this case arnica could be of no use, and I recall the painful sense of mortification I had when she said to me with the naïve egoism of love, "Let us go, my dear. Ah, how awful it is! And you will always go bathing and swimming alone!"

I remember how glaring and hot the sun was, baking the dry earth that crumbled under our feet; how it sparkled on the mirror of the pond; how the big carp struggled on the bank; how a shoal of fish dimpled the pond's surface in the middle; how a hawk floated high up in the sky, hovering over the ducks, who swam quacking and splashing among the reeds in the centre of the water; how the white, curly storm-clouds gathered on the horizon; how the mud brought on to the bank by the net gradually slipped away; and how, as I crossed the dike, I heard the sounds of the washing-bat floating across the pond.

But the blows of the bat ring out as though there were two bats and another chiming in, a third lower in the scale; and that sound frets me, worries me, especially as I know the bat is a bell, and Fyodor Filippitch can't make it stop. And the bat, like an instrument of torture, is crushing my leg, which is chilled. I wake up.

I was waked up, it seemed to me, by our galloping very swiftly, and two voices talking quite close beside me.

"I say, Ignat, eh . . . Ignat!" said the voice of my driver; "take my fare; you've got to go anyway, and why should I go on for nothing—take him!"

The voice of Ignat close beside me answered—

"It's no treat for me to have to answer for a passenger. . . . Will you stand me a pint bottle of vodka?"

"Go on with your pint bottle! . . . A dram, and I'll say done."

"A dram!" shouted another voice: "a likely idea! tire your horses for a dram!"

I opened my eyes. Still the same insufferable wavering snow floating before one's eyes, the same drivers and horses, but beside me I saw a sledge. My driver had overtaken Ignat, and we had been for some time moving alongside. Although the voice from the other sledge advised him not to accept less than a pint, Ignat all at once pulled up his horses.

"Move the baggage in! Done! it's your luck. Stand me a dram when we come to-morrow. Have you much baggage, eh?"

My driver jumped out into the snow with an alacrity quite unlike him, bowed to me, and begged me to get into Ignat's sledge. I was perfectly ready to do so; but evidently the God-fearing peasant was so pleased that he wanted to lavish his gratitude and joy on some one. He bowed and thanked me, Alyoshka, and Ignashka.

"There, thank God too! Why, Lord 'a' mercy, here we've been driving half the night, and don't know ourselves where we're going! He'll take you all right, sir, but my horses are quite done up."

And he moved my things with increased energy. While they were shifting my things, with the wind at my back almost carrying me off my legs, I went towards the second sledge. The sledge was more than a quarter buried in the snow, especially on the side where a cloak had been hung over the two drivers' heads to keep off the wind; under the cloak it was sheltered and snug. The old man was lying just as before with his legs out, while the story-teller was still telling his story: "So at the very time when the General arrived in the king's name, that is, to Mariya in the prison, Mariya says to him, 'General! I don't want you, and I cannot love you, and you are not my lover; my lover is that same prince.' . . . So then"—he was going on, but, seeing me, he paused a moment, and began pulling at his pipe.

"Well, sir, are you come to listen to the tale?" said the other man, whom I have called the counsellor.

"Why, you are nice and cheerful in here!" I said.

"To be sure, it passes the time— anyway, it keeps one from thinking."

"Don't you know, really, where we are now?" This question, it struck me, was not liked by the drivers.

"Why, who's to make out where we are? May be we've got to the Kalmucks altogether," answered the counsellor.

"What are we going to do?" I asked.

"What are we to do? Why, we'll go on, and may be we'll get somewhere," he said in a tone of displeasure.

"Well, but if we don't get there, and the horses can go no further in the snow, what then?"

"What then? Nothing."

"But we may freeze."

"To be sure, we may, for there are no stacks to be seen now; we must have driven right out to the Kalmucks. The chief thing is, we must look about in the snow."

"And aren't you at all afraid of being frozen, sir?" said the old man, in a trembling voice.

Although he seemed to be jeering me, I could see that he was shivering in every bone.

"Yes, it's getting very cold," I said.

"Ah, sir! You should do as I do; every now and then take a run; that would warm you."

"It's first-rate, the way you run after the sledge," said the counsellor.

CHAPTER VII

THE NEW DRIVER

"PLEASE get in: it's all ready!" Alyoshka called to me from the front sledge.

The blizzard was so terrific that it was only by my utmost efforts, bending double and clutching the skirts of my coat in both hands, that I managed to struggle through the whirling snow, which was blown up by the wind under my feet, and to make the few steps that separated me from the sledge. My former driver was kneeling in the middle of the empty sledge, but on seeing me he took off his big cap; whereupon the wind snatched at his hair furiously. He asked me for something for drink, but most likely had not expected me to give him anything extra, for my refusal did not in the least disappoint him. He thanked me for that too, put on his cap, and said to me, "Well, good luck to you, sir!" and tugging at his reins, and clucking to his horses, he drove away from us. After that, Ignashka too, with a swing of his whole body forward, shouted to his horses. Again the sound of the crunching of the hoofs, shouting, and bells replaced the sound of the howling of the wind, which was more audible when we were standing still.

For a quarter of an hour after moving I did not go to sleep, but amused myself by watching the figures of my new driver and horses. Ignashka sat up smartly, incessantly jumped up and down, swinging his arm with the whip over the horses, shouting, knocking one leg against the other, and bending forward to set straight the shaft-horse's breech, which kept slipping to the right side. He was not tall, but seemed to be well built. Over his full coat he had on a cloak not tied in at the waist; the collar of it was open, and his neck was quite bare; his boots were not of felt, but of leather, and his cap was a small one, which he was continually taking off and shifting. His ears had no covering but his hair.

In all his actions could be detected not merely energy, but even more, it struck me, the desire to keep up his own energies. The further we went, the more and more frequently he jumped up and down on the box, shifted his position, slapped one leg against the other, and addressed remarks to me and Alyoshka. It seemed to me he was afraid of losing heart. And there was good reason; though we had good horses, the road became heavier and heavier at every step, and the horses unmistakably moved more unwillingly; he had to use the whip now, and the shaft-horse, a spirited, big, shaggy horse, stumbled twice, though at once taking fright, he darted forward and flung up his shaggy head almost to the very bells. The right trace-horse, whom I could not help watching, noticeably kept the traces slack, together with the long leather tassel of the breech, that shifted and shook up and down on the off-side. He needed the whip, but, like a good, spirited horse he seemed vexed at his own feebleness, and angrily dropped and flung up his head, as though asking for the rein. It certainly was terrible to see the blizzard getting more and more violent, the horses growing weaker, and the road getting worse, while we hadn't a notion where we were and whether we should reach the station, or even a shelter of any sort. And ludicrous and strange it was to hear the bells ringing so gaily and unconcernedly, and Ignashka calling so briskly and jauntily, as though we were driving at midday in sunny, frosty Christmas weather, along some village street on a holiday; and strangest of all it was to think that we were going on all the while and going quickly, anywhere to get away from where we were. Ignashka sang a song, in the vilest falsetto, but so loudly and with breaks in it, filled in by such whistling, that it was odd to feel frightened as one listened to him.

"Hey, hey, what are you splitting your throat for, Ignashka?" I heard the voice of the counsellor. "Do stop it for an hour."

"What?"

"Shut up!"

Ignat ceased. Again all was quiet, and the wind howled and whined, and the whirling snow began to lie thicker on our sledge. The counsellor came up to us.

"Well, what is it?"

"What, indeed; which way are we to go?"

"Who knows?"

"Why, are your feet frozen, that you keep beating them together?"

"They're quite numb."

"You should take a run. There's something over yonder; isn't it a Kalmuck encampment? It would warm your feet, anyway."

"All right. Hold the horses . . . there."

And Ignat ran in the direction indicated.

"One must keep looking and walking round, and one will find something; what's the sense of driving on like a fool?" the counsellor said to me. "See, what a steam the horses are in!"

All the time Ignat was gone—and that lasted so long that I began to be afraid he was lost—the counsellor told me in a calm, self-confident tone, how one must act during a blizzard, how the best thing of all was to unyoke a horse and let it go its own way; that as God is holy, it would lead one right; how one could sometimes see by the stars, and how if he had been driving the leading sledge, we should have been at the station long ago.

"Well, is it?" he asked Ignat, who was coming back, stepping with difficulty almost knee-deep in the snow.

"Yes, it's an encampment," Ignat answered, panting, "but I don't know what sort of a one. We must have come right out to Prolgovsky homestead, mate. We must bear more to the left."

"What nonsense! . . . That's our encampment, behind the village!" retorted the counsellor.

"But I tell you it's not!"

"Why, I've looked, so I know. That's what it will be; or if not that, then it's Tamishevsko. We must keep more to the right, and we shall get out on the big bridge, at the eighth verst, directly."

"I tell you it's not so! Why, I've seen it!" Ignat answered with irritation.

"Hey, mate, and you call yourself a driver!"

"Yes, I do. . . . You go yourself!"

"What should I go for? I know as it is."

Ignat unmistakably lost his temper; without replying, he jumped on the box and drove on.

"I say, my legs are numb; there's no warming them," he said to Alyoshka, clapping his legs together more and more frequently, and knocking off and scraping at the snow, that had got in above his boot-tops.

I felt awfully sleepy.

CHAPTER VIII

SLEEP

"Can I really be beginning to freeze?" I wondered sleepily. "Being frozen always begins by sleepiness, they say. Better be drowned than frozen—let them drag me out in the net; but never mind, I don't care whether it's drowning or freezing, if only that stick, or whatever it is, wouldn't poke me in the back, and I could forget everything."

I lost consciousness for a second.

"How will it all end, though?" I suddenly wondered, opening my eyes for a minute and staring at the white expanse of snow; "how will it end, if we don't come across any stacks, and the horses come to a standstill, which I fancy will happen soon? We shall all be frozen."

I must own that, though I was a little

frightened, the desire that something extraordinary and rather tragic should happen to us was stronger than a little fear. It struck me that it would not be bad if, towards morning, the horses should reach some remote, unknown village with us half-frozen, some of us indeed completely frozen. And dreams of something like that floated with extraordinary swiftness and clearness before my imagination. The horses stop, the snow drifts higher and higher, and now nothing can be seen of the horses but their ears and the yoke; but suddenly Ignashka appears on the top of the snow with his three horses and drives past us. We entreat him, we scream to him to take us with him; but the wind blows away our voice, there is no voice heard. Ignashka laughs, shouts to his horses, whistles, and vanishes from our sight in a deep ravine filled with snow. The old man is on horseback, his elbows jogging up and down, and he tries to gallop away, but cannot move from the spot. My old driver with his big cap rushes at him, drags him to the ground and tramples him in the snow. "You're a sorcerer," he shouts, "you're abusive, we will be lost together." But the old man pops his head out of a snowdrift; he is not so much an old man now as a hare, and he hops away from us. All the dogs are running after him. The counsellor, who is Fyodor Filippitch, says we must all sit round in a ring, that it doesn't matter if the snow does bury us; we shall be warm. And we really are warm and snug; only we are thirsty. I get out a case of wine; I treat all of them to rum with sugar in it, and I drink it myself with great enjoyment. The story-teller tells us some tale about a

rainbow—and over our heads there is a ceiling made of snow and a rainbow. "Now let us make ourselves each a room in the snow and go to sleep;" I say. The snow is soft and warm like fur; I make myself a room and try to get into it, but Fyodor Filippitch, who has seen my money in the wine-case, says, "Stop, give me the money—you have to die any way!" and he seizes me by the leg. I give him the money, and only beg him to let me go; but they will not believe it is all the money, and try to kill me. I clutch at the old man's hand, and with inexpressible delight begin kissing it; the old man's hand is soft and sweet. At first he snatches it away, but then he gives it me, and even strokes me with the other hand. But Fyodor Filippitch approaches and threatens me. I run into my room; now it is not a room, but a long, white corridor, and some one is holding me by the legs. I pull myself away. My boots and stockings, together with part of my skin, are left in the hands of the man who held me. But I only feel cold and ashamed—all the more ashamed as my aunt with her parasol and her homœopathic medicine-chest is coming to meet me, arm in arm with the drowned man. They are laughing, and do not understand the signs I make to them. I fling myself into a sledge, my legs drag in the snow; but the old man pursues me, his elbows jogging up and down. The old man is close upon me, but I hear two bells ringing in front of me, and I know I am safe if I can reach them. The bells ring more and more distinctly; but the old man has overtaken me and fallen with his body on my face, so that I can hardly hear the bells. I snatch his hand again, and begin kissing it, but he is not the old man but the drowned man, and he shouts, "Ignashka, stop, yonder are the Ahmetkin stacks, I do believe! Run and look!" That is too dreadful. No, I had better wake up.

I open my eyes. The wind has blown the skirt of Alyoshka's coat over my face; my knee is uncovered; we are driving over a bare surface of ice, and the chime of the bells with its jangling fifth rings out more distinctly in the air.

I look to see where there is a stack; but instead of stacks, I see now with open eyes a house with a balcony and a turreted wall like a fortress. I feel little interest in examining this house and fortress. I want most to see again the white corridor, along which I was running, to hear the church bell ringing and to kiss the old man's hand. I close my eyes again and fall asleep.

CHAPTER IX

BELLS

I SLEPT soundly; but the chime of the bells was audible all the while, and came into my dreams; at one time in the form of a dog barking and rushing at me, then an organ, of which I am one of the pipes, then French verses which I am composing. Then it seemed that the chime of the bell is an instrument of torture with which my right heel is being continually squeezed. This was so vivid that I woke up and opened my eyes, rubbing my foot. It was beginning to get frostbitten. The night was as light, as dim, as white as ever. The same movement jolted me and the sledge; Ignashka was sitting sideways as before, clapping his legs together. The trace-horse, as before, craning his neck and not lifting his legs high, ran trotting over the deep snow; the tassel bobbed up and down on the breech, and lashed against the horse's belly. The shaft-horse's head, with his mane flying, swayed regularly up and down, tightening and loosening the reins that were fastened to the yoke. But all this was more than ever covered, buried in snow. The snow whirled in front of us, buried the runners on one side, and the horses' legs up to the knees, and was piled up high on our collars and caps. The wind blew first on the right, then on the left, played with my collar, with the skirt of Ignashka's coat, and the trace-horse's mane, and whistled through the yoke and the shafts.

It had become fearfully cold, and I had hardly peeped out of my fur collar when the dry, frozen, whirling snow settled on my eyelashes, my nose and my mouth, and drifted down my neck. I looked round—all was white, and light and snowy; nowhere anything but dim light and snow. I felt seriously alarmed. Alyoshka was asleep at my feet, right at the bottom of the sledge; his whole back was covered by a thick layer of snow. Ignashka was not depressed; he was incessantly tugging at the reins, shouting and clapping his feet together. The bells rang as strangely as ever. The horses were panting, but they still went on, though rather more slowly, and stumbling more and more often. Ignashka jumped up and down again, brandished his gloves, and began singing a song in his shrill, strained voice. Before he had finished the song, he pulled up, flung the reins on the forepart of the sledge, and got down. The wind howled ruthlessly; the snow simply poured as it were in shovelfuls on the skirts of my fur cloak. I looked round; the third sledge was not there (it had been left behind somewhere). Beside the second sledge I could see in the snowy fog the old man hopping from one leg to the other. Ignashka walked three steps away from the sledge, sat down on the snow, undid his belt and began taking off his boots.

"What are you doing?" I asked.

"I must take my boots off; or my feet will be quite frostbitten!" he answered, going on with what he was about.

It was too cold for me to poke my neck out of my fur collar to see what he was doing. I sat up straight, looking at the trace-horse, who stood with one leg outstretched in an attitude of painful exhaustion, shaking his tied-up, snowy tail. The jolt Ignashka gave the sledge in jumping up on the box waked me up.

"Well, where are we now?" I asked. "Shall we go on till morning?"

"Don't you worry yourself, we'll take you all right," he answered. "Now my feet are grandly warm since I shifted my boots."

And he started; the bells began ringing; the sledge began swaying from side to side; and the wind whistled through the runners. And again we set off floating over the boundless sea of snow.

CHAPTER X

HIS FACE

I SLEPT soundly. When I was waked up by Alyoshka kicking me, and opened my eyes, it was morning. It seemed even colder than in the night. No snow was falling from above; but the keen, dry wind was still driving the fine snow along the ground and especially under the runners and the horses' hoofs. To the right the sky in the east was a heavy, dingy blue colour; but bright, orange-red, slanting rays were becoming more and more clearly marked in it Overhead, behind the flying white clouds, faintly tinged with red, the pale blue sky was visible; on the left the clouds were light, bright, and moving. Everywhere around, as far as the eye could see, the country lay under deep, white snow, thrown up into sharp ridges. Here and there could be seen a greyish hillock, where the fine, dry snow had persistently blown by. Not a track of sledge, or man, or beast was visible. The outlines and colours of the driver's back and the horses could be seen clearly and distinctly against the white background. . . . The rim of Ignashka's dark blue cap, his collar, his hair, and even his boots were white. The sledge was completely buried. The grey shaft-horse's head and forelock were covered with snow on the right side; my right trace-horse's legs were buried up to the knee, and all his back, crisp with frozen sweat, was coated with snow on the off-side. The tassel was still dancing in time to any tune one liked to fancy, and the trace-horse stepped to the same rhythm. It was only from his sunken belly, that heaved and fell so often, and his drooping ears that one could see how exhausted he was. Only one new object caught my attention. That was a verst post, from which the snow was falling to the ground, and about which the wind had swept up quite a mountain on the right and kept whirling and shifting the powdery snow from one side to the other. I was utterly amazed to find that we had been driving the whole night with the same horses, twelve hours without stopping or knowing where we were going, and yet had somehow arrived. Our bells chimed more gaily than ever. Ignat kept wrapping himself round and shouting; behind us we heard the snorting of the horses and the ringing of the bells of the sledge in which were the old man and the counsellor; but the man who had been asleep had gone completely astray from us on the steppe. When we had driven on another half-verst, we came upon fresh tracks of a sledge and three horses, not yet covered by the snow, and here and there we saw a red spot of blood, most likely from a horse that had been hurt.

"That's Filip. Why, he's got in before us!" said Ignashka.

And now a little house with a signboard came into sight near the roadside, in the middle of the snow, which buried it almost to the roof and windows. Near the little inn stood a sledge with three grey horses, with their coats crisp with sweat, their legs stiffly stretched out, and their heads drooping. The snow had been cleared about the door, and a spade stood there; but the droning wind still whirled and drifted the snow from the roof.

At the sound of our bells there came out from the door a big, red-faced, red-haired driver, holding a glass of vodka in his hand, and shouting something to us. Ignashka turned to me and asked my permission to stop here; then, for the first time, I saw his face.

CHAPTER XI

SAFE!

HIS face was not swarthy, lean, and straight-nosed, as I had expected, judging from his hair and figure. It was a merry, round face, with quite a pug nose, a large mouth, and round, bright, light blue eyes. His face and neck were red, as though they had been rubbed with a polishing cloth; his eyebrows, long eyelashes, and the down that covered all the lower part of his face were stiffly coated with snow and perfectly white. It was only half a verst from the station, and we stopped.

"Only make haste," I said.

"One minute," answered Ignashka, jumping off the box and going towards Filip.

"Give it here, mate," he said, taking the glove off his right hand and flinging it with the whip on the snow, and throwing back his head, he tossed off the glass of vodka at one gulp.

The innkeeper, probably an old Cossack, came out of the door with a pint bottle in his hand.

"To whom shall I take some?" said he.

Tall Vassily, a thin, flaxen-headed peasant with a goat's beard, and the counsellor, a stout man with light eyebrows and a thick light beard framing his red face, came up, and drank a glass each. The old man, too, was approaching the group, but they did not offer him any, and he moved away to his horses, that were fastened at the back of the sledge, and began stroking one of them on the back.

The old man was just as I had imagined him to be—a thin little man, with a wrinkled, bluish face, a scanty beard, a sharp nose, and decayed, yellow teeth. His cap was a regular driver's cap, perfectly new, but his greatcoat was shabby, smeared with tar, and torn about the shoulders and skirts. It did not cover his knees, and his coarse, hempen under-garment, which was stuffed into his huge, felt boots. He was bent and wrinkled, his face quivering, and his knees trembling. He bustled about the sledge, apparently trying to get warm.

"Why, Mitritch, have a drop; it would warm you finely," the counsellor said to him.

Mitritch gave a shrug. He straightened the breech on his horse, set the yoke right, and came up to me.

"Well, sir," said he, taking his cap off his grey hair, and bowing low, "we've been lost all night along with you, and looking for the road; you might treat me to a glass. Surely, your excellency! Else I've nothing to warm me up," he added with a deprecating smile.

I gave him twenty-five kopecks. The innkeeper brought out a glass, and handed it to the old man. He took off his glove with the whip, and put his black, horny little hand, blue with cold, to the glass; but his thumb was not under his control; he could not hold the glass, and let it drop, spilling the vodka in the snow.

All the drivers laughed.

"I say, Mitritch is so frozen, he can't hold the vodka."

But Mitritch was greatly mortified at having spilt the drink.

They poured him out another glass, however, and put it to his lips. He became more cheerful at once, ran into the inn, lighted a pipe, began grinning, showing his decayed, yellow teeth, and at every word he uttered an oath. After drinking a last glass, the drivers got into their sledges, and we drove on.

The snow became whiter and brighter, so that it made one's eyes ache to look at it. The orange-red streaks spread higher and higher, and grew brighter and brighter in the sky overhead. The red disc of the sun appeared on the horizon through the dark blue clouds. The blue became deeper and more brilliant. Along the road near the station there was a distinct yellowish track, with here and there deep ruts in it. In the tense, frozen air there was a peculiar, refreshing lightness.

My sledge flew along very briskly. The head of the shaft-horse, with his mane floating up on the yoke above, bobbed up and down quickly under the sportsman's bell, the clapper of which did not move freely now, but somehow grated against the sides. The gallant trace-horses, pulling together at the twisted, frozen traces, trotted vigorously, and the tassel danced right under the belly and the breech. Sometimes a trace-horse slipped off the beaten track into a snowdrift, and his eyes were all powdered with snow as he plunged smartly out of it. Ignashka shouted in a cheerful tenor; the dry frost crunched under the runners; behind us we heard the two bells ringing out with a clear, festive note, and the drunken shouts of the drivers. I looked round. The grey, crisp-haired trace-horses, breathing regularly, galloped over the snow with outstretched necks and bits askew. Filip cracked his whip and set his cap straight. The old man lay in the middle of the sledge with his legs up as before.

Two minutes later the sledge was creaking over the swept boards of the approach to the posting-station, and Ignashka turned his merry face, all covered with frost and snow, towards me.

"We've brought you safe after all, sir," said he.